THE
JEEVES COLLECTION

Books by P. G. Wodehouse

Fiction

Aunts Aren't Gentlemen
The Adventures of Sally
Bachelors Anonymous
Barmy in Wonderland
Big Money
Bill the Conqueror
Blandings Castle and
   Elsewhere
Carry On, Jeeves
The Clicking of Cuthbert
Cocktail Time
The Code of the Woosters
The Coming of Bill
Company for Henry
A Damsel in Distress
Do Butlers Burgle Banks?
Doctor Sally
Eggs, Beans and Crumpets
A Few Quick Ones
French Leave
Frozen Assets
Full Moon
Galahad at Blandings
A Gentleman of Leisure
The Girl in Blue
The Girl on the Boat
The Gold Bat
The Head of Kay's
The Heart of a Goof
Heavy Weather
Ice in the Bedroom
If I Were You
Indiscretions of Archie
The Inimitable Jeeves
Jeeves and the Feudal Spirit
Jeeves in the Offing
Jill the Reckless
Joy in the Morning
Laughing Gas
Leave it to Psmith
The Little Nugget
Lord Emsworth and Others
Louder and Funnier
Love Among the Chickens
The Luck of the Bodkins
The Man Upstairs
The Man with Two Left Feet
The Mating Season
Meet Mr Mulliner
Mike and Psmith
Mike at Wrykyn
Money for Nothing
Money in the Bank
Mr Mulliner Speaking
Much Obliged, Jeeves
Mulliner Nights
Not George Washington
Nothing Serious
The Old Reliable
Pearls, Girls and Monty Bodkin
A Pelican at Blandings
Piccadilly Jim
Pigs Have Wings

Plum Pie
The Pothunters
A Prefect's Uncle
The Prince and Betty
Psmith, Journalist
Psmith in the City
Quick Service
Right Ho, Jeeves
Ring for Jeeves
Sam the Sudden
Service with a Smile
The Small Bachelor
Something Fishy
Something Fresh
Spring Fever
Stiff Upper Lip, Jeeves
Summer Lightning
Summer Moonshine
Sunset at Blandings
The Swoop
Tales of St Austin's
Thank You, Jeeves
Ukridge
Uncle Dynamite
Uncle Fred in the Springtime
Uneasy Money
Very Good, Jeeves
The White Feather
William Tell Told Again
Young Men in Spats

Omnibuses

The World of Blandings
The World of Jeeves
The World of Mr Mulliner
The World of Psmith
The World of Ukridge
The World of Uncle Fred
Wodehouse Nuggets
   (edited by Richard Usborne)
The Hollywood Omnibus
Weekend Wodehouse

Paperback Omnibuses

The Golf Omnibus
The Aunts Omnibus
The Drones Omnibus
The Clergy Omnibus
The Jeeves Omnibus 1
The Jeeves Omnibus 2
The Jeeves Omnibus 3
The Jeeves Omnibus 4

Poems

The Parrot and Other Poems

Autobiographical

Wodehouse on Wodehouse
   (comprising Bring on the Girls,
   Over Seventy, Performing Flea)

Letters

Yours, Plum

THE
JEEVES COLLECTION

Stiff Upper Lip, Jeeves
The Inimitable Jeeves
Carry On, Jeeves

P. G. Wodehouse

CHANCELLOR PRESS

A Cresset Press Book produced for Chancellor Press
This edition published in 1992
© in this collection the Trustees of the Estate of P. G. Wodehouse 1992
Stiff Upper Lip, Jeeves © P. G. Wodehouse 1963
The Inimitable Jeeves © P. G. Wodehouse 1923
Carry On, Jeeves © P. G. Wodehouse 1925

ISBN 1–85152–236–0

Printed and bound in Great Britain by
Mackays of Chatham PLC, Chatham, Kent

Contents

STIFF UPPER LIP, JEEVES

1

I marmaladed a slice of toast with something of a flourish, and I don't suppose I have ever come much closer to saying 'Tra-la-la' as I did the lathering, for I was feeling in mid-season form this morning. God, as I once heard Jeeves put it, was in His Heaven and all was right with the world. (He added, I remember, some guff about larks and snails, but that is a side issue and need not detain us.)

It is no secret in the circles in which he moves that Bertram Wooster, though as glamorous as one could wish when night has fallen and the revels get under way, is seldom a ball of fire at the breakfast table. Confronted with the eggs and b., he tends to pick cautiously at them, as if afraid they may leap from the plate and snap at him. Listless, about sums it up. Not much bounce to the ounce.

But today vastly different conditions had prevailed. All had been verve, if that's the word I want, and animation. Well, when I tell you that after sailing through a couple of sausages like a tiger of the jungles tucking into its luncheon coolie I was now, as indicated, about to tackle the toast and marmalade, I fancy I need say no more.

The reason for this improved outlook on the proteins and carbohydrates is not far to seek. Jeeves was back, earning his weekly envelope once more at the old stand. Her butler having come down with an ailment of some sort, my Aunt Dahlia, my good and deserving aunt, had borrowed him for a house party she was throwing at Brinkley Court, her Worcestershire residence, and he had been away for more than a week. Jeeves, of course, is a gentleman's gentleman, not a butler, but if the call comes, he can buttle with the best of them. It's in the blood. His Uncle Charlie is a butler, and no doubt he has picked up many a hint on technique from him.

He came in a little later to remove the debris, and I asked him if he had had a good time at Brinkley.

'Extremely pleasant, thank you, sir.'

'More than I had in your absence. I felt like a child of tender years deprived of its Nannie. If you don't mind me calling you a Nannie.'

'Not at all, sir.'

Though, as a matter of fact, I was giving myself a slight edge, putting it that way. My Aunt Agatha, the one who eats broken bottles and turns into a werewolf at the time of the full moon, generally refers to Jeeves as my keeper.

'Yes, I missed you sorely, and had no heart for whooping it up with the lads at the Drones. From sport to sport they . . . how does that gag go?'

'Sir?'

'I heard you pull it once with reference to Freddie Widgeon, when one of his girls had given him the bird. Something about hurrying.'

'Ah yes, sir. From sport to sport they hurry me, to stifle my regret —'

'And when they win a smile from me, they think that I forget. That was it. Not your own, by any chance?'

'No, sir. An old English drawing-room ballad.'

'Oh? Well, that's how it was with me. But tell me all about Brinkley. How was Aunt Dahlia?'

'Mrs. Travers appeared to be in her customary robust health, sir.'

'And how did the party go off?'

'Reasonably satisfactorily, sir.'

'Only reasonably?'

'The demeanour of Mr. Travers cast something of a gloom on the proceedings. He was low-spirited.'

'He always is when Aunt Dahlia fills the house with guests. I've known even a single foreign substance in the woodwork to make him drain the bitter cup.'

'Very true, sir, but on this occasion I think his despondency was due principally to the presence of Sir Watkyn Bassett.'

'You don't mean that old crumb was there?' I said, Great-Scott-ing, for I knew that if there is one man for whose insides my Uncle Tom has the most vivid distaste, it is this Bassett. 'You astound me, Jeeves.'

'I, too, must confess to a certain surprise at seeing the gentleman at Brinkley Court, but no doubt Mrs. Travers felt it incumbent upon her to return his hospitality. You will recollect that Sir Watkyn recently entertained Mrs. Travers and yourself at Totleigh Towers.'

I winced. Intending, I presumed, merely to refresh my memory, he had touched an exposed nerve. There was some cold coffee left in the pot, and I took a sip to restore my equanimity.

'The word "entertained" is not well chosen, Jeeves. If locking a fellow in his bedroom, as near as a toucher with gyves upon his wrists, and stationing the local police force on the lawn below to ensure that he doesn't nip out of the window at the end of a knotted sheet is your idea of entertaining, it isn't mine, not by a jugful.'

I don't know how well up you are in the Wooster archives, but if you have dipped into them to any extent, you will probably recall the sinister affair of Sir Watkyn Bassett and my visit to his Gloucestershire home. He and my Uncle Tom are rival collectors of what are known as objets d'art, and on one occasion he pinched a silver cow-creamer, as the revolting things are called, from the relation by marriage, and Aunt Dahlia and self went to Totleigh to pinch it back, an enterprise which, though crowned with success, as the expression is, so nearly landed me in the jug that when reminded of that house of horror I still quiver like an aspen, if aspens are the things I'm thinking of.

'Do you ever have nightmares, Jeeves?' I asked, having got through with my bit of wincing.

'Not frequently, sir.'

'Nor me. But when I do, the set-up is always the same. I am back at Totleigh Towers with Sir W. Bassett, his daughter Madeline, Roderick Spode, Stiffy Byng, Gussie Fink-Nottle and the dog Bartholomew, all doing their stuff, and I wake, if you will pardon the expression so soon after breakfast, sweating at every pore. Those were the times that . . . what, Jeeves?'

'Tried men's souls, sir.'

'They certainly did – in spades. Sir Watkyn Bassett, eh?' I said thoughtfully. 'No wonder Uncle Tom mourned and would not be comforted. In his position I'd have been low-spirited myself. Who else were among those present?'

'Miss Bassett, sir, Miss Byng, Miss Byng's dog and Mr. Fink-Nottle.'

'Gosh! Practically the whole Totleigh Towers gang. Not Spode?'

'No, sir. Apparently no invitation had been extended to his lordship.'

'His what?'

'Mr. Spode, if you recall, recently succeeded to the title of Lord Sidcup.'

'So he did. I'd forgotten. But Sidcup or no Sidcup, to me he will always be Spode. There's a bad guy, Jeeves.'

'Certainly a somewhat forceful personality, sir.'

'I wouldn't want him in my orbit again.'

'I can readily understand it, sir.'

'Nor would I willingly foregather with Sir Watkyn Bassett, Madeline Bassett, Stiffy Byng and Bartholomew. I don't mind Gussie. He looks like a fish and keeps newts in a glass tank in his bedroom, but one condones that sort of thing in an old schoolfellow, just as one condones in an old Oxford friend such as the Rev. H.P. Pinker the habit of tripping over his feet and upsetting things. How was Gussie? Pretty bobbish?'

'No, sir. Mr. Fink-Nottle, too, seemed to me low-spirited.'

'Perhaps one of his newts had got tonsilitis or something.'

'It is conceivable, sir.'

'You've never kept newts, have you?'

'No, sir.'

'Nor have I. Nor, to the best of my knowledge, have Einstein, Jack Dempsey and the Archbishop of Canterbury, to name but three others. Yet Gussie revels in their society and is never happier than when curled up with them. It takes all sorts to make a world, Jeeves.'

'It does, indeed, sir. Will you be lunching in?'

'No, I've a date at the Ritz,' I said, and went off to climb into the outer crust of the English gentleman.

As I dressed, my thoughts returned to the Bassetts, and I was still wondering why on earth Aunt Dahlia had allowed the pure air of Brinkley Court to be polluted by Sir Watkyn and associates, when the telephone rang and I went into the hall to answer it.

'Bertie?'

'Oh, hullo, Aunt Dahlia.'

There had been no mistaking that loved voice. As always when we converse on the telephone, it had nearly fractured my ear-drum. This aunt was at one time a prominent figure in hunting circles, and when in the saddle, so I'm told, could make herself heard not only in the field or meadow where she happened to be, but in several adjoining counties. Retired now from active fox-chivvying, she still tends to address a nephew in the tone of voice previously reserved for rebuking hounds for taking time off to chase rabbits.

'So you're up and about, are you?' she boomed. 'I thought you'd be in bed, snoring your head off.'

'It is a little unusual for me to be in circulation at this hour,' I agreed, 'but I rose today with the lark and, I think, the snail. Jeeves!'

'Sir?'

'Didn't you tell me once that snails were early risers?'

'Yes, sir. The poet Browning in his *Pippa Passes*, having established that the hour is seven a.m., goes on to say, "The lark's on the wing, the snail's on the thorn." '

'Thank you, Jeeves. I was right, Aunt Dahlia. When I slid from between the sheets, the lark was on the wing, the snail on the thorn.'

'What the devil are you babbling about?'

'Don't ask me, ask the poet Browning. I was merely apprising you that I was up betimes. I thought it was the least I could do to celebrate Jeeves's return.'

'He got back all right, did he?'

'Looking bronzed and fit.'

'He was in rare form here. Bassett was terrifically impressed.'

I was glad to have this opportunity of solving the puzzle which had been perplexing me.

'Now there,' I said, 'you have touched on something I'd very much like to have information *re*. What on earth made you invite Pop Bassett to Brinkley?'

'I did it for the wife and kiddies.'

I eh-what-ed. 'You wouldn't care to amplify that?' I said. 'It got past me to some extent.'

'For Tom's sake, I mean,' she replied with a hearty laugh that rocked me to my foundations. 'Tom's been feeling rather low of late because of what he calls iniquitous taxation. You know how he hates to give up.'

I did, indeed. If Uncle Tom had his way, the Revenue authorities wouldn't get so much as a glimpse of his money.

'Well, I thought having to fraternize with Bassett would take his mind off it – show him that there are worse things in this world than income tax. Our doctor here gave me the idea. He was telling me about a thing called Hodgkin's Disease that you cure by giving the patient arsenic. The principle's the same. That Bassett really is the limit. When I see you, I'll tell you the story of the black amber statuette. It's a thing he's just bought for his collection. He was showing it to Tom when he was here, gloating over it. Tom suffered agonies, poor old buzzard.'

'Jeeves told me he was low-spirited.'

'So would you be, if you were a collector and another collector you particularly disliked had got hold of a thing you'd have given your cyeteeth to have in your own collection.'

'I see what you mean,' I said, marvelling, as I had often done before, that Uncle Tom could attach so much value to objects which I personally would have preferred not to be found dead in a ditch with. The cow-creamer I mentioned earlier was one of them, being a milk jug shaped like a cow, of all ghastly ideas. I have always maintained fearlessly that the spiritual home of all these fellows who collect things is a padded cell in a loony bin.

'It gave Tom the worst attack of indigestion he's had since he was last lured into eating lobster. And talking of indigestion, I'm coming up to London for the day the day after tomorrow and shall require you to give me lunch.'

I assured her that that should be attended to, and after the exchange of a few more civilities she rang off.

'That was Aunt Dahlia, Jeeves,' I said, coming away from the machine.

'Yes, sir, I fancied I recognized Mrs. Travers's voice.'

'She wants me to give her lunch the day after tomorrow. I think we'd better have it here. She's not keen on restaurant cooking.'

'Very good, sir.'

'What's this black amber statuette thing she was talking about?'

'It is a somewhat long story, sir.'

'Then don't tell me now. If I don't rush, I shall be late for my date.'

I reached for the umbrella and hat, and was heading for the open spaces, when I heard Jeeves give that soft cough of his and, turning, saw that a shadow was about to fall on what had been a day of joyous reunion. In the eye which he was fixing on me I detected the aunt-like gleam which always means that he disapproves of something, and when he said in a soupy tone of voice 'Pardon me, sir, but are you proposing to enter the Ritz Hotel in that hat?' I knew that the time had come when Bertram must show that iron resolution of his which has been so widely publicized.

In the matter of head-joy Jeeves is not in tune with modern progressive thought, his attitude being best described, perhaps, as hidebound, and right from the start I had been asking myself what his reaction would be to the blue Alpine hat with the pink feather in it which I had purchased in his absence. Now I knew. I could see at a g. that he wanted no piece of it.

I, on the other hand, was all for this Alpine lid. I was prepared to concede that it would have been more suitable for rural wear, but against this had to be set the fact that it unquestionably lent a *diablerie* to my appearance, and mine is an appearance that needs all the *diablerie* it can get. In my voice, therefore, as I replied, there was a touch of steel.

'Yes, Jeeves, that, in a nutshell, is what I am proposing to do. Don't you like this hat?'

'No, sir.'

'Well, I do,' I replied rather cleverly, and went out with it tilted just that merest shade over the left eye which makes all the difference.

2

My date at the Ritz was with Emerald Stoker, younger offspring of that pirate of the Spanish Main, old Pop Stoker, the character who once kidnapped me on board his yacht with a view to making me marry his elder daughter Pauline. Long story, I won't go into it now, merely saying that the old fathead had got entirely the wrong angle on the relations between his ewe lamb and myself, we being just good friends, as the expression is. Fortunately it all ended happily, with the popsy linked in matrimony with Marmaduke, Lord Chuffnell, an ancient buddy of mine, and we're still good friends. I put in an occasional week-end with her and Chuffy, and when she comes to London on a shopping binge or whatever it may be, I see to it that she gets her calories. Quite natural, then, that when her sister Emerald came over from America to study painting at the Slade, she should have asked me to keep an eye on her and give her lunch from time to time. Kindly old Bertram, the family friend.

I was a bit late, as I had foreshadowed, in getting to the tryst, and she was already there when I arrived. It struck me, as it did every time I saw her, how strange it is that members of a family can be so unlike each other – how different in appearance, I mean, Member A. so often is from Member B., and for the matter of that Member B. from Member C., if you follow what I'm driving at. Take the Stoker troupe, for instance. To look at them, you'd never have guessed they were united by ties of blood. Old Stoker resembled one of those fellows who play bit parts in gangster pictures: Pauline was of a beauty so radiant that strong men whistled after her in the street; while Emerald, in sharp contra-distinction, was just ordinary, no different from a million other nice girls except perhaps for a touch of the Pekinese about the nose and eyes and more freckles than you usually see.

I always enjoyed putting on the nosebag with her, for there was a sort of motherliness about her which I found restful. She was one of those soothing, sympathetic girls you can take your troubles to, confident of having your hand held and your head patted. I was still a bit ruffled about Jeeves and the Alpine hat and of course told her all about it, and nothing could have been in better taste than her attitude. She said it sounded as if Jeeves must be something like her father – she had never met him – Jeeves, I mean, not her father, whom of course she had met frequently – and she told me I had been quite right in displaying the velvet hand in the iron glove, or rather the other way around, isn't it, because it never did to let oneself be bossed. Her father, she said, always tried to boss everybody, and in her opinion one of these days some haughty spirit was going to haul off and poke him in the nose – which, she said, and I agreed with her, would do him all the good in the world.

I was so grateful for these kind words that I asked her if she would care to come to the theatre on the following night, I knowing where I could get hold of a couple of tickets for a well-spoken-of musical, but she said she couldn't make it.

'I'm going down to the country this afternoon to stay with some people. I'm taking the four o'clock train at Paddington.'

'Going to be there long?'

'About a month.'

'At the same place all the time?'

'Of course.'

She spoke lightly, but I found myself eyeing her with a certain respect. Myself, I've never found a host and hostess who could stick my presence for more than about a week. Indeed, long before that as a general rule the conversation at the dinner table is apt to turn on the subject of how good the train service to London is, those present obviously hoping wistfully that Bertram will avail himself of it. Not to mention the time-tables left in your room with a large cross against the 2.35 and the legend 'Excellent train. Highly recommended.'

'Their name's Bassett.' I started visibly. 'They live in Gloucester-shire.' I started visibly. 'Their house is called –'

'Totleigh Towers?'

She started visibly, making three visible starts in all.

'Oh, do you know them? Well, that's fine. You can tell me about them.'

This surprised me somewhat.

'Why, don't *you* know them?'

'I've only met Miss Bassett. What are the rest of them like?'

It was a subject on which I was a well-informed source, but I hesitated for a moment, asking myself if I ought to reveal to this frail girl what she was letting herself in for. Then I decided that the truth must be told and nothing held back. Cruel to hide the facts from her and allow her to go off to Totleigh Towers unprepared.

'The inmates of the leper colony under advisement,' I said, 'consist of Sir Watkyn Bassett, his daughter Madeline, his niece Stephanie Byng, a chap named Spode who recently took to calling himself Lord Sidcup, and Stiffy Byng's Aberdeen terrier Bartholomew, the last of whom you would do well to watch closely if he gets anywhere near your ankles, for he biteth like a serpent and stingeth like an adder. So you've met Madeline Bassett? What did you think of her?'

She seemed to weigh this. A moment or two passed before she surfaced again. When she spoke, it was with a spot of wariness in her voice.

'Is she a great friend of yours?'

'Far from it.'

'Well, she struck me as a drip.'

'She is a drip.'

'Of course, she's very pretty. You have to hand her that.'

I shook the loaf.

'Looks are not everything. I admit that any redblooded Sultan or Pasha, if offered the opportunity of adding M. Bassett to the personnel of his harem, would jump to it without hesitation, but he would regret his impulsiveness before the end of the first week. She's one of those soppy girls, riddled from head to foot with whimsy. She holds the view that the stars are God's daisy chain, that rabbits are gnomes in attendance on the Fairy Queen, and that every time a fairy blows its wee nose a baby is born, which, as we know, is not the case. She's a drooper.'

'Yes, that's how she seemed to me. Rather like one of the lovesick maidens in *Patience*.'

'Eh?'

'*Patience*. Gilbert and Sullivan. Haven't you ever seen it?'

'Oh yes, now I recollect. My Aunt Agatha made me take her son Thos to it once. Not at all a bad little show, I thought, though a bit highbrow. We now come to Sir Watkyn Bassett, Madeline's father.'

'Yes, she mentioned her father.'

'And well she might.'

'What's he like?'

'One of those horrors from outer space. It may seem a hard thing to say of any man, but I would rank Sir Watkyn Bassett as an even bigger stinker than your father.'

'Would you call Father a stinker?'

'Not to his face, perhaps.'

'He thinks you're crazy.'

'Bless his old heart.'

'And you can't say he's wrong. Anyway, he's not so bad, if you rub him the right way.'

'Very possibly, but if you think a busy man like myself has time to go rubbing your father, either with or against the grain, you are greatly mistaken. The word "stinker", by the way, reminds me that there is one redeeming aspect of life at Totleigh Towers, the presence in the neighbouring village of the Rev. H.P. ("Stinker") Pinker, the local curate. You'll like him. He used to play football for England. But watch out for Spode. He's about eight feet high and has the sort of eye that can open an oyster at sixty paces. Take a line through gorillas you have met, and you will get the idea.'

'You do seem to have some nice friends.'

'No friends of mine. Though I'm fond of young Stiffy and am always prepared to clasp her to my bosom, provided she doesn't start something. But then she always does start something. I think that completes the roster. Oh no, Gussie. I was forgetting Gussie.'

'Who's he?'

'Fellow I've known for years and years. He's engaged to Madeline Bassett. Chap named Gussie Fink-Nottle.'

She uttered a sharp squeak.

'Does he wear horn-rimmed glasses?'

'Yes.'

'And keep newts?'

'In great profusion. Why, do you know him?'

'I've met him. We met at a studio party.'

'I didn't know he ever went to studio parties.'

'He went to this one, and we talked most of the evening. I thought he was a lamb.'

'You mean a fish.'

'I don't mean a fish.'

'He looks like a fish.'

'He does not look like a fish.'

'Well, have it your own way,' I said tolerantly, knowing it was futile to attempt to reason with a girl who had spent an evening vis-à-vis Gussie Fink-Nottle and didn't think he looked like a fish. 'So there you are, that's Totleigh Towers. Wild horses wouldn't drag me there, not that I suppose they would ever try, but you'll probably have a good enough time,' I said, for I didn't wish to depress her unduly. 'It's a beautiful place, and it isn't as if you were going there to pinch a cow-creamer.'

'To what a what?'

'Nothing, nothing. I was just thinking of something,' I said, and turned the conv. to other topics.

She gave me the impression, when we parted, of being a bit pensive, which I could well understand, and I wasn't feeling too unpensive myself. There's a touch of the superstitious in my make-up, and the way the Bassett ménage seemed to be raising its ugly head, if you know what I mean, struck me as sinister. I had a . . . what's the word? . . . begins with a p . . . pre-something . . . presentiment, that's the baby . . . I had a presentiment that I was being tipped off by my guardian angel that Totleigh Towers was trying to come back into my life and that I would be well advised to watch my step and keep an eye skinned.

It was consequently a thoughtful Bertram Wooster who half an hour later sat toying with a stoup of malvoisie in the smoking room of the Drones Club. To the overtures of fellow-members who wanted to hurry me from sport to sport I turned a deaf ear, for I wished to brood. And I was trying to tell myself that all this Totleigh Towers business was purely coincidental and meant nothing, when the smoking-room waiter slid up and informed me that a gentleman stood without, asking to have speech with me. A clerical gentleman named Pinker, he said, and I gave another of my visible starts, the presentiment stronger on the wing than ever.

It wasn't that I had any objection to the sainted Pinker. I loved him like a b. We were up at Oxford together, and our relations have always been on strictly David and Jonathan lines. But while technically not a resident of Totleigh Towers, he helped the Vicar vet the souls of the local yokels in the adjoining village of Totleigh-in-the-Wold, and that was near enough to it to make this sudden popping up of his deepen the apprehension I was feeling. It seemed to me that it only needed Sir Watkyn Bassett, Madeline Bassett, Roderick Spode and the dog Bartholomew to saunter in arm in arm, and I would have a full hand. My respect for my guardian angel's astuteness hit a new high. A gloomy bird, with a marked disposition to take the dark view and make one's flesh creep, but there was no gainsaying that he knew his stuff.

'Bung him in,' I said dully, and in due season the Rev. H.P. Pinker lumbered across the threshold and advancing with outstretched hand tripped over his feet and upset a small table, his almost invariable practice when moving from spot to spot in any room where there's furniture.

3

Which was odd, when you came to think of it, because after representing his University for four years and his country for six on the football field, he still turns out for the Harlequins when he can get a Saturday off from saving souls, and when footballing is as steady on his pins as a hart or roe or whatever the animals are that don't trip over their feet and upset things. I've seen him a couple of times in the arena, and was profoundly impressed by his virtuosity. Rugby football is more or less a sealed book to me, I never having gone in for it, but even I could see that he was good. The lissomness with which he moved hither and thither was most impressive, as was his homicidal ardour when doing what I believe is called tackling. Like the Canadian Mounted Police he always got his man, and when he did so the air was vibrant with the excited cries of morticians in the audience making bids for the body.

He's engaged to be married to Stiffy Byng, and his long years of football should prove an excellent preparation for setting up house with her. The way I look at it is that when a fellow has had pluguglies in cleated boots doing a Shuffle-Off-To-Buffalo on his face Saturday after Saturday since he was a slip of a boy, he must get to fear nothing, not even marriage with a girl like Stiffy, who from early childhood has seldom let the sun go down without starting some loony enterprise calculated to bleach the hair of one and all.

There was plenty and to spare of the Rev. H.P. Pinker. Even as a boy, I imagine, he must have burst seams and broken try-your-weight machines, and grown to man's estate he might have been Roderick Spode's twin brother. Purely in the matter of thews, sinews and tonnage, I mean of course, for whereas Roderick Spode went about seeking whom he might devour and was a consistent menace to pedestrians and traffic, Stinker, though no doubt a fiend in human shape when assisting the Harlequins Rugby football club to dismember some rival troupe of athletes, was in private life a gentle soul with whom a child could have played. In fact, I once saw a child doing so.

Usually when you meet this man of God, you find him beaming. I believe his merry smile is one of the sights of Totleigh-in-the-Wold, as it was of Magdalen College, Oxford, when we were up there together. But now I seemed to note in his aspect a certain gravity, as if he had just discovered a schism in his flock or found a couple of choir boys smoking reefers in the churchyard. He gave me the impression of a two-hundred-pound curate with something on his mind beside his hair. Upsetting another table, he took a seat and said he was glad he had caught me.

'I thought I'd find you at the Drones.'

'You have,' I assured him. 'What brings you to the metrop?'

'I came up for a Harlequins committee meeting.'

'And how were they all?'

'Oh, fine.'

'That's good. I've been worrying myself sick about the Harlequins committee. Well, how have you been keeping, Stinker?'

'I've been all right.'

'Are you free for dinner?'

'Sorry, I've got to get back to Totleigh.'

'Too bad. Jeeves tells me Sir Watkyn and Madeline and Stiffy have been staying with my aunt at Brinkley.'

'Yes.'

'Have they returned?'

'Yes.'

'And how's Stiffy?'

'Oh, fine.'

'And Bartholomew?'

'Oh, fine.'

'And your parishioners? Going strong, I trust?'

'Oh yes, they're fine.'

I wonder if anything strikes you about the slice of give-and-take I've just recorded. No? Oh, surely. I mean, here were we, Stinker Pinker and Bertram Wooster, buddies who had known each other virtually from the egg, and we were talking like a couple of strangers making conversation on a train. At least, he was, and more and more I became convinced that his bosom was full of the perilous stuff that weighs upon the heart, as I remember Jeeves putting it once.

I persevered in my efforts to uncork him.

'Well, Stinker,' I said, 'what's new? Has Pop Bassett given you that vicarage yet?'

This caused him to open up a bit. His manner became more animated.

'No, not yet. He doesn't seem able to make up his mind. One day he says he will, the next day he says he's not so sure, he'll have to think it over.'

I frowned. I disapproved of this shilly-shallying. I could see how it must be throwing a spanner into Stinker's whole foreign policy, putting him in a spot and causing him alarm and despondency. He can't marry Stiffy on a curate's stipend, so they've got to wait till Pop Bassett gives him a vicarage which he has in his gift. And while I personally, though fond of the young gumboil, would run a mile in tight shoes to avoid marrying Stiffy, I knew him to be strongly in favour of signing her up.

'Something always happens to put him off. I think he was about ready to close the deal before he went to stay at Brinkley, but most unfortunately I bumped into a valuable vase of his and broke it. It seemed to rankle rather.'

I heaved a sigh. It's always what Jeeves would call most disturbing to hear that a chap with whom you have plucked the gowans fine, as the expression is, isn't making out as well as could be wished. I was all set to follow this Pinker's career with considerable interest, but the way things were shaping it began to look as if there wasn't going to be a career to follow.

'You move in a mysterious way your wonders to perform, Stinker. I believe you would bump into something if you were crossing the Gobi desert.'

'I've never been in the Gobi desert.'

'Well, don't go. It isn't safe. I suppose Stiffy's sore about this . . . what's the word? . . . Not vaseline . . . Vacillation, that's it. She chafes, I imagine, at this vacillation on Bassett's part and resents him letting "I dare not" wait upon "I would", like the poor cat in the adage. Not my own, that, by the way. Jeeves's. Pretty steamed up, is she?'

'She is rather.'

'I don't blame her. Enough to upset any girl. Pop Bassett has no right to keep gumming up the course of true love like this.'

'No.'

'He needs a kick in the pants.'

'Yes.'

'If I were Stiffy, I'd put a toad in his bed or strychnine in his soup.'

'Yes. And talking of Stiffy, Bertie –'

He broke off, and I eyed him narrowly. There could be no question to my mind that I had been right about that perilous stuff. His bosom was obviously chock full of it.

'There's something the matter, Stinker.'

'No, there isn't. Why do you say that?'

'Your manner is strange. You remind me of a faithful dog looking up into its proprietor's face as if it were trying to tell him something. Are you trying to tell me something?'

He swallowed once or twice, and his colour deepened, which took a bit of doing, for even when his soul is in repose he always looks like a clerical beetroot. It was as though the collar he buttons at the back was choking him. In a hoarse voice he said:

'Bertie.'

'Hullo?'

'Bertie.'

'Still here, old man, and hanging on your lips.'

'Bertie, are you busy just now?'

'Not more than usual.'

'You could get away for a day or two?'

'I suppose one might manage it.'

'Then can you come to Totleigh?'

'To stay with you, do you mean?'

'No, to stay at Totleigh Towers.'

I stared at the man, wide-eyed as the expression is. Had it not been that I knew him to be abstemiousness itself, rarely indulging in anything stronger than a light lager, and not even that during Lent, I should have leaped to the conclusion that there beside me sat a curate who had been having a couple. My eyebrows rose till they nearly disarranged my front hair.

'Stay *where*? Stinker, you're not yourself, or you wouldn't be gibbering like this. You can't have forgotten the ordeal I passed through last time I went to Totleigh Towers.'

'I know. But there's something Stiffy wants you to do for her. She wouldn't tell me what it was, but she said it was most important and that you would have to be on the spot to do it.'

I drew myself up. I was cold and resolute.

'You're crazy, Stinker!'

'I don't see why you say that.'

'Then let me explain where your whole scheme falls to the ground. To begin with, is it likely that after what has passed between us Sir Watkyn B. would issue an invitation to one who has always been to him a pain in the neck to end all pains in the neck? If ever there was a man who was all in favour of me taking the high road while he took the low road, it is this same Bassett. His idea of a happy day is one spent with at least a hundred miles between him and Bertram.'

'Madeline would invite you, if you sent her a wire asking if you could come for a day or two. She never consults Sir Watkyn about guests. It's an understood thing that she has anyone she wants to at the house.'

This I knew to be true, but I ignored the suggestion and proceeded remorselessly.

'In the second place, I know Stiffy. A charming girl whom, as I was telling Emerald Stoker, I am always prepared to clasp to my bosom, at least I would be if she wasn't engaged to you, but one who is a cross between a ticking bomb and a poltergeist. She lacks that balanced judgment which we like to see in girls. She gets ideas, and if you care to call them bizarre ideas, it will be all right with me. I need scarcely remind you that when I last visited Totleigh Towers she egged you on to pinch Constable Eustace Oates's helmet, the one thing a curate should shrink from doing if he wishes to rise to heights in the Church. She is, in short, about as loony a young shrimp as ever wore a wind-swept hair-do. What this commission is that she has in mind for me we cannot say, but going by the form book I see it as something totally unfit for human consumption. Didn't she even hint at its nature?'

'No. I asked, of course, but she said she would rather keep it under her hat till she saw you.'

'She won't see me.'

'You won't come to Totleigh?'

'Not within fifty miles of the sewage dump.'

'She'll be terribly disappointed.'

'You will administer spiritual solace. That's your job. Tell her these things are sent to try us.'

'She'll probably cry.'

'Nothing better for the nervous system. It does something, I forget what, to the glands. Ask any well-known Harley Street physician.'

I suppose he saw that my iron front was not to be shaken, for he made no further attempt to sell the idea to me. With a sigh that seemed to come up from the soles of the feet, he rose, said goodbye, knocked over the glass from which I had been refreshing myself and withdrew.

Knowing how loath Bertram Wooster always is to let a pal down and fail him in his hour of need, you are probably thinking that this distressing scene had left me shaken, but as a matter of fact it had bucked me up like a day at the seaside.

Let's just review the situation. Ever since breakfast my guardian angel had been scaring the pants off me by practically saying in so many words that Totleigh Towers was all set to re-enter my life, and it was now clear that what he had had in mind had been the imminence of this plea to me to go there, he feeling that in a weak moment I might allow myself to be persuaded against my better judgment. The peril was now past. Totleigh Towers had made its spring and missed by a mile, and I no longer had a thing to worry about. It was with a light heart that I joined a group of pleasure-seekers who were playing Darts and cleaned them up with effortless skill. Three o'clock was approaching when I left the club en route for home, and it must have been getting on for half past when I hove alongside the apartment house where I have my abode.

There was a cab standing outside, laden with luggage. From its window Gussie Fink-Nottle's head was poking out, and I remember thinking once again how mistaken Emerald Stoker had been about his appearance. Seeing him steadily, if not whole, I could detect in his aspect no trace of the lamb, but he was looking so like a halibut that if he hadn't been wearing horn-rimmed spectacles, a thing halibuts seldom do, I might have supposed myself to be gazing on something a.w.o.l. from a fishmonger's slab.

I gave him a friendly yodel, and he turned the spectacles in my direction.

'Oh, hullo, Bertie,' he said, 'I've just been calling on you. I left a message with Jeeves. Your aunt told me to tell you she's coming to London the day after tomorrow and she wants you to give her lunch.'

'Yes, she was on the phone to that effect this morning. I suppose she thought you'd forget to notify me. Come in and have some orange juice,' I said, for it is to that muck that he confines himself whilst making whoopee.

He looked at his watch, and his eyes lost the gleam that always comes into them when orange juice is mentioned.

'I wish I could, but I can't,' he sighed. 'I should miss my train. I'm off to Totleigh on the four o'clock at Paddington.'

'Oh, really? Well, look out for a friend of yours, who'll be on it. Emerald Stoker.'

'Stoker? Stoker? Emerald Stoker?'

'Girl with freckles. American. Looks like a Pekinese of the better sort. She tells me she met you at a studio party the other day, and you talked about newts.'

His face cleared.

'Of course, yes. Now I've placed her. I didn't get her name that day. Yes, we had a long talk about newts. She used to keep them herself as a child, only she called them guppies. A most delightful girl. I shall enjoy seeing her again. I don't know when I've met a girl who attracted me more.'

'Except, of course, Madeline.'

His face darkened. He looked like a halibut that's taken offence at a rude remark from another halibut.

'Madeline! Don't talk to me about Madeline! Madeline makes me sick!' he hissed. 'Paddington!' he shouted to the charioteer and was gone with the wind, leaving me gaping after him, all of a twitter.

4

And I'll tell you why I was all of a t. My critique of her when chatting with Emerald Stoker will have shown how allergic I was to this Bassett beazel. She was scarcely less of a pain in the neck to me than I was to her father or Roderick Spode. Nevertheless, there was a grave danger that I might have to take her for better or for worse, as the book of rules puts it.

The facts may be readily related. Gussie, enamoured of the Bassett, would have liked to let her in on the way he felt, but every time he tried to do so his nerve deserted him and he found himself babbling about newts. At a loss to know how to swing the deal, he got the idea of asking me to plead his cause, and when I pleaded it, the Bassett, as pronounced a fathead as ever broke biscuit, thought I was pleading mine. She said she was so sorry to cause me pain, but her heart belonged to Gussie. Which would have been fine, had she not gone on to say that if anything should ever happen to make her revise her conviction that he was a king among men and she was compelled to give him the heave-ho, I was the next in line, and while she could never love me with the same fervour she felt for Gussie, she would do her best to make me happy. I was, in a word, in the position of a Vice-President of the United States of America who, while feeling that he is all right so far, knows that he will be for it at a moment's notice if anything goes wrong with the man up top.

Little wonder, then, that Gussie's statement that Madeline made him sick smote me like a ton of bricks and had me indoors and bellowing for Jeeves before you could say What ho. As had so often happened before, I felt that my only course was to place myself in the hands of a higher power.

'Sir?' he said, manifesting himself.

'A ghastly thing has happened, Jeeves! Disaster looms.'

'Indeed, sir? I am sorry to hear that.'

There's one thing you have to give Jeeves credit for. He lets the dead past bury its d. He and the young master may have had differences about Alpine hats with pink feathers in them, but when he sees the y.m. on the receiving end of the slings and arrows of outrageous fortune, he sinks his dudgeon and comes through with the feudal spirit at its best. So now, instead of being cold and distant and aloof, as a lesser man would have been, he showed the utmost agitation and concern. That is to say, he allowed one eyebrow to rise perhaps an eighth of an inch, which is as far as he ever goes in the way of expressing emotion.

'What would appear to be the trouble, sir?'

I sank into a chair and mopped the frontal bone. Not for many a long day had I been in such a doodah.

'I've just seen Gussie Fink-Nottle.'

'Yes, sir. Mr. Fink-Nottle was here a moment ago.'

'I met him outside. He was in a cab. And do you know what?'

'No, sir.'

'I happened to mention Miss Bassett's name, and he said – follow this closely, Jeeves – he said – I quote – "Don't talk to me about Madeline. Madeline makes me sick." Close quotes.'

'Indeed, sir?'

'Those are not the words of love.'

'No, sir.'

'They are the words of a man who for some reason not disclosed is fed to the front teeth with the adored object. I hadn't time to go into the matter, because a moment later he was off like a scalded cat to Paddington, but it's pretty clear there must have been a rift in the what-d'you-call-it. Begins with an l.'

'Would lute be the word for which you are groping, sir?'

'Possibly. I don't know that I'd care to bet on it.'

'The poet Tennyson speaks of the little rift within the lute, that by and by will make the music mute and ever widening slowly silence all.'

'Then lute it is. And we know what's going to happen if this particular lute goes phut.'

We exchanged significant glances. At least, I gave him a significant glance, and he looked like a stuffed frog, his habit when being discreet. He knows just how I'm situated as regards M. Bassett, but naturally we don't discuss it except by going into the sig-glance-stuffed-frog routine. I mean, you can't talk about a thing like that. I don't know if it would actually come under the head of speaking lightly of a woman's name, but it wouldn't be seemly, and the Woosters are sticklers for seemliness. So, for that matter, are the Jeeveses.

'What ought I to do, do you think?'

'Sir?'

'Don't stand there saying "Sir?" You know as well as I do that a situation has arisen which calls for the immediate coming of all good men to the aid of the party. It is of the essence that Gussie's engagement does not spring a leak. Steps must be taken.'

'It would certainly seem advisable, sir.'

'But what steps? I ought, of course, to hasten to the seat of war and try to start the dove of peace going into its act – have a bash, in other words, at seeing what a calm, kindly man of the world can do to bring the young folks together, if you get what I mean.'

'I apprehend you perfectly, sir. Your role, as I see it, would be that of what the French call the *raisonneur*.'

'You're probably right. But mark this. Apart from the fact that the mere thought of being under the roof of Totleigh Towers again is one that freezes the gizzard, there's another snag. I was talking to Stinker Pinker just now, and he says that Stiffy Byng has something she wants me to do for her. Well, you know the sort of thing Stiffy generally wants people to do. You recall the episode of Constable Oates's helmet?'

'Very vividly, sir.'

'Oates had incurred her displeasure by reporting to her Uncle Watkyn that her dog Bartholomew had spilled him off his bicycle, causing him to fall into a ditch and sustain bruises and contusions, and she persuaded Harold Pinker, a man in holy orders who buttons his collar at the back, to pinch his helmet for her. And that was comparatively mild for Stiffy. There are no limits, literally none, to what she can think of when she gives her mind to it. The imagination boggles at the thought of what she may be cooking up for me.'

'Certainly you may be pardoned for feeling apprehensive, sir.'

'So there you are. I'm on the horns of . . . what are those things you get on the horns of?'

'Dilemmas, sir.'

'That's right. I'm on the horns of a dilemma. Shall I, I ask myself, go and see what I can accomplish in the way of running repairs on the lute, or would it be more prudent to stay put and let nature take its course, trusting to Time, the great healer, to do its stuff?'

'If I might make a suggestion, sir?'

'Press on, Jeeves.'

'Would it not be possible for you to go to Totleigh Towers, but to decline to carry out Miss Byng's wishes?'

I weighed this. It was, I could see, a thought.

'Issue a *nolle prosequi*, you mean? Tell her to go and boil her head?'

'Precisely, sir.'

I eyed him reverently.

'Jeeves,' I said, 'as always, you have found the way. I'll wire Miss Bassett asking if I can come, and I'll wire Aunt Dahlia that I can't give her lunch, as I'm leaving town. And I'll tell Stiffy that whatever she has in mind, she gets no service and co-operation from me. Yes, Jeeves, you've hit it. I'll go to Totleigh, though the flesh creeps at the prospect. Pop Bassett will be there. Spode will be there. Stiffy will be there. The dog Bartholomew will be there. It makes one wonder why so much fuss has been made about those half-a-league half-a-league half-a-league-onward bimbos who rode into the Valley of Death. They weren't going to find Pop Bassett at the other end. Ah well, let us hope for the best.'

'The only course to pursue, sir.'

'Stiff upper lip, Jeeves, what?'

'Indubitably, sir. That, if I may say so, is the spirit.'

5

As Stinker had predicted, Madeline Bassett placed no obstacle in the way of my visiting Totleigh Towers. In response to my invitation-cadging missive she gave me the green light, and an hour or so after her telegram had arrived Aunt Dahlia rang up from Brinkley, full of eagerness to ascertain what the hell, she having just received my wire saying that owing to absence from the metropolis I would be unable to give her the lunch for which she had been budgeting.

Her call came as no surprise. I had anticipated that there might be a certain liveliness on the Brinkley front. The old flesh-and-blood is a genial soul who loves her Bertram dearly, but she is a woman of imperious spirit. She dislikes having her wishes thwarted, and her voice came booming at me like a pack of hounds in full cry.

'Bertie, you foul young blot on the landscape!'

'Speaking.'

'I got your telegram.'

'I thought you would. Very efficient, the gramming service.'

'What do you mean, you're leaving town? You never leave town except to come down here and wallow in Anatole's cooking.'

Her allusion was to her peerless French chef, at the mention of whose name the mouth starts watering automatically. God's gift to the gastric juices I have sometimes called him.

'Where are you going?'

My mouth having stopped watering, I said I was going to Totleigh Towers, and she uttered an impatient snort.

'There's something wrong with this blasted wire. It sounded as if you were saying you were going to Totleigh Towers.'

'I am.'

'To Totleigh *Towers*?'

'I leave this afternoon.'

'What in the world made them invite you?'

'They didn't. I invited myself.'

'You mean you're deliberately seeking the society of Sir Watkyn Bassett? You must be more of an ass than even I have ever thought you. And I speak as a woman who has just had the old bounder in her hair for more than a week.'

I saw her point, and hastened to explain.

'I admit Pop Bassett is a bit above the odds,' I said, 'and unless one is compelled by circumstances it is always wisest not to stir him, but a sharp crisis has been precipitated in my affairs. All is not well between Gussie Fink-Nottle and Madeline Bassett. Their engagement is tottering toward the melting pot, and you know what that engagement means to me. I'm going down there to try to heal the rift.'

'What can you do?'

'My role, as I see it, will be that of what the French call the *raisonneur*.'

'And what does that mean?'

'Ah, there you have me, but that's what Jeeves says I'll be.'

'Are you taking Jeeves with you?'

'Of course. Do I ever stir foot without him?'

'Well, watch out, that's all I say to you, watch out. I happen to know that Bassett is making overtures to him.'

'How do you mean, overtures?'

'He's trying to steal him from you.'

I reeled, and might have fallen, had I not been sitting at the time. 'Incredulous!'

'If you mean incredible, you're wrong. I told you how he had fallen under Jeeves's spell when he was here. He used to follow him with his eyes as he buttled, like a cat watching a duck, as Anatole would say. And one morning I heard him making him a definite proposition. Well? What's the matter with you? Have you fainted?'

I told her that my momentary silence had been due to the fact that her words had stunned me, and she said she didn't see why, knowing Bassett, I should be so surprised.

'You can't have forgotten how he tried to steal Anatole. There isn't anything to which that man won't stoop. He has no conscience whatsoever. When you get to Totleigh, go and see someone called Plank and ask him what he thinks of Sir Watkyn ruddy Bassett. He chiselled this poor devil Plank out of a . . . Oh, hell!' said the aged relative as a voice intoned 'Thur-ree minutes', and she hung up, having made my flesh creep as nimbly as if she had been my guardian angel, on whose talent in that direction I have already touched.

It was still creeping with undiminished gusto as I steered the sports model along the road to Totleigh-in-the-Wold that afternoon. I was convinced, of course, that Jeeves would never dream of severing relations with the old firm, and when urged to do so by this blighted Bassett would stop his ears like the deaf adder, which, as you probably know, made a point of refusing to hear the voice of the charmer, charm he never so wisely. But the catch is that you can be convinced about a thing and nevertheless get pretty jumpy when you muse on it, and it was in no tranquil mood that I eased the Arab steed through the gates of Totleigh Towers and fetched up at the front door.

I don't know if you happen to have come across a hymn, the chorus of which goes:

> Tum tumty tumty tumty
> Tum tiddly om pom isle,
> Where every prospect pleases
> And only man is vile

or words to that effect, but the description would have fitted Totleigh Towers like the paper on the wall. Its façade, its spreading grounds, rolling parkland, smoothly shaven lawns and what not were all just like Mother makes, but what percentage was there in that, when you knew what was waiting for you inside? It's never a damn bit of use a prospect pleasing, if the gang that goes with it lets it down.

This lair of old Bassett's was one of the fairly stately homes of England – not a show place like the joints you read about with three hundred and sixty-five rooms, fifty-two staircases and twelve court-yards, but definitely not a bungalow. He had bought it furnished some time previously from a Lord somebody who needed cash, as so many do these days.

Not Pop Bassett, though. In the evening of his life he had more than a sufficiency. It would not be going too far, indeed, to describe him as stinking rich. For a great part of his adult life he had been a metropolitan police magistrate, and in that capacity once fined me five quid for a mere light-hearted peccadillo on Boat Race Night, when a mild reprimand would more than have met the case. It was shortly after this that a relative died and left him a vast fortune. That, at least, was the story given out. What really happened, of course, was that all through his years as a magistrate he had been trousering the fines, amassing the stuff in sackfuls. Five quid here, five quid there, it soon mounts up.

We had made goodish going on the road, and it wasn't more than about four-forty when I rang the front-door bell. Jeeves took the car to the stables, and the butler – Butterfield was his name, I remembered – led me to the drawing-room.

'Mr. Wooster,' he said, loosing me in.

I was not surprised to find tea in progress, for I had heard the clinking of cups. Madeline Bassett was at the controls, and she extended a drooping hand to me.

'Bertie! How nice to see you.'

I can well imagine that a casual observer, if I had confided to him my qualms at the idea of being married to this girl, would have raised his eyebrows and been at a loss to understand, for she was undeniably an eyeful, being slim, svelte and bountifully equipped with golden hair and all the fixings. But where the casual observer would have been making his bloomer was in overlooking that squashy soupiness of hers, that subtle air she had of being on the point of talking babytalk. She was the sort of girl who puts her hands over a husband's eyes, as he is crawling in to breakfast with a morning head, and says 'Guess who?'

I once stayed at the residence of a newly-married pal of mine, and his bride had had carved in large letters over the fireplace in the drawing-room, where it was impossible to miss it, the legend 'Two Lovers Built This Nest', and I can still recall the look of dumb anguish in the other half of the sketch's eyes every time he came in and saw it. Whether Madeline Bassett, on entering the marital state, would go to such an awful extreme, one could not say, but it seemed most probable, and I resolved that when I started trying to reconcile her and Gussie, I would not scamp my work but would give it everything I had.

'You know Mr. Pinker,' she said, and I perceived that Stinker was present. He was safely wedged in a chair and hadn't, as far as I could see, upset anything yet, but he gave me the impression of a man who was crouching for the spring and would begin to operate shortly. There was a gate-leg table laden with muffins and cucumber sandwiches which I foresaw would attract him like a magnet.

On seeing me, he had started visibly, dropping a plate with half a muffin on it, and his eyes had widened. I knew what he was thinking, of course. He supposed that my presence must be due to a change of heart. Rejoice with me, for I have found the sheep which was lost, he was no doubt murmuring to himself. I mourned in spirit a bit for the poor fish, knowing what a nasty knock he had coming to him when he got on to it that nothing was going to induce me to undertake whatever the foul commission might be that Stiffy had earmarked for me. On that point I was resolved to be firm, no matter what spiritual agonies he and she suffered in the process. I had long since learned that the secret of a happy and successful life was to steer clear of any project masterminded by that young scourge of the species.

The conversation that followed was what you might call . . . I've forgotten the word, but it begins with a d. I mean, with Stinker within earshot Madeline and I couldn't get down to brass tacks, so we just chewed the fat . . . desultory, that's the word I wanted. We just chewed the fat in a desultory way. Stinker said he was there to talk over the forthcoming school treat with Sir Watkyn, and I said 'Oh, is there a school treat coming up?' and Madeline said it was taking place the day after tomorrow and owing to the illness of the vicar Mr. Pinker would be in sole charge, and Stinker winced a bit, as if he didn't like the prospect much.

Madeline asked if I had had a nice drive down, and I said 'Oh, splendid.' Stinker said Stiffy would be so pleased I had come, and I smiled one of my subtle smiles. And then Butterfield came in and said Sir Watkyn could see Mr. Pinker now, and Stinker oozed off. And the moment the door had closed behind curate and butler, Madeline clasped her hands, gave me one of those squashy looks, and said:

'Oh, Bertie, you should not have come here. I had not the heart to deny your pathetic request – I knew how much you yearned to see me again, however briefly, however hopelessly – but was it *wise*? Is it not merely twisting the knife in the wound? Will it not simply cause you needless pain to be near me, knowing we can never be more than just good friends? It is useless, Bertie. You must not hope. I love Augustus.'

Her words, as you may well imagine, were music to my e. She wouldn't, I felt, have come out with anything as definite as this if there had been a really serious spot of trouble between her and Gussie. Obviously that crack of his about her making him sick had been a mere passing what-d'you-call-it, the result of some momentary attack of the pip caused possibly by her saying he smoked too much or something of the sort. Anyway, whatever it was that had rifted the lute was now plainly forgotten and forgiven, and I was saying to myself that, the way things looked, I ought to be able to duck out of here immediately after breakfast tomorrow, when I noticed that a look of pain had spread over her map and that the eyes were dewy.

'It makes me so sad to think of your hopeless love, Bertie,' she said, adding something which I didn't quite catch about moths and stars. 'Life is so tragic, so cruel. But what can I do?'

'Not a thing,' I said heartily. 'Just carry on regardless.'

'But it breaks my heart.'

And with these words she burst into what are sometimes called uncontrollable sobs. She sank into her chair, covering her face with her hands, and it seemed to me that the civil thing to do was to pat her head. This project I now carried out, and I can see, looking back, that it was a mistake. I remember Monty Bodkin of the Drones, who once patted a weeping female on the head, unaware that his betrothed was standing in his immediate rear, drinking the whole thing in, telling me that the catch in this head-patting routine is that, unless you exercise the greatest care, you forget to take your hand off. You just stand there resting it on the subject's bean, and this is apt to cause spectators to purse their lips.

Monty fell into this error and so did I. And the lip-pursing was attended to by Spode, who chanced to enter at this moment. Seeing the popsy bathed in tears, he quivered from stem to stern.

'Madeline!' he yipped. 'What's the matter?'

'It is nothing, Roderick, nothing,' she replied chokingly.

She buzzed off, no doubt to bathe her eyes, and Spode pivoted round and gave me a penetrating look. He had grown a bit, I noticed, since I had last seen him, being now about nine foot seven. In speaking of him to Emerald Stoker I had, if you remember, compared him to a gorilla, and what I had had in mind had been the ordinary run-of-the-mill gorilla, not the large economy size. What he was looking like now was King Kong. His fists were clenched, his eyes glittered, and the dullest observer could have divined that it was in no sunny spirit that he was regarding Bertram.

6

To ease the strain, I asked him if he would have a cucumber sandwich, but with an impassioned gesture he indicated that he was not in the market for cucumber sandwiches, though I could have told him, for I had found them excellent, that he was passing up a good thing.

'A muffin?'

No, not a muffin, either. He seemed to be on a diet.

'Wooster,' he said, his jaw muscles moving freely, 'I can't make up my mind whether to break your neck or not.'

'Not' would have been the way my vote would have been cast, but he didn't give me time to say so.

'I was amazed when I heard from Madeline that you had had the effrontery to invite yourself here. Your motive, of course, was clear. You have come to try to undermine her faith in the man she loves and sow doubts in her mind. Like a creeping snake,' he added, and I was interested to learn that this was what snakes did. 'You had not the elementary decency, when she had made her choice, to accept her decision and efface yourself. You hoped to win her away from Fink-Nottle.'

Feeling that it was about time I said something, I got as far as 'I –', but he shushed me with another of those impassioned gestures. I couldn't remember when I'd met anyone so resolved on hogging the conversation.

'No doubt you will say that your love was so overpowering that you could not resist the urge to tell her of it and plead with her. Utter nonsense. Despicable weakness. Let me tell you, Wooster, that I have loved that girl for years and years, but never by word or look have I so much as hinted it to her. It was a great shock to me when she became engaged to this man Fink-Nottle, but I accepted the situation because I thought that that was where her happiness lay. Though stunned, I kept –'

'A stiff upper lip?'

'– my feelings to myself. I sat –'

'Like Patience on a monument.'

'– tight, and said nothing that would give her a suspicion of how I felt. All that mattered was that she should be happy. If you ask me if I approve of Fink-Nottle as a husband for her, I admit frankly that I do not. To me he seems to possess all the qualities that go to make the perfect pill, and I may add that my opinion is shared by her father. But he is the man she has chosen and I abide by her choice. I do not crawl behind Fink-Nottle's back and try to prejudice her against him.'

'Very creditable.'

'What did you say?'

I said I had said it did him credit. Very white of him, I said I thought it.

'Oh? Well, I suggest to you, Wooster, that you follow my example. And let me tell you that I shall be watching you closely, and I shall expect to see less of this head-stroking you were doing when I came in. If I don't, I'll –'

Just what he proposed to do he did not reveal, though I was able to hazard a guess, for at this moment Madeline returned. Her eyes were pinkish and her general aspect down among the wines and spirits.

'I will show you your room, Bertie,' she said in a pale, saintlike voice, and Spode gave me a warning look.

'Be careful, Wooster, be very careful,' he said as we went out.

Madeline seemed surprised.

'Why did Roderick tell you to be careful?'

'Ah, that we shall never know. Afraid I might slip on the parquet floor, do you think?'

'He sounded as if he was angry with you. Had you been quarrelling?'

'Good heavens, no. Our talk was conducted throughout in an atmosphere of the utmost cordiality.'

'I thought he might be annoyed at your coming here.'

'On the contrary. Nothing could have exceeded the warmth of his "Welcome to Totleigh Towers".'

'I'm so glad. It would pain me so much if you and he were . . . Oh, there's Daddy.'

We had reached the upstairs corridor, and Sir Watkyn Bassett was emerging from his room, humming a light air. It died on his lips as he saw me, and he stood staring at me aghast. He reminded me of one of those fellows who spend the night in haunted houses and are found next morning dead to the last drop with a look of awful horror on their faces.

'Oh, Daddy,' said Madeline. 'I forgot to tell you. I asked Bertie to come here for a few days.'

Pop Bassett swallowed painfully.

'When you say a few days – ?'

'At least a week, I hope.'

'Good God!'

'If not longer.'

'Great heavens!'

'There is tea in the drawing-room, Daddy.'

'I need something stronger than tea,' said Pop Bassett in a low, husky voice, and he tottered off, a broken man. The sight of his head disappearing as he made for the lower regions where the snootful awaited him brought to my mind a poem I used to read as a child. I've forgotten most of it, but it was about a storm at sea and the punch line ran "We are lost," the captain shouted, as he staggered down the stairs.'

'Daddy seems upset about something,' said Madeline.

'He did convey that impression,' I said, speaking austerely, for the old blister's attitude had offended me. I could make allowances for him, because naturally a man of regular habits doesn't like suddenly finding Woosters in his midst, but I did feel that he might have made more of an effort to bear up. Think of the Red Indians, Bassett, I would have said to him, had we been on better terms, pointing out that they were never in livelier spirits than when being cooked on both sides at the stake.

This painful encounter, following so quickly on my conversation, if you could call it a conversation, with Spode, might have been expected to depress me, but this was far from being the case. I was so uplifted by the official news that all was well between M. Bassett and G. Fink-Nottle that I gave it little thought. It's never, of course, the ideal set-up to come to stay at a house where your host shudders to the depths of his being at the mere sight of you and is compelled to rush to where the bottles are and get a restorative, but the Woosters can take the rough with the s., and the bonging of the gong for dinner some little time later found me in excellent fettle. It was to all intents and purposes with a song on my lips that I straightened my tie and made my way to the trough.

Dinner is usually the meal at which you catch Bertram at his best, and certainly it's the meal I always most enjoy. Many of my happiest hours have been passed in the society of the soup, the fish, the pheasant or whatever it may be, the soufflé, the fruits in their season and the spot of port to follow. They bring out the best in me. 'Wooster,' those who know me have sometimes said, 'may be a pretty total loss during the daytime hours, but plunge the world in darkness, switch on the soft lights, uncork the champagne and shove a dinner into him, and you'd be surprised.'

But if I am to sparkle and charm all and sundry, I make one provision – viz. that the company be congenial. And anything less congenial than the Co. on this occasion I have seldom encountered. Sir Watkyn Bassett, who was plainly still much shaken at finding me on the premises, was very far from being the jolly old Squire who makes the party go from the start. Beyond shooting glances at me over his glasses, blinking as if he couldn't bring himself to believe I was real and looking away with a quick shudder, he contributed little or nothing to what I have heard Jeeves call the feast of reason and the flow of soul. Add Spode, strong and silent, Madeline Bassett, mournful and drooping, Gussie, also apparently mournful, and Stiffy, who seemed to be in a kind of daydream, and you had something resembling a wake of the less rollicking type.

Sombre, that's the word I was trying to think of. The atmosphere was sombre. The whole binge might have been a scene from one of those Russian plays my Aunt Agatha sometimes makes me take her son Thos to at the Old Vic in order to improve his mind, which, as is widely known, can do with all the improvement that's coming to it.

It was toward the middle of the meal that, feeling that it was about time somebody said something, I drew Pop Bassett's attention to the table's centrepiece. In any normal house it would have been a bowl of flowers or something of that order, but this being Totleigh Towers it was a small black figure carved of some material I couldn't put a name to. It was so gosh-awful in every respect that I presumed it must be something he had collected recently. My Uncle Tom is always coming back from sales with similar eyesores.

'That's new, isn't it?' I said, and he started violently. I suppose he'd just managed to persuade himself that I was merely a mirage and had been brought up with a round turn on discovering that I was there in the flesh.

'That thing in the middle of the table that looks like the end man in a minstrel show. It's something you got since . . . er . . . since I was here last, isn't it?'

Tactless of me, I suppose, to remind him of that previous visit of mine, and I oughtn't to have brought it up, but these things slip out.

'Yes,' he said, having paused for a moment to shudder. 'It is the latest addition to my collection.'

'Daddy bought it from a man named Plank who lives not far from here at Hockley-cum-Meston,' said Madeline.

'Attractive little bijou,' I said. It hurt me to look at it, but I felt that nothing was to be lost by giving him the old oil. 'Just the sort of thing Uncle Tom would like to have. By Jove,' I said, remembering, 'Aunt Dahlia was speaking to me about it on the phone yesterday, and she told me Uncle Tom would give his eyeteeth to have it in his collection. I'm not surprised. It looks valuable.'

'It's worth a thousand pounds,' said Stiffy, coming out of her coma and speaking for the first time.

'As much as that? Golly!' Amazing, I was thinking, that magistrates could get to be able to afford expenditure on that scale just by persevering through the years fining people and sticking to the money. 'What is it? Soapstone?'

I had said the wrong thing.

'Amber,' Pop Bassett snapped, giving me the sort of look he had given me in heaping measure on the occasion when I had stood in the dock before him at Bosher Street police court. 'Black amber.'

'Of course, yes. That's what Aunt Dahlia said, I recall. She spoke very highly of it, let me tell you, extremely highly.'

'Indeed?'

'Oh, absolutely.'

I had been hoping that this splash of dialogue would have broken the ice, so to speak, and started us off kidding back and forth like the guys and dolls in one of those old-world salons you read about. But no. Silence fell again, and eventually, at long last, the meal came to an end, and two minutes later I was on my way to my room, where I proposed to pass the rest of the evening with an Erle Stanley Gardner I'd brought with me. No sense, as I saw it, in going and mixing with the mob in the drawing-room and having Spode glare at me and Pop Bassett sniff at me and Madeline Bassett as likely as not sing old English folk songs at me till bedtime. I was aware that in executing this quiet sneak I was being guilty of a social *gaffe* which would have drawn raised eyebrows from the author of a book of etiquette, but the great lesson we learn from life is to know when and when not to be in the centre of things.

7

I haven't mentioned it till now, having been all tied up with other matters, but during dinner, as you may well imagine, something had been puzzling me not a little – the mystery, to wit, of what on earth had become of Emerald Stoker.

At that lunch of ours she had told me in no uncertain terms that she was off to Totleigh on the four o'clock train that afternoon, and however leisurely its progress it must have got there by this time, because Gussie had travelled on it and he had fetched up at the joint all right. But I could detect no sign of her on the premises. It seemed to me, sifting the evidence, that only one conclusion could be arrived at, that she had been pulling the Wooster leg.

But why? With what motive? That was what I was asking myself as I sneaked up the stairs to where Erle Stanley Gardner awaited me. If you had cared to describe me as perplexed and bewildered, you would have been perfectly correct.

Jeeves was in my room when I got there, going about his gentleman's gentlemanly duties, and I put my problem up to him.

'Did you ever see a film called *The Vanishing Lady*, Jeeves?'

'No, sir. I rarely attend cinematographic performances.'

'Well, it was about a lady who vanished, if you follow what I mean, and the reason I bring it up is that a female friend of mine has apparently disappeared into thin air, leaving not a wrack behind, as I once heard you put it.'

'Highly mysterious, sir.'

'You said it. I seek in vain for a solution. When I gave her lunch yesterday, she told me she was off on the four o'clock train to go and stay at Totleigh Towers, and the point I want to drive home is that she hasn't arrived. You remember the day I lunched at the Ritz?'

'Yes, sir. You were wearing an Alpine hat.'

'There is no need to dwell on the Alpine hat, Jeeves.'

'No, sir.'

'If you really want to know, several fellows at the Drones asked me where I had got it.'

'No doubt with a view to avoiding your hatter, sir.'

I saw that nothing was to be gained by bandying words. I turned the conversation to a pleasanter and less controversial subject.

'Well, Jeeves, you'll be glad to hear that everything's all right.'

'Sir?'

'About that lute we were speaking of. No rift. Sound as a bell. I have it straight from the horse's mouth that Miss Bassett and Gussie are sweethearts still. The relief is stupendous.'

I hadn't expected him to clap his hands and leap about, because of course he never does, but I wasn't prepared for the way he took this bit of hot news. He failed altogether to string along with my jocund mood.

'I fear, sir, that you are too sanguine. Miss Bassett's attitude may well be such as you have described, but on Mr. Fink-Nottle's side, I am sorry to say there exists no little dissatisfaction and resentment.'

The smile which had been splitting my face faded. It's never easy to translate what Jeeves says into basic English, but I had been able to grab this one off the bat, and what I believe the French call a *frisson* went through me like a dose of salts.

'You mean she's a sweetheart still, but he isn't?'

'Precisely, sir. I encountered Mr. Fink-Nottle in the stable yard as I was putting away the car, and he confided his troubles to me. His story occasioned me grave uneasiness.'

Another *frisson* passed through my frame. I had the unpleasant feeling you get sometimes that centipedes in large numbers are sauntering up and down your spinal column. I feared the worst.

'But what's happened?' I faltered, if faltered's the word.

'I regret to inform you, sir, that Miss Bassett has insisted on Mr. Fink-Nottle adopting a vegetarian diet. His mood is understandably disgruntled and rebellious.'

I tottered. In my darkest hour I had never anticipated anything as bad as this. You wouldn't think it to look at him, because he's small and shrimplike and never puts on weight, but Gussie loves food. Watching him tucking into his rations at the Drones, a tapeworm would raise its hat respectfully, knowing that it was in the presence of a master. Cut him off, therefore, from the roasts and boileds and particularly from cold steak and kidney pie, a dish of which he is inordinately fond, and you turned him into something fit for treasons, stratagems and spoils, as the fellow said – the sort of chap who would break an engagement as soon as look at you. At the moment of my entry I had been about to light a cigarette, and now the lighter fell from my nerveless hand.

'She's made him become a *vegetarian*?'

'So Mr. Fink-Nottle informed me, sir.'

'No chops?'

'No, sir.'

'No steaks?'

'No, sir.'

'Just spinach and similar garbage?'

'So I gather, sir.'

'But why?'

'I understand that Miss Bassett has recently been reading the life of the poet Shelley, sir, and has become converted to his view that the consumption of flesh foods is unspiritual. The poet Shelley held strong opinions on this subject.'

I picked up the lighter in a sort of trance. I was aware that Madeline B. was as potty as they come in the matter of stars and rabbits and what happened when fairies blew their wee noses, but I had never dreamed that her goofiness would carry her to such lengths as this. But as the picture rose before my eyes of Gussie at the dinner table picking with clouded brow at what had unquestionably looked like spinach, I knew that his story must be true. No wonder Gussie in agony of spirit had said that Madeline made him sick. Just so might a python at a Zoo have spoken of its keeper, had the latter suddenly started feeding it cheese straws in lieu of the daily rabbit.

'But this is frightful, Jeeves!'

'Certainly somewhat disturbing, sir.'

'If Gussie is seething with revolt, anything may happen.'

'Yes, sir.'

'Is there nothing we can do?'

'It might be possible for you to reason with Miss Bassett, sir. You would have a talking point. Medical research has established that the ideal diet is one in which animal and vegetable foods are balanced. A strict vegetarian diet is not recommended by the majority of doctors, as it lacks sufficient protein and in particular does not contain the protein which is built up of the amino-acids required by the body. Competent observers have traced some cases of mental disorder to this shortage.'

'You'd tell her that?'

'It might prove helpful, sir.'

'I doubt it,' I said, blowing a despondent smoke ring. 'I don't think it would sway her.'

'Nor on consideration do I, sir. The poet Shelley regarded the matter from the humanitarian standpoint rather than that of bodily health.

He held that we should show reverence for other life forms, and it is his views that Miss Bassett has absorbed.'

A hollow groan escaped me.

'Curse the poet Shelley! I hope he trips over a loose shoelace and breaks his ruddy neck.'

'Too late, sir. He is no longer with us.'

'Blast all vegetables!'

'Yes, sir. Your concern is understandable. I may mention that the cook expressed herself in a somewhat similar vein when I informed her of Mr. Fink-Nottle's predicament. Her heart melted in sympathy with his distress.'

I was in no mood to hear about cooks' hearts, soluble or otherwise, and I was about to say so, when he proceeded.

'She instructed me to apprise Mr. Fink-Nottle that if he were agreeable to visiting the kitchen at some late hour when the household had retired for the night, she would be happy to supply him with cold steak and kidney pie.'

It was as if the sun had come smiling through the clouds or the long shot on which I had placed my wager had nosed its way past the opposition in the last ten yards and won by a short head. For the peril that had threatened to split the Bassett-Fink-Nottle axis had been averted. I knew Gussie from soup to nuts. Cut him off from the proteins and the amino-acids, and you soured his normally amiable nature, turning him into a sullen hater of his species who asked nothing better than to bite his n. and dearest and bite them good. But give him this steak and kidney pie outlet, thus allowing him to fulfil what they call his legitimate aspirations, and chagrin would vanish and he would become his old lovable self once more. The dark scowl would be replaced by the tender simper, the acid crack by the honeyed word, and all would be hotsy-totsy once more with his love life. My bosom swelled with gratitude to the cook whose quick thinking had solved the problem and brought home the bacon.

'Who is she, Jeeves?'

'Sir?'

'This life-saving cook. I shall want to give her a special mention in my evening prayers.'

'She is a woman of the name of Stoker, sir.'

'*Stoker*? Did you say Stoker?'

'Yes, sir.'

'Odd!'

'Sir?'

'Nothing. Just a rather strange coincidence. Have you told Gussie?'

'Yes, sir. I found him most co-operative. He plans to present himself in the kitchen shortly after midnight. Cold steak and kidney pie is, of course, merely a palliative –'

'On the contrary. It's Gussie's favourite dish. I've known him to order it even on curry day at the Drones. He loves the stuff.'

'Indeed, sir? That is very gratifying.'

'Gratifying is the word. What a lesson this teaches us, Jeeves, never to despair, never to throw in the towel and turn our face to the wall, for there is always hope.'

'Yes, sir. Would you be requiring anything further?'

'Not a thing, thanks. My cup runneth over.'

'Then I will be saying good night, sir.'

'Good night, Jeeves.'

After he had gone, I put in about half an hour on my Erle Stanley Gardner, but I found rather a difficulty in following the thread and keeping my attention on the clues. My thoughts kept straying to this epoch-making cook. Strange, I felt, that her name should be Stoker. Some relation, perhaps.

I could picture the woman so exactly. Stout, red-faced, spectacled, a little irritable, perhaps, if interrupted when baking a cake or thinking out a sauce, but soft as butter at heart. No doubt something in Gussie's wan aspect had touched her. 'That boy needs feeding up, poor little fellow', or possibly she was fond of goldfish and had been drawn to him because he reminded her of them. Or she may have been a Girl Guide. At any rate, whatever the driving motive behind her day's good deed, she had deserved well of Bertram, and I told myself that a thumping tip should reward her on my departure. Purses of gold should be scattered, and with a lavish hand.

I was musing thus and feeling more benevolent every minute, when who should blow in but Gussie in person, and I had been right in picturing his aspect as wan. He wore the unmistakable look of a man who has been downing spinach for weeks.

I took it that he had come to ask me what I was doing at Totleigh Towers, a point on which he might naturally be supposed to be curious, but that didn't seem to interest him. He plunged without delay into as forceful a denunciation of the vegetable world as I've ever heard, oddly enough being more bitter about Brussels sprouts and broccoli than about spinach, which I would have expected him to feature. It was some considerable time before I could get a word in, but when I did my voice dripped with sympathy.

'Yes, Jeeves was telling me about that,' I said, 'and my heart bled for you.'

'And so it jolly well ought to have done – in buckets – if you've a spark of humanity in you,' he retorted warmly. 'Words cannot describe the agonies I've suffered, particularly when staying at Brinkley Court.'

I nodded. I knew just what an ordeal it must have been. With Aunt Dahlia's peerless chef wielding the skillet, the last place where you want to be on a vegetarian diet is Brinkley. Many a time when enjoying the old relative's hospitality I've regretted that I had only one stomach to give to the evening's bill of fare.

'Night after night I had to refuse Anatole's unbeatable eatables, and when I tell you that two nights in succession he gave us those *Mignonettes de Poulet Petit Duc* of his and on another occasion his *Timbales de Ris de Veau Toulousiane*, you will appreciate what I went through.'

It being my constant policy to strew a little happiness as I go by, I hastened to point out the silver lining in the c's.

'Your sufferings must have been terrible,' I agreed. 'But courage, Gussie. Think of the cold steak and kidney pie.'

I had struck the right note. His drawn face softened.

'Jeeves told you about that?'

'He said the cook had it all ready and waiting for you, and I remember thinking at the time that she must be a pearl among women.'

'That is not putting it at all too strongly. She's an angel in human shape. I spotted her solid merits the moment I saw her.'

'You've seen her?'

'Of course I've seen her. You can't have forgotten that talk we had when I was in the cab, about to start off for Paddington. Though why you should have got the idea that she looks like a Pekinese is more than I can imagine.'

'Eh? Who?'

'Emerald Stoker. She doesn't look in the least like a Pekinese.'

'What's Emerald Stoker got to do with it?'

He seemed surprised.

'Didn't she tell you?'

'Tell me what?'

'That she was on her way here to take office as the Totleigh Towers cook.'

I goggled. I thought for a moment that the privations through which he was passing must have unhinged this newt-fancier's brain.

'Did you say *cook*?'

'I'm surprised she didn't tell you. I suppose she felt that you weren't to be trusted to keep her secret. She would, of course, have spotted you as a babbler from the outset. Yes, she's the cook all right.'

'But *why* is she the cook?' I said, getting down to the *res* in that direct way of mine.

'She explained that fully to me on the train. It appears that she's dependent on a monthly allowance from her father in New York, and normally she gets by reasonably comfortably on this. But early this month she was unfortunate in her investments on the turf. Sunny Jim in the three o'clock at Kempton Park.'

I recalled the horse to which he referred. Only prudent second thoughts had kept me from having a bit on it myself.

'The animal ran sixth in a field of seven and she lost her little all. She was then faced with the alternative of applying to her father for funds, which would have necessitated a full confession of her rash act, or of seeking some gainful occupation which would tide her over till, as she put it, the United States Marines arrived.'

'She could have touched me or her sister Pauline.'

'My good ass, a girl like that doesn't borrow money. Much too proud. She decided to become a cook. She tells me she didn't hesitate more than about thirty seconds before making her choice.'

I wasn't surprised. To have come clean to the paternal parent would have been to invite hell of the worst description. Old Stoker was not the type of father who laughs indulgently when informed by a daughter that she has lost her chemise and foundation garments at the races. I don't suppose he has ever laughed indulgently in his life. I've never seen him even smile. Apprised of his child's goings-on, he would unquestionably have blown his top and reduced her to the level of a fifth-rate power. I have been present on occasions when the old gawd-help-us was going good, and I can testify that his boiling point is low. Quite rightly had she decided that silence was best.

It was quite a load off my mind to be able to file away the Emerald Stoker mystery in my case book as solved, for I dislike being baffled and the thing had been weighing on me, but there were one or two small points to be cleared up.

'How did she happen to come to Totleigh?'

'I must have been responsible for that. During our talk at that studio party I remember mentioning that Sir Watkyn was in the market for a cook, and I suppose I must have given her his address, for she applied for the post and got it. These American girls have such enterprise.'

'Is she enjoying her job?'

'Thoroughly, according to Jeeves. She's teaching the butler Rummy.'

'I hope she skins him to the bone.'

'No doubt she will when he is sufficiently advanced to play for money. And she tells me she loves to cook. What's her cooking like?'

I could answer that. She had once or twice given me dinner at her flat, and the browsing had been impeccable.

'It melts in the mouth.'

'It hasn't melted in mine,' said Gussie bitterly. 'Ah well,' he added, a softer light coming into his eyes, 'there's always that steak and kidney pie.'

And on this happier note he took his departure.

8

It was pretty late when I finished the perusal of my Erle Stanley Gardner and later when I woke from the light doze into which I had fallen on closing the volume. Totleigh Towers had long since called it a day, and all was still throughout the house except for a curious rumbling noise proceeding from my interior. After bending an ear to this for awhile I was able to see what was causing it. I had fed sparsely at the dinner table, with the result that I had become as hungry as dammit.

I don't know if you have had the same experience, but a thing I've always found about myself is that it takes very little to put me off my feed. Let the atmosphere at lunch or dinner be what you might call difficult, and my appetite tends to dwindle. I've often had this happen when breaking bread with my Aunt Agatha, and it had happened again at tonight's meal. What with the strain of constantly catching Pop Bassett's eye and looking hastily away and catching Spode's and looking hastily away and catching Pop's again, I had done far less than justice to Emerald Stoker's no doubt admirable offerings. You read stories sometimes where someone merely toys with his food or even pushes away his plate untasted, and that substantially was what I had done. So now this strange hollow feeling, as if some hidden hand had scooped out my insides with a tablespoon.

This imperative demand for sustenance had probably been coming on during my Erle Stanley Gardnering, but I had been so intent on trying to keep tabs on the murder gun and the substitute gun and the gun which Perry Mason had buried in the shrubbery that I hadn't noticed it. Only now had the pangs of hunger really started to throw their weight about, and more and more clearly as they did so there rose before my eyes the vision of that steak and kidney pie which was lurking in the kitchen, and it was as though I could hear a soft voice calling to me 'Come and get it.'

It's odd how often you find that out of evil cometh good, as the expression is. Here was a case in point. I had always thought of my previous visit to Totleigh Towers as a total loss. I saw now that I had been wrong. It had been an ordeal testing the nervous system to the utmost, but there was one thing about it to be placed on the credit side of the ledger. I allude to the fact that it had taught me the way to the kitchen. The route lay down the stairs, through the hall, into the dining-room and through the door at the end of the last named. Beyond the door I presumed that there was some sort of passage or corridor and then you were in the steak and kidney pie zone. A simple journey, not to be compared for complexity with some I had taken at night in my time.

With the Woosters to think is to act, and scarcely more than two minutes later I was on my way.

It was dark on the stairs and just as dark, if not darker, in the hall. But I was making quite satisfactory progress and was about half-way through the latter, when an unforeseen hitch occurred. I bumped into a human body, the last thing I had expected to encounter en route, and for an instant . . . well, I won't say that everything went black, because everything was black already, but I was considerably perturbed. My heart did one of those spectacular leaps Nijinsky used to do in the Russian Ballet, and I was conscious of a fervent wish that I could have been elsewhere.

Elsewhere, however, being just where I wasn't, I had no option but to grapple with this midnight marauder, and when I did so I was glad to find that he was apparently one who had stunted his growth by smoking as a boy. There was a shrimp-like quality about him which I found most encouraging. It seemed to me that it would be an easy task to throttle him into submission, and I was getting down to it with a hearty good will when my hand touched what were plainly spectacles and at the same moment a stifled 'Hey, look out for my glasses!' told me my diagnosis had been all wrong. This was no thief in the night, but an old crony with whom in boyhood days I had often shared my last bar of milk chocolate.

'Oh, hullo, Gussie,' I said. 'Is that you? I thought you were a burglar.'

There was a touch of asperity in his voice as he replied:

'Well, I wasn't.'

'No, I see that now. Pardonable mistake, though, you must admit.'

'You nearly gave me heart failure.'

'I, too, was somewhat taken aback. No one more surprised than the undersigned when you suddenly popped up. I thought I had a clear track.'

'Where to?'

'Need you ask? The steak and kidney pie. If you've left any.'

'Yes, there's quite a bit left.'

'Was it good?'

'Delicious.'

'Then I think I'll be getting along. Good night, Gussie. Sorry you were troubled.'

Continuing on my way, I think I must have lost my bearings a little. Shaken, no doubt, by the recent encounter. These get-togethers take their toll. At any rate, to cut a long story s., what happened was that as I felt my way along the wall I collided with what turned out to be a grandfather clock, for the existence of which I had not budgeted, and it toppled over with a sound like the delivery of several tons of coal through the roof of a conservatory. Glass crashed, pulleys and things parted from their moorings, and as I stood trying to separate my heart from the front teeth in which it had become entangled, the lights flashed on and I beheld Sir Watkyn Bassett.

It was a moment fraught with embarrassment. It's bad enough to be caught by your host prowling about his house after hours even when said host is a warm admirer and close personal friend, and I have, I think, made it clear that Pop Bassett was not one of my fans. He could barely stand the sight of me by daylight, and I suppose I looked even worse to him at one o'clock in the morning.

My feeling of having been slapped between the eyes with a custard pie was deepened by the spectacle of his dressing-gown. He was a small man . . . you got the impression, seeing him, that when they were making magistrates there wasn't enough material left over when they came to him . . . and for some reason not easy to explain it nearly always happens that the smaller the ex-magistrate, the louder the dressing-gown. His was a bright purple number with yellow frogs, and I am not deceiving my public when I say that it smote me like a blow, rendering me speechless.

Not that I'd have felt chatty even if he had been upholstered in something quiet in dark blue. I don't believe you can ever be completely at your ease in the company of someone before whom you've stood in the dock saying 'Yes, your worship' and 'No, your worship' and being told by him that you're extremely lucky to get off with a fine and not fourteen days without the option. This is particularly so if you have just smashed a grandfather clock whose welfare is no doubt very near his heart. At any rate, be that as it may, he was the one to open the conversation, not me.

'Good God!' he said, speaking with every evidence of horror. 'You!'

A thing I never know, and probably never will, is what to say when somebody says 'You!' to me. A mild 'Oh, hullo' was the best I could do on this occasion, and I felt at the time it wasn't good. Better, of course, than 'What ho, there, Bassett!' but nevertheless not good.

'Might I ask what you are doing here at this hour, Mr. Wooster?'

Well, I might have laughed a jolly laugh and replied 'Upsetting grandfather clocks', keeping it light, as it were, if you know what I mean, but something told me it wouldn't go so frightfully well. I had what amounted to an inspiration.

'I came down to get a book. I'd finished my Erle Stanley Gardner and I couldn't seem to drop off to sleep, so I came to see if I couldn't pick up something from your shelves. And in the dark I bumped into the clock.'

'Indeed?' he said, putting a wealth of sniffiness into the word. A thing about this undersized little son of a bachelor I ought to have mentioned earlier is that during his career on the bench he was one of those unpleasant sarcastic magistrates who get themselves so disliked by the criminal classes. You know the type. Their remarks are generally printed in the evening papers with the word 'laughter' after them in brackets, and they count the day lost when they don't make some unfortunate pickpocket or some wretched drunk and disorderly feel like a piece of cheese. I know that on the occasion when we stood face to face in Bosher Street police court he convulsed the audience with three solid jokes at my expense in the first two minutes, bathing me in confusion. 'Indeed?' he said. 'Might I inquire why you were conducting your literary researches in the dark? It would surely have been well within the scope of even your limited abilities to press a light switch.'

He had me there, of course. The best I could say was that I hadn't thought of it, and he sniffed a nasty sniff, as much as to suggest that I was just the sort of dead-from-the-neck-up dumb brick who wouldn't have thought of it. He then turned to the subject of the clock, one which I would willingly have left unventilated. He said he had always valued it highly, it being more or less the apple of his eye.

'My father bought it many years ago. He took it everywhere with him.'

Here again I might have lightened things by asking him if his parent wouldn't have found it simpler to have worn a wrist-watch, but I felt once more that he was not in the mood.

'My father was in the Diplomatic service, and was constantly transferred from one post to another. He was never parted from the clock. It accompanied him in perfect safety from Rome to Vienna, from Vienna to Paris, from Paris to Washington, from Washington to Lisbon. One would have said it was indestructible. But it had still to pass the supreme test of encountering Mr. Wooster, and that was too much for it. It did not occur to Mr. Wooster . . . one cannot think of everything . . . that light may be obtained by pressing a light switch, so he –'

Here he broke off, not so much because he had finished what he had to say as because at this point in the conversation I sprang on to the top of a large chest which stood some six or seven feet distant from the spot where we were chewing the fat. I may have touched the ground once while in transit, but not more than once and that once not willingly. A cat on hot bricks could not have moved with greater nippiness.

My motives in doing so were founded on a solid basis. Toward the later stages of his observations on the clock I had gradually become aware of a curious sound, as if someone in the vicinity was gargling mouthwash, and looking about me I found myself gazing into the eyes of the dog Bartholomew, which were fixed on me with the sinister intentness which is characteristic of this breed of animal. Aberdeen terriers, possibly owing to their heavy eyebrows, always seem to look at you as if they were in the pulpit of the church of some particularly strict Scottish sect and you were a parishioner of dubious reputation sitting in the front row of the stalls.

Not that I noticed his eyes very much, my attention being riveted on his teeth. He had an excellent set and was baring them, and all I had ever heard of his tendency to bite first and ask questions afterwards passed through my mind in a flash. Hence the leap for life. The Woosters are courageous, but they do not take chances.

Pop Bassett was plainly nonplussed, and it was only when his gaze, too, fell upon Bartholomew that he abandoned what must have been his original theory, that Bertram had cracked under the strain and would do well to lose no time in seeing a good mental specialist. He eyed Bartholomew coldly and addressed him as if he had been up before him in his police court.

'Go away, sir! Lie down, sir! Go away!' he said, rasping, if that's the word.

Well, I could have told him that you can't talk to an Aberdeen terrier in that tone of voice for, except perhaps for Doberman pinschers, there is no breed of dog quicker to take offence.

'Really, the way my niece allows this infernal animal to roam at large about the –'

'House' I suppose he was about to say, but the word remained unspoken. It was a moment for rapid action, not for speech. The gargling noise had increased in volume, and Bartholomew was flexing his muscles and getting under way. He moved, he stirred, he seemed to feel the rush of life along his keel, as the fellow said, and Pop Bassett with a lissomness of which I would not have suspected him took to himself the wings of the dove and floated down beside me on the chest. Whether he clipped a second or two off my time I cannot say, but I rather think he did.

'This is intolerable!' he said as I moved courteously to make room for him, and I could see the thing from his point of view. All he asked from life, now that he had made his pile, was to be as far away as possible from Bertram Wooster, and here he was cheek by jowl, as you might say, on a rather uncomfortable chest with him. A certain peevishness was inevitable.

'Not too good,' I agreed. 'Unquestionably open to criticism, the animal's behaviour.'

'He must be off his head. He knows me perfectly well. He sees me every day.'

'Ah,' I said, putting my finger on the weak spot in his argument, 'but I don't suppose he's ever seen you in that dressing-gown.'

I had been too outspoken. He let me see at once that he had taken umbrage.

'What's wrong with my dressing-gown?' he demanded hotly.

'A bit on the bright side, don't you think?'

'No, I do not.'

'Well, that's how it would strike a highly-strung dog.'

I paused here to chuckle softly, and he asked what the devil I was giggling about. I put him abreast.

'I was merely thinking that I wish we *could* strike the highly-strung dog. The trouble on these occasions is that one is always weaponless. It was the same some years ago when an angry swan chased self and friend on to the roof of a sort of boathouse building at my Aunt Agatha's place in Hertfordshire. Nothing would have pleased us better than to bung a brick at the bird, or slosh him with a boathook, but we had no brick and were short of boathooks. We had to wait till Jeeves came along, which he eventually did in answer to our cries. It would have thrilled you to have seen Jeeves on that occasion. He advanced dauntlessly and —'

'Mr. Wooster!'

'Speaking.'

'Kindly spare me your reminiscences.'

'I was merely saying —'

'Well, don't.'

Silence fell. On my part, a wounded silence, for all I'd tried to do was take his mind off things with entertaining chit-chat. I moved an inch or two away from him in a marked manner. The Woosters do not force their conversation on the unwilling.

All this time Bartholomew had been trying to join us, making a series of energetic springs. Fortunately Providence in its infinite wisdom had given Scotties short legs, and though full of the will to win he could accomplish nothing constructive. However much an Aberdeen terrier may bear 'mid snow and ice a banner with the strange device Excelsior, he nearly always has to be content with dirty looks and the sharp, passionate bark.

Some minutes later my fellow-rooster came out of the silence. No doubt the haughtiness of my manner had intimidated him, for there was a mildness in his voice which had not been there before.

'Mr. Wooster.'

I turned coldly.

'Were you addressing me, Bassett?'

'There must be something we can do.'

'You might fine the animal five pounds.'

'We cannot stay here all night.'

'Why not? What's to stop us?'

This held him. He relapsed into silence once more. And we were sitting there like a couple of Trappist monks, when a voice said 'Well, for heaven's sake!' and I perceived that Stiffy was with us.

Not surprising, of course, that she should have turned up sooner or later. If Scotties come, I ought to have said to myself, can Stiffy be far behind?

9

Considering that so substantial a part of her waking hours is devoted to thrusting innocent bystanders into the soup, Stiffy is far prettier than she has any right to be. She's on the small side – petite, I believe, is the technical term – and I have always felt that when she and Stinker walk up the aisle together, if they ever do, their disparity in height should be good for a laugh or two from the ringside pews. The thought has occurred to me more than once that the correct response for Stinker to make, when asked by the M.C. if he is prepared to take this Stephanie to be his wedded wife, would be, 'Why, certainly, what there is of her.'

'What on earth do you two think you're doing?' she inquired, not unnaturally surprised to see her uncle and an old friend in our current position. 'And why have you been upsetting the furniture?'

'That was me,' I said. 'I bumped into the grandfather clock. I'm as bad as Stinker, aren't I, bumping into things, ha-ha.'

'Less of the ha-ha,' she riposted warmly. 'And don't mention yourself in the same breath as my Harold. Well, that doesn't explain why you're sitting up there like a couple of buzzards on a tree top.'

Pop Bassett intervened, speaking at his sniffiest. Her comparison of him to a buzzard, though perfectly accurate, seemed to have piqued him.

'We were savagely attacked by your dog.'

'Not so much attacked,' I said, 'as given nasty looks. We didn't vouchsafe him time to attack us, deeming it best to get out of his sphere of influence before he could settle down to work. He's been trying to get at us for the last two hours, at least it seems like two hours.'

She was quick to defend the dumb chum.

'Well, how can you blame the poor angel? Naturally he thought you were international spies in the pay of Moscow. Prowling about the house at this time of night. I can understand Bertie doing it, because he was dropped on the head as a baby, but I'm surprised at you, Uncle Watkyn. Why don't you go to bed?'

'I shall be delighted to go to bed,' said Pop Bassett stiffly, 'if you will kindly remove this animal. He is a public menace.'

'Very highly-strung,' I put in. 'We were remarking on it only just now.'

'He's all right, if you don't go out of your way to stir him up. Get back to your basket, Bartholomew, you bounder,' said Stiffy, and such was the magic of her personality that the hound turned on its heel without a word and passed into the night.

Pop Bassett climbed down from the chest, and directed a fishy magisterial look at me.

'Good night, Mr. Wooster. If there is any more of my furniture you wish to break, pray consider yourself at perfect liberty to indulge your peculiar tastes,' he said, and he, too, passed into the night.

Stiffy looked after him with a thoughtful eye.

'I don't believe Uncle Watkyn likes you, Bertie. I noticed the way he kept staring at you at dinner, as if appalled. Well, I don't wonder your arrival hit him hard. It did me. I've never been so surprised in my life as when you suddenly bobbed up like a corpse rising to the surface of a sheet of water. Harold told me he had pleaded with you to come here, but nothing would induce you. What made you change your mind?'

In my previous sojourn at Totleigh Towers circumstances had compelled me to confide in this young prune my position as regarded her cousin Madeline, so I had no hesitation now in giving her the low-down.

'I learned that there was trouble between Madeline and Gussie, due, I have since been informed, to her forcing him to follow in the footsteps of the poet Shelley and become a vegetarian, and I felt that I might accomplish something as a *raisonneur*.'

'As a whatonneur?'

'I thought that would be a bit above your head. It's a French expression meaning, I believe, though I would have to check with Jeeves, a calm kindly man of the world who intervenes when a rift has occurred between two loving hearts and brings them together again. Very essential in the present crisis.'

'You mean that if Madeline hands Gussie the pink slip, she'll marry you?'

'That, broadly, is about the strength of it. And while I admire and respect Madeline, I'm all against the idea of having her smiling face peeping at me over the coffee pot for the rest of my life. So I came along here to see what I could do.'

'Well, you couldn't have come at a better moment. Now you're here, you can get cracking on that job Harold told you I want you to do for me.'

I saw that the time had come for some prompt in-the-bud-nipping.

'Include me out. I won't touch it. I know you and your jobs.'

'But this is something quite simple. You can do it on your head. And you'll be bringing sunshine and happiness into the life of a poor slob who can do with a bit of both. Were you ever a Boy Scout?'

'Not since early boyhood.'

'Then you've lots of leeway to make up in the way of kind deeds. This'll be a nice start for you. The facts are as follows.'

'I don't want to hear them.'

'You would prefer that I recalled Bartholomew and told him to go on where he left off?'

She had what Jeeves had called a talking point.

'Very well. Tell me all. But briefly.'

'It won't take long, and then you can be off to beddy-bye. You remember that little black statuette thing on the table at dinner.'

'Ah yes, the eyesore.'

'Uncle Watkyn bought it from a man called Plank.'

'So I gathered.'

'Well, do you know what he paid him for it?'

'A thousand quid, didn't you say?'

'No, I didn't. I said it was worth that. But he got it out of this poor blighter Plank for a fiver.'

'You're kidding.'

'No, I'm not. He paid him five pounds. He makes no secret of it. When we were at Brinkley, he was showing the thing to Mr. Travers and telling him all about it . . . how he happened to see it on Plank's mantelpiece and spotted how valuable it was and told Plank it was worth practically nothing but he would give him five pounds for it because he knew how hard up he was. He gloated over how clever he had been, and Mr. Travers writhed like an egg whisk.'

I could well believe it. If there's one thing that makes a collector spit blood, it's hearing about another collector getting a bargain.

'How do you know Plank was hard up?'

'Well, would he have let the thing go for a fiver if he wasn't?'

'Something in that.'

'You can't say Uncle Watkyn isn't a dirty dog.'

'I would never dream of saying he isn't — and always has been — the dirtiest of dogs. It bears out what I have frequently maintained, that there are no depths to which magistrates won't stoop. I don't wonder you look askance. Your Uncle Watkyn stands revealed as a chiseller of the lowest type. But nothing to be done about it, of course.'

'I don't know so much about that.'

'Why, have you tried doing anything?'

'In a sort of way. I arranged that Harold should preach a very strong sermon on Naboth's Vineyard. Not that I suppose you've ever heard of Naboth's Vineyard.'

I bridled. She had offended my *amour propre*.

'I doubt if there's a man in London and the home counties who has the facts relating to Naboth's Vineyard more thoroughly at his fingertips than me. The news may not have reached you, but when at school I once won a prize for Scripture Knowledge.'

'I bet you cheated.'

'Not at all. Sheer merit. Did Stinker co-operate?'

'Yes, he thought it was a splendid idea and went about sucking throat pastilles for a week, so as to be in good voice. The set-up was the same as the play in *Hamlet*. You know. With which to catch the conscience of the king and all that.'

'Yes, I see the strategy all right. How did it all work out?'

'It didn't. Harold lives in the cottage of Mrs. Bootle, the postman's wife, where they only have oil lamps, and the sermon was on a table with a lamp on it, and he bumped into the table and upset the lamp and it burned the sermon and he hadn't time to write it out again, so he had to dig out something on another topic from the old stockpile. He was terribly disappointed.'

I pursed my lips, and was on the point of saying that of all the web-footed muddlers in existence H.P. Pinker took the well-known biscuit, when it occurred to me that it might possibly hurt her feelings, and I desisted. The last thing I wanted was to wound the child, particularly when I remembered that crack of hers about recalling Bartholomew.

'So we've got to handle the thing another way, and that's where you come in.'

I smiled a tolerant smile.

'I can see where you're heading,' I said. 'You want me to go to your Uncle Watkyn and slip a jack under his better self. "Play the game, Bassett," you want me to say, "Let conscience be your guide, Bassett," trying to drive it into his nut how wrong it is to put over a fast one on the widow and the orphan. I am assuming for purposes of argument that Plank is an orphan, though possibly not a widow. But my misguided young shrimp, do you really suppose that Pop Bassett looks on me as a friend and counsellor to whom he is always willing to lend a ready ear? You yourself were stressing only a moment ago how allergic he was to the Wooster charm. It's no good me talking to him.'

'I don't want you to.'

'Then what do you want me to do?'

'I want you to pinch the thing and return it to Plank, who will then sell it to Mr. Travers at a proper price. The idea of Uncle Watkyn only giving him a fiver for it! We can't have him getting away with raw work like that. He needs a sharp lesson.'

I smiled another tolerant smile. The young boll weevil amused me. I was thinking how right I had been in predicting that any job assigned by her to anyone would be unfit for human consumption.

'Well, really, Stiffy!'

The quiet rebuke in my voice ought to have bathed her in shame and remorse, but it didn't. She came back at me strongly.

'I don't know what you're Well-really-ing about. You're always pinching things, aren't you? Policemen's helmets and things like that.'

I inclined the bean. It was true that I had once lived in Arcady.

'There is,' I was obliged to concede, 'a certain substance in what you say. I admit that in my time I may have removed a lid or two from the upper stories of members of the constabulary –'

'Well, then.'

'– but only on Boat Race Night and when the heart was younger than it is as of even date. It was an episode of the sort that first brought me and your Uncle Watkyn together. But you can take it from me that the hot blood has cooled and I'm a reformed character. My answer to your suggestion is No.'

'No?'

'N-ruddy-o,' I said, making it clear to the meanest intelligence. 'Why don't you pinch the thing yourself?'

'It wouldn't be any good. I couldn't take it to Plank. I'm confined to barracks. Bartholomew bit the butler, and the sins of the Scottie are visited upon its owner. I do think you might reconsider, Bertie.'

'Not a hope.'

'You're a blighter!'

'But a blighter who knows his own mind and is not to be shaken by argument or plea, however specious.'

She was silent for a space. Then she gave a little sigh.

'Oh, dear,' she said. 'And I did hope I wouldn't have to tell Madeline about Gussie.'

I gave another of those visible starts of mine. I've seldom heard words I liked the sound of less. Fraught with sinister significance they seemed to me.

'Do you know what happened tonight, Bertie? I was roused from sleep about an hour ago, and what do you think roused me? Stealthy footsteps, no less. I crept out of my room, and I saw Gussie sneaking down the stairs. All was darkness, of course, but he had a little torch and it shone on his spectacles. I followed him. He went to the kitchen. I peered in, and there was the cook shovelling cold steak and kidney pie into him like a stevedore loading a grain ship. And the thought flashed into my mind that if Madeline heard of this, she would give him the bum's rush before he knew what had hit him.'

'But a girl doesn't give a fellow the bum's rush just because she's told him to stick to the sprouts and spinach and she hears that he's been wading into the steak and kidney pie,' I said, trying to reassure myself but not getting within several yards of it.

'I bet Madeline would.'

And so, thinking it over, did I. You can't judge goofs like Madeline Bassett by ordinary standards. What the normal popsy would do and what she would do in any given circumstances were two distinct and separate things. I had not forgotten the time when she had severed relations with Gussie purely because through no fault of his own he got stinko when about to present the prizes at Market Snodsbury Grammar School.

'You know how high her ideals are. Yes, sir, if someone were to drop an incautious word to her about tonight's orgy, those wedding bells would not ring out. Gussie would be at liberty, and she would start looking about her for somebody else to fill the vacant spot. I really think you'll have to reconsider that decision of yours, Bertie, and do just this one more bit of pinching.'

'Oh, my sainted aunt!'

I spoke as harts do when heated in the chase and panting for cooling streams. It would have been plain to a far less astute mind than mine that this blighted Byng had got me by the short hairs and was in a position to dictate tactics and strategy.

Blackmail, of course, but the gentler sex love blackmail. Not once but on several occasions has my Aunt Dahlia bent me to her will by threatening that if I didn't play ball she would bar me from her table, thus dashing Anatole's lunches and dinners from my lips. Show me a delicately nurtured female, and I will show you a ruthless Napoleon of Crime prepared without turning a hair to put the screws on some unfortunate male whose services she happens to be in need of. There ought to be a law.

'It looks as if the die were cast,' I said reluctantly.

'It is,' she assured me.

'You're really adamant?'

'Couldn't be more so. My heart bleeds for Plank, and I'm going to see that justice is done.'

'Right ho, then. I'll have a crack at it.'

'That's my little man. The whole thing's so frightfully easy and simple. All you have to do is lift the thing off the dining-room table and smuggle it over to Plank. Think how his face'll light up when you walk in on him with it. "My hero!" I expect he'll say.'

And with a laugh which, though silvery, grated on my ear like a squeaking slate pencil, she buzzed off.

10

Proceeding to my room and turning in between the sheets, I composed myself for sleep, but I didn't get a lot of it and what I did get was much disturbed by dreams of being chased across difficult country by sharks, some of them looking like Stiffy, some like Sir Watkyn Bassett, others like the dog Bartholomew. When Jeeves came shimmering in next morning with the breakfast tray, I lost no time in supplying him with full information *re* the harrow I found myself the toad under.

'You see the posish, Jeeves,' I concluded. 'When the loss of the thing is discovered and the hue and cry sets in, who will be the immediate suspect? Wooster, Bertram. My name in this house is already mud, and the men up top will never think of looking further for the guilty party. On the other hand, if I refuse to sit in, Stiffy will consider herself scorned, and we all know what happens when you scorn a woman. She'll tell Madeline Bassett that Gussie has been at the steak and kidney pie, and ruin and desolation will ensue. I see no way of beating the game.'

To my surprise, instead of raising an eyebrow the customary eighth of an inch and saying 'Most disturbing, sir,' he came within an ace of smiling. That is to say, the left corner of his mouth quivered almost imperceptibly before returning to position one.

'You cannot accede to Miss Byng's request, sir.'

I took an astonished sip of coffee. I couldn't follow his train of thought. It seemed to me that he couldn't have been listening.

'But if I don't, she'll squeal to the F.B.I.'

'No, sir, for the lady will be forced to admit that it is physically impossible for you to carry out her wishes. The statuette is no longer at large. It has been placed in Sir Watkyn's collection room behind a stout steel door.'

'Good Lord! How do you know?'

'I chanced to pass the dining-room, sir, and inadvertently overheard a conversation between Sir Watkyn and his lordship.'

'Call him Spode.'

'Very good, sir. Mr. Spode was observing to Sir Watkyn that he had not at all liked the interest you displayed in the figurine at dinner last night.'

'I was just giving Pop B. the old salve in the hope of sweetening the atmosphere a bit.'

'Precisely, sir, but your statement that the object was "just the sort of thing Uncle Tom would like to have" made a deep impression on Mr. Spode. Remembering the unfortunate episode of the cow-creamer, which did so much to mar the pleasantness of your previous visit to Totleigh Towers, he informed Sir Watkyn that he had revised his original view that you were here to attempt to lure Miss Bassett from Mr. Fink-Nottle, and that he was now convinced that your motive in coming to the house had to do with the figurine, and that you were planning to purloin it on Mr. Travers's behalf. Sir Watkyn, who appeared much moved, accepted the theory in toto, all the more readily because of an encounter which he said he had had with you in the early hours of this morning.'

I nodded.

'Yes, we got together in the hall at, I suppose, about one a.m. I had gone down to see if I could get a bit of that steak and kidney pie.'

'I quite understand, sir. It was an injudicious thing to do, if I may say so, but the claims of steak and kidney pie are of course paramount. It was immediately after this that Sir Watkyn fell in with Mr. Spode's suggestion that the statuette be placed under lock and key in the collection room. I presume that it is now there, and when it is explained to Miss Byng that only by means of burglar's tools or a flask of trinitrotoluol could you obtain access to it and that neither of these is in your possession, I am sure the lady will see reason and recede from her position.'

Only the circumstance of my being in bed at the moment kept me from dancing a few carefree steps.

'You speak absolute sooth, Jeeves. This lets me out.'

'Completely, sir.'

'Perhaps you wouldn't mind going and explaining the position of affairs to Stiffy now. You can tell the story so much better than I could, and she ought to be given the low-down as soon as possible. I don't know where she is at this time of day, but you'll find her messing about somewhere, I've no doubt.'

'I saw Miss Byng in the garden with Mr. Pinker, sir. I think she was trying to prepare him for his approaching ordeal.'

'Eh?'

'If you recall, sir, owing to the temporary indisposition of the vicar, Mr. Pinker will be in sole charge of the school treat tomorrow, and he views the prospect with not unnatural qualms. There is a somewhat lawless element among the school children of Totleigh-in-the-Wold, and he fears the worst.'

'Well, tell Stiffy to take a couple of minutes off from the pep talk and listen to your communiqué.'

'Very good, sir.'

He was absent quite a time – so long, in fact, that I was dressed when he returned.

'I saw Miss Byng, sir.'

'And – ?'

'She is still insistent that you restore the statuette to Mr. Plank.'

'She's cuckoo. I can't get into the collection room.'

'No, sir, but Miss Byng can. She informs me that not long ago Sir Watkyn chanced to drop his key, and she picked it up and omitted to apprise him. Sir Watkyn had another key made, but the original remains in Miss Byng's possession.'

I clutched the brow.

'You mean she can get into the room any time she feels like it?'

'Precisely, sir. Indeed, she has just done so.'

And so saying he fished the eyesore from an inner pocket and handed it to me.

'Miss Byng suggests that you take the object to Mr. Plank after luncheon. In her droll way she said the meal – I quote her words – would put the necessary stuffing into you and nerve you for the . . . It is somewhat early, sir, but shall I get you a little brandy?'

'Not a little, Jeeves,' I said. 'Fetch the cask.'

I don't know how Emerald Stoker was with brush and palette, never having seen any of her output, but she unquestionably had what it takes where cooking was concerned, and any householder would have been glad to sign her up for the duration. The lunch she provided was excellent, everything most toothsome.

But with this ghastly commission of Stiffy's on the agenda paper, I had little appetite for her offerings. The brow was furrowed, the manner distrait, the stomach full of butterflies.

'Jeeves,' I said as he accompanied me to my car at the conclusion of the meal, speaking rather peevishly, perhaps, for I was not my usual sunny self, 'doesn't it strike you as odd that, with infant mortality so rife, a girl like Stiffy should have been permitted to survive into the early twenties? Some mismanagement there. What's the tree I read about somewhere that does you in if you sit under it?'

'The Upas tree, sir.'

'She's a female Upas tree. It's not safe to come near her. Disaster on every side is what she strews. And another thing. It's all very well for her to say . . . glibly?'

'Or airily, sir. The words are synonymous.'

'It's all very well for her to say glibly or airily "Take this blasted eyesore to Plank," but how do I find him? I can't go rapping on every door in Hockley-cum-Meston, saying "Excuse me, are you Plank?" It'd be like looking for a needle in a haystack.'

'A very colourful image, sir. I appreciate your difficulty. I would suggest tnat you proceed to the local post office and institute inquiries there. Post office officials invariably have information at their disposal as to the whereabouts of dwellers in the vicinity.'

He had not erred. Braking the car in the Hockley-cum-Meston High Street, I found that the post office was one of those shops you get in villages, where in addition to enjoying the postal facilities you can purchase cigarettes, pipe tobacco, wool, lollipops, string, socks, boots, overalls, picture postcards and bottles containing yellow non-alcoholic drinks, probably fizzy. In answer to my query the old lady behind the counter told me I would find Plank up at the big house with the red shutters about half a mile further back along the road. She seemed a bit disappointed that information was all I was after and that I had no intention of buying a pair of socks or a ball of string, but she bore up philosophically, and I toddled back to the car.

I remembered the house she had spoken of, having passed it on my way. Imposing mansion with a lot of land. This Plank, I took it, would be some sort of labourer on the estate. I pictured him as a sturdy, gnarled old fellow whose sailor son had brought home the eyesore from one of his voyages, and neither of them had had the foggiest that it was valuable. 'I'll put it on the mantelpiece, Dad,' no doubt the son had said. 'It'll look well up there,' to which the old gaffer had replied 'Aye, lad, gormed if 'twon't look gradely on the mantel-piece.' Or words to that effect. I can't do the dialect, of course. So they had shoved it on the mantelpiece, and then along had come Sir Watkyn Bassett with his smooth city ways and made suckers out of parent and offspring. Happening all the time, that sort of thing.

I reached the house and was about to knock on the door, when there came bustling up an elderly gentleman with a square face, much tanned as if he had been sitting out in the sun quite a lot without his parasol.

'Oh, there you are,' he said. 'Hope I haven't kept you waiting. We were having football practice, and I lost track of the time. Come in, my dear fellow, come in.'

I need scarcely say that this exuberant welcome to one who, whatever his merits, was a total stranger warmed my heart quite a good deal.

It was with the feeling that his attitude did credit to Gloucestershire hospitality that I followed him through a hall liberally besprinkled with the heads of lions, leopards, gnus and other fauna into a room with french windows opening on the front garden. Here he left me while he went off to fetch drinks, his first question having been Would I care for one for the tonsils, to which I had replied with considerable enthusiasm that I would. When he returned, he found me examining the photographs on the wall. The one on which my eye was resting at the moment was a school football group, and it was not difficult to spot the identity of the juvenile delinquent holding the ball and sitting in the middle.

'You?' I said.

'That's me,' he replied. 'My last year at school. I skippered the side that season. That's old Scrubby Willoughby sitting next to me. Fast wing threequarter, but never would learn to give the reverse pass.'

'He wouldn't?' I said, shocked. I hadn't the remotest what he was talking about, but he had said enough to show me that this Willoughby must have been a pretty dubious character, and when he went on to tell me that poor old Scrubby had died of cirrhosis of the liver in the Federal Malay States, I wasn't really surprised. I imagine these fellows who won't learn to give the reverse pass generally come to a fairly sticky end.

'Chap on my other side is Smiler Todd, prop forward.'

'Prop forward, eh?'

'And a very good one. Played for Cambridge later on. You fond of Rugger?'

'I don't think I know him.'

'Rugby football.'

'Oh, ah. No, I've never gone in for it.'

'You haven't?'

'No.'

'Good God!'

I could see that I had sunk pretty low in his estimation, but he was a host and managed to fight down the feeling of nausea with which my confession had afflicted him.

'I've always been mad keen on Rugger. Didn't get much of it after leaving school, as they stationed me in West Africa. Tried to teach the natives there the game, but had to give it up. Too many deaths, with the inevitable subsequent blood feuds. Retired now and settled down here. I'm trying to make Hockley-cum-Meston the best football village in these parts, and I will say for the lads that they're coming on nicely. What we need is a good prop forward, and I can't find one. But you don't want to hear all this. You want to know about my

Brazilian expedition.'

'Oh, have you been to Brazil?'

I seemed to have said the wrong thing, as one so often does. He stared.

'Didn't you know I'd been to Brazil?'

'Nobody tells me anything.'

'I should have thought they'd have briefed you at the office. Seems silly to send a reporter all the way down here without telling him what they're sending him for.'

I'm pretty astute, and I saw there had been a mix-up somewhere.

'Were you expecting a reporter?'

'Of course I was. Aren't you from the *Daily Express*?'

'Sorry, no.'

'I thought you must be the chap who was coming to interview me about my Brazilian explorations.'

'Oh, you're an explorer?'

Again I had said the wrong thing. He was plainly piqued.

'What did you think I was? Does the name Plank mean nothing to you?'

'Is your name Plank?'

'Of course it is.'

'Well, what a very odd coincidence,' I said, intrigued. 'I'm looking for a character called Plank. Not you, somebody else. The bimbo I want is a sturdy tiller of the soil, probably gnarled, with a sailor son. As you have the same name as him, you'll probably be interested in the story I'm about to relate. I have here,' I said, producing the black amber thing, 'a what-not.'

He gaped at it.

'Where did you get that? That's the bit of native sculpture I picked up on the Congo and then sold to Sir Watkyn Bassett.'

I was amazed.

'*You* sold it to him?'

'Certainly.'

'Well, shiver my timbers!'

I was conscious of a Boy Scoutful glow. I liked this Plank, and I rejoiced that it was in my power to do him as good a turn as anyone had ever done anybody. God bless Bertram Wooster, I felt he'd be saying in another couple of ticks. For the first time I was glad that Stiffy had sent me on this mission.

'Then I'll tell you what,' I said. 'If you'll just give me five pounds –'

I broke off. He was looking at me with a cold, glassy stare, as no doubt he had looked at the late lions, leopards and gnus whose remains were to be viewed on the walls of the outer hall. Fellows at the Drones who have tried to touch Ooofy Prosser, the club millionaire, for a trifle to see them through till next Wednesday have described him to me as looking just like that.

'Oh, so that's it!' he said, and even Pop Bassett could not have spoken more nastily. 'I've got your number now. I've met your sort all over the world. You won't get any five pounds, my man. You sit where you are and don't move. I'm going to call the police.'

'It will not be necessary, sir,' said a respectful voice, and Jeeves entered through the french window.

11

His advent drew from me a startled goggle and, I rather think, a cry of amazement. Last man I'd expected to see, and how he had got here defeated me. I've sometimes felt that he must dematerialize himself like those fellows in India – fakirs, I think they're called – who fade into thin air in Bombay and turn up five minutes later in Calcutta or points west with all the parts reassembled.

Nor could I see how he had divined that the young master was in sore straits and in urgent need of his assistance, unless it was all done by what I believe is termed telepathy. Still, here he was, with his head bulging at the back and on his face that look of quiet intelligence which comes from eating lots of fish, and I welcomed his presence. I knew from experience what a wizard he was at removing the oppressed from the soup, and the soup was what I was at this point in my affairs deeply immersed in.

'Major Plank?' he said.

Plank, too, was goggling.

'Who on earth are you?'

'Chief Inspector Witherspoon, sir, of Scotland Yard. Has this man been attempting to obtain money from you?'

'Just been doing that very thing.'

'As I suspected. We have had our eye on him for a long time, but till now have never been able to apprehend him in the act.'

'Notorious crook, is he?'

'Precisely, sir. He is a confidence man of considerable eminence in the underworld, who makes a practice of calling at houses and extracting money from their owners with some plausible story.'

'He does more than that. He pinches things from people and tries to sell them. Look at that statuette he's holding. It's a thing I sold to Sir Watkyn Bassett, who lives at Totleigh-in-the-Wold, and he had the cool cheek to come here and try to sell it to me for five pounds.'

'Indeed, sir? With your permission I will impound the object.'

'You'll need it as evidence?'

'Exactly, sir. I shall now take him to Totleigh Towers and confront him with Sir Watkyn.'

'Yes, do. That'll teach him. Nasty hangdog look the fellow's got. I suspected from the first he was wanted by the police. Had him under observation for a long time, have you?'

'For a very long time, sir. He is known to us at the Yard as Alpine Joe, because he always wears an Alpine hat.'

'He's got it with him now.'

'He never moves without it.'

'You'd think he'd have the sense to adopt some rude disguise.'

'You would indeed, sir, but the mental processes of a man like that are hard to follow.'

'Then there's no need for me to phone the local police?'

'None, sir. I will take him into custody.'

'You wouldn't like me to hit him over the head first with a Zulu knobkerrie?'

'Unnecessary, sir.'

'It might be safer.'

'No, sir, I am sure he will come quietly.'

'Well, have it your own way. But don't let him give you the slip.'

'I will be very careful, sir.'

'And shove him into a dungeon with dripping walls and see to it that he is well gnawed by rats.'

'Very good, sir.'

What with all the stuff about reverse passes and prop forwards, plus the strain of seeing gentlemen's personal gentlemen appear from nowhere and of having to listen to that loose talk about Zulu knobkerries, the Wooster bean was not at its best as we moved off, and there was nothing in the way of conversational give-and-take until we had reached my car, which I had left at the front gate.

'Chief Inspector *who*?' I said, recovering a modicum of speech as we arrived at our objective.

'Witherspoon, sir.'

'Why Witherspoon? On the other hand,' I added, for I like to look on both sides of a thing, 'why not Witherspoon? However, that is not germane to the issue and can be reserved for discussion later. The real point – the nub – the thing that should be threshed out immediately – is how on earth do you come to be here?'

'I anticipated that my arrival might occasion you a certain surprise, sir. I hastened after you directly I learned of the revelation Sir Watkyn had made to Miss Byng, for I foresaw that your interview with Major

Plank would be embarrassing, and I hoped to be able to intercept you before you could establish communication with him.'

Practically all of this floated past me.

'How do you mean, the revelation Pop Bassett made to Stiffy?'

'It occurred shortly after luncheon, sir. Miss Byng informs me that she decided to approach Sir Watkyn and make a last appeal to his better feelings. As you are aware, the matter of the statuette has always been one that affected her deeply. She thought that if she reproached Sir Watkyn with sufficient vehemence, something constructive might result. Greatly to her astonishment, she had hardly begun to speak when Sir Watkyn, chuckling heartily, asked her if she could keep a secret. He then revealed that there was no foundation for the story he had told Mr. Travers and that in actual fact he had paid Major Plank a thousand pounds for the object.'

It took me perhaps a quarter of a minute to sort all this out.

'A thousand quid?'

'Yes, sir.'

'Not a fiver?'

'No, sir.'

'You mean he lied to Uncle Tom?'

'Yes, sir.'

'What on earth did he do that for?'

I thought he would say he hadn't a notion, but he didn't.

'I think Sir Watkyn's motive was obvious, sir.'

'Not to me.'

'He acted from a desire to exasperate Mr. Travers. Mr. Travers is a collector, and collectors are never pleased when they learn that a rival collector has acquired at an insignificant price an *objet d'art* of great value.'

It penetrated. I saw what he meant. The discovery that Pop Bassett had got hold of a thousand-quid thingummy for practically nothing would have been gall and w. to Uncle Tom. Stiffy had described him as writhing like an egg whisk, and I could well believe it. It must have been agony for the poor old buster.

'You've hit it, Jeeves. It's just what Pop Bassett would do. Nothing would please him better than to spoil Uncle Tom's day. What a man, Jeeves!'

'Yes, sir.'

'Would you like to have a mind like his?'

'No, sir.'

'Nor me. It just shows how being a magistrate saps the moral fibre. I remember thinking as I stood before him in the dock that he had a shifty eye and that I wouldn't trust him as far as I could throw an elephant. I suppose all magistrates are like that.'

'There may be exceptions, sir.'

'I doubt it. Twisters, every one of them. So my errand was...what, Jeeves?'

'Bootless, sir.'

'Bootless? It doesn't sound right, but I suppose you know. Well, I wish the news you've just sprung could have broken before I presented myself *chez* Plank. I would have been spared a testing ordeal.'

'I can appreciate the nervous strain you must have undergone, sir. It is unfortunate that I was not able to arrive earlier.'

'How did you arrive at all? That's what's puzzling me. You can't have walked.'

'No, sir. I borrowed Miss Byng's car. I left it some little distance down the road and proceeded to the house on foot. Hearing voices, I approached the french window and listened, and was thus enabled to intervene at the crucial moment.'

'Very resourceful.'

'Thank you, sir.'

'I should like to express my gratitude. And when I say gratitude, I mean heartfelt gratitude.'

'Not at all, sir. It was a pleasure.'

'But for you, Plank would have had me in the local calaboose in a matter of minutes. Who is he, by the way? I got the impression that he was an explorer of sorts.'

'Yes, sir.'

'Pretty far-flung, I gathered.'

'Extremely, sir. He has recently returned from an expedition into the interior of Brazil. He inherited the house where he resides from a deceased godfather. He breeds cocker spaniels, suffers somewhat from malaria and eats only non-fattening protein bread.'

'You seem to have got him taped all right.'

'I made inquiries at the post office, sir. The person behind the counter was most informative. I also learned that Major Plank is an enthusiast on Rugby football and is hoping to make Hockley-cum-Meston invincible on the field.'

'Yes, so he was telling me. You aren't a prop forward, are you, Jeeves?'

'No, sir. Indeed, I do not know what the term signifies.'

'I don't, either, except that it's something a team has to have if it's hoping to do down the opposition at Rugby football. Plank, I believe, has searched high and low for one, but his errand has been bootless.

Rather sad, when you come to think of it. All that money, all those cocker spaniels, all that protein bread, but no prop forward. Still, that's life.'

'Yes indeed, sir.'

I slid behind the steering wheel, and told him to hop in.

'But I was forgetting. You've got Stiffy's car. Then I'll be driving on. The sooner I get this statuette thing back into her custody, the better.'

He didn't shake his head, because he never shakes his head, but he raised the south-east corner of a warning eyebrow.

'If you will pardon the suggestion, sir, I think it would be more advisable for me to take the object to Miss Byng. It would scarcely be prudent for you to enter the environs of Totleigh Towers with it on your person. You might encounter his lordship . . . I should say Mr. Spode.'

I well-I'll-be-dashed. He had surprised me.

'Surely you aren't suggesting that he would frisk me?'

'I think it highly possible, sir. In the conversation which I overheard, Mr. Spode gave me the impression of being prepared to stop at nothing. If you will give me the object, I will see that Miss Byng restores it to the collection room at the earliest possible moment.'

I mused, but not for long. I was only too pleased to get rid of the beastly thing.

'Very well, if you say so. Here you are. Though I think you're wronging Spode.'

'I think not, sir.'

And blow me tight if he wasn't right. Scarcely had I steered the car into the stable yard, when a solid body darkened the horizon, and there was Spode, looking like Chief Inspector Witherspoon about to make a pinch.

'Wooster!' he said.

'Speaking,' I said.

'Get out of that car,' he said. 'I'm going to search it.'

12

I was conscious of a thrill of thankfulness for Jeeves's prescience, if prescience is the word I want. I mean that uncanny knack he has of peering into the future and forming his plans and schemes well ahead of time. But for his thoughtful diagnosis of the perils that lay before me, I should at this juncture have been deep in the mulligatawny and no hope of striking for the shore. As it was, I was able to be nonchalant, insouciant and debonair. I was like the fellow I once heard Jeeves speak of who was armed so strong in honesty that somebody's threats passed by him as the idle wind, which he respected not. I think if Spode had been about three feet shorter and not so wide across the shoulders, I would have laughed a mocking laugh and quite possibly have flicked my cambric handkerchief in his face.

He was eyeing me piercingly, little knowing what an ass he was going to feel before yonder sun had set.

'I have just searched your room.'

'You have? You surprise me. Looking for something, were you?'

'You know what I'm looking for. That amber statuette you said your uncle would be so glad to have.'

'Oh, that? I understood it was in the collection room.'

'Who told you that?'

'A usually well-informed source.'

'Well, it is no longer in the collection room. Somebody has removed it.'

'Most extraordinary.'

'And when I say "somebody", I mean a slimy sneak thief of the name of Wooster. The thing isn't in your bedroom, so if it is not in your car, you must have it on you. Turn out your pockets.'

I humoured his request, largely influenced by the fact that there was so much of him. A Singer midget would have found me far less obliging. The contents having been placed before him, he snorted in a disappointed way, as if he had hoped for better things, and dived into the car, opening drawers and looking under cushions. And Stiffy, coming along at this moment, drank in his vast trouser seat with a curious eye.

'What goes on?' she asked.

This time I did laugh that mocking laugh. It seemed to be indicated.

'You know that black eyesore thing that was on the dinner table? Apparently it's disappeared, and Spode has got the extraordinary idea that I've pinched it and am holding it . . . what's the word . . . Not incognito . . . Incommunicado, that's it. He thinks I'm holding it incommunicado.'

'He does?'

'So he says.'

'Man must be an ass.'

Spode wheeled around, flushed with his excesses. I was pleased to see that while looking under the seat he had got a bit of oil on his nose. He eyed Stiffy bleakly.

'Did you call me an ass?'

'Certainly I did. I was taught by a long series of governesses always to speak the truth. The idea of accusing Bertie of taking that statuette.'

'It does sound silly,' I agreed. 'Bizarre is perhaps the word.'

'The thing's in Uncle Watkyn's collection room.'

'It is not in the collection room.'

'Who says so?'

'I say so.'

'Well, I say it is. Go and look, if you don't believe me. Stop that, Bartholomew, you blighted dog!' bellowed Stiffy, abruptly changing the subject, and she hastened off on winged feet to confer with the hound, who had found something in, I presumed, the last stages of decay and was rolling on it. I could follow her train of thought. Scotties at their best are niffy. Add to their natural bouquet the aroma of a dead rat or whatever it was, and you have a mixture too rich for the human nostril. There was a momentary altercation, and Bartholomew, cursing a good deal as was natural, was hauled off tubwards.

A minute or two later Spode returned with most of the stuffing removed from his person.

'I seem to have done you an injustice, Wooster,' he said, and I was amazed that he had it in him to speak so meekly.

The Woosters are always magnanimous. We do not crush the vanquished beneath the iron heel.

'Oh, was the thing there all right?'

'Er – yes. Yes, it was.'

'Ah well, we all make mistakes.'

'I could have sworn it had gone.'

'But wasn't the door locked?'

'Yes.'

'Reminds you of one of those mystery stories, doesn't it, where there's a locked room with no windows, and blowed if one fine morning you don't find a millionaire inside with a dagger of Oriental design sticking in his wishbone. You've got some oil on your nose.'

'Oh, have I?' he said, feeling.

'Now you've got it on your cheek. I'd go and join Bartholomew in the bath tub if I were you.'

'I will. Thank you, Wooster.'

'Not at all, Spode, or rather, Sidcup. Don't spare the soap.'

I suppose there's nothing that braces one more thoroughly than the spectacle of the forces of darkness stubbing their toe, and the heart was light as I made my way to the house. What with this and what with that, it was as though a great weight had rolled off me. Birds sang, insects buzzed, and I felt that what they were trying to say was 'All is well. Bertram has come through.'

But a thing I've often noticed is that when I've got something off my mind, it pretty nearly always happens that Fate sidles up and shoves on something else, as if curious to see how much the traffic will bear. It went into its act on the present occasion. Feeling that I needed something else to worry about, it spat on its hands and got down to it, allowing Madeline Bassett to corner me as I was passing through the hall.

Even if she had been her normal soupy self, she would have been the last person I wanted to have a word with, but this she was far from being. Something had happened to remove the droopiness, and her eyes had a gleam in them which filled me with a nameless fear. She was obviously all steamed up for some reason, and it was plain that what she was about to say was not going to make the last of the Woosters clap his hands in glee and start chanting hosannas like the Cherubim and Seraphim, if I've got the names right. A moment later she revealed what it was that was eating her, dishing it out without what I believe is called preamble.

'I am furious with Augustus!' she said, and my heart stood still. It was as if the Totleigh Towers spectre, if there was one, had laid an icy hand on it.

'Why, what's happened?'

'He was very rude to Roderick.'

This seemed incredible. Nobody but an all-in wrestling champion would be rude to a fellow as big as Spode.

'Surely not?'

'I mean he was very rude *about* Roderick. He said he was sick and tired of seeing him clumping about the place as if it belonged to him, and hadn't he got a home of his own, and if Daddy had an ounce more sense than a billiard ball he would charge him rent. He was most offensive.'

My h. stood stiller. It is not stretching the facts to say that I was appalled and all of a doodah. It just showed, I was telling myself, what a vegetarian diet can do to a chap, changing him in a flash from a soft boiled to a hard boiled egg. I have no doubt the poet Shelley's circle noticed the same thing with the poet Shelley.

I tried to pour oil on the troubled w's.

'Probably just kidding, don't you think?'

'No, I don't.'

'He didn't say it with a twinkle in his eye?'

'No.'

'Nor with a light laugh?'

'No.'

'You might not have noticed it. Very easy to miss, these light laughs.'

'He meant every word he said.'

'Then it was probably just a momentary spasm of what-d'you-call-it. Irritability. We all have them.'

She ground a tooth or two. At least, it looked as if that was what she was doing.

'It was nothing of the kind. He was harsh and bitter, and he has been like that for a long time. I noticed it first at Brinkley. One morning we had walked in the meadows and the grass was all covered with little wreaths of mist, and I said Didn't he sometimes feel that they were the elves' bridal veils, and he said sharply, "No, never," adding that he had never heard such a silly idea in his life.'

Well, of course, he was perfectly correct, but it was no good pointing that out to a girl like Madeline Bassett.

'And that evening we were watching the sunset, and I said sunsets always made me think of the Blessed Damozel leaning out from the gold bar of heaven, and he said "Who?" and I said "The Blessed Damozel," and he said, "Never heard of her". And he said that sunsets made him sick and so did the Blessed Damozel and he had a pain in his inside.'

I saw that the time had come to be a *raisonneur*.

'This was at Brinkley?'

'Yes.'

'I see. After you had made him become a vegetarian. Are you sure,' I said, raisonneuring like nobody's business, 'that you were altogether wise in confining him to spinach and what not? Many a proud spirit rebels when warned off the proteins. And I don't know if you know it, but medical research has established that the ideal diet is one in which animal and vegetable foods are balanced. It's something to do with the something acids required by the body.'

I won't say she actually snorted, but the sound she uttered was certainly on the borderline of the snort.

'What nonsense!'

'It's what doctors say.'

'Which doctors?'

'Well-known Harley Street physicians.'

'I don't believe it. Thousands of people are vegetarians and enjoy perfect health.'

'Bodily health, yes,' I said, cleverly seizing on the debating point. 'But what of the soul? If you suddenly steer a fellow off the steaks and chops, it does something to his soul. My Aunt Agatha once made my Uncle Percy be a vegetarian, and his whole nature became soured. Not,' I was forced to admit, 'that it wasn't fairly soured already, as anyone's would be who was in constant contact with my Aunt Agatha. I bet you'll find that that's all that's wrong with Gussie. He simply wants a mutton chop or two under his belt.'

'Well, he's not going to have them. And if he continues to behave like a sulky child, I shall know what to do about it.'

I remember Stinker Pinker telling me once that toward the end of his time at Oxford he was down in Bethnal Green spreading the light, and a costermonger kicked him in the stomach. He said it gave him a strange, confused, dreamlike feeling, and that's what these ominous words of M. Bassett's gave me now. She had spoken them from between teeth which, if not actually clenched, were the next thing to it, and it was as if the substantial boot of a vendor of blood oranges and bananas had caught me squarely in the solar plexus.

'Er – what will you do about it?'

'Never mind.'

I put out a cautious feeler.

'Suppose . . . not that it's likely to happen, of course . . . but suppose Gussie, maddened by abstinence, were to go off and tuck into . . . well, to take an instance at random, cold steak and kidney pie, what would be the upshot?'

I had never supposed that she had it in her to give anyone a piercing look, but that is what she gave me now. I don't think even Aunt Agatha's eyes have bored more deeply into me.

'Are you telling me, Bertie, that Augustus has been eating steak and kidney pie?'

'Good heavens, no. It was just a thingummy.'

'I don't understand you.'

'What do they call questions that aren't really questions? Begins with an h. Hypothetical, that's the word. It was just a hypothetical question.'

'Oh? Well, the answer to it is that if I found that Augustus had been eating the flesh of animals slain in anger, I would have nothing more to do with him,' she said, and she biffed off, leaving me a spent force and a mere shell of my former self.

13

The following day dawned bright and fair. At least I suppose it did. I didn't see it dawning myself, having dropped off into a troubled slumber some hours before it got its nose down to it, but when the mists of sleep cleared and I was able to attend to what was going on, sunshine was seeping through the window and the ear detected the chirping of about seven hundred and fifty birds, not one of whom, unlike me, appeared to have a damn thing on his or her mind. As carefree a bunch as I've ever struck, and it gave me the pip to listen to them, for melancholy had marked me for her own, as the fellow said, and all this buck and heartiness simply stepped up the gloom in which my yesterday's chat with Madeline Bassett had plunged me.

As may well be imagined, her obiter dicta, as I believe they're called, had got right in amongst me. This, it was plain, was no mere lovers' tiff, to be cleaned up with a couple of tears and a kiss or two, but a real Class A rift which, if prompt steps were not taken through the proper channels, would put the lute right out of business and make it as mute as a drum with a hole in it. And the problem of how those steps were to be taken defeated me. Two iron wills had clashed. On the one hand we had Madeline's strong anti-flesh-food bias, on the other Gussie's firm determination to get all the cuts off the joint that were coming to him. What, I asked myself, would the harvest be, and I was still shuddering at the thought of what the future might hold, when Jeeves trickled in with the morning cup of tea.

'Eh?' I said absently, as he put it on the table. Usually I spring at the refreshing fluid like a seal going after a slice of fish. Preoccupied, if you know what I mean. Or distrait, if you care to put it that way.

'I was saying that we are fortunate in having a fine day for the school treat, sir.'

I sat up with a jerk, upsetting the cuppa as deftly as if I'd been the Rev. H.P. Pinker.

'Is it today?'

'This afternoon, sir.'

I groaned one of those hollow ones.

'It needed but this, Jeeves.'

'Sir?'

'The last straw. I'd enough on my mind already.'

'There is something disturbing you, sir?'

'You're right there is. Hell's foundations are quivering. What do you call it when a couple of nations start off by being all palsy-walsy and then begin calling each other ticks and bounders?'

'Relations have deteriorated would be the customary phrase, sir.'

'Well, relations have deteriorated between Miss Bassett and Gussie. He, as we know, was already disgruntled, and now she's disgruntled, too. She has taken exception to a derogatory crack he made about the sunset. She thinks highly of sunsets, and he told her they made him sick. Can you believe this?'

'Quite readily, sir. Mr. Fink-Nottle was commenting to me on the sunset yesterday evening. He said it looked so like a slice of underdone beef that it tortured him to see it. One can appreciate his feelings.'

'I dare say, but I wish he'd keep them to himself. He also appears to have spoken disrespectfully of the Blessed Damozel. Who's the Blessed Damozel, Jeeves? I don't seem to have heard of her.'

'The heroine of a poem by the late Dante Gabriel Rossetti, sir. She leaned out from the gold bar of Heaven.'

'Yes, I gathered that. That much was specified.'

'Her eyes were deeper than the depths of waters stilled at even. She had three lilies in her hand, and the stars in her hair were seven.'

'Oh, were they? Well, be that as it may, Gussie said she made him sick, too, and Miss Bassett's as sore as a sunburned neck.'

'Most disturbing, sir.'

'Disturbing is the word. If things go on the way they are, no bookie would give odds of less than a hundred to eight on this betrothal lasting another week. I've seen betrothals in my time, many of them, but never one that looked more likely to come apart at the seams than that of Augustus Fink-Nottle and Madeline, daughter of Sir Watkyn and the late Lady Bassett. The suspense is awful. Who was the chap I remember reading about somewhere, who had a sword hanging over him attached to a single hair?'

'Damocles, sir. It is an old Greek legend.'

'Well, I know just how he felt. And with this on my mind, I'm expected to attend a ruddy school treat. I won't go.'

'Your absence may cause remark, sir.'

'I don't care. They won't get a smell of me. I'm oiling out, and let them make of it what they will.'

Apart from anything else, I was remembering the story I had heard Pongo Twistleton tell one night at the Drones, illustrative of how unbridled passions are apt to become at these binges. Pongo got mixed up once in a school treat down in Somersetshire, and his description of how, in order to promote a game called 'Is Mr. Smith at Home?' he had had to put his head in a sack and allow the younger generation to prod him with sticks had held the smoking-room spellbound. At a place like Totleigh, where even on normal days human life was not safe, still worse excesses were to be expected. The glimpse or two I had had of the local Dead End kids had told me how tough a bunch they were and how sedulously they should be avoided by the man who knew what was good for him.

'I shall nip over to Brinkley in the car and have lunch with Uncle Tom. You at my side, I hope?'

'Impossible, I fear, sir. I have promised to assist Mr. Butterfield in the tea tent.'

'Then you can tell me all about it.'

'Very good, sir.'

'If you survive.'

'Precisely, sir.'

It was a nice easy drive to Brinkley, and I got there well in advance of the luncheon hour. Aunt Dahlia wasn't there, having, as foreshadowed, popped up to London for the day, and Uncle Tom and I sat down alone to a repast in Anatole's best vein. Over the *Suprême de Foie Gras au Champagne* and the *Neige aux Perles des Alpes* I placed him in possession of the facts relating to the black amber statuette thing, and his relief at learning that Pop Bassett hadn't got a thousand-quid *objet d'art* for a fiver was so profound and the things he said about Pop B. so pleasing to the ear that by the time I started back my dark mood had become sensibly lightened and optimism had returned to its throne.

After all, I reminded myself, it wasn't as if Gussie was going to be indefinitely under Madeline's eye. In due season he would buzz back to London and there would be able to tuck into the beefs and muttons till his ribs squeaked, confident that not a word of his activities would reach her. The effect of this would be to refill him with sweetness and light, causing him to write her loving letters which would carry him along till she emerged from this vegetarian phase and took up stamp collecting or something. I know the other sex and their sudden enthusiasms. They get these crazes and wallow in them for awhile, but they soon become fed up and turn to other things. My Aunt Agatha once went in for politics, but it only took a few meetings at which she got the bird from hecklers to convince her that the cagey thing to do was to stay at home and attend to her fancy needlework, giving the whole enterprise a miss.

It was getting on for what is called the quiet evenfall when I anchored at Totleigh Towers. I did my usual sneak to my room, and I had been there a few minutes when Jeeves came in.

'I saw you arrive, sir,' he said, 'and I thought you might be in need of refreshment.'

I assured him that his intuition had not led him astray, and he said he would bring me a whisky-and-s. immediately.

'I trust you found Mr. Travers in good health, sir.'

I was able to reassure him there.

'He was a bit low when I blew in, but on receipt of my news about the what-not blossomed like a flower. It would have done you good to have heard what he had to say about Pop Bassett. And talking of Pop Bassett, how did the school treat go off?'

'I think the juvenile element enjoyed the festivities, sir.'

'How about you?'

'Sir?'

'You were all right? They didn't put your head in a sack and prod you with sticks?'

'No, sir. My share in the afternoon's events was confined to assisting in the tea tent.'

'You speak lightly, Jeeves, but I've known some dark work to take place in school treat tea tents.'

'It is odd that you should say that, sir, for it was while partaking of tea that a lad threw a hard-boiled egg at Sir Watkyn.'

'And hit him?'

'On the left cheek-bone, sir. It was most unfortunate.'

I could not subscribe to this.

'I don't know why you say "unfortunate". Best thing that could have happened, in my opinion. The very first time I set eyes on Pop Bassett, in the picturesque environment of Bosher Street police court, I remember saying to myself that there sat a man to whom it would do all the good in the world to have hard-boiled eggs thrown at him. One of my crowd on that occasion, a lady accused of being drunk and disorderly and resisting the police, did on receipt of her sentence, throw her boot at him, but with a poor aim, succeeding only in beaning the magistrate's clerk. What's the boy's name?'

'I could not say, sir. His actions were cloaked in anonymity.'

'A pity. I would have liked to reward him by sending camels bearing apes, ivory and peacocks to his address. Did you see anything of Gussie in the course of the afternoon?'

'Yes, sir. Mr. Fink-Nottle, at Miss Bassett's insistence, played a large part in the proceedings and was, I am sorry to say, somewhat roughly handled by the younger revellers. Among other vicissitudes that he underwent, a child entangled its all-day sucker in his hair.'

'That must have annoyed him. He's fussy about his hair.'

'Yes, sir, he was visibly incensed. He detached the sweetmeat and threw it from him with a good deal of force, and by ill luck it struck Miss Byng's dog on the nose. Affronted by what he presumably mistook for an unprovoked assault, the animal bit Mr. Fink-Nottle in the leg.'

'Poor old Gussie!'

'Yes, sir.'

'Still, into each life some rain must fall.'

'Precisely, sir. I will go and bring your whisky-and-soda.'

He had scarcely gone, when Gussie blew in, limping a little but otherwise showing no signs of what Jeeves had called the vicissitudes he had undergone. He seemed, indeed, above rather than below his usual form, and I remember the phrase 'the bulldog breed' passed through my mind. If Gussie was a sample of young England's stamina and fortitude, it seemed to me that the country's future was secure. It is not every nation that can produce sons capable of grinning, as he was doing, so shortly after being bitten by Aberdeen terriers.

'Oh, there you are, Bertie,' he said. 'Jeeves told me you were back. I looked in to borrow some cigarettes.'

'Go ahead.'

'Thanks,' he said, filling his case. 'I'm taking Emerald Stoker for a walk.'

'You're *what*?'

'Or a row on the river. Whichever she prefers.'

'But, Gussie –'

'Oh, before I forget. Pinker is looking for you. He says he wants to see you about something important.'

'Never mind about Stinker. You can't take Emerald Stoker for walks.'

'Can't I? Watch me.'

'But –'

'Sorry, no time to talk now. I don't want to keep her waiting. So long, I must be off.'

He left me plunged in thought, and not agreeable thought either. I think I have made it clear to the meanest i. that my whole future depended on Augustus Fink-Nottle sticking to the straight and narrow path and not blotting his copybook, and I could not but feel that by taking Emerald Stoker for walks he was skidding off the straight and narrow path and blotting his c. in no uncertain manner. That, at least, was, I was pretty sure, how an idealistic beazel like Madeline Bassett, already rendered hot under the collar by his subversive views on sunsets and Blessed Damozels, would regard it. It is not too much to say that when Jeeves returned with the whisky-and-s., he found me all of a twitter and shaking on my stem.

I would have liked to put him abreast of this latest development, but, as I say, there are things we don't discuss, so I merely drank deep of the flowing bowl and told him that Gussie had just been a pleasant visitor.

'He tells me Stinker Pinker wants to see me about something.'

'No doubt with reference to the episode of Sir Watkyn and the hard-boiled egg, sir.'

'Don't tell me it was Stinker who threw it.'

'No, sir, the miscreant is believed to have been a lad in his early teens. But the young fellow's impulsive action has led to unfortunate consequences. It has caused Sir Watkyn to entertain doubts as to the wisdom of entrusting a vicarage to a curate incapable of maintaining order at a school treat. Miss Byng, while confiding this information to me, appeared greatly distressed. She had supposed – I quote her verbatim – that the thing was in the bag, and she is naturally much disturbed.'

I drained my glass and lit a moody gasper. If Totleigh Towers wanted to turn me into a cynic, it was going the right way about it.

'There's a curse on this house, Jeeves. Broken blossoms and shattered hopes wherever you look. It seems to be something in the air. The sooner we're out of here, the better. I wonder if we couldn't –'

I had been about to add 'make our getaway tonight', but at this moment the door flew open and Spode came bounding in, wiping the words from my lips and causing me to raise an eyebrow or two. I resented this habit he was developing of popping up out of a trap at me every other minute like a Demon King in pantomime, and only the fact that I couldn't think of anything restrained me from saying something pretty stinging. As it was, I wore the mask and spoke with the suavity of the perfect host.

'Ah, Spode. Come on in and take a few chairs,' I said, and was on the point of telling him that we Woosters kept open house, when he interrupted me with the uncouth abruptness so characteristic of these human gorillas. Roderick Spode may have had his merits, though I had never been able to spot them, but his warmest admirer couldn't have called him couth.

14

'Have you seen Fink-Nottle?' he said.

I didn't like the way he spoke or the way he was looking. The lips, I noted, were twitching, and the eyes glittered with what I believe is called a baleful light. It seemed pretty plain to me that it was in no friendly spirit that he was seeking Gussie, so I watered down the truth a bit, as the prudent man does on these occasions.

'I'm sorry, no. I've only just got back from my uncle's place over Worcestershire way. Some urgent family business came up and I had to go and attend to it, so unfortunately missed the school treat. A great disappointment. You haven't seen Gussie, have you, Jeeves?'

He made no reply, possibly because he wasn't there. He generally slides discreetly off when the young master is entertaining the quality, and you never see him go. He just evaporates.

'Was it something important you wanted to see him about?'

'I want to break his neck.'

My eyebrows, which had returned to normal, rose again. I also, if I remember rightly, pursed my lips.

'Well, really, Spode! Is this not becoming a bit thick? It's not so long ago that you were turning over in your mind the idea of breaking mine. I think you should watch yourself in this matter of neck-breaking and check the urge before it gets too strong a grip on you. No doubt you say to yourself that you can take it or leave it alone, but isn't there the danger of the thing becoming habit-forming? Why do you want to break Gussie's neck?'

He ground his teeth, at least that's what I think he did to them, and was silent for a space. Then, though there wasn't anyone within earshot but me, he lowered his voice.

'I can speak frankly to you, Wooster, because you, too, love her.'

'Eh? Who?' I said. It should have been 'whom', I suppose, but that didn't occur to me at the time.

'Madeline, of course.'

'Oh, Madeline?'

'As I told you, I have always loved her, and her happiness is very dear to me. It is everything to me. To give her a moment's pleasure I would cut myself in pieces.'

I couldn't follow him there, but before I could go into the question of whether girls enjoy seeing people cut themselves in pieces he had resumed.

'It was a great shock to me when she became engaged to this man Fink-Nottle, but I accepted the situation because I thought that that was where her happiness lay. Though stunned, I kept silent.'

'Very white.'

'I said nothing that would give her a suspicion of how I felt.'

'Very pukka.'

'It was enough for me that she should be happy. Nothing else mattered. But when Fink-Nottle turns out to be a libertine –'

'Who, Gussie?' I said, surprised. 'The last chap I'd have attached such a label to. Pure as the driven s., I'd have thought, if not purer. What makes you think Gussie's a libertine?'

'The fact that less than ten minutes ago I saw him kissing the cook,' said Spode through the teeth which I'm pretty sure he was grinding, and he dived out of the door and was gone.

How long I remained motionless, like a ventriloquist's dummy whose ventriloquist has gone off to the local and left it sitting, I cannot say. Probably not so very long, for when life returned to the rigid limbs and I legged it for the open spaces to try to find Gussie and warn him of this V-shaped depression which was coming his way, Spode was still in sight. He was disappearing in a nor'-nor'-easterly direction, so, not wanting to hobnob with him again while he was in this what you might call difficult mood, I pushed off sou'-sou'-west, and found that I couldn't have set my course more shrewdly. There was a sort of yew alley or rhododendron walk or some such thing confronting me, and as I entered it I saw Gussie. He was standing in a kind of trance, and his fatheadedness in standing when he ought to have been running like a rabbit smote me like a blow and lent an extra emphasis to the 'Hoy!' with which I accosted him.

He turned, and as I approached him I noted that he seemed even more braced than when last seen. The eyes behind the horn-rimmed spectacles gleamed with a brighter light, and a smile wreathed his lips. He looked like a fish that's just learned that its rich uncle in Australia has pegged out and left it a packet.

'Ah, Bertie,' he said, 'we decided to go for a walk, not a row. We thought it might be a little chilly on the water. What a beautiful evening, Bertie, is it not?'

I couldn't see eye to eye with him there.

'It strikes you as that, does it? It doesn't me.'

He seemed surprised.

'In what respect do you find it not up to sample?'

'I'll tell you in what respect I find it not up to sample. What's all this I hear about you and Emerald Stoker? Did you kiss her?'

The Soul's Awakening expression on his face became intensified. Before my revolted eyes Augustus Fink-Nottle definitely smirked.

'Yes, Bertie, I did, and I'll do it again if it's the last thing I do. What a girl, Bertie! So kind, so sympathetic. She's my idea of a thoroughly womanly woman, and you don't see many of them around these days. I hadn't time when I was in your room to tell you about what happened at the school treat.'

'Jeeves told me. He said Bartholomew bit you.'

'And how right he was. The bounder bit me to the bone. And do you know what Emerald Stoker did? Not only did she coo over me like a mother comforting a favourite child, but she bathed and bandaged my lacerated leg. She was a ministering angel, the nearest thing to Florence Nightingale you could hope to find. It was shortly after she had done the swabbing and bandaging that I kissed her.'

'Well, you shouldn't have kissed her.'

Again he showed surprise. He had thought it, he said, a pretty sound idea.

'But you're engaged to Madeline.'

I had hoped with these words to start his conscience working on all twelve cylinders, but something seemed to have gone wrong with the machinery, for he remained as calm and unmoved as the fish on ice he so closely resembled.

'Ah, Madeline,' he said. 'I was about to touch on Madeline. Shall I tell you what's wrong with Madeline Bassett? No heart. That's where she slips up. Lovely to look at, but nothing *here*,' he said, tapping the left side of his chest. 'Do you know how she reacted to that serious flesh wound of mine? She espoused Bartholomew's cause. She said the whole thing was my fault. She accused me of having teased the little blister. In short, she behaved like a louse. How different from Emerald Stoker. Do you know what Emerald Stoker did?'

'You told me.'

'I mean in addition to binding up my wounds. She went straight off to the kitchen and cut me a package of sandwiches. I have them here,' said Gussie, exhibiting a large parcel and eyeing it reverently. 'Ham,' he added in a voice that throbbed with emotion. 'She made them for me with her own hands, and I think it was her thoughtfulness even more than her divine sympathy that showed me that she was the only girl in the world for me. The scales fell from my eyes, and I saw that what I had once felt for Madeline had been just a boyish infatuation. What I feel for Emerald Stoker is the real thing. In my opinion she stands alone, and I shall be glad if you will stop going about the place saying that she looks like a Pekinese.'

'But, Gussie –'

He silenced me with an imperious wave of the ham sandwiches.

'It's no good your saying "But, Gussie". The trouble with you, Bertie, is that you haven't got it in you to understand true love. You're a mere butterfly flitting from flower to flower and sipping, like Freddie Widgeon and the rest of the halfwits of whom the Drones Club is far too full. A girl to you is just the plaything of an idle hour, and anything in the nature of a grand passion is beyond you. I'm different. I have depth. I'm a marrying man.'

'But you can't marry Emerald Stoker.'

'Why not? We're twin souls.'

I thought for a moment of giving him a word-portrait of old Stoker, to show him the sort of father-in-law he would be getting if he carried through the project he had in mind, but I let it go. Reason told me that a fellow who for months had been expecting to draw Pop Bassett as a father-in-law was not going to be swayed by an argument like that. However frank my description of him, Stoker could scarcely seem anything but a change for the better.

I stood there at a loss, and was still standing there at a loss, when I heard my name called and looking behind me saw Stinker and Stiffy. They were waving hands and things, and I gathered that they had come to thresh out with me the matter of Sir Watkyn Bassett and the hard-boiled egg.

The last thing I would have wished at this crucial point in my affairs was an interruption, for all my faculties should have been concentrated on reasoning with Gussie and trying to make him see the light, but it has often been said of Bertram Wooster that when a buddy in distress is drawn to his attention he forgets self. No matter what his commitments elsewhere, the distressed buddy has only to beckon and he is with him. With a brief word to Gussie that I would be back at an early date to resume our discussion, I hurried to where Stiffy and Stinker stood.

'Talk quick,' I said. 'I'm in conference. Too long to tell you all about it, but a serious situation has arisen. As, according to Jeeves, one has with you. From what he told me I gathered that the odds against Stinker clicking as regards that vicarage have lengthened. More letting-I-dare-not-wait-upon-I-would-ness on Pop Bassett's part, he gave me to understand. Too bad.'

'Of course, one can see it from Sir Watkyn's point of view,' said Stinker, who, if he has a fault besides bumping into furniture and upsetting it, is always far too tolerant in his attitude toward the dregs of humanity. 'He thinks that if I'd drilled the distinction between right and wrong more vigorously into the minds of the Infants Bible Class, the thing wouldn't have happened.'

'I don't see why not,' said Stiffy.

Nor did I. In my opinion, no amount of Sunday afternoon instruction would have been sufficient to teach a growing boy not to throw hard-boiled eggs at Sir Watkyn Bassett.

'But there's nothing I can do about it, is there?' I said.

'You bet there is,' said Stiffy. 'We haven't lost all hope of sweetening him. The great thing is to let his nervous system gradually recover its poise, and what we came to see you about, Bertie, was to tell you on no account to go near him till he's had a chance to simmer down. Don't seek him out. Leave him alone. The sight of you does something to him.'

'No more than the sight of him does to me,' I riposted warmly. I resented the suggestion that I had nothing better to do with my time than fraternize with ex-magistrates. 'Certainly I'll avoid his society. It'll be a pleasure. Is that all?'

'That's all.'

'Then I'll be getting back to Gussie,' I said, and was starting to move off, when Stiffy uttered a sharp squeak.

'Gussie! That reminds me. There's something I wanted to tell him, something of vital concern to him, and I can't think how it slipped my mind. Gussie,' she called, and Gussie, seeming to wake abruptly from a daydream, blinked and came over. 'What are you doing hanging about here, Gussie?'

'Who, me? I was discussing something with Bertie, and he said he'd be back, when at liberty, to go into it further.'

'Well, let me tell you that you've no time for discussing things with Bertie.'

'Eh?'

'Or for saying "Eh?" I met Roderick just now, and he asked me if I knew where you were, because he wants to tear you limb from limb owing to his having seen you kiss the cook.'

Gussie's jaw fell with a dull thud.

'You never told me that,' he said to me, and one spotted the note of reproach in his voice.

'No, sorry, I forgot to mention it. But it's true. You'd better start coping. Run like a hare, is my advice.'

He took it. Standing not on the order of his going, as the fellow said, he dashed off as if shot from a gun, and was making excellent time when he was brought up short by colliding with Spode, who had at that moment entered left centre.

15

It's always disconcerting to have even as small a chap as Gussie take you squarely in the midriff, as I myself can testify, having had the same experience down in Washington Square during a visit to New York. Washington Square is bountifully supplied with sad-eyed Italian kids who whizz to and fro on roller skates, and one of them, proceeding on his way with lowered head, rammed me in the neighbourhood of the third waistcoat button at a high rate of m.p.h. It gave me a strange Where-am-I feeling, and I imagine Spode's sensations were somewhat similar. His breath escaped him in a sharp 'Oof!' and he swayed like some forest tree beneath the woodman's axe. But unfortunately Gussie had paused to sway, too, and this gave him time to steady himself on even keel and regroup his forces. Reaching out a hamlike hand, he attached it to the scruff of Gussie's neck and said 'Ha!'

'Ha!' is one of those things it's never easy to find the right reply to – it resembles 'You!' in that respect – but Gussie was saved the necessity of searching for words by the fact that he was being shaken like a cocktail in a manner that precluded speech, if precluded is the word I want. His spectacles fell off and came to rest near where I was standing. I picked them up with a view to returning them to him when he had need of them, which I could see would not be immediately.

As this Fink-Nottle was a boyhood friend, with whom, as I have said, I had frequently shared my last bar of milk chocolate, and as it was plain that if someone didn't intervene pretty soon he was in danger of having all his internal organs shaken into a sort of macédoine or hash, the thought of taking some steps to put an end to this distressing scene naturally crossed my mind. The problem presenting several points of interest was, of course, what steps to take. My tonnage was quite insufficient to enable me to engage Spode in hand-to-hand conflict, and I toyed with the idea of striking him on the back of the head with a log of wood. But this project was rendered null and void by the fact that there were no logs of wood present. These yew alleys or rhododendron walks provide twigs and fallen leaves, but nothing in the shape of logs capable of being used as clubs. And I had just decided that something might be accomplished by leaping on Spode's back and twining my arms around his neck, when I heard Stiffy cry 'Harold!'

One gathered what she was driving at. Gussie was no particular buddy of hers, but she was a tender-hearted young prune and one always likes to save a fellow creature's life, if possible. She was calling on Stinker to get into the act and save Gussie's. And a quick look at him showed me that he was at a loss to know how to proceed. He stood there passing a finger thoughtfully over his chin, like a cat in an adage.

I knew what was stopping him getting into action. It was not . . . it's on the tip of my tongue . . . begins with a p . . . I've heard Jeeves use the word . . . pusillanimity, that's it, meaning broadly that a fellow is suffering from a pronounced case of cold feet . . . it was not, as I was saying when I interrupted myself, pusillanimity that held him back. Under normal conditions lions could have taken his correspondence course, and had he encountered Spode on the football field, he would have had no hesitation in springing at his neck and twisting it into a lovers' knot. The trouble was that he was a curate, and the brass hats of the Church look askance at curates who swat the parishioners. Sock your flock, and you're sunk. So now he shrank from intervening, and when he did intervene, it was merely with the soft word that's supposed to turn away wrath.

'I say, you know, what?' he said.

I could have told him he was approaching the thing from the wrong angle. When a gorilla like Spode is letting his angry passions rise, there is little or no percentage in the mild remonstrance. Seeming to realize this, he advanced to where the blighter was now, or so it appeared, trying to strangle Gussie and laid a hand on his shoulder. Then, seeing that this, too, achieved no solid results, he pulled. There was a rending sound, and the clutching hand relaxed its grip.

I don't know if you've ever tried detaching a snow leopard of the Himalayas from its prey – probably not, as most people don't find themselves out that way much – but if you did, you would feel fairly safe in budgeting for a show of annoyance on the animal's part. It was the same with Spode. Incensed at what I suppose seemed to him this unwarrantable interference with his aims and objects, he hit Stinker on the nose, and all the doubts that had been bothering that man of God vanished in a flash.

I should imagine that if there's one thing that makes a fellow forget that he's in holy orders, it's a crisp punch on the beezer. A moment before, Stinker had been all concern about the disapproval of his superiors in the cloth, but now, as I read his mind, he was saying to himself 'To hell with my superiors in the cloth,' or however a curate would put it, 'Let them eat cake.'

It was a superb spectacle while it lasted, and I was able to understand what people meant when they spoke of the Church Militant. A good deal to my regret it did not last long. Spode was full of the will to win, but Stinker had the science. It was not for nothing that he had added a Boxing Blue to his Football Blue when at the old Alma Mater. There was a brief mix-up, and the next thing one observed was Spode on the ground, looking like a corpse which had been in the water several days. His left eye was swelling visibly, and a referee could have counted a hundred over him without eliciting a response.

Stiffy, with a brief 'At-a-boy!', led Stinker off, no doubt to bathe his nose and staunch the vital flow, which was considerable, and I handed Gussie his glasses. He stood twiddling them in a sort of trance, and I made a suggestion which I felt was in his best interests.

'Not presuming to dictate, Gussie, but wouldn't it be wise to remove yourself before Spode comes to? From what I know of him, I think he's one of those fellows who wake up cross.'

I have seldom seen anyone move quicker. We were out of the yew alley, if it was a yew alley, or the rhododendron walk, if that's what it was, almost before the words had left my lips. We continued to set a good pace, but eventually we slowed up a bit, and he was able to comment on the recent scene.

'That was a ghastly experience, Bertie,' he said.

'Can't have been at all pleasant,' I agreed.

'My whole past life seemed to flash before me.'

'That's odd. You weren't drowning.'

'No, but the principle's the same. I can tell you I was thankful when Pinker made his presence felt. What a splendid chap he is.'

'One of the best.'

'That's what today's Church needs, more curates capable of hauling off and letting fellows like Spode have it where it does most good. One feels so safe when he's around.'

I put a point which seemed to have escaped his notice.

'But he won't always be around. He has Infants Bible Classes and Mothers Meetings and all that sort of thing to occupy his time. And don't forget that Spode, though crushed to earth, will rise again.'

His jaw sagged a bit.

'I never thought of that.'

'If you take my advice, you'll clear out and go underground for a while. Stiffy would lend you her car.'

'I believe you're right,' he said, adding something about out of the mouths of babes and sucklings which I thought a bit offensive. 'I'll leave this evening.'

'Without saying goodbye.'

'Of course without saying goodbye. No, don't go that way. Keep bearing to the left. I want to go to the kitchen garden. I told Em I'd meet her there.'

'You told *who?*'

'Emerald Stoker. Who did you think I meant? She had to go to the kitchen garden and gather beans and things for tonight's dinner.'

And there, sure enough, she was with a large basin in her hands, busy about her domestic duties.

'Here's Bertie, Em,' said Gussie, and she whisked round, spilling a bean or two.

I was disturbed to see how every freckle on her face lit up as she looked at him, as if she were gazing on some lovely sight, which was far from being the case. In me she didn't seem much interested. A brief 'Hullo, Bertie' appeared to cover it as far as I was concerned, her whole attention being earmarked for Gussie. She was staring at him as a mother might have stared at a loved child who had shown up at the home after a clash with one of the neighbourhood children. Until then I had been too agitated to notice how dishevelled his encounter with Spode had left him, but I now saw that his general appearance was that of something that has been passed through a wringer.

'What . . . *what* have you been doing to yourself?' she ejaculated, if that's the word. 'You look like a devastated area.'

'Inevitable in the circs,' I said. 'He's been having a spot of unpleasantness with Spode.'

'Is that the man you were telling me about? The human gorilla?'

'That's the one.'

'What happened?'

'Spode tried to shake the stuffing out of him.'

'You poor precious lambkin,' said Emerald, addressing Gussie, not me. 'Gosh, I wish I had him here for a minute. I'd teach him!'

And by what I have always thought an odd coincidence her wish was granted. A crashing sound like that made by a herd of hippopotami going through the reeds on a river bank attracted my notice and I beheld Spode approaching at a rate of knots with the obvious intention of resuming at as early a date as possible his investigations into the colour of Gussie's insides which Stinker's intervention had compelled him to file under the head of unfinished business. In predicting that this menace, though crushed to earth, would rise again, I had been perfectly correct.

There seemed to me a strong resemblance in the newcomer's manner to that of those Assyrians who, so we learn from sources close to them, came down like a wolf on the fold with their cohorts all gleaming with purple and gold. He could have walked straight into their camp, and they would have laid down the red carpet for him, recognizing him instantly as one of the boys.

But where the Assyrians had had the bulge on him was that they weren't going to find in the fold a motherly young woman with strong wrists and a basin in her hands. This basin appeared to be constructed of some thickish form of china, and as Spode grabbed Gussie and started to go into the old shaking routine it descended on the back of his head with what some call a dull and others a sickening thud. It broke into several fragments, but by that time its mission had been accomplished. His powers of resistance sapped, no doubt, by his recent encounter with the Rev. H.P. Pinker, Spode fell to earth he knew not where and lay there looking peaceful. I remember thinking at the time that this was not his lucky day, and it just showed, I thought, that it's always a mistake to be a louse in human shape, as he had been from birth, because sooner or later retribution is bound to overtake you. As I recall Jeeves putting it once, the mills of God grind slowly, but they grind exceeding small, or words to that effect.

For a space Emerald Stoker stood surveying her handiwork with a satisfied smile on her face, and I didn't blame her for looking a bit smug, for she had unquestionably fought the good fight. Then suddenly, with a quick 'Oh, golly!' she was off like a nymph surprised while bathing, and a moment later I understood what had caused this mobility. She had seen Madeline Bassett approaching, and no cook likes to have to explain to her employer why she has been bonneting her employer's guests with china basins.

As Madeline's eyes fell on the remains, they widened to the size of golf balls and she looked at Gussie as if he had been a mass murderer she wasn't very fond of.

'What have you been doing to Roderick?' she demanded.

'Eh?' said Gussie.

'I said, What have you done to Roderick?'

Gussie adjusted his spectacles and shrugged a shoulder.

'Oh, that? I merely chastised him. The fellow had only himself to blame. He asked for it, and I had to teach him a lesson.'

'You brute!'

'Not at all. He had the option of withdrawing. He must have foreseen what would happen when he saw me remove my glasses. When I remove my glasses, those who know what's good for them take to the hills.'

'I hate you, I hate you!' cried Madeline, a thing I didn't know anyone ever said except in the second act of a musical comedy.

'You do?' said Gussie.

'Yes, I do. I loathe you.'

'Then in that case,' said Gussie, 'I shall now eat a ham sandwich.'

And this he proceeded to do with a sort of wolfish gusto that sent cold shivers down my spine, and Madeline shrieked sharply.

'This is the end!' she said, another thing you don't often hear.

When things between two once loving hearts have hotted up to this extent, it is always the prudent course for the innocent bystander to edge away, and this I did. I started back to the house, and in the drive I met Jeeves. He was at the wheel of Stiffy's car. Beside him, looking like a Scotch elder rebuking sin, was the dog Bartholomew.

'Good evening, sir,' he said. 'I have been taking this little fellow to the veterinary surgeon. Miss Byng was uneasy because he bit Mr. Fink-Nottle. She was afraid he might have caught something. I am glad to say the surgeon has given him a clean bill of health.'

'Jeeves,' I said, 'I have a tale of horror to relate.'

'Indeed, sir?'

'The lute is mute,' I said, and as briefly as possible put him in possession of the facts. When I had finished, he agreed that it was most disturbing.

'But I fear there is nothing to be done, sir.'

I reeled. I have grown so accustomed to seeing Jeeves solve every problem, however sticky, that this frank confession of his inability to deliver the goods unmanned me.

'You're baffled?'

'Yes, sir.'

'At a loss?'

'Precisely, sir. Possibly at some future date a means of adjusting matters will occur to me, but at the moment, I regret to say, I can think of nothing. I am sorry, sir.'

I shrugged the shoulders. The iron had entered into my soul, but the upper lip was stiff.

'It's all right, Jeeves. Not your fault if a thing like this lays you a stymie. Drive on, Jeeves,' I said, and he drove on. The dog Bartholomew gave me an unpleasantly superior look as they moved off, as if asking me if I were saved.

I pushed along to my room, the only spot in this joint of terror where anything in the nature of peace and quiet was to be had, not that even there one got much of it. The fierce rush of life at Totleigh Towers had got me down, and I wanted to be alone.

I suppose I must have sat there for more than half an hour, trying to think what was to be done for the best, and then out of what I have heard Jeeves describe as the welter of emotions one coherent thought emerged, and that was that if I didn't shortly get a snifter, I would expire in my tracks. It was now the cocktail hour, and I knew that, whatever his faults, Sir Watkyn Bassett provided aperitifs for his guests. True, I had promised Stiffy that I would avoid his society, but I had not anticipated then that this emergency would arise. It was a straight choice between betraying her trust and perishing where I sat, and I decided on the former alternative.

I found Pop Bassett in the drawing-room with a well-laden tray at his elbow and hurried forward, licking my lips. To say that he looked glad to see me would be overstating it, but he offered me a life-saver and I accepted it gratefully. An awkward silence of about twenty minutes followed, and then, just as I had finished my second and was fishing for the olive, Stiffy entered. She gave me a quick reproachful look, and I could see that her trust in Bertram's promises would never be the same again, but it was to Pop Bassett that she directed her attention.

'Hullo, Uncle Watkyn.'

'Good evening, my dear.'

'Having a spot before dinner?'

'I am.'

'You think you are,' said Stiffy, 'but you aren't, and I'll tell you why. There isn't going to be any dinner. The cook's eloped with Gussie Fink-Nottle.'

16

I wonder if you have ever noticed a rather peculiar thing, viz. how differently the same news item can affect two different people? I mean, you tell something to Jones and Brown, let us say, and while Jones sits plunged in gloom and looking licked to a splinter, Brown gives three rousing cheers and goes into a buck-and-wing dance. And the same thing is true of Smith and Robinson. Often struck me as curious, that has.

It was so now. Listening to the recent heated exchanges between Madeline Bassett and Gussie hadn't left me what you might call optimistic, but the heart bowed down with weight of woe to weakest hope will cling, as the fellow said, and I had tried to tell myself that their mutual love, though admittedly having taken it on the chin at the moment, might eventually get cracking again, causing all to be forgotten and forgiven. I mean to say, remorse has frequently been known to set in after a dust-up between a couple of troth-plighters, with all that Sorry-I-was-cross and Can-you-ever-forgive-me stuff, and love, after being down in the cellar for a time with no takers, perks up and carries on again as good as new. Oh, blessings on the falling-out that all the more endears is the way I heard Jeeves put it once.

But at Stiffy's words this hope collapsed as if it had been struck on the back of the head with a china basin containing beans, and I sank forward in my chair, the face buried in the hands. It is always my policy to look on the bright side, but in order to do this you have to have a bright side to look on, and under existing conditions there wasn't one. This, as Madeline Bassett would have said, was the end. I had come to this house as a raisonneur to bring the young folks together, but however much of a raisonneur you are, you can't bring young folks together if one of them elopes with somebody else. You are not merely hampered, but shackled. So now, as I say, I sank forward in my chair, the f. buried in the h.

To Pop Bassett, on the other hand, this bit of front page news had plainly come as rare and refreshing fruit. My face being buried as stated, I couldn't see if he went into a buck-and-wing dance, but I should think it highly probable that he did a step or two, for when he spoke you could tell from the timbre of his voice that he was feeling about as pepped up as a man can feel without bursting.

One could understand his fizziness, of course. Of all the prospective sons-in-law in existence, Gussie, with the possible exception of Bertram Wooster, was the one he would have chosen last. He had viewed him with concern from the start, and if he had been living back in the days when fathers called the shots in the matter of their daughters' marriages, would have forbidden the banns without a second thought.

Gussie once told me that when he, Gussie, was introduced to him, Bassett, as the fellow who was to marry his, Bassett's, offspring, he, Bassett, had stared at him with his jaw dropping and then in a sort of strangled voice had said '*What!*' Incredulously, if you see what I mean, as if he were hoping that they were just playing a jolly practical joke on him and that in due course the real chap would jump out from behind a chair and say 'April fool!' And when he, Bassett, at last got on to it that there was no deception and that Gussie was really what he had drawn, he went off into a corner and sat there motionless, refusing to speak when spoken to.

Little wonder, then, that Stiffy's announcement had bucked him up like a dose of Doctor Somebody's Tonic Swamp Juice, which acts directly on the red corpuscles and imparts a gentle glow.

'Eloped?' he gurgled.

'That's right.'

'With the cook?'

'With none other. That's why I said there wasn't going to be any dinner. We shall have to make do with hard-boiled eggs, if there are any left over from the treat.'

The mention of hard-boiled eggs made Pop Bassett wince for a moment, and one could see that his thoughts had flitted back to the tea tent, but he was far too happy to allow sad memories to trouble him for long. With a wave of the hand he dismissed dinner as something that didn't matter one way or the other. The Bassetts, the wave suggested, could rough it if they had to.

'Are you sure of your facts, my dear?'

'I met them as they were starting off. Gussie said he hoped I wouldn't mind him borrowing my car.'

'You reassured him, I trust?'

'Oh, yes. I said "That's all right, Gussie. Help yourself." '

'Good girl. Good girl. An excellent response. Then they have really gone?'

'With the wind.'

'And they plan to get married?'

'As soon as Gussie can get a special licence. You have to apply to the Archbishop of Canterbury, and I'm told he stings you for quite a bit.'

'Money well spent.'

'That's how Gussie feels. He told me he was dropping the cook at Bertie's aunt's place and then going on to London to confer with the Archbish. He's full of zeal.'

This extraordinary statement that Gussie was landing Emerald Stoker on Aunt Dahlia brought my head up with a jerk. I found myself speculating on how the old flesh-and-blood was going to take the intrusion, and it gave me rather an awed feeling to think how deep Gussie's love for his Em must be, to make him face such fearful risks. The aged relative has a strong personality and finds no difficulty, when displeased, in reducing the object of her displeasure to a spot of grease in a matter of minutes. I am told that sportsmen whom in her hunting days she had occasion to rebuke for riding over hounds were never the same again and for months would go about in a sort of stupor, starting at sudden noises.

My head being now up, I was able to see Pop Bassett, and I found that he was regarding me with an eye so benevolent that I could hardly believe that this was the same ex-magistrate with whom I had so recently been hobnobbing, if you can call it hobnobbing when a couple of fellows sit in a couple of chairs for twenty minutes without saying a word to each other. It was plain that joy had made him the friend of all the world, even to the extent of allowing him to look at Bertram without a shudder. He was more like something out of Dickens than anything human.

'Your glass is empty, Mr. Wooster,' he cried buoyantly, 'may I refill it?'

I said he might. I had had two, which is generally my limit, but with my aplomb shattered as it was I felt that a third wouldn't hurt. Indeed, I would have been willing to go even more deeply into the thing. I once read about a man who used to drink twenty-six martinis before dinner, and the conviction was beginning to steal over me that he had had the right idea.

'Roderick tells me,' he proceeded, as sunny as if a crack of his had been greeted with laughter in court, 'that the reason you were unable to be with us at the school treat this afternoon was that urgent family business called you to Brinkley Court. I trust everything turned out satisfactorily?'

'Oh yes, thanks.'

'We all missed you, but business before pleasure, of course. How was your uncle? You found him well, I hope?'

'Yes, he was fine.'

'And your aunt?'

'She had gone to London.'

'Indeed? You must have been sorry not to have seen her. I know few women I admire more. So hospitable. So breezy. I have seldom enjoyed anything more than my recent visit to her house.'

I think his exuberance would have led him to continue in the same strain indefinitely, but at this point Stiffy came out of the thoughtful silence into which she had fallen. She had been standing there regarding him with a speculative eye, as if debating within herself whether or not to start something, and now she gave the impression that her mind was made up.

'I'm glad to see you so cheerful, Uncle Watkyn. I was afraid my news might have upset you.'

'Upset me!' said Pop Bassett incredulously. 'Whatever put that idea in your head?'

'Well, you're short one son-in-law.'

'It is precisely that that has made this the happiest day of my life.'

'Then you can make it the happiest of mine,' said Stiffy, striking while the iron was h. 'By giving Harold that vicarage.'

Most of my attention, as you may well imagine, being concentrated on contemplating the soup in which I was immersed, I cannot say whether or not Pop Bassett hesitated, but if he did, it was only for an instant. No doubt for a second or two the vision of that hard-boiled egg rose before him and he was conscious again of the resentment he had been feeling at Stinker's failure to keep a firm hand on the junior members of his flock, but the thought that Augustus Fink-Nottle was not to be his son-in-law drove the young cleric's shortcomings from his mind. Filled with the milk of human kindness so nearly to the brim that you could almost hear it sloshing about inside him, he was in no shape to deny anyone anything. I really believe that if at this point in the proceedings I had tried to touch him for a fiver, he would have parted without a cry.

'Of course, of course, of course, of course,' he said, carolling like one of Jeeves's larks on the wing. 'I am sure that Pinker will make an excellent vicar.'

'The best,' said Stiffy. 'He's wasted as a curate. No scope. Running under wraps. Unleash him as a vicar, and he'll be the talk of the Established Church. He's as hot as a pistol.'

'I have always had the highest opinion of Harold Pinker.'

'I'm not surprised. All the nibs feel the same. They know he's got what it takes. Very sound on doctrine, and can preach like a streak.'

'Yes, I enjoy his sermons. Manly and straightforward.'

'That's because he's one of these healthy outdoor open air men. Muscular Christianity, that's his dish. He used to play football for England.'

'Indeed?'

'He was what's called a prop forward.'

'Really?'

At the words 'prop forward' I had, of course, started visibly. I hadn't known that that's what Stinker was, and I was thinking how ironical life could be. I mean to say, there was Plank searching high and low for a forward of this nature, saying to himself that he would pretty soon have to give up the hopeless quest, and here was I in a position to fill the bill for him, but owing to the strained condition of our relations unable to put him on to this good thing. Very sad, I felt, and the thought occurred to me, as it had often done before, that one ought to be kind even to the very humblest, because you never know when they may not come in useful.

'Then may I tell Harold that the balloon's going up?' said Stiffy.

'I beg your pardon?'

'I mean it's official about this vicarage?'

'Certainly, certainly, certainly.'

'Oh, Uncle Watkyn! How can I thank you?'

'Quite all right, my dear,' said Pop Bassett, more Dickensy than ever. 'And now,' he went on, parting from his moorings and making for the door, 'you will excuse me, Stephanie, and you, Mr. Wooster. I must go to Madeline and —'

'Congratulate her?'

'I was about to say dry her tears.'

'If any.'

'You think she will not be in a state of dejection?'

'Would any girl be, who's been saved by a miracle from having to marry Gussie Fink-Nottle?'

'True. Very true,' said Pop Bassett, and he was out of the room like one of those wing threequarters who, even if they can't learn to give the reverse pass, are fast.

If there had been any uncertainty as to whether Sir Watkyn Bassett had done a buck-and-wing dance, there was none about Stiffy doing one now. She pirouetted freely, and the dullest eye could discern that it was only the fact that she hadn't one on that kept her from strewing roses from her hat. I had seldom seen a young shrimp so above herself. And I, having Stinker's best interests at heart, packed all my troubles in the old kitbag for the time being and rejoiced with her. If there's one thing Bertram Wooster is and always has been nippy at, it's forgetting his personal worries when a pal is celebrating some stroke of good fortune.

For some time Stiffy monopolized the conversation, not letting me get a word in edgeways. Women are singularly gifted in this respect. The frailest of them has the lung power of a gramophone record and the flow of speech of a Regimental Sergeant Major. I have known my Aunt Agatha to go on calling me names long after you would have supposed that both breath and inventiveness would have given out.

Her theme was the stupendous bit of good luck which was about to befall Stinker's new parishioners, for they would be getting not only the perfect vicar, a saintly character who would do the square thing by their souls, but in addition the sort of vicar's wife you dream about. It was only when she paused after drawing a picture of herself doling out soup to the deserving poor and asking in a gentle voice after their rheumatism that I was able to rise to a point of order. In the midst of all the joyfulness and back-slapping a sobering thought had occurred to me.

'I agree with you,' I said, 'that this would appear to be the happy ending, and I can quite see how you have arrived at the conclusion that it's the maddest merriest day of all the glad new year, but there's something you ought to give a thought to, and it seems to me you're overlooking it.'

'What's that? I didn't think I'd missed anything.'

'This promise of Pop Bassett's to give you the vicarage.'

'All in order, surely? What's your kick?'

'I was only thinking that, if I were you, I'd get it in writing.'

This stopped her as if she had bumped into a prop forward. The ecstatic animation faded from her face, to be replaced by the anxious look and the quick chewing of the lower lip. It was plain that I had given her food for thought.

'You don't think Uncle Watkyn would double-cross us?'

'There are no limits to what your foul Uncle Watkyn can do, if the mood takes him,' I responded gravely. 'I wouldn't trust him an inch. Where's Stinker?'

'Out on the lawn, I think.'

'Then get hold of him and bring him here and have Pop Bassett embody the thing in the form of a letter.'

'I suppose you know you're making my flesh creep?'

'Merely pointing out the road to safety.'

She mused awhile, and the lower lip got a bit more chewing done to it.

'All right,' she said at length. 'I'll fetch Harold.'

'And it wouldn't hurt to bring a couple of lawyers, too,' I said as she whizzed past me.

It was about five minutes later, as I was falling into a reverie and brooding once more on the extreme stickiness of my affairs, that Jeeves came in and told me I was wanted on the telephone.

17

I paled beneath my tan.

'Who is it, Jeeves?'

'Mrs. Travers, sir.'

Precisely what I had feared. It was, as I have indicated, an easy drive from Totleigh Towers to Brinkley Court and in his exhilarated state Gussie would no doubt have kept a firm foot on the accelerator and given the machine all the gas at his disposal. I presumed that he and girl friend must have just arrived, and that this telephone call was Aunt Dahlia what-the-helling. Knowing how keenly the old bean resented being the recipient of anything in the nature of funny business, into which category Gussie's butting in uninvited with his Em in attendance would unquestionably fall, I braced myself for the coming storm with as much fortitude as I could muster.

You might say, of course, that his rash act was no fault of mine and had nothing to do with me, but it's practically routine for aunts to blame nephews for everything that happens. It seems to be what nephews are for. It was only by an oversight, I have always felt, that my Aunt Agatha omitted to hold me responsible a year or two ago when her son, young Thos, nearly got sacked from the scholastic institution which he attends for breaking out at night in order to go and shy for coconuts at the local amusement park.

'How did she seem, Jeeves?'

'Sir?'

'Did she give you the impression that she was splitting a gusset?'

'Not particularly, sir. Mrs. Travers's voice is always robust. Would there be any reason why she should be splitting the gusset to which you refer?'

'You bet there would. No time to tell you now, but the skies are darkening and the air is full of V-shaped depressions off the coast of Iceland.'

'I am sorry, sir.'

'Nor are you the only one. Who was the fellow – or fellows, for I believe there was more than one – who went into the burning fiery furnace?'

'Shadrach, Meshach and Abednego, sir.'

'That's right. The names were on the tip of my tongue. I read about them when I won my Scripture Knowledge prize at school. Well, I know just how they must have felt. Aunt Dahlia?' I said, for I had now reached the instrument.

I had been expecting to have my ear scorched with well-chosen words, but to my surprise she seemed in merry mood. There was no suggestion of recrimination in her voice.

'Hullo there, you young menace to western civilization,' she boomed. 'How are you? Still ticking over?'

'To a certain extent. And you?'

'I'm fine. Did I interrupt you in the middle of your tenth cocktail?'

'My third,' I corrected. 'I usually stay steady at two, but Pop Bassett insisted on replenishing my glass. He's a bit above himself at the moment and very much the master of the revels. I wouldn't put it past him to have an ox roasted whole in the market place, if he can find an ox.'

'Stinko, is he?'

'Not perhaps stinko, but certainly effervescent.'

'Well, if you can suspend your drunken orgy for a minute or two, I'll tell you the news from home. I got back from London a quarter of an hour ago, and what do you think I found waiting on the mat? That newt-collecting freak Spink-Bottle, accompanied by a girl who looks like a Pekinese with freckles.'

I drew a deep breath and embarked on my speech for the defence. If Bertram was to be put in the right light, now was the moment. True, her manner so far had been affable and she had given no sign of being about to go off with a bang, but one couldn't be sure that that wasn't because she was just biding her time. It's never safe to dismiss aunts lightly at times like this.

'Yes,' I said, 'I heard he was on his way, complete with freckled human Pekinese. I am sorry, Aunt Dahlia, that you should have been subjected to this unwarrantable intrusion, and I would like to make it abundantly clear that it was not the outcome of any advice or encouragement from me. I was in total ignorance of his intentions. Had he confided in me his purpose of inflicting his presence on you, I should have –'

Here I paused, for she had asked me rather brusquely to put a sock in it.

'Stop babbling, you ghastly young gas-bag. What's all this silver-tongued-orator stuff about?'

'I was merely expressing my regret that you should have been subjected –'

'Well, don't. There's no need to apologize. I couldn't be more pleased. I admit that I'm always happier when I don't have Spink-Bottle breathing down the back of my neck and taking up space in the house which I require for other purposes, but the girl was as welcome as manna in the wilderness.'

Having won that prize for Scripture Knowledge I was speaking of, I had no difficulty in grasping her allusion. She was referring to an incident which occurred when the children of Israel were crossing some desert or other and were sorely in need of refreshment, rations being on the slender side. And they were just saying to one another how well a spot of manna would go down and regretting that there was none in the quartermaster's stores, when blowed if a whole wad of the stuff didn't descend from the skies, just making their day.

Her words had of course surprised me somewhat, and I asked her why Emerald Stoker had been as welcome as manna in the w.

'Because her arrival brought sunshine into a stricken home. There couldn't have been a smoother piece of timing. You didn't see Anatole when you were over here this afternoon, did you?'

'No. Why?'

'I was wondering if you had noticed anything wrong with him. Shortly after you left he developed a *mal au foie* or whatever he called it and took to his bed.'

'I'm sorry.'

'So was Tom. He was looking forward gloomily to a dinner cooked by the kitchen maid, who, though a girl of many sterling merits, always adopts the scorched earth policy when preparing a meal, and you know what his digestion's like. Conditions looked dark, and then Spink-Bottle suddenly revealed that this Pekinese of his was an experienced chef, and she's taken over. Who is she? Do you know anything about her?'

I was, of course, able to supply the desired information.

'She's the daughter of a well-to-do American millionaire called Stoker, who, I imagine, will be full of strange oaths when he hears she's married Gussie, the latter being, as you will concede, not everybody's cup of tea.'

'So he isn't going to marry Madeline Bassett?'

'No, the fixture has been scratched.'

'That's definite, is it?'

'Yes.'

'You can't have been much success as a raisonneur.'

'No.'

'Well, I think she'll make Spink-Bottle a good wife. Seems a very nice girl.'

'Few better.'

'But this leaves you in rather a spot, doesn't it? If Madeline Bassett is now at large, won't she expect you to fill in?'

'That, aged relative, is the fear that haunts me.'

'Has Jeeves nothing to suggest?'

'He says he hasn't. But I've known him on previous occasions to be temporarily baffled and then suddenly to wave his magic wand and fix everything up. So I haven't entirely lost hope.'

'No, I expect you'll wriggle out of it somehow, as you always do. I wish I had a fiver for every time you've been within a step of the altar rails and have managed to escape unscathed. I remember you telling me once that you had faith in your star.'

'Quite. Still, it's no good trying to pretend that peril doesn't loom. It looms like the dickens. The corner in which I find myself is tight.'

'And you would like to get that way, too, I suppose? All right, you can get back to your orgy when I've told you why I rang you up.'

'Haven't you?' I said, surprised.

'Certainly not. You don't catch me wasting time and money chatting with you about your amours. Here is the nub. You know that black amber thing of Bassett's?'

'The statuette? Of course.'

'I want to buy it for Tom. I've come into a bit of money. The reason I went to London today was to see my lawyer about a legacy someone's left me. Old school friend, if that's of any interest to you. It works out at about a couple of thousand quid, and I want you to get that statuette for me.'

'It's going to be pretty hard to get away with it.'

'Oh, you'll manage. Go as high as fifteen hundred pounds, if you have to. I suppose you couldn't just slip it in your pocket? It would save a lot of overhead. But probably that's asking too much of you, so tackle Bassett and get him to sell it.'

'Well, I'll do my best. I know how much Uncle Tom covets that statuette. Rely on me, Aunt Dahlia.'

'That's my boy.'

I returned to the drawing-room in somewhat pensive mood, for my relations with Pop Bassett were such that it was going to be embarrassing trying to do business with him, but I was relieved that the aged relative had dismissed the idea of purloining the thing. Surprised, too, as well as relieved, because the stern lesson association with her over the years has taught me is that when she wants to do a loved husband a good turn, she is seldom fussy about the methods employed to that end. It was she who had initiated, if that's the word I want,

the theft of the cow-creamer, and you would have thought she would
have wanted to save money on the current deal. Her view has always
been that if a collector pinches something from another collector, it
doesn't count as stealing, and of course there may be something in it.
Pop Bassett, when at Brinkley, would unquestionably have looted
Uncle Tom's collection, had he not been closely watched. These
collectors have about as much conscience as the smash-and-grab
fellows for whom the police are always spreading dragnets.

I was musing along these lines and trying to think what would be
the best way of approaching Pop, handicapped as I would be by the
fact that he shuddered like a jelly in a high wind every time he saw
me and preferred when in my presence to sit and stare before him
without uttering, when the door opened, and Spode came in.

18

The first thing that impressed itself on the senses was that he had about as spectacular a black eye as you could meet with in a month of Sundays, and I found myself at a momentary loss to decide how it was best to react to it. I mean, some fellows with bunged-up eyes want sympathy, others prefer that you pretend that you've noticed nothing unusual in their appearance. I came to the conclusion that it was wisest to greet him with a careless 'Ah, Spode,' and I did so, though I suppose, looking back, that 'Ah, Sidcup' would have been more suitable, and it was as I spoke that I became aware that he was glaring at me in a sinister manner with the eye that wasn't closed. I have spoken of these eyes of his as being capable of opening an oyster at sixty paces, and even when only one of them was functioning the impact of his gaze was disquieting. I have known my Aunt Agatha's gaze to affect me in the same way.

'I was looking for you, Wooster,' he said.

He uttered the words in the unpleasant rasping voice which had once kept his followers on the jump. Before succeeding to his new title he had been one of those Dictators who were fairly common at one time in the metropolis, and had gone about with a mob of underlings wearing black shorts and shouting 'Heil, Spode!' or words along those general lines. He gave it up when he became Lord Sidcup, but he was still apt to address all and sundry as if he were ticking off some erring member of his entourage whose shorts had got a patch on them.

'Oh, were you?' I said.

'I was.' He paused for a moment, continuing to give me the eye, then he said 'So!'

'So!' is another of those things, like 'You!' and 'Ha!', which it's never easy to find the right answer to. Nothing in the way of a come-back suggested itself to me, so I merely lit a cigarette in what I intended to be a nonchalant manner, though I may have missed it by a considerable margin, and he proceeded.

'So I was right!'

'Eh?'

'In my suspicions.'

'Eh?'

'They have been confirmed.'

'Eh?'

'Stop saying "Eh?", you miserable worm, and listen to me.'

I humoured him. You might have supposed that having so recently seen him knocked base over apex by the Rev. H.P. Pinker and subsequently laid out cold by Emerald Stoker and her basin of beans I would have regarded him with contempt as pretty small-time stuff and rebuked him sharply for calling me a miserable worm, but the idea never so much as crossed my mind. He had suffered reverses, true, but they had left him with his spirit unbroken and the muscles of his brawny arms just as much like iron bands as they had always been, and the way I looked at it was that if he wanted me to go easy on the word 'Eh?' he had only to say so.

Continuing to pierce me with the eye that was still on duty, he said:

'I happened to be passing through the hall just now.'

'Oh?'

'I heard you talking on the telephone.'

'Oh?'

'You were speaking to your aunt.'

'Oh?'

'Don't keep saying "Oh?", blast you.'

Well, these restrictions were making it a bit hard for me to hold up my end of the conversation, but there seemed nothing to be done about it. I maintained a rather dignified silence, and he resumed his remarks.

'Your aunt was urging you to steal Sir Watkyn's amber statuette.'

'She wasn't!'

'Pardon me. I thought you would try to deny the charge, so I took the precaution of jotting down your actual words. The statuette was mentioned and you said "It's going to be pretty hard to get away with it." She then presumably urged you to spare no effort, for you said "Well, I'll do my best. I know how much Uncle Tom covets that statuette. Rely on me, Aunt Dahlia." What the devil are you gargling about?'

'Not gargling,' I corrected. 'Laughing lightly. Because you've got the whole thing wrong, though I must say the way you've managed to record the dialogue does you a good deal of credit. Do you use shorthand?'

'How do you mean I've got it wrong?'

'Aunt Dahlia was asking me to try to buy the thing from Sir Watkyn.'

He snorted and said 'Ha!' and I thought it a bit unjust that he should say 'Ha!' if I wasn't allowed to say 'Eh?' and 'Oh?' There should always be a certain give and take in these matters, or where are you?

'Do you expect me to believe that?'

'Don't you believe it?'

'No, I don't. I'm not an ass.'

This, of course, was a debatable point, as I once heard Jeeves describe it, but I didn't press it.

'I know that aunt of yours,' he proceeded. 'She would steal the filling out of your back teeth if she thought she could do it without detection.' He paused for a moment, and I knew that he was thinking of the cow-creamer. He had always – and, I must admit, not without reason – suspected the old flesh-and-blood of being the motive force behind its disappearance, and I imagine it had been a nasty knock to him that nothing could be proved. 'Well, I strongly advise you, Wooster, not to let her make a catspaw of you this time, because if you're caught, as you certainly will be, you'll be for it. Don't think that Sir Watkyn will hush the thing up to avoid a scandal. You'll go to prison, that's where you'll go. He dislikes you intensely, and nothing would please him more than to be able to give you a long stretch without the option.'

I thought this showed a vindictive spirit in the old wart hog and one that I deplored, but I felt it would be injudicious to say so. I merely nodded understandingly. I was thankful that there was no danger of this contingency, as Jeeves would have called it, arising. Strong in the knowledge that nothing would induce me to pinch their ruddy statuette, I was able to remain calm and nonchalant, or as calm and nonchalant as you can be when a fellow eight foot six in height with one eye bunged up and the other behaving like an oxyacetylene blowpipe is glaring at you.

'Yes, sir,' said Spode, 'it'll be chokey for you.'

And he was going on to say that he would derive great pleasure from coming on visiting days and making faces at me through the bars, when Pop Bassett returned.

But a very different Bassett from the fizzy rejoicer who had exited so short a while before. Then he had been all buck and beans, as any father would have been whose daughter was not going to marry Gussie Fink-Nottle. Now his face was drawn and his general demeanour that of an incautious luncher who discovers when there is no time to draw back that he has swallowed a rather too elderly oyster.

'Madeline tells me,' he began. Then he saw Spode's eye, and broke off. It was the sort of eye which, even if you have a lot on your mind, you can't help noticing. 'Good gracious, Roderick,' he said, 'did you have a fall?'

'Fall, my foot,' said Spode, 'I was socked by a curate.'

'Good heavens! What curate?'

'There's only one in these parts, isn't there?'

'You mean you were assaulted by Mr. Pinker? You astound me, Roderick.'

Spode spoke with genuine feeling.

'Not half as much as he astounded *me*. He was more or less of a revelation to me, I don't mind telling you, because I didn't know curates had left hooks like that. He's got a knack of feinting you off balance and then coming in with a sort of corkscrew punch which it's impossible not to admire. I must get him to teach it to me some time.'

'You speak as though you bore him no animosity.'

'Of course I don't. A very pleasant little scrap with no ill feeling on either side. I've nothing against Pinker. The one I've got it in for is the cook. She beaned me with a china basin. From behind, of all unsporting things. If you'll excuse me, I'll go and have a word with that cook.'

He was so obviously looking forward to telling Emerald Stoker what he thought of her that it gave me quite a pang to have to break it to him that his errand would be bootless.

'You can't,' I pointed out. 'She is no longer with us.'

'Don't be an ass. She's in the kitchen, isn't she?'

'I'm sorry, no. She's eloped with Gussie Fink-Nottle. A wedding has been arranged and will take place as soon as the Archbish of Canterbury lets him have a special licence.'

Spode reeled. He had only one eye to stare at me with, but he got all the mileage out of it that was possible.

'Is that true?'

'Absolutely.'

'Well, that makes up for everything. If Madeline's back in circula-tion . . . Thank you for telling me, Wooster, old chap.'

'Don't mention it, Spode, old man, or, rather, Lord Sidcup, old man.'

For the first time Pop Bassett appeared to become aware that the slight, distinguished-looking young fellow standing on one leg by the sofa was Bertram.

'Mr. Wooster,' he said. Then he stopped, swallowed once or twice and groped his way to the table where the drinks were. His manner was feverish. Having passed a liberal snootful down the hatch, he was able to resume. 'I have just seen Madeline.'

'Oh, yes?' I said courteously. 'How is she?'

'Off her head, in my opinion. She says she is going to marry you.'

Well, I had more or less steeled myself to something along these lines, so except for quivering like a stricken blancmange and letting my lower jaw fall perhaps six inches I betrayed no sign of discomposure, in which respect I differed radically from Spode, who reeled for the second time and uttered a cry like that of a cinnamon bear that has stubbed its toe on a passing rock.

'You're joking!'

Pop Bassett shook his head regretfully. His face was haggard.

'I wish I were, Roderick. I am not surprised that you are upset. I feel the same myself. I am distraught. I can see no light on the horizon. When she told me, it was as if I had been struck by a thunderbolt.'

Spode was staring at me, aghast. Even now, it seemed, he was unable to take in the full horror of the situation. There was incredulity in his one good eye.

'But she can't marry *that*!'

'She seems resolved to.'

'But he's worse than that fishfaced blighter.'

'I agree with you. Far worse. No comparison.'

'I'll go and talk to her,' said Spode, and left us before I could express my resentment at being called *that*.

It was perhaps fortunate that only half a minute later Stiffy and Stinker entered, for if I had been left alone with Pop Bassett, I would have been hard put to it to hit on a topic of conversation calculated to interest, elevate and amuse.

19

Stinker's nose, as was only to be expected, had swollen a good deal since last heard from, but he seemed in excellent spirits, and Stiffy couldn't have been merrier and brighter. Both were obviously thinking in terms of the happy ending, and my heart bled freely for the unfortunate young slobs. I had observed Pop Bassett closely while Spode was telling him about Stinker's left hook, and what I had read on his countenance had not been encouraging.

These patrons of livings with vicarages to bestow always hold rather rigid views as regards the qualifications they demand from the curates they are thinking of promoting to fields of higher activity, and left hooks, however adroit, are not among them. If Pop Bassett had been a fight promoter on the look-out for talent and Stinker a promising novice anxious to be put on his next programme for a six-round preliminary bout, he would no doubt have gazed on him with a kindly eye. As it was, the eye he was now directing at him was as cold and bleak as if an old crony had been standing before him in the dock, charged with having moved pigs without a permit or failed to abate a smoky chimney. I could see trouble looming, and I wouldn't have risked a bet on the happy e. even at the most liberal odds.

The stickiness of the atmosphere, so patent to my keener sense, had not communicated itself to Stiffy. No voice was whispering in her ear that she was about to be let down with a thud which would jar her to the back teeth. She was all smiles and viv-whatever-the-word-is, plainly convinced that the signing on the dotted line was now a mere formality.

'Here we are, Uncle Watkyn,' she said, beaming freely.

'So I see.'

'I've brought Harold.'

'So I perceive.'

'We've talked it over, and we think we ought to have the thing embodied in the form of a letter.'

Pop Bassett's eye grew colder and bleaker, and the feeling I had that we were all back in Bosher Street police court deepened. Nothing, it seemed to me, was needed to complete the illusion except a magistrate's clerk with a cold in the head, a fug you could cut with a knife and a few young barristers hanging about hoping for dock briefs.

'I fear I do not understand you,' he said.

'Oh, come, Uncle Watkyn, you know you're brighter than that. I'm talking about Harold's vicarage.'

'I was not aware that Mr. Pinker had a vicarage.'

'The one you're going to give him, I mean.'

'Oh?' said Pop Bassett, and I have seldom heard an 'Oh?' that had a nastier sound. 'I have just seen Roderick,' he added, getting down to the *res*.

At the mention of Spode's name Stiffy giggled, and I could have told her it was a mistake. There is a time for girlish frivolity, and a time when it is misplaced. It had not escaped my notice that Pop Bassett had begun to swell like one of those curious circular fish you catch down in Florida, and in addition to this he was rumbling as I imagine volcanoes do before starting in on the neighbouring house-holders and making them wish they had settled elsewhere.

But even now Stiffy seemed to have no sense of impending doom. She uttered another silvery laugh. I've noticed this slowness in getting hep to atmospheric conditions in other girls. The young of the gentler sex never appear to realize that there are moments when the last thing required by their audience is the silvery laugh.

'I'll bet he had a shiner.'

'I beg your pardon?'

'Was his eye black?'

'It was.'

'I thought it would be. Harold's strength is as the strength of ten, because his heart is pure. Well, how about that embodying letter? I have a fountain pen. Let's get the show on the road.'

I was expecting Pop Bassett to give an impersonation of a bomb falling on an ammunition dump, but he didn't. Instead, he continued to exhibit that sort of chilly stiffness which you see in magistrates when they're fining people five quid for boyish peccadilloes.

'You appear to be under a misapprehension, Stephanie,' he said in the metallic voice he had once used when addressing the prisoner Wooster. 'I have no intention of entrusting Mr. Pinker with a vicarage.'

Stiffy took it big. She shook from wind-swept-hair-do to shoe-sole, and if she hadn't clutched at Stinker's arm might have taken a toss. One could understand her emotion. She had been coasting along, confident that she had it made, and suddenly out of a blue and smiling sky these words of doom. No doubt it was the suddenness and unexpectedness of the wallop that unmanned her, if you can call it unmanning when it happens to a girl. I suppose she was feeling very much as Spode had felt when Emerald Stoker's basin had connected with his occiput. Her eyes bulged, and her voice came out in a passionate squeak.

'But, Uncle Watkyn! You promised!'

I could have told her she was wasting her breath trying to appeal to the old buzzard's better feelings, because magistrates, even when ex, don't have any. The tremolo in her voice might have been expected to melt what is usually called a heart of stone, but it had no more effect on Pop Bassett than the chirping of the household canary.

'Provisionally only,' he said. 'I was not aware, when I did so, that Mr. Pinker had brutally assaulted Roderick.'

At these words Stinker, who had been listening to the exchanges in a rigid sort of way, creating the illusion that he had been stuffed by a good taxidermist, came suddenly to life, though as all he did was make a sound like the last drops of water going out of a bath tub, it was hardly worth the trouble and expense. He succeeded, however, in attracting Pop Bassett's attention, and the latter gave him the eye.

'Yes, Mr. Pinker?'

It was a moment or two before Stinker followed up the gurgling noise with speech. And even then it wasn't much in the way of speech. He said:

'I – er – He – er –'

'Proceed, Mr. Pinker.'

'It was – I mean it wasn't –'

'If you could make yourself a little plainer, Mr. Pinker, it would be of great assistance to our investigations into the matter under discussion. I must confess to finding you far from lucid.'

It was the type of crack he had been accustomed in the old Bosher Street days to seeing in print with 'laughter' after it in brackets, but on this occasion it fell flatter than a Dover sole. It didn't get a snicker out of me, nor out of Stinker, who merely knocked over a small china ornament and turned a deeper vermilion, while Stiffy came back at him in great shape.

'There's no need to talk like a magistrate, Uncle Watkyn.'

'I beg your pardon?'

'In fact, it would be better if you stopped talking at all and let me explain. What Harold's trying to tell you is that he didn't brutally assault Roderick, Roderick brutally assaulted him.'

'Indeed? That was not the way I heard the story.'

'Well, it's the way it happened.'

'I am perfectly willing to hear your version of the deplorable incident.'

'All right, then. Here it comes. Harold was cooing to Roderick like a turtle dove, and Roderick suddenly hauled off and plugged him squarely on the beezer. If you don't believe me, take a look at it. The poor angel spouted blood like a Versailles fountain. Well, what would you have expected Harold to do? Turn the other nose?'

'I would have expected him to remember his position as a clerk in holy orders. He should have complained to me, and I would have seen to it that Roderick made ample apology.'

A sound like the shot heard round the world rang through the room. It was Sniffy snorting.

'Apology!' she cried, having got the snort out of her system. 'What's the good of apologies? Harold took the only possible course. He sailed in and laid Roderick out cold, as anyone would have done in his place.'

'Anyone who had not his cloth to think of.'

'For goodness' sake, Uncle Watkyn, a fellow can't be thinking of cloth all the time. It was an emergency. Roderick was murdering Gussie Fink-Nottle.'

'And Mr. Pinker *stopped* him? Great heavens!'

There was a pause while Pop Bassett struggled with his feelings. Then Stiffy, as Stinker had done with Spode, had a shot at the honeyed word. She had spoken of Stinker cooing to Spode like a turtle dove, and if memory served me aright that was just how he had cooed, and it was of a cooing turtle dove that she now reminded me. Like most girls, she can always get a melting note into her voice if she thinks there's any percentage to be derived from it.

'It's not like you, Uncle Watkyn, to go back on your solemn promise.'

I could have corrected her there. I would have thought it was just like him.

'I can't believe it's really you who's doing this cruel thing to me. It's so unlike you. You have always been so kind to me. You have made me love and respect you. I have come to look on you as a second father. Don't louse the whole thing up now.'

A powerful plea, which with any other man would undoubtedly have brought home the bacon. With Pop Bassett it didn't get to first base. He had been looking like a man with no bowels – of compassion, I mean of course – and he went on looking like one.

'If by that peculiar expression you intend to imply that you are expecting me to change my mind and give Mr. Pinker this vicarage,

I must disappoint you. I shall do no such thing. I consider that he has shown himself unfit to be a vicar, and I am surprised that after what has occurred he can reconcile it with his conscience to continue his duties as a curate.'

Strong stuff, of course, and it drew from Stinker what may have been a hollow groan or may have been a hiccup. I myself looked coldly at the old egg and I rather think I curled my lip, though I should say it was very doubtful if he noticed my scorn, for his attention was earmarked for Stiffy. She had turned almost as scarlet as Stinker, and I heard a distinct click as her front teeth met. It was through these teeth (clenched) that she spoke.

'So that's how you feel about it?'

'It is.'

'Your decision is final?'

'Quite final.'

'Nothing will move you?'

'Nothing.'

'I see,' said Stiffy, having chewed the lower lip for a space in silence. 'Well, you'll be sorry.'

'I disagree with you.'

'You will. Just wait. Bitter remorse is coming to you, Uncle Watkyn. Never underestimate the power of a woman,' said Stiffy, and with a choking sob – though there again it may have been a hiccup – she rushed from the room.

She had scarcely left us when Butterfield entered, and Pop Bassett eyed him with the ill-concealed petulance with which men of testy habit eye butlers who butt in at the wrong moment.

'Yes, Butterfield? What is it, what is it?'

'Constable Oates desires a word with you, sir.'

'Who?'

'Police Constable Oates, sir.'

'What does he want?'

'I gather that he has a clue to the identity of the boy who threw a hard-boiled egg at you, sir.'

The words acted on Pop Bassett as I'm told the sound of bugles acts on war-horses, not that I've ever seen a war-horse. His whole demeanour changed in a flash. His face lit up, and there came into it the sort of look you see on the faces of bloodhounds when they settle down to the trail. He didn't actually say 'Whoopee!' but that was probably because the expression was not familiar to him. He was out of the room in a matter of seconds, Butterfield lying some lengths behind, and Stinker, who had been replacing a framed photograph which he had knocked off a neighbouring table, addressed me in what you might call a hushed voice.

'I say, Bertie, what do you think Stiffy meant when she said that?'

I, too, had been speculating as to what the young pipsqueak had had in mind. A sinister thing to say, it seemed to me. Those words 'Just wait' had had an ominous ring. I weighed his question gravely.

'Difficult to decide,' I said, 'it may be one thing, or it may be another.'

'She has such an impulsive nature.'

'Very impulsive.'

'It makes me uneasy.'

'Why you? Pop B's the one who ought to be feeling uneasy. Knowing her as I do, if I were in his place –'

The sentence I had begun would, if it had come to fruition, have concluded with the words 'I'd pack a few necessaries in a suitcase and go to Australia,' but as I was about to utter them I chanced to glance out of the window and they froze on my lips.

The window looked on the drive, and from where I was standing I got a good view of the front steps, and when I saw what was coming up those front steps, my heart leaped from its base.

It was Plank. There was no mistaking that square, tanned face and that purposeful walk of his. And when I reflected that in about a couple of ticks Butterfield would be showing him into the drawing-room where I stood and we would meet once more, I confess that I was momentarily at a loss to know how to proceed.

My first thought was to wait till he had got through the front door and then nip out of the window, which was conveniently open. That, I felt, was what Napoleon would have done. And I was just about to get the show on the road, as Stiffy would have said, when I saw the dog Bartholomew coming sauntering along, and I knew that I would be compelled to revise my strategy from the bottom up. You can't go climbing out of windows under the eyes of an Aberdeen terrier so prone as Bartholomew was always to think the worst. In due season, no doubt, he would learn that what he had taken for a burglar escaping with the swag had been in reality a harmless guest of the house and would be all apologies, but by that time my lower slopes would be as full of holes as a Swiss cheese.

Falling back on my second line of defence, I slid behind the sofa with a muttered, 'Not a word to a soul, Stinker. Chap I don't want to meet,' and was nestling there like a turtle in its shell, when the door opened.

20

It's pretty generally recognized at the Drones Club and elsewhere that Bertram Wooster is a man who knows how to keep the chin up and the upper lip stiff, no matter how rough the going may be. Beneath the bludgeonings of Fate, his head is bloody but unbowed, as the fellow said. In a word, he can take it.

But I must admit that as I crouched in my haven of refuge I found myself chafing not a little. Life at Totleigh Towers, as I mentioned earlier, had got me down. There seemed no way of staying put in the darned house. One was either soaring like an eagle on to the top of chests or whizzing down behind sofas like a diving duck, and apart from the hustle and bustle of it all that sort of thing wounds the spirit and does no good to the trouser crease. And so, as I say, I chafed.

I was becoming increasingly bitter about this man Plank and the tendency he seemed to be developing of haunting me like a family spectre. I couldn't imagine what he was doing here. Whatever the faults of Totleigh Towers, I had supposed that, when there, one would at least be free from his society. He had an excellent home in Hockley-cum-Meston, and one sought in vain for an explanation of why the hell he didn't stay in it.

My disapproval extended to the personnel of the various native tribes he had encountered in the course of his explorations. On his own showing, he had for years been horning in uninvited on the aborigines of Brazil, the Congo and elsewhere, and not one of them apparently had had the enterprise to get after him with a spear or to say it with poisoned darts from the family blowpipe. And these were fellows who called themselves savages. Savages, forsooth! The savages in the books I used to read in my childhood would have had him in the Obituary column before he could say 'What ho', but with the ones you get nowadays it's all slackness and laissez-faire. Can't be bothered. Leave it to somebody else. Let George do it. One sometimes wonders what the world's coming to.

From where I sat my range of vision was necessarily a bit restricted, but I was able to see a pair of Empire-building brogue shoes, so I assumed that when the door had opened it was Butterfield showing him in, and this surmise was confirmed a moment later when he spoke. His was a voice which, once heard, lingers in the memory.

'Afternoon,' he said.

'Good afternoon,' said Stinker.

'Warm day.'

'Very warm.'

'What's been going on here? What are all those tents and swings and things in the park?'

Stinker explained that the annual school treat had only just concluded, and Plank expressed his gratification at having missed it. School treats, he said, were dashed dangerous things, always to be avoided by the shrewd, as they were only too apt to include competitions for bonny babies.

'Did you have a competition for bonny babies?'

'Yes, we did, as a matter of fact. The mothers always insist on it.'

'The mothers are the ones you want to watch out for,' said Plank. 'I'm not saying the little beasts aren't bad enough themselves, dribbling out of the side of their mouths at you and all that sort of thing, but it's the mothers who constitute the really grave peril. Look,' he said, and I think he must at this point have pulled up a trouser leg. 'See that scar on my calf? That's what I got in Peru once for being fool enough to let myself be talked into judging a competition for bonny babies. The mother of one of the Honourably Mentioneds spiked me in the leg with a native dagger as I was stepping down from the judge's stand after making my speech. Hurt like sin, I can assure you, and still gives me a twinge when the weather's wet. Fellow I know is fond of saying that the hand that rocks the cradle rules the world. Whether this is so or not I couldn't tell you, but it certainly knows how to handle a Peruvian dagger.'

I found myself revising to some extent the rather austere opinion I had formed of the slackness and lack of ginger of the modern native. The males might have lost their grip in recent years, but the female element, it seemed, still had the right stuff in them, though of course where somebody like Plank is concerned, a stab in the fleshy part of the leg is only a step in the right direction, merely scratching the surface as you might say.

Plank continued chatty. 'You live in these parts?' he said.

'Yes, I live in the village.'

'Totleigh?'

'Yes.'

'Don't run a Rugger club in Totleigh, do you?'

Stinker replied in the negative. The Totleigh-in-the-Wold athletes, he said, preferred the Association code, and Plank, probably shuddering, said 'Good God!'

'You ever played Rugger?'

'A little.'

'You should take it up seriously. No finer sport. I'm trying to make the Hockley-cum-Meston team the talk of Gloucestershire. I coach the boys daily, and they're coming along very nicely, very nicely indeed. What I need is a good prop forward.'

What he got was Pop Bassett, who came bustling in at this moment. He Good-afternoon-Plank-ed, and Plank responded in suitable terms.

'Very nice of you to look me up, Plank,' said Pop. 'Will you have something to drink?'

'Ah,' said Plank, and you could see that he meant it.

'I would ask you to stay to dinner, but unfortunately one of my guests has eloped with the cook.'

'Dashed sensible of him, if he was going to elope with anyone. Very hard to find these days, cooks.'

'It has of course completely disorganized our domestic arrangements. Neither my daughter nor my niece is capable of preparing even the simplest meal.'

'You'll have to go to the pub.'

'It seems the only solution.'

'If you were in West Africa, you could drop in and take pot luck with a native chief.'

'I am not in West Africa,' said Pop Bassett, speaking, I thought, a little testily, and I could understand him feeling a bit miffed. It's always annoying when you're up against it and people tell you what a jolly time you could be having if you weren't and how topping everything would be if you were somewhere where you aren't.

'I dined out a good deal in West Africa,' said Plank. 'Capital dinners some of those fellows used to give me, I remember, though there was always the drawback that you could never be sure the main dish wasn't one of their wives' relations, broiled over a slow fire and disguised in some native sauce. Took the edge off your appetite, unless you were feeling particularly peckish.'

'So I would be disposed to imagine.'

'All a matter of taste, of course.'

'Quite. Was there something you particularly wished to see me about, Plank?'

'No, nothing that I can think of.'

'Then if you will excuse me, I will be getting back to Madeline.'

'Who's Madeline?'

'My daughter. Your arrival interrupted me in a serious talk I was having with her.'

'Something wrong with the girl?'

'Something extremely wrong. She is contemplating making a disastrous marriage.'

'All marriages are disastrous,' said Plank, who gave one the impression, reading between the lines, that he was a bachelor. 'They lead to bonny babies, and bonny babies lead to bonny baby competitions. I was telling this gentleman here of an experience I had in Peru and showing him the scar on my leg, the direct result of being ass enough to judge one of these competitions. Would you care to see the scar on my leg?'

'Some other time, perhaps.'

'Any time that suits you. Why is this marriage you say she's contemplating so disastrous?'

'Because Mr. Wooster is not a suitable husband for her.'

'Who's Mr. Wooster?'

'The man she wishes to marry. A typical young wastrel of the type so common nowadays.'

'I used to know a fellow called Wooster, but I don't suppose it can be the same chap, because my Wooster was eaten by a crocodile on the Zambesi the other day, which rather rules him out. All right, Bassett, you pop back to the girl and tell her from me that if she's going to start marrying every Tom, Dick and Harry she comes across, she ought to have her head examined. If she'd seen as many native chiefs' wives as I have, she wouldn't be wanting to make such an ass of herself. Dickens of a life they lead, those women. Nothing to do but grind maize meal and have bonny babies. Right ho, Bassett, don't let me keep you.'

There came the sound of a closing door as Pop Bassett sped on his way, and Plank turned his attention to Stinker. He said:

'I didn't tell that old ass, because I didn't want him sticking around in here talking his head off, but as a matter of fact I did come about something special. Do you happen to know where I can find a chap called Pinker?'

'My name's Pinker.'

'Are you sure? I thought Bassett said it was Wooster.'

'No, Wooster's the one who's going to marry Sir Watkyn's daughter.'

'So he is. It all comes back to me now. I wonder if you can be the fellow I want. The Pinker I'm after is a curate.'

'I'm a curate.'

'You are? Yes, by Jove, you're perfectly right. I see your collar buttons at the back. You're not H. P. Pinker by any chance?'

'Yes.'

'Prop forward for Oxford and England a few years ago?'

'Yes.'

'Well, would you be interested in becoming a vicar?'

There was a crashing sound, and I knew that Stinker in his emotion must have upset his customary table. After a while he said in a husky voice that the one thing he wanted was to get his hooks on a vicarage or words to that effect, and Plank said he was glad to hear it.

'My chap at Hockley-cum-Meston is downing tools now that his ninetieth birthday is approaching, and I've been scouring the countryside for a spare. Extraordinarily difficult the quest has been, because what I wanted was a vicar who was a good prop forward, and it isn't often you find a parson who knows one end of a football from the other. I've never seen you play, I'm sorry to say, because I've been abroad so much, but with your record you must obviously be outstanding. So you can take up your duties as soon as old Bellamy goes into storage. When I get home, I'll embody the thing in the form of a letter.'

Stinker said he didn't know how to thank him, and Plank said that was all right, no need of any thanks.

'I'm the one who ought to be grateful. We're all right at half-back and three-quarters, but we lost to Upper Bleaching last year simply because our prop forward proved a broken reed. This year we'll show 'em. Amazing bit of luck finding you, and I could never have done it if it hadn't been for a friend of mine, a Chief Inspector Witherspoon of Scotland Yard. He phoned me just now and told me you were to be found at Totleigh-in-the-Wold. He said if I called at Totleigh Towers, they would give me your address. Extraordinary how these Scotland Yard fellows nose things out. The result of years of practise, I suppose. What was that noise?'

Stinker said he had heard nothing.

'Sort of gasping noise. Seemed to come from behind that sofa. Take a look.'

I was aware for a moment of Stinker's face peering down at me; then he turned away.

'There's nothing behind the sofa,' he said, very decently imperilling his immortal soul by falsifying the facts on behalf of a pal.

'Thought it might be a dog being sick,' said Plank.

And I suppose it had sounded rather like that. The revelation of Jeeves's black treachery had shaken me to my foundations, causing me to forget that in the existing circs silence was golden. A silly thing to do, of course, to gasp like that, but, dash it, if for years you have nursed a gentleman's personal gentleman in your bosom and out of a blue sky you find that he has deliberately sicked Brazilian explorers on to you, I maintain that you're fully entitled to behave like a dog in the throes of nausea. I could make nothing of his scurvy conduct, and was so stunned that for a minute or two I lost the thread of the conversation. When the mists cleared, Plank was speaking, and the subject had been changed.

'I wonder how Bassett is getting on with that daughter of his. Do you know anything of this chap Wooster?'

'He's one of my best friends.'

'Bassett doesn't seem too fond of him.'

'No.'

'Ah well, we all have our likes and dislikes. Which of the two girls is this Madeline he was speaking of? I've never met them, but I've seen them around. Is she the little squirt with the large blue eyes?'

I should imagine Stinker didn't care overmuch for hearing his loved one described as a little squirt, though reason must have told him that that was precisely what she was, but he replied without heat.

'No, that's Sir Watkyn's niece, Stephanie Byng.'

'Byng? Now why does that name seem to ring a bell? Oh yes, of course. Old Johnny Byng, who was with me on one of my expeditions. Red-haired fellow, haven't seen him for years. He was bitten by a puma, poor chap, and they tell me he still hesitates in a rather noticeable manner before sitting down. Stephanie Byng, eh? You know her, of course?'

'Very well.'

'Nice girl?'

'That's how she seems to me, and if you don't mind, I'll be going and telling her the good news.'

'What good news?'

'About the vicarage.'

'Oh, ah, yes. You think she'll be interested?'

'I'm sure she will. We're going to be married.'

'Good God! No chance of getting out of it?'

'I don't want to get out of it.'

'Amazing! I once hitch-hiked all the way from Johannesburg to Cape Town to avoid getting married, and here you are seeming quite pleased at the prospect. Oh well, no accounting for tastes. All right, you run along. And I suppose I'd better have a word with Bassett before I leave. Fellow bores me stiff, but one has to be civil.'

The door closed and silence fell, and after waiting a few minutes, just in case, I felt it was safe to surface. And I had just done so and was limbering up the limbs, which had become somewhat cramped, when the door opened and Jeeves came in carrying a tray.

21

'Good evening, sir,' he said. 'Would you care for an appetizer? I was obliging Mr. Butterfield by bringing them. He is engaged at the moment in listening at the door of the room where Sir Watkyn is in conference with Miss Bassett. He tells me he is compiling his Memoirs, never misses an opportunity of gathering suitable material.'

I gave the man one of my looks. My face was cold and hard, like a School Treat egg. I can't remember a time when I've been fuller of righteous indignation.

'What I want, Jeeves, is not a slab of wet bread with a dead sardine on it —'

'Anchovy, sir.'

'Or anchovy. I am in no mood to split straws. I require an explanation, and a categorical one, at that.'

'Sir?'

'You can't evade the issue by saying "Sir?". Answer me this, Jeeves, with a simple Yes or No. Why did you tell Plank to come to Totleigh Towers?'

I thought the query would crumple him up like a damp sock, but he didn't so much as shuffle a foot.

'My heart was melted by Miss Byng's tale of her misfortunes, sir. I chanced to encounter the young lady and found her in a state of considerable despondency as the result of Sir Watkyn's refusal to bestow a vicarage on Mr. Pinker. I perceived immediately that it was within my power to alleviate her distress. I had learned at the post office at Hockley-cum-Meston that the incumbent there was retiring shortly, and being cognizant of Major Plank's desire to strengthen the Hockley-cum-Meston forward line, I felt that it would be an excellent idea to place him in communication with Mr. Pinker. In order to be in a position to marry Miss Byng, Mr. Pinker requires a vicarage, and in order to compete successfully with rival villages in the football arena Major Plank is in need of a vicar with Mr. Pinker's wide experience as a prop forward. Their interests appeared to me to be identical.'

'Well, it worked all right. Stinker has clicked.'

'He is to succeed Mr. Bellamy as incumbent at Hockley-cum-Meston?'

'As soon as Bellamy calls it a day.'

'I am very happy to hear it, sir.'

I didn't reply for a while, being obliged to attend to a sudden touch of cramp.

This ironed out, I said, still icy:

'You may be happy, but I haven't been for the last quarter of an hour or so, nestling behind the sofa and expecting Plank at any moment to unmask me. It didn't occur to you to envisage what would happen if he met me?'

'I was sure that your keen intelligence would enable you to find a means of avoiding him, sir, as indeed it did. You concealed yourself behind the sofa?'

'On all fours.'

'A very shrewd manoeuvre on your part, if I may say so, sir. It showed a resource and swiftness of thought which it would be difficult to overpraise.'

My iciness melted. It is not too much to say that I was mollified. It's not often that I'm given the old oil in this fashion, most of my circle, notably my Aunt Agatha, being more prone to the slam than the rave. And it was only after I had been savouring that 'keen intelligence' gag, if savouring is the word I want, for some moments that I suddenly remembered that marriage with Madeline Bassett loomed ahead, and I gave a start so visible that he asked me if I was feeling unwell.

I shook the loaf.

'Physically, no, Jeeves. Spiritually, yes.'

'I do not quite understand you, sir.'

'Well, here is the news, and this is Bertram Wooster reading it. I'm going to be married.'

'Indeed, sir?'

'Yes, Jeeves, married. The banns are as good as up.'

'Would it be taking a liberty if I were to ask —'

'Who to? You don't need to ask. Gussie Fink-Nottle has eloped with Emerald Stoker, thus creating a . . . what is it?'

'Would vacuum be the word you are seeking, sir?'

'That's right. A vacuum which I shall have to fill. Unless you can think of some way of getting me out of it.'

'I will devote considerable thought to the matter, sir.'

'Thank you, Jeeves,' I said, and would have spoken further, but at this moment I saw the door opening and speechlessness supervened. But it wasn't, as I had feared, Plank, it was only Stiffy.

'Hullo, you two,' she said. 'I'm looking for Harold.'

I could see at a g. that Jeeves had been right in describing her demeanour as despondent. The brow was clouded and the general appearance that of an overwrought soul. I was glad to be in a position to inject a little sunshine into her life. Pigeon-holing my own troubles for future reference, I said:

'He's looking for you. He has a strange story to relate. You know about Plank?'

'What about him?'

'I'll tell you what about him. Plank to you hitherto has been merely a shadowy figure who hangs out at Hockley-cum-Meston and sells black amber statuettes to people, but he has another side to him.'

She betrayed a certain impatience.

'If you think I'm interested in Plank —'

'Aren't you?'

'No, I'm not.'

'You will be. He has, as I was saying, another side to him. He is a landed proprietor with vicarages in his gift, and to cut a long story down to a short-short, as one always likes to do when possible, he has just given one to Stinker.'

I had been right in supposing that the information would have a marked effect on her dark mood. I have never actually seen a corpse spring from its bier and start being the life and soul of the party, but I should imagine that its deportment would closely resemble that of this young Byng as the impact of my words came home to her. A sudden light shot into her eyes, which, as Plank had correctly said, were large and blue, and an ecstatic 'Well, Lord love a duck!' escaped her. Then doubts seemed to creep in, for the eyes clouded over again.

'Is this true?'

'Absolutely official.'

'You aren't pulling my leg?'

I drew myself up rather haughtily.

'I wouldn't dream of pulling your leg. Do you think Bertram Wooster is the sort of chap who thinks it funny to raise people's hopes, only to . . . what, Jeeves?'

'Dash them to the ground, sir.'

'Thank you, Jeeves.'

'Not at all, sir.'

'You may take this information as coming straight from the mouth of the stable cat. I was present when the deal went through. Behind the sofa, but present.'

She still seemed at a loss.

'But I don't understand. Plank has never met Harold.'

'Jeeves brought them together.'

'Did you, Jeeves?'

'Yes, miss.'

' 'At-a-boy!'

'Thank you, miss.'

'And he's really given Harold a vicarage?'

'The vicarage of Hockley-cum-Meston. He's embodying it in the form of a letter tonight. At the moment there's a vicar still vicking, but he's infirm and old and wants to turn it up as soon as they can put on an understudy. The way things look, I should imagine that we shall be able to unleash Stinker on the Hockley-cum-Meston souls in the course of the next few days.'

My simple words and earnest manner had resolved the last of her doubts. The misgivings she may have had as to whether this was the real ginger vanished. Her eyes shone more like twin stars than anything, and she uttered animal cries and danced a few dance steps. Presently she paused, and put a question.

'What's Plank like?'

'How do you mean, what's he like?'

'He hasn't a beard, has he?'

'No, no beard.'

'That's good, because I want to kiss him, and if he had a beard, it would give me pause.'

'Dismiss the notion,' I urged, for Plank's psychology was an open book to me. The whole trend of that confirmed bachelor's conversation had left me with the impression that he would find it infinitely preferable to be spiked in the leg with a native dagger than to have popsies covering his upturned face with kisses. 'He'd have a fit.'

'Well, I must kiss somebody. Shall I kiss you, Jeeves?'

'No, thank you, miss.'

'You, Bertie?'

'I'd rather you didn't.'

'Then I've a good mind to go and kiss Uncle Watkyn, louse of the first water though he has recently shown himself.'

'How do you mean, recently?'

'And having kissed him I shall tell him the news and taunt him vigorously with having let a good thing get away from him. I shall tell him that when he declined to avail himself of Harold's services he was like the Indian.'

I did not get her drift.

'What Indian?'

'The base one my governesses used to make me read about, the poor simp whose hand . . . How does it go, Jeeves?'

'Threw a pearl away richer than all his tribe, miss.'

'That's right. And I shall tell him I hope the vicar he does get will be a weed of a man who has a chronic cold in the head and bleats. Oh, by the way, talking of Uncle Watkyn reminds me. I shan't have any use for this now.'

And so speaking she produced the black amber eyesore from the recesses of her costume like a conjuror taking a rabbit out of a hat.

22

It was as if she had suddenly exhibited a snake of the lowest order. I gazed at the thing, appalled. It needed but this to put the frosting on the cake.

'Where did you get that?' I asked in a voice that was low and trembled.

'I pinched it.'

'What on earth did you do that for?'

'Perfectly simple. The idea was to go to Uncle Watkyn and tell him he wouldn't get it back unless he did the square thing by Harold. Power politics, don't they call it, Jeeves?'

'Or blackmail, miss.'

'Yes, or blackmail, I suppose. But you can't be too nice in your methods when you're dealing with the Uncle Watkyns of this world. But now that Plank has eased the situation and made our paths straight, of course I shan't need it, and I suppose the shrewd thing is to return it to store before its absence is noted. Go and put it in the collection room, Bertie. Here's the key.'

I recoiled as if she had offered me the dog Bartholomew. Priding myself as I do on being a preux chevalier, I like to oblige the delicately nurtured when it's feasible, but there are moments when only a *nolle prosequi* will serve, and I recognized this as one of them. The thought of making the perilous passage she was suggesting gave me goose pimples.

'I'm not going near the ruddy collection room. With my luck, I'd find your Uncle Watkyn there, arm in arm with Spode, and it wouldn't be too easy to explain what I was doing there and how I'd got in. Besides, I can't go roaming about the place with Plank on the premises.'

She laughed one of those silvery ones, a practice to which, as I have indicated, she was far too much addicted.

'Jeeves told me about you and Plank. Very funny.'

'I'm glad you think so. We personally were not amused.'

Jeeves, as always, found the way.

'If you will give the object to me, miss, I will see that it is restored to its place.'

'Thank you, Jeeves. Well, good-bye all. I'm off to find Harold,' said Stiffy, and she withdrew, dancing on the tips of her toes.

I shrugged a shoulder.

'Women, Jeeves!'

'Yes, sir.'

'What a sex!'

'Yes, sir.'

'Do you remember something I said to you about Stiffy on our previous visit to Totleigh Towers?'

'Not at the moment, no, sir.'

'It was on the occasion when she landed me with Police Constable Oates's helmet just as my room was about to be searched by Pop Bassett and his minions. Dipping into the future, I pointed out that Stiffy, who is pure padded cell from the foundations up, was planning to marry the Rev. H.P. Pinker, himself as pronounced a goop as ever preached about the Hivites and Hittites, and I speculated, if you recall, as to what their offspring, if any, would be like.'

'Ah yes, sir, I recollect now.'

'Would they, I asked myself, inherit the combined loopiness of two such parents?'

'Yes, sir, you were particularly concerned, I recall, for the well-being of the nurses, governesses, private schoolmasters and public school-masters who would assume the charge of them.'

'Little knowing that they were coming up against something hotter than mustard. Exactly. The thought still weighs heavy upon me. However, we haven't leisure to go into the subject now. You'd better take that ghastly object back where it belongs without delay.'

'Yes, sir. If it were done when 'twere done, then 'twere well it were done quickly,' he said, making for the door, and I thought, as I had so often thought before, how neatly he put these things.

It seemed to me that the time had now come to adopt the strategy which I had had in mind right at the beginning – viz. to make my getaway via the window. With Plank at large in the house and likely at any moment to come winging back to where the drinks were, safety could be obtained only by making for some distant yew alley or rhododendron walk and remaining ensconced there till he had blown over. I hastened to the window, accordingly, and picture my chagrin and dismay on finding that Bartholomew, instead of continuing his stroll, had decided to take a siesta on the grass immediately below. I had actually got one leg over the sill before he was drawn to my attention. In another half jiffy I should have dropped on him as the gentle rain from heaven upon the spot beneath.

I had no difficulty in recognizing the situation as what the French call an *impasse*, and as I stood pondering what to do for the best, footsteps sounded without, and feeling that 'twere well it were done quickly I made for the sofa once more, lowering my previous record by perhaps a split second.

I was surprised, as I lay nestling in my little nook, by the complete absence of dialogue that ensued. Hitherto, all my visitors had started chatting from the moment of their entry, and it struck me as odd that I should now be entertaining a couple of deaf mutes. Peeping cautiously out, however, I found that I had been mistaken in supposing that I had with me a brace of guests. It was Madeline alone who had blown in. She was heading for the piano, and something told me that it was her intention to sing old folk songs, a pastime to which, as I have indicated, she devoted not a little of her leisure. She was particularly given to indulgence in this nuisance when her soul had been undergoing an upheaval and required soothing, as of course it probably did at this juncture.

My fears were realized. She sang two in rapid succession, and the thought that this sort of thing would be a permanent feature of our married life chilled me to the core. I've always been what you might call allergic to old folk songs, and the older they are, the more I dislike them.

Fortunately, before she could start on a third she was interrupted. Clumping footsteps sounded, the door handle turned, heavy breathing made itself heard, and a voice said 'Madeline!' Spode's voice, husky with emotion.

'Madeline,' he said, 'I've been looking for you everywhere.'

'Oh, Roderick! How is your eye?'

'Never mind my eye,' said Spode. 'I didn't come here to talk about eyes.'

'They say a piece of beefsteak reduces the swelling.'

'Nor about beefsteaks. Sir Watkyn has told me the awful news about you and Wooster. Is it true you're going to marry him?'

'Yes, Roderick, it is true.'

'But you can't love a half-baked, half-witted ass like Wooster,' said Spode, and I thought the remark extremely offensive. Pick your words more carefully, Spode, I might have said, rising and confronting him. However, for one reason and another I didn't, but continued to nestle and I heard Madeline sigh, unless it was the draught under the sofa.

'No, Roderick, I do not love him. He does not appeal to the essential me. But I feel it is my duty to make him happy.'

'Tchah!' said Spode, or something that sounded like that. 'Why on earth do you want to go about making worms like Wooster happy?'

'He loves me, Roderick. You must have seen that dumb, worshipping look in his eyes as he gazes at me.'

'I've something better to do than peer into Wooster's eyes. Though I can well imagine they look dumb. We've got to have this thing out, Madeline.'

'I don't understand you, Roderick.'

'You will.'

'Ouch!'

I think on the cue 'You will' he must have grabbed her by the wrist, for the word 'Ouch!' had come through strong and clear, and this suspicion was confirmed when she said he was hurting her.

'I'm sorry, sorry,' said Spode. 'But I refuse to allow you to ruin your life. You can't marry this man Wooster. I'm the one you're going to marry.'

I was with him heart and soul, as the expression is. Nothing would ever make me really fond of Roderick Spode, but I liked the way he was talking. A little more of this, I felt, and Bertram would be released from his honourable obligations. I wished he had thought of taking this firm line earlier.

'I've loved you since you were so high.'

Not being able to see him, I couldn't ascertain how high that was, but I presumed he must have been holding his hand not far from the floor. A couple of feet, would you say? About that, I suppose.

Madeline was plainly moved. I heard her gurgle.

'I know, Roderick, I know.'

'You guessed my secret?'

'Yes, Roderick. How sad life is!'

Spode declined to string along with her in this view.

'Not a bit of it. Life's fine. At least, it will be if you give this blighter Wooster the push and marry me.'

'I have always been devoted to you, Roderick.'

'Well, then?'

'Give me time to think.'

'Carry on. Take all the time you need.'

'I don't want to break Bertie's heart.'

'Why not? Do him good.'

'He loves me so dearly.'

'Nonsense. I don't suppose he has ever loved anything in his life except a dry martini.'

'How can you say that? Did he not come here because he found it impossible to stay away from me?'

'No, he jolly well didn't. Don't let him fool you on that point. He came here to pinch that black amber statuette of your father's.'

'What!'

'That's what. In addition to being half-witted, he's a low thief.'

'It can't be true!'

'Of course it's true. His uncle wants the thing for his collection. I heard him plotting with his aunt on the telephone not half an hour ago. "It's going to be pretty hard to get away with it," he was saying, "but I'll do my best. I know how much Uncle Tom covets that statuette." He's always stealing things. The very first time I met him, in an antique shop in the Brompton Road, he as near as a toucher got away with your father's umbrella.'

A monstrous charge, and one which I can readily refute. He and Pop Bassett and I were, I concede, in the antique shop in the Brompton Road to which he had alluded, but the umbrella sequence was purely one of those laughable misunderstandings. Pop Bassett had left the blunt instrument propped against a seventeenth-century chair, and what caused me to take it up was the primeval instinct which makes a man without an umbrella, as I happened to be that morning, reach out unconsciously for the nearest one in sight, like a flower turning to the sun. The whole thing could have been explained in two words, but they hadn't let me say even one, and the slur had been allowed to rest on me.

'You shock me, Roderick!' said Madeline.

'Yes, I thought it would make you sit up.'

'If this is really so, if Bertie is really a thief –'

'Well?'

'Naturally I will have nothing more to do with him. But I can't believe it.'

'I'll go and fetch Sir Watkyn,' said Spode. 'Perhaps you'll believe him.'

For several minutes after he had clumped out, Madeline must have stood in a reverie, for I didn't hear a sound out of her. Then the door opened, and the next thing that came across was a cough which I had no difficulty in recognizing.

23

It was that soft cough of Jeeves's which always reminds me of a very old sheep clearing its throat on a distant mountain top. He coughed it at me, if you remember, on the occasion when I first swam into his ken wearing the Alpine hat. It generally signifies disapproval, but I've known it to occur also when he's about to touch on a topic of a delicate nature. And when he spoke, I knew that that was what he was going to do now, for there was a sort of hushed note in his voice.

'I wonder if I might have a moment of your time, miss?'

'Of course, Jeeves.'

'It is with reference to Mr. Wooster.'

'Oh, yes?'

'I must begin by saying that I chanced to be passing the door when Lord Sidcup was speaking to you and inadvertently overheard his lordship's observations on the subject of Mr. Wooster. His lordship has a carrying voice. And I find myself in a somewhat equivocal position, torn between loyalty to my employer and a natural desire to do my duty as a citizen.'

'I don't understand you, Jeeves,' said Madeline, which made two of us.

He coughed again.

'I am anxious not to take a liberty, miss, but if I may speak frankly –'

'Please do.'

'Thank you, miss. His lordship's words seemed to confirm a rumour which is circulating in the servants' hall that you are contemplating a matrimonial union with Mr. Wooster. Would it be indiscreet of me if I were to inquire if this is so?'

'Yes, Jeeves, it is quite true.'

'If you will pardon me for saying so, I think you are making a mistake.'

Well spoken, Jeeves, you are on the right lines, I was saying to myself, and I hoped he was going to rub it in. I waited anxiously for Madeline's reply, a little afraid that she would draw herself to her full height and dismiss him from her presence. But she didn't. She merely said again that she didn't understand him.

'If I might explain, miss. I am loath to criticize my employer, but I feel that you should know that he is a kleptomaniac.'

'What!'

'Yes, miss. I had hoped to be able to preserve his little secret, as I have always done hitherto, but he has now gone to lengths which I cannot countenance. In going through his effects this afternoon I discovered this small black figure, concealed beneath his underwear.'

I heard Madeline utter a sound like a dying soda-water syphon.

'But that belongs to my father!'

'If I may say so, nothing belongs to anyone if Mr. Wooster takes a fancy to it.'

'Then Lord Sidcup was right?'

'Precisely, miss.'

'He said Mr. Wooster tried to steal my father's umbrella.'

'I heard him, and the charge was well founded. Umbrellas, jewellery, statuettes, they are all grist to Mr. Wooster's mill. I do not think he can help it. It is a form of mental illness. But whether a jury would take that view, I cannot say.'

Madeline went into the soda-syphon routine once more.

'You mean he might be sent to prison?'

'It is a contingency that seems to me far from remote.'

Again I felt that he was on the right lines. His trained senses told him that if there's one thing that puts a girl off marrying a chap, it is the thought that the honeymoon may be spoiled at any moment by the arrival of Inspectors at the love nest, come to scoop him in for larceny. No young bride likes that sort of thing, and you can't blame her if she finds herself preferring to team up with someone like Spode, who, though a gorilla in fairly human shape, is known to keep strictly on the right side of the law. I could almost hear Madeline's thoughts turning in this direction, and I applauded Jeeves's sound grip on the psychology of the individual, as he calls it.

Of course, I could see that all this wasn't going to make my position in the Bassett home any too good, but there are times when only the surgeon's knife will serve. And I had the sustaining thought that if ever I got out from behind this sofa I could sneak off to where my car waited champing at the bit and drive off Londonwards without stopping to say goodbye and thanks for a delightful visit. This would obviate – is it obviate? – all unpleasantness.

Madeline continued shaken.

'Oh dear, Oh dear!' she said.

'Yes, miss.'

'This has come as a great shock.'

'I can readily appreciate it, miss.'

'Have you known of this long?'

'Ever since I entered Mr. Wooster's employment.'

'Oh dear, Oh dear! Well, thank you, Jeeves.'

'Not at all, miss.'

I think Jeeves must have shimmered off after this, for silence fell and nothing happened except that my nose began to tickle. I would have given ten quid to have been able to sneeze, but this of course was outside the range of practical politics. I just crouched there, thinking of this and that, and after quite a while the door opened once more, this time to admit something in the nature of a mob scene. I could see three pairs of shoes, and deduced that they were those of Spode, Pop Bassett and Plank. Spode, it will be recalled, had gone to fetch Pop, and Plank presumably had come along for the ride, hoping no doubt for something moist at journey's end.

Spode was the first to speak, and his voice rang with the triumph that comes into the voices of suitors who have caught a dangerous rival bending.

'Here we are,' he said. 'I've brought Sir Watkyn to support my statement that Wooster is a low sneak thief who goes about snapping up everything that isn't nailed down. You agree, Sir Watkyn?'

'Of course I do, Roderick. It's only a month or so ago that he and that aunt of his stole my cow-creamer.'

'What's a cow-creamer?' asked Plank.

'A silver cream jug, one of the gems of my collection.'

'They got away with it, did they?'

'They did.'

'Ah,' said Plank. 'Then in that case I think I'll have a whisky and soda.'

Pop Bassett was warming to his theme. His voice rose above the hissing of Plank's syphon.

'And it was only by the mercy of Providence that Wooster didn't make off with my umbrella that day in the Brompton Road. If that young man has one defect more marked than another, it is that he appears to be totally ignorant of the distinction between *meum* and *tuum*. He came up before me in my court once, I remember, charged with having stolen a policeman's helmet, and it is a lasting regret to me that I merely fined him five pounds.'

'Mistaken kindness,' said Spode.

'So I have always felt, Roderick. A sharper lesson might have done him all the good in the world.'

'Never does to let these fellows off lightly,' said Plank. 'I had a servant chap in Mozambique who used to help himself to my cigars, and I foolishly overlooked it because he assured me he had got religion and everything would be quite all right from now on. And it wasn't a week later that he skipped out, taking with him a box of Havanas and my false teeth, which he sold to one of the native chiefs in the neighbourhood. Cost me a case of trade gin and two strings of beads to get them back. Severity's the only thing. The iron hand. Anything else is mistaken for weakness.'

Madeline gave a sob, at least it sounded like a sob.

'But, Daddy.'

'Well?'

'I don't think Bertie can help himself.'

'My dear child, it is precisely his habit of helping himself to everything he can lay his hands on that we are criticizing.'

'I mean, he's a kleptomaniac.'

'Eh? Who told you that?'

'Jeeves.'

'That's odd. How did the subject come up?'

'He told me when he gave me this. He found it in Bertie's room. He was very worried about it.'

There was a spot of silence – of a stunned nature, I imagine. Then Pop Bassett said 'Good heavens!' and Spode said 'Good Lord!' and Plank said, 'Why, that's that little thingummy I sold you, Bassett, isn't it?' Madeline gave another sob, and my nose began to tickle again.

'Well, this is astounding!' said Pop. 'He found it in Wooster's room, you say?'

'Concealed beneath his underwear.'

Pop Bassett uttered a sound like the wind going out of a dying duck.

'How right you were, Roderick! You said his motive in coming here was to steal this. But how he got into the collection room I cannot understand.'

'These fellows have their methods.'

'Seems to be a great demand for that thing,' said Plank. 'There was a young slab of damnation with a criminal face round at my place only yesterday trying to sell it to me.'

'Wooster!'

'No, it wasn't Wooster. My fellow's name was Alpine Joe.'

'Wooster would naturally adopt a pseudonym.'

'I suppose he would. I never thought of that.'

'Well, after this –' said Pop Bassett.

'Yes, after this,' said Spode, 'you're certainly not going to marry the man, Madeline. He's worse than Fink-Nottle.'

'Who's Fink-Nottle?' asked Plank.

'The one who eloped with Stoker,' said Pop.

'Who's Stoker?' asked Plank. I don't think I've ever come across a fellow with a greater thirst for information.

'The cook.'

'Ah yes. I remember you telling me. Knew what he was doing, that chap. I'm strongly opposed to anyone marrying anybody, but if you're going to marry someone, you unquestionably save something from the wreck by marrying a woman who knows what to do with a joint of beef. There was a fellow I knew in the Federated Malay States who –'

It would probably have been a diverting anecdote, but Spode didn't let him get on with it any further. Addressing Madeline, he said:

'What you're going to do is marry me, and I don't want any argument. How about it, Madeline?'

'Yes, Roderick. I will be your wife.'

Spode uttered a whoop which made my nose tickle worse than ever.

'That's the stuff! That's how I like to hear you talk! Come on out into the garden. I have much to say to you.'

I imagine that at this juncture he must have folded her in his embrace and hustled her out, for I heard the door close. And as it did so Pop Bassett uttered a whoop somewhat similar in its intensity to the one that had proceeded from the Spode lips. He was patently boomps-a-daisy, and one could readily understand why. A father whose daughter, after nearly marrying Gussie Fink-Nottle and then nearly marrying me, sees the light and hooks on to a prosperous member of the British aristocracy is entitled to rejoice. I didn't like Spode and would have been glad at any time to see a Peruvian matron spike him in the leg with her dagger, but there was no denying that he was hot stuff matrimonially.

'Lady Sidcup!' said Pop, rolling the words round his tongue like vintage port.

'Who's Lady Sidcup?' asked Plank, anxious, as always, to keep abreast.

'My daughter will shortly be. One of the oldest titles in England. That was Lord Sidcup who has just left us.'

'I thought his name is Roderick.'

'His Christian name is Roderick.'

'Ah!' said Plank. 'Now I've got it. Now I have the whole picture. Your daughter was to have married someone called Fink-Nottle?'

'Yes.'

'Then she was to have married this chap Wooster or Alpine Joe, as the case may be?'

'Yes.'

'And now she's going to marry Lord Sidcup?'

'Yes.'

'Clear as crystal,' said Plank. 'I knew I should get it threshed out in time. Simply a matter of concentration and elimination. You approve of this marriage? As far,' he added, 'as one can approve of any marriage.'

'I most certainly do.'

'Then I think this calls for another whisky-and-soda.'

'I will join you,' said Pop Bassett.

It was at this point, unable to hold it back any longer, that I sneezed.

'I knew there was something behind that sofa,' said Plank, rounding it and subjecting me to the sort of look he had once given native chiefs who couldn't grasp the rules of Rugby football. 'Odd sounds came from that direction. Good God, it's Alpine Joe.'

'It's Wooster!'

'Who's Wooster? Oh, you told me, didn't you? What steps do you propose to take?'

'I have rung for Butterfield.'

'Who's Butterfield?'

'My butler.'

'What do you want a butler for?'

'To tell him to bring Oates.'

'Who's Oates?'

'Our local policeman. He is having a glass of whisky in the kitchen.'

'Whisky!' said Plank thoughtfully, and as if reminded of something went to the side table.

The door opened.

'Oh, Butterfield, will you tell Oates to come here.'

'Very good, Sir Watkyn.'

'Bit out of condition, that chap,' said Plank, eyeing Butterfield's retreating back. 'Wants a few games of Rugger to put him in shape. What are you going to do about this Alpine Joe fellow? You going to charge him?'

'I certainly am. No doubt he assumed that I would shrink from causing a scandal, but he was wrong. I shall let the law take its course.'

'Quite right. Soak him to the utmost limit. You're a Justice of the Peace, aren't you?'

'I am, and intend to give him twenty-eight days in the second division.'

'Or sixty? Nice round number, sixty. You couldn't make it six months, I suppose?'

'I fear not.'

'No, I imagine you have a regular tariff. Ah, well, twenty-eight days is better than nothing.'

'Police Constable Oates,' said Butterfield in the doorway.

24

I don't know why it is, but there's something about being hauled off to a police bin that makes you feel a bit silly. At least, that's how it always affects me. I mean, there you are, you and the arm of the Law, toddling along side by side, and you feel that in a sense he's your host and you ought to show an interest and try to draw him out. But it's so difficult to hit on anything in the nature of an exchange of ideas, and conversation never really flows. I remember at my private school, the one I won a prize for Scripture Knowledge at, the Rev. Aubrey Upjohn, the top brass, used to take us one by one for an educational walk on Sunday afternoons, and I always found it hard to sparkle when my turn came to step out at his side. It was the same on this occasion, when I accompanied Constable Oates to the village coop. It's no good my pretending the thing went with a swing, because it didn't.

Probably if I'd been one of the topnotchers, about to do a ten years stretch for burglary or arson or what not, it would have been different, but I was only one of the small fry who get twenty-eight days in the second division, and I couldn't help thinking the officer was looking down on me. Not actually sneering, perhaps, but aloof in his manner, as if feeling I wasn't much for a cop to get his teeth into.

And, of course, there was another thing. Speaking of my earlier visit to Totleigh Towers, I mentioned that when Pop Bassett immured me in my room, he stationed the local police force on the lawn below to see that I didn't nip out of the window. That local police force was this same Oates, and as it was raining like the dickens at the time, no doubt the episode had rankled. Only a very sunny constable can look with an indulgent eye on the fellow responsible for his getting the nastiest cold in the head of his career.

At any rate, he showed himself now a man of few words, though good at locking people up in cells. There was only one at the Totleigh-in-the-Wold emporium, and I had it all to myself, a cosy little apartment with a window, not barred but too small to get out of, a grille in the door, a plank bed and that rather powerful aroma of drunks and disorderlies which you always find in these homes from home. Whether it was superior or inferior to the one they had given me at Bosher Street, I was unable to decide. Not much in it either way, it seemed to me.

To say that when I turned in on the plank bed I fell into a dreamless sleep would be deceiving my public. I passed a somewhat restless night. I could have sworn, indeed, that I didn't drop off at all, but I suppose I must have done, because the next thing I knew sunlight was coming through the window and mine host was bringing me breakfast.

I got outside it with an appetite unusual with me at such an early hour, and at the conclusion of the meal I fished out an old envelope and did what I have sometimes done before when the bludgeonings of Fate were up and about to any extent – viz. make a list of Credits and Debits, as I believe Robinson Crusoe used to. The idea being to see whether I was ahead of or behind the game at moment of going to press.

The final score worked out as follows:

Credit	Debit
Not at all a bad breakfast, that. Coffee quite good. I was surprised.	Don't always be thinking of your stomach, you jailbird.
Who's a jailbird?	You're a jailbird.
Well, yes, I suppose I am, if you care to put it that way. But I am innocent. My hands are clean.	More than your face is.
Not looking my best, what?	You look like something the cat brought in.
A bath will put that right.	And you'll get one in prison.
You really think it'll come to that?	Well, you heard what Pop Bassett said.
I wonder what it's like, doing twenty-eight days? Hitherto, I've always just come for the night.	You'll hate it. It'll bore you stiff.
I don't know so much. They give you a cake of soap and a hymnbook, don't they?	What's the good of a cake of soap and a hymnbook?

I'll be able to whack up some sort
of indoor game with them. And
don't forget that I've not got to
marry Madeline Bassett. Let's
hear what you have to say to that.

And the Debit account didn't utter. I had baffled it.

Yes, I felt, as I hunted around in case there might be a crumb of
bread which I had overlooked, that amply compensated me for the
vicissitudes I was undergoing. And I had been musing along these
lines for a while, getting more and more reconciled to my lot, when
a silvery voice spoke, making me jump like a startled grasshopper. I
couldn't think where it was coming from at first, and speculated for
a moment on the possibility of it being my guardian angel, though I
had always thought of him, I don't know why, as being of the male
sex. Then I saw something not unlike a human face at the grille, and
a closer inspection told me that it was Stiffy.

I Hullo-there-ed cordially, and expressed some surprise at finding
her on the premises.

'I wouldn't have thought Oates would have let you in. It isn't
Visitors Day, is it?'

She explained that the zealous officer had gone up to the house to
see her Uncle Watkyn and that she had sneaked in when he had legged
it.

'Oh, Bertie,' she said, 'I wish I could slip you in a file.'

'What would I do with a file?'

'Saw through the bars, of course, ass.'

'There aren't any bars.'

'Oh, aren't there? That's a difficulty. We'll have to let it go, then.
Have you had breakfast?'

'Just finished.'

'Was it all right?'

'Fairly toothsome.'

'I'm glad to hear that, because I'm weighed down with remorse.'

'You are? Why?'

'Use the loaf. If I hadn't pinched that statuette thing, none of this
would have happened.'

'Oh, I wouldn't worry.'

'But I do worry. Shall I tell Uncle Watkyn that you're innocent,
because I was the guilty party? You ought to have your name cleared.'

I put the bee on this suggestion with the greatest promptitude.

'Certainly not. Don't dream of it.'

'But don't you want your name cleared?'

'Not at the expense of you taking the rap.'

'Uncle Watkyn wouldn't send me to chokey.'

'I dare say not, but Stinker would learn all and would be shocked to the core.'

'Coo! I didn't think of that.'

'Think of it now. He wouldn't be able to help asking himself if it was a prudent move for a vicar to link his lot with yours. Doubts, that's what he'd have, and qualms. It isn't as if you were going to be a gangster's moll. The gangster would be all for you swiping everything in sight and would encourage you with word and gesture, but it's different with Stinker. When he marries you, he'll want you to take charge of the parish funds. Apprise him of the facts, and he won't have an easy moment.'

'I see what you mean. Yes, you have a point there.'

'Picture his jumpiness if he found you near the Sunday offertory bag. No, secrecy and silence is the only course.'

She sighed a bit, as if her conscience was troubling her, but she saw the force of my reasoning.

'I suppose you're right, but I do hate the idea of you doing time.'

'There are compensations.'

'Such as?'

'I am saved from the scaffold.'

'The – ? Oh, I see what you mean. You get out of marrying Madeline.'

'Exactly, and, as I remember telling you once, I am implying nothing derogatory to Madeline when I say that the thought of being united to her in bonds of holy wedlock was one that gave your old friend shivers down the spine. The fact is in no way to her discredit. I should feel just the same about marrying many of the world's noblest women. There are certain females whom one respects, admires, reveres, but only from a distance, and it is to this group that Madeline belongs.'

And I was about to develop this theme, with possibly a reference to those folk songs, when a gruff voice interrupted our *tête-à-tête*, if you can call a thing a *tête-à-tête* when the two of you are on opposite sides of an iron grille. It was Constable Oates, returned from his excursion. Stiffy's presence displeased him, and he spoke austerely.

'What's all this?' he demanded.

'What's all what?' riposted Stiffy with spirit, and I remember thinking that she rather had him there.

'It's against regulations to talk to the prisoner, Miss.'

'Oates,' said Stiffy, 'you're an ass.'

This was profoundly true, but it seemed to annoy the officer. He resented the charge, and said so, and Stiffy said she didn't want any back chat from him.

'You road company rozzers make me sick. I was only trying to cheer him up.'

It seemed to me that the officer gave a bitter snort, and a moment later he revealed why he had done so.

'It's me that wants cheering up,' he said morosely, 'I've just seen Sir Watkyn and he says he isn't pressing the charge.'

'What!' I cried.

'What!' yipped Stiffy.

'That's what,' said the constable, and you could see that while there was sunshine above, there was none in his heart. I could sympathize with him, of course. Naturally nothing makes a member of the Force sicker than to have a criminal get away from him. He was in rather the same position as some crocodile on the Zambesi or some puma in Brazil would have been, if it had earmarked Plank for its lunch and seen him shin up a high tree.

'Shackling the police, that's what I call it,' he said, and I think he spat on the floor. I couldn't see him, of course, but I was aware of a spit-like sound.

Stiffy whooped, well pleased, and I whooped myself, if I remember correctly. For all the bold front I had been putting up, I had never in my heart really liked the idea of rotting for twenty-eight days in a dungeon cell. Prison is all right for a night, but you don't want to go overdoing the thing.

'Then what are we waiting for?' said Stiffy. 'Get a move on, officer. Fling wide those gates.'

Oates flung them, not attempting to conceal his chagrin and disappointment, and I passed with Stiffy into the great world outside the prison walls.

'Goodbye, Oates,' I said as we left, for one always likes to do the courteous thing. 'It's been nice meeting you. How are Mrs. Oates and the little ones?'

His only reply was a sound like a hippopotamus taking its foot out of the mud on a river bank, and I saw Stiffy frown, as though his manner offended her.

'You know,' she said, as we reached the open spaces, 'we really ought to do something about Oates, something that would teach him that we're not put into this world for pleasure alone. I can't suggest what offhand, but if we put our heads together, we could think of something. You ought to stay on, Bertie, and help me bring his ginger hairs in sorrow to the grave.'

I raised an eyebrow.

'As the guest of your Uncle Watkyn?'

'You could muck in with Harold. There's a spare room at that cottage place of his.'

'Sorry, no.'

'You won't stay on?'

'I will not. I intend to put as many miles as possible in as short a time as possible between Totleigh-in-the-Wold and myself. And it's no good your using that expression "lily-livered poltroon", because I am adamant.'

She made what I believe is called a *moue*. It's done by pushing the lips out and drawing them in again.

'I thought it wouldn't be any use asking you. No spirit, that's your trouble, no enterprise. I'll have to get Harold to do it.'

And as I stood shuddering at the picture her words conjured up, she pushed off, exhibiting dudgeon. And I was still speculating as to what tureen of soup she was planning to land the sainted Pinker in and hoping that he would have enough sense to stay out of it, when Jeeves drove up in the car, a welcome sight.

'Good morning, sir,' he said. 'I trust you slept well.'

'Fitfully, Jeeves. Those plank beds are not easy on the fleshy parts.'

'So I would be disposed to imagine, sir. And your disturbed night has left you ruffled, I am sorry to see. You are far from *soigné*.'

I could, I suppose, have said something about 'Way down upon the *soigné* river,' but I didn't. My mind was occupied with deeper thoughts. I was in pensive mood.

'You know, Jeeves,' I said, 'one lives and learns.'

'Sir?'

'I mean, this episode has been a bit of an eye-opener to me. It has taught me a lesson. I see now what a mistake one makes in labelling someone as a ruddy Gawd-help-us just because he normally behaves like a ruddy Gawd-help-us. Look closely, and we find humanity in the unlikeliest places.'

'A broadminded view, sir.'

'Take this Sir W. Bassett. In my haste, I have always pencilled him in as a hellhound without a single redeeming quality. But what do I find? He has this softer side to him. Having got Bertram out on a limb, he does not, as one would have expected, proceed to saw it off, but tempers justice with mercy, declining to press the charge. It has touched me a good deal to discover that under that forbidding exterior there lies a heart of gold. Why are you looking like a stuffed frog, Jeeves? Don't you agree with me?'

'Not altogether, sir, when you attribute Sir Watkyn's leniency to sheer goodness of heart. There were inducements.'

'I don't dig you, Jeeves.'

'I made it a condition that you be set at liberty, sir.'

My inability to dig him became intensified. He seemed to me to be talking through the back of his neck, the last thing you desire in a personal attendant.

'How do you mean, condition? Condition of what?'

'Of my entering his employment, sir. I should mention that during my visit to Brinkley Court Sir Watkyn very kindly expressed appreciation of the manner in which I performed my duties and made me an offer to leave your service and enter his. This offer, conditional upon your release, I have accepted.'

The police station at Totleigh-in-the-Wold is situated in the main street of that village, and from where we were standing I had a view of the establishments of a butcher, a baker, a grocer and a publican licensed to sell tobacco, ales and spirits. And as I heard these words, this butcher, this baker, this grocer and this publican seemed to pirouette before my eyes as if afflicted with St. Vitus dance.

'You're leaving me?' I gasped, scarcely able to b. my e.

The corner of his mouth twitched. He seemed to be about to smile, but of course thought better of it.

'Only temporarily, sir.'

Again I was unable to dig him.

'Temporarily?'

'I think it more than possible that after perhaps a week or so differences will arise between Sir Watkyn and myself, compelling me to resign my position. In that event, if you are not already suited, sir, I shall be most happy to return to your employment.'

I saw all. It was a ruse, and by no means the worst of them. His brain enlarged by constant helpings of fish, he had seen the way and found a formula acceptable to all parties. The mists cleared from before my eyes, and the butcher, the baker, the grocer and the publican licensed to sell tobacco, ales and spirits switched back again to what is called the status quo.

A rush of emotion filled me.

'Jeeves,' I said, and if my voice shook, what of it? We Woosters are but human, 'you stand alone. Others abide our question, but you don't, as the fellow said. I wish there was something I could do to repay you.'

He coughed that sheep-like cough of his.

'There does chance to be a favour it is within your power to bestow, sir.'

'Name it, Jeeves. Ask of me what you will, even unto half my kingdom.'

'If you could see your way to abandoning your Alpine hat, sir.'

I ought to have seen it coming. That cough should have told me. But I hadn't, and the shock was severe. For an instant I don't mind admitting that I reeled.

'You would go as far as that?' I said, chewing the lower lip.

'It was merely a suggestion, sir.'

I took the hat off and gazed at it. The morning sunlight played on it, and it had never looked so blue, its feather so pink.

'I suppose you know you're breaking my heart?'

'I am sorry, sir.'

I sighed. But, as I have said, the Woosters can take it.

'Very well, Jeeves. So be it.'

I gave him the hat. It made me feel like a father reluctantly throwing his child from the sledge to divert the attention of the pursuing wolf pack, as I believe happens all the time in Russia in the winter months, but what would you?

'You propose to burn this Alpine hat, Jeeves?'

'No, sir. To present it to Mr. Butterfield. He thinks it will be of assistance to him in his courtship.'

'His what?'

'Mr. Butterfield is courting a widowed lady in the village, sir.'

This surprised me.

'But surely he was a hundred and four last birthday?'

'He is well stricken in years, yes, sir, but nevertheless –'

'There's life in the old dog yet?'

'Precisely, sir.'

My heart melted. I ceased to think of self. It had just occurred to me that in the circumstances I would be unable to conclude my visit by tipping Butterfield. The hat would fill that gap.

'All right, Jeeves, give him the lid, and heaven speed his wooing. You might tell him that from me.'

'I will make a point of doing so. Thank you very much, sir.'

'Not at all, Jeeves.'

THE INIMITABLE JEEVES

1

Jeeves Exerts the old Cerebellum

'Morning, Jeeves,' I said.

'Good morning, sir,' said Jeeves.

He put the good old cup of tea softly on the table by my bed, and I took a refreshing sip. Just right, as usual. Not too hot, not too sweet, not to weak, not too strong, not too much milk, and not a drop spilled in the saucer. A most amazing cove, Jeeves. So dashed competent in every respect. I've said it before, and I'll say it again. I mean to say, take just one small instance. Every other valet I've ever had used to barge into my room in the morning while I was still asleep, causing much misery: but Jeeves seems to know when I'm awake by a sort of telepathy. He always floats in with the cup exactly two minutes after I come to life. Makes a deuce of a lot of difference to a fellow's day.

'How's the weather, Jeeves?'

'Exceptionally clement, sir.'

'Anything in the papers?'

'Some slight friction threatening in the Balkans, sir. Otherwise, nothing.'

'I say, Jeeves, a man I met at the club last night told me to put my shirt on Privateer for the two o'clock race this afternoon. How about it?'

'I should not advocate it, sir. The stable is not sanguine.'

That was enough for me. Jeeves knows. How, I couldn't say, but he knows. There was a time when I would laugh lightly, and go ahead, and lose my little all against his advice, but not now.

'Talking of shirts,' I said, 'have those mauve ones I ordered arrived yet?'

'Yes, sir. I sent then back.'

'Sent them back?'

'Yes, sir. They would not have become you.'

Well, I must say I'd thought fairly highly of those shirtings, but I bowed to superior knowledge. Weak? I don't know. Most fellows, no doubt, are all for having their valets confine their activities to creasing trousers and what not without trying to run the home; but it's different with Jeeves. Right from the first day he came to me, I have looked on him as a sort of guide, philosopher, and friend.

'Mr Little rang up on the telephone a few moments ago, sir. I informed him that you were not yet awake.'

'Did he leave a message?'

'No, sir. He mentioned that he had a matter of importance to discuss with you, but confided no details.'

'Oh, well, I expect I shall be seeing him at the club.'

'No doubt, sir.'

I wasn't what you might call in a fever of impatience. Bingo Little is a chap I was at school with, and we see a lot of each other still. He's the nephew of old Mortimer Little, who retired from business recently with a goodish pile. (You've probably heard of Little's Liniment – It Limbers Up the Legs.) Bingo biffs about London on a pretty comfortable allowance given him by his uncle, and leads on the whole a fairly unclouded life. It wasn't likely that anything which he described as a matter of importance would turn out to be really so frightfully important. I took it that he had discovered some new brand of cigarette which he wanted me to try, or something like that, and didn't spoil my breakfast by worrying.

After breakfast I lit a cigarette and went to the open window to inspect the day. It certainly was one of the best and brightest.

'Jeeves,' I said.

'Sir?' said Jeeves. He had been clearing away the breakfast things, but at the sound of the young master's voice cheesed it courteously.

'You were absolutely right about the weather. It is a juicy morning.'

'Decidedly, sir.'

'Spring and all that.'

'Yes, sir.'

'In the spring, Jeeves, a livelier iris gleams upon the burnished dove.'

'So I have been informed, sir.'

'Right ho! Then bring me my whangee, my yellowest shoes, and the old green Homburg. I'm going into the park to do pastoral dances.'

I don't know if you know that sort of feeling you get on these days round about the end of April and the beginning of May, when the sky's a light blue, with cotton-wool clouds,and there's a bit of breeze blowing from the west? Kind of uplifted feeling. Romantic, if you know what I mean. I'm not much of a ladies' man, but on this particular morning it seemed to me that what I really wanted was some charming girl to buzz up and ask me to save her from assassins or something. So that it was a bit of an anti-climax when I merely ran into young Bingo Little, looking perfectly foul in a crimson satin tie decorated with horseshoes.

'Hallo, Bertie,' said Bingo.

'My God, man!' I gargled. 'The cravat! The gent's neckwear! Why? For what reason?'

'Oh, the tie?' He blushed. 'I – er – I was given it.'

He seemed embarrassed, so I dropped the subject. We toddled along a bit, and sat down on a couple of chairs by the Serpentine.

'Jeeves tells me you want to talk to me about something,' I said.

'Eh?' said Bingo, with a start. 'Oh yes, yes. Yes.'

I waited for him to unleash the topic of the day, but he didn't seem to want to get along. Conversation languished. He stared straight ahead of him in a glassy sort of manner.

'I say, Bertie,' he said, after a pause of about an hour and a quarter.

'Hallo!'

'Do you like the name Mabel?'

'No.'

'No?'

'No.'

'You don't think there's a kind of music in the word, like the wind rustling gently through the tree-tops?'

'No.'

He seemed disappointed for a moment; then cheered up.

'Of course, you wouldn't. You always were a fatheaded worm without any soul, weren't you?'

'Just as you say. Who is she? Tell me all.'

For I realized now that poor old Bingo was going through it once again. Ever since I have known him – and we were at school together – he has been perpetually falling in love with someone, generally in the spring, which seems to act on him like magic. At school he had the finest collection of actresses' photographs of anyone of his time; and at Oxford his romantic nature was a byword.

'You'd better come along and meet her at lunch,' he said, looking at his watch.

'A ripe suggestion,' I said. 'Where are you meeting her? At the Ritz?'

'Near the Ritz.'

He was geographically accurate. About fifty yards east of the Ritz there is one of those blighted tea-and-bun shops you see dotted about all over London, and into this, if you'll believe me, young Bingo dived like a homing rabbit; and before I had time to say a word we were wedged in at a table, on the brink of a silent pool of coffee left there by an early luncher.

I'm bound to say I couldn't quite follow the development of the scenario. Bingo, while not absolutely rolling in the stuff, has always had a fair amount of the ready. Apart from what he got from his uncle, I knew that he had finished up the jumping season well on the right side of the ledger. Why, then, was he lunching the girl at this God-forsaken eatery? It couldn't be because he was hard up.

Just then the waitress arrived. Rather a pretty girl.

'Aren't we going to wait – ?' I started to say to Bingo, thinking it somewhat thick that, in addition to asking a girl to lunch with him in a place like this, he should fling himself on the foodstuffs before she turned up, when I caught sight of his face, and stopped.

The man was goggling. His entire map was suffused with a rich blush. He looked like the Soul's Awakening done in pink.

'Hullo, Mabel!' he said, with a sort of gulp.

'Hallo!' said the girl.

'Mabel,' said Bingo, 'this is Bertie Wooster, a pal of mine.'

'Pleased to meet you,' she said. 'Nice morning.'

'Fine,' I said.

'You see I'm wearing the tie,' said Bingo.

'It suits you beautiful,' said the girl.

Personally, if anyone had told me that a tie like that suited me, I should have risen and struck them on the mazzard, regardless of their age and sex; but poor old Bingo simply got all flustered with gratification, and smirked in the most gruesome manner.

'Well, what's it going to be today?' asked the girl, introducing the business touch into the conversation.

Bingo studied the menu devoutly.

'I'll have a cup of cocoa, cold veal and ham pie, slice of fruit cake, and a macaroon. Same for you, Bertie?'

I gazed at the man, revolted. That he could have been a pal of mine all these years and think me capable of insulting the old tum with this sort of stuff cut me to the quick.

'Or how about a bit of hot steak-pudding, with a sparkling limado to wash it down?' said Bingo.

You know, the way love can change a fellow is really frightful to contemplate. This chappie before me, who spoke in that absolutely careless way of macaroons and limado, was the man I had seen in happier days telling the head-waiter at Claridge's exactly how he wanted the chef to prepare the *sole frite augourmet aux champignons*, and saying he would jolly well sling it back if it wasn't just right. Ghastly! Ghastly!

A roll and butter and a small coffee seemed the only things on the list that hadn't been specially prepared by the nastier-minded members of the Borgia family for people they had a particular grudge against, so I chose them, and Mabel hopped it.

'Well?' said Bingo rapturously.

I took it that he wanted my opinion of the female poisoner who had just left us.

'Very nice,' I said.

He seemed dissatisfied.

'You don't think she's the most wonderful girl you ever saw?' he said wistfully.

'Oh, absolutely!' I said, to appease the blighter. 'Where did you meet her?'

'At a subscription dance at Camberwell.'

'What on earth were you doing at a subscription dance at Camberwell?'

'Your man Jeeves asked me if I would buy a couple of tickets. It was in aid of some charity or other.'

'Jeeves? I didn't know he went in for that sort of thing.'

'Well, I suppose he has to relax a bit every now and then. Anyway, he was there, swinging a dashed efficient shoe. I hadn't meant to go at first, but I turned up for a lark. Oh, Bertie, think what I might have missed!'

'What might you have missed?' I asked, the old lemon being slightly clouded.

'Mabel, you chump. If I hadn't gone I shouldn't have met Mabel.'

'Oh, ah!'

At this point Bingo fell into a species of trance, and only came out of it to wrap himself round the pie and the macaroon.

'Bertie,' he said, 'I want your advice.'

'Carry on.'

'At least, not your advice, because that wouldn't be much good to anybody. I mean, you're a pretty consummate old ass, aren't you? Not that I want to hurt your feelings, of course.'

'No, no, I see that.'

'What I wish you would do is to put the whole thing to that fellow Jeeves of yours, and see what he suggests. You've often told me that he has helped other pals of yours out of messes. From what you tell me, he's by way of being the brains of the family.'

'He's never let me down yet.'

'Then put my case to him.'

'What case?'

'My problem.'

'What problem?'

'Why, you poor fish, my uncle, of course. What do you think my uncle's going to say to all this? If I sprang it on him cold, he'd tie himself in knots on the hearthrug.'

'One of these emotional johnnies, eh?'

'Somehow or other his mind has got to be prepared to receive the news. But how?'

'Ah!'

'That's a lot of help, that "ah"! You see, I'm pretty well dependent on the old boy. If he cut off my allowance, I should be very much in the soup. So you put the whole binge to Jeeves and see if he can't scare up a happy ending somehow. Tell him my future is in his hands, and that, if the wedding bells ring out, he can rely on me, even unto half my kingdom. Well, call it ten quid. Jeeves would exert himself with ten quid on the horizon, what?'

'Undoubtedly,' I said.

I wasn't in the least surprised at Bingo wanting to lug Jeeves into his private affairs like this. It was the first thing I would have thought of doing myself if I had been in any hole of any description. As I have frequently had occasion to observe, he is a bird of the ripest intellect, full of bright ideas. If anybody could fix things for poor old Bingo, he could.

I stated the case to him that night after dinner.

'Jeeves.'

'Sir?'

'Are you busy just now?'

'No, sir.'

'I mean, not doing anything in particular?'

'No, sir. It is my practice at this hour to read some improving book; but, if you desire my services, this can easily be postponed, or indeed, abandoned altogether.'

'Well, I want your advice. It's about Mr Little.'

'Young Mr Little, sir, or the elder Mr Little, his uncle, who lives in Pounceby Gardens?'

Jeeves seemed to know everything. Most amazing thing. I'd been pally with Bingo practically all my life, and yet I didn't remember having heard that his uncle lived anywhere in particular.

'How did you know he lived in Pounceby Gardens?' I said.

'I am on terms of some intimacy with the elder Mr Little's cook, sir. In fact, there is an understanding.'

I'm bound to say that this gave me a bit of a start. Somehow I'd never thought of Jeeves going in for that sort of thing.

'Do you mean you're engaged?'

'It may be said to amount to that, sir.'

'Well, well!'

'She is a remarkably excellent cook, sir,' said Jeeves, as though he felt called on to give some explanation. 'What was it you wished to ask me about Mr Little?'

I sprang the details on him.

'And that's how the matter stands, Jeeves,' I said. 'I think we ought to rally round a trifle and help poor old Bingo put the thing through. Tell me about old Mr Little. What sort of a chap is he?'

'A somewhat curious character, sir. Since retiring from business he has become a great recluse, and now devotes himself almost entirely to the pleasures of the table.'

'Greedy hog, you mean?'

'I would not, perhaps, take the liberty of describing him in precisely those terms, sir. He is what is usually called a gourmet. Very particular about what he eats, and for that reason sets a high value on Miss Watson's services.

'The cook?'

'Yes, sir.'

'Well, it looks to me as though our best plan would be to shoot young Bingo in on him after dinner one night. Melting mood, I mean to say, and all that.'

'The difficulty is, sir, that at the moment Mr Little is on a diet, owing to an attack of gout.'

'Things begin to look wobbly.'

'No, sir, I fancy that the elder Mr Little's misfortune may be turned to the younger Mr Little's advantage. I was speaking only the other day to Mr Little's valet, and he was telling me that it has become his principle duty to read to Mr Little in the evenings. If I were in your place, sir, I should send young Mr Little to read to his uncle.'

'Nephew's devotion, you mean? Old man touched by kindly action, what?'

'Partly that, sir. But I would rely more on young Mr Little's choice of literature.'

'That's no good. Jolly old Bingo has a kind face, but when it comes to literature he stops at the *Sporting Times*.'

'That difficulty may be overcome. I would be happy to select books for Mr Little to read. Perhaps I might explain my idea a little further.'

'I can't say I quite grasp it yet.'

'The method which I advocate is what, I believe, the advertisers call Direct Suggestion, sir, consisting as it does of driving an idea home by constant repetition. You may have had experience of the system?'

'You mean they keep on telling you that some soap or other is the best, and after a bit you come under the influence and charge round the corner and buy a cake?'

'Exactly, sir. The same method was the basis of all the most valuable propaganda during the recent war. I see no reason why it should not be adopted to bring about the desired result with regard to the subject's views on class distinctions. If young Mr Little were to read day after day to his uncle a series of narratives in which marriage with young persons of an inferior social status was held up as both feasible and admirable, I fancy it would prepare the elder Mr Little's mind for the reception of the information that his nephew wishes to marry a waitress in a tea-shop.'

'*Are* there any books of that sort nowadays? The only ones I ever see mentioned in the papers are about married couples who find life grey, and can't stick each other at any price.'

'Yes, sir, there are a great many, neglected by the reviewers but widely read. You have never encountered *All for Love*, by Rosie M. Banks?'

'No.'

'Nor, *A Red, Red Summer*, by the same author?'

'No.'

'I have an aunt, sir, who owns an almost complete set of Rosie M. Banks'. I could easily borrow as many volumes as young Mr Little might require. They make very light, attractive reading.'

'Well, it's worth trying.'

'I should certainly recommend the scheme, sir.'

'All right, then. Toddle round to your aunt's tomorrow and grab a couple of the fruitiest. We can but have a dash at it.'

'Precisely, sir.'

2

No Wedding Bells for Bingo

Bingo reported three days later that Rosie M. Banks was the goods and beyond a question the stuff to give the troops. Old Little had jibbed somewhat at first at the proposed change of literary diet, he not being much of a lad for fiction and having stuck hitherto exclusively to the heavier monthly reviews; but Bingo had got chapter one of *All for Love* past his guard before he knew what was happening and after that there was nothing to it. Since then they had finished *A Red, Red Summer Rose*, *Madcap Myrtle* and *Only a Factory Girl*, and were half-way through *The Courtship of Lord Strathmorlick*.

Bingo told me all this in a husky voice over an egg beaten up in sherry. The only blot on the thing from his point of view was that it wasn't doing a bit of good to the old vocal cords, which were beginning to show signs of cracking under the strain. He had been looking his symptoms up in a medical dictionary, and he thought he had got 'clergyman's throat'. But against this you had to set the fact that he was making an undoubted hit in the right quarter, and also that after the evening's reading he always stayed on to dinner; and, from what he told me, the dinners turned out by old Little's cook had to be tasted to be believed. There were tears in the old blighter's eyes as he got on the subject of the clear soup. I suppose to a fellow who for weeks had been tackling macaroons and limado it must have been like Heaven.

Old Little wasn't able to give any practical assistance at these banquets, but Bingo said that he came to the table and had his whack of arrowroot, and sniffed the dishes, and told stories of *entrées* he had had in the past, and sketched out scenarios of what he was going to do to the bill of fare in the future, when the doctor put him in shape; so I suppose he enjoyed himself, too, in a way. Anyhow, things seemed to be buzzing along quite satisfactorily, and Bingo said he had got an idea which, he thought, was going to clinch the thing. He wouldn't tell me what it was, but he said it was a pippin.

'We make progress, Jeeves,' I said.

'That is very satisfactory, sir.'

'Mr Little tells me that when he came to the big scene in *Only a Factory Girl*, his uncle gulped like a stricken bullpup.'

'Indeed, sir?'

'Where Lord Claude takes the girl in his arms, you know, and says – '

'I am familiar with the passage, sir. It is distinctly moving. It was a great favourite of my aunt's.'

'I think we're on the right track.'

'It would seem so, sir.'

'In fact, this looks like being another of your successes. I've always said, and I always shall say, that for sheer brains, Jeeves, you stand alone. All the other great thinkers of the age are simply in the crowd, watching you go by.'

'Thank you very much, sir. I endeavour to give satisfaction.'

About a week after this, Bingo blew in with the news that his uncle's gout had ceased to trouble him, and that on the morrow he would be back at the old stand working away with knife and fork as before.

'And, by the way,' said Bingo, 'he wants you to lunch with him tomorrow.'

'Me? Why me? He doesn't know I exist.'

'Oh, yes, he does. I've told him about you.'

'What have you told him?'

'Oh, various things. Anyhow, he wants to meet you. And take my tip, laddie – you go! I should think lunch tomorrow would be something special.'

I don't know why it was, but even then it struck me that there was something dashed odd – almost sinister, if you know what I mean – about young Bingo's manner. The old egg had the air of one who has something up his sleeve.

'There is more in this than meets the eye,' I said. 'Why should your uncle ask a fellow to lunch whom he's never seen?'

'My dear old fathead, haven't I just said that I've been telling him all about you – that you're my best pal – at school together, and all that sort of thing?'

'But even then – and another thing. Why are you so dashed keen on my going?'

Bingo hesitated for a moment.

'Well, I told you I'd got an idea. This is it. I want you to spring the news on him. I haven't the nerve myself.'

'What! I'm hanged if I do!'

'And you call yourself a pal of mine!'

'Yes, I know; but there are limits.'

'Bertie,' said Bingo reproachfully, 'I saved your life once.'

'When?'

'Didn't I? It must have been some other fellow, then. Well, anyway, we were boys together and all that. You can't let me down.'

'Oh, all right,' I said. 'But, when you say you haven't nerve enough for any dashed thing in the world, you misjudge yourself. A fellow who – '

'Cheerio!' said young Bingo. 'One-thirty tomorrow. Don't be late.'

I'm bound to say that the more I contemplated the binge, the less I liked it. It was all very well for Bingo to say that I was slated for a magnificent lunch; but what good is the best possible lunch to a fellow if he is slung out into the street on his ear during the soup course? However, the word of a Wooster is his bond and all that sort of rot, so at one-thirty next day I tottered up the steps of No. 16, Pounceby Gardens, and punched the bell. And half a minute later I was in the drawing-room, shaking hands with the fattest man I have ever seen in my life.

The motto of the Little family was evidently 'variety'. Young Bingo is long and thin and hasn't had a superfluous ounce on him since we first met; but the uncle restored the average and a bit over. The hand which grasped mine wrapped it round and enfolded it till I began to wonder if I'd ever get it out without excavating machinery.

'Mr Wooster, I am gratified – I am proud – I am honoured.'

It seemed to me that young Bingo must have boosted me to some purpose.

'Oh, ah!' I said.

He stepped back a bit, still hanging to the good right hand.

'You are very young to have accomplished so much!'

I couldn't follow the train of thought. The family, especially my Aunt Agatha, who has savaged me incessantly from childhood up, have always rather made a point of the fact that mine is a wasted life, and that, since I won the prize at my first school for the best collection of wild flowers made during the summer holidays, I haven't done a dam' thing to land me on the nation's scroll of fame. I was wondering if he couldn't have got me mixed up with someone else, when the telephone bell rang outside in the hall, and the maid came in to say that I was wanted. I buzzed down, and found it was young Bingo.

'Hallo!' said young Bingo. 'So you've got there? Good man! I knew I could rely on you. I say, old crumpet, did my uncle seem pleased to see you?'

'Absolutely all over me. I can't make it out.'

'Oh, that's all right. I just rang up to explain. The fact is, old man, I know you won't mind, but I told him that you were the author of those books I've been reading to him.'

'What!'

'Yes, I said that "Rosie M. Banks" was your pen-name, and you didn't want it generally known, because you were a modest, retiring sort of chap. He'll listen to you now. Absolutely hang on your words. A brightish idea, what? I doubt if Jeeves in person could have thought up a better one than that. Well, pitch it strong, old lad, and keep steadily before you the fact that I must have my allowance raised. I can't possibly marry on what I've got now. If this film is to end with the slow fade-out on the embrace, at least double is indicated. Well, that's that. Cheerio!'

And he rang off. At that moment the gong sounded, and the genial host came tumbling downstairs like the delivery of a ton of coals.

I always look back to that lunch with a sort of aching regret. It was the lunch of a lifetime, and I wasn't in a fit state to appreciate it. Subconsciously, if you know what I mean, I could see it was pretty special, but I had got the wind up to such a frightful extent over the ghastly situation in which young Bingo had landed me that its deeper meaning never really penetrated. Most of the time I might have been eating sawdust for all the good it did me.

Old Little struck the literary note right from the start.

'My nephew has probably told you that I have been making a close study of your books of late?' he began.

'Yes. He did mention it. How – er – how did you like the bally things?'

He gazed reverently at me.

'Mr Wooster, I am not ashamed to say that the tears came into my eyes as I listened to them. It amazes me that a man as young as you can have been able to plumb human nature so surely to its depths; to play with so unerring a hand on the quivering heartstrings of your reader; to write novels so true, so human, so moving, so vital!'

'Oh, it's just a knack,' I said.

The good old persp. was bedewing my forehead by this time in a pretty lavish manner. I don't know when I've been so rattled.

'Do you find the room a trifle warm?'

'Oh, no, no, rather not. Just right.'

'Then it's the pepper. If my cook has a fault – which I am not prepared to admit – it is that she is inclined to stress the pepper a trifle in her made dishes. By the way, do you like her cooking?'

I was so relieved that we had got off the subject of my literary output that I shouted approval in a ringing baritone.

'I am delighted to hear it, Mr Wooster. I may be prejudiced, but to my mind that woman is a genius.'

'Absolutely!' I said.

'She has been with me seven years, and in all that time I have not known her guilty of a single lapse from the highest standard. Except once, in the winter of 1917, when a purist might have condemned a certain mayonnaise of hers as lacking in creaminess. But one must make allowances. There had been several air-raids about that time, and no doubt the poor woman was shaken. But nothing is perfect in this world, Mr Wooster, and I have had my cross to bear. For seven years I have lived in constant apprehension lest some evilly-disposed person might lure her from my employment. To my certain knowledge she has received offers, lucrative offers, to accept service elsewhere. You may judge of my dismay, Mr Wooster, when only this morning the bolt fell. She gave notice!'

'Good Lord!'

'Your consternation does credit, if I may say so, to the heart of the author of *A Red, Red Summer Rose*. But I am thankful to say the worst has not happened. The matter has been adjusted. Jane is not leaving me.'

'Good egg!'

'Good egg, indeed – though the expression is not familiar to me. I do not remember having come across it in your books. And, speaking of your books, may I say that what has impressed me about them even more than the moving poignancy of the actual narrative, is your philosophy of life. If there were more men like you, Mr Wooster, London would be a better place.'

This was dead opposite to my Aunt Agatha's philosophy of life, she having always rather given me to understand that it is the presence in it of chappies like me that makes London more or less of a plague spot; but I let it go.

'Let me tell you, Mr Wooster, that I appreciate your splendid defiance of the outworn fetishes of a purblind social system. I appreciate it! *You* are big enough to see that rank is but the guinea stamp and that, in the magnificent words of Lord Bletchmore in *Only a Factory Girl*, "Be her origin ne'er so humble, a good woman is the equal of the finest lady on earth!" '

'I say! Do you think that?'

'I do, Mr Wooster. I am ashamed to say that there was a time when I was like other men, a slave to the idiotic convention which we call Class Distinction. But, since I read your book – '

I might have known it. Jeeves had done it again.

'You think it's all right for a chappie in what you might call a certain social position to marry a girl of what you might describe as the lower classes?'

'Most assuredly I do, Mr Wooster.'

I took a deep breath, and slipped him the good news.

'Young Bingo – your nephew, you know – wants to marry a waitress,' I said.

'I honour him for it,' said old Little.

'You don't object?'

'On the contrary.'

I took another deep breath and shifted to the sordid side of the business.

'I hope you won't think I'm butting in, don't you know,' I said, 'but – er – well, how about it?'

'I fear I do not quite follow you.'

'Well, I mean to say, his allowance and all that. The money you're good enough to give him. He was rather hoping that you might see your way to jerking up the total a bit.'

Old Little shook his head regretfully.

'I fear that can hardly be managed. You see, a man in my position is compelled to save every penny. I will gladly continue my nephew's existing allowance, but beyond that I cannot go. It would not be fair to my wife.'

'What! But you're not married?'

'Not yet. But I propose to enter upon that holy state almost immediately. The lady who for years has cooked so well for me honoured me by accepting my hand this very morning.' A cold gleam of triumph came into his eye. 'Now let 'em try to get her away from me!' he muttered defiantly.

'Young Mr Little has been trying frequently during the afternoon to reach you on the telephone, sir,' said Jeeves that night, when I got home.

'I'll bet he has,' I said. I had sent poor old Bingo an outline of the situation by messenger-boy shortly after lunch.

'He seemed a trifle agitated.'

'I don't wonder, Jeeves,' I said, 'so brace up and bite the bullet. I'm afraid I've bad news for you.

'That scheme of yours – reading those books to old Mr Little and all that – has blown out a fuse.'

'They did not soften him?'

'They did. That's the whole bally trouble. Jeeves, I'm sorry to say that *fiancée* of yours – Miss Watson, you know – the cook, you know – well, the long and the short of it is that she's chosen riches instead of honest worth, if you know what I mean.'

'Sir?'

'She's handed you the mitten and gone and got engaged to old Mr Little!'

'Indeed, sir?'

'You don't seem much upset.'

'The fact is, sir, I had anticipated some such outcome.'

I stared at him. 'Then what on earth did you suggest the scheme for?'

'To tell you the truth, sir, I was not wholly averse from a severance of my relations with Miss Watson. In fact, I greatly desired it. I respect Miss Watson exceedingly, but I have seen for a long time that we were not suited. Now, the *other* young person with whom I have an understanding – '

'Great Scott, Jeeves! There isn't another?'

'Yes, sir.'

'How long has this been going on?'

'For some weeks, sir. I was greatly attracted by her when I first met her at a subscription dance at Camberwell.'

'My sainted aunt! Not – '

Jeeves inclined his head gravely.

'Yes, sir. By an odd coincidence it is the same young person that young Mr Little – I have placed the cigarettes on the small table. Good night, sir.'

3

Aunt Agatha Speaks her Mind

I suppose in the case of a chappie of really fine fibre and all that sort of thing, a certain amount of gloom and anguish would have followed this dishing of young Bingo's matrimonial plans. I mean, if mine had been a noble nature, I would have been all broken up. But, what with one thing and another, I can't let it weigh on me very heavily. The fact that less than a week after he had had the bad news I came on young Bingo dancing like an untamed gazelle at Ciro's helped me to bear up.

A resilient bird, Bingo. He may be down, but he is never out. While these little love-affairs of his are actually on, nobody could be more earnest and blighted; but once the fuse has blown out and the girl has handed him his hat and begged him as a favour never to let her see him again, up he bobs as merry and bright as ever. If I've seen it happen once, I've seen it happen a dozen times.

So I didn't worry about Bingo. Or about anything else, as a matter of fact. What with one thing and another, I can't remember ever having been chirpier than at about this period in my career. Everything seemed to be going right. On three separate occasions horses on which I'd invested a sizeable amount won by lengths instead of sitting down to rest in the middle of the race, as horses usually do when I've got money on them.

Added to this, the weather continued topping to a degree; my new socks were admitted on all sides to be just the kind that mother makes; and to round it all off, my Aunt Agatha had gone to France and wouldn't be on hand to snooter me for at least another six weeks. And, if you knew my Aunt Agatha, you'd agree that that alone was happiness enough for anyone.

It suddenly struck me so forcibly, one morning while I was having my bath, that I hadn't a worry on earth that I began to sing like a bally nightingale as I sploshed the sponge about. It seemed to me that everything was absolutely for the best in the best of all possible worlds.

But have you ever noticed a rummy thing about life? I mean the
way something always comes along to give it you in the neck at the
very moment when you're feeling most braced about things in general. No sooner had I dried the old limbs and shoved on the suiting
and toddled into the sitting-room than the blow fell. There was a
letter from Aunt Agatha on the mantelpiece.

'Oh gosh!' I said when I'd read it.

'Sir?' said Jeeves. He was fooling about in the background on
some job or other.

'It's from my Aunt Agatha, Jeeves. Mrs Gregson, you know.'

'Yes, sir?'

'Ah, you wouldn't speak in that light, careless tone if you knew
what was in it,' I said with a hollow, mirthless laugh. 'The curse has
come upon us, Jeeves. She wants me to go and join her at – what's
the name of the dashed place? – at Roville-sur-mer. Oh, hang it
all!'

'I had better be packing, sir?'

'I suppose so.'

To people who don't know my Aunt Agatha I find it extraordinarily
difficult to explain why it is that she has always put the wind up me
to such a frightful extent. I mean, I'm not dependent on her financially or anything like that. It's simply personality, I've come to the
conclusion. You see, all through my childhood and when I was a
kid at school she was always able to turn me inside out with a single
glance, and I haven't come out from under the 'fluence yet. We run
to height a bit in our family, and there's about five-foot-nine of Aunt
Agatha, topped off with a beaky nose, an eagle eye, and a lot of grey
hair, and the general effect is pretty formidable. Anyway, it never
even occurred to me for a moment to give her the miss-in-baulk on
this occasion. If she said I must go to Roville, it was all over except
buying the tickets.

'What's the idea, Jeeves? I wonder why she wants me.'

'I could not say, sir.'

Well, it was no good talking about it. The only gleam of consolation, the only bit of blue among the clouds, was the fact that at
Roville I should at last be able to wear the rather fruity cummerbund
I had bought six months ago and had never had the nerve to put
on. One of those silk contrivances, you know, which you tie round
your waist instead of a waistcoat, something on the order of a sash
only more substantial. I had never been able to muster up the
courage to put it on so far, for I knew that there would be trouble

with Jeeves when I did, it being a pretty brightish scarlet. Still, at a place like Roville, presumably dripping with the gaiety and *joie de vivre* of France, it seemed to me that something might be done.

Roville, which I reached early in the morning after a beastly choppy crossing and a jerky night in the train, is a fairly nifty spot where a chappie without encumbrances in the shape of aunts might spend a somewhat genial week or so. It is like all these French places, mainly sands and hotels and casinos. The hotel which had had the bad luck to draw Aunt Agatha's custom was the Splendide, and by the time I got there there wasn't a member of the staff who didn't seem to be feeling it deeply. I sympathized with them. I've had experience of Aunt Agatha at hotels before. Of course, the real rough work was all over when I arrived, but I could tell by the way everyone grovelled before her that she had started by having her first room changed because it hadn't a southern exposure and her next because it had a creaking wardrobe and that she had said her say on the subject of the cooking, the waiting, the chambermaiding and everything else, with perfect freedom and candour. She had got the whole gang nicely under control by now. The manager, a whiskered cove who looked like a bandit, simply tied himself into knots whenever she looked at him.

All this triumph had produced a sort of grim geniality in her, and she was almost motherly when we met.

'I am so glad you were able to come, Bertie,' she said. 'The air will do you so much good. Far better for you than spending your time in stuffy London night clubs.'

'Oh, ah,' I said.

'You will meet some pleasant people, too. I want to introduce you to a Miss Hemmingway and her brother, who have become great friends of mine. I am sure you will like Miss Hemmingway. A nice, quiet girl, so different from so many of the bold girls one meets in London nowadays. Her brother is curate at Chipley-in-the-Glen in Dorsetshire. He tells me they are connected with the Kent Hemmingways. A very good family. She is a charming girl.'

I had a grim foreboding of an awful doom. All this boosting was so unlike Aunt Agatha, who normally is one of the most celebrated right-and-left-hand knockers in London society. I felt a clammy suspicion. And, by Jove, I was right.

'Aline Hemmingway,' said Aunt Agatha, 'is just the girl I should like to see you marry, Bertie. You ought to be thinking of getting married. Marriage might make something of you. And I could not wish you a better wife than dear Aline. She would be such a good influence in your life.'

'Here, I say!' I chipped in at this juncture, chilled to the marrow.

'Bertie!' said Aunt Agatha, dropping the motherly manner for a bit and giving me the cold eye.

'Yes, but I say – '

'It is young men like you, Bertie, who make the person with the future of the race at heart despair. Cursed with too much money, you fritter away in idle selfishness a life which might have been made useful, helpful and profitable. You do nothing but waste your time on frivolous pleasures. You are simply an anti-social animal, a drone. Bertie, it is imperative that you marry.'

'But, dash it all – '

'Yes! You should be breeding children to – '

'No, really, I say, please!' I said, blushing richly. Aunt Agatha belongs to two or three of these women's clubs, and she keeps forgetting she isn't in the smoking-room.

'Bertie,' she resumed, and would no doubt have hauled up her slacks at some length, had we not been interrupted. 'Ah, here they are!' she said. 'Aline, dear!'

And I perceived a girl and a chappie bearing down on me, smiling in a pleased sort of manner.

'I want you to meet my nephew, Bertie Wooster,' said Aunt Agatha. 'He has just arrived. Such a surprise! I had no notion that he intended coming to Roville.'

I gave the couple the wary up-and-down, feeling like a cat in the middle of a lot of hounds. Sort of trapped feeling, you know what I mean. An inner voice was whispering that Bertram was up against it.

The brother was a small round cove with a face rather like a sheep. He wore pince-nez, his expression was benevolent, and he had on one of those collars which button at the back.

'Welcome to Roville, Mr Wooster,' he said.

'Oh, Sidney!' said the girl. 'Doesn't Mr Wooster remind you of Canon Blenkinsop, who came to Chipley to preach last Easter?'

'My dear! The resemblance is most striking!'

They peered at me for a while as if I were something in a glass case, and I goggled back and had a good look at the girl. There's no doubt about it, she was different from what Aunt Agatha had called the bold girls one meets in London nowadays. No bobbed

hair and gaspers about *her*! I don't know when I've met anybody
who looked so – respectable is the only word. She had on a kind of
plain dress, and her hair was plain, and her face was sort of mild
and saint-like. I don't pretend to be a Sherlock Holmes or anything
of that order, but the moment I looked at her I said to myself, 'The
girl plays the organ in a village church!'

Well, we gazed at one another for a bit, and there was a certain
amount of chit-chat, and then I tore myself away. But before I went
I had been booked up to take brother and girl for a nice drive that
afternoon. And the thought of it depressed me to such an extent
that I felt there was only one thing to be done. I went straight back
to my room, dug out the cummerbund, and draped it round the old
tum. I turned round and Jeeves shied like a startled mustang.

'I beg your pardon, sir,' he said in a sort of hushed voice. 'You
are surely not proposing to appear in public in that thing?'

'The cummerbund?' I said in a careless, debonair way, passing it
off. 'Oh, rather!'

'I should not advise it, sir, really I shouldn't.'

'Why not?'

'The effect, sir, is loud in the extreme.'

I tackled the blighter squarely. I mean to say, nobody knows better
than I do that Jeeves is a master mind and all that, but, dash it, a
fellow must call his soul his own. You can't be a serf to your valet.
Besides, I was feeling pretty low and the cummerbund was the only
thing which could cheer me up.

'You know, the trouble with you, Jeeves,' I said, 'is that you're
too – what's the word I want? – too bally insular. You can't realize
that you aren't in Piccadilly all the time. In a place like this a bit of
colour and touch of the poetic is expected of you. Why, I've just
seen a fellow downstairs in a morning suit of yellow velvet.'

'Nevertheless, sir – '

'Jeeves,' I said firmly, 'my mind is made up. I am feeling a little
low-spirited and need cheering. Besides, what's wrong with it? This
cummerbund seems to me to be called for. I consider that it has
rather a Spanish effect. A touch of the hidalgo. Sort of Vicente y
Blasco What's-his-name stuff. The jolly old hidalgo off to the bull
fight.'

'Very good, sir,' said Jeeves coldly.

Dashed upsetting, this sort of thing. If there's one thing that gives
me the pip, it's unpleasantness in the home; and I could see that
relations were going to be fairly strained for a while. And, coming

on top of Aunt Agatha's bombshell about the Hemmingway girl, I
don't mind confessing it made me feel more or less as though nobody
loved me.

The drive that afternoon was about as mouldy as I had expected.
The curate chappie prattled on of this and that; the girl admired
the view; and I got a headache early in the proceedings which started
at the sole of my feet and got worse all the way up. I tottered back
to my room to dress for dinner, feeling like a toad under the harrow.
If it hadn't been for that cummerbund business earlier in the day I
could have sobbed on Jeeves's neck and poured out all my troubles
to him. Even as it was, I couldn't keep the thing entirely to myself.

'I say, Jeeves,' I said.

'Sir?'

'Mix me a stiffish brandy and soda.'

'Yes, sir.'

'Stiffish, Jeeves. Not too much soda, but splash the brandy about
a bit.'

'Very good, sir.'

After imbibing, I felt a shade better.

'Jeeves,' I said.

'Sir?'

'I rather fancy I'm in the soup, Jeeves.'

'Indeed, sir?'

I eyed the man narrowly. Dashed aloof his manner was. Still
brooding over the cummerbund.

'Yes. Right up to the hocks,' I said, suppressing the pride of the
Woosters and trying to induce him to be a bit matier. 'Have you
seen a girl popping about here with a parson brother?'

'Miss Hemmingway, sir? Yes, sir.'

'Aunt Agatha wants me to marry her.'

'Indeed, sir?'

'Well, what about it?'

'Sir?'

'I mean, have you anything to suggest?'

'No, sir.'

The blighter's manner was so cold and unchummy that I bit the
bullet and had a dash at being airy.

'Oh, well, tra-la-la!' I said.

'Precisely, sir,' said Jeeves.

And that was, so to speak, that.

4

Pearls Mean Tears

I remember – it must have been when I was at school because I don't go in for that sort of thing very largely nowadays – reading a poem or something about something or other in which there was a line which went, if I've got it rightly, 'Shades of the prison house begin to close upon the growing boy.' Well, what I'm driving at is that during the next two weeks that's exactly how it was with me. I mean to say, I could hear the wedding bells chiming faintly in the distance and getting louder and louder every day, and how the deuce to slide out of it was more than I could think. Jeeves, no doubt, could have dug up a dozen brainy schemes in a couple of minutes, but he was still aloof and chilly and I couldn't bring myself to ask him point-blank. I mean, he could see easily enough that the young master was in a bad way and, if that wasn't enough to make him overlook the fact that I was still gleaming brightly about the waist-band, well, what it amounted to was that the old feudal spirit was dead in the blighter's bosom and there was nothing to be done about it.

It really was rummy the way the Hemmingway family had taken to me. I wouldn't have said off-hand that there was anything particularly fascinating about me – in fact, most people look on me as rather an ass; but there was no getting away from the fact that I went like a breeze with this girl and her brother. They didn't seem happy if they were away from me. I couldn't move a step, dash it, without one of them popping out from somewhere and freezing on. In fact, I'd got into the habit now of retiring to my room when I wanted to take it easy for a bit. I had managed to get a rather decent suite on the third floor, looking down on to the promenade.

I had gone to earth in my suite one evening and for the first time that day was feeling that life wasn't so bad after all. Right through the day from lunch-time I'd had the Hemmingway girl on my hands, Aunt Agatha having shooed us off together immediately after the midday meal. The result was, as I looked down on the lighted promenade and saw all the people popping happily about on their way to dinner and the Casino and what not, a kind of wistful feeling came over me. I couldn't help thinking how dashed happy I could have contrived to be in this place if only Aunt Agatha and the other blisters had been elsewhere.

I heaved a sigh, and at that moment there was a knock at the door.

'Someone at the door, Jeeves,' I said.

'Yes, sir.'

He opened the door, and in popped Aline Hemmingway and her brother. The last persons I had expected. I really had thought that I could be alone for a minute in my own room.

'Oh, hallo!' I said.

'Oh, Mr Wooster!' said the girl in a gasping sort of way. 'I don't know how to begin.'

Then I noticed that she appeared considerably rattled, and as for the brother, he looked like a sheep with a secret sorrow.

This made me sit up and take notice. I had supposed that this was just a social call, but apparently something had happened to give them a jolt. Though I couldn't see why they should come to me about it.

'Is anything up?' I said.

'Poor Sidney – it was my fault – I ought never to have let him go there alone,' said the girl. Dashed agitated.

At this point the brother, who after shedding a floppy overcoat and parking his hat on a chair had been standing by wrapped in the silence, gave a little cough, like a sheep caught in the mist on a mountain top.

'The fact is, Mr Wooster,' he said, 'a sad, a most deplorable thing has occurred. This afternoon, while you were so kindly escorting my sist-ah, I found the time hang a little heavy upon my hands and I was tempted to – ah – gamble at the Casino.'

I looked at the man in a kindlier spirit than I had been able to up to date. This evidence that he had sporting blood in his veins made him seem more human, I'm bound to say. If only I'd known earlier that he went in for that sort of thing, I felt that we might have had a better time together.

'Oh!' I said. 'Did you click?'

He sighed heavily.

'If you mean was I successful, I must answer in the negative. I rashly persisted in the view that the colour red, having appeared no fewer than seven times in succession, must inevitably at no distant date give place to black. I was in error. I lost my little all, Mr Wooster.'

'Tough luck,' I said.

'I left the Casino,' proceeded the chappie, 'and returned to the hotel. There I encountered one of my parishioners, a Colonel Musgrave, who chanced to be holiday-making over here. I – er – induced him to cash me a cheque for one hundred pounds on my little account in my London bank.'

'Well, that was all to the good, what?' I said, hoping to induce the poor fish to look on the bright side. 'I mean, bit of luck finding someone to slip it into first crack out of the box.'

'On the contrary, Mr Wooster, it did but make matters worse. I burn with shame as I make the confession, but I immediately went back to the Casino and lost the entire sum – this time under the mistaken supposition that the colour black was, as I believe the expression is, due for a run.'

'I say!' I said. 'You *are* having a night out!'

'And,' concluded the chappie, 'the most lamentable feature of the whole affair is that I have no funds in the bank to meet the cheque when presented.'

I'm free to confess that, though I realized by this time that all this was leading up to a touch and that my ear was shortly going to be bitten in no uncertain manner, my heart warmed to the poor prune. Indeed, I gazed at him with no little interest and admiration. Never before had I encountered a curate so genuinely all to the mustard. Little as he might look like one of the lads of the village, he certainly appeared to be real tabasco, and I wished he had shown me this side of his character before.

'Colonel Musgrave,' he went on, gulping somewhat, 'is not a man who would be likely to overlook the matter. He is a hard man. He will expose me to my vic-ah. My vic-ah is a hard man. In short, Mr Wooster, if Colonel Musgrave presents that cheque I shall be ruined. And he leaves for England tonight.'

The girl, who had been standing by biting her handkerchief and gurgling at intervals while the brother got the above off his chest, now started in once more.

'Mr Wooster,' she cried, 'won't you, won't you help us? Oh, do say you will! We must have the money to get back the cheque from Colonel Musgrave before nine o'clock – he leaves on the nine-twenty. I was at my wits' end what to do when I remembered how kind you had always been. Mr Wooster, will you lend Sidney the money and take these as security?' And before I knew what she was doing she had dived into her bag, produced a case, and opened it. 'My pearls,' she said. 'I don't know what they are worth – they were a present from my poor father – '

'Now, alas, no more – ' chipped in the brother.

'But I know they must be worth ever so much more than the amount we want.'

Dashed embarrassing. Made me feel like a pawnbroker. More than a touch of popping the watch about the whole business.

'No, I say, really,' I protested. 'There's no need of any security, you know, or any rot of that kind. Only too glad to let you have the money. I've got it on me, as a matter of fact. Rather luckily drew some this morning.'

And I fished it out and pushed it across. The brother shook his head.

'Mr Wooster,' he said, 'we appreciate your generosity, your beautiful, heartening confidence in us, but we cannot permit this.'

'What Sidney means,' said the girl, 'is that you really don't know anything about us when you come to think of it. You mustn't risk lending all this money without any security at all to two people who, after all, are almost strangers. If I hadn't thought that you would be quite business-like about this I would never have dared to come to you.'

'The idea of – er – pledging the pearls at the local Mont de Pieté was, you will readily understand, repugnant to us,' said the brother.

'If you will just give me a receipt, as a matter of form – '

'Oh, right-o!'

I wrote out the receipt and handed it over, feeling more or less of an ass.

'Here you are,' I said.

The girl took the piece of paper, shoved it in her bag, grabbed the money and slipped it to brother Sidney, and then, before I knew what was happening, she had darted at me, kissed me, and legged it from the room.

I'm bound to say the thing rattled me. So dashed sudden and unexpected. I mean, a girl like that. Always been quiet and demure and what not – by no means the sort of female you'd have expected to go about the place kissing fellows. Through a sort of mist I could see that Jeeves had appeared from the background and was helping the brother on with his coat; and I remember wondering idly how the dickens a man could bring himself to wear a coat like that, it being more like a sack than anything else. Then the brother came up to me and grasped my hand.

'I cannot thank you sufficiently, Mr Wooster!'

'Oh, not at all.'

'You have saved my good name. Good name in man or woman, dear my lord,' he said, massaging the fin with some fervour, 'is the immediate jewel of their souls. Who steals my purse steals trash. 'Twas mine, 'tis his, and has been slave to thousands. But he that filches my good name robs me of that which enriches not him and makes me poor indeed. I thank you from the bottom of my heart. Good night, Mr Wooster.'

'Good night, old thing,' I said.

I blinked at Jeeves as the door shut. 'Rather a sad affair, Jeeves,' I said.

'Yes, sir.'

'Luckily I happened to have all that money handy.'

'Well – er – yes, sir.'

'You speak as though you didn't think much of it.'

'It is not my place to criticize your actions, sir, but I will venture to say that I think you behaved a little rashly.'

'What, lending that money?'

'Yes, sir. These fashionable French watering places are notoriously infested by dishonest characters.'

This was a bit too thick.

'Now look here, Jeeves,' I said. 'I can stand a lot but when it comes to your casting asp-whatever-the-word-is on a bird in Holy Orders – '

'Perhaps I am over-suspicious, sir. But I have seen a great deal of these resorts. When I was in the employment of Lord Frederick Ranelagh, shortly before I entered your service, his lordship was very neatly swindled by a criminal known, I believe, by the soubriquet of Soapy Sid, who scraped acquaintance with us in Monte Carlo with the assistance of a female accomplice. I have never forgotten the circumstances.'

'I don't want to butt in on your reminiscences, Jeeves,' I said, coldly, 'but you're talking through your hat. How can there have been anything fishy about the business? They've left me the pearls, haven't they? Very well, then, think before you speak. You had better be tooling down to the desk now and having these things shoved in the hotel safe.' I picked up the case and opened it. 'Oh, Great Scott!'

The bally thing was empty!

'Oh, my Lord!' I said, staring. 'Don't tell me there's been dirty work at the crossroads after all!'

'Precisely, sir. It was in exactly the same manner that Lord Frederick was swindled on the occasion to which I have alluded. While his female accomplice was gratefully embracing his lordship, Soapy Sid substituted a duplicate case for the one containing the pearls and went off with the jewels, the money and the receipt. On the strength of the receipt he subsequently demanded from his lordship the return of the pearls, and his lordship, not being able to produce them, was obliged to pay a heavy sum in compensation. It is a simple but effective ruse.'

I felt as if the bottom had dropped out of things with a jerk.

'Soapy Sid? Sid! *Sidney*! Brother Sidney! Why, by Jove, Jeeves, do you think that parson was Soapy Sid?'

'Yes, sir.'

'But it seems extraordinary. Why, his collar buttoned at the back – I mean, he would have deceived a bishop. Do you really think he was Soapy Sid?'

'Yes, sir. I recognized him directly he came into the room.'

I stared at the blighter.

'You recognized him?'

'Yes, sir.'

'Then, dash it all,' I said, deeply moved. 'I think you might have told me.'

'I thought it would save disturbance and unpleasantness if I merely extracted the case from the man's pocket as I assisted him with his coat, sir. Here it is.'

He laid another case on the table beside the dud one, and, by Jove, you couldn't tell them apart. I opened it, and there were the good old pearls, as merry and bright as dammit, smiling up at me. I gazed feebly at the man. I was feeling a bit overwrought.

'Jeeves,' I said. 'You're an absolute genius!'

'Yes, sir.'

Relief was surging over me in great chunks by now. Thanks to Jeeves I was not going to be called on to cough up several thousand quid.

'It looks to me as though you have saved the old home. I mean, even a chappie endowed with the immortal rind of dear old Sid is hardly likely to have the nerve to come back and retrieve these little chaps.'

'I should imagine not, sir.'

'Well, then – Oh, I say, you don't think they are just paste or anything like that?'

'No, sir. These are genuine pearls and extremely valuable.'

'Well, then, dash it, I'm on velvet. Absolutely reclining on the good old plush! I may be down a hundred quid but I'm up a jolly good string of pearls. Am I right or wrong?'

'Hardly that, sir. I think that you will have to restore the pearls.'

'What! To Sid? Not while I have my physique!'

'No, sir. To their rightful owner.'

'But who is their rightful owner?'

'Mrs Gregson, sir.'

'What! How do you know?'

'It was all over the hotel an hour ago that Mrs Gregson's pearls had been abstracted. I was speaking to Mrs Gregson's maid shortly before you came in and she informed me that the manager of the hotel is now in Mrs Gregson's suite.'

'And having a devil of a time, what?'

'So I should be disposed to imagine, sir.'

The situation was beginning to unfold before me.

'I'll go and give them back to her, eh? It'll put me one up, what?'

'Precisely, sir. And, if I may make the suggestion, I think it might be judicious to stress the fact that they were stolen by—.'

'Great Scott! By the dashed girl she was hounding me on to marry, by Jove!'

'Exactly, sir.'

'Jeeves,' I said, 'this is going to be the biggest score off my jolly old relative that has ever occurred in the world's history.'

'It is not unlikely, sir.'

'Keep her quiet for a bit, what? Make her stop snootering me for a while?'

'It should have that effect, sir.'

'Golly!' I said, bounding for the door.

Long before I reached Aunt Agatha's lair I could tell that the hunt was up. Divers chappies in hotel uniform and not a few chambermaids of sorts were hanging about in the corridor, and through the panels I could hear a mixed assortment of voices, with Aunt Agatha's topping the lot. I knocked but no one took any notice, so I trickled in. Among those present I noticed a chambermaid in hysterics, Aunt

Agatha with her hair bristling and the whiskered cove who looked like a bandit, the hotel manager fellow.

'Oh, hallo!' I said. 'Hallo-allo-allo!'

Aunt Agatha shooshed me away. No welcoming smile for Bertram.

'Don't bother me now, Bertie,' she snapped, looking at me as if I were more or less the last straw.

'Something up?'

'Yes, yes, yes! I've lost my pearls.'

'Pearls? Pearls? Pearls?' I said. 'No, really. Dashed annoying. Where did you see them last?'

'What does it matter where I saw them last? They have been stolen.'

Here Wilfred the Whisker King, who seemed to have been taking a rest between rounds, stepped into the ring again and began to talk rapidly in French. Cut to the quick he seemed. The chambermaid whooped in the corner.

'Sure you've looked everywhere?' I said.

'Of course I've looked everywhere.'

'Well, you know, I've often lost a collar stud and – '

'Do try not to be so maddening, Bertie! I have enough to bear without your imbecilities. Oh, be quiet! Be quiet!' she shouted in the sort of voice used by sergeant-majors and those who call the cattle home across the Sands of Dee. And such was the magnetism of her forceful personality that Wilfred subsided as if he had run into a wall. The chambermaid continued to go strong.

'I say,' I said, 'I think there's something the matter with this girl. Isn't she crying or something? You may not have spotted it, but I'm rather quick at noticing things.'

'She stole my pearls! I am convinced of it.'

This started the whisker specialist off again, and in about a couple of minutes Aunt Agatha had reached the frozen grande-dame stage and was putting the last of the bandits through it in the voice she usually reserves for snubbing waiters in restaurants.

'I tell you, my good man, for the hundredth time – '

'I say,' I said, 'don't want to interrupt you and all that sort of thing, but these aren't the little chaps by any chance, are they?'

I pulled the pearls out of my pocket and held them up.

'These look like pearls, what?'

I don't know when I've had a more juicy moment. It was one of those occasions about which I shall prattle to my grandchildren – if I ever have any, which at the moment of going to press seems more or less of a hundred-to-one shot. Aunt Agatha simply deflated before my eyes. It reminded me of when I once saw some chappies letting the gas out of a balloon.

'Where – where – where – ' she gurgled.

'I got them from your friend, Miss Hemmingway.'

Even now she didn't get it.

'From Miss Hemmingway. Miss *Hemmingway*! But – but how did they come into her possession?'

'How?' I said. 'Because she jolly well stole them. Pinched them! Swiped them! Because that's how she makes her living, dash it – palling up to unsuspicious people in hotels and sneaking their jewellery. I don't know what her alias is, but her bally brother, the chap whose collar buttons at the back, is known in criminal circles as Soapy Sid.'

She blinked.

'Miss Hemmingway a thief! I – I – ' She stopped and looked feebly at me. 'But how did you manage to recover the pearls, Bertie dear?'

'Never mind,' I said crisply. 'I have my methods.' I dug out my entire stock of manly courage, breathed a short prayer and let her have it right in the thorax.

'I must say, Aunt Agatha, dash it all,' I said severely, 'I think you have been infernally careless. There's a printed notice in every bedroom in this place saying that there's a safe in the manager's office, where jewellery and valuables ought to be placed, and you absolutely disregarded it. And what's the result? The first thief who came along simply walked into your room and pinched your pearls. And instead of admitting that it was all your fault, you started biting this poor man here in the gizzard. You have been very, very unjust to this poor man.'

'Yes, yes,' moaned the poor man.

'And this unfortunate girl, what about her? Where does she get off? You've accused her of stealing the things on absolutely no evidence. I think she would be jolly well advised to bring an action for – for whatever it is and soak you for substantial damages.'

'*Mais oui, mais ouis, c'est trop fort!*' shouted the Bandit Chief, backing me up like a good 'un. And the chambermaid looked up inquiringly, as if the sun was breaking through the clouds.

'I shall recompense her,' said Aunt Agatha feebly.

'If you take my tip you jolly well will, and that eftsoons or right speedily. She's got a cast-iron case, and if I were her I wouldn't take a penny under twenty quid. But what gives me the pip most is the way you've unjustly abused this poor man here and tried to give his hotel a bad name – '

'Yes, by damn! It's too bad! cried the whiskered marvel. 'You careless old woman! You give my hotel bad names, would you or wasn't it? Tomorrow you leave my hotel, by great Scotland!'

And more to the same effect, all good, ripe stuff. And presently having said his say he withdrew, taking the chambermaid with him, the latter with a crisp tenner clutched in a vice-like grip. I suppose she and the bandit split it outside. A French hotel manager wouldn't be likely to let real money wander away from him without counting himself in on the division.

I turned to Aunt Agatha, whose demeanour was now rather like that of one who, picking daisies on the railway, has just caught the down express in the small of the back.

'I don't want to rub it in, Aunt Agatha,' I said coldly, 'but I should just like to point out before I go that the girl who stole your pearls is the girl you've been hounding me on to marry ever since I got here. Good heavens! Do you realize that if you had brought the thing off I should probably have had children who would have sneaked my watch while I was dandling them on my knee? I'm not a complaining sort of chap as a rule, but I must say that another time I do think you might be more careful how you go about egging me on to marry females.'

I gave her one look, turned on my heel and left the room.

'Ten o'clock, a clear night, and all's well, Jeeves,' I said, breezing back into the good old suite.

'I am gratified to hear it, sir.'

'If twenty quid would be any use to you, Jeeves – '

'I am much obliged, sir.'

There was a pause. And then – well, it was a wrench, but I did it. I unstripped the cummerbund and handed it over.

'Do you wish me to press this, sir?'

I gave the thing one last, longing look. It had been very dear to me.

'No,' I said, 'take it away; give it to the deserving poor – I shall never wear it again.'

'Thank you very much, sir,' said Jeeves.

5

The Pride of the Woosters is Wounded

If there's one thing I like, it's a quiet life. I'm not one of those fellows who get all restless and depressed if things aren't happening to them all the time. You can't make it too placid for me. Give me regular meals, a good show with decent music every now and then, and one or two pals to totter round with, and I ask no more.

That is why the jar, when it came, was such a particularly nasty jar. I mean, I'd returned from Roville with a sort of feeling that from now on nothing could occur to upset me. Aunt Agatha, I imagined, would require at least a year to recover from the Hemmingway affair: and apart from Aunt Agatha there isn't anybody who really does much in the way of harrying me. It seemed to me that the skies were blue, so to speak, and no clouds in sight.

I little thought . . . Well, look here, what happened was this, and I ask you if it wasn't enough to rattle anybody.

Once a year Jeeves takes a couple of weeks' vacation and biffs off to the sea or somewhere to restore his tissues. Pretty rotten for me, of course, while he's away. But it has to be stuck, so I stick it; and I must admit that he usually manages to get hold of a fairly decent fellow to look after me in his absence.

Well, the time had come round again, and Jeeves was in the kitchen giving the understudy a few tips about his duties. I happened to want a stamp or something, and I toddled down the passage to ask him for it. The silly ass had left the kitchen door open, and I hadn't gone two steps when his voice caught me squarely in the eardrum.

'You will find Mr Wooster,' he was saying to the substitute chappie, 'an exceedingly pleasant and amiable young gentleman, but not intelligent. By no means intelligent. Mentally he is negligible – quite negligible.'

Well, I mean to say, what!

I suppose, strictly speaking, I ought to have charged in and ticked the blighter off properly in no uncertain voice. But I doubt whether it's humanly possible to tick Jeeves off. Personally, I didn't even have a dash at it. I merely called for my hat and stick in a marked manner and legged it. But the memory rankled, if you know what I mean. We Woosters do not lightly forget. At least, we do – some things – appointments, and people's birthdays, and letters to post, and all that – but not an absolute bally insult like the above. I brooded like the dickens.

I was still brooding when I dropped in at the oyster-bar at Buck's for a quick bracer. I needed a bracer rather particularly at the moment, because I was on my way to lunch with Aunt Agatha. A pretty frightful ordeal, believe me or believe me not, even though I took it that after what had happened at Roville she would be in a fairly subdued and amiable mood. I had just had one quick and another rather slower, and was feeling about as cheerio as was possible under the circs, when a muffled voice hailed me from the north-east, and, turning round, I saw young Bingo Little propped up in a corner, wrapping himself round a sizeable chunk of bread and cheese.

'Hallo-allo-allo!' I said. 'Haven't seen you for ages. You've not been in here lately, have you?'

'No. I've been living out in the country.'

'Eh?' I said, for Bingo's loathing for the country was well known. 'Whereabouts?'

'Down in Hampshire, at a place called Ditteredge.'

'No, really? I know some people who've got a house there. The Glossops. Have you met them?'

'Why, that's where I'm staying!' said young Bingo. 'I'm tutoring the Glossop kid.'

'What for?' I said. I couldn't seem to see young Bingo as a tutor. Though, of course, he did get a degree of sorts at Oxford, and I suppose you can always fool some of the people some of the time.

'What for? For money, of course! An absolute sitter came un-stitched in the second race at Haydock Park,' said young Bingo, with some bitterness, 'and I dropped my entire month's allowance. I hadn't the nerve to touch my uncle for any more, so it was a case of buzzing round to the agents and getting a job. I've been down there three weeks.'

'I haven't met the Glossop kid.'

'Don't!' advised Bingo, briefly.

'The only one of the family I really know is the girl.' I had hardly spoken these words when the most extraordinary change came over young Bingo's face. His eyes bulged, his cheeks flushed, and his Adam's apple hopped about like one of those india-rubber balls on the top of the fountain in a shooting-gallery.

'Oh, Bertie!' he said, in a strangled sort of voice.

I looked at the poor fish anxiously. I knew that he was always falling in love with someone, but it didn't seem possible that even he could have fallen in love with Honoria Glossop. To me the girl was simply nothing more nor less than a pot of poison. One of those dashed large, brainy, strenuous, dynamic girls you see so many of these days. She had been at Girton, where, in addition to enlarging her brain to the most frightful extent, she had gone in for every kind of sport and developed the physique of a middle-weight catch-as-catch-can wrestler. I'm not sure she didn't box for the Varsity while she was up. The effect she had on me whenever she appeared was to make me want to slide into a cellar and lie low till they blew the All Clear.

Yet here was young Bingo obviously all for her. There was no mistaking it. The love light was in the blighter's eyes.

'I worship her, Bertie! I worship the very ground she treads on!' continued the patient, in a loud, penetrating voice. Fred Thompson and one or two fellows had come in, and McGarry, the chappie behind the bar, was listening with his ears flapping. But there's no reticence about Bingo. He always reminds me of the hero of a musical comedy who takes the centre of the stage, gathers the boys round him in a circle, and tells them all about his love at the top of his voice.

'Have you told her?'

'No, I haven't the nerve. But we walk together in the garden most evenings, and it sometimes seems to me that there is a look in her eyes.'

'I know that look. Like a sergeant-major.'

'Nothing of the kind! Like a tender goddess.'

'Half a second, old thing,' I said. 'Are you sure we're talking about the same girl? The one I mean is Honoria. Perhaps there's a younger sister or something I've not heard of?'

'Her name is Honoria,' bawled Bingo reverently.

'And she strikes you as a tender goddess?'

'She does.'

'God bless you!' I said.

'She walks in beauty like the night of cloudless climes and starry skies; and all that's best of dark and bright meet in her aspect and her eyes. Another bit of bread and cheese,' he said to the lad behind the bar.

'You're keeping your strength up,' I said.

'This is my lunch. I've got to meet Oswald at Waterloo at one-fifteen, to catch the train back. I brought him up to town to see the dentist.'

'Oswald? Is that the kid?'

'Yes. Pestilential to a degree.'

'Pestilential! That reminds me, I'm lunching with my Aunt Agatha. I'll have to pop off now, or I'll be late.'

I hadn't seen Aunt Agatha since that little affair of the pearls; and, while I didn't anticipate any great pleasure from gnawing a bone in her society, I must say that there was one topic of conversation I felt pretty confident she wouldn't touch on, and that was the subject of my matrimonial future. I mean, when a woman's made a bloomer like the one Aunt Agatha made at Roville, you'd naturally think that a decent shame would keep her off it for, at any rate, a month or two.

But women beat me. I mean to say, as regards nerve. You'll hardly credit it, but she actually started in on me with the fish. Absolutely with the fish, I give you my solemn word. We'd hardly exchanged a word about the weather, when she let me have it without a blush.

'Bertie,' she said, 'I've been thinking again about you and how necessary it is that you should get married. I quite admit that I was dreadfully mistaken in my opinion of that terrible, hypocritical girl at Roville, but this time there is no danger of an error. By great good luck I have found the very wife for you, a girl whom I have only recently met, but whose family is above suspicion. She has plenty of money, too, though that does not matter in your case. The great point is that she is strong, self-reliant and sensible, and will counterbalance the deficiencies and weaknesses of your character. She has met you; and, while there is naturally much in you of which she disapproves, she does not dislike you. I know this, for I have sounded her – guardedly, of course – and I am sure you have only to make the first advance –'

'Who is it?' I would have said it long before, but the shock had made me swallow a bit of roll the wrong way, and I had only just finished turning purple and trying to get a bit of air back into the old windpipe. 'Who is it?'

'Sir Roderick Glossop's daughter, Honoria.'

'No, no!' I cried, paling beneath the tan.

'Don't be silly, Bertie. She is just the wife for you.'

'Yes, but look here – '

'She will mould you.'

'But I don't want to be moulded.'

Aunt Agatha gave me the kind of look she used to give me when I was a kid and had been found in the jam cupboard.

'Bertie! I hope you are not going to be troublesome.'

'Well, but I mean – '

'Lady Glossop has very kindly invited you to Ditteredge Hall for a few days. I told her you would be delighted to come down tomorrow.'

'I'm sorry, but I've got a dashed important engagement tomorrow.'

'What engagement?'

'Well – er – '

'You have no engagement. And, even if you had, you must put it off. I shall be very seriously annoyed, Bertie, if you do not go to Ditteredge Hall tomorrow.'

'Oh, right-o!' I said.

It wasn't two minutes after I had parted from Aunt Agatha before the old fighting spirit of the Woosters reasserted itself. Ghastly as the peril was which loomed before me, I was conscious of a rummy sort of exhilaration. It was a tight corner, but the tighter the corner, I felt, the more juicily should I score off Jeeves when I got myself out of it without a bit of help from him. Ordinarily, of course, I should have consulted him and trusted to him to solve the difficulty; but after what I had heard him saying in the kitchen, I was dashed if I was going to demean myself. When I got home I addressed the man with light abandon.

'Jeeves,' I said, 'I'm in a bit of a difficulty.'

'I'm sorry to hear that, sir.'

'Yes, quite a bad hole. In fact, you might say on the brink of a precipice, and faced by an awful doom.'

'If I could be of any assistance, sir – '

'Oh, no. No, no. Thanks very much, but no, no. I won't trouble you. I've no doubt I shall be able to get out of it by myself.'

'Very good, sir.'

So that was that. I'm bound to say I'd have welcomed a bit more curiosity from the fellow, but that is Jeeves all over. Cloaks his emotions, if you know what I mean.

Honoria was away when I got to Ditteredge on the following afternoon. Her mother told me that she was staying with some people named Braythwayt in the neighbourhood, and would be back next day, bringing the daughter of the house with her for a visit. She said I would find Oswald out in the grounds, and such is a mother's love that she spoke as if that were a bit of a boost for the grounds and an inducement to go there.

Rather decent, the grounds at Ditteredge. A couple of terraces, a bit of lawn with a cedar on it, a bit of shrubbery, and finally a small but goodish lake with a stone bridge running across it. Directly I'd worked my way round the shrubbery I spotted young Bingo leaning against the bridge smoking a cigarette. Sitting on the stone-work, fishing, was a species of kid whom I took to be Oswald the Plague-Spot.

Bingo was both surprised and delighted to see me, and introduced me to the kid. If the latter was surprised and delighted too, he concealed it like a diplomat. He just looked at me, raised his eye-brows slightly, and went on fishing. He was one of those supercilious striplings who give you the impression that you went to the wrong school and that your clothes don't fit.

'This is Oswald,' said Bingo.

'What,' I replied cordially, 'could be sweeter? How are you?'

'Oh, all right,' said the kid.

'Nice place, this.'

'Oh, all right,' said the kid.

'Having a good time fishing?'

'Oh, all right,' said the kid.

Young Bingo led me off to commune apart.

'Doesn't jolly old Oswald's incessant flow of prattle make your head ache sometimes?' I asked.

Bingo sighed.

'It's a hard job.'

'What's a hard job?'

'Loving him.'

'Do you love him?' I asked, surprised. I shouldn't have thought it could be done.

'I try to,' said young Bingo, 'for Her sake. She's coming back tomorrow, Bertie.'

'So I heard.'

'She is coming, my love, my own – '

'Absolutely,' I said. 'But touching on young Oswald once more.

Do you have to be with him all day? How do you manage to stick it?'

'Oh, he doesn't give much trouble. When we aren't working he sits on that bridge all the time, trying to catch tiddlers.'

'Why don't you shove him in?'

'Shove him in?'

'It seems to me distinctly the thing to do,' I said, regarding the stripling's back with a good deal of dislike. 'It would wake him up a bit, and make him take an interest in things.'

Bingo shook his head a bit wistfully.

'Your proposition attracts me,' he said, 'but I'm afraid it can't be done. You see, She would never forgive me. She is devoted to the little brute.'

'Great Scott!' I cried. 'I've got it!' I don't know if you know that feeling when you get an inspiration, and tingle all down your spine from the soft collar as now worn to the very soles of the old Waukeesis? Jeeves, I suppose, feels that way more or less all the time, but it isn't often it comes to me. But now all Nature seemed to be shouting at me. 'You've clicked!' and I grabbed young Bingo by the arm in a way that must have made him feel as if a horse had bitten him. His finely-chiselled features were twisted with agony and what not, and he asked me what the dickens I thought I was playing at.

'Bingo,' I said, 'what would Jeeves have done?'

'How do you mean, what would Jeeves have done?'

'I mean what would he have advised in a case like yours? I mean you wanting to make a hit with Honoria Glossop and all that. Why, take it from me, he would have shoved you behind that clump of bushes over there; he would have got me to lure Honoria on to the bridge somehow; then, at the proper time, he would have told me to give the kid a pretty hefty jab in the small of the back, so as to shoot him into the water; and then you would have dived in and hauled him out. How about it?'

'You didn't think that out by yourself, Bertie?' said young Bingo, in a hushed sort of voice.

'Yes, I did. Jeeves isn't the only fellow with ideas.'

'But it's absolutely wonderful.'

'Just a suggestion.'

'The only objection I can see is that it would be so dashed awkward for you. I mean to say, suppose the kid turned round and said you had shoved him in, that would make you frightfully unpopular with Her.'

'I don't mind risking that.'

The man was deeply moved.

'Bertie, this is noble.'

'No, no.'

He clasped my hand silently, then chuckled like the last drop of water going down the waste pipe in a bath.

'Now what?' I said.

'I was only thinking,' said young Bingo, 'how fearfully wet Oswald will get. Oh, happy day!'

6

The Hero's Reward

I don't know if you've noticed it, but it's rummy how nothing in this world ever seems to be absolutely perfect. The drawback to this otherwise singularly fruity binge was, of course, the fact that Jeeves wouldn't be on the spot to watch me in action. Still, apart from that there wasn't a flaw. The beauty of the thing was, you see, that nothing could possibly go wrong. You know how it is, as a rule, when you want to get Chappie A on Spot B at exactly the same moment when Chappie C is on Spot D. There's always a chance of a hitch. Take the case of a general, I mean to say, who's planning out a big movement. He tells one regiment to capture the hill with the windmill on it at the exact moment when another regiment is taking the bridgehead or something down in the valley; and everything gets all messed up. And then, when they're chatting the thing over in camp that night, the colonel of the first regiment says, 'Oh, sorry! Did you say the hill with the windmill? I thought you said the one with the flock of sheep?' And there you are! But in this case, nothing like that could happen, because Oswald and Bingo would be on the spot right along, so that all I had to worry about was getting Honoria there in due season. And I managed that all right, first shot, by asking her if she would come for a stroll in the grounds with me, as I had something particular to say to her.

She had arrived shortly after lunch in the car with the Braythwayt girl. I was introduced to the latter, a tallish girl with blue eyes and fair hair. I rather took to her – she was so unlike Honoria – and, if I had been able to spare the time, I shouldn't have minded talking to her for a bit. But business was business – I had fixed it up with Bingo to be behind the bushes at three sharp, so I got hold of Honoria and steered her out through the grounds in the direction of the lake.

'You're very quiet, Mr Wooster,' she said.

Made me jump a bit. I was concentrating pretty tensely at the moment. We had just come in sight of the lake, and I was casting a keen eye over the ground to see that everything was in order. Everything appeared to be as arranged. The kid Oswald was hunched up on the bridge; and, as Bingo wasn't visible, I took it that he had got into position. My watch made it two minutes after the hour.

'Eh?' I said. 'Oh, ah, yes. I was just thinking.'

'You said you had something important to say to me.'

'Absolutely!' I had decided to open the proceedings by sort of paving the way for young Bingo. I mean to say, without actually mentioning his name, I wanted to prepare the girl's mind for the fact that, surprising as it might seem, there was someone who had long loved her from afar and all that sort of rot. 'It's like this,' I said. 'It may sound rummy and all that, but there's somebody who's frightfully in love with you and so forth – a friend of mine, you know.'

'Oh, a friend of yours?'

'Yes.'

She gave a kind of a laugh.

'Well, why doesn't he tell me so?'

'Well, you see, that's the sort of chap he is. Kind of shrinking, diffident kind of fellow. Hasn't got the nerve. Thinks you so much above him, don't you know. Looks on you as a sort of goddess. Worships the ground you tread on, but can't whack up the ginger to tell you so.'

'This is very interesting.'

'Yes. He's not a bad chap, you know, in his way. Rather an ass, perhaps, but well-meaning. Well, that's the posish. You might just bear it in mind, what?'

'How funny you are!'

She chucked back her head and laughed with considerable vim. She had a penetrating sort of laugh. Rather like a train going into a tunnel. It didn't sound over-musical to me, and on the kid Oswald it appeared to jar not a little. He gazed at us with a good deal of dislike.

'I wish the dickens you wouldn't make that row,' he said. 'Scaring all the fish away.'

It broke the spell a bit. Honoria changed the subject.

'I do wish Oswald wouldn't sit on the bridge like that,' she said. 'I'm sure it isn't safe. He might easily fall in.'

'I'll go and tell him,' I said.

I suppose the distance between the kid and me at this juncture was about five yards, but I got the impression that it was nearer a hundred. And, as I started to toddle across the intervening space, I had a rummy feeling that I'd done this very thing before. Then I remembered. Years ago, at a country-house party, I had been roped in to play the part of a butler in some amateur theatricals in aid of some ghastly charity or other; and I had had to open the proceedings by walking across the empty stage from left upper entrance and shoving a tray on a table down right. They had impressed it on me at rehearsals that I mustn't take the course at a quick heel-and-toe, like a chappie finishing strongly in a walking-race; and the result was that I kept the brakes on to such an extent that it seemed to me as if I was never going to get to the bally table at all. The stage seemed to stretch out in front of me like a trackless desert, and there was a kind of breathless hush as if all Nature had paused to concentrate its attention on me personally. Well, I felt just like that now. I had a kind of dry gulping in my throat, and the more I walked the farther away the kid seemed to get, till suddenly I found myself standing just behind him without quite knowing how I'd got there.

'Hallo!' I said, with a sickly sort of grin – wasted on the kid, because he didn't bother to turn round and look at me. He merely wiggled his left ear in a rather peevish manner. I don't know when I've met anybody in whose life I appeared to mean so little.

'Hallo!' I said. 'Fishing?'

I laid my hand in a sort of elderly-brotherly way on his shoulder.

'Here, look out!' said the kid, wobbling on his foundations.

It was one of those things that want doing quickly or not at all. I shut my eyes and pushed. Something seemed to give. There was a scrambling sound, a kind of yelp, a scream in the offing, and a splash. And so the long day wore on, so to speak.

I opened my eyes. The kid was just coming to the surface.

'Help!' I shouted, cocking an eye on the bush from which young Bingo was scheduled to emerge.

Nothing happened. Young Bingo didn't emerge to the slightest extent whatever.

'I say! Help!' I shouted again.

I don't want to bore you with reminiscences of my theatrical career, but I must just touch once more on that appearance of mine as the butler. The scheme on that occasion had been that when I put the tray on the table the heroine would come on and say a few words to get me off. Well, on the night the misguided female forgot to stand by, and it was a full minute before the search-party located her and shot her on to the stage. And all that time I had to stand there, waiting. A rotten sensation, believe me, and this was just the same, only worse. I understood what these writer-chappies mean when they talk about time standing still.

Meanwhile, the kid Oswald was presumably being cut off in his prime, and it began to seem to me that some sort of steps ought to be taken about it. What I had seen of the lad hadn't particularly endeared him to me, but it was undoubtedly a bit thick to let him pass away. I don't know when I have seen anything more grubby and unpleasant than the lake as viewed from the bridge; but the thing apparently had to be done. I chucked off my coat and vaulted over.

It seems rummy that water should be so much wetter when you go into it with your clothes on than when you're just bathing, but take it from me that it is. I was only under about three seconds, I suppose, but I came up feeling like the bodies you read of in the paper which 'had evidently been in the water several days'. I felt clammy and bloated.

At this point the scenario struck another snag. I had assumed that directly I came to the surface I should get hold of the kid and steer him courageously to shore. But he hadn't waited to be steered. When I had finished getting the water out of my eyes and had time to look round, I saw him about ten yards away, going strongly and using, I think, the Australian crawl. The spectacle took all the heart out of me. I mean to say, the whole essence of a rescue, if you know what I mean, is that the party of the second part shall keep fairly still and on one spot. If he starts swimming off on his own account and can obviously give you at least forty yards in the hundred, where are you? The whole thing falls through. It didn't seem to me that there was much to be done except get ashore, so I got ashore. By the time I had landed, the kid was half-way to the house. Look at it from whatever angle you like, the thing was a wash-out.

I was interrupted in my meditations by a noise like the Scotch express going under a bridge. It was Honoria Glossop laughing. She was standing at my elbow, looking at me in a rummy manner.

'Oh, Bertie, you are funny!' she said. And even in that moment there seemed to me something sinister in the words. She had never called me anything except 'Mr Wooster' before. 'How wet you are!'

'Yes, I am wet.'

'You had better hurry into the house and change.'

'Yes.'

I wrung a gallon or two of water out of my clothes.

'You *are* funny!' she said again. 'First proposing in that extraordinary roundabout way, and then pushing poor little Oswald into the lake so as to impress me by saving him.'

I managed to get the water out of my throat sufficiently to try to correct this fearful impression.

'No, no!'

'He said you pushed him in, and I saw you do it. Oh, I'm not angry, Bertie. I think it was too sweet of you. But I'm quite sure it's time that I took you in hand. You certainly want someone to look after you. You've been seeing too many moving-pictures. I suppose the next thing you would have done would have been to set the house on fire so as to rescue me.' She looked at me in a proprietary sort of way. 'I think,' she said, 'I shall be able to make something of you, Bertie. It is true yours has been a wasted life up to the present, but you are still young, and there is a lot of good in you.'

'No, really there isn't.'

'Oh, yes, there is. It simply wants bringing out. Now you run straight up to the house and change your wet clothes, or you will catch cold.'

And, if you know what I mean, there was a sort of motherly note in her voice which seemed to tell me, even more than her actual words, that I was for it.

As I was coming downstairs after changing, I ran into young Bingo, looking festive to a degree.

'Bertie!' he said. 'Just the man I wanted to see. Bertie, a wonderful thing has happened.'

'You blighter!' I cried. 'What became of you? Do you know – '

'Oh, you mean about being in those bushes? I hadn't time to tell you about that. It's all off.'

'All off?'

'Bertie, I was actually starting to hide in those bushes when the most extraordinary thing happened. Walking across the lawn I saw the most radiant, the most beautiful girl in the world. There is none like her, none. Bertie, do you believe in love at first sight? You do believe in love at first sight, don't you, Bertie, old man? Directly I saw her she seemed to draw me like a magnet. I seemed to forget everything. We two were alone in a world of music and sunshine. I joined her. I got into conversation. She is a Miss Braythwayt, Bertie – Daphne Braythwayt. Directly our eyes met, I realized that what I had imagined to be love for Honoria Glossop had been a mere passing whim. Bertie, you do believe in love at first sight, don't you? She is so wonderful, so sympathetic. Like a tender goddess – '

At this point I left the blighter.

Two days later I got a letter from Jeeves.

' – The weather,' it ended, 'continues fine. I have had one exceedingly enjoyable bathe.'

I gave one of those hollow, mirthless laughs, and went downstairs to join Honoria. I had an appointment with her in the drawing-room. She was going to read Ruskin to me.

7

Introducing Claude and Eustace

The blow fell precisely at one-forty-five (summer time). Spenser, Aunt Agatha's butler, was offering me the fried potatoes at the moment, and such was my emotion that I lofted six of them on to the sideboard with the spoon. Shaken to the core, if you know what I mean.

Mark you, I was in a pretty enfeebled condition already. I had been engaged to Honoria Glossop nearly two weeks, and during all that time not a day had passed without her putting in some heavy work in the direction of what Aunt Agatha had called 'moulding' me. I had read solid literature till my eyes bubbled; we had legged it together through miles of picture-galleries; and I had been compelled to undergo classical concerts to an extent you would hardly believe. All in all, therefore, I was in no fit state to receive shocks, especially shocks like this. Honoria had lugged me round to lunch at Aunt Agatha's, and I had just been saying to myself, 'Death, where is thy jolly old sting?' when she hove the bomb.

'Bertie,' she said, suddenly, as if she had just remembered it, 'what is the name of that man of yours – your valet?'

'Eh? Oh, Jeeves.'

'I think he's a bad influence for you,' said Honoria. 'When we are married, you must get rid of Jeeves.'

It was at this point that I jerked the spoon and sent six of the best and crispest sailing on to the sideboard, with Spenser gambolling after them like a dignified old retriever.

'Get rid of Jeeves!' I gasped.

'Yes. I don't like him.'

'*I* don't like him,' said Aunt Agatha.

'But I can't. I mean – why, I couldn't carry on for a day without Jeeves.'

'You will have to,' said Honoria. 'I don't like him at all.'

'*I* don't like him at all,' said Aunt Agatha. 'I never did.'

Ghastly, what? I'd always had an idea that marriage was a bit of a wash-out, but I'd never dreamed that it demanded such frightful sacrifices from a fellow. I passed the rest of the meal in a sort of stupor.

The scheme had been, if I remember, that after lunch I should go off and caddy for Honoria on a shopping tour down Regent Street; but when she got up and started collecting me and the rest of her things, Aunt Agatha stopped her.

'You run along, dear,' she said. 'I want to say a few words to Bertie.'

So Honoria legged it, and Aunt Agatha drew up her chair and started in.

'Bertie,' she said, 'dear Honoria does not know it, but a little difficulty has arisen about your marriage.'

'By Jove! Not really?' I said, hope starting to dawn.

'Oh, it's nothing at all, of course. It is only a little exasperating. The fact is, Sir Roderick is being rather troublesome.'

'Thinks I'm not a good bet? Wants to scratch the fixture? Well, perhaps he's right.'

'Pray do not be so absurd, Bertie. It is nothing so serious as that. But the nature of Sir Roderick's profession unfortunately makes him – over-cautious.'

I didn't get it.

'Over-cautious?'

'Yes. I suppose it is inevitable. A nerve specialist with his extensive practice can hardly help taking a rather warped view of humanity.'

I got what she was driving at now. Sir Roderick Glossop, Honoria's father, is always called a nerve specialist, because it sounds better, but everybody knows that he's really a sort of janitor to the loony-bin. I mean to say, when your uncle the Duke begins to feel the strain a bit and you find him in the blue drawing-room sticking straws in his hair, old Glossop is the first person you send for. He toddles round, gives the patient the once-over, talks about over-excited nervous systems, and recommends complete rest and seclusion and all that sort of thing. Practically every posh family in the country has called him in at one time or another, and I suppose that, being in that position – I mean constantly having to sit on people's heads while their nearest and dearest phone to the asylum to send round the wagon – does tend to make a chappie take what you might call a warped view of humanity.

'You mean he thinks I may be a loony, and he doesn't want a loony son-in-law?' I said.

Aunt Agatha seemed rather peeved than otherwise at my deadly intelligence.

'Of course, he does not think anything so ridiculous. I told you he was simply exceedingly cautious. He wants to satisfy himself that you are perfectly normal.' Here she paused, for Spenser had come in with the coffee. When he had gone, she went on: 'He appears to have got hold of some extraordinary story about your having pushed his son Oswald into the lake at Ditteredge Hall. Incredible, of course. Even you would hardly do a thing like that.'

'Well, I did sort of lean against him, you know, and he shot off the bridge.'

'Oswald definitely accuses you of having pushed him into the water. That has disturbed Sir Roderick, and unfortunately it has caused him to make inquiries, and he has heard about your poor Uncle Henry.'

She eyed me with a good deal of solemnity, and I took a grave sip of coffee. We were peeping into the family cupboard and having a look at the good old skeleton. My late Uncle Henry, you see, was by way of being the blot on the Wooster escutcheon. An extremely decent chappie personally, and one who had always endeared himself to me by tipping me with considerable lavishness when I was at school; but there's no doubt he did at times do rather rummy things, notably keeping eleven pet rabbits in his bedroom; and I suppose a purist might have considered him more or less off his onion. In fact, to be perfectly frank, he wound up his career, happy to the last and completely surrounded by rabbits, in some sort of a home.

'Is is very absurd, of course,' continued Aunt Agatha. 'If any of the family had inherited poor Henry's eccentricity – and it was nothing more – it would have been Claude and Eustace, and there could not be two brighter boys.'

Claude and Eustace were twins, and had been kids at school with me in my last summer term. Casting my mind back, it seemed to me that 'bright' just about described them. The whole of that term, as I remembered, had been spent in getting them out of a series of frightful rows.

'Look how well they are doing at Oxford. Your Aunt Emily had a letter from Claude only the other day saying that they hoped to be elected shortly to a very important college club, called The Seekers.'

'Seekers?' I couldn't recall any club of the name in my time at Oxford. 'What do they seek?'

'Claude did not say. Truth or knowledge, I should imagine. It is evidently a very desirable club to belong to, for Claude added that Lord Rainsby, the Earl of Datchet's son, was one of his fellow candidates. However, we are wandering from the point, which is that Sir Roderick wants to have a quiet talk with you quite alone. Now I rely on you, Bertie, to be – I won't say intelligent, but at least sensible. Don't giggle nervously; try to keep that horrible glassy expression out of your eyes; don't yawn or fidget; and remember that Sir Roderick is the president of the West London branch of the anti-gambling league, so please do not talk about horse-racing. He will lunch with you at your flat tomorrow at one-thirty. Please remember that he drinks no wine, strongly disapproves of smoking, and can only eat the simplest food, owing to an impaired digestion. Do not offer him coffee, for he considers it the root of half the nerve-trouble in the world.'

'I should think a dog-biscuit and a glass of water would about meet the case, what?'

'Bertie!'

'Oh, all right. Merely persiflage.'

'Now it is precisely that sort of idiotic remark that would be calculated to arouse Sir Roderick's worst suspicions. Do please try to refrain from any misguided flippancy when you are with him. He is a very serious-minded man ... Are you going? Well, please remember all I have said. I rely on you, and, if anything goes wrong, I shall never forgive you.'

'Right-o!' I said.

And so home, with a jolly day to look forward to.

I breakfasted pretty late next morning and went for a stroll afterwards. It seemed to me that anything I could do to clear the old lemon ought to be done, and a bit of fresh air generally relieves that rather foggy feeling that comes over a fellow early in the day. I had taken a stroll in the park, and got back as far as Hyde Park Corner, when some blighter sloshed me between the shoulder-blades. It was young Eustace, my cousin. He was arm-in-arm with two other fellows, the one on the outside, being my cousin Claude and the one in the middle a pink-faced chappie with light hair and an apologetic sort of look.

'Bertie, old egg!' said young Eustace affably.

'Hallo!' I said, not frightfully chirpily.

'Fancy running into you, the one man in London who can support us in the style we are accustomed to! By the way, you've never met the old Dog-Face, have you? Dog-Face, this is my cousin Bertie. Lord Rainsby – Mr Wooster. We've just been round to your flat, Bertie. Bitterly disappointed that you were out, but were hospitably entertained by old Jeeves. That man's a corker, Bertie. Stick to him.'

'What are you doing in London?' I asked.

'Oh, buzzing round. We're just up for the day. Flying visit, strictly unofficial. We oil back on the three-ten. And now, touching that lunch you very decently volunteered to stand us, which shall it be? Ritz? Savoy? Carlton? Or, if you're a member of Ciro's or the Embassy, that would do just as well.'

'I can't give you lunch. I've got an engagement myself. And, by Jove,' I said, taking a look at my watch, 'I'm late.' I hailed a taxi. 'Sorry.'

'As man to man, then,' said Eustace, 'lend us a fiver.'

I hadn't time to stop and argue. I unbelted the fiver and hopped into the cab. It was twenty to two when I got to the flat. I bounded into the sitting-room, but it was empty.

Jeeves shimmied in.

'Sir Roderick has not yet arrived, sir.'

'Good egg!' I said. 'I thought I should find him smashing up the furniture.' My experience is that the less you want a fellow, the more punctual he's bound to be, and I had had a vision of the old lad pacing the rug in my sitting-room, saying 'He cometh not!' and generally hotting up. 'Is everything in order?'

'I fancy you will find the arrangements quite satisfactory, sir.'

'What are you giving us?'

'Cold consommé, a cutlet, and a savoury, sir. With lemon-squash, iced.'

'Well, I don't see how that can hurt him. Don't go getting carried away by the excitement of the thing and start bringing in coffee.'

'No, sir.'

'And don't let your eyes get glassy, because, if you do, you're apt to find yourself in a padded cell before you know where you are.'

'Very good, sir.'

There was a ring at the bell.

'Stand by, Jeeves,' I said. 'We're off!'

8

Sir Roderick Comes to Lunch

I had met Sir Roderick Glossop before, of course, but only when I was with Honoria; and there is something about Honoria which makes almost anybody you meet in the same room seem sort of under-sized and trivial by comparison. I had never realized till this moment what an extraordinarily formidable old bird he was. He had a pair of shaggy eyebrows which gave his eyes a piercing look which was not at all the sort of thing a fellow wanted to encounter on an empty stomach. He was fairly tall and fairly broad, and he had the most enormous head, with practically no hair on it, which made it seem bigger and much more like the dome of St Paul's. I suppose he must have taken about a nine or something in hats. Shows what a rotten thing it is to let your brain develop too much.

'What ho! What ho! What ho!' I said, trying to strike the genial note, and then had a sudden feeling that that was just the sort of thing I had been warned not to say. Dashed difficult it is to start things going properly on an occasion like this. A fellow living in a London flat is so handicapped. I mean to say, if I had been the young squire greeting the visitor in the country, I could have said, 'Welcome to Meadowsweet Hall!' or something zippy like that. It sounds silly to say 'Welcome to Number 6A, Crichton Mansions, Berkeley Street, W.'

'I am afraid I am a little late,' he said, as we sat down. 'I was detained at my club by Lord Alastair Hungerford, the Duke of Ramfurline's son. His Grace, he informed me, had exhibited a renewal of the symptoms which have been causing the family so much concern. I could not leave him immediately. Hence my unpunctuality, which I trust has not discommoded you.'

'Oh, not at all. So the Duke is off his rocker, what?'

'The expression which you use is not precisely the one I should have employed myself with reference to the head of perhaps the noblest family in England, but there is no doubt that cerebral excitement does, as you suggest, exist in no small degree.' He sighed as well as he could with his mouth full of cutlet. 'A profession like mine is a great strain, a great strain.'

'Must be.'

'Sometimes I am appalled at what I see around me.' He stopped suddenly and sort of stiffened. 'Do you keep a cat, Mr Wooster?'

'Eh? What? Cat? No, no cat.'

'I was conscious of a distinct impression that I had heard a cat mewing either in the room or very near to where we are sitting.'

'Probably a taxi or something in the street.'

'I fear I do not follow you.'

'I mean to say, taxis squawk, you know. Rather like cats in a sort of way.'

'I had not observed the resemblance,' he said, rather coldly.

'Have some lemon-squash,' I said. The conversation seemed to be getting rather difficult.

'Thank you. Half a glassful, if I may.' The hell-brew appeared to buck him up, for he resumed in a slightly more pally manner. 'I have a particular dislike for cats. But I was saying – Oh, yes. Sometimes I am positively appalled at what I see around me. It is not only the cases which come under my professional notice, painful as many of those are. It is what I see as I go about London. Sometimes it seems to me that the whole world is mentally unbalanced. This very morning, for example, a most singular and distressing occurrence took place as I was driving from my house to the club. The day being clement, I had instructed my chauffeur to open my laudaulette, and I was leaning back, deriving no little pleasure from the sunshine, when our progress was arrested in the middle of the thoroughfare by one of those blocks in the traffic which are inevitable in so congested a system as that of London.'

I suppose I had been letting my mind wander a bit, for when he stopped and took a sip of lemon-squash I had a feeling that I was listening to a lecture and was expected to say something.

'Hear, hear!' I said.

'I beg your pardon?'

'Nothing, nothing. You were saying – '

'The vehicles proceeding in the opposite direction had also been temporarily arrested, but after a moment they were permitted to proceed. I had fallen into a meditation, when suddenly the most extraordinary thing took place. My hat was snatched abruptly from my head! And as I looked back I perceived it being waved in a kind of feverish triumph from the interior of a taxicab, which, even as I looked, disappeared through a gap in the traffic and was lost to sight.'

I didn't laugh, but I distinctly heard a couple of my floating ribs part from their moorings under the strain.

'Must have been meant for a practical joke,' I said. 'What?'

This suggestion didn't seem to please the old boy.

'I trust,' he said, 'I am not deficient in an appreciation of the humorous, but I confess that I am at a loss to detect anything akin to pleasantry in the outrage. The action was beyond all question that of a mentally unbalanced subject. These mental lesions may express themselves in almost any form. The Duke of Ramfurline, to whom I had occasion to allude just now, is under the impression – this is in the strictest confidence – that he is a canary: and his seizure today, which so perturbed Lord Alastair, was due to the fact that a careless footman had neglected to bring him his morning lump of sugar. Cases are common, again, of men waylaying women and cutting off portions of their hair. It is from a branch of this latter form of mania that I should be disposed to imagine that my assailant was suffering. I can only trust that he will be placed under proper control before he – Mr Wooster, there *is* a cat close at hand! It is *not* in the street! The mewing appears to come from the adjoining room.'

This time I had to admit there was no doubt about it. There was a distinct sound of mewing coming from the next room. I punched the bell for Jeeves, who drifted in and stood waiting with an air of respectful devotion.

'Sir?'

'Oh, Jeeves,' I said. 'Cats! What about it? Are there any cats in the flat?'

'Only the three in your bedroom, sir.'

'What!'

'Cats in his bedroom!' I heard Sir Roderick whisper in a kind of stricken way, and his eyes hit me amidships like a couple of bullets.

'What do you mean,' I said, 'only the three in my bedroom?'

'The black one, the tabby and the small lemon-coloured animal, sir.'

'What on earth – ?'

I charged round the table in the direction of the door. Unfortunately, Sir Roderick had just decided to edge in that direction himself, with the result that we collided in the doorway with a good deal of force, and staggered out into the hall together. He came smartly out of the clinch and grabbed an umbrella from the rack.

'Stand back!' he shouted, waving it overhead. 'Stand back, sir! I am armed!'

It seemed to me that the moment had come to be soothing.

'Awfully sorry I barged into you,' I said. 'Wouldn't have had it happen for worlds. I was just dashing out to have a look into things.'

He appeared a trifle reassured, and lowered the umbrella. But just then the most frightful shindy started in the bedroom. It sounded as though all the cats in London, assisted by delegates from outlying suburbs, had got together to settle their differences once for all. A sort of augmented orchestra of cats.

'This noise is unendurable,' yelled Sir Roderick. 'I cannot hear myself speak.'

'I fancy, sir,' said Jeeves respectfully, 'that the animals may have become somewhat exhilarated as the result of having discovered the fish under Mr Wooster's bed.'

The old boy tottered.

'Fish! Did I hear you rightly?'

'Sir?'

'Did you say that there was a fish under Mr Wooster's bed?'

'Yes, sir.'

Sir Roderick gave a low moan, and reached for his hat and stick.

'You aren't going?' I said.

'Mr Wooster, I *am* going! I prefer to spend my leisure time in less eccentric society.'

'But I say. Here, I must come with you. I'm sure the whole business can be explained. Jeeves, my hat.'

Jeeves rallied round. I took the hat from him and shoved it on my head.

'Good heavens!'

Beastly shock it was! The bally thing had absolutely engulfed me, if you know what I mean. Even as I was putting it on I got a sort of impression that it was a trifle roomy; and no sooner had I let it go than it settled down over my ears like a kind of extinguisher.

'I say! This isn't my hat!'

'It is *my* hat!' said Sir Roderick in about the coldest, nastiest voice I'd ever heard. 'The hat which was stolen from me this morning as I drove in my car.'

'But –'

I suppose Napoleon or somebody like that would have been equal to the situation, but I'm bound to say it was too much for me. I just stood there goggling in a sort of coma, while the old boy lifted the hat off me and turned to Jeeves.

'I should be glad, my man,' he said, 'if you would accompany me a few yards down the street. I wish to ask you some questions.'

'Very good, sir.'

'Here, but, I say – !' I began, but he left me standing. He stalked out, followed by Jeeves. And at that moment the row in the bedroom started again, louder than ever.

I was about fed up with the whole thing. I mean, cats in your bedroom – a bit thick, what? I didn't know how the dickens they had got in, but I was jolly well resolved that they weren't going to stay picnicking there any longer. I flung open the door. I got a momentary flash of about a hundred and fifteen cats of all sizes and colours scrapping in the middle of the room, and then they all shot past me with a rush and out of the front door; and all that was left of the mob-scene was the head of a whacking big fish, lying on the carpet and staring up at me in a rather austere sort of way, as if it wanted a written explanation and apology.

There was something about the thing's expression that absolutely chilled me, and I withdrew on tiptoe and shut the door. And, as I did so, I bumped into someone.

'Oh, sorry!' he said.

I spun round. It was the pink-faced chappie, Lord Something or other, the fellow I had met with Claude and Eustace.

'I say,' he said apologetically, 'awfully sorry to bother you, but those weren't my cats I met just now legging it downstairs, were they? They looked like my cats.'

'They came out of my bedroom.'

'Then they *were* my cats!' he said sadly. 'Oh, dash it.'

'Did you put cats in my bedroom?'

'Your man, what's-his-name, did. He rather decently said I could keep them there till my train went. I'd just come to fetch them. And now they've gone! Oh, well, it can't be helped, I suppose. I'll take the hat and the fish, anyway.'

I was beginning to dislike this chappie.

'Did you put that bally fish there, too?'

'No, that was Eustace's. The hat was Claude's.'

I sank limply into a chair.

'I say, you couldn't explain this, could you?' I said. The chappie gazed at me in mild surprise.

'Why, don't you know all about it? I say!' He blushed profusely. 'Why, if you don't know about it, I shouldn't wonder if the whole thing didn't seem rummy to you.'

'Rummy is the word.'

'It was for The Seekers, you know?'

'The Seekers?'

'Rather a blood club, you know, up at Oxford, which your cousins and I are rather keen on getting into. You have to pinch something, you know, to get elected. Some sort of a souvenir, you know. A policeman's helmet, you know, or a door-knocker or something, you know. The room's decorated with the things at the annual dinner, and everybody makes speeches and all that sort of thing. Rather jolly! Well, we wanted rather to make a sort of special effort and do the thing in style, if you understand, so we came up to London to see if we couldn't pick up something here that would be a bit out of the ordinary. And we had the most amazing luck right from the start. Your cousin Claude managed to collect a quite decent top-hat out of a passing car and your cousin Eustace got away with a really goodish salmon or something from Harrods, and I snaffed three excellent cats all in the first hour. We were fearfully braced, I can tell you. And then the difficulty was to know where to park the things till our train went. You look so beastly conspicuous, you know, tooling about London with a fish and a lot of cats. And then Eustace remembered you, and we all came on here in a cab. You were out, but your man said it would be all right. When we met you, you were in such a hurry that we hadn't time to explain. Well, I think I'll be taking the hat, if you don't mind.'

'It's gone.'

'Gone?'

'The fellow you pinched it from happened to be the man who was lunching here. He took it away with him.'

'Oh, I say! Poor old Claude will be upset. Well, how about the goodish salmon or something?'

'Would you care to view the remains?' He seemed all broken up when he saw the wreckage.

'I doubt if the committee would accept that,' he said sadly. 'There isn't a frightful lot of it left, what?'

'The cats ate the rest.'

He sighed deeply.

'No cats, no fish, no hat. We've had all our trouble for nothing.

I do call that hard! And on top of that – I say, I hate to ask you, but you couldn't lend me a tenner, could you?'

'A tenner? What for?'

'Well, the fact is, I've got to pop round and bail Claude and Eustace out. They've been arrested.'

'Arrested!'

'Yes. You see, what with the excitement of collaring the hat and the salmon or something, added to the fact that we had rather a festive lunch, they got a bit above themselves, poor chaps, and tried to pinch a motor-lorry. Silly, of course, because I don't see how they could have got the thing to Oxford and shown it to the committee. Still, there wasn't any reasoning with them, and when the driver started making a fuss, there was a bit of a mix-up, and Claude and Eustace are more or less languishing in Vine Street police station till I pop round and bail them out. So if you could manage a tenner – Oh, thanks, that's fearfully good of you. It would have been too bad to leave them there, what? I mean, they're both such frightfully good chaps, you know. Everybody likes them up at the Varsity. They're fearfully popular.'

'I bet they are!' I said.

When Jeeves came back, I was waiting for him on the mat. I wanted speech with the blighter.

'Well?' I said.

'Sir Roderick asked me a number of questions, sir, respecting your habits and mode of life, to which I replied guardedly.'

'I don't care about that. What I want to know is why you didn't explain the whole thing to him right at the start? A word from you would have put everything clear.'

'Yes, sir.'

'Now he's gone off thinking me a loony.'

'I should not be surprised, from his conversation with me, sir, if some such idea had not entered his head.'

I was just starting to speak, when the telephone bell rang. Jeeves answered it.

'No, madam, Mr Wooster is not in. No, madam, I do not know when he will return. No, madam, he left no message. Yes, madam, I will inform him.' He put back the receiver. 'Mrs Gregson, sir.'

Aunt Agatha! I had been expecting it. Ever since the luncheon-party had blown out a fuse, her shadow had been hanging over me, so to speak.

'Does she know? Already?'

'I gather that Sir Roderick has been speaking to her on the telephone, sir, and – '

'No wedding bells for me, what?'

Jeeves coughed.

'Mrs Gregson did not actually confide in me, sir, but I fancy that some such thing may have occurred. She seemed decidedly agitated, sir.'

It's a rummy thing, but I'd been so snootered by the old boy and the cats and the fish and the hat and the pink-faced chappie and all the rest of it that the bright side simply hadn't occurred to me till now. By Jove, it was like a bally weight rolling off my chest! I gave a yelp of pure relief.

'Jeeves!' I said, 'I believe you worked the whole thing!'

'Sir?'

'I believe you had the jolly old situation in hand right from the start.'

'Well, sir, Spenser, Mrs Gregson's butler, who inadvertently chanced to overhear something of your conversation when you were lunching at the house, did mention certain of the details to me; and I confess that, though it may be a liberty to say so, I entertained hopes that something might occur to prevent the match. I doubt if the young lady was entirely suitable to you, sir.'

'And she would have shot you out on your ear five minutes after the ceremony.'

'Yes, sir. Spenser informed me that she had expressed some such intention. Mrs Gregson wishes you to call upon her immediately, sir.'

'She does, eh? What do you advise, Jeeves?'

'I think a trip abroad might prove enjoyable, sir.'

I shook my head. 'She'd come after me.'

'Not if you went far enough afield, sir. There are excellent boats leaving every Wednesday and Saturday for New York.'

'Jeeves,' I said, 'you are right, as always. Book the tickets.'

9

A Letter of Introduction

You know, the longer I live, the more clearly I see that half the trouble in this bally world is caused by the light-hearted and thoughtless way in which chappies dash off letters of introduction and hand them to other chappies to deliver to chappies of the third part. It's one of those things that make you wish you were living in the Stone Age. What I mean to say is, if a fellow in those days wanted to give anyone a letter of introduction, he had to spend a month or so carving it on a large-sized boulder, and the chances were that the other chappie got so sick of lugging the thing round in the hot sun that he dropped it after the first mile. But nowadays it's so easy to write letters of introduction that everybody does it without a second thought, with the result that some perfectly harmless cove like myself gets in the soup.

Mark you, all the above is what you might call the result of my riper experience. I don't mind admitting that in the first flush of the thing, so to speak, when Jeeves told me – this would be about three weeks after I'd landed in America – that a blighter called Cyril Bassington-Bassington had arrived and I found that he had brought a letter of introduction to me from Aunt Agatha . . . where was I? Oh, yes . . . I don't mind admitting, I was saying, that just at first I was rather bucked. You see, after the painful events which had resulted in my leaving England I hadn't expected to get any sort of letter from Aunt Agatha which would pass the censor, so to speak. And it was a pleasant surprise to open this one and find it almost civil. Chilly, perhaps, in parts, but on the whole quite tolerably polite. I looked on the thing as a hopeful sign. Sort of olive branch, you know. Or do I mean orange blossom? What I'm getting at is that the fact that Aunt Agatha was writing to me without calling me names seemed, more or less, like a step in the direction of peace.

And I was all for peace, and that right speedily. I'm not saying a word against New York, mind you. I liked the place, and was having quite a ripe time there. But the fact remains that a fellow who's been used to London all his life does get a trifle homesick on a foreign strand, and I wanted to pop back to the cosy old flat in Berkeley Street – which could only be done when Aunt Agatha had simmered down and got over the Glossop episode. I know that London is a biggish city, but, believe me, it isn't half big enough for any fellow to live in with Aunt Agatha when she's after him with the old hatchet. And so I'm bound to say I looked on this chump Bassington-Bassington, when he arrived, more or less as a Dove of Peace, and was all for him.

He would seem from contemporary accounts to have blown in one morning at seven-forty-five, that being the ghastly sort of hour they shoot you off the liner in New York. He was given the respectful raspberry by Jeeves, and told to try again about three hours later, when there would be a sporting chance of my having sprung from my bed with a glad cry to welcome another day and all that sort of thing. Which was rather decent of Jeeves, by the way, for it so happened that there was a slight estrangement, a touch of coldness, a bit of a row in other words, between us at the moment because of some rather priceless purple socks which I was wearing against his wishes: and a lesser man might easily have snatched at the chance of getting back at me a bit by loosing Cyril into my bedchamber at a moment when I couldn't have stood a two-minutes' conversation with my dearest pal. For until I have had my early cup of tea and have brooded on life for a bit absolutely undisturbed, I'm not much of a lad for the merry chit-chat.

So Jeeves very sportingly shot Cyril out into the crisp morning air, and didn't let me know of his existence till he brought his card in with the Bohea.

'And what might all this be, Jeeves?' I said, giving the thing the glassy gaze.

'The gentleman has arrived from England, I understand, sir. He called to see you earlier in the day.'

'Good Lord, Jeeves! You don't mean to say the day starts earlier than this?'

'He desired me to say he would return later, sir.'

'I've never heard of him. Have *you* ever heard of him, Jeeves?'

'I am familiar with the name Bassington-Bassington, sir. There are three branches of the Bassington-Bassington family – the Shropshire Bassington-Bassingtons, the Hampshire Bassington-Bassingtons, and the Kent Bassington-Bassingtons.'

'England seems pretty well stocked up with Bassington-Bassingtons.'

'Tolerably so, sir.'

'No chance of a sudden shortage, I mean, what?'

'Presumably not, sir.'

'And what sort of a specimen is this one?'

'I could not say, sir, on such short acquaintance.'

'Will you give me a sporting two to one, Jeeves, judging from what you have seen of him, that this chappie is not a blighter or an excrescence?'

'No, sir. I should not care to venture such liberal odds.'

'I knew it. Well, the only thing that remains to be discovered is what kind of a blighter he is.'

'Time will tell, sir. The gentleman brought a letter for you, sir.'

'Oh, he did, did he?' I said, and grasped the communication. And then I recognized the handwriting. 'I say, Jeeves, this is from my Aunt Agatha!'

'Indeed, sir?'

'Don't dismiss it in that light way. Don't you see what this means? She says she wants me to look after this excrescence while he's in New York. By Jove, Jeeves, if I only fawn on him a bit, so that he sends back a favourable report to headquarters, I may yet be able to get back to England in time for Goodwood. Now is certainly the time for all good men to come to the aid of the party, Jeeves. We must rally round and cosset this cove in no uncertain manner.'

'Yes, sir.'

'He isn't going to stay in New York long,' I said, taking another look at the letter. 'He's headed for Washington. Going to give the nibs there the once-over, apparently, before taking a whirl at the Diplomatic Service. I should say that we can win this lad's esteem and affection with a lunch and a couple of dinners, what?'

'I fancy that should be entirely adequate, sir.'

'This is the jolliest thing that's happened since we left England. It looks to me as if the sun were breaking through the clouds.'

'Very possibly, sir.'

He started to put out my things, and there was an awkward sort of silence.

'Not those socks, Jeeves,' I said, gulping a bit but having a dash at the careless, off-hand tone. 'Give me the purple ones.'

'I beg your pardon, sir?'

'Those jolly purple ones.'

'Very good, sir.'

He lugged them out of the drawer as if he were a vegetarian fishing a caterpillar out of the salad. You could see he was feeling deeply. Deuced painful and all that, this sort of thing, but a chappie has got to assert himself every now and then. Absolutely.

I was looking for Cyril to show up again any time after breakfast, but he didn't appear: so towards one o'clock I trickled out to the Lambs Club, where I had an appointment to feed the Wooster face with a cove of the name of Caffyn I'd got pally with since my arrival – George Caffyn, a fellow who wrote plays and what not. I'd made a lot of friends during my stay in New York, the city being crammed with bonhomous lads who one and all extended a welcoming hand to the stranger in their midst.

Caffyn was a bit late, but bobbed up finally, saying that he had been kept at a rehearsal of his new musical comedy, *Ask Dad*; and we started in. We had just reached the coffee, when the waiter came up and said that Jeeves wanted to see me.

Jeeves was in the waiting-room. He gave the socks one pained look as I came in, then averted his eyes.

'Mr Bassington-Bassington has just telephoned, sir.'

'Oh?'

'Yes, sir.'

'Where is he?'

'In prison, sir.'

I reeled against the wallpaper. A nice thing to happen to Aunt Agatha's nominee on his first morning under my wing, I did *not* think!

'In prison!'

'Yes, sir. He said on the telephone that he had been arrested and would be glad if you could step round and bail him out.'

'Arrested! What for?'

'He did not favour me with his confidence in that respect, sir.'

'This is a bit thick, Jeeves.'

'Precisely, sir.'

I collected old George, who very decently volunteered to stagger along with me, and we hopped into a taxi. We sat around at the police station for a bit on a wooden bench in a sort of ante-room, and presently a policeman appeared, leading in Cyril.

'Hallo! Hallo! Hallo!' I said. 'What?'

My experience is that a fellow never really looks his best just after he's come out of a cell. When I was up at Oxford, I used to have a regular job bailing out a pal of mine who never failed to get pinched every Boat Race night, and he always looked like something that had been dug up by the roots. Cyril was in pretty much the same sort of shape. He had a black eye and a torn collar, and altogether was nothing to write home about – especially if one was writing to Aunt Agatha. He was a thin, tall chappie with a lot of light hair and pale-blue goggly eyes which made him look like one of the rarer kinds of fish.

'I got your message,' I said.

'Oh, are you Bertie Wooster?'

'Absolutely. And this is my pal George Caffyn. Writes plays and what not, don't you know.'

We all shook hands, and the policeman, having retrieved a piece of chewing-gum from the underside of a chair, where he had parked it against a rainy day, went off into a corner and began to contemplate the infinite.

'This is a rotten country,' said Cyril.

'Oh, I don't know, you know, don't you know!' I said.

'We do our best,' said George.

'Old George is an American,' I explained. 'Writes plays, don't you know, and what not.'

'Of course, I didn't invent the country,' said George. 'That was Columbus. But I shall be delighted to consider any improvements you may suggest and lay them before the proper authorities.'

'Well, why don't the policemen in New York dress properly?'

George took a look at the chewing officer across the room.

'I don't see anything missing,' he said.

'I mean to say, why don't they they wear helmets like they do in London? Why do they look like postmen? It isn't fair on a fellow. Makes it dashed confusing. I was simply standing on the pavement, looking at things, when a fellow who looked like a postman prodded me in the ribs with a club. I didn't see why I should have postmen prodding me. Why the dickens should a fellow come three thousand miles to be prodded by postmen?'

'The point is well taken,' said George. 'What did you do?'

'I gave him a shove, you know. I've got a frightfully hasty temper, you know. All the Bassington-Bassingtons have got frightfully hasty tempers, don't you know! And then he biffed me in the eye and tugged me off to this beastly place.'

'I'll fix it, old son,' I said. And I hauled out the bank-roll and went off to open negotiations, leaving Cyril to talk to George. I don't mind admitting that I was a bit perturbed. There were furrows in the old brow, and I had a kind of foreboding feeling. As long as this chump stayed in New York, I was responsible for him: and he didn't give me the impression of being the species of cove a reasonable chappie would care to be responsible for for more than about three minutes.

I mused with a considerable amount of tensity over Cyril that night, when I had got home and Jeeves had brought me the final whisky. I couldn't help feeling that this first visit of his to America was going to be one of those times that try men's souls and what not. I hauled out Aunt Agatha's letter of introduction and re-read it, and there was no getting away from the fact that she undoubtedly appeared to be somewhat wrapped up in this blighter and to consider it my mission in life to shield him from harm while on the premises. I was deuced thankful that he had taken such a liking for George Caffyn, old George being a steady sort of cove. After I had got him out of his dungeon-cell, he and George had gone off together, as chummy as brothers, to watch the afternoon rehearsal of *Ask Dad*. There was some talk, I gathered, of their dining together. I felt pretty easy in my mind while George had his eye on him.

I had got about as far as this in my meditations, when Jeeves came in with a telegram. At least, it wasn't a telegram: it was a cable – from Aunt Agatha, and this is what it said:

Has Cyril Bassington-Bassington called yet? On no account introduce him into theatrical circles. Vitally important. Letter follows.

I read it a couple of times.

'This is rummy, Jeeves!'

'Yes, sir?'

'Very rummy and dashed disturbing!'

'Will there be anything further tonight, sir?'

Of course, if he was going to be as bally unsympathetic as that there was nothing to be done. My idea had been to show him the cable and ask his advice. But if he was letting those purple socks rankle to that extent, the good old *noblesse oblige* of the Woosters couldn't lower itself to the extent of pleading with the man. Absolutely not. So I gave it a miss.

'Nothing more, thanks.'

'Good night, sir.'

'Good night.'

He floated away, and I sat down to think the thing over. I had
been directing the best efforts of the old bean to the problem for a
matter of half an hour, when there was a ring at the bell. I went to
the door, and there was Cyril, looking pretty festive.

'I'll come in for a bit if I may,' he said. 'Got something rather
priceless to tell you.'

He curveted past me into the sitting-room, and when I got there
after shutting the front door I found him reading Aunt Agatha's
cable and giggling in a rummy sort of manner. 'Oughtn't to have
looked at this, I suppose. Caught sight of my name and read it
without thinking. I say, Wooster, old friend of my youth, this is
rather funny. Do you mind if I have a drink? Thanks awfully and
all that sort of rot. Yes, it's rather funny, considering what I came
to tell you. Jolly old Caffyn has given me a small part in that musical
comedy of his, *Ask Dad*. Only a bit, you know, but quite tolerably
ripe. I'm feeling frightfully braced, don't you know!'

He drank his drink, and went on. He didn't seem to notice that
I wasn't jumping about the room, yapping with joy.

'You know, I've always wanted to go on the stage, you know,' he
said. 'But my jolly old guv'nor wouldn't stick it at any price. Put the
old Waukeesi down with a bang, and turned bright purple whenever
the subject was mentioned. That's the real reason why I came over
here, if you want to know. I knew there wasn't a chance of my being
able to work this stage wheeze in London without somebody getting
on to it and tipping off the guv'nor, so I rather brainily sprang the
scheme of popping over to Washington to broaden my mind. There's
nobody to interfere on this side, you see, so I can go right ahead!'

I tried to reason with the poor chump.

'But your guv'nor will have to know some time.'

'That'll be all right. I shall be the jolly old star by then, and he
won't have a leg to stand on.'

'It seems to me he'll have one leg to stand on while he kicks me
with the other.'

'Why, where do you come in? What have you got to do with it?'

'I introduced you to George Caffyn.'

'So you did, old top, so you did. I'd quite forgotten. I ought to
have thanked you before. Well, so long. There's an early rehearsal
of *Ask Dad* tomorrow morning, and I must be toddling. Rummy the
thing should be called *Ask Dad*, when that's just what I'm not going
to do. See what I mean, what, what? Well, pip-pip!'

'Toodle-oo!' I said sadly, and the blighter scudded off. I dived for the phone and called up George Caffyn.

'I say, George, what's all this about Cyril Bassington-Bassington?'

'What about him?'

'He tells me you've given him a part in your show.'

'Oh, yes. Just a few lines.'

'But I've just had fifty-seven cables from home telling me on no account to let him go on the stage.'

'I'm sorry. But Cyril is just the type I need for that part. He's simply got to be himself.'

'It's pretty tough on me, George, old man. My Aunt Agatha sent this blighter over with a letter of introduction to me, and she will hold me responsible.'

'She'll cut you out of her will?'

'It isn't a question of money. But – of course, you've never met my Aunt Agatha, so it's rather hard to explain. But she's a sort of human vampire-bat, and she'll make things most fearfully unpleasant for me when I go back to England. She's the kind of woman who comes and rags you before breakfast, don't you know.'

'Well, don't go back to England, then. Stick here and become President.'

'But, George, old top – !'

'Good night!'

'But, I say, George, old man!'

'You didn't get my last remark. It was "Good night!" You Idle Rich may not need any sleep, but I've got to be bright and fresh in the morning. God bless you!'

I felt as if I hadn't a friend in the world. I was so jolly well worked up that I went and banged on Jeeves's door. It wasn't a thing I'd have cared to do as a rule, but it seemed to me that now was the time for all good men to come to the aid of the party, so to speak, and that it was up to Jeeves to rally round the young master, even if it broke up his beauty-sleep.

Jeeves emerged in a brown dressing gown.

'Sir?'

'Deuced sorry to wake you up, Jeeves, and what not, but all sorts of dashed disturbing things have been happening.'

'I was not asleep. It is my practice, on retiring, to read a few pages of some instructive book.'

'That's good! What I mean to say is, if you've just finished exercising the old bean, it's probably in mid-season form for tackling problems. Jeeves, Mr Bassington-Bassington is going on the stage!'

'Indeed, sir?'

'Ah! The thing doesn't hit you! You don't get it properly! Here's the point. All his family are most fearfully dead against his going on the stage. There's going to be no end of trouble if he isn't headed off. And, what's worse, my Aunt Agatha will blame *me*, you see.'

'I see, sir.'

'Well, can't you think of some way of stopping him?'

'Not, I confess, at the moment, sir.'

'Well, have a stab at it.'

'I will give the matter my best consideration, sir. Will there be anything further tonight?'

'I hope not! I've had all I can stand already.'

'Very good, sir.'

He popped off.

10

Startling Dressiness of a Lift Attendant

The part which old George had written for the chump Cyril took up about two pages of typescript; but it might have been Hamlet, the way that poor, misguided pinhead worked himself to the bone over it. I suppose, if I heard him read his lines once, I did it a dozen times in the first couple of days. He seemed to think that my only feeling about the whole affair was one of enthusiastic admiration, and that he could rely on my support and sympathy. What with trying to imagine how Aunt Agatha was going to take this thing, and being woken up out of the dreamless in the small hours every other night to give my opinion of some new bit of business which Cyril had invented, I became more or less the good old shadow. And all the time Jeeves remained still pretty cold and distant about the purple socks. It's this sort of thing that ages a chappie, don't you know, and makes his youthful *joie-de-vivre* go a bit groggy at the knees.

In the middle of it Aunt Agatha's letter arrived. It took her about six pages to do justice to Cyril's father's feelings in regard to his going on the stage and about six more to give me a kind of sketch of what she would say, think, and do if I didn't keep him clear of injurious influences while he was in America. The letter came by the afternoon mail, and left me with a pretty firm conviction that it wasn't a thing I ought to keep to myself. I didn't even wait to ring the bell: I whizzed for the kitchen, bleating for Jeeves, and butted into the middle of a regular tea-party of sorts. Seated at the table were a depressed-looking cove who might have been a valet or something, and a boy in a Norfolk suit. The valet-chappie was drinking a whisky and soda, and the boy was being tolerably rough with some jam and cake.

'Oh, I say, Jeeves!' I said. 'Sorry to interrupt the feast of reason and flow of soul and so forth, but – '

At this juncture the small boy's eye hit me like a bullet and stopped me in my tracks. It was one of those cold, clammy, accusing sort of eyes – the kind that makes you reach up to see if your tie is straight: and he looked at me as if I were some sort of unnecessary product which Cuthbert the Cat had brought in after a ramble among the local ash-cans. He was a stoutish infant with a lot of freckles and a good deal of jam on his face.

'Hallo! Hallo! Hallo!' I said. 'What?' There didn't seem much else to say.

The stripling stared at me in a nasty sort of way through the jam. He may have loved me at first sight, but the impression he gave me was that he didn't think a lot of me and wasn't betting much that I would improve a great deal on acquaintance. I had a kind of feeling that I was about as popular with him as a cold Welsh rarebit.

'What's your name?' he asked.

'My name? Oh, Wooster, don't you know, and what not.'

'My pop's richer than you are!'

That seemed to be all about me. The child having said his say, started in on the jam again. I turned to Jeeves:

'I say, Jeeves, can you spare a moment? I want to show you something.'

'Very good, sir.' We toddled into the sitting-room.

'Who is your little friend, Sidney the Sunbeam, Jeeves?'

'The young gentleman, sir?'

'It's a loose way of describing him, but I know what you mean.'

'I trust I was not taking a liberty in entertaining him, sir?'

'Not a bit. If that's your idea of a large afternoon, go ahead.'

'I happened to meet the young gentleman taking a walk with his father's valet, sir, whom I used to know somewhat intimately in London, and I ventured to invite them both to join me here.'

'Well, never mind about him, Jeeves. Read this letter.'

He gave it the up-and-down.

'Very disturbing, sir!' was all he could find to say.

'What are we going to do about it?'

'Time may provide a solution, sir.'

'On the other hand, it mayn't, what?'

'Extremely true, sir.'

We'd got as far as this, when there was a ring at the door. Jeeves shimmered off, and Cyril blew in, full of good cheer and blitheringness.

'I say, Wooster, old thing,' he said, 'I want your advice. You know this jolly old part of mine. How ought I to dress it? What I mean is, the first act scene is laid in an hotel of sorts, at about three in the afternoon. What ought I to wear, do you think?'

I wasn't feeling fit for a discussion of gent's suitings.

'You'd better consult Jeeves,' I said.

'A hot and by no means unripe idea! Where is he?'

'Gone back to the kitchen, I suppose.'

'I'll smite the good old bell, shall I? Yes. No?'

'Right-o!'

Jeeves poured silently in.

'Oh, I say, Jeeves,' began Cyril, 'I just wanted to have a syllable or two with you. It's this way – Hallo, who's this?'

I then perceived that the stout stripling had trickled into the room after Jeeves. He was standing near the door looking at Cyril as if his worst fears had been realized. There was a bit of a silence. The child remained there, drinking Cyril in for about half a minute; then he gave his verdict:

'Fish-face!'

'Eh? What?' said Cyril.

The child, who had evidently been taught at his mother's knee to speak the truth, made his meaning a trifle clearer.

'You've a face like a fish!'

He spoke as if Cyril was more to be pitied than censured, which I am bound to say I thought rather decent and broadminded of him. I don't mind admitting that, whenever I looked at Cyril's face, I always had a feeling that he couldn't have got that way without its being mostly his own fault. I found myself warming to this child. Absolutely, don't you know. I liked his conversation.

It seemed to take Cyril a moment or two really to grasp the thing, and then you could hear the blood of the Bassington-Bassingtons begin to sizzle.

'Well, I'm dashed!' he said. 'I'm dashed if I'm not!'

'I wouldn't have a face like that,' proceeded the child, with a good deal of earnestness, 'not if you gave me a million dollars.' He thought for a moment, then corrected himself. 'Two million dollars!' he added.

Just what occurred then I couldn't exactly say, but the next few minutes were a bit exciting. I take it that Cyril must have made a dive for the infant. Anyway, the air seemed pretty well congested with arms and legs and things. Something bumped into the Wooster waistcoat just around the third button, and I collapsed on to the settee and rather lost interest in things for the moment. When I had unscrambled myself, I found that Jeeves and the child had retired and Cyril was standing in the middle of the room snorting a bit.

'Who's that frightful little brute, Wooster?'

'I don't know. I never saw him before today.'

'I gave him a couple of tolerably juicy buffets before he legged it. I say, Wooster, that kid said a dashed odd thing. He yelled out something about Jeeves promising him a dollar if he called me – er – what he said.'

It sounded pretty unlikely to me.

'What would Jeeves do that for?'

'It struck me as rummy, too.'

'Where would be the sense of it?'

'That's what I can't see.'

'I mean to say, it's nothing to Jeeves what sort of face you have!'

'No!' said Cyril. He spoke a little coldly, I fancied. I don't know why. 'Well, I'll be popping. Toodle-oo!'

'Pip-pip!'

It must have been about a week after this rummy little episode that George Caffyn called me up and asked me if I would care to go and see a run-through of his show. *Ask Dad*, it seemed, was to open out of town in Schenectady on the following Monday, and this was to be a sort of preliminary dress-rehearsal. A preliminary dress-rehearsal, old George explained, was the same as a regular dress-rehearsal inasmuch as it was apt to look like nothing on earth and last into the small hours, but more exciting because they wouldn't be timing the piece and consequently all the blighters who on these occasions let their angry passions rise would have plenty of scope for interruptions, with the result that a pleasant time would be had by all.

The thing was billed to start at eight o'clock, so I rolled up at ten-fifteen, so as not to have too long to wait before they began. The dress-parade was still going on. George was on the stage, talking to a cove in shirt-sleeves and an absolutely round chappie with big spectacles and a practically hairless dome. I had seen George with the latter merchant once or twice at the club, and I knew that he was Blumenfield, the manager. I waved to George, and slid into a seat at the back of the house, so as to be out of the way when the fighting started. Presently George hopped down off the stage and came and joined me, and fairly soon after that the curtain went down. The chappie at the piano whacked out a well-meant bar or two, and the curtain went up again.

I can't quite recall what the plot of *Ask Dad* was about, but I do know that it seemed able to jog along all right without much help from Cyril. I was rather puzzled at first. What I mean is, through brooding on Cyril and hearing him in his part and listening to his views on what ought and what ought not to be done, I suppose I had got a sort of impression rooted in the old bean that he was pretty well the backbone of the show, and that the rest of the company didn't do much except go on and fill in when he happened to be off the stage. I sat there for nearly half an hour, waiting for him to make his entrance, until I suddenly discovered he had been on from the start. He was, in fact, the rummy-looking plug-ugly who was now leaning against a potted palm a couple of feet from the O.P. side, trying to appear intelligent while the heroine sang a song about Love being like something which for the moment has slipped my memory. After the second refrain he began to dance in company with a dozen other equally weird birds. A painful spectacle for one who could see a vision of Aunt Agatha reaching for the hatchet and old Bassington-Bassington senior putting on his strongest pair of hob-nailed boots. Absolutely!

The dance had just finished, and Cyril and his pals had shuffled off into the wings when a voice spoke from the darkness on my right.

'Pop!'

Old Blumenfield clapped his hands, and the hero, who had just been about to get the next line off his diaphragm, cheesed it. I peered into the shadows. Who should it be but Jeeves's little playmate with the freckles! He was now strolling down the aisle with his hands in his pockets as if the place belonged to him. An air of respectful attention seemed to pervade the building.

'Pop,' said the stripling, 'that number's no good.' Old Blumenfield beamed over his shoulder.

'Don't you like it, darling?'

'It gives me a pain.'

'You're dead right.'

'You want something zippy there. Something with a bit of jazz to it!'

'Quite right my boy. I'll make a note of it. All right. Go on!'

I turned to George, who was muttering to himself in rather an overwrought way.

'I say, George, old man, who the dickens is that kid?'

Old George groaned a bit hollowly, as if things were a trifle thick.

'I didn't know he had crawled in! It's Blumenfield's son. Now we're going to have a Hades of a time!'

'Does he always run things like this?'

'Always!'

'But why does old Blumenfield listen to him?'

'Nobody seems to know. It may be pure fatherly love, or he may regard him as a mascot. My own idea is that he thinks the kid has exactly the amount of intelligence of the average member of the audience, and that what makes a hit with him will please the general public. While, conversely, what he doesn't like will be too rotten for anyone. The kid is a pest, a wart, and a pot of poison, and should be strangled!'

The rehearsal went on. The hero got off his line. There was a slight outburst of frightfulness between the stage-manager and a Voice named Bill that came from somewhere near the roof, the subject under discussion being where the devil Bill's 'ambers' were at that particular juncture. Then things went on again until the moment arrived for Cyril's big scene.

I was still a trifle hazy about the plot, but I had got on to the fact that Cyril was some sort of an English peer who had come over to America doubtless for the best reasons. So far he had only had two lines to say. One was 'Oh, I say!' and the other was 'Yes, by Jove!'; but I seemed to recollect, from hearing him read his part, that pretty soon he was due rather to spread himself. I sat back in my chair and waited for him to bob up.

He bobbed up about five minutes later. Things had got a bit stormy by that time. The Voice and the stage-director had had another of their love-feasts – this time something to do with why Bills' 'blues' weren't on the job or something. And, almost as soon as that was over, there was a bit of unpleasantness because a flower-pot fell off a window-ledge and nearly brained the hero. The atmosphere was consequently more or less hotted up when Cyril, who had been hanging about at the back of the stage, breezed down centre and toed the mark for his most substantial chunk of entertainment. The heroine had been saying something – I forget what – and all the chorus, with Cyril at their head, had begun to surge round her in the restless sort of way those chappies always do when there's a number coming along.

Cyril's first line was, 'Oh, I say, you know, you mustn't say that, really!' and it seemed to me he passed it over the larynx with a goodish deal of vim and *je-ne-sais-quoi*. But, by Jove, before the heroine had time for the come-back, our little friend with the freckles had risen to lodge a protest.

'Pop!'

'Yes, darling?'

'That one's no good.'

'Which one, darling?'

'The one with a face like a fish.'

'But they all have faces like fish, darling.'

The child seemed to see the justice of this objection. He became more definite.

'The ugly one.'

'Which ugly one? That one?' said old Blumenfield, pointing to Cyril.

'Yep! He's rotten!'

'I thought so myself.'

'He's a pill!'

'You're dead right, my boy. I've noticed it for some time.'

Cyril had been gaping a bit while these few remarks were in progress. He now shot down to the footlights. Even from where I was sitting, I could see that these harsh words had hit the old Bassington-Bassington family pride a frightful wallop. He started to get pink in the ears, and then in the nose, and then in the cheeks, till in about a quarter of a minute he looked pretty much like an explosion in a tomato cannery on a sunset evening.

'What the deuce do you mean?'

'What the deuce do *you* mean?' shouted old Blumenfield. 'Don't yell at me across the footlights!'

'I've a dashed good mind to come down and spank that little brute!'

'What!'

'A dashed good mind!'

Old Blumenfield swelled like a pumped-up tyre. He got rounder than ever.

'See here, mister – I don't know your darn name – !'

'My name's Bassington-Bassington, and the jolly old Bassington-Bassingtons – I mean the Bassington-Bassingtons aren't accustomed – '

Old Blumenfield told him in a few brief words pretty much what he thought of the Bassington-Bassingtons and what they weren't accustomed to. The whole strength of the company rallied round to enjoy his remarks. You could see them jutting out from the wings and protruding from behind trees.

'You got to work good for my pop!' said the stout child, waggling his head reprovingly at Cyril.

'I don't want any bally cheek from you!' said Cyril, gurgling a bit.

'What's that?' barked old Blumenfield. 'Don't you understand that this boy is my son?'

'Yes, I do,' said Cyril. 'And you both have my sympathy!'

'You're fired!' bellowed old Blumenfield, swelling a good bit more. 'Get out of my theatre!'

About half past ten next morning, just after I had finished lubricating the good old interior with a soothing cup of Oolong, Jeeves filtered into my bedroom, and said that Cyril was waiting to see me in the sitting-room.

'How does he look, Jeeves?'

'Sir?'

'What does Mr Bassington-Bassington look like?'

'It is hardly my place, sir, to criticize the facial peculiarities of your friends.'

'I don't mean that. I mean, does he appear peeved and what not?'

'Not noticeably, sir. His manner is tranquil.'

'That's rum!'

'Sir?'

'Nothing. Show him in, will you?'

I'm bound to say I had expected to see Cyril showing a few more traces of last night's battle. I was looking for a bit of the overwrought soul and the quivering ganglions, if you know what I mean. He seemed pretty ordinary and quite fairly cheerful.

'Hallo, Wooster, old thing!'

'Cheero!'

'I just looked in to say goodbye.'

'Goodbye?'

'Yes. I'm off to Washington in an hour.' He sat down on the bed. 'You know, Wooster, old top,' he went on, 'I've been thinking it all over, and really it doesn't seem quite fair to the jolly old guv'nor, my going on the stage and so forth. What do you think?'

'I see what you mean.'

'I mean to say, he sent me over here to broaden my jolly old mind and words to that effect, don't you know, and I can't help thinking it would be a bit of a jar for the old boy if I gave him the bird and went on the stage instead. I don't know if you understand me, but what I mean to say is, it's a sort of question of conscience.'

'Can you leave the show without upsetting everything?'

'Oh, that's all right. I've explained everything to old Blumenfield, and he quite sees my position. Of course, he's sorry to lose me – said he didn't see how he could fill my place and all that sort of thing – but, after all, even if it does land him in a bit of a hole, I think I'm right in resigning my part, don't you?'

'Oh, absolutely.'

'I thought you'd agree with me. Well, I ought to be shifting. Awfully glad to have seen something of you, and all that sort of rot. Pip-pip!'

'Toodle-oo!'

He sallied forth, having told all those bally lies with the clear, blue, pop-eyed gaze of a young child. I rang for Jeeves. You know, ever since last night I had been exercising the old bean to some extent, and a good deal of light had dawned upon me.

'Jeeves!'

'Sir?'

'Did you put that pie-faced infant up to bally-ragging Mr Bassington-Bassington?'

'Sir?'

'Oh, you know what I mean. Did you tell him to get Mr Bassington-Bassington sacked from the *Ask Dad* company?'

'I would not take such a liberty, sir.' He started to put out my clothes. 'It is possible that young Master Blumenfield may have gathered from casual remarks of mine that I did not consider the stage altogether a suitable sphere for Mr Bassington-Bassington.'

'I say, Jeeves, you know, you're a bit of a marvel.'

'I endeavour to give satisfaction, sir.'

'And I'm frightfully obliged, if you know what I mean. Aunt Agatha would have had sixteen or seventeen fits if you hadn't headed him off.'

'I fancy there might have been some little friction and unpleasantness, sir. I am laying out the blue suit with the thin red stripe, sir. I fancy the effect will be pleasing.'

It's a rummy thing, but I had finished breakfast and gone out and got as far as the lift before I remembered what it was that I had meant to do to reward Jeeves for his really sporting behaviour in this matter of the chump Cyril. It cut me to the heart to do it, but I had decided to give him his way and let those purple socks pass out of my life. After all, there are times when a cove must make sacrifices. I was just going to nip back and break the glad news to him, when the lift came up, so I thought I would leave it till I got home.

The coloured chappie in charge of the lift looked at me, as I hopped in, with a good deal of quiet devotion and what not.

'I wish to thank yo', suh,' he said, 'for yo' kindness.'

'Eh? What?'

'Misto' Jeeves done give them purple socks, as you told him. Thank yo' very much, suh!'

I looked down. The blighter was a blaze of mauve from the ankle-bone southward. I don't know when I've seen anything so dressy.

'Oh, ah! Not at all! Right-o! Glad you like them!' I said.

Well, I mean to say, what? Absolutely!

11

Comrade Bingo

The thing really started in the park – at the Marble Arch end – where weird birds of every description collect on Sunday afternoons and stand on soap-boxes and make speeches. It isn't often you'll find me there, but it so happened that on the Sabbath after my return to the good old metrop. I had a call to pay in Manchester Square, and, taking a stroll round in that direction so as not to arrive too early, I found myself right in the middle of it.

Now that the Empire isn't the place it was, I always think the park on a Sunday is the centre of London, if you know what I mean. I mean to say, that's the spot that makes the returned exile really sure he's back again. After what you might call my enforced sojourn in New York I'm bound to say that I stood there fairly lapping it all up. It did me good to listen to the lads giving tongue and realize that all had ended happily and Bertram was home again.

On the edge of the mob farthest away from me a gang of top-hatted chappies were starting an open-air missionary service; nearer at hand an atheist was letting himself go with a good deal of vim, though handicapped a bit by having no roof to his mouth; while in front of me there stood a little group of serious thinkers with a banner labelled 'Heralds of the Red Dawn'; and as I came up, one of the heralds, a bearded egg in a slouch hat and a tweed suit, was slipping it into the Idle Rich with such breadth and vigour that I paused for a moment to get an earful. While I was standing there somebody spoke to me.

'Mr Wooster, surely?'

Stout chappie. Couldn't place him for a second. Then I got him. Bingo Little's uncle, the one I had lunch with at the time when young Bingo was in love with that waitress at the Piccadilly bun-shop. No wonder I hadn't recognized him at first. When I had seen him last he had been a rather sloppy old gentleman – coming down to lunch, I remember, in carpet slippers and a velvet smoking-jacket; whereas now dapper simply wasn't the word. He absolutely gleamed in the sunlight in a silk hat, morning coat, lavender spats and sponge-bag trousers, as now worn. Dressy to a degree.

'Oh, hallo!' I said. 'Going strong?'

'I am in excellent health, I thank you. And you?'

'In the pink. Just been over to America.'

'Ah! Collecting local colour for one of your delightful romances?'

'Eh?' I had to think a bit before I got on to what he meant. 'Oh, no,' I said. 'Just felt I needed a change. Seen anything of Bingo lately?' I asked quickly, being desirous of heading the old thing off what you might call the literary side of my life.

'Bingo?'

'Your nephew.'

'Oh, Richard? No, not very recently. Since my marriage a little coolness seems to have sprung up.'

'Sorry to hear that. So you've married since I saw you, what? Mrs Little all right?'

'My wife is happily robust. But – er – *not* Mrs Little. Since we last met a gracious Sovereign has been pleased to bestow on me a signal mark of his favour in the shape of – ah – a peerage. On the publication of the last Honours List I became Lord Bittlesham.'

'By Jove! Really? I say, heartiest congratulations. That's the stuff to give the troops, what? Lord Bittlesham?' I said. 'Why, you're the owner of Ocean Breeze.'

'Yes. Marriage has enlarged my horizon in many directions. My wife is interested in horse-racing, and I now maintain a small stable. I understand that Ocean Breeze is fancied, as I am told the expression is, for a race which will take place at the end of the month at Goodwood, the Duke of Richmond's seat in Sussex.'

'The Goodwood Cup. Rather! I've got my chemise on it for one.'

'Indeed? Well, I trust the animal will justify your confidence. I know little of these matters myself, but my wife tells me that it is regarded in knowledgeable circles as what I believe is termed a snip.'

At this moment I suddenly noticed that the audience was gazing in our direction with a good deal of interest, and I saw that the bearded chappie was pointing at us.

'Yes, look at them! Drink them in!' he was yelling, his voice rising above the perpetual-motion fellow's and beating the missionary service all to nothing. 'There you see two typical members of the class which has down-trodden the poor for centuries. Idlers! Non-producers! Look at the tall thin one with the face like a motor-mascot. Has he ever done an honest day's work in his life? No! A prowler, a trifler, and a blood-sucker! And I bet he still owes his tailor for those trousers!'

He seemed to me to be verging on the personal, and I didn't think a lot of it. Old Bittlesham, on the other hand, was pleased and amused.

'A great gift of expression these fellows have,' he chuckled. 'Very trenchant.'

'And the fat one!' proceeded the chappie. 'Don't miss him. Do you know who that is? That's Lord Bittlesham! One of the worst. What has he ever done except eat four square meals a day? His god is his belly, and he sacrifices burnt-offerings to it. If you opened that man now you would find enough lunch to support ten working-class families for a week.'

'You know, that's rather well put,' I said, but the old boy didn't seem to see it. He had turned a brightish magenta and was bubbling like a kettle on the boil.

'Come away, Mr Wooster,' he said. 'I am the last man to oppose the right of free speech, but I refuse to listen to this vulgar abuse any longer.'

We legged it with quiet dignity, the chappie pursuing us with his foul innuendoes to the last. Dashed embarrassing.

Next day I looked in at the club, and found young Bingo in the smoking-room.

'Hallo, Bingo,' I said, toddling over to his corner full of *bonhomie*, for I was glad to see the chump. 'How's the boy?'

'Jogging along.'

'I saw your uncle yesterday.'

Young Bingo unleashed a grin that split his face in half.

'I know you did, you trifler. Well, sit down, old thing, and suck a bit of blood. How's the prowling these days?'

'Good Lord! You weren't there!'

'Yes, I was.'

'I didn't see you.'

'Yes, you did. But perhaps you didn't recognize me in the shrubbery.'

'The shrubbery?'

'The beard, my boy. Worth every penny I paid for it. Defies detection. Of course, it's a nuisance having people shouting "Beaver!" at you all the time, but one's got to put up with that.'

I goggled at him.

'I don't understand.'

'It's a long story. Have a martini or a small gore-and-soda, and I'll tell you all about it. Before we start, give me your honest opinion. Isn't she the most wonderful girl you ever saw in your puff?'

He had produced a photograph from somewhere, like a conjurer taking a rabbit out of a hat, and was waving it in front of me. It appeared to be a female of sorts, all eyes and teeth.

'Oh, Great Scott!' I said. 'Don't tell me you're in love again.'

He seemed aggrieved.

'What do you mean – again?'

'Well, to my certain knowledge you've been in love with at least half a dozen girls since the spring, and it's only July now. There was that waitress and Honoria Glossop and – '

'Oh, tush! Not to say pish! Those girls? Mere passing fancies. This is the real thing.'

'Where did you meet her?'

'On top of a bus. Her name is Charlotte Corday Rowbotham.'

'My God!'

'It's not her fault, poor child. Her father had her christened that because he's all for the Revolution, and it seems that the original Charlotte Corday used to go about stabbing oppressors in their baths, which entitles her to consideration and respect. You must meet old Rowbotham, Bertie. A delightful chap. Wants to massacre the *bourgeosie*, sack Park Lane and disembowel the hereditary aristocracy. Well, nothing could be fairer than that, what? But about Charlotte. We were on top of the bus, and it started to rain. I offered her my umbrella, and we chatted of this and that. I fell in love and got her address, and a couple of days later I bought the beard and toddled round and met the family.'

'But why the beard?'

'Well, she had told me all about her father on the bus, and I saw that to get any footing at all in the home I should have to join these Red Dawn blighters; and naturally, if I was to make speeches in the park, where at any moment I might run into a dozen people I knew, something in the nature of a disguise was indicated. So I bought the beard, and, by Jove, old boy, I've become dashed attached to the thing. When I take it off to come in here, for instance, I feel absolutely nude. It's done me a lot of good with old Rowbotham. He thinks I'm a Bolshevist of sorts who has to go about disguised because of the police. You really must meet old Rowbotham, Bertie. I tell you what, are you doing anything tomorrow afternoon?'

'Nothing special. Why?'

'Good! Then you can have us all to tea at your flat. I had promised to take the crowd to Lyons' Popular Café after a meeting we're holding down in Lambeth, but I can save money this way; and, believe me, laddie, nowadays, as far as I'm concerned, a penny saved is a penny earned. My uncle told you he'd got married?'

'Yes. And he said there was a coolness between you.'

'Coolness? I'm down to zero. Ever since he married he's been launching out in every direction and economizing on *me*. I suppose that peerage cost the old devil the deuce of a sum. Even baronetcies have gone up frightfully nowadays, I'm told. And he's started a racing-stable. By the way, put your last collar stud on Ocean Breeze for the Goodwood Cup. It's a cert.'

'I'm going to.'

'It can't lose. I mean to win enough on it to marry Charlotte with. You're going to Goodwood, of course?'

'Rather!'

'So are we. We're holding a meeting on Cup day just outside the paddock.'

'But, I say, aren't you taking frightful risks? Your uncle's sure to be at Goodwood. Suppose he spots you? He'll be fed to the gills if he finds out that you're the fellow who ragged him in the park.'

'How the deuce is he to find out? Use your intelligence, you prowling inhaler of red corpuscles. If he didn't spot me yesterday, why should he spot me at Goodwood? Well, thanks for your cordial invitation for tomorrow, old thing. We shall be delighted to accept. Do us well, laddie, and blessings shall reward you. By the way, I may have misled you by using the word "tea". None of your wafer slices of bread-and-butter. We're good trenchermen, we of the Revolution. What we shall require will be something on the order of scrambled eggs, muffins, jam, ham, cake and sardines. Expect us at five sharp.'

'But, I say, I'm not quite sure – '

'Yes, you are. Silly ass, don't you see that this is going to do you a bit of good when the Revolution breaks loose? When you see old Rowbotham sprinting up Piccadilly with a dripping knife in each hand, you'll be jolly thankful to be able to remind him that he once ate your tea and shrimps. There will be four of us Charlotte, self, the old man, and Comrade Butt. I suppose he will insist on coming along.'

'Who the devil's Comrade Butt?'

'Did you notice a fellow standing on my left in our little troupe yesterday? Small, shrivelled chap. Looks like a haddock with lung-trouble. That's Butt. My rival, dash him. He's sort of semi-engaged to Charlotte at the moment. Till I came along he was the blue-eyed boy. He's got a voice like a foghorn, and old Rowbotham thinks a lot of him. But, hang it, if I can't thoroughly encompass this Butt and cut him out and put him where he belongs among the discards – well, I'm not the man I was, that's all. He may have a big voice, but he hasn't my gift of expression. Thank heaven I was once cox of my college boat. Well, I must be pushing now. I say, you don't know how I could raise fifty quid somehow, do you?'

'Why don't you work?'

'Work?' said young Bingo, surprised. 'What, me? No, I shall have to think of some way. I must put at least fifty on Ocean Breeze. Well, see you tomorrow. God bless you, old sort, and don't forget the muffins.'

I don't know why, ever since I first knew him at school, I should have felt a rummy feeling of responsibility for young Bingo. I mean to say, he's not my son (thank goodness) or my brother or anything like that. He's got absolutely no claim on me at all, and yet a large-sized chunk of my existence seems to be spent in fussing over him like a bally old hen and hauling him out of the soup. I suppose it must be some rare beauty in my nature or something. At any rate, this latest affair of his worried me. He seemed to be doing his best to marry into a family of pronounced loonies, and how the deuce he thought he was going to support even a mentally afflicted wife on nothing a year beat me. Old Bittlesham was bound to knock off his allowance if he did anything of the sort and, with a fellow like young Bingo, if you knocked off his allowance, you might just as well hit him on the head with an axe and make a clean job of it.

'Jeeves,' I said, when I got home, 'I'm worried.'

'Sir?'

'About Mr Little. I won't tell you about it now, because he's bringing some friends of his to tea tomorrow, and then you will be able to judge for yourself. I want you to observe closely, Jeeves, and form your decision.'

'Very good, sir.'

'And about the tea. Get in some muffins.'

'Yes, sir.'

'And some jam, ham, cake, scrambled eggs, and five or six wagon-loads of sardines.'

'Sardines, sir?' said Jeeves, with a shudder.

'Sardines.'

There was an awkward pause.

'Don't blame me, Jeeves,' I said. 'It isn't my fault.'

'No, sir.'

'Well, that's that.'

'Yes, sir.'

I could see the man was brooding tensely.

I've found, as a general rule in life, that the things you think are going to be the scaliest nearly always turn out not so bad after all; but it wasn't that way with Bingo's tea-party. From the moment he invited himself I felt that the thing was going to be blue round the edges, and it was. And I think the most gruesome part of the whole affair was the fact that, for the first time since I'd known him, I saw Jeeves come very near to being rattled. I suppose there's a chink in everyone's armour, and young Bingo found Jeeves's right at the drop of the flag when he breezed in with six inches or so of brown beard hanging on to his chin. I had forgotten to warn Jeeves about the beard, and it came on him absolutely out of a blue sky. I saw the man's jaw drop, and he clutched at the table for support. I don't blame him, mind you. Few people have ever looked fouler than young Bingo in the fungus. Jeeves paled a little; then the weakness passed and he was himself again. But I could see that he had been shaken.

Young Bingo was too busy introducing the mob to take much notice. They were a very C3 collection. Comrade Butt looked like one of the things that come out of dead trees after the rain; moth-eaten was the word I should have used to describe old Rowbotham; and as for Charlotte, she seemed to take me straight into another and a dreadful world. It wasn't that she was exactly bad-looking. In fact, if she had knocked off starchy foods and done Swedish exercises for a bit, she might have been quite tolerable. But there was too much of her. Billowy curves. Well-nourished, perhaps, expresses it best. And, while she may have had a heart of gold, the thing you noticed about her first was that she had a tooth of gold. I know that young Bingo, when in form, could fall in love with practically anything of the other sex; but this time I couldn't see any excuse for him at all.

'My friend, Mr Wooster,' said Bingo, completing the ceremonial.

Old Rowbotham looked at me and then he looked round the room, and I could see he wasn't particularly braced. There's nothing of absolutely Oriental luxury about the old flat, but I have managed to make myself fairly comfortable, and I suppose the surroundings jarred him a bit.

'Mr Wooster?' said old Rowbotham. 'May I say Comrade Wooster?'

'I beg your pardon?'

'Are you of the movement?'

'Well – er – '

'Do you yearn for the Revolution?'

'Well, I don't know that I exactly yearn. I mean to say, as far as I can make out, the whole hub of the scheme seems to be to massacre coves like me; and I don't mind owning I'm not frightfully keen on the idea.'

'But I'm talking him round,' said Bingo. 'I'm wrestling with him. A few more treatments ought to do the trick.'

Old Rowbotham looked at me a bit doubtfully.

'Comrade Little has great eloquence,' he admitted.

'I think he talks something wonderful,' said the girl, and young Bingo shot a glance of such succulent devotion at her that I reeled in my tracks. It seemed to depress Comrade Butt a good deal too. He scowled at the carpet and said something about dancing on volcanoes.

'Tea is served, sir,' said Jeeves.

'Tea, Pa!' said Charlotte, starting at the word like the old warhorse who hears the bugle; and we got down to it.

Funny how one changes as the years roll on. At school, I remember, I would cheerfully have sold my soul for scrambled eggs and sardines at five in the afternoon; but somehow, since reaching man's estate, I had rather dropped out of the habit; and I'm bound to admit I was appalled to a goodish extent at the way the sons and daughter of the Revolution shoved their heads down and went for the foodstuffs. Even Comrade Butt cast off his gloom for a space and immersed his whole being in scrambled eggs, only coming to the surface at intervals to grab another cup of tea. Presently the hot water gave out, and I turned to Jeeves.

'More hot water.'

'Very good, sir.'

'Hey! What's this? What's this?' Old Rowbotham had lowered his cup and was eyeing us sternly. He tapped Jeeves on the shoulder. 'No servility, my lad; no servility!'

'I beg your pardon, sir?'

'Don't call me "sir." Call me Comrade. Do you know what you are, my lad? You're an absolute relic of an exploded feudal system.'

'Very good, sir.'

'If there's one thing that makes my blood boil in my veins – '

'Have another sardine,' chipped in young Bingo – the first sensible thing he'd done since I had known him. Old Rowbotham took three and dropped the subject, and Jeeves drifted away. I could see by the look of his back what he felt.

At last, just as I was beginning to feel that it was going on for ever, the thing finished. I woke up to find the party getting ready to leave.

Sardines and about three quarters of tea had mellowed old Rowbotham. There was quite a genial look in his eye as he shook my hand.

'I must thank you for your hospitality, Comrade Wooster,' he said.

'Oh, not at all! Only too glad – '

'Hospitality?' snorted the man Butt, going off in my ear like a depth-charge. He was scowling in a morose sort of manner at young Bingo and the girl, who were giggling together by the window. 'I wonder the food didn't turn to ashes in our mouths! Eggs! Muffins! Sardines! All wrung from the bleeding lips of the starving poor!'

'Oh, I say! What a beastly idea!'

'I will send you some literature on the subject of the Cause,' said old Rowbotham. 'And soon, I hope, we shall see you at one of our little meetings.'

Jeeves came in to clear away, and found me sitting among the ruins. It was all very well for Comrade Butt to knock the food, but he had pretty well finished the ham; and if you had shoved the remainder of the jam into the bleeding lips of the starving poor it would hardly have made them sticky.

'Well, Jeeves,' I said, 'how about it?'

'I would prefer to express no opinion, sir.'

'Jeeves, Mr Little is in love with that female.'

'So I gathered, sir. She was slapping him in the passage.'

I clutched my brow.

'Slapping him?'

'Yes, sir. Roguishly.'

'Great Scott! I didn't know it had got as far as that. How did Comrade Butt seem to be taking it? Or perhaps he didn't see?'

'Yes, sir, he observed the entire proceedings. He struck me as extremely jealous.'

'I don't blame him. Jeeves, what are we to do?'

'I could not say, sir.'

'It's a bit thick.'

'Very much so, sir.'

And that was all the consolation I got from Jeeves.

12

Bingo has a Bad Goodwood

I had promised to meet young Bingo next day, to tell him what I thought of his infernal Charlotte, and I was mooching slowly up St James's Street, trying to think how the dickens I could explain to him, without hurting his feelings, that I considered her one of the world's foulest, when who should come toddling out of the Devonshire Club but old Bittlesham and Bingo himself. I hurried on and overtook them.

'What ho!' I said.

The result of this simple greeting was a bit of a shock. Old Bittlesham quivered from head to foot like a poleaxed blancmange. His eyes were popping and his face had gone sort of greenish.

'Mr Wooster!' He seemed to recover somewhat, as if I wasn't the worst thing that could have happened to him. 'You gave me a severe start.'

'Oh, sorry.'

'My uncle,' said young Bingo in a hushed, bedside sort of voice, 'isn't feeling quite himself this morning. He's had a threatening letter.'

'I go in fear of my life,' said old Bittlesham.

'Threatening letter?'

'Written,' said old Bittlesham, 'in an uneducated hand and couched in terms of uncompromising menaces. Mr Wooster, do you recall a sinister, bearded man who assailed me in no measured terms in Hyde Park last Sunday?'

I jumped, and shot a look at young Bingo. The only expression on his face was one of grave, kindly concern.

'Why – ah – yes,' I said. 'Bearded man. Chap with a beard.'

'Could you identify him, if necessary?'

'Well, I – er – how do you mean?'

'The fact is, Bertie,' said Bingo, 'we think this man with the beard is at the bottom of all this business. I happened to be walking late last night through Pounceby Gardens, where Uncle Mortimer lives, and as I was passing the house a fellow came hurrying down the steps in a furtive sort of way. Probably he had just been shoving the letter in at the front door. I noticed that he had a beard. I didn't think any more of it, however, until this morning, when Uncle Mortimer showed me the letter he had received and told me about the chap in the park. I'm going to make inquiries.'

'The police should be informed,' said Lord Bittlesham.

'No,' said young Bingo firmly, 'not at this stage of the proceedings. It would hamper me. Don't you worry, Uncle; I think I can track this fellow down. You leave it all to me. I'll pop you into a taxi now, and go and talk it over with Bertie.'

'You're a good boy, Richard,' said old Bittlesham, and we put him in a passing cab and pushed off. I turned and looked young Bingo squarely in the eyeball.

'Did you send that letter?' I said.

'Rather! You ought to have seen it, Bertie! One of the best gent's ordinary threatening letters I ever wrote.'

'But where's the sense of it?'

'Bertie, my lad,' said Bingo, taking me earnestly by the coat-sleeve, 'I had an excellent reason. Posterity may say of me what it will, but one thing it can never say – that I have not a good solid business head. Look here!' He waved a bit of paper in front of my eyes.

'Great Scott!' It was a cheque – an absolute, dashed cheque for fifty of the best, signed Bittlesham, and made out to the order of R. Little.

'What's that for?'

'Expenses,' said Bingo, pouching it. 'You don't suppose an investigation like this can be carried on for nothing, do you! I now proceed to the bank and startle them into a fit with it. Later I edge round to my bookie and put the entire sum on Ocean Breeze. What you want in situations of this kind, Bertie, is tact. If I had gone to my uncle and asked him for fifty quid, would I have got it? No! But by exercising tact – Oh! by the way, what do you think of Charlotte?'

'Well – er – '

Young Bingo massaged my sleeve affectionately.

'I know, old man, I know. Don't try to find words. She bowled you over, eh? Left you speechless, what? *I* know! That's the effect she has on everybody. Well, I leave you here, laddie. Oh, before we part – Butt! What of Butt? Nature's worst blunder, don't you think?'

'I must say I've seen cheerier souls.'

'I think I've got him licked, Bertie. Charlotte is coming to the Zoo with me this afternoon. Alone. And later on to the pictures. That looks like the beginning of the end, what? Well, toodle-oo, friend of my youth. If you've nothing better to do this morning, you might take a stroll along Bond Street and be picking out a wedding present.'

I lost sight of Bingo after that. I left messages a couple of times at the club, asking him to ring me up, but they didn't have any effect. I took it that he was too busy to respond. The Sons of the Red Dawn also passed out of my life, though Jeeves told me he had met Comrade Butt one evening and had a brief chat with him. He reported Butt as gloomier than ever. In the competition for the bulging Charlotte, Butt had apparently gone right back in the betting.

'Mr Little would appear to have eclipsed him entirely, sir,' said Jeeves.

'Bad news, Jeeves; bad news.'

'Yes, sir.'

'I suppose what it amounts to, Jeeves, is that, when young Bingo really takes his coat off and starts in, there is no power of God or man that can prevent him making a chump of himself.'

'It would seem so, sir,' said Jeeves.

Then Goodwood came along, and I dug out the best suit and popped down.

I never know, when I'm telling a story, whether to cut the thing down to plain facts or whether to drool on and shove in a lot of atmosphere, and all that. I mean, many a cove would no doubt edge into the final spasm of this narrative with a long description of Goodwood, featuring the blue sky, the rolling prospect, the joyous crowds of pickpockets, and the parties of the second part who were having the pockets picked, and – in a word, what not. But better give it a miss, I think. Even if I wanted to go into details about the bally meeting I don't think I'd have the heart to. The thing's too recent. The anguish hasn't had time to pass. You see, what happened was that Ocean Breeze (curse him!) finished absolutely nowhere for the Cup. Believe me, nowhere.

These are the times that try men's souls. It's never pleasant to be caught in the machinery when a favourite comes unstitched, and in the case of this particular dashed animal, one had come to look on the running of the race as a pure formality, a sort of quaint, old-world ceremony to be gone through before one sauntered up to the bookie and collected. I had wandered out of the paddock to try and forget, when I bumped into old Bittlesham: and he looked so rattled and purple, and his eyes were standing out of his head at such an angle, that I simply pushed my hand out and shook his in silence.

'Me, too,' I said. 'Me, too. How much did *you* drop?'

'Drop?'

'On Ocean Breeze.'

'I did not bet on Ocean Breeze.'

'What! You owned the favourite for the Cup, and didn't back it!'

'I never bet on horse-racing. It is against my principles. I am told that the animal failed to win the contest.'

'Failed to win! Why, he was so far behind that he nearly came in first in the next race.'

'Tut!' said old Bittlesham.

'Tut is right,' I agreed. Then the rumminess of the thing struck me. 'But if you haven't dropped a parcel over the race,' I said, 'why are you looking so rattled?'

'That fellow is here!'

'What fellow?'

'That bearded man.'

It will show you to what an extent the iron had entered into my soul when I say that this was the first time I had given a thought to young Bingo. I suddenly remembered now that he had told me he would be at Goodwood.

'He is making an inflammatory speech at this very moment, specifically directed at me. Come! Where that crowd is.' He lugged me along and, by using his weight scientifically, got us into the front rank. 'Look! Listen!'

Young Bingo was certainly tearing off some ripe stuff. Inspired by the agony of having put his little all on a stumer that hadn't finished in the first six, he was fairly letting himself go on the subject of the blackness of the hearts of plutocratic owners who allowed a trusting public to imagine a horse was the real goods when it couldn't trot the length of its stable without getting its legs crossed and sitting down to rest. He then went on to draw what I'm bound to say was a most moving picture of a working man's home, due to this dishonesty. He showed us the working man, all optimism and simple trust, believing every word he read in the papers about Ocean Breeze's form; depriving his wife and children of food in order to back the brute; going without beer so as to be able to cram an extra bob on; robbing the baby's money-box with a hatpin on the eve of the race; and finally getting let down with a thud. Dashed impressive it was. I could see old Rowbotham nodding his head gently, while poor old Butt glowered at the speaker with ill-concealed jealousy. The audience ate it.

'But what does Lord Bittlesham care,' shouted Bingo, 'if the poor working man loses his hard-earned savings? I tell you, friends and comrades, you may talk, and you may argue and you may cheer, and you may pass resolutions, but what you need is Action! Action! The world won't be a fit place for honest men to live in till the blood of Lord Bittlesham and his kind flows down the gutters of Park Lane!'

Roars of approval from the populace, most of whom, I suppose, had had their little bit on blighted Ocean Breeze, and were feeling it deeply. Old Bittlesham bounded over to a large, sad policeman who was watching the proceedings, and appeared to be urging him to rally round. The policeman pulled at his moustache, and smiled gently, but that was as far as he seemed inclined to go; and old Bittlesham came back to me, puffing not a little.

'It's monstrous! The man definitely threatens my personal safety, and that policeman declines to interfere. Said it was just talk! Talk! It's monstrous!'

'Absolutely,' I said, but I can't say it seemed to cheer him up much.

Comrade Butt had taken the centre of the stage now. He had a voice like the Last Trump, and you could hear every word he said, but somehow he didn't seem to be clicking. I suppose the fact was he was too impersonal, if that's the word I want. After Bingo's speech the audience was in the mood for something a good deal snappier than just general remarks abut the Cause. They had started to heckle the poor blighter pretty freely, when he stopped in the middle of a sentence, and I saw that he was staring at old Bittlesham.

The crowd thought he had dried up.

'Suck a lozenge,' shouted someone.

Comrade Butt pulled himself together with a jerk, and even from where I stood I could see the nasty gleam in his eye.

'Ah,' he yelled, 'you may mock, comrades; you may jeer and sneer; and you may scoff; but let me tell you that the movement is spreading every day and every hour. Yes, even amongst the so-called upper classes it's spreading. Perhaps you'll believe me when I tell you that here, today, on this very spot, we have in our little band one of our most earnest workers, the nephew of that very Lord Bittlesham whose name you were hooting but a moment ago.'

And before old Bingo had a notion of what was up, he had reached out a hand and grabbed the beard. It came off all in once piece, and, well as Bingo's speech had gone, it was simply nothing compared with the hit made by this bit of business. I heard old Bittlesham give one short, sharp snort of amazement at my side, and then any remarks he may have made were drowned in thunders of applause.

I'm bound to say that in this crisis young Bingo acted with a good deal of decision and character. To grab Comrade Butt by the neck and try to twist his head off was with him the work of a moment. But before he could get any results the sad policeman, brightening up like magic, had charged in, and the next minute he was shoving his way back through the crowd, with Bingo in his right hand and Comrade Butt in his left.

'Let me pass, sir, please,' he said, civilly, as he came up against old Bittlesham, who was blocking the gangway.

'Eh?' said old Bittlesham, still dazed.

At the sound of his voice young Bingo looked up quickly from under the shadow of the policeman's right hand, and as he did so all the stuffing seemed to go out of him with a rush. For an instant he drooped like a bally lily, and then shuffled brokenly on. His air was the air of a man who has got it in the neck properly.

Sometimes when Jeeves has brought in my morning tea and shoved it on the table beside my bed, he drifts silently from the room and leaves me to go to it: at other times he sort of shimmies respectfully in the middle of the carpet, and then I know that he wants a word or two. On the day after I had got back from Goodwood I was lying on my back, staring at the ceiling, when I noticed that he was still in my midst.

'Oh, hallo,' I said. 'Yes?'

'Mr Little called earlier in the morning, sir.'

'Oh, by Jove, what? Did he tell you about what happened?'

'Yes, sir. It was in connection with that that he wished to see you. He proposes to retire to the country and remain there for some little while.'

'Dashed sensible.'

'That was my opinion, also, sir. There was, however, a slight financial difficulty to be overcome. I took the liberty of advancing him ten pounds on your behalf to meet current expenses. I trust that meets with your approval, sir?'

'Oh, of course. Take a tenner off the dressing-table.'

'Very good, sir.'

'Jeeves,' I said.

'Sir?'

'What beats me is how the dickens the thing happened. I mean, how did the chappie Butt ever get to know who he was?'

Jeeves coughed.

'There, sir, I fear I may have been somewhat to blame.'

'You? How?'

'I fear I may carelessly have disclosed Mr Little's identity to Mr Butt on the occasion when I had that conversation with him.'

I sat up.

'What?'

'Indeed, now that I recall the incident, sir, I distinctly remember saying that Mr Little's work for the Cause really seemed to me to deserve something in the nature of public recognition. I greatly regret having been the means of bringing about a temporary estrangement between Mr Little and his lordship. And I am afraid there is another aspect to the matter. I am also responsible for the breaking off of relations between Mr Little and the young lady who came to tea here.'

I sat up again. It's a rummy thing, but the silver lining had absolutely escaped my notice till then.

'Do you mean to say it's off?'

'Completely, sir. I gathered from Mr Little's remarks that his hopes in that direction may now be looked on as definitely quenched. If there were no other obstacle, the young lady's father, I am informed by Mr Little, now regards him as a spy and a deceiver.'

'Well, I'm dashed.'

'I appear inadvertently to have caused much trouble, sir.'

'Jeeves!' I said.

'Sir?'

'How much money is there on the dressing-table?'

'In addition to the ten-pound note which you instructed me to take, sir, there are two five-pound notes, three one-pounds, a ten shillings, two half-crowns, a florin, four shillings, a sixpence, and a halfpenny, sir.'

'Collar it all,' I said. 'You've earned it.'

13

The Great Sermon Handicap

After Goodwood's over, I generally find that I get a bit restless. I'm not much of a lad for the birds and the trees and the great open spaces as a rule, but there's no doubt that London's not at its best in August, and rather tends to give me the pip and make me think of popping down into the country till things have bucked up a trifle. London, about a couple of weeks after that spectacular finish of young Bingo's which I've just been telling you about, was empty and smelled of burning asphalt. All my pals were away, most of the theatres were shut, and they were taking up Piccadilly in large spadefuls.

It was most infernally hot. As I sat in the old flat one night trying to muster up energy enough to go to bed, I felt I couldn't stand it much longer: and when Jeeves came in with the tissue-restorers on a tray I put the thing to him squarely.

'Jeeves,' I said, wiping the brow and gasping like a stranded goldfish, 'it's beastly hot.'

'The weather *is* oppressive, sir.'

'Not all the soda, Jeeves.'

'No, sir.'

'I think we've had about enough of the metrop. for the time being, and require a change. Shift-ho, I think, Jeeves, what?'

'Just as you say, sir. There is a letter on the tray, sir.'

'By Jove, Jeeves, that was practically poetry. Rhymed, did you notice?' I opened the letter. 'I say, this is rather extraordinary.'

'Sir?'

'You know Twing Hall?'

'Yes, sir.'

'Well, Mr Little is there.'

'Indeed, sir?'

'Absolutely in the flesh. He's had to take another of those tutoring jobs.'

After that fearful mix-up at Goodwood, when young Bingo Little, a broken man, had touched me for a tenner and whizzed silently off into the unknown, I had been all over the place, asking mutual friends if they had heard anything of him, but nobody had. And all the time he had been at Twing Hall. Rummy. And I'll tell you why it was rummy. Twing Hall belongs to old Lord Wickhammersley, a great pal of my guv'nor's when he was alive, and I have a standing invitation to pop down there when I like. I generally put in a week or two some time in the summer, and I was thinking of going there before I read the letter.

'And what's more, Jeeves, my cousin Claude, and my cousin Eustace – you remember them?'

'Very vividly, sir.'

'Well, they're down there, too, reading for some exam or other with the vicar. I used to read with him myself at one time. He's known far and wide as a pretty hot coach for those of fairly feeble intellect. Well, when I tell you he got *me* through Smalls, you'll gather that he's a bit of a hummer. I call this most extraordinary.'

I read the letter again. It was from Eustace. Claude and Eustace are twins, and more or less generally admitted to be the curse of the human race.

The Vicarage,

Twing, Glos.

Dear Bertie,

Do you want to make a bit of money? I hear you had a bad Goodwood, so you probably do. Well, come down here quick and get in on the biggest sporting event of the season. I'll explain when I see you, but you can take it from me it's all right.

Claude and I are with a reading-party at old Heppenstall's. There are nine of us, not counting your pal Bingo Little, who is tutoring the kid up at the Hall.

Don't miss this golden opportunity, which may never occur again. Come and join us.

Yours,

EUSTACE.

I handed this to Jeeves. He studied it thoughtfully.

'What do you make of it? A rummy communication, what?'

'Very high-spirited young gentlemen, sir, Mr Claude and Mr Eustace. Up to some game, I should be disposed to imagine.'

'Yes. But what game, do you think?'

'It is impossible to say, sir. Did you observe that the letter continues over the page?'

'Eh, what?' I grabbed the thing. This was what was on the other side of the last page:

SERMON HANDICAP
RUNNERS AND BETTING
PROBABLE STARTERS

Rev. Joseph Tucker (Badgwick), scratch.
Rev. Leonard Starkie (Stapleton), scratch.
Rev. Alexander Jones (Upper Bingley), receives three minutes.
Rev. W. Dix (Little Clickton-on-the-Wold), receives five minutes.
Rev. Francis Heppenstall (Twing), receives eight minutes.
Rev. Cuthbert Dibble (Boustead Parva), receives nine minutes.
Rev. Orlo Hough (Boustead Magna), receives nine minutes.
Rev. J. J. Roberts (Fale-by-the-Water), receives ten minutes.
Rev. G. Hayward (Lower Bingley), receives twelve minutes.
Rev. James Bates (Gandle-by-the-Hill), receives fifteen minutes.
(*The above have arrived.*)

Prices: 5–2, Tucker, Starkie; 3–1, Jones; 9–2, Dix; 6–1, Heppenstall, Dibble, Hough; 100–8 any other.

It baffled me.
'Do you understand it, Jeeves?'
'No, sir.'
'Well, I think we ought to have a look into it, anyway, what?'
'Undoubtedly, sir.'
'Right-o, then. Pack our spare dickey and a toothbrush in a neat brown-paper parcel, send a wire to Lord Wickhammersley to say we're coming, and buy two tickets on the five-ten at Paddington tomorrow.'

The five-ten was late as usual, and everybody was dressing for dinner when I arrived at the Hall. It was only by getting into my evening things in record time and taking the stairs to the dining-room in a couple of bounds that I managed to dead-heat with the soup. I slid into the vacant chair, and found that I was sitting next to old Wickhammersley's youngest daughter, Cynthia.

'Oh, hallo, old thing,' I said.

Great pals we've always been. In fact, there was a time when I had an idea I was in love with Cynthia. However, it blew over. A

dashed pretty and lively and attractive girl, mind you, but full of
ideals and all that. I may be wronging her, but I have an idea that
she's the sort of girl who would want a fellow to carve out a career
and what not. I know I've heard her speak favourably of Napoleon.
So what with one thing and another the jolly old frenzy sort of
petered out, and now we're just pals. I think she's a topper, and she
thinks me next door to a loony, so everything's nice and matey.

'Well, Bertie, so you've arrived?'

'Oh, yes, I've arrived. Yes, here I am. I say, I seem to have plunged
into the middle of quite a young dinner-party. Who are all these
coves?'

'Oh, just people from round about. You know most of them. You
remember Colonel Willis, and the Spencers – '

'Of course, yes. And there's old Heppenstall. Who's the other
clergyman next to Mrs Spencer?'

'Mr Hayward, from Lower Bingley.'

'What an amazing lot of clergymen there are round here. Why,
there's another, next to Mrs Willis.'

'That's Mr Bates, Mr Heppenstall's nephew. He's an assistant-
master at Eton. He's down here during the summer holidays, acting
as locum tenens for Mr Spettigue, the rector of Gandle-by-the-
Hill.'

'I thought I knew his face. He was in his fourth year at Oxford
when I was a fresher. Rather a blood. Got his rowing-blue and all
that.' I took another look round the table, and spotted young Bingo.
'Ah, there he is,' I said. 'There's the old egg.'

'There's who?'

'Young Bingo Little. Great pal of mine. He's tutoring your
brother, you know.'

'Good gracious! Is he a friend of yours?'

'Rather! Known him all my life.'

'Then tell me, Bertie, is he at all weak in the head?'

'Weak in the head?'

'I don't mean simply because he's a friend of yours. But he's so
strange in his manner.'

'How do you mean?'

'Well, he keeps looking at me so oddly.'

'Oddly? How? Give me an imitation.'

'I can't in front of all these people.'

'Yes, you can. I'll hold my napkin up.'

'All right, then. Quick. There!'

Considering that she had only about a second and a half to do it in, I must say it was a jolly fine exhibition. She opened her mouth and eyes pretty wide and let her jaw drop sideways, and managed to look so like a dyspeptic calf that I recognized the symptoms immediately.

'Oh, that's all right,' I said. 'No need to be alarmed. He's simply in love with you.'

'In love with me. Don't be absurd.'

'My dear old thing, you don't know young Bingo. He can fall in love with *anybody*.'

'Thank you!'

'Oh, I didn't mean it that way, you know. I don't wonder at his taking to you. Why, I was in love with you myself once.'

'Once? Ah! And all that remains now are the cold ashes? This isn't one of your tactful evenings, Bertie.'

'Well, my dear sweet thing, dash it all, considering that you gave me the bird and nearly laughed yourself into a permanent state of hiccoughs when I asked you – '

'Oh, I'm not reproaching you. No doubt there were faults on both sides. He's very good-looking, isn't he?'

'Good-looking? Bingo? Bingo good-looking? No, I say, come now, really!'

'I mean, compared with some people,' said Cynthia.

Some time after this, Lady Wickhammersley gave the signal for the females of the species to leg it, and they duly stampeded. I didn't get a chance of talking to young Bingo when they'd gone, and later, in the drawing-room, he didn't show up. I found him eventually in his room, lying on the bed with his feet on the rail, smoking a toofah. There was a notebook on the counterpane beside him.

'Hallo, old scream,' I said.

'Hallo, Bertie,' he replied, in what seemed to me rather a moody, distrait sort of manner.

'Rummy finding you down here. I take it your uncle cut off your allowance after that Goodwood binge and you had to take this tutoring job to keep the wolf from the door?'

'Correct,' said young Bingo tersely.

'Well, you might have let your pals know where you were.'

He frowned darkly.

'I didn't want them to know where I was. I wanted to creep away and hide myself. I've been through a bad time, Bertie, these last weeks. The sun ceased to shine – '

'That's curious. We've had gorgeous weather in London.'

'The birds ceased to sing – '

'What birds?'

'What the devil does it matter what birds?' said young Bingo, with some asperity. 'Any birds. The birds round about here. You don't expect me to specify them by their pet names, do you? I tell you, Bertie, it hit me hard at first, very hard.'

'What hit you?' I simply couldn't follow the blighter.

'Charlotte's calculated callousness.'

'Oh, ah!' I've seen poor old Bingo through so many unsuccessful love-affairs that I'd almost forgotten there was a girl mixed up with that Goodwood business. Of course! Charlotte Corday Rowbotham. And she had given him the raspberry, I remembered, and gone off with Comrade Butt.

'I went through torments. Recently, however, I've – er – bucked up a bit. Tell me, Bertie, what are you doing down here? I didn't know you knew these people.'

'Me? Why, I've known them since I was a kid.'

Young Bingo put his feet down with a thud.

'Do you mean to say you've known Lady Cynthia all that time?'

'Rather! She can't have been seven when I met her first.'

'Good Lord!' said young Bingo. He looked at me for the first time as though I amounted to something, and swallowed a mouthful of smoke the wrong way. 'I love that girl, Bertie,' he went on, when he'd finished coughing.

'Yes. Nice girl, of course.'

He eyed me with pretty deep loathing.

'Don't speak of her in that horrible casual way. She's an angel. An angel! Was she talking about me at all at dinner, Bertie?'

'Oh, yes.'

'What did she say?'

'I remember one thing. She said she thought you good-looking.'

Young Bingo closed his eyes in a sort of ecstasy. Then he picked up the notebook.

'Pop off now, old man, there's a good chap,' he said in a hushed, far-away voice. 'I've got a bit of writing to do.'

'Writing?'

'Poetry, if you must know. I wish the dickens,' said young Bingo, not without some bitterness, 'she had been christened something except Cynthia. There isn't a dam' word in the language it rhymes

with. Ye gods, how I could have spread myself if she had only been
called Jane!'

Bright and early next morning, as I lay in bed blinking at the sunlight
on the dressing-table and wondering when Jeeves was going to show
up with a cup of tea, a heavy weight descended on my toes, and the
voice of young Bingo polluted the air. The blighter had apparently
risen with the lark.

'Leave me,' I said, 'I would be alone. I can't see anybody till I've
had my tea.'

'When Cynthia smiles,' said young Bingo, 'the skies are blue; the
world takes on a roseate hue; birds in the garden trill and sing, and
Joy is king of everything, when Cynthia smiles.' He coughed, changing gears. 'When Cynthia frowns – '

'What the devil are you talking about?'

'I'm reading you my poem. The one I wrote to Cynthia last night.
I'll go on, shall I?'

'No!'

'No?'

'No. I haven't had my tea.'

At this moment Jeeves came in with the good old beverage, and
I sprang on it with a glad cry. After a couple of sips things looked
a bit brighter. Even young Bingo didn't offend the eye to quite such
an extent. By the time I'd finished the first cup I was a new man,
so much so that I not only permitted but encouraged the poor fish
to read the rest of the bally thing, and even went so far as to criticize
the scansion of the fourth line of the fifth verse. We were still
arguing the point when the door burst open and in blew Claude and
Eustace. One of the things which discourages me about rural life is
the frightful earliness with which events begin to break loose. I've
stayed at places in the country where they've jerked me out of the
dreamless at about six-thirty to go for a jolly swim in the lake. At
Twing, thank heaven, they know me, and let me breakfast in bed.

The twins seemed pleased to see me.

'Good old Bertie!' said Claude.

'Stout fellow!' said Eustace. 'The Rev. told us you had arrived. I
thought that letter of mine would fetch you.'

'You can always bank on Bertie,' said Claude. 'A sportsman to
the finger-tips. Well, has Bingo told you about it?'

'Not a word. He's been – '

'We've been talking,' said Bingo hastily, 'of other matters.'

Claude pinched the last slice of thin bread-and-butter, and Eustace poured himself out a cup of tea.

'It's like this, Bertie,' said Eustace, settling down cosily. 'As I told you in my letter, there are nine of us marooned in this desert spot, reading with old Heppenstall. Well, of course, nothing is jollier than sweating up the Classics when it's a hundred in the shade, but there does come a time when you begin to feel the need of a little relaxation; and, by Jove, there are absolutely no facilities for relaxation in this place whatever. And then Steggles got this idea. Steggles is one of our reading-party, and, between ourselves, rather a worm as a general thing. Still, you have to give him credit for getting this idea.'

'What idea?'

'Well, you know how many parsons there are round about here. There are about a dozen hamlets within a radius of six miles, and each hamlet has a church and each church has a parson and each parson preaches a sermon every Sunday. Tomorrow week – Sunday the twenty-third – we're running off the great Sermon Handicap. Steggles is making the book. Each parson is to be clocked by a reliable steward of the course, and the one that preaches the longest sermon wins. Did you study the race-card I sent you?'

'I couldn't understand what it was all about.'

'Why, you chump, it gives the handicaps and the current odds on each starter. I've got another one here, in case you've lost yours. Take a careful look at it. It gives you the thing in a nutshell. Jeeves, old son, do you want a sporting flutter?'

'Sir?' said Jeeves, who had just meandered in with my breakfast.

Claude explained the scheme. Amazing the way Jeeves grasped it right off. But he merely smiled in a paternal sort of way.

'Thank you, sir, I think not.'

'Well, you're with us, Bertie, aren't you?' said Claude, sneaking a roll and a slice of bacon. 'Have you studied that card? Well, tell me, does anything strike you about it?'

Of course it did. It had struck me the moment I looked at it.

'Why, it's a sitter for old Heppenstall,' I said. 'He's got the event sewed up in a parcel. There isn't a parson in the land who could give him eight minutes. Your pal Steggles must be an ass, giving him a handicap like that. Why, in the days when I was with him, old Heppenstall never used to preach under half an hour, and there was one sermon of his on Brotherly Love which lasted forty-five minutes if it lasted a second. Has he lost his vim lately, or what is it?'

'Not a bit of it,' said Eustace. 'Tell him what happened, Claude.'

'Why,' said Claude, 'the first Sunday we were here, we all went to Twing church, and old Heppenstall preached a sermon that was well under twenty minutes. This is what happened. Steggles didn't notice it, and the Rev. didn't notice it himself, but Eustace and I both spotted that he had dropped a chunk of at least half a dozen pages out of his sermon-case as he was walking up to the pulpit. He sort of flickered when he got to the gap in the manuscript, but carried on all right, and Steggles went away with the impression that twenty minutes or a bit under was his usual form. The next Sunday we heard Tucker and Starkie, and they both went well over the thirty-five minutes, so Steggles arranged the handicapping as you see on the card. You must come into this, Bertie. You see, the trouble is that I haven't a bean, and Eustace hasn't a bean, and Bingo Little hasn't a bean, so you'll have to finance the syndicate. Don't weaken! It's just putting money in all our pockets. Well, we'll have to be getting back now. Think the thing over, and phone me later in the day. And, if you let us down, Bertie, may a cousin's curse – Come on, Claude, old thing.'

The more I studied the scheme, the better it looked.

'How about it, Jeeves?' I said.

Jeeves smiled gently, and drifted out.

'Jeeves has no sporting blood,' said Bingo.

'Well, I have. I'm coming into this. Claude's quite right. It's like finding money by the wayside.'

'Good man!' said Bingo. 'Now I can see daylight. Say I have a tenner on Heppenstall, and cop; that'll give me a bit in hand to back Pink Pill with in the two o'clock at Gatwick the week after next; cop on that, put the pile on Musk-Rat for the one-thirty at Lewes, and there I am with a nice little sum to take to Alexandra Park on September the tenth, when I've got a tip straight from the stable.'

It sounded like a bit out of *Smiles's Self-Help*.

'And then,' said young Bingo, 'I'll be in a position to go to my uncle and beard him in his lair somewhat. He's quite a bit of a snob, you know, and when he hears that I'm going to marry the daughter of an earl – '

'I say, old man,' I couldn't help saying, 'aren't you looking ahead rather far?'

'Oh, that's all right. It's true nothing's actually settled yet, but she practically told me the other day she was fond of me.'

'What!'

'Well, she said that the sort of man she liked was the self-reliant, manly man with strength, good looks, character, ambition, and initiative.'

'Leave me, laddie,' I said. 'Leave me to my fried egg.'

Directly I'd got up I went to the phone, snatched Eustace away from his morning's work, and instructed him to put a tenner on the Twing flier at current odds for each of the syndicate; and after lunch Eustace rang me up to say that he had done business at a snappy seven-to-one, the odds having lengthened owing to a rumour in knowledgeable circles that the Rev. was subject to hay-fever, and was taking big chances strolling in the paddock behind the Vicarage in the early mornings. And it was dashed lucky, I thought next day, that we had managed to get the money on in time, for on the Sunday morning old Heppenstall fairly took the bit between his teeth, and gave us thirty-six solid minutes on Certain Popular Superstitions. I was sitting next to Steggles in the pew, and I saw him blench visibly. He was a little rat-faced fellow, with shifty eyes and a suspicious nature. The first thing he did when he emerged into the open air was to announce, formally, that anyone who fancied the Rev. could now be accommodated at fifteen-to-eight on, and he added, in a rather nasty manner, that if he had his way, this sort of in-and-out running would be brought to the attention of the Jockey Club, but that he supposed that there was nothing to be done about it. This ruinous price checked the punters at once, and there was little money in sight. And so matters stood till just after lunch on Tuesday afternoon, when, as I was strolling up and down in front of the house with a cigarette, Claude and Eustace came bursting up the drive on bicycles, dripping with momentous news.

'Bertie,' said Claude, deeply agitated, 'unless we take immediate action and do a bit of quick thinking, we're in the cart.'

'What's the matter?'

'G. Hayward's the matter,' said Eustace morosely. 'The Lower Bingley starter.'

'We never even considered him,' said Claude. 'Somehow or other, he got overlooked. It's always the way. Steggles overlooked him. We all overlooked him. But Eustace and I happened by the merest fluke to be riding through Lower Bingley this morning, and there was a wedding on at the church, and it suddenly struck us that it wouldn't be a bad move to get a line on G. Hayward's form, in case he might be a dark horse.'

'And it was jolly lucky we did,' said Eustace. 'He delivered an address of twenty-six minutes by Claude's stop-watch. At a village wedding, mark you! What'll we do when he really extends himself!'

'There's only one thing to be done, Bertie,' said Claude. 'You must spring some more funds, so that we can hedge on Hayward and save ourselves.'

'But – '

'Well, it's the only way out.'

'But I say, you know, I hate the idea of all that money we put on Heppenstall being chucked away.'

'What else can you suggest? You don't suppose the Rev. can give this absolute marvel a handicap and win, do you?'

'I've got it!' I said.

'What?'

'I see a way by which we can make it safe for our nominee. I'll pop over this afternoon, and ask him as a personal favour to preach that sermon of his on Brotherly Love on Sunday.'

Claude and Eustace looked at each other, like those chappies in the poem, with a wild surmise.

'It's a scheme,' said Claude.

'A jolly brainy scheme,' said Eustace. 'I didn't think you had it in you, Bertie.'

'But even so,' said Claude, 'fizzer as that sermon no doubt is, will it be good enough in the face of a four-minute handicap?'

'Rather!' I said. 'When I told you it lasted forty-five minutes, I was probably understating it. I should call it – from my recollection of the thing – nearer fifty.'

'Then carry on,' said Claude.

I toddled over in the evening and fixed the thing up. Old Heppenstall was most decent about the whole affair. He seemed pleased and touched that I should have remembered the sermon all these years, and said he had once or twice had an idea of preaching it again, only it had seemed to him, on reflection, that it was perhaps a trifle long for a rustic congregation.

'And in these restless times, my dear Wooster,' he said, 'I fear that brevity in the pulpit is becoming more and more desiderated by even the bucolic churchgoer, who one might have supposed would be less afflicted with the spirit of hurry and impatience than his metropolitan brother. I have had many arguments on the subject with my nephew, young Bates, who is taking my old friend Spettigue's cure over at Gandle-by-the-Hill. His view is that a sermon nowadays should be a bright, brisk, straight-from-the shoulder address, never lasting more than ten or twelve minutes.'

'Long?' I said. 'Why, my goodness! You don't call that Brotherly Love sermon of yours *long*, do you?'

'It takes fully fifty minutes to deliver.'

'Surely not?'

'Your incredulity, my dear Wooster, is extremely flattering – far more flattering, of course, than I deserve. Nevertheless, the facts are as I have stated. You are sure that I would not be well advised to make certain excisions and eliminations? You do not think it would be a good thing to cut, to prune? I might, for example, delete the rather exhaustive excursus into the family life of the early Assyrians?'

'Don't touch a word of it, or you'll spoil the whole thing,' I said earnestly.

'I am delighted to hear you say so, and I shall preach the sermon without fail next Sunday morning.'

What I have always said, and what I always shall say, is, that this ante-post betting is a mistake, an error, and a mug's game. You can never tell what's going to happen. If fellows would only stick to the good old SP there would be fewer young men go wrong. I'd hardly finished my breakfast on the Saturday morning, when Jeeves came to my bedside to say that Eustace wanted me on the telephone.

'Good Lord, Jeeves, what's the matter, do you think?'

I'm bound to say I was beginning to get a bit jumpy by this time.

'Mr Eustace did not confide in me, sir.'

'Has he got the wind up?'

'Somewhat vertically, sir, to judge by his voice.'

'Do you know what I think, Jeeves? Something's gone wrong with the favourite.'

'Which is the favourite, sir?'

'Mr Heppenstall. He's gone to odds on. He was intending to preach a sermon on Brotherly Love which would have brought him home by lengths. I wonder if anything's happened to him.'

'You could ascertain, sir, by speaking to Mr Eustace on the telephone. He is holding the wire.'

'By Jove, yes!'

I shoved on a dressing gown, and flew downstairs like a mighty, rushing wind. The moment I heard Eustace's voice I knew we were for it. It had a croak of agony in it.

'Bertie?'

'Here I am.'

'Deuce of a time you've been. Bertie, we're sunk. The favourite's blown up.'

'No!'

'Yes. Coughing in his stable all last night.'

'What!'

'Absolutely! Hay-fever.'

'Oh, my sainted aunt!'

'The doctor is with him now, and it's only a question of minutes before he's officially scratched. That means the curate will show up at the post instead, and he's no good at all. He is being offered at a hundred-to-six, but no takers. What shall we do?'

I had to grapple with the thing for a moment in silence.

'Eustace.'

'Hallo?'

'What can you get on G. Hayward?'

'Only four to one now. I think there's been a leak, and Steggles has heard something. The odds shortened late last night in a significant manner.'

'Well, four to one will clear us. Put another fiver all round on G. Hayward for the syndicate. That'll bring us out on the right side of the ledger.'

'If he wins.'

'What do you mean? I thought you considered him a cert, bar Heppenstall.'

'I'm beginning to wonder,' said Eustace gloomily, 'if there's such a thing as a cert, in this world. I'm told the Rev. Joseph Tucker did an extraordinarily fine trial gallop at a mothers' meeting over at Badgwick yesterday. However, it seems our only chance. So-long.'

Not being one of the official stewards, I had my choice of churches next morning, and naturally I didn't hesitate. The only drawback to going to Lower Bingley was that it was ten miles away, which meant an early start, but I borrowed a bicycle from one of the grooms and tooled off. I had only Eustace's word for it that G. Hayward was such a stayer, and it might have been that he had showed too flattering form at that wedding where the twins had heard him preach; but any misgivings I may have had disappeared the moment he got into the pulpit. Eustace had been right. The man was a trier. He was a tall, rangy-looking greybeard, and he went off from the start with a nice, easy action, pausing and clearing his throat at the end of each sentence, and it wasn't five minutes before I realized that here was the winner. His habit of stopping dead and looking round the church at intervals was worth minutes to us, and in the home stretch we gained no little advantage owing to his dropping his pince-nez and having to grope for them. At the twenty-minute mark he had merely settled down. Twenty-five minutes saw him going strong. And when he finally finished with a good burst, the clock showed thirty-five minutes fourteen seconds. With the handicap which he had been given, this seemed to me to make the event easy for him, and it was with much *bonhomie* and goodwill to all men that I hopped on to the old bike and started back to the Hall for lunch.

Bingo was talking on the phone when I arrived.

'Fine! Splendid! Topping!' he was saying. 'Eh? Oh, we needn't worry about him. Right-o, I'll tell Bertie.' He hung up the receiver and caught sight of me. 'Oh, hallo, Bertie; I was just talking to Eustace. It's all right, old man. The report from Lower Bingley has just got in. G. Hayward romps home.'

'I knew he would. I've just come from there.'

'Oh, were you there? I went to Badgwick. Tucker ran a splendid race, but the handicap was too much for him. Starkie had a sore throat and was nowhere. Roberts, of Fale-by-the-Water, ran third. Good old G. Hayward!' said Bingo affectionately, and we strolled out on to the terrace.

'Are all the returns in, then?' I asked.

'All except Gandle-by-the-Hill. But we needn't worry about Bates. He never had a chance. By the way, poor old Jeeves loses his tenner. Silly ass!'

'Jeeves? How do you mean?'

'He came to me this morning, just after you had left, and asked me to put a tenner on Bates for him. I told him he was a chump, and begged him not to throw his money away, but he would do it.'

'I beg your pardon, sir. This note arrived for you just after you had left the house this morning.'

Jeeves had materialized from nowhere, and was standing at my elbow.

'Eh? What? Note?'

'The Reverend Mr Heppenstall's butler brought it over from the Vicarage, sir. It came too late to be delivered to you at the moment.'

Young Bingo was talking to Jeeves like a father on the subject of betting against the form-book. The yell I gave made him bite his tongue in the middle of a sentence.

'What the dickens is the matter?' he asked, not a little peeved.

'We're dished! Listen to this!'

I read him the note:

> The Vicarage,
>
> Twing, Glos.
>
> *My Dear Wooster,*
>
> *As you may have heard, circumstances over which I have no control will prevent my preaching the sermon on Brotherly Love for which you made such a flattering request. I am unwilling, however, that you shall be disappointed, so, if you will attend divine service at Gandle-by-the-Hill this morning, you will hear my sermon preached by young Bates, my nephew. I have lent him the manuscript at his urgent desire, for, between ourselves, there are wheels within wheels. My nephew is one of the candidates for the headmastership of a well-known public school, and the choice has narrowed down between him and one rival.*
>
> *Late yesterday evening James received private information that the head of the Board of Governors of the school proposed to sit under him this Sunday in order to judge of the merits of his preaching, a most important item in swaying the Board's choice. I acceded to his plea that I lend him my sermon on Brotherly Love, of which, like you, he apparently retains a vivid recollection. It would have been too late for him to compose a sermon of suitable length in place of this brief address which – mistakenly, in my opinion – he had designed to deliver to his rustic flock, and I wished to help the boy.*
>
> *Trusting that his preaching of the sermon will supply you with as pleasant memories as you say you have of mine, I remain,*
>
> *Cordially yours,*
>
> F. HEPPENSTALL.
>
> *PS – The hay-fever has rendered my eyes unpleasantly weak for the time being, so I am dictating this letter to my butler, Brookfield, who will convey it to you.*

I don't know when I've experienced a more massive silence than the one that followed my reading of this cheery epistle. Young Bingo gulped once or twice, and practically every known emotion came and went on his face. Jeeves coughed one soft, low, gentle cough like a sheep with a blade of grass stuck in its throat, and then stood gazing serenely at the landscape. Finally young Bingo spoke.

'Great Scott!' he whispered hoarsely. 'An SP job!'

'I believe that is the technical term, sir,' said Jeeves.

'So you had inside information, dash it!' said young Bingo.

'Why, yes, sir,' said Jeeves. 'Brookfield happened to mention the contents of the note to me when he brought it. We are old friends.'

Bingo registered grief, anguish, rage, despair and resentment.

'Well, all I can say,' he cried, 'is that it's a bit thick! Preaching another man's sermon! Do you call that honest? Do you call that playing the game?'

'Well, my dear old thing,' I said, 'be fair. It's quite within the rules. Clergymen do it all the time. They aren't expected always to make up the sermons they preach.'

Jeeves coughed again, and fixed me with an expressionless eye.

'And in the present case, sir, if I may be permitted to take the liberty of making the observation, I think we should make allowances. We should remember that the securing of this headmastership meant everything to the young couple.'

'Young couple? What young couple?'

'The Reverend James Bates, sir, and Lady Cynthia. I am informed by her ladyship's maid that they have been engaged to be married for some weeks – provisionally, so to speak; and his lordship made his consent conditional on Mr Bates securing a really important and remunerative position.'

Young Bingo turned a light green.

'Engaged to be married!'

'Yes, sir.'

There was a silence.

'I think I'll go for a walk,' said Bingo.

'But, my dear old thing,' I said, 'it's just lunch-time. The gong will be going any minute now.'

'I don't want any lunch!' said Bingo.

14
The Purity of the Turf

After that, life at Twing jogged along pretty peacefully for a bit.
Twing is one of those places where there isn't a frightful lot to do
nor any very hectic excitement to look forward to. In fact, the only
event of any importance on the horizon, as far as I could ascertain,
was the annual village school-treat. One simply filled in the time by
loafing about the grounds, playing a bit of tennis, and avoiding young
Bingo as far as was humanly possible.

This last was a very necessary move if you wanted a happy life,
for the Cynthia affair had jarred the unfortunate mutt to such an
extent that he was always waylaying one and decanting his anguished
soul. And when, one morning, he blew into my bedroom while I
was toying with a bit of breakfast, I decided to take a firm line from
the start. I could stand having him moaning all over me after dinner,
and even after lunch; but at breakfast, no. We Woosters are ami-
ability itself, but there is a limit.

'Now look here, old friend,' I said. 'I know your bally heart is
broken and all that, and at some future time I shall be delighted to
hear all about it, but – '

'I didn't come to talk about that.'

'No? Good egg!'

'The past,' said young Bingo, 'is dead. Let us say no more about
it.'

'Right-o!'

'I have been wounded to the very depths of my soul, but don't
speak about it.'

'I won't.'

'Ignore it. Forget it.'

'Absolutely!'

I hadn't seen him so dashed reasonable for days.

'What I came to see you about this morning, Bertie,' he said,
fishing a sheet of paper out of his pocket, 'was to ask if you would
care to come in on another little flutter.'

If there is one thing we Woosters are simply dripping with, it is sporting blood. I bolted the rest of my sausage, and sat up and took notice.

'Proceed,' I said. 'You interest me strangely, old bird.'

Bingo laid the paper on the bed.

'On Monday week,' he said, 'you may or may not know, the annual village school-treat takes place. Lord Wickhammersley lends the Hall grounds for the purpose. There will be games and a conjurer, and coco-nut shies, and tea in a tent. And also sports.'

'I know. Cynthia was telling me.'

Young Bingo winced.

'Would you mind not mentioning that name? I am not made of marble.'

'Sorry!'

'Well, as I was saying, this jamboree is slated for Monday week. The question is, Are we on?'

'How do you mean, "Are we on?"?'

'I am referring to the sports. Steggles did so well out of the Sermon Handicap that he has decided to make a book on these sports. Punters can be accommodated at ante-post odds or starting price, according to their preference. I think we ought to look into it,' said young Bingo.

I pressed the bell.

'I'll consult Jeeves. I don't touch any sporting proposition without his advice. Jeeves,' I said, as he drifted in, 'rally round.'

'Sir?'

'Stand by. We want your advice.'

'Very good, sir.'

'State your case, Bingo.'

Bingo stated his case.

'What about it, Jeeves?' I said. 'Do we go in?'

Jeeves pondered to some extent.

'I am inclined to favour the idea, sir.'

That was good enough for me. 'Right,' I said. 'Then we will form a syndicate and bust the Ring. I supply the money, you supply the brains, and Bingo – what do you supply, Bingo?'

'If you will carry me, and let me settle up later,' said young Bingo, 'I think I can put you in the way of winning a parcel on the Mothers' Sack Race.'

'All right. We will put you down as Inside Information. Now what are the events?'

Bingo reached for his paper and consulted it.

'Girls' Under Fourteen Fifty-Yard Dash seems to open the proceedings.'

'Anything to say about that, Jeeves?'

'No, sir. I have no information.'

'What's the next?'

'Boys' and Girls' Mixed Animal Potato Race, All Ages.'

This was a new one to me. I had never heard of it at any of the big meetings.

'What's that?'

'Rather sporting,' said young Bingo. 'The competitors enter in couples, each couple being assigned an animal cry and a potato. For instance, let's suppose that you and Jeeves entered. Jeeves would stand at a fixed point holding a potato. You would have your head in a sack, and you would grope about trying to find Jeeves and making a noise like a cat; Jeeves also making a noise like a cat. Other competitors would be making noises like cows and pigs and dogs, and so on, and groping about for *their* potato-holders, who would also be making noises like cows and pigs and dogs and so on – '

I stopped the poor fish.

'Jolly if you're fond of animals,' I said, 'but on the whole – '

'Precisely, sir,' said Jeeves. 'I wouldn't touch it.'

'Too open, what?'

'Exactly, sir. Very hard to estimate form.'

'Carry on, Bingo. Where do we go from there?'

'Mothers' Sack Race.'

'Ah! That's better. This is where you know something.'

'A gift for Mrs Penworthy, the tobacconist's wife,' said Bingo confidently. 'I was in at her shop yesterday, buying cigarettes, and she told me she had won three times at fairs in Worcestershire. She only moved to these parts a short time ago, so nobody knows about her. She promised me she would keep herself dark, and I think we could get a good price.'

'Risk a tenner each way, Jeeves, what?'

'I think so, sir.'

'Girls' Open Egg and Spoon Race,' read Bingo.

'How about that?'

'I doubt if it would be worthwhile to invest, sir,' said Jeeves. 'I am told it is a certainty for last year's winner, Sarah Mills, who will doubtless start an odds-on favourite.'

'Good, is she?'

'They tell me in the village that she carries a beautiful egg, sir.'

'Then there's the Obstacle Race,' said Bingo. 'Risky, in my opinion. Like betting on the Grand National. Fathers' Hat-Trimming Contest – another speculative event. That's all except for the Choir-Boys' Hundred Yards Handicap, for a pewter mug presented by the vicar – open to all whose voices have not broken before the second Sunday in Epiphany. Willie Chambers won last year, in a canter, receiving fifteen yards. This time he will probably be handicapped out of the race. I don't know what to advise.'

'If I might make a suggestion, sir.'

I eyed Jeeves with interest. I don't know that I'd ever seen him look so nearly excited.

'You've got something up your sleeve?'

'I have, sir.'

'Red-hot?'

'That precisely describes it, sir. I think I may confidently assert that we have the winner of the Choir-Boys' Handicap under this very roof, sir. Harold, the page-boy.'

'Page-boy? Do you mean the tubby little chap in buttons one sees bobbing about here and there? Why, dash it, Jeeves, nobody has a greater respect for your knowledge of form than I have, but I'm hanged if I can see Harold catching the judge's eye. He's practically circular, and every time I've seen him he's been leaning up against something, half asleep.'

'He receives thirty yards, sir, and could win from scratch. The boy is a flier.'

'How do you know?'

Jeeves coughed, and there was a dreamy look in his eye.

'I was as much astonished as yourself, sir, when I first became aware of the lad's capabilities. I happened to pursue him one morning with the intention of fetching him a clip on the side of the head – '

'Great Scott, Jeeves! You?'

'Yes, sir. The boy is of an outspoken disposition, and had made an opprobrious remark respecting my personal appearance.'

'What did he say about your appearance?'

'I have forgotten, sir,' said Jeeves, with a touch of austerity. 'But it was opprobrious. I endeavoured to correct him, but he outdistanced me by yards and made good his escape.'

'But, I say, Jeeves, this is sensational. And yet – if he's such a sprinter, why hasn't anybody in the village found it out? Surely he plays with the other boys?'

'No, sir. As his lordship's page-boy, Harold does not mix with the village lads.'

'Bit of a snob, what?'

'He is somewhat acutely alive to the existence of class distinctions, sir.'

'You're absolutely certain he's such a wonder?' said Bingo. 'I mean, it wouldn't do to plunge unless you're sure.'

'If you desire to ascertain the boy's form by personal inspection, sir, it will be a simple matter to arrange a secret trial.'

'I'm bound to say I should feel easier in my mind,' I said.

'Then if I may take a shilling from the money on your dressing-table – '

'What for?'

'I propose to bribe the lad to speak slightingly of the second footman's quint, sir. Charles is somewhat sensitive on the point, and should undoubtedly make the lad extend himself. If you will be at the first-floor passage-window, overlooking the back door, in half an hour's time – '

I don't know when I've dressed in such a hurry. As a rule, I'm what you might call a slow and careful dresser: I like to linger over the tie and see that the trousers are just so; but this morning I was all worked up. I just shoved on my things anyhow, and joined Bingo at the window with a quarter of an hour to spare.

The passage-window looked down on to a broad sort of paved courtyard, which ended after about twenty yards in an archway through a high wall. Beyond this archway you got to a strip of the drive, which curved round for another thirty yards or so, till it was lost behind a thick shrubbery. I put myself in the stripling's place and thought what steps I would take with a second footman after me. There was only one thing to do – leg it for the shrubbery and take cover; which meant that at least fifty yards would have to be covered – an excellent test. If good old Harold could fight off the second footman's challenge long enough to allow him to reach the bushes, there wasn't a choir-boy in England who could give him thirty yards in the hundred. I waited, all of a twitter, for what seemed like hours, and then suddenly there was a confused noise without, and something round and blue and buttony shot through the back door and buzzed for the archway like a mustang. And about two seconds later out came the second footman, going his hardest.

There was nothing to it. Absolutely nothing. The field never had a chance. Long before the footman reached the half-way mark, Harold was in the bushes, throwing stones. I came away from the window thrilled to the marrow; and when I met Jeeves on the stairs I was so moved that I nearly grasped his hand.

'Jeeves,' I said, 'no discussion! The Wooster shirt goes on this boy!'

'Very good, sir,' said Jeeves.

The worst of these country meetings is that you can't plunge as heavily as you would like when you get a good thing, because it alarms the Ring. Steggles, though pimpled, was, as I have indicated, no chump, and if I had invested all I wanted to he would have put two and two together. I managed to get a good solid bet down for the syndicate, however, though it did make him look thoughtful. I heard in the next few days that he had been making searching inquiries in the village concerning Harold; but nobody could tell him anything, and eventually he came to the conclusion, I suppose, that I must be having a long shot on the strength of that thirty-yards start. Public opinion wavered between Jimmy Goode, receiving ten yards, at seven-to-two, and Alexander Bartlett, with six yards start, at eleven-to-four. Willie Chambers, scratch, was offered to the public at two-to-one but found no takers.

We were taking no chances on the big event, and directly we had got our money on at a nice hundred-to-twelve, Harold was put into strict training. It was a wearing business, and I can understand now why most of the big trainers are grim, silent men, who look as though they had suffered. The kid wanted constant watching. It was no good talking to him about honour and glory and how proud his mother would be when he wrote and told her he had won a real cup – the moment blighted Harold discovered that training meant knocking off pastry, taking exercise, and keeping away from the cigarettes, he was all against it, and it was only by unceasing vigilance that we managed to keep him in any shape at all. It was the diet that was the stumbling-block. As far as exercise went, we could generally arrange for a sharp dash every morning with the assistance of the second footman. It ran into money, of course, but that couldn't be helped. Still, when a kid has simply to wait till the butler's back is turned to have the run of the pantry, and has only to nip into the smoking-room to collect a handful of the best Turkish, training becomes a rocky job. We could only hope that on the day his natural stamina would pull him through.

And then one evening young Bingo came back from the links with a disturbing story. He had been in the habit of giving Harold mild exercise in the afternoons by taking him out as a caddie.

At first he seemed to think it humorous, the poor chump! He bubbled over with merry mirth as he began his tale.

'I say, rather funny this afternoon,' he said. 'You ought to have seen Steggles's face.'

'Seen Steggles's face? What for?'

'When he saw young Harold sprint, I mean.'

I was filled with a grim foreboding of an awful doom.

'Good heavens! You didn't let Harold sprint in front of Steggles?'

Young Bingo's jaw dropped.

'I never thought of that,' he said, gloomily. 'It wasn't my fault. I was playing a round with Steggles, and after we'd finished we went into the club-house for a drink, leaving Harold with the clubs outside. In about five minutes we came out, and there was the kid on the gravel practising swings with Steggle's driver and a stone. When he saw us coming, the kid dropped the club and was over the horizon like a streak. Steggles was absolutely dumbfounded. And I must say it was a revelation to me. The kid certainly gave of his best. Of course, it's a nuisance in a way; but I don't see, on second thoughts,' said Bingo, brightening up, 'what it matters. We're in at a good price. We've nothing to lose by the kid's form becoming known. I take it he will start odds-on, but that doesn't affect us.'

I looked at Jeeves. Jeeves looked at me.

'It affects us all right if he doesn't start at all.'

'Precisely, sir.'

'What do you mean?' asked Bingo.

'If you ask me,' I said, 'I think Steggles will try to nobble him before the race.'

'Good Lord! I never thought of that!' Bingo blenched. 'You don't think he would really do it?'

'I think he would have a jolly good try. Steggles is a bad man. From now on, Jeeves, we must watch Harold like hawks.'

'Undoubtedly, sir.'

'Ceaseless vigilance, what?'

'Precisely, sir.'

'You wouldn't care to sleep in his room, Jeeves?'

'No, sir, I should not.'

'No, nor would I, if it comes to that. But dash it all,' I said, 'we're letting ourselves get rattled! We're losing our nerve. This won't do. How can Steggles possibly get at Harold, even if he wants to?'

There was no cheering young Bingo up. He's one of those birds who simply leap at the morbid view, if you give them half a chance.

'There are all sorts of ways of nobbling favourites,' he said, in a sort of death-bed voice. 'You ought to read some of the racing novels. In *Pipped on the Post* Lord Jasper Maulevereras near as a toucher outed Bonny Betsy by bribing the head lad to slip a cobra into her saddle the night before the Derby!'

'What are the chances of a cobra biting Harold, Jeeves?'

'Slight, I should imagine, sir. And in such an event, knowing the boy as intimately as I do, my anxiety would be entirely for the snake.'

'Still, unceasing vigilance, Jeeves.'

'Most certainly, sir.'

I must say I got a bit fed up with young Bingo in the next few days. It's all very well for a fellow with a big winner in his stable to exercise proper care, but in my opinion Bingo overdid it. The blighter's mind appeared to be absolutely saturated with racing fiction; and in stories of that kind, as far as I could make out, no horse is ever allowed to start in a race without at least a dozen attempts to put it out of action. He stuck to Harold like a plaster. Never let the unfortunate kid out of his sight. Of course, it meant a lot to the poor old egg if he could collect on this race, because it would give him enough money to chuck his tutoring job and get back to London; but all the same, he needn't have woken me up at three in the morning twice running – once to tell me we ought to cook Harold's food ourselves to prevent doping: the other time to say that he had heard mysterious noises in the shrubbery. But he reached the limit, in my opinion, when he insisted on my going to evening service on Sunday, the day before the sports.

'Why on earth?' I said, never being much of a lad for evensong.

'Well, I can't go myself. I shan't be here. I've got to go to London today with young Egbert.' Egbert was Lord Wickhammersley's son, the one Bingo was tutoring. 'He's going for a visit down in Kent, and I've got to see him off at Charing Cross. It's an infernal nuisance. I shan't be back till Monday afternoon. In fact, I shall miss most of the sports, I expect. Everything, therefore, depends on you, Bertie.'

'But why should either of us go to evening service?'

'Ass! Harold sings in the choir, doesn't he?'

'What about it? I can't stop him dislocating his neck over a high note, if that's what you're afraid of.'

'Fool! Steggles sings in the choir too. There may be dirty work after the service.'

'What absolute rot!'

'Is it?' said young Bingo. 'Well, let me tell you that in *Jenny, the Girl Jockey*, the villain kidnapped the boy who was to ride the favourite the night before the big race, and he was the only one who understood and could control the horse, and if the heroine hadn't dressed up in riding things and – '

'Oh, all right, all right. But, if there's any danger, it seems to me the simplest thing would be for Harold not to turn out on Sunday evening.'

'He must turn out. You seem to think the infernal kid is a monument of rectitude, beloved by all. He's got the shakiest reputation of any kid in the village. He's played hookey from the choir so often that the vicar told him, if one more thing happened, he would fire him out. Nice chumps we should look if he was scratched the night before the race!'

Well, of course, that being so, there was nothing for it but to toddle along.

There's something about evening service in a country church that makes a fellow feel drowsy and peaceful. Sort of end-of-a-perfect-day feeling. Old Heppenstall was up in the pulpit, and he has a kind of regular, bleating delivery that assists thought. They had left the door open, and the air was full of a mixed scent of trees and honeysuckle and mildew and villagers' Sunday clothes. As far as the eye could reach, you could see farmers propped up in restful attitudes, breathing heavily; and the children in the congregation who had fidgeted during the earlier part of the proceedings were now lying back in a surfeited sort of coma. The last rays of the setting sun shone through the stained-glass windows, birds were twittering in the trees, the women's dresses crackled gently in the stillness. Peaceful. That's what I'm driving at. I felt peaceful. Everybody felt peaceful. And that is why the explosion, when it came, sounded like the end of all things.

I call it an explosion, because that was what it seemed like when it broke loose. One moment a dreamy hush was all over the place, broken only by old Heppenstall talking about our duty to our neighbours; and then, suddenly, a sort of piercing, shrieking squeal that got you right between the eyes and ran all the way down your spine and out at the soles of your feet.

'EE-ee-ee-ee-ee! Oo-ee! Ee-ee-ee-ee!'

It sounded like about six hundred pigs having their tails twisted simultaneously, but it was simply the kid Harold, who appeared to be having some species of fit. He was jumping up and down and slapping at the back of his neck. And about every other second he would take a deep breath and give out another of the squeals.

Well, I mean, you can't do that sort of thing in the middle of the sermon during evening service without exciting remark. The congregation came out of its trance with a jerk, and climbed on the pews to get a better view. Old Heppenstall stopped in the middle of a sentence and spun round. And a couple of vergers with great presence of mind bounded up the aisle like leopards, collected Harold, still squealing, and marched him out. They disappeared into the vestry, and I grabbed my hat and legged it round to the stage-door, full of apprehension and what not. I couldn't think what the deuce could have happened, but somewhere dimly behind the proceedings there seemed to me to lurk the hand of the blighter Steggles.

By the time I got there and managed to get someone to open the door, which was locked, the service seemed to be over. Old Heppenstall was standing in the middle of a crowd of choir-boys and vergers and sextons and what not, putting the wretched Harold through it with no little vim. I had come in at the tail-end of what must have been a fairly fruity oration.

'Wretched boy! How dare you – '

'I got a sensitive skin!'

'This is no time to talk about your skin – '

'Somebody put a beetle down my back!'

'Absurd!'

'I felt it wriggling – '

'Nonsense!'

'Sounds pretty thin, doesn't it?' said someone at my side.

It was Steggles, dash him. Clad in a snowy surplice or cassock, or whatever they call it, and wearing an expression of grave concern, the blighter had the cold, cynical crust to look me in the eyeball without a blink.

'Did you put a beetle down his neck?' I cried.

'Me!' said Steggles. 'Me!'

Old Heppenstall was putting on the black cap.

'I do not credit a word of your story, wretched boy! I have warned you before, and now the time has come to act. You cease from this moment to be a member of my choir. Go, miserable child!'

Steggles plucked at my sleeve.

'In that case,' he said, 'those bets, you know – I'm afraid you lose your money, dear old boy. It's a pity you didn't put it on SP. I always think SP's the only safe way.'

I gave him one look. Not a bit of good, of course.

'And they talk about the Purity of the Turf!' I said. And I meant it to sting, by Jove!

Jeeves received the news bravely, but I think the man was a bit rattled beneath the surface.

'An ingenious young gentleman, Mr Steggles, sir.'

'A bally swindler, you mean.'

'Perhaps that would be a more exact description. However, these things will happen on the Turf, and it is useless to complain.'

'I wish I had your sunny disposition, Jeeves!'

Jeeves bowed.

'We now rely, then, it would seem, sir, almost entirely on Mrs Penworthy. Should she justify Mr Little's encomiums and show real class in the Mothers' Sack Race, our gains will just balance our losses.'

'Yes; but that's not much consolation when you've been looking forward to a big win.'

'It is just possible that we may still find ourselves on the right side of the ledger after all, sir. Before Mr Little left, I persuaded him to invest a small sum for the syndicate of which you were kind enough to make me a member, sir, on the Girls' Egg and Spoon Race.'

'On Sarah Mills?'

'No, sir. On a long-priced outsider. Little Prudence Baxter, sir, the child of his lordship's head gardener. Her father assures me she has a very steady hand. She is accustomed to bring him a mug of beer from the cottage each afternoon, and he informs me she has never spilled a drop.'

Well, that sounded as though young Prudence's control was good. But how about speed? With seasoned performers like Sarah Mills entered, the thing practically amounted to a classic race, and in these big events you must have speed.

'I am aware that it is what is termed a long shot,' sir. Still, I thought it judicious.'

'You backed here for a place, too, of course?'

'Yes, sir. Each way.'

'Well, I suppose it's all right. I've never known you make a bloomer yet.'

'Thank you very much, sir.'

I'm bound to say that, as a general rule, my idea of a large afternoon would be to keep as far away from a village school-treat as possible. A sticky business. But with such grave issues toward, if you know what I mean, I sank my prejudices on this occasion and rolled up. I found the proceedings about as scaly as I had expected. It was a warm day, and the hall grounds were a dense, practically liquid mass of peasantry. Kids seethed to and fro. One of them, a small girl of sorts, grabbed my hand and hung on to it as I clove my way through the jam to where the Mothers' Sack Race was to finish. We hadn't been introduced, but she seemed to think I would do as well as anyone else to talk to about the rag-doll she had won in the Lucky Dip, and she rather spread herself on the topic.

'I'm going to call it Gertrude,' she said. 'And I shall undress it every night and put it to bed, and wake it up in the morning and dress it, and put it to bed at night, and wake it up next morning and dress it – '

'I say, old thing,' I said, 'I don't want to hurry you and all that, but you couldn't condense it a bit, could you? I'm rather anxious to see the finish of this race. The Wooster fortunes are by way of hanging on it.'

'I'm going to run in a race soon,' she said, shelving the doll for the nonce and descending to ordinary chit-chat.

'Yes?' I said. Distrait, if you know what I mean, and trying to peer through the chinks in the crowd. 'What race is that?'

'Egg 'n' Spoon.'

'No really? Are you Sarah Mills?'

'Na-ow!' Registering scorn. 'I'm Prudence Baxter.'

Naturally this put our relations on a different footing. I gazed at her with considerable interest. One of the stable. I must say she didn't look much of a flier. She was short and round. Bit out of condition, I thought.

'I say,' I said, 'that being so, you mustn't dash about in the hot sun and take the edge off yourself. You must conserve your energies, old friend. Sit down here in the shade.'

'Don't want to sit down.'

'Well, take it easy, anyhow.'

The kid flitted to another topic like a butterfly hovering from flower to flower.

'I'm a good girl,' she said.

'I bet you are. I hope you're a good egg-and-spoon racer, too.'

'Harold's a bad boy. Harold squealed in church and isn't allowed to come to the treat. I'm glad,' continued this ornament of her sex, wrinkling her nose virtuously, 'because he's a bad boy. He pulled my hair, Friday. Harold isn't coming to the treat! Harold isn't coming to the treat! Harold isn't coming to the treat!' she chanted, making a regular song of it.

'Don't rub it in, my dear old gardener's daughter,' I pleaded. 'You don't know it, but you've hit on a rather painful subject.'

'Ah Wooster, my dear fellow! So you have made friends with this little lady?'

It was old Heppenstall, beaming pretty profusely. Life and soul of the party.

'I am delighted, my dear Wooster,' he went on, 'quite delighted at the way you young men are throwing yourselves into the spirit of this little festivity of ours.'

'Oh, yes?' I said.

'Oh, yes! Even Rupert Steggles. I must confess that my opinion of Rupert Steggles has materially altered for the better this afternoon.'

Mine hadn't. But I didn't say so.

'I have always considered Rupert Steggles, between ourselves, a rather self-centred youth, by no means the kind who would put himself out to further the enjoyment of his fellows. And yet twice within the last half-hour I have observed him escorting Mrs Penworthy, our worthy tobacconist's wife, to the refreshment.'

I left him standing. I shook off the clutching hand of the Baxter kid and hared it rapidly to the spot where the Mothers' Sack Race was just finishing. I had a horrid presentiment that there had been more dirty work at the crossroads. The first person I ran into was young Bingo. I grabbed him by the arm.

'Who won?'

'I don't know. I didn't notice.' There was bitterness in the chappie's voice. 'It wasn't Mrs Penworthy, dash her! Bertie, that hound Steggles is nothing more nor less than one of our leading snakes. I don't know how he heard about her, but he must have got on to it that she was dangerous. Do you know what he did? He lured that miserable woman into the refreshment-tent five minutes before the race and brought her out so weighed down with cake and tea that she blew up in the first twenty yards. Just rolled over and lay there! Well, thank goodness, we still have Harold!'

I gaped at the poor chump.

'Harold! Haven't you heard?'

'Heard?' Bingo turned a delicate green. 'Heard what? I haven't heard anything. I only arrived five minutes ago. Came here straight from the station. What has happened? Tell me!'

I slipped him the information. He stared at me for a moment in a ghastly sort of way, then with a hollow groan, tottered away and was lost in the crowd. A nasty knock, poor chap. I didn't blame him for being upset.

They were clearing the decks now for the Egg and Spoon Race, and I thought I might as well stay where I was and watch the finish. Not that I had much hope. Young Prudence was a good conversationalist, but she didn't seem to me to be the build for a winner.

As far as I could see through the mob, they got off to a good start. A short, red-haired child was making the running with a freckled blonde second, and Sarah Mills lying up an easy third. Our nominee was straggling along with the field, well behind the leaders. It was not hard even as early as this to spot the winner. There was a grace, a practised precision, in the way Sarah Mills held her spoon that told its own story. She was cutting out a good pace, but her egg didn't even wobble. A natural egg-and-spooner, if ever there was one.

Class will tell. Thirty yards from the tape, the red-haired kid tripped over her feet and shot her egg on to the turf. The freckled blonde fought gamely, but she had run herself out half-way down the straight, and Sarah Mills came past and home on a tight rein by several lengths, a popular winner. The blonde was second. A sniffing female in blue gingham beat a pie-faced kid in pink for the place-money, and Prudence Baxter, Jeeves's long shot, was either fifth or sixth, I couldn't see which.

And then I was carried along with the crowd to where old Heppenstall was going to present the prizes. I found myself standing next to the man Steggles.

'Hallo, old chap!' he said, very bright and cheery. 'You've had a bad day, I'm afraid.'

I looked at him with silent scorn. Lost on the blighter, of course.

'It's not been a good meeting for any of the big punters,' he went on. 'Poor old Bingo Little went down badly over that Egg and Spoon Race.'

I hadn't been meaning to chat with the fellow, but I was startled.

'How do you mean badly?' I said. 'We – he only had a small bet on.'

'I don't know what you call small. He had thirty quid each way on the Baxter kid.'

The landscape reeled before me.

'What!'

'Thirty quid at ten to one. I thought he must have heard something, but apparently not. The race went by the form-book all right.'

I was trying to do sums in my head. I was just in the middle of working out the syndicate's losses, when old Heppenstall's voice came sort of faintly to me out of the distance. He had been pretty fatherly and debonair when ladling out the prizes for the other events, but now he had suddenly grown all pained and grieved. He peered sorrowfully at the multitude.

'With regard to the Girls' Egg and Spoon Race, which has just concluded,' he said, 'I have a painful duty to perform. Circumstances have arisen which it is impossible to ignore. It is not too much to say that I am stunned.'

He gave the populace about five seconds to wonder why he was stunned, then went on.

'Three years ago, as you are aware, I was compelled to expunge from the list of events at this annual festival the Fathers' Quarter-Mile, owing to reports coming to my ears of wagers taken and given on the result at the village inn and a strong suspicion that on at least one occasion the race had actually been sold by the speediest runner. That unfortunate occurrence shook my faith in human nature, I admit – but still there was one event at least which I confidently expected to remain untainted by the miasma of professionalism. I allude to the Girls' Egg and Spoon Race. It seems, alas, that I was too sanguine.'

He stopped again, and wrestled with his feelings.

'I will not weary you with the unpleasant details. I will merely say that before the race was run a stranger in our midst, the manservant of one of the guests at the Hall – I will not specify with more particularity – approached several of the competitors and presented each of them with five shillings on condition that they – er – finished. A belated sense of remorse has led him to confess to me what he did, but it is too late. The evil is accomplished, and retribution must take its course. It is no time for half-measures. I must be firm. I rule that Sarah Mills, Jane Parker, Bessie Clay, and Rosie Jukes, the first four to pass the winning-post, have forfeited their amateur status and are disqualified, and this handsome work-bag, presented by Lord Wickhammersley, goes, in consequence, to Prudence Baxter. Prudence, step forward!'

15

The Metropolitan Touch

Nobody is more alive than I am to the fact that young Bingo Little is in many respects a sound old egg. In one way and another he has made life pretty interesting for me at intervals ever since we were at school. As a companion for a cheery hour I think I would choose him before anybody. On the other hand, I'm bound to say that there are things about him that could be improved. His habit of falling in love with every second girl he sees is one of them; and another is his way of letting the world in on the secrets of his heart. If you want shrinking reticence, don't go to Bingo, because he's got about as much of it as a soap advertisement.

I mean to say – well, here's the telegram I got from him one evening in November, about a month after I'd got back to town from my visit to Twing Hall:

> *I say Bertie old man I am in love at last. She is the most wonderful girl Bertie old man. This is the real thing at last Bertie. Come here at once and bring Jeeves. Oh I say you know that tobacco shop in Bond Street on the left side as you go up. Will you get me a hundred of their special cigarettes and send them to me here. I have run out. I know when you see her you will think she is the most wonderful girl. Mind you bring Jeeves. Don't forget the cigarettes.*
>
> BINGO.

It had been handed in at Twing Post Office. In other words, he had submitted that frightful rot to the goggling eye of a village post-mistress who was probably the mainspring of local gossip and would have the place ringing with the news before nightfall. He couldn't have given himself away more completely if he had hired the town crier. When I was a kid, I used to read stories about knights and vikings and that species of chappie who would get up without a blush in the middle of a crowded banquet and loose off a song about how perfectly priceless they thought their best girl. I've often felt that those days would have suited young Bingo down to the ground.

Jeeves had brought the thing in with the evening drink, and I slung it over to him.

'It's about due, of course,' I said. 'Young Bingo hasn't been in love for at least a couple of months. I wonder who it is this time?'

'Miss Mary Burgess, sir,' said Jeeves, 'the niece of the Reverend Mr Heppenstall. She is staying at Twing Vicarage.'

'Great Scott!' I knew that Jeeves knew practically everything in the world, but this sounded like second-sight. 'How do you know that?'

'When we were visiting Twing Hall in the summer, sir, I formed a somewhat close friendship with Mr Heppenstall's butler. He is good enough to keep me abreast of the local news from time to time. From his account, sir, the young lady appears to be a very estimable young lady. Of a somewhat serious nature, I understand. Mr Little is very *épris*, sir. Brookfield, my correspondent, writes that last week he observed him in the moonlight at an advanced hour gazing up at his window.'

'Whose window! Brookfield's?'

'Yes, sir. Presumably under the impression that it was the young lady's.'

'But what the deuce is he doing at Twing at all?'

'Mr Little was compelled to resume his old position as tutor to Lord Wickhammersley's son at Twing Hall, sir. Owing to having been unsuccessful in some speculations at Hurst Park at the end of October.'

'Good Lord, Jeeves! Is there anything you don't know?'

'I couldn't say, sir.'

I picked up the telegram.

'I suppose he wants us to go down and help him out a bit?'

'That would appear to be his motive in dispatching the message, sir.'

'Well, what shall we do? Go?'

'I would advocate it, sir. If I may say so, I think that Mr Little should be encouraged in this particular matter.'

'You think he's picked a winner this time?'

'I hear nothing but excellent reports of the young lady, sir. I think it is beyond question that she would be an admirable influence for Mr Little, should the affair come to a happy conclusion. Such a union would also, I fancy, go far to restore Mr Little to the good graces of his uncle, the young lady being well connected and possessing private means. In short, sir, I think that if there is anything that we can do we should do it.'

'Well, with you behind him,' I said, 'I don't see how he can fail to click.'

'You are very good, sir,' said Jeeves. 'The tribute is much appreciated.'

Bingo met us at Twing station next day, and insisted on my sending Jeeves on in the car with the bags while he and I walked. He started in about the female the moment we had begun to hoof it.

'She is very wonderful, Bertie. She is not one of these flippant, shallow-minded modern girls. She is sweetly grave and beautifully earnest. She reminds me of – what is the name I want?'

'Marie Lloyd?'

'Saint Cecilia,' said young Bingo, eyeing me with a good deal of loathing. 'She reminds me of Saint Cecilia. She makes me yearn to be a better, nobler, deeper, broader man.'

'What beats me,' I said, following up a train of thought, 'is what principle you pick them on. The girls you fall in love with, I mean. I mean to say, what's your system? As far as I can see, no two of them are alike. First it was Mabel the waitress, then Honoria Glossop, then that fearful blister Charlotte Corday Rowbotham – '

I own that Bingo had the decency to shudder. Thinking of Charlotte always made me shudder, too.

'You don't seriously mean, Bertie, that you are intending to compare the feeling I have for Mary Burgess, the holy devotion, the spiritual – '

'Oh, all right, let it go,' I said. 'I say, old lad, aren't we going rather a long way round?'

Considering that we were supposed to be heading for Twing Hall, it seemed to me that we were making a longish job of it. The Hall is about two miles from the station by the main road, and we had cut off down a lane, gone across country for a bit, climbed a stile or two, and were now working our way across a field that ended in another lane.

'She sometimes takes her little brother for a walk round this way,' explained Bingo. 'I thought we would meet her and bow, and you could see her, you know, and then we would walk on.'

'Of course,' I said, 'that's enough excitement for anyone, and undoubtedly a corking reward for tramping three miles out of one's way over ploughed fields with tight boots, but don't we do anything else? Don't we tack on to the girl and buzz along with her?'

'Good Lord!' said Bingo, honestly amazed. 'You don't suppose I've got nerve enough for that, do you? I just look at her from afar off and all that sort of thing. Quick! Here she comes! No, I'm wrong!'

It was like that song of Harry Lauder's where he's waiting for the girl and says 'This is her-r-r. No, it's a rabbut.' Young Bingo made me stand there in the teeth of a nor'-east half-gale for ten minutes, keeping me on my toes with a series of false alarms, and I was just thinking of suggesting that we should lay off and give the rest of the proceedings a miss, when round the corner there came a fox-terrier, and Bingo quivered like an aspen. Then there hove in sight a small boy, and he shook like a jelly. Finally, like a star whose entrance has been worked up by the *personnel* of the *ensemble*, a girl appeared, and his emotion was painful to witness. His face got so red that, what with his white collar and the fact that the wind had turned his nose blue, he looked more like a French flag than anything else. He sagged from the waist upwards, as if he had been filleted.

He was just raising his fingers limply to his cap when he suddenly saw that the girl wasn't alone. A chappie in clerical costume was also among those present, and the sight of him didn't seem to do Bingo a bit of good. His face got redder and his nose bluer, and it wasn't till they had nearly passed that he managed to get hold of his cap.

The girl bowed, the curate said, 'Ah, Little. Rough weather,' the dog barked, and then they toddled on and the entertainment was over.

The curate was a new factor in the situation to me. I reported his movements to Jeeves when I got to the Hall. Of course, Jeeves knew all about it already.

'That is the Reverend Mr Wingham, Mr Heppenstall's new curate, sir. I gathered from Brookfield that he is Mr Little's rival, and at the moment the young lady appears to favour him. Mr Wingham has the advantage of being on the premises. He and the young lady play duets after dinner, which acts as a bond. Mr Little on these occasions, I understand, prowls about in the road, chafing visibly.'

'That seems to be all the poor fish is able to do, dash it. He can chafe all right, but there he stops. He's lost his pep. He's got no dash. Why, when we met her just now, he hadn't even the common manly courage to say "Good evening"!'

'I gather that Mr Little's affection is not unmingled with awe, sir.'

'Well, how are we to help a man when he's such a rabbit as that? Have you anything to suggest? I shall be seeing him after dinner, and he's sure to ask first thing what you advise.'

'In my opinion, sir, the most judicious course for Mr Little to pursue would be to concentrate on the young gentleman.'

'The small brother? How do you mean?'

'Make a friend of him, sir – take him for walks and so forth.'

'It doesn't sound one of your red-hottest ideas. I must say I expected something fruitier than that.'

'It would be a beginning, sir, and might lead to better things.'

'Well, I'll tell him. I liked the look of her, Jeeves.'

'A thoroughly estimable young lady, sir.'

I slipped Bingo the tip from the stable that night, and was glad to observe that it seemed to cheer him up.

'Jeeves is always right,' he said. 'I ought to have thought of it myself. I'll start in tomorrow.'

It was amazing how the chappie bucked up. Long before I left for town it had become a mere commonplace for him to speak to the girl. I mean he didn't simply look stuffed when they met. The brother was forming a bond that was a dashed sight stronger than the curate's duets. She and Bingo used to take him for walks together. I asked Bingo what they talked about on these occasions, and he said Wilfred's future. The girl hoped that Wilfred would one day become a curate, but Bingo said no, there was something about curates he didn't quite like.

The day we left, Bingo came to see us off with Wilfred frisking about him like an old college chum. The last I saw of them, Bingo was standing him chocolates out of the slot-machine. A scene of peace and cheery goodwill. Dashed promising, I thought.

Which made it all the more of a jar, about a fortnight later, when his telegram arrived. As follows:

> Bertie old man I say Bertie could you possibly come down here at once. Everything gone wrong hang it all. Dash it Bertie you simply must come. I am in a state of absolute despair and heart-broken. Would you mind sending another hundred of those cigarettes. Bring

Jeeves when you come Bertie. You simply must come Bertie. I rely on you. Don't forget to bring Jeeves.

BINGO.

For a chap who's perpetually hard-up, I must say that young Bingo is the most wasteful telegraphist I ever struck. He's got no notion of condensing. The silly ass simply pours out his wounded soul at twopence a word, or whatever it is, without a thought.

'How about it, Jeeves?' I said. 'I'm getting a bit fed. I can't go chucking all my engagements every second week in order to biff down to Twing and rally round young Bingo. Send him a wire telling him to end it all in the village pond.'

'If you could spare me for the night, sir, I should be glad to run down and investigate.'

'Oh, dash it! Well, I suppose there's nothing else to be done. After all, you're the fellow he wants. All right, carry on.'

Jeeves got back late the next day.

'Well?' I said.

Jeeves appeared perturbed. He allowed his left eyebrow to flicker upwards in a concerned sort of manner.

'I have done what I could, sir,' he said, 'but I fear Mr Little's chances do not appear bright. Since our last visit, sir, there has been a decidedly sinister and disquieting development.'

'Oh, what's that?'

'You may remember Mr Steggles, sir – the young gentleman who was studying for an examination with Mr Heppenstall at the Vicarage?'

'What's Steggles got to do with it?' I asked.

'I gather from Brookfield, sir, who chanced to overhear a conversation, that Mr Steggles is interesting himself in the affair.'

'Good Lord! What, making a book on it?'

'I understand that he is accepting wagers from those in his immediate circle, sir. Against Mr Little, whose chances he does not seem to fancy.'

'I don't like that, Jeeves.'

'No, sir. It is sinister.'

'From what I know of Steggles there will be dirty work.'

'It has already occurred, sir.'

'Already?'

'Yes, sir. It seems that, in pursuance of the policy which he has been good enough to allow me to suggest to him, Mr Little escorted

Master Burgess to the church bazaar, and there met Mr Steggles, who was in the company of young Master Heppenstall, the Reverend Mr Heppenstall's second son, who is home from Rugby just now, having recently recovered from an attack of mumps. The encounter took place in the refreshment-room, where Mr Steggles was at that moment entertaining Master Heppenstall. To cut a long story short, sir, the two gentlemen became extremely interested in the hearty manner in which the lads were fortifying themselves; and Mr Steggles offered to back his nominee in a weight-for-age eating contest against Master Burgess for a pound a side. Mr Little admitted to me that he was conscious of a certain hesitation as to what the upshot might be, should Miss Burgess get to hear of the matter, but his sporting blood was too much for him and he agreed to the contest. This was duly carried out, both lads exhibiting the utmost willingness and enthusiasm, and eventually Master Burgess justified Mr Little's confidence by winning, but only after a bitter struggle. Next day both contestants were in considerable pain; inquiries were made and confessions extorted, and Mr Little – I learn from Brookfield, who happened to be near the door of the drawing-room at the moment – had an extremely unpleasant interview with the young lady, which ended in her desiring him never to speak to her again.'

There's no getting away from the fact that, if ever a man required watching, it's Steggles. Machiavelli could have taken his correspondence course.

'It was a put-up job, Jeeves!' I said. 'I mean, Steggles worked the whole thing on purpose. It's his old nobbling game.'

'There would seem to be no doubt about that, sir.'

'Well, he seems to have dished poor old Bingo all right.'

'That is the prevalent opinion, sir. Brookfield tells me that down in the village at the Cow and Horses seven to one is being freely offered on Mr Wingham and finding no takers.'

'Good Lord! Are they betting about it down in the village, too?'

'Yes, sir. And in adjoining hamlets also. The affair has caused widespread interest. I am told that there is a certain sporting reaction in even so distant a spot as Lower Bingley.'

'Well, I don't see what there is to do. If Bingo is such a chump – '

'One is fighting a losing battle, I fear, sir, but I did venture to indicate to Mr Little a course of action which might prove of advantage. I recommended him to busy himself with good works.'

'Good works?'

'About the village, sir. Reading to the bedridden – chatting with the sick – that sort of thing, sir. We can but trust that good results will ensue.'

'Yes, I suppose so,' I said doubtfully. 'But, by gosh, if I was a sick man I'd hate to have a loony like young Bingo coming and gibbering at my bedside.'

'There *is* that aspect of the matter, sir,' said Jeeves.

I didn't hear a word from Bingo for a couple of weeks, and I took it after while that he had found the going too hard and had chucked in the towel. And then, one night not long before Christmas, I came back to the flat pretty latish, having been out dancing at the Embassy. I was fairly tired, having swung a practically non-stop shoe from shortly after dinner till two AM, and bed seemed to be indicated. Judge of my chagrin and all that sort of thing, therefore, when, tottering to my room and switching on the light, I observed the foul features of young Bingo all over the pillow. The blighter had appeared from nowhere and was in my bed, sleeping like an infant with a sort of happy, dreamy smile on his map.

A bit thick I mean to say! We Woosters are all for the good old medieval hosp. and all that, but when it comes to finding chappies collaring your bed, the thing becomes a trifle too mouldy. I hove a shoe, and Bingo sat up, gurgling.

"'s matter? 's matter?' said young Bingo.

'What the deuce are you doing in my bed?' I said.

'Oh, hallo, Bertie! So there you are!'

'Yes, here I am. What are you doing in my bed?'

'I came up to town for the night on business.'

'Yes, but what are you doing in my bed?'

'Dash it all, Bertie,' said young Bingo querulously, 'don't keep harping on your beastly bed. There's another made up in the spare room. I saw Jeeves make it with my own eyes. I believe he meant it for me, but I knew what a perfect host you were, so I just turned in here. I say, Bertie, old man,' said Bingo, apparently fed up with the discussion about sleeping-quarters, 'I see daylight.'

'Well, it's getting on for three in the morning.'

'I was speaking figuratively, you ass. I meant that hope has begun to dawn. About Mary Burgess, you know. Sit down and I'll tell you all about it.'

'I won't. I'm going to sleep.'

'To begin with,' said young Bingo, settling himself comfortably against the pillows and helping himself to a cigarette from my private box, 'I must once again pay a marked tribute to good old Jeeves. A modern Solomon. I was badly up against it when I came to him for advice, but he rolled up with a tip which has put me – I use the term advisedly and in a conservative spirit – on velvet. He may have told you that he recommended me to win back the lost ground by busying myself with good works? Bertie, old man,' said young Bingo earnestly, 'for the last two weeks I've been comforting the sick to such an extent that, if I had a brother and you brought him to me on a sick-bed at this moment, by Jove, old man, I'd heave a brick at him. However, though it took it out of me like the deuce, the scheme worked splendidly. She softened visibly before I'd been at it a week. Started to bow again when we met in the street, and so forth. About a couple of days ago she distinctly smiled – in a sort of faint, saint-like kind of way, you know – when I ran into her outside the Vicarage. And yesterday – I say, you remember that curate chap, Wingham? Fellow with a long nose.'

'Of course I remember him. Your rival.'

'Rival?' Bingo raised his eyebrows. 'Oh, well, I suppose you could have called him that at one time. Though it sounds a little far-fetched.'

'Does it?' I said, stung by the sickening complacency of the chump's manner. 'Well, let me tell you that the last I heard was that at the Cow and Horses in Twing village and all over the place as far as Lower Bingley they were offering seven to one on the curate and finding no takers.'

Bingo started violently and sprayed cigarette-ash all over my bed.

'Betting!' he gargled. 'Betting! You don't mean that they're betting on this holy, sacred . . . Oh, I say, dash it all! Haven't people any sense of decency and reverence? Is nothing safe from their beastly, sordid graspingness? I wonder,' said young Bingo thoughtfully, 'if there's a chance of my getting any of that seven-to-one money? Seven to one! What a price! Who's offering it, do you know? Oh, well, I suppose it wouldn't do. No, I suppose it wouldn't be quite the thing.'

'You seem, dashed confident,' I said. 'I'd always thought that Wingham – '

'Oh, I'm not worried about him,' said Bingo. 'I was just going to tell you. Wingham's got the mumps, and won't be out and about for weeks. And, jolly as that is in itself, it's not all. You see, he was producing the Village School Christmas Entertainment, and now I've taken over the job. I went to old Heppenstall last night and clinched the contract. Well, you see what that means. It means that I shall be absolutely the centre of the village life and thought for three solid weeks, with a terrific triumph to wind up with. Everybody looking up to me and fawning on me, don't you see, and all that. It's bound to have a powerful effect on Mary's mind. It will show her that I am capable of serious effort; that there is a solid foundation of worth in me; that, mere butterfly as she may once have thought me, I am in reality – '

'Oh, all right, let it go!'

'It's a big thing, you know, this Christmas Entertainment. Old Heppenstall is very much wrapped up in it. Nibs from all over the countryside rolling up. The Squire present, with family. A big chance for me, Bertie, my boy, and I mean to make the most of it. Of course, I'm handicapped a bit by not having been in on the thing from the start. Will you credit it that that uninspired doughnut of a curate wanted to give the public some rotten little fairy play out of a book for children published about fifty years ago without one good laugh or the semblance of a gag in it? It's too late to alter the thing entirely, but at least I can jazz it up. I'm going to write them in something zippy to brighten the thing up a bit.'

'You can't write.'

'Well, when I say write, I mean pinch. That's why I've popped up to town. I've been to see that revue, *Cuddle Up!* at the Palladium, tonight. Full of good stuff. Of course, it's rather hard to get anything in the nature of a big spectacular effect in the Twing Village Hall, with no scenery to speak of and a chorus of practically imbecile kids of ages ranging from nine to fourteen, but I think I see my way. Have you seen *Cuddle Up!?*'

'Yes. Twice.'

'Well, there's some good stuff in the first act, and I can lift practically all the numbers. Then there's that show at the Palace. I can see the *matinée* of that tomorrow before I leave. There's sure to be some decent bits in that. Don't you worry about my not being able to write a hit. Leave it to me, laddie, leave it to me. And now, my dear old chap,' said young Bingo, snuggling down cosily, 'you mustn't keep me up talking all night. It's all right for you fellows who have nothing to do, but I'm a busy man. Good night, old thing. Close the door quietly after you and switch out the light. Breakfast, about ten tomorrow, I suppose, what? Right-o. Good night.'

For the next three weeks I didn't see Bingo. He became a sort of

Voice Heard Off, developing a habit of ringing me up on long-distance and consulting me on various points arising at rehearsal, until the day when he got me out of bed at eight in the morning to ask whether I thought *Merry Christmas!* was a good title. I told him then that this nuisance must now cease, and after that he cheesed it, and practically passed out of my life, till one afternoon when I got back to the flat to dress for dinner and found Jeeves inspecting a whacking big poster sort of thing which he had draped over the back of an armchair.

'Good Lord, Jeeves!' I said. I was feeling rather weak that day, and the thing shook me. 'What on earth's that?'

'Mr Little sent it to me, sir, and desired me to bring it to your notice.'

'Well, you've certainly done it!'

I took another look at the object. There was no doubt about it, he caught the eye. It was about seven feet long, and most of the lettering in about as bright red ink as I ever struck.

This was how it ran:

Twing Village Hall,
Friday, December 23rd,
Richard Little
presents
A New and Original Revue
Entitled
What Ho, Twing!!
Book by
Richard Little
Lyrics by
Richard Little
Music by
Richard Little
With the Full Twing Juvenile
Company and Chorus.
Scenic Effects by
Richard Little
Produced by
Richard Little

'What do you make of it, Jeeves?' I said.

'I confess I am a little doubtful, sir. I think Mr Little would have done better to follow my advice and confine himself to good works about the village.'

'You think the thing will be a frost?'

'I could not hazard a conjecture, sir. But my experience has been that what pleases the London public is not always so acceptable to the rural mind. The metropolitan touch sometimes proves a trifle too exotic for the provinces.'

'I suppose I ought to go down and see the dashed thing?'

'I think Mr Little would be wounded were you not present, sir.'

The Village Hall at Twing is a smallish building, smelling of apples. It was full when I turned up on the evening of the twenty-third, for I had purposely timed myself to arrive not long before the kick-off. I had had experience of onc or two of these binges, and didn't want to run any risk of coming early and finding myself shoved into a seat in one of the front rows where I wouldn't be able to execute a quiet sneak into the open air half-way through the proceedings, if the occasion seemed to demand it. I secured a nice strategic position near the door at the back of the hall.

From where I stood I had a good view of the audience. As always on these occasions, the first few rows were occupied by the Nibs – consisting of the Squire, a fairly mauve old sportsman with white whiskers, his family, a platoon of local parsons and perhaps a couple of dozen of prominent pew-holders. Then came a dense squash of what you might call the lower middle classes. And at the back, where I was, we came down with a jerk in the social scale, this end of the hall being given up almost entirely to a collection of frankly Tough Eggs, who had rolled up not so much for any love of the drama as because there was a free tea after the show. Take it for all in all, a representative gathering of Twing life and thought. The Nibs were whispering in a pleased manner to each other, the Lower Middles were sitting up very straight, as if they'd been bleached, and the Tough Eggs whiled away the time by cracking nuts and exchanging low rustic wheezes. The girl, Mary Burgess, was at the piano playing a waltz. Beside her stood the curate, Wingham, apparently recovered. The temperature, I should think, was about a hundred and twenty-seven.

Somebody jabbed me heartily in the lower ribs, and I perceived the man Steggles.

'Hallo!' he said. 'I didn't know you were coming down.'

I didn't like the chap, but we Woosters can wear the mask. I beamed a bit.

'Oh, yes,' I said. 'Bingo wanted me to roll up and see his show.'

'I hear he's giving us something pretty ambitious,' said the man Steggles. 'Big effects and all that sort of thing.'

'I believe so.'

'Of course, it means a lot to him, doesn't it? He's told you about the girl, of course?'

'Yes. And I hear you're laying seven to one against him,' I said, eyeing the blighter a trifle austerely.

He didn't even quiver.

'Just a little flutter to relieve the monotony of country life,' he said. 'But you've got the facts a bit wrong. It's down in the village that they're laying seven to one. I can do you better than that, if you feel in a speculative mood. How about a tenner at a hundred to eight?'

'Good Lord! Are you giving that?'

'Yes. Somehow,' said Steggles meditatively, 'I have a sort of feeling, a kind of premonition that something's going to go wrong tonight. You know what Little is. A bungler, if ever there was one. Something tells me that this show of his is going to be a frost. And if it is, of course, I should think it would prejudice the girl against him pretty badly. His standing always was rather shaky.'

'Are you going to try and smash up the show?' I said sternly.

'Me!' said Steggles. 'Why, what could I do? Half a minute, I want to go and speak to a man.'

He buzzed off, leaving me distinctly disturbed. I could see from the fellow's eye that he was meditating some of his customary rough stuff, and I thought Bingo ought to be warned. But there wasn't time and I couldn't get at him. Almost immediately after Steggles had left me the curtain went up.

Except as a prompter, Bingo wasn't much in evidence in the early part of the performance. The thing at the outset was merely one of those weird dramas which you dig out of books published around Christmas time and entitled *Twelve Little Plays for the Tots*, or something like that. The kids drooled on in the usual manner, the booming voice of Bingo ringing out from time to time behind the scenes when the fatheads forgot their lines; and the audience was settling down into the sort of torpor usual on these occasions, when the first of Bingo's interpolated bits occurred. It was that number which What's-her-name sings in that revue at the Palace – you would recognize the tune if I hummed it, but I can never get hold of the dashed thing. It always got three encores at the Palace, and it went well now, even with a squeaky-voiced child jumping on and off the key like a chamois of the Alps leaping from crag to crag. Even the Tough Eggs liked it. At the end of the second refrain the entire house was shouting for an encore, and the kid with the voice like a slate-pencil took a deep breath and started to let it go once more.

At this point all the lights went out.

I don't know when I've had anything so sudden and devastating happen to me before. They didn't flicker. They just went out. The hall was in complete darkness.

Well, of course, that sort of broke the spell, as you might put it. People started to shout directions, and the Tough Eggs stamped their feet and settled down for a pleasant time. And, of course, young Bingo had to make an ass of himself. His voice suddenly shot at us out of the darkness.

'Ladies and gentlemen, something has gone wrong with the lights – '

The Tough Eggs were tickled by this bit of information straight from the stable. They took it up as a sort of battle-cry. Then, after about five minutes, the lights went up again, and the show was resumed.

It took ten minutes after that to get the audience back into its state of coma, but eventually they began to settle down, and everything was going nicely when a small boy with a face like a turbot edged out in front of the curtain, which had been lowered after a pretty painful scene about a wishing-ring or a fairy's curse or something of that sort, and started to sing that song of George Thingummy's out of *Cuddle Up!* You know the one I mean. 'Always Listen to Mother, Girls!' it's called, and he gets the audience to join in and sing the refrain. Quite a ripeish ballad, and one which I myself have frequently sung in my bath with not a little vim; but by no means – as anyone but a perfect sapheaded prune like young Bingo would have known – by no means the sort of thing for a children's Christmas entertainment in the old village hall. Right from the start of the first refrain the bulk of the audience had begun to stiffen in their seats and fan themselves, and the Burgess girl at the piano was accompanying in a stunned, mechanical sort of way, while the curate at her side averted his gaze in a pained manner. The Tough Eggs, however, were all for it.

At the end of the second refrain the kid stopped and began to sidle towards the wings. Upon which the following brief duologue took place:

YOUNG BINGO (*Voice heard, off, ringing against the rafters*): 'Go on!'

THE KID (*coyly*): 'I don't like to.'

YOUNG BINGO (*still louder*): 'Go on, you little blighter, or I'll slay you!'

I suppose the kid thought it over swiftly and realized that Bingo, being in a position to get at him, had better be conciliated, whatever the harvest might be; for he shuffled down to the front and, having shut his eyes and giggled hysterically, said: 'Ladies and gentlemen, I will now call upon Squire Tressidder to oblige by singing the refrain!'

You know, with the most charitable feelings towards him, there are moments when you can't help thinking that young Bingo ought to be in some sort of a home. I suppose, poor fish, he had pictured this as the big punch of the evening. He had imagined, I take it, that the Squire would spring jovially to his feet, rip the song off his chest, and all would be gaiety and mirth. Well, what happened was simply that old Tressidder – and, mark you, I'm not blaming him – just sat where he was, swelling and turning a brighter purple every second. The lower middle classes remained in frozen silence, waiting for the roof to fall. The only section of the audience that really seemed to enjoy the idea was the Tough Eggs, who yelled with enthusiasm. It was jam for the Tough Eggs.

And then the lights went out again.

When they went up, some minutes later, they disclosed the Squire marching stiffly out at the head of his family, fed up to the eyebrows; the Burgess girl at the piano with a pale, set look; and the curate gazing at her with something in his expression that seemed to suggest that, although all this was no doubt deplorable, he had spotted the silver lining.

The show went on once more. There were great chunks of Plays-for-the-Tots dialogue, and then the girl at the piano struck up the prelude to that Orange-Girl number that's the big hit of the Palace revue. I took it that this was to be Bingo's smashing act one finale. The entire company was on the stage, and a clutching hand had appeared round the edge of the curtain, ready to pull at the right moment. It looked like the finale all right. It wasn't long before I realized that it was something more. It was the finish.

I take it you know that Orange number at the Palace? It goes:

Oh, won't you something something oranges,
  My something oranges,
  My something oranges;
Oh, won't you something something something I forget,
Something something something tumty tumty yet:
Oh –

or words to that effect. It's a dashed clever lyric, and the tune's good, too; but the thing that made the number was the business where the girls take oranges out of their baskets, you know, and toss them lightly to the audience. I don't know if you've ever noticed it, but it always seems to tickle an audience to bits when they get things thrown at them from the stage. Every time I've been to the Palace the customers have simply gone wild over this number.

But at the Palace, of course, the oranges are made of yellow wool, and the girls don't so much chuck them as drop them limply into the first and second rows. I began to gather that the business was going to be treated rather differently tonight when a dashed great chunk of pips and mildew sailed past my ear and burst on the wall behind me. Another landed with a squelch on the neck of one of the Nibs in the third row. And then a third took me right on the tip of the nose, and I kind of lost interest in the proceedings for a while.

When I had scrubbed my face and got my eye to stop watering for a moment, I saw that the evening's entertainment had begun to resemble one of Belfast's livelier nights. The air was thick with shrieks and fruit. The kids on the stage, with Bingo buzzing distractedly to and fro in their midst, were having the time of their lives. I suppose they realized that this couldn't go on for ever, and were making the most of their chances. The Tough Eggs had begun to pick up all the oranges that hadn't burst and were shooting them back, so that the audience got it both coming and going. In fact, take it all round, there was a certain amount of confusion; and, just as things had begun really to hot up, out went the lights again.

It seemed to me about my time for leaving, so I slid for the door. I was hardly outside when the audience began to stream out. They surged about me in twos and threes, and I've never seen a public body so dashed unanimous on any point. To a man – and to a woman – they were cursing poor old Bingo; and there was a large and rapidly growing school of thought which held that the best thing to do would be to waylay him as he emerged and splash him about in the village pond a bit.

There were such a dickens of a lot of these enthusiasts and they looked so jolly determined that it seemed to me that the only matey thing to do was to go behind and warn young Bingo to turn his coat-collar up and breeze off snakily by some side exit. I went behind, and found him sitting on a box in the wings, perspiring pretty freely and looking more or less like the spot marked with a cross where the accident happened. His hair was standing up and his ears were hanging down, and one harsh word would undoubtedly have made him burst into tears.

'Bertie,' he said hollowly, as he saw me, 'it was that blighter Steggles! I caught one of the kids before he could get away and got it all out of him. Steggles substituted real oranges for the balls of wool which with infinite sweat and at a cost of nearly a quid I had specially prepared. Well, I will now proceed to tear him limb from limb. It'll be something to do.'

I hated to spoil his day-dreams, but it had to be.

'Good heavens, man,' I said, 'you haven't time for frivolous amusements now. You've got to get out. And quick!'

'Bertie,' said Bingo in a dull voice, 'she was here just now. She said it was all my fault and that she would never speak to me again. She said she had always suspected me of being a heartless practical joker, and now she knew. She said – Oh, well, she ticked me off properly.'

'That's the least of your troubles,' I said. It seemed impossible to rouse the poor zib to a sense of his position. 'Do you realize that about two hundred of Twing's heftiest are waiting for you outside to chuck you into the pond?'

'No!'

'Absolutely!'

For a moment the poor chap seemed crushed. But only for a moment. There has always been something of the good old English bulldog breed about Bingo. A strange, sweet smile flickered for an instant over his face.

'It's all right,' he said. 'I can sneak out through the cellar and climb over the wall at the back. They can't intimidate *me*!'

It couldn't have been more than a week later when Jeeves, after he had brought me my tea, gently steered me away from the sporting

page of the *Morning Post* and directed my attention to an announcement in the engagements and marriages column.

It was a brief statement that a marriage had been arranged and
would shortly take place between the Hon. and Rev. Hubert
Wingham, third son of the Right Hon. the Earl of Sturridge, and
Mary, only daughter of the late Matthew Burgess, of Weatherly
Court, Hants.

'Of course,' I said, after I had given it the east-to-west, 'I expected
this, Jeeves.'

'Yes, sir.'

'She would never forgive him what happened that night.'

'No, sir.'

'Well,' I said, as I took a sip of the fragrant and steaming, 'I don't
suppose it will take old Bingo long to get over it. It's about the
hundred and eleventh time this sort of thing has happened to him.
You're the man I'm sorry for.'

'Me, sir?'

'Well, dash it all, you can't have forgotten what a deuce of a lot
of trouble you took to bring the thing off for Bingo. It's too bad that
all your work should have been wasted.'

'Not entirely wasted, sir.'

'Eh?'

'It is true that my efforts to bring about the match between Mr
Little and the young lady were not successful, but I still look back
upon the matter with a certain satisfaction.'

'Because you did your best, you mean?'

'Not entirely, sir, though of course that thought also gives me
pleasure. I was alluding more particularly to the fact that I found
the affair financially remunerative.'

'Financially remunerative? What do you mean?'

'When I learned that Mr Steggles had interested himself in the
contest, sir, I went shares with my friend Brookfield and bought the
book which had been made on the issue by the landlord of the Cow
and Horses. It has proved a highly profitable investment. Your
breakfast will be ready almost immediately, sir. Kidneys on toast and
mushrooms. I will bring it when you ring.'

16

The Delayed Exit of Claude and Eustace

The feeling I had when Aunt Agatha trapped me in my lair that morning and spilled the bad news was that my luck had broken at last. As a rule, you see, I'm not lugged into Family Rows. On the occasions when Aunt is calling to Aunt like mastodons bellowing across primeval swamps and Uncle James's letter about Cousin Mabel's peculiar behaviour is being shot round the family circle ('Please read this carefully and send it on to Jane'), the clan has a tendency to ignore me. It's one of the advantages I get from being a bachelor – and, according to my nearest and dearest, practically a half-witted bachelor at that. 'It's no good trying to get Bertie to take the slightest interest' is more or less the slogan, and I'm bound to say I'm all for it. A quiet life is what I like. And that's why I felt that the Curse had come upon me, so to speak, when Aunt Agatha sailed into my sitting-room while I was having a placid cigarette and started to tell me about Claude and Eustace.

'Thank goodness,' said Aunt Agatha, 'arrangements have at last been made about Eustace and Claude.'

'Arrangements?' I said, not having the foggiest.

'They sail on Friday for South Africa. Mr Van Alstyne, a friend of poor Emily's, has given them berths in his firm at Johannesburg, and we are hoping that they will settle down there and do well.'

I didn't get the thing at all.

'Friday? The day after tomorrow, do you mean?'

'Yes.'

'For South Africa?'

'Yes. They leave on the *Edinburgh Castle*.'

'But what's the idea? I mean, aren't they in the middle of their term at Oxford?'

Aunt Agatha looked at me coldly.

'Do you positively mean to tell me, Bertie, that you take so little interest in the affairs of your nearest relatives that you are not aware that Claude and Eustace were expelled from Oxford over a fortnight ago?'

'No, really?'

'You are hopeless, Bertie. I should have thought that even you – '

'Why were they sent down?'

'They poured lemonade on the Junior Dean of their college . . . I see nothing amusing in the outrage, Bertie.'

'No, no, rather not,' I said hurriedly. 'I wasn't laughing. Choking. Got something stuck in my throat, you know.'

'Poor Emily,' went on Aunt Agatha, 'being one of those doting mothers who are the ruin of their children, wished to keep the boys in London. She suggested that they might cram for the Army. But I was firm. The Colonies are the only place for wild youths like Eustace and Claude. So they sail on Friday. They have been staying for the last two weeks with your Uncle Clive in Worcestershire. They will spend tomorrow night in London and catch the boat-train on Friday morning.'

'Bit risky, isn't it? I mean, aren't they apt to cut loose a bit tomorrow night if they're left all alone in London?'

'They will not be left alone. They will be in your charge.'

'Mine!'

'Yes. I wish you to put them up in your flat for the night, and see that they do not miss the train in the morning.'

'Oh, I say, no!'

'Bertie!'

'Well, I mean, quite jolly coves both of them, but I don't know. They're rather nuts, you know . . . Always glad to see them, of course, but when it comes to putting them up for the night – '

'Bertie, if you are so sunk in callous self-indulgence that you cannot even put yourself to this trifling inconvenience for the sake of – '

'Oh, all right,' I said. 'All right.'

It was no good arguing, of course. Aunt Agatha always makes me feel as if I had gelatine where my spine ought to be. She's one of those forceful females. I should think Queen Elizabeth I must have been something like her. When she holds me with her glittering eye and says, 'Jump to it, my lad', or words to that effect, I make it so without further discussion.

When she had gone, I rang for Jeeves to break the news to him.

'Oh, Jeeves,' I said, 'Mr Claude and Mr Eustace will be staying here tomorrow night.'

'Very good, sir.'

'I'm glad you think so. To me the outlook seems black and scaly. You know what those two lads are!'

'Very high-spirited young gentlemen, sir.'

'Blisters, Jeeves. Undeniable blisters. It's a bit thick!'

'Would there by anything further, sir?'

At that, I'm bound to say, I drew myself up a trifle haughtily. We Woosters freeze like the dickens when we seek sympathy and meet with cold reserve. I knew what was up, of course. For the last day or so there had been a certain amount of coolness in the home over a pair of jazzy spats which I had dug up while exploring in the Burlington Arcade. Some dashed brainy cove, probably the chap who invented those coloured cigarette-cases, had recently had the rather topping idea of putting out a line of spats on the same system. I mean to say, instead of the ordinary grey and white, you can now get them in your regimental or school colours. And, believe me, it would have taken a chappie of stronger fibre than I am to resist the pair of Old Etonian spats which had smiled up at me from inside the window. I was inside the shop, opening negotiations, before it had even occurred to me that Jeeves might not approve. And I must say he had taken the thing a bit hardly. The fact of the matter is, Jeeves, though in many ways the best valet in London, is too conservative. Hide-bound, if you know what I mean, and an enemy to Progress.

'Nothing further, Jeeves,' I said, with quiet dignity.

'Very good, sir.'

He gave one frosty look at the spats and biffed off. Dash him!

Anything merrier and brighter than the Twins, when they curvetted into the old flat while I was dressing for dinner the next night, I have never struck in my whole puff. I'm only about half a dozen years older than Claude and Eustace, but in some rummy manner they always make me feel as if I were well on in the grandfather class and just waiting for the end. Almost before I realized they were in the place, they had collared the best chairs, pinched a couple of my special cigarettes, poured themselves out a whisky-and-soda apiece, and started to prattle with the gaiety and abandon of two birds who had achieved their life's ambition instead of having come a most frightful purler and being under sentence of exile.

'Hallo, Bertie, old thing,' said Claude. 'Jolly decent of you to put us up.'

'Oh, no,' I said. 'Only wish you were staying a good long time.'

'Hear that, Eustace? He wishes we were staying a good long time.'

'I expect it will seem a good long time,' said Eustace, philosophically.

'You heard about the binge, Bertie? Our little bit of trouble, I mean?'

'Oh, yes. Aunt Agatha was telling me.'

'We leave our country for our country's good,' said Eustace.

'And let there be no moaning at the bar,' said Claude, 'when I put out to sea. What did Aunt Agatha tell you?'

'She said you poured lemonade on the Junior Dean.'

'I wish the deuce,' said Claude, annoyed, 'that people would get these things right. It wasn't the Junior Dean. It was the Senior Tutor.'

'And it wasn't lemonade,' said Eustace. 'It was soda-water. The dear old thing happened to be standing just under our window while I was leaning out with a siphon in my hand. He looked up, and – well, it would have been chucking away the opportunity of a life-time if I hadn't let him have it in the eyeball.'

'Simply chucking it away,' agreed Claude.

'Might never have occurred again,' said Eustace.

'Hundred to one against it,' said Claude.

'Now, what,' said Eustace, 'do you propose to do, Bertie, in the way of entertaining the handsome guests tonight?'

'My idea was to have a bit of dinner in the flat,' I said. 'Jeeves is getting it ready now.'

'And afterwards?'

'Well, I thought we might chat of this and that, and then it struck me that you would probably like to turn in early, as your train goes about ten or something, doesn't it?'

The twins looked at each other in a pitying sort of way.

'Bertie,' said Eustace, 'you've got the programme nearly right, but not quite. I envisage the evening's events thus: We will toddle along to Ciro's after dinner. It's an extension night, isn't it? Well, that will see us through till about two-thirty or three.'

'After which, no doubt,' said Claude, 'the Lord will provide.'

'But I thought you would want to get a good night's rest.'

'Good night's rest!' said Eustace. 'My dear old chap, you don't for a moment imagine that we are dreaming of going to *bed* tonight, do you?'

I suppose the fact of the matter is, I'm not the man I was. I mean, those all-night vigils don't seem to fascinate me as they used to a few years ago. I can remember the time, when I was up at Oxford, when a Covent Garden ball till six in the morning, with breakfast at the Hammams and probably a free fight with a few selected costermongers to follow, seemed to me what the doctor ordered. But nowadays two o'clock is about my limit; and by two o'clock the twins were just settling down and beginning to go nicely.

As far as I can remember, we went on from Ciro's to play chemmy with some fellows I don't recall having met before, and it must have been about nine in the morning when we fetched up again at the flat. By which time, I'm bound to admit, as far as I was concerned the first careless freshness was beginning to wear off a bit. In fact, I'd just got enough strength to say goodbye to the twins, wish them a pleasant voyage and a happy and successful career in South Africa, and stagger into bed. The last I remember was hearing the blighters chanting like larks under the cold shower, breaking off from time to time to shout to Jeeves to rush along the eggs and bacon.

It must have been about one in the afternoon when I woke. I was feeling more or less like something the Pure Food Committee had rejected, but there was one bright thought which cheered me up, and that was that about now the twins would be leaning on the rail of the liner, taking their last glimpse of the dear old homeland. Which made it all the more of a shock when the door opened and Claude walked in.

'Hallo, Bertie!' said Claude. 'Had a nice refreshing sleep? Now, what about a good old bite of lunch?'

I'd been having so many distorted nightmares since I had dropped off to sleep that for half a minute I thought this was simply one more of them, and the worst of the lot. It was only when Claude sat down on my feet that I got on to the fact that this was stern reality.

'Great Scott! What on earth are you doing here?' I gurgled.

Claude looked at me reproachfully.

'Hardly the tone I like to hear in a host, Bertie,' he said reprovingly. 'Why, it was only last night that you were saying you wished I was stopping a good long time. Your dream has come true. I am.'

'But why aren't you on your way to South Africa?'

'Now that,' said Claude, 'is a point I rather thought you would want to have explained. It's like this, old man. You remember that girl you introduced me to at Ciro's last night?'

'Which girl?'

'There was only one,' said Claude coldly. 'Only one that counted, that is to say. Her name was Marion Wardour. I danced with her a good deal, if you remember.'

I began to recollect in a hazy sort of way. Marion Wardour has been a pal of mine for some time. A very good sort. She's playing in that show at the Apollo at the moment. I remembered now that she had been at Ciro's with a party the night before, and the twins had insisted on being introduced.

'We are soul-mates, Bertie,' said Claude. 'I found it out quite early in the PM, and the more thought I've given to the matter the more convinced I've become. It happens like that now and then, you know. Two hearts that beat as one, I mean, and all that sort of thing. So the long and the short of it is that I gave old Eustace the slip at Waterloo and slid back here. The idea of going to South Africa and leaving a girl like that in England doesn't appeal to me a bit. I'm for all thinking imperially and giving the Colonies a leg-up and all that sort of thing; but it can't be done. After all,' said Claude reasonably, 'South Africa has got along all right without me up to now, so why shouldn't it stick it?'

'But what about Van Alstyne, or whatever his name is? He'll be expecting you to turn up.'

'Oh, he'll have Eustace. That'll satisfy him. Very sound fellow, Eustace. Probably end up by being a magnate of some kind. I shall watch his future progress with considerable interest. And now you must excuse me for a moment, Bertie. I want to go and hunt up Jeeves and get him to mix me one of those pick-me-ups of his. For some reason which I can't explain, I've got a slight headache this morning.'

And, believe me or believe me not, the door had hardly closed behind him when in blew Eustace with a shining morning face that made me ill to look at.

'Oh, my aunt!' I said.

Eustace started to giggle pretty freely.

'Smooth work, Bertie, smooth work!' he said. 'I'm sorry for poor old Claude, but there was no alternative. I eluded his vigilance at Waterloo and snaked off in a taxi. I suppose the poor old ass is wondering where the deuce I've got to. But it couldn't be helped. If you really seriously expected me to go slogging off to South Africa, you shouldn't have introduced me to Miss Wardour last night. I want to tell you all about that, Bertie. I'm not a man,' said Eustace, sitting down on the bed, 'who falls in love with every girl he sees. I suppose "strong, silent", would be the best description you could find for me. But when I do meet my affinity I don't waste time. I – '

'Oh, heaven! Are you in love with Marion Wardour, too?'

'Too? What do you mean, "too"?'

I was going to tell him about Claude, when the blighter came in in person, looking like a giant refreshed. There's no doubt that Jeeves's pick-me-ups will produce immediate results in anything short of an Egyptian mummy. It's something he puts in them – the Worcester sauce or something. Claude had revived like a watered flower, but he nearly had a relapse when he saw his bally brother goggling at him over the bed-rail.

'What on earth are you doing here?' he said.

'What on earth are *you* doing here?' said Eustace.

'Have you come back to inflict your beastly society upon Miss Wardour?'

'Is that why you've come back?'

They thrashed the subject out a bit further.

'Well,' said Claude at last. 'I suppose it can't be helped. If you're here, you're here. May the best man win!'

'Yes, but dash it all!' I managed to put in at this point. 'What's the idea? Where do you think you're going to stay if you stick on in London?'

'Why, here,' said Eustace, surprised.

'Where else?' said Claude, raising his eyebrows.

'You won't object to putting us up, Bertie?' said Eustace.

'Not a sportsman like you,' said Claude.

'But, you silly asses, suppose Aunt Agatha finds out that I'm hiding you when you ought to be in South Africa? Where do I get off?'

'Where *does* he get off?' Claude asked Eustace.

'Oh, I expect he'll manage somehow,' said Eustace to Claude.

'Of course,' said Claude, quite cheered up. '*He'll* manage.'

'Rather!' said Eustace. 'A resourceful chap like Bertie! Of course he will.'

'And now,' said Claude, shelving the subject, 'what about that bite of lunch we were discussing a moment ago, Bertie? That stuff good old Jeeves slipped into me just now has given me what you might call an appetite. Something in the nature of six chops and a batter pudding would about meet the case, I think.'

I suppose every chappie in the world has black periods in his life to which he can't look back without the smouldering eye and the silent shudder. Some coves, if you can judge by the novels you read nowadays, have them practically all the time; but, what with enjoying a sizeable private income and a topping digestion, I'm bound to say it isn't very often I find my own existence getting a flat tyre. That's why this particular epoch is one that I don't think about more often than I can help. For the days that followed the unexpected resurrection of the blighted twins were so absolutely foul that the old nerves began to stick out of my body a foot long and curling at the ends. All of a twitter, believe me. I imagine the fact of the matter is that we Woosters are so frightfully honest and open and all that, that it gives us the pip to have to deceive.

All was quiet along the Potomac for about twenty-four hours, and then Aunt Agatha trickled in to have a chat. Twenty minutes earlier and she would have found the twins gaily shoving themselves outside a couple of rashers and an egg. She sank into a chair, and I could see that she was not in her usual sunny spirits.

'Bertie,' she said, 'I am uneasy.'

So was I. I didn't know how long she intended to stop, or when the twins were coming back.

'I wonder,' she said, 'if I took too harsh a view towards Claude and Eustace.'

'You couldn't.'

'What do you mean?'

'I – er – mean it would be so unlike you to be harsh to anybody, Aunt Agatha.' And not bad, either. I mean, quick – like that – without thinking. It pleased the old relative, and she looked at me with slightly less loathing than she usually does.

'It is nice of you to say that, Bertie, but what I was thinking was, are they *safe*?'

'Are they *what*?'

It seemed such a rummy adjective to apply to the twins, they being about as innocuous as a couple of sprightly young tarantulas.

'Do you think all is well with them?'

'How do you mean?'

Aunt Agatha eyed me almost wistfully.

'Has it ever occurred to you, Bertie,' she said, 'that your Uncle George may be psychic?'

She seemed to me to be changing the subject.

'Psychic?'

'Do you think it is possible that he could *see* things not visible to the normal eye?'

I thought it dashed possible, if not probable. I don't know if you've ever met my Uncle George. He's a festive old egg who wanders from club to club continually having a couple with other festive old eggs. When he heaves in sight, waiters brace themselves up and the wine-steward toys with his corkscrew. It was my Uncle George who discovered that alcohol was a food well in advance of modern medical thought.

'Your Uncle George was dining with me last night, and he was quite shaken. He declares that, while on his way from the Devonshire Club to Boodle's he suddenly saw the phantasm of Eustace.'

'The what of Eustace?'

'The phantasm. The wraith. It was so clear that he thought for an instant that it was Eustace himself. The figure vanished round a corner, and when Uncle George got there nothing was to be seen. It is all very queer and disturbing. It had a marked effect on poor George. All through dinner he touched nothing but barley-water, and his manner was quite disturbed. You do think those poor, dear boys are safe, Bertie? They have not met with some horrible accident?'

It made my mouth water to think of it, but I said no, I didn't think they had met with any horrible accident. I thought Eustace *was* a horrible accident, and Claude about the same, but I didn't say so. And presently she biffed off, still worried.

When the twins came in, I put it squarely to the blighters. Jolly as it was to give Uncle George shocks, they must not wander at large about the metrop.

'But, my dear old soul,' said Claude. 'Be reasonable. We can't have our movements hampered.'

'Out of the question,' said Eustace.

'The whole essence of the thing, if you understand me,' said Claude, 'is that we should be at liberty to flit hither and thither.'

'Exactly,' said Eustace. 'Now hither, now thither.'

'But, damn it – '

'Bertie!' said Eustace reprovingly. 'Not before the boy!'

'Of course, in a way I see his point,' said Claude. 'I suppose the solution of the problem would be to buy a couple of disguises.'

'My dear old chap!' said Eustace, looking at him with admiration. 'The brightest idea on record. Not your own, surely?'

'Well, as a matter of fact, it was Bertie who put it into my head.'

'Me!'

'You were telling me the other day about old Bingo Little and the beard he bought when he didn't want his uncle to recognize him.'

'If you think I'm going to have you two excrescences popping in and out of my flat in beards – '

'Something in that,' agreed Eustace. 'We'll make it whiskers, then.'

'And false noses,' said Claude.

'And, as you say, false noses. Right-o, then, Bertie, old chap, that's a load off your mind. We don't want to be any trouble to you while we're paying you this little visit.'

And, when I went buzzing round to Jeeves for consolation, all he would say was something about Young Blood. No sympathy.

'Very good, Jeeves,' I said. 'I shall go for a walk in the park. Kindly put me out the Old Etonian spats.'

'Very good, sir.'

It must have been a couple of days after that that Marion Wardour rolled in at about the hour of tea. She looked warily round the room before sitting down.

'Your cousins not at home, Bertie?' she said.

'No, thank goodness!'

'Then I'll tell you where they are. They're in my sitting-room, glaring at each other from opposite corners, waiting for me to come in. Bertie, this has got to stop.'

'You're seeing a good deal of them, are you?'

Jeeves came in with the tea, but the poor girl was so worked up that she didn't wait for him to pop off before going on with her complaint. She had an absolutely hunted air, poor thing.

'I can't move a step without tripping over one or both of them,' she said. 'Generally both. They've taken to calling together, and they just settle down grimly and try to sit each other out. It's wearing me to a shadow.'

'I know,' I said sympathetically. 'I know.'

'Well, what's to be done?'

'It beats me. Couldn't you tell your maid to say you are not at home?'

She shuddered slightly.

'I tried that once. They camped on the stairs, and I couldn't get out all the afternoon. And I had a lot of particularly important engagements. I wish you would persuade them to go to South Africa, where they seem to be wanted.'

'You must have made the dickens of an impression on them.'

'I should say I have. They've started giving me presents now. At least Claude has. He insisted on my accepting this cigarette-case last night. Came round to the theatre and wouldn't go away till I took it. It's not a bad one, I must say.'

It wasn't. It was a distinctly fruity concern in gold with a diamond stuck in the middle. And the rummy thing was that I had a notion I'd seen something very like it before somewhere. How the deuce Claude had been able to dig up the cash to buy a thing like that was more than I could imagine.

Next day was a Wednesday, and as the object of their devotion had a *matinée*, the twins were, so to speak, off duty. Claude had gone with his whiskers on to Hurst Park, and Eustace and I were in the flat, talking. At least, he was talking and I was wishing he would go.

'The love of a good woman, Bertie,' he was saying, 'must be a wonderful thing. Sometimes . . . Good Lord! What's that?'

The front door had opened, and from out in the hall there came the sound of Aunt Agatha's voice asking if I was in. Aunt Agatha has one of those high, penetrating voices, but this was the first time I'd ever been thankful for it. There was just about two seconds to clear the way for her, but it was long enough for Eustace to dive under the sofa. His last shoe had just disappeared when she came in.

She had a worried look. It seemed to me about this time that everybody had.

'Bertie,' she said, 'what are your immediate plans?'

'How do you mean? I'm dining tonight with – '

'No, no, I don't mean tonight. Are you busy for the next few days? But, of course you are not,' she went on, not waiting for me to answer. 'You never have anything to do. Your whole life is spent in idle – but we can go into that later. What I came for this afternoon was to tell you that I wish you to go with your poor Uncle George to Harrogate for a few weeks. The sooner you can start, the better.'

This appeared to me to approximate so closely to the frozen limit that I uttered a yelp of protest. Uncle George is all right, but he won't do. I was trying to say as much when she waved me down.

'If you are not entirely heartless, Bertie, you will do as I ask you. Your poor Uncle George has had a severe shock.'

'What, another?'

'He feels that only complete rest and careful medical attendance can restore his nervous system to its normal poise. It seems that in the past he has derived benefit from taking the waters at Harrogate, and he wishes to go there now. We do not think he ought to be alone, so I wish you to accompany him.'

'But, I say!'

'Bertie!'

There was a lull in the conversation.

'What shock has he had?' I asked.

'Between ourselves,' said Aunt Agatha, lowering her voice in an impressive manner, 'I incline to think that the whole affair was the outcome of an over-excited imagination. You are one of the family, Bertie, and I can speak freely to you. You know as well as I do that your poor Uncle George has for many years *not* been a – he has – er – developed a bit of a habit – how shall I put it?'

'Shifting it a bit?'

'I beg your pardon?'

'Mopping up the stuff to some extent?'

'I dislike your way of putting it exceedingly, but I must confess that he has not been, perhaps, as temperate as he should. He is highly-strung, and . . . Well, the fact is, that he has had a shock.'

'Yes, but what?'

'That is what it is so hard to induce him to explain with any precision. With all his good points, your poor Uncle George is apt to become incoherent when strongly moved. As far as I could gather, he appears to have been the victim of a burglary.'

'Burglary!'

'He says that a strange man with whiskers and a peculiar nose entered his rooms in Jermyn Street during his absence and stole some of his property. He says that he came back and found the man in his sitting-room. He immediately rushed out of the room and disappeared.'

'Uncle George?'

'No, the man. And, according to your Uncle George, he had stolen a valuable cigarette-case. But, as I say, I am inclined to think that the whole thing was imagination. He has not been himself since the day when he fancied that he saw Eustace in the street. So I should like you, Bertie, to be prepared to start for Harrogate with him not later than Saturday.'

She popped off, and Eustace crawled out from under the sofa. The blighter was strongly moved. So was I, for the matter of that. The idea of several weeks with Uncle George at Harrogate seemed to make everything go black.

'So that's where he got that cigarette-case, dash him!' said Eustace bitterly. 'Of all the dirty tricks! Robbing his own flesh and blood! That fellow ought to be in chokey.'

'He ought to be in South Africa,' I said. 'And so ought you.'

And with an eloquence which rather surprised me, I hauled up my slacks for perhaps ten minutes on the subject of his duty to his family and what not. I appealed to his sense of decency. I boosted South Africa with vim. I said everything I could think of, much of it twice over. But all the blighter did was to babble about his dashed brother's baseness in putting one over on him in the matter of the cigarette-case. He seemed to think that Claude, by slinging in the handsome gift, had got right ahead of him: and there was a painful scene when the latter came back from Hurst Park. I could hear them talking half the night, long after I had tottered off to bed. I don't know when I've met fellows who could do with less sleep than those two.

After this, things became a bit strained at the flat owing to Claude and Eustace not being on speaking terms. I'm all for a certain chumminess in the home, and it was wearing to have to live with two fellows who wouldn't admit that the other one was on the map at all.

One felt the thing couldn't go on like that for long, and, by Jove, it didn't. But, if anyone had come to me the day before and told me what was going to happen, I should simply have smiled wanly. I mean, I'd got so accustomed to thinking that nothing short of a dynamite explosion could ever dislodge those two nestlers from my midst that, when Claude sidled up to me on the Friday morning and told me his bit of news, I could hardly believe I was hearing right.

'Bertie,' he said, 'I've been thinking it over.'

'What over?' I said.

'The whole thing. This business of staying in London when I ought to be in South Africa. It isn't fair,' said Claude warmly. 'It isn't right. And the long and the short of it is, Bertie, old man, I'm leaving tomorrow.'

I reeled in my tracks.

'You are?' I gasped.

'Yes. If,' said Claude, 'you won't mind sending old Jeeves out to buy a ticket for me. I'm afraid I'll have to stick you for the passage money, old man. You don't mind?'

'Mind!' I said, clutching his hand fervently.

'That's all right, then. Oh, I say, you won't say a word to Eustace about this, will you?'

'But isn't he going, too?'

Claude shuddered.

'No, thank heaven! The idea of being cooped up on board a ship with that blighter gives me the pip just to think of it. No, not a word to Eustace. I say, I suppose you can get me a berth all right at such short notice?'

'Rather!' I said. Sooner than let this opportunity slip, I would have bought the bally boat.

'Jeeves,' I said, breezing into the kitchen. 'Go out on first speed to the Union-Castle offices and book a berth on tomorrow's boat for Mr Claude. He is leaving us, Jeeves.'

'Yes, sir.'

'Mr Claude does not wish any mention of this to be made to Mr Eustace.'

'No, sir. Mr Eustace made the same proviso when he desired me to obtain a berth on tomorrow's boat for himself.'

I gaped at the man.

'Is he going, too?'

'Yes, sir.'

'This is rummy.'

'Yes, sir.'

Had circumstances been other than they were, I would at this juncture have unbent considerably towards Jeeves. Frisked round him a bit and whooped to a certain extent, and what not. But those spats still formed a barrier, and I regret to say that I took the opportunity of rather rubbing it in a bit on the man. I mean, he'd been so dashed aloof and unsympathetic, though perfectly aware that the young master was in the soup and that it was up to him to rally round, that I couldn't help pointing out how the happy ending had been snaffled without any help from him.

'So that's that, Jeeves,' I said. 'The episode is concluded. I knew things would sort themselves out if one gave them time and didn't get rattled. Many chaps in my place would have got rattled, Jeeves.'

'Yes, sir.'

'Gone rushing about, I mean, asking people for help and advice and so forth.'

'Very possibly, sir.'

'But not me, Jeeves.'

'No, sir.'

I left him to brood on it.

Even the thought that I'd got to go to Harrogate with Uncle George couldn't depress me that Saturday when I gazed about the old flat and realized that Claude and Estace weren't in it. They had slunk off stealthily and separately immediately after breakfast, Eustace to catch the boat-train at Waterloo, Claude to go round to the garage where I kept my car. I didn't want any chance of the two meeting at Waterloo and changing their minds, so I had suggested to Claude that he might find it pleasanter to drive down to Southampton.

I was lying back on the old settee, gazing peacefully up at the flies on the ceiling and feeling what a wonderful world this was, when Jeeves came in with a letter.

'A messenger-boy has brought this, sir.'

I opened the envelope, and the first thing that fell out was a five-pound note.

'Great Scott!' I said. 'What's all this?'

The letter was scribbled in pencil, and was quite brief;

Dear Bertie,

Will you give enclosed to your man, and tell him I wish I could make it more. He has saved my life. This is the first happy day I've had for a week.

Yours,

M.W.

Jeeves was standing holding out the fiver, which had fluttered to the floor.

'You'd better stick to it,' I said. 'It seems to be for you.'

'Sir?'

'I say that fiver is for you, apparently. Miss Wardour sent it.'

'That was extremely kind of her, sir.'

'What the dickens is she sending you fivers for? She says you saved her life.'

Jeeves smiled gently.

'She over-estimates my services, sir.'

'But what *were* your services, dash it?'

'It was in the matter of Mr Claude and Mr Eustace, sir. I was hoping that she would not refer to the matter, as I did not wish you to think that I had been taking a liberty.'

'What do you mean?'

'I chanced to be in the room while Miss Wardour was complaining with some warmth of the manner in which Mr Claude and Mr Eustace were thrusting their society upon her. I felt that in the circumstances it might be excusable if I suggested a slight ruse to enable her to dispense with their attentions.'

'Good Lord! You don't mean to say you were at the bottom of their popping off, after all!'

Silly ass it made me feel. I mean, after rubbing it in to him like that about having clicked without his assistance.

'It occurred to me that, were Miss Wardour to inform Mr Claude and Mr Eustace independently that she proposed sailing for South Africa to take up a theatrical engagement, the desired effect might be produced. It appears that my anticipations were correct, sir. The young gentlemen ate it, if I may use the expression.'

'Jeeves,' I said – we Woosters may make bloomers, but we are never too proud to admit it – 'you stand alone!'

'Thank you very much, sir.'

'Oh, but I say!' A ghastly thought had struck me. 'When they get on the boat and find she isn't there, won't they come buzzing back?'

'I anticipated that possibility, sir. At my suggestion, Miss Wardour informed the young gentlemen that she proposed to travel overland to Madeira and join the vessel there.'

'And where do they touch after Madeira?'

'Nowhere, sir.'

For a moment I just lay back, letting the idea of the thing soak in. There seemed to me to be only one flaw.

'The only pity is,' I said, 'that on a large boat like that they will be able to avoid each other. I mean, I should have liked to feel that Claude was having a good deal of Eustace's society and vice versa.'

'I fancy that that will be so, sir. I secured a two-berth state-room. Mr Claude will occupy one berth, Mr Eustace the other.'

I sighed with pure ecstasy. It seemed a dashed shame that on this joyful occasion I should have to go off to Harrogate with my Uncle George.

'Have you started packing yet, Jeeves?' I asked.

'Packing, sir?'

'For Harrogate. I've got to go there today with Sir George.'

'Of course, yes, sir. I forgot to mention it. Sir George rang up on the telephone this morning while you were still asleep, and said that he had changed his plans. He does not intend to go to Harrogate.'

'Oh, I say, how absolutely topping!'

'I thought you might be pleased, sir.'

'What made him change his plans? Did he say?'

'No, sir. But I gather from his man, Stevens, that he is feeling much better and does not now require a rest-cure. I took the liberty of giving Stevens the recipe for that pick-me-up of mine, of which you have always approved so much. Stevens tells me that Sir George informed him this morning that he is feeling a new man.'

Well, there was only one thing to do, and I did it. I'm not saying it didn't hurt, but there was no alternative.

'Jeeves,' I said, 'those spats.'

'Yes, sir?'

'You really dislike them?'

'Intensely, sir.'

'You don't think time might induce you to change your views?'

'No, sir.'

'All right, then. Very well. Say no more. You may burn them.'

'Thank you very much, sir. I have already done so. Before breakfast this morning. A quiet grey is far more suitable, sir. Thank you, sir.'

17
Bingo and The Little Woman

It must have been a week or so after the departure of Claude and Eustace that I ran into young Bingo Little in the smoking-room of the Senior Liberal Club. He was lying back in an armchair with his mouth open and a sort of goofy expression in his eyes, while a grey-bearded cove in the middle distance watched him with so much dislike that I concluded that Bingo had pinched his favourite seat. That's the worst of being in a strange club – absolutely without intending it, you find yourself constantly trampling upon the vested interests of the Oldest Inhabitants.

'Hallo, face,' I said.

'Cheerio, ugly,' said young Bingo, and we settled down to have a small one before lunch.

Once a year the committee of the Drones decides that the old club could do with a wash and brush-up, so they shoo us out and dump us down for a few weeks at some other institution. This time we were roosting at the Senior Liberal, and personally I had found the strain pretty fearful. I mean, when you've got used to a club where everything's nice and cheery, and where, if you want to attract a chappie's attention, you heave a piece of bread at him, it kind of damps you to come to a place where the youngest member is about eighty-seven and it isn't considered good form to talk to anyone unless you and he were through the Peninsular War together. It was a relief to come across Bingo. We started to talk in hushed voices.

'This club,' I said, 'is the limit.'

'It is the eel's eyebrows,' agreed young Bingo. 'I believe that old boy over by the window has been dead three days, but I don't like to mention it to anyone.'

'Have you lunched here yet?'

'No. Why?'

'They have waitresses instead of waiters.'

'Good Lord! I thought that went out with the armistice.' Bingo mused a moment, straightening his tie absently. 'Er – pretty girls?' he said.

'No.'

He seemed disappointed, but pulled round.

'Well, I've heard that the cooking's the best in London.'

'So they say. Shall we be going in?'

'All right. I expect,' said young Bingo, 'that at the end of the meal – or possibly at the beginning – the waitress will say, "Both together, sir?" Reply the affirmative. I haven't a bean.'

'Hasn't your uncle forgiven you yet?'

'Not yet, confound him!'

I was sorry to hear the row was still on. I resolved to do the poor old thing well at the festive board, and I scanned the menu with some intentness when the girl rolled up with it.

'How would this do you, Bingo?' I said at length. 'A few plovers' eggs to weigh in with, a cup of soup, a touch of cold salmon, some cold curry, and a splash of gooseberry tart and cream with a bite of cheese to finish?'

I don't know that I had expected the man actually to scream with delight, though I had picked the items from my knowledge of his pet dishes, but I had expected him to say something. I looked up, and found that his attention was elsewhere. He was gazing at the waitress with the look of a dog that's just remembered where its bone was buried.

She was a tallish girl with sort of soft, soulful brown eyes. Nice figure and all that. Rather decent hands, too. I didn't remember having seen her about before, and I must say she raised the standard of the place quite a bit.

'How about it, laddie?' I said, being all for getting the order booked and going on to the serious knife-and-fork work.

'Eh?' said young Bingo absently.

I recited the programme once more.

'Oh, yes, fine!' said Bingo. 'Anything, anything.' The girl pushed off, and he turned to me with protruding eyes. 'I thought you said they weren't pretty, Bertie!' he said reproachfully.

'Oh, my heavens!' I said. 'You surely haven't fallen in love again – and with a girl you've only just seen?'

'There are times, Bertie,' said young Bingo, 'when a look is enough – when, passing through a crowd, we meet somebody's eye and something seems to whisper – '

At this point the plovers' eggs arrived, and he suspended his remarks in order to swoop on them with some vigour.

'Jeeves,' I said that night when I got home, 'stand by.'

'Sir?'

'Burnish the old brain and be alert and vigilant. I suspect that Mr Little will be calling round shortly for sympathy and assistance.'

'Is Mr Little in trouble, sir?'

'Well you might call it that. He's in love. For about the fifty-third time. I ask you, Jeeves, as man to man, did you ever see such a chap?'

'Mr Little is certainly warm-hearted, sir.'

'Warm-hearted! I should think he has to wear asbestos vests. Well, stand by, Jeeves.'

'Very good, sir.'

And sure enough, it wasn't ten days before in rolled the old ass, bleating for volunteers to step one pace forward and come to the aid of the party.

'Bertie,' he said, 'if you are a pal of mine, now is the time to show it.'

'Proceed, old gargoyle,' I replied. 'You have our ear.'

'You remember giving me lunch at the Senior Liberal some days ago. We were waited on by a – '

'I remember. Tall, lissom, female.'

He shuddered somewhat.

'I wish you wouldn't talk of her like that, dash it all. She's an angel.'

'All right. Carry on.'

'I love her.'

'Right-o! Push along.'

'For goodness' sake don't bustle me. Let me tell you the story in my own way. I love her, as I was saying, and I want you, Bertie, old boy, to pop round to my uncle and do a bit of diplomatic work. That allowance of mine must be restored, and dashed quick, too. What's more, it must be increased.'

'But look here,' I said, being far from keen on the bally business, 'why not wait a while?'

'Wait? What's the good of waiting?'

'Well, you know what generally happens when you fall in love. Something goes wrong with the works and you get left. Much better tackle your uncle after the whole thing's fixed and settled.'

'It *is* fixed and settled. She accepted me this morning.'

'Good Lord! That's quick work. You haven't known her two weeks.'

'Not in this life, no,' said young Bingo. 'But she has a sort of idea that we must have met in some previous existence. She thinks I must have been a king in Babylon when she was a Christian slave. I can't say I remember it myself, but there may be something in it.'

'Great Scott!' I said. 'Do waitresses really talk like that?'

'How should *I* know how waitresses talk?'

'Well, you ought to by now. The first time I ever met your uncle was when you hounded me on to ask him if he would rally round to help you marry that girl Mabel in the Piccadilly bun-shop.'

Bingo started violently. A wild gleam came into his eyes. And before I knew what he was up to he had brought down his hand with a most frightful whack on my summer trousering, causing me to leap like a young ram.

'Here!' I said.

'Sorry,' said Bingo. 'Excited. Carried away. You've given me an idea, Bertie.' He waited till I had finished massaging the limb, and resumed his remarks. 'Can you throw your mind back to that occasion, Bertie? Do you remember the frightfully subtle scheme I worked? Telling him you were What's-her-name, the woman who wrote those books, I mean?'

It wasn't likely I'd forget. The ghastly thing was absolutely seared into my memory.

'That is the line of attack,' said Bingo. 'That is the scheme. Rosie M. Banks forward once more.'

'It can't be done, old thing. Sorry, but it's out of the question. I couldn't go through all that again.'

'Not for me?'

'Not for a dozen more like you.'

'I never thought,' said Bingo sorrowfully, 'to hear those words from Bertie Wooster!'

'Well, you've heard them now,' I said. 'Paste them in your hat.'

'Bertie, we were at school together.'

'It wasn't my fault.'

'We've been pals for fifteen years.'

'I know. It's going to take me the rest of my life to live it down.'

'Bertie, old man,' said Bingo, drawing up his chair closer and starting to knead my shoulder-blade, 'listen! Be reasonable!'

And of course, dash it, at the end of ten minutes I'd allowed the blighter to talk me round. It's always the way. Anyone can talk me round. If I were in a Trappist monastery, the first thing that would happen would be that some smooth performer would lure me into some frightful idiocy against my better judgement by means of the deaf-and-dumb language.

'Well, what do you want me to do?' I said, realizing that it was hopeless to struggle.

'Start off by sending the old boy an autographed copy of your latest effort with a flattering inscription. That will tickle him to death. Then you pop round and put it across.'

'What *is* my latest?'

'*The Woman who Braved All*,' said young Bingo. 'I've seen it all over the place. The shop windows and bookstalls are full of nothing but it. It looks to me from the picture on the jacket the sort of book any chappie would be proud to have written. Of course, he will want to discuss it with you.'

'Ah!' I said, cheering up. 'That dishes the scheme, doesn't it? I don't know what the bally thing is about.'

'You will have to read it, naturally.'

'Read it! No, I say – '

'Bertie, we were at school together.'

'Oh, right-o! Right-o!' I said.

'I knew I could rely on you. You have a heart of gold. Jeeves,' said young Bingo, as the faithful servitor rolled in, 'Mr Wooster has a heart of gold.'

'Very good, sir,' said Jeeves.

Bar a weekly wrestle with the *Pink 'Un* and an occasional dip into the form-book I'm not much of a lad for reading, and my sufferings as I tackled *The Woman* (curse her!) *who Braved All* were pretty fearful. But I managed to get through it, and only just in time, as it happened, for I'd hardly reached the bit where their lips met in one long, slow kiss and everything was still but for the gentle sighing of the breeze in the laburnum, when a messenger-boy brought a note from old Bittlesham asking me to trickle round to lunch.

I found the old boy in a mood you could only describe as melting. He had a copy of the book on the table beside him and kept turning the pages in the intervals of dealing with things in aspic and what not.

'Mr Wooster,' he said, swallowing a chunk of trout, 'I wish to congratulate you. I wish to thank you. You go from strength to strength. I have read *All for Love*; and I have read *Only a Factory*

Girl; I know *Madcap Myrtle* by heart. But this – this is your bravest and best. It tears the heartstrings.'

'Yes?'

'Indeed yes! I have read it three times since you most kindly sent me the volume – I wish to thank you once more for the charming inscription – and I think I may say that I am a better, sweeter, deeper man. I am full of human charity and kindliness towards my species.'

'No, really?'

'Indeed, indeed I am.'

'Towards the whole species?'

'Towards the whole species.'

'Even young Bingo?' I said, trying him pretty high.

'My nephew? Richard?' He looked a bit thoughtful, but stuck it like a man and refused to hedge. 'Yes, even towards Richard. Well . . . that is to say . . . perhaps . . . yes, even towards Richard.'

'That's good, because I wanted to talk about him. He's pretty hard up, you know.'

'In straitened circumstances?'

'Stony. And he could use a bit of the right stuff paid every quarter, if you felt like unbelting.'

He mused a while and got through a slab of cold guinea hen before replying. He toyed with the book, and it fell open at page two hundred and fifteen. I couldn't remember what was on page two hundred and fifteen, but it must have been something tolerably zippy, for his expression changed and he gazed up at me with misty eyes, as if he'd taken a shade too much mustard with his last bite of ham.

'Very well, Mr Wooster,' he said. 'Fresh from a perusal of this noble work of yours, I cannot harden my heart. Richard shall have his allowance.'

'Stout fellow!' I said. Then it occurred to me that the expression might strike a chappie who weighed seventeen stone as a bit personal. 'Good egg, I mean. That'll take a weight off his mind. He wants to get married, you know.'

'I did not know. And I am not sure that I altogether approve. Who is the lady?'

'Well, as matter of fact, she's a waitress.'

He leaped in his seat.

'You don't say so, Mr Wooster! This is remarkable. This is most cheering. I had not given the boy credit for such tenacity of purpose. An excellent trait in him which I had not hitherto suspected. I recollect clearly that, on the occasion when I first had the pleasure of making your acquaintance, nearly eighteen months ago, Richard was desirous of marrying this same waitress.'

I had to break it to him.

'Well, not absolutely this same waitress. In fact, quite a different waitress. Still, a waitress, you know.'

The light of avuncular affection died out of the old boy's eyes.

'H'm!' he said a bit dubiously. 'I had supposed that Richard was displaying the quality of constancy which is so rare in the modern young man. I – I must think it over.'

So we left it at that, and I came away and told Bingo the position of affairs.

'Allowance OK,' I said. 'Uncle's blessing a trifle wobbly.'

'Doesn't he seem to want the wedding bells to ring out?'

'I left him thinking it over. If I were a bookie, I should feel justified in offering a hundred to eight against.'

'You can't have approached him properly. I might have known you would muck it up,' said young Bingo. Which, considering what I had been through for his sake, struck me as a good bit sharper than a serpent's tooth.

'It's awkward,' said young Bingo. 'It's infernally awkward. I can't tell you all the details at the moment, but . . . yes, it's awkward.'

He helped himself absently to a handful of my cigars and pushed off.

I didn't see him again for three days. Early in the afternoon of the third day he blew in with a flower in his buttonhole and a look on his face as if someone had hit him behind the ear with a stuffed eel skin.

'Hallo, Bertie.'

'Hallo, old turnip. Where have you been all this while?'

'Oh, here and there! Ripping weather we're having, Bertie.'

'Not bad.'

'I see the Bank Rate is down again.'

'No, really?'

'Disturbing news from Lower Silesia, what?'

'Oh, dashed!'

He pottered about the room for a bit, babbling at intervals. The boy seemed cuckoo.

'Oh, I say, Bertie!' he said suddenly, dropping a vase which he had picked off the mantelpiece and was fiddling with. 'I know what it was I wanted to tell you. I'm married.'

18

All's Well

I stared at him. That flower in his buttonhole... That dazed look... Yes, he had all the symptoms: and yet the thing seemed incredible. The fact is, I suppose, I'd seen so many of young Bingo's love-affairs start off with a whoop and a rattle and poof themselves out half-way down the straight that I couldn't believe he had actually brought it off at last.

'Married!'

'Yes. This morning at a registrar's in Holborn. I've just come from the wedding breakfast.'

I sat up in my chair. Alert. The man of affairs. It seemed to me that this thing wanted threshing out in all its aspects.

'Let's get this straight,' I said. 'You're really married?'

'Yes.'

'The same girl you were in love with the day before yesterday?'

'What do you mean?'

'Well, you know what you're like. Tell me, what made you commit this rash act?'

'I wish the deuce you wouldn't talk like that. I married her because I love her, dash it. The best little woman,' said young Bingo, 'in the world.'

'That's all right, and deuced creditable, I'm sure. But have you reflected what your uncle's going to say? The last I saw of him, he was by no means in a confetti-scattering mood.'

'Bertie,' said Bingo, 'I'll be frank with you. The little woman rather put it up to me, if you know what I mean. I told her how my uncle felt about it, and she said that we must part unless I loved her enough to brave the old boy's wrath and marry her right away. So I had no alternative. I bought a buttonhole and went to it.'

'And what do you propose to do now?'

'Oh, I've got it all planned out! After you've seen my uncle and broken the news – '

'What!'

'After you've – '

'You don't mean to say you think you're going to lug *me* into it?'

He looked at me like Lillian Gish coming out of a swoon.

'Is this Bertie Wooster talking?' he said, pained.

'Yes, it jolly well is.'

'Bertie, old man,' said Bingo, patting me gently here and there, 'reflect! We were at school – '

'Oh, all right!'

'Good man! I knew I could rely on you. She's waiting down below in the hall. We'll pick her up and dash round to Pounceby Gardens right away.'

I had only seen the bride before in her waitress kit, and I was rather expecting that on her wedding day she would have launched out into something fairly zippy in the way of upholstery. The first gleam of hope I had felt since the start of this black business came to me when I saw that, instead of being all velvet and scent and flowery hat, she was dressed in dashed good taste. Quiet. Nothing loud. So far as looks went, she might have stepped straight out of Berkeley Square.

'This is my old pal, Bertie Wooster, darling,' said Bingo. 'We were at school together, weren't we, Bertie?'

'We were!' I said. 'How do you do? I think we – er – met at lunch the other day, didn't we?'

'Oh yes! How do you do?'

'My uncle eats out of Bertie's hand,' explained Bingo. 'So he's coming round with us to start things off and kind of pave the way. Hi, taxi!'

We didn't talk much on the journey. Kind of tense feeling. I was glad when the cab stopped at old Bittlesham's wigwam and we all hopped out. I left Bingo and wife in the hall while I went upstairs to the drawing-room, and the butler toddled off to dig out the big chief.

While I was prowling about the room waiting for him to show up, I suddenly caught sight of the bally *Woman who Braved All* lying on one of the tables. It was open at page two hundred and fifteen, and a passage heavily marked in pencil caught my eye. And directly I read it I saw that it was all to the mustard and was going to help me in my business.

This was the passage:

'What can prevail' – Millicent's eyes flashed as she faced the stern old man – 'What can prevail against a pure and all-consuming love? Neither principalities nor powers, my lord, nor all the puny prohibitions of guardians and parents. I love your son, Lord Mindermere, and nothing can keep us apart. Since time first began this love of ours was fated, and who are you to put yourself against the decrees of Fate?'

The earl looked at her keenly from beneath his bushy eyebrows.

'Humph!' he said.

Before I had time to refresh my memory as to what Millicent's come-back had been to that remark, the door opened and old Bittlesham rolled in. All over me, as usual.

'My dear Mr Wooster, this is an unexpected pleasure. Pray take a seat. What can I do for you?'

'Well, the fact is, I'm more or less in the capacity of a jolly old ambassador at the moment. Representing young Bingo, you know.'

His geniality sagged a trifle, I thought, but he didn't heave me out, so I pushed on.

'The way I always look at it,' I said, 'is that it's dashed difficult for anything to prevail against what you might call a pure and all-consuming love. I mean, can it be done? I doubt it.'

My eyes didn't exactly flash as I faced the stern old man, but I sort of waggled my eyebrows. He puffed a bit and looked doubtful.

'We discussed this matter at our last meeting, Mr Wooster. And on that occasion – '

'Yes. But there have been developments, as it were, since then. The fact of the matter is,' I said, coming to the point, 'this morning young Bingo went and jumped off the dock.'

'Good heavens!' He jerked himself to his feet with his mouth open. 'Why? Where? Which dock?'

I saw that he wasn't quite on.

'I was speaking metaphorically,' I explained, 'if that's the word I want. I mean he got married.'

'Married!'

'Absolutely hitched up. I hope you aren't ratty about it, what? Young blood, you know. Two loving hearts, and all that.'

He panted in a rather overwrought way.

'I am greatly disturbed by your news. I – I consider that I have been – er – defied. Yes, defied.'

'But who are you to pit yourself against the decrees of Fate?' I said, taking a look at the prompt book out of the corner of my eye. 'Eh?'

'You see, this love of theirs was fated. Since time began, you know.'

I'm bound to admit that if he'd said 'Humph!' at this juncture, he would have had me stymied. Luckily it didn't occur to him. There was a silence, during which he appeared to brood a bit. Then his eye fell on the book and he gave a sort of start.

'Why, bless my soul, Mr Wooster, you have been quoting!'

'More or less.'

'I thought your words sounded familiar.' His whole appearance changed and he gave a sort of gurgling chuckle. 'Dear me, dear me, you know my weak spot!' He picked up the book and buried himself in it for quite a while. I began to think he had forgotten I was there. After a bit, however, he put it down again, and wiped his eyes. 'Ah, well!' he said.

I shuffled my feet and hoped for the best.

'Ah, well,' he said again. 'I must not be like Lord Windermere, must I, Mr Wooster? Tell me, did you draw that haughty old man from a living model?'

'Oh, no! Just thought of him and bunged him down, you know.'

'Genius!' murmured old Bittlesham. 'Genius! Well, Mr Wooster, you have won me over. Who, as you say, am I to put myself against the decrees of Fate? I will write to Richard tonight and inform him of my consent to his marriage.'

'You can slip him the glad news in person,' I said. 'He's waiting downstairs, with wife complete. I'll pop down and send them up. Cheerio, and thanks very much. Bingo will be most awfully bucked.'

I shot out and went downstairs. Bingo and Mrs were sitting on a couple of chairs like patients in a dentist's waiting-room.

'Well?' said Bingo eagerly.

'All over except the hand-clasping,' I replied, slapping the old crumpet on the back. 'Charge up and get matey. Toodle-oo, old things. You know where to find me, if wanted. A thousand congratulations, and all that sort of rot.'

And I pipped, not wishing to be fawned upon.

You never can tell in this world. If ever I felt that something attempted, something done had earned a night's repose, it was when I got back to the flat and shoved my feet up on the mantelpiece and started to absorb the cup of tea which Jeeves had brought in. Used as I am to seeing Life's sitters blow up in the home stretch and finish nowhere, I couldn't see any cause for alarm in this affair of young Bingo's. All he had to do when I left him in Pounceby Gardens was to walk upstairs with the little missus and collect the blessing. I was so convinced of this that when, about half an hour later, he came galloping into my sitting-room, all I thought was that he wanted to thank me in broken accents and tell me what a good chap I had been. I merely beamed benevolently on the old creature as he entered, and was just going to offer him a cigarette when I observed that he seemed to have something on his mind. In fact, he looked as if something solid had hit him in the solar plexus.

'My dear old soul,' I said, 'what's up?'

Bingo plunged about the room.

'I *will* be calm!' he said, knocking over an occasional table. 'Calm, dammit!' He upset a chair.

'Surely nothing has gone wrong?'

Bingo uttered one of those hollow, mirthless yelps.

'Only every bally thing that could go wrong. What do you think happened after you left us? You know that beastly book you insisted on sending my uncle?'

It wasn't the way I should have put it myself, but I saw the poor old bean was upset for some reason or other, so I didn't correct him.

'*The Woman who Braved All?*' I said. 'It came in dashed useful. It was by quoting bits out of it that I managed to talk him round.'

'Well, it didn't come in useful when we got into the room. It was lying on the table, and after we had started to chat a bit and everything was going along nicely the little woman spotted it. "Oh, have you read this, Lord Bittlesham?" she said. "Three times already," said my uncle. "I'm so glad," said the little woman. "Why, are you also an admirer of Rosie M. Banks?" asked the old boy, beaming. "I *am* Rosie M. Banks!" said the little woman.'

'Oh, my aunt! Not really?'

'Yes.'

'But how could she be? I mean, dash it, she was slinging the foodstuffs at the Senior Liberal Club.'

Bingo gave the settee a moody kick.

'She took the job to collect material for a book she's writing called *Mervyn Keene, Clubman*.'

'She might have told you.'

'It made such a hit with her when she found that I loved her for herself alone, despite her humble station, that she kept it under her hat. She meant to spring it on me later on, she said.'

'Well, what happened then?'

'There was the dickens of a painful scene. The old boy nearly got apoplexy. Called her an imposter. They both started talking at once at the top of their voices, and the thing ended with the little woman buzzing off to her publishers to collect proofs as a preliminary to getting a written apology from the old boy. What's going to happen now, I don't know. Apart from the fact that my uncle will be as mad as a wet hen when he finds out that he has been fooled, there's going to be a lot of trouble when the little woman discovers that we worked the Rosie M. Banks wheeze with a view to trying to get me married to somebody else. You see, one of the things that first attracted her to me was the fact that I had never been in love before.'

'Did you tell her that?'

'Yes.'

'Great Scott!'

'Well, I hadn't been . . . not really in love. There's all the difference in the world between . . . Well, never mind that. What am I going to do? That's the point.'

'I don't know.'

'Thanks,' said young Bingo. 'That's a lot of help.'

Next morning he rang me up on the phone just after I'd got the bacon and eggs into my system – the one moment of the day, in short, when a chappie wishes to muse on life absolutely undisturbed.

'Bertie!'

'Hallo?'

'Things are hotting up.'

'What's happened now?'

'My uncle has given the little woman's proofs the once-over and admits her claim. I've just been having five snappy minutes with him on the telephone. He says that you and I made a fool of him, and he could hardly speak, he was so shirty. Still, he made it clear all right that my allowance has gone phut again.'

'I'm sorry.'

'Don't waste time being sorry for me,' said young Bingo grimly. 'He's coming to call on you today to demand a personal explanation.'

'Great Scott!'

'And the little woman is coming to call on you to demand a personal explanation.'

'Good Lord!'

'I shall watch your future career with some considerable interest,' said young Bingo.

I bellowed for Jeeves.

'Jeeves!'

'Sir?'

'I'm in the soup.'

'Indeed, sir?'

I sketched out the scenario for him.

'What would you advise?'

'I think if I were you, sir, I would accept Mr Pitt-Waley's invitation immediately. If you remember, sir, he invited you to shoot with him in Norfolk this week.'

'So he did! By Jove, Jeeves, you're always right. Meet me at the station with my things the first train after lunch. I'll go and lie low at the club for the rest of the morning.'

'Would you require my company on this visit, sir?'

'Do you want to come?'

'If I might suggest it, sir, I think it would be better if I remained here and kept in touch with Mr Little. I might possibly hit upon some method of pacifying the various parties, sir.'

'Right-o! But, if you do, you're a marvel.'

I didn't enjoy myself much in Norfolk. It rained most of the time, and when it wasn't raining I was so dashed jumpy that I couldn't hit a thing. By the end of the week I couldn't stand it any longer. Too bally absurd, I mean, being marooned miles away in the country just because young Bingo's uncle and wife wanted to have a few words with me. I made up my mind that I would pop back and do the strong, manly thing by lying low in my flat and telling Jeeves to inform everybody who called that I wasn't at home.

I sent Jeeves a telegram saying I was coming, and drove straight to Bingo's place when I reached town. I wanted to find out the general posish of affairs. But apparently the man was out. I rang a couple of times but nothing happened, and I was just going to leg it when I heard the sound of footsteps inside and the door opened. It wasn't one of the cheeriest moments of my career when I found myself peering into the globular face of Lord Bittlesham.

'Oh, er, hallo!' I said. And there was a bit of a pause.

I don't quite know what I had been expecting the old boy to do if, by bad luck, we should ever meet again, but I had a sort of general idea that he would turn fairly purple and start almost immediately to let me have it in the gizzard. It struck me as somewhat rummy, therefore, when he simply smiled weakly. A sort of frozen smile it was. His eyes kind of bulged and he swallowed once or twice.

'Er . . .' he said.

I waited for him to continue, but apparently that was all there was.

'Bingo in?' I said, after a rather embarrassing pause.

He shook his head and smiled again. And then, suddenly, just as the flow of conversation had begun to slacken once more, I'm dashed if he didn't make a sort of lumbering leap back into the flat and bang the door.

I couldn't understand it. But, as it seemed that the interview, such as it was, was over, I thought I might as well be shifting. I had just started down the steps when I met young Bingo, charging up three steps at a time.

'Hallo, Bertie!' he said. 'Where did you spring from? I thought you were out of town?'

'I've just got back. I looked in on you to see how the land lay.'

'How do you mean?'

'Why, all that business, you know.'

'Oh, that!' said young Bingo airily. 'That was all settled days ago. The dove of peace is flapping its wings all over the place. Everything's as right as it can be. Jeeves fixed it all up. He's a marvel, that man, Bertie, I've always said so. Put the whole thing straight in half a minute with one of those brilliant ideas of his.'

'This is topping!'

'I knew you'd be pleased.'

'Congratulate you.'

'Thanks.'

'What did Jeeves do? I couldn't think of any solution of the bally thing myself.'

'Oh, he took the matter in hand and smoothed it all out in a second! My uncle and the little woman are tremendous pals now. They gas away by the hour together about literature and all that. He's always dropping in for a chat.'

This reminded me.

'He's in there now,' I said. 'I say, Bingo, how *is* your uncle these days?'

336 The Inimitable Jeeves

'Much as usual. How do you mean?'

'I mean he hasn't been feeling the strain of things a bit, has he? He seemed rather strange in his manner just now.'

'Why, have you met him?'

'He opened the door when I rang. And then, after he had stood goggling at me for a bit, he suddenly banged the door in my face. Puzzled me, you know. I mean, I could have understood it if he'd ticked me off and all that, but dash it, the man seemed absolutely scared.'

Young Bingo laughed a care-free laugh.

'Oh, that's all right!' he said. 'I forgot to tell you about that. Meant to write, but kept putting it off. He thinks you're a loony.'

'He – what!'

'Yes. That was Jeeves's idea, you know. It's solved the whole problem splendidly. He suggested that I should tell my uncle that I had acted in perfectly good faith in introducing you to him as Rosie M. Banks; that I had repeatedly had it from your own lips that you were, and that I didn't see any reason why you shouldn't be. The idea being that you were subject to hallucinations and generally potty. And then we got hold of Sir Roderick Glossop – you remember, the old boy whose kid you pushed into the lake that day down at Ditteredge Hall – and he rallied round with his story of how he had come to lunch with you and found your bedroom full up with cats and fish, and how you had pinched his hat while you were driving past his car in a taxi, and all that, you know. It just rounded the whole thing off nicely. I always say, and I always shall say, that you've only got to stand on Jeeves, and Fate can't touch you.'

I can stand a good deal, but there are limits.

'Well, of all the dashed bits of nerve I ever – '

Bingo looked at me astonished.

'You aren't *annoyed*?' he said.

'Annoyed! At having half London going about under the impression that I'm off my chump? Dash it all – '

'Bertie,' said Bingo, 'you amaze and wound me. If I had dreamed that you would object to doing a trifling good turn to a fellow who's been a pal or yours for fifteen years – '

'Yes, but, look here – '

'Have you forgotten,' said young Bingo, 'that we were at school together?'

I pushed on to the old flat, seething like the dickens. One thing I was jolly certain of, and that was that this was where Jeeves and I parted company. A topping valet, of course, none better in London, but I wasn't going to allow that to weaken me. I buzzed into the flat like an east wind . . . and there was the box of cigarettes on the small table and the illustrated weekly papers on the big table and my slippers on the floor, and every dashed thing so bally *right*, if you know what I mean, that I started to calm down in the first two seconds. It was like one of those moments in a play where the chappie, about to steep himself in crime, suddenly hears the soft, appealing strains of the old melody he learned at his mother's knee. Softened, I mean to say. That's the word I want. I was softened.

And then through the doorway there shimmered good old Jeeves in the wake of a tray full of the necessary ingredients, and there was something about the mere look of the man -

However, I steeled the old heart and had a stab at it.

'I have just met Mr Little, Jeeves,' I said.

'Indeed, sir?'

'He – er – he told me you had been helping him.'

'I did my best, sir. And I am happy to say that matters now appear to be proceeding smoothly. Whisky, sir?'

'Thanks. Er – Jeeves.'

'Sir?'

'Another time – '

'Sir?'

'Oh, nothing . . . Not all the soda, Jeeves.'

'Very good, sir.'

He started to drift out.

'Oh, Jeeves!'

'Sir?'

'I wish . . . that is . . . I think . . . I mean . . . Oh, nothing!'

'Very good, sir. The cigarettes are at your elbow, sir. Dinner will be ready at a quarter to eight precisely, unless you desire to dine out?'

'No. I'll dine in.'

'Yes, sir.'

'Jeeves!'

'Sir?'

'Oh, nothing!' I said.

'Very good, sir,' said Jeeves.

Carry on, Jeeves

To
Bernard le Strange

1

JEEVES TAKES CHARGE

Now, touching this business of old Jeeves – my man, you know – how do we stand? Lots of people think I'm much too dependent on him. My Aunt Agatha, in fact, has even gone so far as to call him my keeper. Well, what I say is: Why not? The man's a genius. From the collar upwards he stands alone. I gave up trying to run my own affairs within a week of his coming to me. That was about half a dozen years ago, directly after the rather rummy business of Florence Craye, my Uncle Willoughby's book, and Edwin, the Boy Scout.

The thing really began when I got back to Easeby, my uncle's place in Shropshire. I was spending a week or so there, as I generally did in the summer; and I had to break my visit to come back to London to get a new valet. I had found Meadowes, the fellow I had taken to Easeby with me, sneaking my silk socks, a thing no bloke of spirit could stick at any price. It transpiring, moreover, that he had looted a lot of other things here and there about the place, I was reluctantly compelled to hand the misguided blighter the mitten and go to London to ask the registry office to dig up another specimen for my approval. They sent me Jeeves.

I shall always remember the morning he came. It so happened that the night before I had been present at a rather cheery little supper, and I was feeling pretty rocky. On top of this I was trying to read a book Florence Craye had given me. She had been one of the house-party at Easeby, and two or three days before I left we had got engaged. I was due back at the end of the week, and I knew she would expect me to have finished the book by then. You see, she was particularly keen on boosting me up a bit nearer her own plane of intellect. She was a girl with a wonderful profile, but steeped to the gills in serious purpose. I can't give you a better idea of the way things stood than by telling you that the book she'd given me to read was called *Types of Ethical Theory*, and that when I opened it at random I struck a page beginning:

The postulate or common understanding involved in speech is certainly co-extensive, in the obligation it carries, with the social organism of which language is the instrument, and the ends of which it is an effort to subserve.

All perfectly true, no doubt; but not the sort of thing to spring on a lad with a morning head.

I was doing my best to skim through this bright little volume when the bell rang. I crawled off the sofa and opened the door. A kind of darkish sort of respectful Johnnie stood without.

'I was sent by the agency, sir,' he said. 'I was given to understand that you require a valet.'

I'd have preferred an undertaker; but I told him to stagger in, and he floated noiselessly through the doorway like a healing zephyr. That impressed me from the start. Meadowes had had flat feet and used to clump. This fellow didn't seem to have any feet at all. He just streamed in. He had a grave, sympathetic face, as if he, too, knew what it was to sup with the lads.

'Excuse me, sir,' he said gently.

Then he seemed to flicker, and wasn't there any longer. I heard him moving about in the kitchen, and presently he came back with a glass on a tray.

'If you would drink this, sir,' he said, with a kind of bedside manner, rather like the royal doctor shooting the bracer into the sick prince. 'It is a little preparation of my own invention. It is the Worcester Sauce that gives it its colour. The raw egg makes it nutritious. The red pepper gives it its bite. Gentlemen have told me they have found it extremely invigorating after a late evening.'

I would have clutched at anything that looked like a lifeline that morning. I swallowed the stuff. For a moment I felt as if somebody had touched off a bomb inside the old bean and was strolling down my throat with a lighted torch, and then everything seemed suddenly to get all right. The sun shone in through the window; birds twittered in the tree-tops; and, generally speaking, hope dawned once more.

'You're engaged!' I said, as soon as I could say anything.

I perceived clearly that this cove was one of the world's workers, the sort no home should be without.

'Thank you, sir. My name is Jeeves.'

'You can start in at once?'

'Immediately, sir.'

'Because I'm due down at Easeby, in Shropshire, the day after tomorrow.'

'Very good, sir.' He looked past me at the mantelpiece. 'That is an excellent likeness of Lady Florence Craye, sir. It is two years since I saw her ladyship. I was at one time in Lord Worplesdon's employment. I tendered my resignation because I could not see eye to eye with his lordship in his desire to dine in dress trousers, a flannel shirt, and a shooting coat.'

He couldn't tell me anything I didn't know about the old boy's eccentricity. This Lord Worplesdon was Florence's father. He was the old buster who, a few years later, came down to breakfast one morning, lifted the first cover he saw, said 'Eggs! Eggs! Eggs! Damn all eggs!' in an overwrought sort of voice, and instantly legged it for France, never to return to the bosom of his family. This, mind you, being a bit of luck for the bosom of the family, for old Worplesdon had the worst temper in the county.

I had known the family ever since I was a kid, and from boyhood up this old boy had put the fear of death into me. Time, the great healer, could never remove from my memory the occasion when he found me – then a stripling of fifteen – smoking one of his special cigars in the stables. He got after me with a hunting-crop just at the moment when I was beginning to realize that what I wanted most on earth was solitude and repose, and chased me more than a mile across difficult country. If there was a flaw, so to speak, in the pure joy of being engaged to Florence, it was the fact that she rather took after her father, and one was never certain when she might erupt. She had a wonderful profile, though.

'Lady Florence and I are engaged, Jeeves,' I said.

'Indeed, sir?'

You know, there was a kind of rummy something about his manner. Perfectly all right and all that, but not what you'd call chirpy. It somehow gave me the impression that he wasn't keen on Florence. Well, of course, it wasn't my business. I supposed that while he had been valeting old Worplesdon she must have trodden on his toes in some way. Florence was a dear girl, and, seen sideways, most awfully good-looking; but if she had a fault it was a tendency to be a bit imperious with the domestic staff.

At this point in the proceedings there was another ring at the front door. Jeeves shimmered out and came back with a telegram. I opened it. It ran:

> Return immediately. Extremely urgent. Catch first train. Florence.

'Rum!' I said.

'Sir?'

'Oh, nothing!'

It shows how little I knew Jeeves in those days that I didn't go a bit deeper into the matter with him. Nowadays I would never dream of reading a rummy communication without asking him what he thought of it. And this one was devilish odd. What I mean is, Florence knew I was going back to Easeby the day after tomorrow, anyway; so why the hurry call? Something must have happened, of course; but I couldn't see what on earth it could be.

'Jeeves,' I said, 'we shall be going down to Easeby this afternoon. Can you manage it?'

'Certainly, sir.'

'You can get your packing done and all that?'

'Without any difficulty, sir. Which suit will you wear for the journey?'

'This one.'

I had on a rather sprightly young check that morning, to which I was a good deal attached; I fancied it, in fact, more than a little. It was perhaps rather sudden till you got used to it, but, nevertheless, an extremely sound effort, which many lads at the club and elsewhere had admired unrestrainedly.

'Very good, sir.'

Again there was that kind of rummy something in his manner. It was the way he said it, don't you know. He didn't like the suit. I pulled myself together to assert myself. Something seemed to tell me that, unless I was jolly careful and nipped this lad in the bud, he would be starting to boss me. He had the aspect of a distinctly resolute blighter.

Well, I wasn't going to have any of that sort of thing, by Jove! I'd seen so many cases of fellows who had become perfect slaves to their valets. I remember poor old Aubrey Fothergill telling me – with absolute tears in his eyes, poor chap! – one night at the club, that he had been compelled to give up a favourite pair of brown shoes simply because Meekyn, his man, disapproved of them. You have to keep these fellows in their place, don't you know. You have to work the good old iron-hand-in-the-velvet-glove wheeze. If you give them a what's-its-name, they take a thingummy.

'Don't you like this suit, Jeeves?' I said coldly.

'Oh, yes, sir.'

'Well, what don't you like about it?'

'It is a very nice suit, sir.'

'Well, what's wrong with it? Out with it, dash it!'

'If I might make the suggestion, sir, a simple brown or blue, with a hint of some quiet twill – '

'What absolute rot!'

'Very good, sir.'

'Perfectly blithering, my dear man!'

'As you say, sir.'

I felt as if I had stepped on the place where the last stair ought to have been, but wasn't. I felt defiant, if you know what I mean, and there didn't seem anything to defy.

'All right, then,' I said.

'Yes, sir.'

And then he went away to collect his kit, while I started in again on *Types of Ethical Theory* and took a stab at a chapter headed 'Idiopsychological Ethics'.

Most of the way down in the train that afternoon, I was wondering what could be up at the other end. I simply couldn't see what could have happened. Easeby wasn't one of those country houses you read about in the society novels, where young girls are lured on to play baccarat and then skinned to the bone of their jewellery, and so on. The house-party I had left had consisted entirely of law-abiding birds like myself.

Besides, my uncle wouldn't have let anything of that kind go on in his house. He was a rather stiff, precise sort of old boy, who liked a quiet life. He was just finishing a history of the family or something, which he had been working on for the last year, and didn't stir much from the library. He was rather a good instance of what they say about its being a good scheme for a fellow to sow his wild oats. I'd been told that in his youth Uncle Willoughby had been a bit of a bounder. You would never have thought it to look at him now.

When I got to the house, Oakshott, the butler, told me that Florence was in her room, watching her maid pack. Apparently there was a dance on at a house about twenty miles away that night, and she was motoring over with some of the Easeby lot and would be away some nights. Oakshott said she had told him to tell her the moment I arrived; so I trickled into the smoking-room and waited, and presently in she came. A glance showed me that she was perturbed, and even peeved. Her eyes had a goggly look, and altogether she appeared considerably pipped.

'Darling!' I said, and attempted the good old embrace; but she side-stepped like a bantam-weight.

'Don't!'

'What's the matter?'

'Everything's the matter! Bertie, you remember asking me, when you left, to make myself pleasant to your uncle?'

'Yes.'

The idea being, of course, that as at that time I was more or less dependent on Uncle Willoughby I couldn't very well marry without his approval. And though I knew he wouldn't have any objection to Florence, having known her father since they were at Oxford together, I hadn't wanted to take any chances; so I had told her to make an effort to fascinate the old boy.

'You told me it would please him particularly if I asked him to read me some of his history of the family.'

'Wasn't he pleased.'

'He was delighted. He finished writing the thing yesterday afternoon, and read me nearly all of it last night. I have never had such a shock in my life. The book is an outrage. It is impossible. It is horrible!'

'But, dash it, the family weren't so bad as all that.'

'It is not a history of the family at all. Your uncle has written his reminiscences! He calls them "Recollections of a Long Life"!'

I began to understand. As I say, Uncle Willoughby had been somewhat on the tabasco side as a young man, and it began to look as if he might have turned out something pretty fruity if he had started recollecting his long life.

'If half of what he has written is true,' said Florence, 'your uncle's youth must have been perfectly appalling. The moment we began to read he plunged straight into a most scandalous story of how he and my father were thrown out of a music-hall in 1887!'

'Why?'

'I decline to tell you why.'

It must have been something pretty bad. It took a lot to make them chuck people out of music-halls in 1887.

'Your uncle specifically states that father had drunk a quart and a half of champagne before beginning the evening,' she went on. 'The book is full of stories like that. There is a dreadful one about Lord Emsworth.'

'Lord Emsworth? Not the one we know? Not the one at Blandings?'

A most respectable old Johnnie, don't you know. Doesn't do a thing nowadays but dig in the garden with a spud.

'The very same. That is what makes the book so unspeakable. It is full of stories about people one knows who are the essence of propriety today, but who seem to have behaved, when they were in London in the eighties, in a manner that would not have been tolerated in the fo'c'sle of a whaler. Your uncle seems to remember everything disgraceful that happend to anybody when he was in his early twenties. There is a story about Sir Stanley Gervase-Gervase at Rosherville Gardens which is ghastly in its perfection of detail. It seems that Sir Stanley – but I can't tell you!'

'Have a dash!'

'No!'

'Oh, well, I shouldn't worry. No publisher will print the book if it's as bad as all that.'

'On the contrary, your uncle told me that all negotiations are settled with Riggs and Ballinger, and he's sending off the manuscript tomorrow for immediate publication. They make a special thing of that sort of book. They published Lady Carnaby's *Memories of Eighty Interesting Years*.'

'I read 'em!'

'Well, then, when I tell you that Lady Carnaby's Memories are simply not to be compared with your uncle's Recollections, you will understand my state of mind. And Father appears in nearly every story in the book! I am horrified at the things he did when he was a young man!'

'What's to be done?'

'The manuscript must be intercepted before it reaches Riggs and Ballinger, and destroyed!'

I sat up.

This sounded rather sporting.

'How are you going to do it?' I inquired.

'How can I do it? Didn't I tell you the parcel goes off tomorrow? I am going to the Murgatroyds' dance tonight and shall not be back till Monday. You must do it. That is why I telegraphed to you.'

'What!'

She gave me a look.

'Do you mean to say you refuse to help me, Bertie?'

'No; but – I say!'

'It's quite simple.'

'But even if I – What I mean is – Of course, anything I can do – but – if you know what I mean – '

'You say you want to marry me, Bertie?'

'Yes, of course; but still – '

For a moment she looked exactly like her old father.

'I will never marry you if those Recollections are published.'

'But, Florence, old thing!'

'I mean it. You may look on it as a test, Bertie. If you have the resource and courage to carry this thing through, I will take it as evidence that you are not the vapid and shiftless person most people think you. If you fail, I shall know that your Aunt Agatha was right

when she called you a spineless invertebrate and advised me strongly
not to marry you. It will be perfectly simple for you to intercept the
manuscript, Bertie. It only requires a little resolution.'

'But suppose Uncle Willoughby catches me at it? He'd cut me off
with a bob.'

'If you care more for your uncle's money than for me – '

'No, no! Rather not!'

'Very well, then. The parcel containing the manuscript will, of
course, be placed on the hall table tomorrow for Oakshott to take
to the village with the letters. All you have to do is to take it away and
destroy it. Then your uncle will think it has been lost in the post.'

It sounded thin to me.

'Hasn't he got a copy of it?'

'No; it has not been typed. He is sending the manuscript just as
he wrote it.'

'But he could write it over again.'

'As if he would have the energy!'

'But – '

'If you are going to do nothing but make absurd objections,
Bertie – '

'I was only pointing things out.'

'Well, don't! Once and for all, will you do me this quite simple
act of kindness?'

The way she put it gave me an idea.

'Why not get Edwin to do it? Keep it in the family, kind of, don't
you know. Besides, it would be a boon to the kid.'

A jolly bright idea it seemed to me. Edwin was her young brother,
who was spending his holidays at Easeby. He was a ferret-faced
kid, whom I had disliked since birth. As a matter of fact, talking
of Recollections and Memories, it was young blighted Edwin who,
nine years before, had led his father to where I was smoking his
cigar and caused all the unpleasantness. He was fourteen now and
had just joined the Boy Scouts. He was one of those thorough kids,
and took his responsibilities pretty seriously. He was always in a sort
of fever because he was dropping behind schedule with his daily acts
of kindness. However hard he tried, he'd fall behind; and then you
would find him prowling about the house, setting such a clip to try
and catch up with himself that Easeby was rapidly becoming a perfect
hell for man and beast.

The idea didn't seem to strike Florence.

'I shall do nothing of the kind, Bertie. I wonder you can't appreciate the compliment I am paying you – trusting you like this.'

'Oh, I see that all right, but what I mean is, Edwin would do it so much better than I would. These Boy Scouts are up to all sorts of dodges. They spoor, don't you know, and take cover and creep about, and what not.'

'Bertie, will you or will you not do this perfectly trivial thing for me? If not, say so now, and let us end this farce of pretending that you care a snap of the fingers for me.'

'Dear old soul, I love you devotedly!'

'Then will you or will you not – '

'Oh, all right,' I said. 'All right! All right!'

And then I tottered forth to think it over. I met Jeeves in the passage just outside.

'I beg your pardon, sir. I was endeavouring to find you.'

'What's the matter?'

'I felt that I should tell you, sir, that somebody had been putting black polish on your brown walking shoes.'

'What! Who? Why?'

'I could not say, sir.'

'Can anything be done with them?'

'Nothing, sir.'

'Damn!'

'Very good, sir.'

I've often wondered since then how these murderer fellows manage to keep in shape while they're contemplating their next effort. I had a much simpler sort of job on hand, and the thought of it rattled me to such an extent in the night watches that I was a perfect wreck next day. Dark circles under the eyes – I give you my word! I had to call on Jeeves to rally round with one of those life-savers of his.

From breakfast on I felt like a bag-snatcher at a railway station. I had to hang about waiting for the parcel to be put on the hall table, and it wasn't put. Uncle Willoughby was a fixture in the library, adding the finishing touches to the great work, I supposed, and the more I thought the thing over the less I liked it. The chances against my pulling it off seemed about three to two, and the thought of what would happen if I didn't gave me cold shivers down the spine. Uncle Willoughby was a pretty mild sort of old boy, as a rule, but I've known him to cut up rough, and, by Jove, he was scheduled to extend himself if he caught me trying to get away with his life work.

It wasn't till nearly four that he toddled out of the library with the parcel under his arm, put it on the table, and toddled off again. I was hiding a bit to the south-east at the moment, behind a suit of armour.

I bounded out and legged it for the table. Then I nipped upstairs to hide the swag. I charged in like a mustang and nearly stubbed my toe on young blighted Edwin, the Boy Scout. He was standing at the chest of drawers, confound him, messing about with my ties.

'Hallo!' he said.

'What are you doing here?'

'I'm tidying your room. It's my last Saturday's act of kindness.'

'Last Saturday's.'

'I'm five days behind. I was six till last night, but I polished your shoes.'

'Was it you – '

'Yes. Did you see them? I just happened to think of it. I was in here, looking round. Mr Berkeley had this room while you were away. He left this morning. I thought perhaps he might have left something in it that I could have sent on. I've often done acts of kindness that way.'

'You must be a comfort to one and all!'

It became more and more apparent to me that this infernal kid must somehow be turned out eftsoons or right speedily. I had hidden the parcel behind my back, and I didn't think he had seen it; but I wanted to get at that chest of drawers quick, before anyone else came along.

'I shouldn't bother about tidying the room,' I said.

'I like tidying it. It's not a bit of trouble – really.'

'But it's quite tidy now.'

'Not so tidy as I shall make it.'

This was getting perfectly rotten. I didn't want to murder the kid, and yet there didn't seem any other way of shifting him. I pressed down the mental accelerator. The old lemon throbbed fiercely. I got an idea.

'There's something much kinder than that which you could do,' I said. 'You see that box of cigars? Take it down to the smoking-room and snip off the ends for me. That would save me no end of trouble. Stagger along, laddie.'

He seemed a bit doubtful; but he staggered. I shoved the parcel into a drawer, locked it, trousered the key, and felt better. I might be a chump, but, dash it, I could out-general a mere kid with a face like a ferret. I went downstairs again. Just as I was passing the smoking-room door out curveted Edwin. It seemed to me that if he wanted to do a real act of kindness he would commit suicide.

'I'm snipping them,' he said.

'Snip on! Snip on!'

'Do you like them snipped much, or only a bit?'
'Medium.'
'All right. I'll be getting on, then.'
'I should.'
And we parted.

Fellows who know all about that sort of thing – detectives, and so on – will tell you that the most difficult thing in the world is to get rid of the body. I remember, as a kid, having to learn by heart a poem about a bird by the name of Eugene Aram, who had the deuce of a job in this respect. All I can recall of the actual poetry is the bit that goes:

> Tum-tum, tum-tum, tum-tumty-tum,
> I slew him, tum-tum tum!

But I recollect that the poor blighter spent much of his valuable time dumping the corpse into ponds and burying it, and what not, only to have it pop out at him again. It was about an hour after I had shoved the parcel into the drawer when I realized that I had let myself in for just the same sort of thing.

Florence had talked in an airy sort of way about destroying the manuscript; but when one came down to it, how the deuce can a chap destroy a great chunky mass of paper in somebody else's house in the middle of summer? I couldn't ask to have a fire in my bedroom, with the thermometer in the eighties. And if I didn't burn the thing, how else could I get rid of it? Fellows on the battlefield eat dispatches to keep them from falling into the hands of the enemy, but it would have taken me a year to eat Uncle Willoughby's Recollections.

I'm bound to say the problem absolutely baffled me. The only thing seemed to be to leave the parcel in the drawer and hope for the best.

I don't know whether you have ever experienced it, but it's a dashed unpleasant thing having a crime on one's conscience. Towards the end of the day the mere sight of the drawer began to depress me. I found myself getting all on edge; and once when Uncle Willoughby trickled silently into the smoking-room when I was alone there and spoke to me before I knew he was there, I broke the record for the sitting high jump.

I was wondering all the time when Uncle Willoughby would sit up and take notice. I didn't think he would have time to suspect that anything had gone wrong till Saturday morning, when he would be expecting, of course, to get the acknowledgement of the manuscript from the publishers. But early on Friday evening he came out of the library as I was passing and asked me to step in. He was looking considerably rattled.

'Bertie,' he said – he always spoke in a precise sort of pompous kind of way – 'an exceedingly disturbing thing has happened. As you know, I dispatched the manuscript of my book to Messrs Riggs and Ballinger, the publishers, yesterday afternoon. It should have reached them by the first post this morning. Why I should have been uneasy I cannot say, but my mind was not altogether at rest respecting the safety of the parcel. I therefore telephoned to Messrs Riggs and Ballinger a few moments back to make inquiries. To my consternation they informed me that they were not yet in receipt of my manuscript.'

'Very rum!'

'I recollect distinctly placing it myself on the hall table in good time to be taken to the village. But here is a sinister thing. I have spoken to Oakshott, who took the rest of the letters to the post office, and he cannot recall seeing it there. He is, indeed, unswerving in his assertions that when he went to the hall to collect the letters there was no parcel among them.'

'Sounds funny!'

'Bertie, shall I tell you what I suspect?'

'What's that?'

'The suspicion will no doubt sound to you incredible, but it alone seems to fit the facts as we know them. I incline to the belief that the parcel has been stolen.'

'Oh, I say! Surely not!'

'Wait! Hear me out. Though I have said nothing to you before, or to anyone else, concerning the matter, the fact remains that during the past few weeks a number of objects – some valuable, others not – have disappeared in this house. The conclusion to which one is irresistibly impelled is that we have a kleptomaniac in our midst. It is a peculiarity of kleptomania, as you are no doubt aware, that the subject is unable to differentiate between the intrinsic values of objects. He will purloin an old coat as readily as a diamond ring, or a tobacco pipe costing but a few shillings with the same eagerness as a purse of gold. The fact that this manuscript of mine could be of no possible value to any outside person convinces me that – '

'But, Uncle, one moment; I know all about those things that were stolen. It was Meadowes, my man, who pinched them. I caught him snaffling my silk socks. Right in the act, by Jove!'

He was tremendously impressed.

'You amaze me, Bertie! Send for the man at once and question him.'

'But he isn't here. You see, directly I found that he was a sock-sneaker I gave him the boot. That's why I went to London – to get a new man.'

'Then, if the man Meadowes is no longer in the house it could not be he who purloined my manuscript. The whole thing is inexplicable.'

After which we brooded for a bit. Uncle Willoughby pottered about the room, registering baffledness, while I sat sucking at a cigarette, feeling rather like a chappie I'd once read about in a book, who murdered another cove and hid the body under the dining-room table, and then had to be the life and soul of a dinner party, with it there all the time. My guilty secret oppressed me to such an extent that after a while I couldn't stick it any longer. I lit another cigarette and started for a stroll in the grounds, by way of cooling off.

It was one of those still evenings you get in the summer, when you can hear a snail clear its throat a mile away. The sun was sinking over the hills and the gnats were fooling about all over the place, and everything smelled rather topping - what with the falling dew and so on – and I was just beginning to feel a little soothed by the peace of it all when suddenly I heard my name spoken.

'It's about Bertie.'

It was the loathsome voice of young blighted Edwin! For a moment I couldn't locate it. Then I realized that it came from the library. My stroll had taken me within a few yards of the open window.

I had often wondered how those Johnnies in books did it – I mean the fellows with whom it was the work of a moment to do about a dozen things that ought to have taken them about ten minutes. But, as a matter of fact, it was the work of a moment with me to chuck away my cigarette, swear a bit, leap about ten yards, dive into a bush that stood near the library window, and stand there with my ears flapping. I was as certain as I've ever been of anything that all sorts of rotten things were in the offing.

'About Bertie?' I heard Uncle Willoughby say.

'About Bertie and your parcel. I heard you talking to him just now. I believe he's got it.'

When I tell you that just as I heard these frightful words a fairly substantial beetle of sorts dropped from the bush down the back of my neck, and I couldn't even stir to squash the same, you will understand that I felt pretty rotten. Everything seemed against me.

'What do you mean, boy? I was discussing the disappearance of my manuscript with Bertie only a moment back, and he professed himself as perplexed by the mystery as myself.'

'Well, I was in his room yesterday afternoon, doing him an act of kindness, and he came in with a parcel. I could see it, though he tried to keep it behind his back. And then he asked me to go to the smoking-room and snip some cigars for him; and about two minutes afterwards he came down – and he wasn't carrying anything. So it must be in his room.'

I understand they deliberately teach these dashed Boy Scouts to cultivate their powers of observation and deduction and what not. Devilish thoughtless and inconsiderate of them, I call it. Look at the trouble it causes.

'It sounds incredible,' said Uncle Willoughby, thereby bucking me up a trifle.

'Shall I go and look in his room?' asked young blighted Edwin. 'I'm sure the parcel's there.'

'But what could be his motive for perpetrating this extraordinary theft?'

'Perhaps he's a – what you said just now.'

'A kleptomaniac? Impossible!'

'It might have been Bertie who took all those things from the very start,' suggested the little brute hopefully. 'He may be like Raffles.'

'Raffles?'

'He's a chap in a book who went about pinching things.'

'I cannot believe that Bertie would – ah – go about pinching things.'

'Well, I'm sure he's got the parcel. I'll tell you what you might do. You might say that Mr Berkeley wired that he had left something here. He had Bertie's room, you know. You might say you wanted to look for it.'

'That would be possible. I – '

I didn't wait to hear any more. Things were getting too hot. I sneaked softly out of my bush and raced for the front door. I sprinted up to my room and made for the drawer where I had put the parcel. And then I found I hadn't the key. It wasn't for the deuce of a time that I recollected I had shifted it to my evening trousers the night before and must have forgotten to take it out again.

Where the dickens were my evening things? I had looked all over the place before I remembered that Jeeves must have taken them away to brush. To leap at the bell and ring it was, with me, the work of a moment. I had just rung it when there was a footstep outside, and in came Uncle Willoughby.

'Oh, Bertie,' he said, without a blush, 'I have – ah – received a telegram from Berkeley, who occupied this room in your absence, asking me to forward him his – er – his cigarette-case, which, it would appear, he inadvertently omitted to take with him when he left the house. I cannot find it downstairs; and it has, therefore, occurred to me that he may have left it in this room. I will – er – just take a look round.'

It was one of the most disgusting spectacles I've ever seen – this white-haired old man, who should have been thinking of the hereafter, standing there lying like an actor.

'I haven't seen it anywhere,' I said.

'Nevertheless, I will search. I must – ah – spare no effort.'

'I should have seen it if it had been here – what?'

'It may have escaped your notice. It is – er – possibly in one of the drawers.'

He began to nose about. He pulled out drawer after drawer, pottering round like an old bloodhound, and babbling from time to time about Berkeley and his cigarette-case in a way that struck me as perfectly ghastly. I just stood there, losing weight every moment.

Then he came to the drawer where the parcel was.

'This appears to be locked,' he said, rattling the handle.

'Yes; I shouldn't bother about that one. It – it's – er – locked, and all that sort of thing.'

'You have not the key?'

A soft, respectful voice spoke behind me.

'I fancy, sir, that this must be the key you require. It was in the pocket of your evening trousers.'

It was Jeeves. He had shimmered in, carrying my evening things, and was standing there holding out the key. I could have massacred the man.

'Thank you,' said my uncle.

'Not at all, sir.'

The next moment Uncle Willoughby had opened the drawer. I shut my eyes.

'No,' said Uncle Willoughby, 'there is nothing here. The drawer is empty. Thank you, Bertie. I hope I have not disturbed you. I fancy – er – Berkeley must have taken his case with him after all.'

When he had gone I shut the door carefully. Then I turned to Jeeves. The man was putting my evening things out on a chair.

'Er – Jeeves!'

'Sir?'

'Oh, nothing.'

It was deuced difficult to know how to begin.

'Er – Jeeves!'

'Sir?'

'Did you – Was there – Have you by chance – '

'I removed the parcel this morning, sir.'

'Oh – ah – why?'

'I considered it more prudent, sir.'

I mused for a while.

'Of course, I suppose all this seems tolerably rummy to you, Jeeves?'

'Not at all, sir. I chanced to overhear you and Lady Florence speaking of the matter the other evening, sir.'

'Did you, by Jove?'

'Yes, sir.'

'Well – er – Jeeves, I think that, on the whole, if you were to – as it were – freeze on to that parcel until we get back to London – '

'Exactly, sir.'

'And then we might – er – so to speak – chuck it away somewhere – what?'

'Precisely, sir.'

'I'll leave it in your hands.'

'Entirely, sir.'

'You know, Jeeves, you're by way of being rather a topper.'

'I endeavour to give satisfaction, sir.'

'One in a million, by Jove!'

'It is very kind of you to say so, sir.'

'Well, that's about all, then, I think.'

'Very good, sir.'

Florence came back on Monday. I didn't see her till we were all having tea in the hall. It wasn't till the crowd had cleared away a bit that we got a chance of having a word together.

'Well, Bertie?' she said.

'It's all right.'

'You have destroyed the manuscript?'

'Not exactly; but – '

'What do you mean?'

'I mean I haven't absolutely – '

'Bertie, your manner is furtive!'

'It's all right. It's this way – '

And I was just going to explain how things stood when out of the library came leaping Uncle Willoughby, looking as braced as a two-year-old. The old boy was a changed man.

'A most remarkable thing, Bertie! I have just been speaking with Mr Riggs on the telephone, and he tells me he received my manuscript by the first post this morning. I cannot imagine what can have caused the delay. Our postal facilities are extremely inadequate in the rural districts. I shall write to headquarters about it. It is insufferable if valuable parcels are to be delayed in this fashion.'

I happened to be looking at Florence's profile at the moment, and at this juncture she swung round and gave me a look that went right through me like a knife. Uncle Willoughby meandered back to the library, and there was a silence that you could have dug bits out of with a spoon.

'I can't understand it,' I said at last. 'I can't understand it, by Jove!'

'I can. I can understand it perfectly, Bertie. Your heart failed you. Rather than risk offending your uncle you – '

'No, no! Absolutely!'

'You preferred to lose me rather than risk losing the money. Perhaps you did not think I meant what I said. I meant every word. Our engagement is ended.'

'But – I say!'

'Not another word!'

'But, Florence, old thing!'

'I do not wish to hear any more. I see now that your Aunt Agatha was perfectly right. I consider that I have had a very lucky escape. There was a time when I thought that, with patience, you might be moulded into something worth while. I see now that you are impossible!'

And she popped off, leaving me to pick up the pieces. When I had collected the debris to some extent I went to my room and rang for Jeeves. He came in looking as if nothing had happened or was ever going to happen. He was the calmest thing in captivity.

'Jeeves!' I yelled. 'Jeeves, that parcel has arrived in London!'

'Yes, sir?'

'Did you send it?'

'Yes, sir. I acted for the best, sir. I think that both you and Lady Florence overestimate the danger of people being offended at being mentioned in Sir Willoughby's Recollections. It has been my experience, sir, that the normal person enjoys seeing his or her name in print, irrespective of what is said about them. I have an aunt, sir, who a few years ago was a martyr to swollen limbs. She tried Walkinshaw's Supreme Ointment and obtained considerable relief – so much so that she sent them an unsolicited testimonial. Her pride at seeing her photograph in the daily papers in connexion with descriptions of her lower limbs before taking, which were nothing less than revolting, was so intense that it led me to believe that publicity, of whatever sort, is what nearly everybody desires. Moreover, if you have ever studied psychology, sir, you will know that respectable old gentlemen are by no means averse to having it advertised that they were extremely wild in their youth. I have an uncle – '

I cursed his aunts and his uncles and him and all the rest of the family.

'Do you know that Lady Florence has broken off her engagement with me?'

'Indeed, sir?'

Not a bit of sympathy! I might have been telling him it was a fine day.

'You're sacked!'

'Very good, sir.'

He coughed gently.

'As I am no longer in your employment, sir, I can speak freely without appearing to take a liberty. In my opinion you and Lady Florence were quite unsuitably matched. Her ladyship is of a highly determined and arbitrary temperament, quite opposed to your own. I was in Lord Worplesdon's service for nearly a year, during which time I had ample opportunities of studying her ladyship. The opinion of the servants' hall was far from favourable to her. Her ladyship's temper caused a good deal of adverse comment among us. It was at times quite impossible. You would not have been happy, sir!'

'Get out!'

'I think you would also have found her educational methods a little trying, sir. I have glanced at the book her ladyship gave you – it has been lying on your table since our arrival – and it is, in my opinion, quite unsuitable. You would not have enjoyed it. And I have it from her ladyship's own maid, who happened to overhear a conversation between her ladyship and one of the gentlemen staying here – Mr Maxwell, who is employed in an editorial capacity by one of the reviews – that it was her intention to start you almost immediately upon Nietzsche. You would not enjoy Nietzsche, sir. He is fundamentally unsound.'

'Get out!'

'Very good, sir.'

It's rummy how sleeping on a thing often makes you feel quite different about it. It's happened to me over and over again. Somehow or other, when I woke next morning the old heart didn't feel half so broken as it had done. It was a perfectly topping day, and there was something about the way the sun came in at the window and the row the birds were kicking up in the ivy that made me half wonder whether Jeeves wasn't right. After all, though she had a wonderful profile, was it such a catch being engaged to Florence Craye as the casual observer might imagine? Wasn't there something in what Jeeves had said about her character? I began to realize that my ideal wife was something quite different, something a lot more clinging and drooping and prattling, and what not.

I had got as far as this in thinking the thing out when that *Types of Ethical Theory* caught my eye. I opened it, and I give you my honest word this was what hit me:

Of the two antithetic terms in the Greek philosophy one only was real and self-subsisting; and that one was Ideal Thought as opposed to that which it has to penetrate and mould. The other, corresponding to our Nature, was in itself phenomenal, unreal, without any permanent footing, having no predicates that held true for two moments together; in short, redeemed from negation only by including indwelling realities appearing through.

Well – I mean to say – what? And Nietzsche, from all accounts, a lot worse than that!

'Jeeves,' I said, when he came in with my morning tea, 'I've been thinking it over. You're engaged again.'

'Thank you, sir.'

I sucked down a cheerful mouthful. A great respect for this bloke's judgement began to soak through me.

'Oh, Jeeves,' I said; 'about that check suit.'

'Yes, sir?'

'Is it really a frost?'

'A trifle too bizarre, sir, in my opinion.'

'But lots of fellows have asked me who my tailor is.'

'Doubtless in order to avoid him, sir.'

'He's supposed to be one of the best men in London.'

'I am saying nothing against his moral character, sir.'

I hesitated a bit. I had a feeling that I was passing into this chappie's clutches, and that if I gave in now I should become just like poor old Aubrey Fothergill, unable to call my soul my own. On the other hand, this was obviously a cove of rare intelligence, and it would be a comfort in a lot of ways to have him doing the thinking for me. I made up my mind.

'All right, Jeeves,' I said. 'You know! Give the bally thing away to somebody!'

He looked down at me like a father gazing tenderly at the way-ward child.

'Thank you, sir. I gave it to the under-gardener last night. A little more tea, sir?'

2

THE ARTISTIC CAREER
OF CORKY

You will notice, as you flit through these reminiscences of mine, that from time to time the scene of action is laid in and around the city of New York; and it is just possible that this may occasion the puzzled look and the start of surprise. 'What,' it is possible that you may ask yourselves, 'is Bertram doing so far from his beloved native land?'

Well, it's a fairly longish story; but, reefing it down a bit and turning it for the nonce into a two-reeler, what happened was that my Aunt Agatha on one occasion sent me over to America to try to stop young Gussie, my cousin, marrying a girl on the vaudeville stage, and I got the whole thing so mixed up that I decided it would be a sound scheme to stop on in New York for a bit instead of going back and having long, cosy chats with her about the affair.

So I sent Jeeves out to find a decent flat, and settled down for a spell of exile.

I'm bound to say New York's a most sprightly place to be exiled in. Everybody was awfully good to me, and there seemed to be plenty of things going on so, take it for all in all, I didn't undergo any frightful hardships. Blokes introduced me to other blokes, and so on and so forth, and it wasn't long before I knew squads of the right sort, some who rolled in the stuff in houses up by the Park, and others who lived with the gas turned down mostly around Washington Square – artists and writers and so forth. Brainy coves.

Corky, the bird I am about to treat of, was one of the artists. A portrait-painter, he called himself, but as a matter of fact his score up to date had been nil. You see, the catch about portrait-painting – I've looked into the thing a bit – is that you can't start painting portraits till people come along and ask you to, and they won't come and ask you to until you've painted a lot first. This makes it kind of difficult, not to say tough, for the ambitious youngster.

Corky managed to get along by drawing an occasional picture for the comic papers – he had rather a gift for funny stuff when he got a good idea – and doing bedsteads and chairs and things for the advertisements. His principal source of income, however, was derived from biting the ear of a rich uncle – one Alexander Worple, who was in the jute business. I'm a bit foggy as to what jute is, but it's apparently something the populace is pretty keen on, for Mr Worple had made quite an indecently large stack of it.

Now, a great many fellows think that having a rich uncle is a pretty soft snap; but, according to Corky, such is not the case. Corky's uncle was a robust sort of cove, who looked like living for ever. He was fifty-one, and it seemed as if he might go to par. It was not this, however, that distressed poor Corky, for he was not bigoted and had no objection to the man going on living. What Corky kicked at was the way the above Worple used to harry him.

Corky's uncle, you see, didn't want him to be an artist. He didn't think he had any talent in that direction. He was always urging him to chuck Art and go into the jute business and start at the bottom and work his way up. And what Corky said was that, while he didn't know what they did at the bottom of a jute business, instinct told him that it was something too beastly for words. Corky, moreover, believed in his future as an artist. Some day, he said, he was going to make a hit. Meanwhile, by using the utmost tact and persuasiveness, he was inducing his uncle to cough up very grudgingly a small quarterly allowance.

He wouldn't have got this if his uncle hadn't had a hobby. Mr Worple was peculiar in this respect. As a rule, from what I've observed, the American captain of industry doesn't do anything out of business hours. When he has put the cat out and locked up the office for the night, he just relapses into a state of coma from which he emerges only to start being a captain of industry again. But Mr Worple in his spare time was what is known as an ornithologist. He had written a book called *American Birds*, and was writing another, to be called *More American Birds*. When he had finished that, the presumption was that he would begin a third, and keep on till the supply of American birds gave out. Corky used to go to him about once every three months and let him talk about American birds. Apparently you could do what you liked with old Worple if you gave him his head first on his pet subject, so these little chats used to make Corky's allowance all right for the time being. But it was pretty rotten for the poor chap. There was the frightful suspense, you see, and, apart from that, birds, except when broiled and in the society of a cold bottle, bored him stiff.

To complete the character-study of Mr Worple, he was a man of extremely uncertain temper, and his general tendency was to think that Corky was a poor chump and that whatever step he took in any direction on his own account was just another proof of his innate idiocy. I should imagine Jeeves feels very much the same about me.

So when Corky trickled into my apartment one afternoon, shooing a girl in front of him, and said, 'Bertie, I want you to meet my fiancée, Miss Singer,' the aspect of the matter which hit me first was precisely the one which he had come to consult me about. The very first words I spoke were, 'Corky, how about your uncle?'

The poor chap gave one of those mirthless laughs. He was looking anxious and worried, like a man who has done the murder all right but can't think what the deuce to do with the body.

'We're so scared, Mr Wooster,' said the girl. 'We were hoping that you might suggest a way of breaking it to him.'

Muriel Singer was one of those very quiet, appealing girls who have a way of looking at you with their big eyes as if they thought you were the greatest thing on earth and wondered that you hadn't got on to it yet yourself. She sat there in a sort of shrinking way, looking at me as if she were saying to herself, 'Oh, I do hope this great strong man isn't going to hurt me.' She gave a fellow a protective kind of feeling, made him want to stroke her hand and say, 'There, there, little one!' or words to that effect. She made me feel that there was nothing I wouldn't do for her. She was rather like one of those innocent-tasting American drinks which creep imperceptibly into your system so that, before you know what you're doing, you're starting out to reform the world by force if necessary and pausing on your way to tell the large man in the corner that, if he looks at you like that, you will knock his head off. What I mean is, she made me feel alert and dashing, like a knight-errant or something of that kind. I felt that I was with her in this thing to the limit.

'I don't see why your uncle shouldn't be most awfully bucked,' I said to Corky. 'He will think Miss Singer the ideal wife for you.'

Corky declined to cheer up.

'You don't know him. Even if he did like Muriel, he wouldn't admit it. That's the sort of pig-headed ass he is. It would be a matter of principle with him to kick. All he would consider would be that I had gone and taken an important step without asking his advice, and he would raise Cain automatically. He's always done it.'

I strained the old bean to meet this emergency.

'You want to work it so that he makes Miss Singer's acquaintance without knowing that you know her. Then you come along –'

'But how can I work it that way?'

I saw his point. That was the catch.

'There's only one thing to do,' I said.

'What's that?'

'Leave it to Jeeves.'

And I rang the bell.

'Sir? said Jeeves, kind of manifesting himself. One of the rummy things about Jeeves is that, unless you watch like a hawk, you very seldom see him come into a room. He's like one of those weird birds in India who dissolve themselves into thin air and nip through space in a sort of disembodied way and assemble the parts again just where they want them. I've got a cousin who's what they call a Theosophist, and he says he's often nearly worked the thing himself, but couldn't quite bring it off, probably owing to having fed in his boyhood on the flesh of animals slain in anger and pie.

The moment I saw the man standing there, registering respectful attention, a weight seemed to roll off my mind. I felt like a lost child who spots his father in the offing.

'Jeeves,' I said, 'we want your advice.'

'Very good, sir.'

I boiled down Corky's painful case into a few well-chosen words.

'So you see what it amounts to, Jeeves. We want you to suggest some way by which Mr Worple can make Miss Singer's acquaintance without getting on to the fact that Mr Corcoran already knows her. Understand?'

'Perfectly, sir.'

'Well, try to think of something.'

'I have thought of something already, sir.'

'You have!'

'The scheme I would suggest cannot fail of success, but it has what may seem to you a drawback, sir, in that it requires a certain financial outlay.'

'He means,' I translated to Corky, 'that he has got a pippin of an idea, but it's going to cost a bit.'

Naturally the poor chap's face dropped, for this seemed to dish the whole thing. But I was still under the influence of the girl's melting gaze, and I saw that this was where I started in as the knight-errant.

'You can count on me for all that sort of thing, Corky,' I said. 'Only too glad. Carry on, Jeeves.'

'I would suggest, sir, that Mr Corcoran take advantage of Mr Worple's attachment to ornithology.'

'How on earth did you know that he was fond of birds?'

'It is the way these New York apartments are constructed, sir. Quite unlike our London houses. The partitions between the rooms are of the flimsiest nature. With no wish to overhear, I have sometimes heard Mr Corcoran expressing himself with a generous strength on the subject I have mentioned.'

'Oh! Well?'

'Why should not the young lady write a small volume, to be entitled – let us say – *The Children's Book of American Birds* and dedicate it to Mr Worple? A limited edition could be published at Your expense, sir, and a great deal of the book would, of course, be given over to eulogistic remarks concerning Mr Worple's own larger treatise on the same subject. I should recommend the dispatching of a presentation copy to Mr Worple, immediately on publication, accompanied by a letter in which the young lady asks to be allowed to make the acquaintance of one to whom she owes so much. This would, I fancy, produce the desired result, but as I say, the expense involved would be considerable.'

I felt like the proprietor of a performing dog on the vaudeville stage when the tyke has just pulled off his trick without a hitch. I had betted on Jeeves all along, and I had known that he wouldn't let me down. It beats me sometimes why a man with his genius is satisfied to hang around pressing my clothes and what not. If I had half Jeeves's brain I should have a stab at being Prime Minister or something.

'Jeeves,' I said, 'that is absolutely ripping! One of your very best efforts.'

'Thank you, sir.'

The girl made an objection.

'But I'm sure I couldn't write a book about anything. I can't even write good letters.'

'Muriel's talents,' said Corky, with a little cough, 'lie more in the direction of the drama, Bertie. I didn't mention it before, but one of our reasons for being a trifle nervous as to how Uncle Alexander will receive the news is that Muriel is in the chorus of that show *Choose Your Exit* at the Manhattan. It's absurdly unreasonable, but we both feel that the fact might increase Uncle Alexander's natural tendency to kick like a steer.'

I saw what he meant. I don't know why it is – one of these psychology sharps could explain it, I suppose – but uncles and aunts, as a class, are always dead against the drama, legitimate or otherwise. They don't seem able to stick it at any price.

But Jeeves had a solution, of course.

'I fancy it would be a simple matter, sir, to find some impecunious author who would be glad to do the actual composition of the volume for a small fee. It is only necessary that the young lady's name should appear on the title page.'

'That's true,' said Corky. 'Sam Patterson would do it for a hundred dollars. He writes a novelette, three short stories, and ten thousand words of a serial for one of the all-fiction magazines under different names every month. A little thing like this would be nothing to him. I'll get after him right away.'

'Fine!'

'Will that be all, sir?' said Jeeves. 'Very good, sir. Thank you, sir.'

I always used to think that publishers has to be devilish intelligent fellows, loaded down with the grey matter; but I've got their number now. All a publisher has to do is to write cheques at intervals, while a lot of deserving and industrious chappies rally round and do the real work. I know, because I have been one myself. I simply sat tight in the old flat with a fountain-pen, and in due season a topping, shiny book came along.

I happened to be down at Corky's place when the first copies of *The Children's Book of American Birds* bobbed up. Muriel Singer was there, and we were talking of things in general when there was a bang at the door and the parcel was delivered.

It was certainly some book. It had a red cover with a fowl of some species on it, and underneath the girl's name in gold letters. I opened a copy at random.

'Often of a spring morning,' it said at the top of page twenty-one, 'as you wander through the fields, you will hear the sweet-toned, carelessly-flowing warble of the purple finch linnet. When you are older you must read all about him in Mr Alexander Worple's wonderful book, *American Birds*.'

You see. A boost for the uncle right away. And only a few pages later there he was in the limelight again in connexion with the yellow-billed cuckoo. It was great stuff. The more I read, the more I admired the chap who had written it and Jeeves's genius in putting us on to the wheeze. I didn't see how the uncle could fail to drop. You can't call a chap the world's greatest authority on the yellow-billed cuckoo without rousing a certain disposition towards chumminess in him.

'It's a cert!' I said.

'An absolute cinch!' said Corky.

And a day or two later he meandered up the Avenue to my flat to tell me that all was well. The uncle had written Muriel a letter so dripping with the milk of human kindness that if he hadn't known

Mr Worple's handwriting Corky would have refused to believe him the author of it. Any time it suited Miss Singer to call, said the uncle, he would be delighted to make her acquaintance.

Shortly after this I had to go out of town. Divers sound sportsmen had invited me to pay visits to their country places, and it wasn't for several months that I settled down in the city again. I had been wondering a lot, of course, about Corky, whether it all turned out right, and so forth, and my first evening in New York, happening to pop into a quiet sort of little restaurant which I go to when I don't feel inclined for the bright lights, I found Muriel Singer there, sitting by herself at a table near the door. Corky, I took it, was out telephoning. I went up and passed the time of day.

'Well, well, well, what?' I said.

'Why, Mr Wooster! How do you do?'

'Corky around?'

'I beg your pardon?'

'You're waiting for Corky, aren't you?'

'Oh, I didn't understand. No, I'm not waiting for him.'

It seemed to me that there was a sort of something in her voice, a kind of thingummy, you know.

'I say, you haven't had a row with Corky, have you?'

'A row.'

'A spat, don't you know – little misunderstanding – faults on both sides – er – and all that sort of thing.'

'Why, whatever makes you think that?'

'Oh, well, as it were, what? What I mean is – I thought you usually dined with him before you went to the theatre.'

'I've left the stage now.'

Suddenly the whole thing dawned on me. I had forgotten what a long time I had been away.

'Why, of course, I see now! You're married!'

'Yes.'

'How perfectly topping! I wish you all kinds of happiness.'

'Thank you so much. Oh, Alexander,' she said, looking past me, 'this is a friend of mine – Mr Wooster.'

I spun round. A bloke with a lot of stiff grey hair and a red sort of healthy face was standing there. Rather a formidable Johnnie, he looked, though peaceful at the moment.

'I want you to meet my husband, Mr Wooster. Mr Wooster is a friend of Bruce's, Alexander.'

The old boy grasped my hand warmly, and that was all that

kept me from hitting the floor in a heap. The place was rocking. Absolutely.

'So you know my nephew, Mr Wooster?' I heard him say. 'I wish you would try to knock a little sense into him and make him quit this playing at painting. But I have an idea that he is steadying down. I noticed it first that night he came to dinner with us, my dear, to be introduced to you. He seemed altogether quieter and more serious. Something seemed to have sobered him. Perhaps you will give us the pleasure of your company at dinner tonight, Mr Wooster? Or have you dined?'

I said I had. What I needed then was air, not dinner. I felt that I wanted to get into the open and think this thing out.

When I reached my flat I heard Jeeves moving about in his lair. I called him.

'Jeeves,' I said, 'now is the time for all good men to come to the aid of the party. A stiff b-and-s first of all, and then I've a bit of news for you.'

He came back with a tray and a long glass.

'Better have one yourself, Jeeves. You'll need it.'

'Later on, perhaps, thank you, sir.'

'All right. Please yourself. But you're going to get a shock. You remember my friend, Mr Corcoran?'

'Yes, sir.'

'And the girl who was to slide gracefully into his uncle's esteem by writing the book on birds?'

'Perfectly, sir.'

'Well, she's slid. She's married the uncle.'

He took it without blinking. You can't rattle Jeeves.

'That was always a development to be feared, sir.'

'You don't mean to tell me that you were expecting it?'

'It crossed my mind as a possibility.'

'Did it, by Jove! Well, I think you might have warned us!'

'I hardly liked to take the liberty, sir.'

Of course, as I saw after I had had a bite to eat and was in a calmer frame of mind, what had happened wasn't my fault, if you came down to it. I couldn't be expected to foresee that the scheme, in itself a cracker-jack, would skid into the ditch as it had done; but all the same I'm bound to admit that I didn't relish the idea of meeting Corky again until time, the great healer, had been able to get in a bit of soothing work. I cut Washington Square out absolutely for the next few months. I gave it the complete miss-in-baulk. And then, just when

I was beginning to think I might safely pop down in that direction and gather up the dropped threads, so to speak, time, instead of working the healing wheeze, went and pulled the most awful bone and put the lid on it. Opening the paper one morning, I read that Mrs Alexander Worple had presented her husband with a son and heir.

I was so dashed sorry for poor old Corky that I hadn't the heart to touch my breakfast. I was bowled over. Absolutely. It was the limit.

I hardly knew what to do. I wanted, of course, to rush down to Washington Square and grip the poor blighter silently by the hand; and then, thinking it over, I hadn't the nerve. Absent treatment seemd the touch. I gave it him in waves.

But after a month or so I began to hesitate again. It struck me that it was playing it a bit low-down on the poor chap, avoiding him like this just when he probably wanted his pals to surge round him most. I pictured him sitting in his lonely studio with no company but his bitter thoughts, and the pathos of it got me to such an extent that I bounded straight into a taxi and told the driver to go all out for the studio.

I rushed in, and there was Corky, hunched up at the easel, painting away, while on the model throne sat a severe-looking female of middle age, holding a baby.

A fellow has to be ready for that sort of thing.

'Oh, ah!' I said, and started to back out.

Corky looked over his shoulder.

'Hallo, Bertie. Don't go. We're just finishing for the day. That will be all this afternoon,' he said to the nurse, who got up with the baby and decanted it into a perambulator which was standing in the fairway.

'At the same hour tomorrow, Mr Corcoran?'

'Yes, please.'

'Good afternoon.'

'Good afternoon.'

Corky stood there, looking at the door, and then he turned to me and began to get it off his chest. Fortunately, he seemed to take it for granted that I knew all about what had happened, so it wasn't as awkward as it might have been.

'It's my uncle's idea,' he said. 'Muriel doesn't know about it yet. The portrait's to be a surprise for her on her birthday. The nurse takes the kid out ostensibly to get a breather, and they beat it down here. If you want an instance of the irony of fate, Bertie, get acquainted with this. Here's the first commission I have ever had to paint a portrait, and the sitter is that human poached egg that has butted in and bounced me out of my inheritance. Can you beat it! I call it rubbing the thing in to expect me to spend my afternoons gazing into the ugly face of a little brat who to all intents and purposes has hit me behind the ear with a black-jack and swiped all I possess. I can't refuse to paint the portrait, because if I did my uncle would stop my allowance; yet every time I look up and catch that kid's vacant eye, I suffer agonies. I tell you, Bertie, sometimes when he gives me a patronizing glance and then turns away and is sick, as if it revolted him to look at me, I come within an ace of occupying the entire front page of the evening papers as the latest murder sensation. There are moments when I can almost see the headlines: "Promising Young Artist Beans Baby With Axe".'

I patted his shoulder silently. My sympathy for the poor old scout was too deep for words.

I kept away from the studio for some time after that, because it didn't seem right of me to intrude on the poor chappie's sorrow. Besides, I'm bound to say that nurse intimidated me. She reminded me so infernally of Aunt Agatha. She was the same gimlet-eyed type.

But one afternoon Corky called me on the phone.

'Bertie!'

'Hallo?'

'Are you doing anything this afternoon?'

'Nothing special.'

'You couldn't come down here, could you?'

'What's the trouble? Anything up?'

'I've finished the portrait.'

'Good boy! Stout work!'

'Yes.' His voice sounded rather doubtful. 'The fact is, Bertie, it doesn't look quite right to me. There's something about it – My uncle's coming in half an hour to inspect it, and – I don't know why it is, but I kind of feel I'd like your moral support!'

I began to see that I was letting myself in for something. The sympathetic cooperation of Jeeves seemed to me to be indicated.

'You think he'll cut up rough?'

'He may.'

I threw my mind back to the red-faced chappie I had met at the restaurant, and tried to picture him cutting up rough. It was only too easy. I spoke to Corky firmly on the telephone.

'I'll come,' I said.

'Good!'

'But only if I may bring Jeeves.'

'Why Jeeves? What's Jeeves got to do with it? Who wants Jeeves? Jeeves is the fool who suggested the scheme that has led – '

'Listen, Corky, old top! If you think I am going to face that uncle of yours without Jeeves's support, you're mistaken. I'd sooner go into a den of wild beasts and bite a lion on the back of the neck.'

'Oh, all right,' said Corky. Not cordially, but he said it; so I rang for Jeeves, and explained the situation.

'Very good, sir,' said Jeeves.

We found Corky near the door, looking at the picture with one hand up in a defensive sort of way, as if he thought it might swing on him.

'Stand right where you are, Bertie,' he said, without moving. 'Now, tell me honestly, how does it strike you?'

The light from the big window fell right on the picture. I took a good look at it. Then I shifted a bit nearer and took another look. Then I went back to where I had been at first, because it hadn't seemed quite so bad from there.

'Well?' said Corky anxiously.

I hesitated a bit.

'Of course, old man, I only saw the kid once, and then only for a moment, but – but it *was* an ugly sort of kid, wasn't it, if I remember rightly?'

'As ugly as that?'

I looked again, and honesty compelled me to be frank.

'I don't see how it could have been, old chap.'

Poor old Corky ran his fingers through his hair in a temperamental sort of way. He groaned.

'You're quite right, Bertie. Something's gone wrong with the darned thing. My private impression is that, without knowing it, I've worked that stunt that Sargent used to pull – painting the soul of the sitter. I've got through the mere outward appearance, and have put the child's soul on canvas.'

'But could a child of that age have a soul like that? I don't see how he could have managed it in the time. What do you think, Jeeves?'

'I doubt it, sir.'

'It – it sort of leers at you, doesn't it?'

'You've noticed that, too?' said Corky.

'I don't see how one could help noticing.'

'All I tried to do was to give the little brute a cheerful expression. But, as it has worked out, he looks positively dissipated.'

'Just what I was going to suggest, old man. He looks as if he were in the middle of a colossal spree, and enjoying every minute of it. Don't you think so, Jeeves?'

'He has a decidedly inebriated air, sir.'

Corky was starting to say something, when the door opened and the uncle came in.

For about three seconds all was joy, jollity and goodwill. The old boy shook hands with me, slapped Corky on the back, said he didn't think he had ever seen such a fine day, and whacked his leg with his stick. Jeeves had projected himself into the background, and he didn't notice him.

'Well, Bruce, my boy; so the portrait is really finished, is it – really finished? Well, bring it out. Let's have a look at it. This will be a wonderful surprise for your aunt. Where is it? Let's – '

And then he got it – suddenly, when he wasn't set for the punch; and he rocked back on his heels.

'Oosh!' he exclaimed. And for perhaps a minute there was one of the scaliest silences I've ever run up against.

'Is this a practical joke?' he said at last, in a way that set about sixteen draughts cutting through the room at once.

I thought it was up to me to rally round old Corky.

'You want to stand a bit farther away from it,' I said.

'You're perfectly right!' he snorted. 'I do! I want to stand so far away from it that I can't see the thing with a telescope!' He turned on Corky like an untamed tiger of the jungle who has just located a chunk of meat. 'And this – this – is what you have been wasting your time and my money for all these years! A painter! I wouldn't let you paint a house of mine. I gave you this commission, thinking that you were a competent worker, and this – this – this extract from a comic supplement is the result!' He swung towards the door, lashing his tail and growling to himself. 'This ends it. If you wish to continue this foolery of pretending to be an artist because you want an excuse for idleness, please yourself. But let me tell you this. Unless you report at my office on Monday morning, prepared to abandon all this idiocy and start in at the bottom of the business to work your way up, as you should have done half a dozen years ago, not another cent – not another cent – not another – Boosh!'

Then the door closed and he was no longer with us. And I crawled out of the bomb-proof shelter.

'Corky, old top!' I whispered faintly.

Corky was standing staring at the picture. His face was set. There was a hunted look in his eye.

'Well, that finishes it!' he muttered brokenly.

'What are you going to do?'

'Do? What can I do? I can't stick on here if he cuts off supplies. You heard what he said. I shall have to go to the office on Monday.'

I couldn't think of a thing to say. I knew exactly how he felt about the office. I don't know when I've been so infernally uncomfortable. It was like hanging round trying to make conversation to a pal who's just been sentenced to twenty years in quod.

And then a soothing voice broke the silence.

'If I might make a suggestion, sir!'

It was Jeeves. He had slid from the shadows and was gazing gravely at the picture. Upon my word, I can't give you a better idea of the shattering effect of Corky's Uncle Alexander when in action than by saying that he had absolutely made me forget for the moment that Jeeves was there.

'I wonder if I have ever happened to mention to you, sir, a Mr Digby Thistleton, with whom I was once in service? Perhaps you have met him? He was a financier. He is now Lord Bridgworth. It was a favourite saying of his that there is always a way. The first time I heard him use the expression was after the failure of a patent depilatory which he promoted.'

'Jeeves,' I said, 'what on earth are you talking about?'

'I mentioned Mr Thistleton, sir, because his was in some respects a parallel case to the present one. His depilatory failed, but he did not despair. He put it on the market again under the name of Hair-o, guaranteed to produce a full crop of hair in a few months. It was advertised, if you remember, sir, by a humorous picture of a billiard ball, before and after taking, and made such a substantial fortune that Mr Thistleton was soon afterwards elevated to the peerage for services to his Party. It seems to me that, if Mr Corcoran looks into the matter, he will find, like Mr Thistleton, that there is always a way. Mr Worple himself suggested the solution of the difficulty. In the heat of the moment he compared the portrait to an extract from a coloured comic supplement. I consider the suggestion a very valuable one, sir. Mr Corcoran's portrait may not have pleased Mr Worple as a likeness of his only child, but I have no doubt that editors would gladly consider it as a foundation for a series of humorous drawings. If Mr Corcoran will allow me to make the suggestion, his talent has always been for the humorous. There is something about this picture – something bold and vigorous, which arrests the attention. I feel sure it would be highly popular.'

Corky was glaring at the picture, and making a sort of dry, sucking noise with his mouth. He seemed completely over-wrought.

And then suddenly he began to laugh in a wild way.

'Corky, old man!' I said, massaging him tenderly. I feared the poor blighter was hysterical.

He began to stagger about all over the floor.

'He's right! The man's absolutely right! Jeeves, you're a life-saver. You've hit on the greatest idea of the age. Report at the office on Monday! Start at the bottom of the business! I'll buy the business if I feel like it. I know the man who runs the comic section of the *Sunday Star*. He'll eat this thing. He was telling me only the other day how hard it was to get a good new series. He'll give me anything I ask for a real winner like this. I've got a gold mine. Where's my hat? I've got an income for life! Where's that confounded hat? Lend me a fiver, Bertie. I want to take a taxi down to Park Row!'

Jeeves smiled paternally. Or, rather, he had a kind of paternal muscular spasm about the mouth, which is the nearest he ever gets to smiling.

'If I might make the suggestion, Mr Corcoran – for a title of the series which you have in mind – "The Adventures of Baby Blobbs".'

Corky and I looked at the picture, then at each other in an awed way. Jeeves was right. There could be no other title.

'Jeeves,' I said. It was a few weeks later, and I had just finished looking at the comic section of the *Sunday Star*. 'I'm an optimist. I always have been. The older I get, the more I agree with Shakespeare and those poet Johnnies about it always being darkest before the dawn and there's a silver lining and what you lose on the swings you make up on the roundabouts. Look at Mr Corcoran, for instance. There was a fellow, one would have said, clear up to the eyebrows in the soup. To all appearances he had got it right in the neck. Yet look at him now. Have you seen these pictures?'

'I took the liberty of glancing at them before bringing them to you, sir. Extremely diverting.'

'They have made a big hit, you know.'

'I anticipated it sir.'

I leaned back against the pillows.

'You know, Jeeves, you're a genius. You ought to be drawing a commission on these things.'

'I have nothing to complain of in that respect, sir. Mr Corcoran has been most generous. I am putting out the brown suit, sir.'

'No, I think I'll wear the blue with the faint red stripe.'

'Not the blue with the faint red stripe, sir.'
'But I rather fancy myself in it.'
'Not the blue with the faint red stripe, sir.'
'Oh, all right, have it your own way.'
'Very good, sir. Thank you, sir.'

3

JEEVES AND THE UNBIDDEN GUEST

I'm not absolutely certain of my facts, but I rather fancy it's Shakespeare – or, if not, it's some equally brainy bird – who says that it's always just when a fellow is feeling particularly braced with things in general that Fate sneaks up behind him with the bit of lead piping. And what I'm driving at is that the man is perfectly right. Take, for instance, the business of Lady Malvern and her son Wilmot. That was one of the scaliest affairs I was ever mixed up with, and a moment before they came into my life I was just thinking how thoroughly all right everything was.

I was still in New York when the thing started, and it was about the time of year when New York is at its best. It was one of those topping mornings, and I had just climbed out from under the cold shower, feeling like a million dollars. As a matter of fact, what was bucking me up more than anything was the fact that the day before I had asserted myself with Jeeves – absolutely asserted myself, don't you know. You see, the way things had been going on I was rapidly becoming a dashed serf. The man had jolly well oppressed me. I didn't so much mind when he made me give up one of my new suits, because Jeeves's judgement about suits is sound and can generally be relied upon.

But I as near as a toucher rebelled when he wouldn't let me wear a pair of cloth-topped boots which I loved like a couple of brothers. And, finally, when he tried to tread on me like a worm in the matter of a hat, I put the Wooster foot down and showed him in no uncertain manner who was who.

It's a long story, and I haven't time to tell you now, but the nub of the thing was that he wanted me to wear the White House Wonder – as worn by President Coolidge – when I had set my heart on the Broadway Special, much patronized by the Younger Set; and the end of the matter was that, after a rather painful scene, I bought the Broadway Special. So that's how things were on this particular morning, and I was feeling pretty manly and independent.

Well, I was in the bathroom, wondering what there was going to be for breakfast while I massaged the spine with a rough towel and sang slightly, when there was a tap at the door. I stopped singing and opened the door an inch.

'What ho, without there!' I said.

'Lady Malvern has called, sir.'

'Eh?'

'Lady Malvern, sir. She is waiting in the sitting-room.'

'Pull yourself together, Jeeves, my man,' I said rather severely, for I bar practical jokes before breakfast. 'You know perfectly well there's no-one waiting for me in the sitting-room. How could there be when it's barely ten o'clock yet?'

'I gathered from her ladyship, sir, that she had landed from an ocean liner at an early hour this morning.'

This made the thing a bit more plausible. I remembered that when I had arrived in America about a year before, the proceedings had begun at some ghastly hour like six, and that I had been shot out on to a foreign shore considerably before eight.

'Who the deuce is Lady Malvern, Jeeves?'

'Her ladyship did not confide in me, sir.'

'Is she alone?'

'Her ladyship is accompanied by a Lord Pershore, sir. I fancy that his lordship would be her ladyship's son.'

'Oh, well, put out rich raiment of sorts, and I'll be dressing.'

'Our heather-mixture lounge is in readiness, sir.'

'Then lead me to it.'

While I was dressing I kept trying to think who on earth Lady Malvern could be. It wasn't till I had climbed through the top of my shirt and was reaching out for the studs that I remembered.

'I've placed her, Jeeves. She's a pal of my Aunt Agatha.'

'Indeed, sir?'

'Yes. I met her at lunch one Sunday before I left London. A very vicious specimen. Writes books. She wrote a book on social conditions in India when she came back from the Durbar.'

'Yes, sir? Pardon me, sir, but not that tie.'

'Eh?'

'Not that tie with the heather-mixture lounge, sir.'

It was a shock to me. I thought I had quelled the fellow. It was rather a solemn moment. What I mean is, if I weakened now, all my good work the night before would be thrown away. I braced myself.

'What's wrong with this tie? I've seen you give it a nasty look before. Speak out like a man! What's the matter with it?'

'Too ornate, sir.'

'Nonsense! A cheerful pink. Nothing more.'

'Unsuitable, sir.'

'Jeeves, this is the tie I wear!'

'Very good, sir.'

Dashed unpleasant. I could see that the man was wounded. But I was firm. I tied the tie, got into the coat and waistcoat, and went into the sitting-room.

'Hullo-ullo-ullo!' I said. 'What?'

'Ah! How do you do, Mr Wooster? You have never met my son Wilmot, I think? Motty, darling, this is Mr Wooster.'

Lady Malvern was a hearty, happy, healthy, overpowering sort of dashed female, not so very tall but making up for it by measuring about six feet from the O.P. to the Prompt Side. She fitted into my biggest armchair as if it had been built round her by someone who knew they were wearing arm-chairs tight about the hips that season. She had bright, bulging eyes and a lot of yellow hair, and when she spoke she showed about fifty-seven front teeth. She was one of those women who kind of numb a fellow's faculties. She made me feel as if I were ten years old and had been brought into the drawing-room in my Sunday clothes to say how-d'you-do. Altogether by no means the sort of thing a chappie would wish to find in his sitting-room before breakfast.

Motty, the son, was about twenty-three, tall and thin and meek-looking. He had the same yellow hair as his mother, but he wore it plastered down and parted in the middle. His eyes bulged, too, but they weren't bright. They were a dull grey with pink rims. His chin gave up the struggle about half-way down, and he didn't appear to have any eyelashes. A mild, furtive, sheepish sort of blighter, in short.

'Awfully glad to see you,' I said, though this was far from the case, for already I was beginning to have a sort of feeling that dirty work was threatening in the offing. 'So you've popped over, eh? Making a long stay in America?'

'About a month. Your aunt gave me your address and told me to be sure to call on you.'

I was glad to hear this, for it seemed to indicate that Aunt Agatha was beginning to come round a bit. As I believe I told you before, there had been some slight unpleasantness between us, arising from the occasion when she had sent me over to New York to disentangle my cousin Gussie from the clutches of a girl on the music-hall stage. When I tell you that by the time I had finished my operations Gussie had not only married the girl but had gone on the Halls himself and was doing well, you'll understand that relations were a trifle strained between aunt and nephew.

I simply hadn't dared to go back and face her, and it was a relief to find that time had healed the wound enough to make her tell her pals to call on me. What I mean is, much as I liked America, I didn't want to have England barred to me for the rest of my natural; and, believe me, England is a jolly sight too small for anyone to live in with Aunt Agatha, if she's really on the war-path. So I was braced at hearing these words and smiled genially on the assemblage.

'Your aunt said that you would do anything that was in your power to be of assistance to us.'

'Rather! Oh, rather. Absolutely.'

'Thank you so much. I want you to put dear Motty up for a little while.'

I didn't get this for a moment.

'Put him up! For my clubs?'

'No, no! Darling Motty is essentially a home bird. Aren't you, Motty, darling?'

Motty, who was sucking the knob of his stick, uncorked himself.

'Yes, Mother,' he said, and corked himself up again.

'I should not like him to belong to clubs. I mean put him up here. Have him to live with you while I am away.'

These frightful words trickled out of her like honey. The woman simply didn't seem to understand the ghastly nature of her proposal. I gave Motty the swift east-to-west. He was sitting with his mouth nuzzling the stick, blinking at the wall. The thought of having this planted on me for an indefinite period appalled me. Absolutely appalled me, don't you know. I was just starting to say that the shot wasn't on the board at any price, and that the first sign Motty gave of trying to nestle into my little home I would yell for the police, when she went on, rolling placidly over me, as it were.

There was something about this woman that sapped one's will-power.

'I am leaving New York by the midday train, as I have to pay a visit to Sing-Sing prison. I am extremely interested in prison conditions in America. After that I work my way gradually across to the coast, visiting the points of interest on the journey. You see, Mr Wooster, I am in America principally on business. No doubt you read my book, *India and the Indians*? My publishers are anxious for me to write a companion volume on the United States. I shall not be able to spend more than a month in the country, as I have to get back for the season, but a month should be ample. I was less than a month in India, and my dear friend Sir Roger Cremorne wrote his *America from Within* after a stay of only two weeks. I should love to take Motty with me, but the poor boy gets so sick when he travels by train. I shall have to pick him up on my return.'

From where I sat I could see Jeeves in the dining-room, laying the breakfast table. I wished I could have had a minute with him alone. I felt certain that he would have been able to think of some way of putting a stop to this woman.

'It will be such a relief to know that Motty is safe with you, Mr Wooster. I know what the temptations of a great city are. Hitherto dear Motty has been sheltered from them. He has lived quietly with me in the country. I know that you will look after him carefully, Mr Wooster. He will give very little trouble.' She talked about the poor blighter as if he wasn't there. Not that Motty seemed to mind. He had stopped chewing his walking-stick and was sitting there with his mouth open. 'He is a vegetarian and a teetotaller and is devoted to reading. Give him a nice book and he will be quite contented.' She got up. 'Thank you so much, Mr Wooster. I don't know what I should have done without your help. Come, Motty. We have just time to see a few of the sights before my train goes. But I shall have to rely on you for most of my information about New York, darling. Be sure to keep your eyes open and take notes of your impressions. It will be such a help. Goodbye, Mr Wooster. I will send Motty back early in the afternoon.'

They went out, and I howled for Jeeves.

'Jeeves!'

'Sir?'

'What's to be done? You heard it all, didn't you? You were in the dining-room most of the time. That pill is coming to stay here.'

'Pill, sir?'

'The excrescence.'

'I beg your pardon, sir?'

I looked at Jeeves sharply. This sort of thing wasn't like him. Then I understood. The man was really upset about that tie. He was trying to get his own back.

'Lord Pershore will be staying here from tonight, Jeeves,' I said coldly.

'Very good, sir. Breakfast is ready, sir.'

I could have sobbed into the bacon and eggs. That there wasn't any sympathy to be got out of Jeeves was what put the lid on it. For a moment I almost weakened and told him to destroy the hat and tie if he didn't like them, but I pulled myself together again. I was dashed if I was going to let Jeeves treat me like a bally one-man chain-gang.

But, what with brooding on Jeeves and brooding on Motty, I was in a pretty reduced sort of state. The more I examined the situation, the more blighted it became. There was nothing I could do. If I slung Motty out, he would report to his mother, and she would pass it on to Aunt Agatha, and I didn't like to think what would happen then. Sooner or later I should be wanting to go back to England, and I didn't want to get there and find Aunt Agatha waiting on the quay for me with a stuffed eelskin. There was absolutely nothing for it but to put the fellow up and make the best of it.

About midday Motty's luggage arrived, and soon afterwards a large parcel of what I took to be nice books. I brightened up a little when I saw it. It was one of those massive parcels and looked as if it had enough in it to keep him busy for a year. I felt a trifle more cheerful, and I got my Broadway Special and stuck it on my head, and gave the pink tie a twist, and reeled out to take a bite of lunch with one or two of the lads at a neighbouring hostelry; and what with excellent browsing and sluicing and cheery conversation and what not, the afternoon passed quite happily. By dinner time I had almost forgotten Motty's existence.

I dined at the club and looked in at a show afterwards, and it wasn't till fairly late that I got back to the flat. There were no signs of Motty, and I took it that he had gone to bed.

It seemed rummy to me, though, that the parcel of nice books was still there with the string and paper on it. It looked as if Motty, after seeing Mother off at the station, had decided to call it a day.

Jeeves came in with the nightly whisky and soda. I could tell by the chappie's manner that he was still upset.

'Lord Pershore gone to bed, Jeeves?' I asked, with reserved hauteur and what not.

'No sir. His lordship has not yet returned.'

'Not returned? What do you mean?'

'His lordship came in shortly after six-thirty, and, having dressed, went out again.'

At this moment there was a noise outside the front door, a sort of scrabbling noise, as if somebody were trying to paw his way through the woodwork. Then a sort of thud.

'Better go and see what that is, Jeeves.'

'Very good, sir.'

He went out and came back again.

'If you would not mind stepping this way, sir, I think we might be able to carry him in.'

'Carry him in?'

'His lordship is lying on the mat, sir.'

I went to the front door. The man was right. There was Motty huddled up outside on the floor. He was moaning a bit.

'He's had some sort of dashed fit,' I said. I took another look. 'Jeeves! Someone's been feeding him meat!'

'Sir?'

'He's a vegetarian, you know. He must have been digging into a steak or something. Call up a doctor!'

'I hardly think it will be necessary, sir. If you would take his lordship's legs, while I – '

'Great Scott, Jeeves! You don't think – he can't be – '

'I am inclined to think so, sir.'

And, by Jove, he was right! Once on the right track, you couldn't mistake it. Motty was under the surface. Completely sozzled.

It was the deuce of a shock.

'You never can tell, Jeeves!'

'Very seldom, sir.'

'Remove the eye of authority and where are you?'

'Precisely, sir.'

'Where is my wandering boy tonight and all that sort of thing, what?'

'It would seem so, sir.'

'Well, we had better bring him in, eh?'

'Yes, sir.'

So we lugged him in, and Jeeves put him to bed, and I lit a cigarette and sat down to think the thing over. I had a kind of foreboding. It seemed to me that I had let myself in for something pretty rocky.

Next morning, after I had sucked down a thoughtful cup of tea, I went into Motty's room to investigate. I expected to find the fellow a wreck, but there he was, sitting up in bed, quite chirpy, reading *Gingery Stories*.

'What ho!' I said.

'What ho!' said Motty.

'What ho! What ho!'

'What ho! What ho! What ho!'

After that it seemed rather difficult to go on with the conversation.

'How are you feeling this morning?' I asked.

'Topping!' replied Motty, blithely and with abandon. 'I say, you know, that fellow of yours – Jeeves, you know – is a corker. I had a most frightful headache when I woke up, and he brought me a sort of rummy dark drink, and it put me right again at once. Said it was his own invention. I must see more of that lad. He seems to me distinctly one of the ones.'

I couldn't believe that this was the same blighter who had sat and sucked his stick the day before.

'You ate something that disagreed with you last night, didn't you?' I said, by way of giving him a chance to slide out of it if he wanted to. But he wouldn't have it at any price.

'No!' he replied firmly. 'I didn't do anything of the kind. I drank too much. Much too much. Lots and lots too much. And, what's more, I'm going to do it again. I'm going to do it every night. If ever you see me sober, old top,' he said, with a kind of holy exaltation, 'tap me on the shoulder and say, "Tut! tut!" and I'll apologize and remedy the defect.'

'But I say, you know, what about me?'

'What about you?'

'Well, I'm, so to speak, as it were, kind of responsible for you. What I mean to say is, if you go doing this sort of thing I'm apt to get in the soup somewhat.'

'I can't help your troubles,' said Motty firmly. 'Listen to me, old thing: this is the first time in my life that I've had a real chance to yield to the temptations of a great city. What's the use of a great city having temptations if fellows don't yield to them? Makes it so bally discouraging for the great city. Besides, Mother told me to keep my eyes open and collect impressions.'

I sat on the edge of the bed. I felt dizzy.

'I know just how you feel, old dear,' said Motty consolingly. 'And, if my principles would permit it, I would simmer down for your sake. But duty first! This is the first time I've been let out alone, and I mean to make the most of it. We're only young once. Why interfere with life's morning? Young man, rejoice in thy youth! Tra-la! What ho!'

Put like that, it did seem reasonable.

'All my bally life, dear boy,' Motty went on, 'I've been cooped up in the ancestral home at Much Middlefold, in Shropshire, and till you've been cooped up in Much Middlefold you don't know what cooping is. The only time we get any excitement is when one of the choir-boys is caught sucking chocolate during the sermon. When that happens, we talk about it for days. I've got a month of New York, and I mean to store up a few happy memories for the long winter evenings. This is my only chance to collect a past, and I'm going to do it. Now tell me, old sport, as man to man, how does one get in touch with that very decent bird Jeeves? Does one ring a bell or shout a bit? I should like to discuss the subject of a good stiff b-and-s with him.'

I had had a sort of vague idea, don't you know, that if I stuck close to Motty and went about the place with him, I might act as a bit of a damper on the gaiety. What I mean is, I thought that if, when he was being the life and soul of the party, he were to catch my reproving eye he might ease up a trifle on the revelry. So the next night I took him along to supper with me. It was the last time. I'm a quiet, peaceful sort of bloke who has lived all his life in London, and I can't stand the pace these swift sportsmen from the rural districts set. What I mean to say is, I'm all for rational enjoyment and so forth, but I think a chappie makes himself conspicuous when he throws soft-boiled eggs at the electric fan. And decent mirth and all that sort of thing are all right, but I do bar dancing on tables and having to dash all over the place dodging waiters, managers, and chuckers-out, just when you want to sit still and digest.

Directly I managed to tear myself away that night and get home, I made up my mind that this was jolly well the last time that I went about with Motty. The only time I met him late at night after that was once when I passed the door of a fairly low-down sort of restaurant and had to step aside to dodge him as he sailed through the air *en route* for the opposite pavement, with a muscular looking sort of fellow peering out after him with a kind of gloomy satisfaction.

In a way, I couldn't help sympathizing with the chap. He had about four weeks to have the good time that ought to have been spread over about ten years, and I didn't wonder at his wanting to be pretty busy. I should have been just the same in his place. Still, there was no denying that it was a bit thick. If it hadn't been for the thought of Lady Malvern and Aunt Agatha in the background, I should have regarded Motty's rapid work with an indulgent smile. But I couldn't get rid of the feeling that, sooner or later, I was the lad who was scheduled to get it behind the ear. And what with brooding on this prospect, and sitting up in the old flat waiting for the familiar footstep, and putting it to bed when it got there, and stealing into the sick-chamber next morning to contemplate the wreckage, I was beginning to lose weight. Absolutely becoming the good old shadow, I give you my honest word. Starting at sudden noises and what not.

And no sympathy from Jeeves. That was what cut me to the quick.

The man was still thoroughly pipped about the hat and tie, and simply wouldn't rally round. One morning I wanted comforting so much that I sank the pride of the Woosters and appealed to the fellow direct.

'Jeeves,' I said, 'this is getting a bit thick!'

'Sir?'

'You know what I mean. This lad seems to have chucked all the principles of a well-spent boyhood. He has got it up his nose!'

'Yes, sir.'

'Well, I shall get blamed, don't you know. You know what my Aunt Agatha is.'

'Yes, sir.'

'Very well, then.'

I waited a moment, but he wouldn't unbend.

'Jeeves,' I said, 'haven't you any scheme up your sleeve for coping with this blighter?'

'No, sir.'

And he shimmered off to his lair. Obstinate devil! So dashed absurd, don't you know. It wasn't as if there was anything wrong with that Broadway Special hat. It was a remarkably priceless effort, and much admired by the lads. But, just because he preferred the White House Wonder, he left me flat.

It was shortly after this that young Motty got the idea of bringing pals back in the small hours to continue the gay revels in the home. This was where I began to crack under the strain. You see, the part of town where I was living wasn't the right place for that sort of thing. I knew lots of chappies down Washington Square way who started the evening at about two a.m. – artists and writers and so forth who frolicked considerably till checked by the arrival of the morning milk. That was all right. They like that sort of thing down there. The neighbours can't get to sleep unless there's someone dancing Hawaiian dances over their heads. But on Fifty-seventh Street the atmosphere wasn't right, and when Motty turned up at three in the morning with a collection of hearty lads, who only stopped singing their college song when they started singing 'The Old Oaken Bucket', there was a marked peevishness among the old settlers in the flats. The management was extremely terse over the telephone at breakfast-time, and took a lot of soothing.

The next night I came home early, after a lonely dinner at a place which I'd chosen because there didn't seem any chance of meeting Motty there. The sitting-room was quite dark, and I was just moving to switch on the light, when there was a sort of explosion and something collared hold of my trouser-leg. Living with Motty had reduced me to such an extent that I was simply unable to cope with this thing. I jumped backward with a loud yell of anguish, and tumbled out into the hall just as Jeeves came out of his den to see what the matter was.

'Did you call, sir?'

'Jeeves! There's something in there that grabs you by the leg!'

'That would be Rollo, sir.'

'Eh?'

'I would have warned you of his presence, but I did not hear you come in. His temper is a little uncertain at present, as he had not yet settled down.'

'Who the deuce is Rollo?'

'His lordship's bull-terrier, sir. His lordship won him in a raffle, and tied him to the leg of the table. If you will allow me, sir, I will go in and switch on the light.'

There really is nobody like Jeeves. He walked straight into the sitting-room, the biggest feat since Daniel and the lions' den, without a quiver. What's more, his magnetism or whatever they call it was such that the dashed animal, instead of pinning him by the leg, calmed down as if he had had a bromide, and rolled over on his back with all his paws in the air. If Jeeves had been his rich uncle he couldn't have been more chummy. Yet directly he caught sight of me again, he got all worked up and seemed to have only one idea in life – to start chewing me where he had left off.

'Rollo is not used to you yet, sir,' said Jeeves, regarding the bally quadruped in an admiring sort of way. 'He is an excellent watch-dog.'

'I don't want a watch-dog to keep me out of my rooms.'

'No, sir.'

'Well, what am I to do?'

'No doubt in time the animal will learn to discriminate, sir. He will learn to distinguish your peculiar scent.'

'What do you mean – my peculiar scent? Correct the impression that I intend to hang about in the hall while life slips by, in the hope that one of these days that dashed animal will decide that I smell all right.' I thought for a bit. 'Jeeves!'

'Sir?'

'I'm going away – tomorrow morning by the first train. I shall go and stop with Mr Todd in the country.'

'Do you wish me to accompany you, sir?'

'No.'

'Very good, sir.'

'I don't know when I shall be back. Forward my letters.'
'Yes, sir.'

As a matter of fact, I was back within the week. Rocky Todd, the pal I went to stay with, is a rummy sort of a chap who lives all alone in the wilds of Long Island, and likes it; but a little of that sort of thing goes a long way with me. Dear old Rocky is one of the best, but after a few days in his cottage in the woods, miles away from anywhere, New York, even with Motty on the premises, began to look pretty good to me. The days down on Long Island have forty-eight hours in them; you can't go to sleep at night because of the bellowing of the crickets; and you have to walk two miles for a drink and six for an evening paper. I thanked Rocky for his kind hospitality, and caught the only train they have down in those parts. It landed me in New York about dinner-time. I went straight to the old flat. Jeeves came out of his lair. I looked round cautiously for Rollo.

'Where's that dog, Jeeves? Have you got him tied up?'

'The animal is no longer here, sir. His lordship gave him to the porter, who sold him. His lordship took a prejudice against the animal on account of being bitten by him in the calf of the leg.'

I don't think I've ever been so bucked by a bit of news. I felt I had misjudged Rollo. Evidently, when you got to know him better, he had a lot of good in him.

'Fine!' I said. 'Is Lord Pershore in, Jeeves?'

'No, sir.'

'Do you expect him back to dinner?'

'No, sir.'

'Where is he?'

'In prison, sir.'

'In prison!'

'Yes, sir.'

'You don't mean – in prison?'

'Yes, sir.'

I lowered myself into a chair.

'Why?' I said.

'He assaulted a constable, sir.'

'Lord Pershore assaulted a constable!'

'Yes, sir.'

I digested this.

'But, Jeeves, I say! This is frightful!'

'Sir?'

'What will Lady Malvern say when she finds out?'

'I do not fancy that her ladyship will find out, sir.'

'But she'll come back and want to know where he is.'

'I rather fancy, sir, that his lordship's bit of time will have run out by then.'

'But supposing it hasn't?'

'In that event, sir, it may be judicious to prevaricate a little.'

'How?'

'If I might make the suggestion, sir, I should inform her ladyship that his lordship has left for a short visit to Boston.'

'Why Boston?'

'Very interesting and respectable centre, sir.'

'Jeeves, I believe you've hit it.'

'I fancy so, sir.'

'Why, this is really the best thing that could have happened. If this hadn't turned up to prevent him, young Motty would have been in a sanatorium by the time Lady Malvern got back.'

'Exactly, sir.'

The more I looked at it in that way, the sounder this prison wheeze seemed to me. There was no doubt in the world that prison was just what the doctor ordered for Motty. It was the only thing that could have pulled him up. I was sorry for the poor blighter, but after all, I reflected, a fellow who had lived all his life with Lady Malvern, in a small village in the interior of Shropshire, wouldn't have much to kick at in a prison. Altogether, I began to feel absolutely braced again. Life became like what the poet Johnnie says – one grand, sweet song. Things went on so comfortably and peacefully for a couple of weeks that I give you my word that I'd almost forgotten such a person as Motty existed. The only flaw in the scheme of things was that Jeeves was still pained and distant. It wasn't anything he said, or did, mind you, but there was a rummy something about him all the time. Once when I was tying the pink tie I caught sight of him in the looking-glass. There was a kind of grieved look in his eyes.

And then Lady Malvern came back, a good bit ahead of schedule. I hadn't been expecting her for days. I'd forgotten how time had been slipping along. She turned up one morning while I was still in bed sipping tea and thinking of this and that. Jeeves flowed in with the announcement that he had just loosed her into the sitting-room. I draped a few garments round me and went in.

There she was, sitting in the same arm chair, looking as massive as ever. The only difference was that she didn't uncover the teeth as she had done the first time.

'Good morning,' I said. 'So you've got back, what?'

'I have got back.'

There was something sort of bleak about her tone, rather as if she had swallowed an east wind. This I took to be due to the fact that she probably hadn't breakfasted. It's only after a bit of breakfast that I'm able to regard the world with that sunny cheeriness which makes a fellow the universal favourite. I'm never much of a lad till I've engulfed an egg or two and a beaker of coffee.

'I suppose you haven't breakfasted?'

'I have not yet breakfasted.'

'Won't you have an egg or something? Or a sausage or something? Or something?'

'No, thank you.'

She spoke as if she belonged to an anti-sausage society or a league for the suppression of eggs. There was a bit of a silence.

'I called on you last night,' she said, 'but you were out.'

'Awfully sorry. Had a pleasant trip?'

'Extremely, thank you.'

'See everything? Niagara Falls, Yellowstone Park, and the jolly old Grand Canyon, and what not?'

'I saw a great deal.'

There was another slight *frappé* silence. Jeeves floated silently into the dining-room and began to lay the breakfast-table.

'I hope Wilmot was not in your way, Mr Wooster?'

I had been wondering when she was going to mention Motty.

'Rather not! Great pals. Hit it off splendidly.'

'You were his constant companion, then?'

'Absolutely. We were always together. Saw all the sights, don't you know. We'd take in the Museum of Art in the morning, and have a bit of lunch at some good vegetarian place, and then toddle along to a sacred concert in the afternoon, and home to an early dinner. We usually played dominoes after dinner. And then the early bed and the refreshing sleep. We had a great time. I was awfully sorry when he went away to Boston.'

'Oh! Wilmot is in Boston?'

'Yes. I ought to have let you know, but of course we didn't know where you were. You were dodging all over the place like a snipe – I mean, don't you know, dodging all over the place, and we couldn't get at you. Yes, Motty went off to Boston.'

'You're sure he went to Boston?'

'Oh, absolutely.' I called out to Jeeves, who was now messing about in the next room with forks and so forth: 'Jeeves, Lord Pershore didn't change his mind about going to Boston, did he?'

'No, sir.'

'I thought I was right. Yes, Motty went to Boston.'

'Then how do you account, Mr Wooster, for the fact that when I went yesterday afternoon to Blackwell's Island prison, to secure material for my book, I saw poor, dear Wilmot there, dressed in a striped suit, seated beside a pile of stones with a hammer in his hands?'

I tried to think of something to say, but nothing came. A fellow has to be a lot broader about the forehead than I am to handle a jolt like this. I strained the old bean till it creaked, but between the collar and the hair parting nothing stirred. I was dumb. Which was lucky, because I wouldn't have had a chance to get any persiflage out of my system. Lady Malvern collared the conversation. She had been bottling it up, and now it came out with a rush.

'So this is how you have looked after my poor, dear boy, Mr Wooster! So this is how you have abused my trust! I left him in your charge, thinking that I could rely on you to shield him from evil. He came to you innocent, unversed in the ways of the world, confiding, unused to the temptations of a large city, and you led him astray!'

I hadn't any remarks to make. All I could think of was the picture of Aunt Agatha drinking all this in and reaching out to sharpen the hatchet against my return.

'You deliberately – '

Far away in the misty distance a soft voice spoke:

'If I might explain, your ladyship.'

Jeeves had projected himself in from the dining room and materialized on the rug. Lady Malvern tried to freeze him with a look, but you can't do that sort of thing to Jeeves. He is look-proof.

'I fancy, your ladyship, that you may have misunderstood Mr Wooster, and that he may have given you the impression that he was in New York when his lordship was – removed. When Mr Wooster informed your ladyship that his lordship had gone to Boston, he was relying on the version I had given him of his lordship's movements. Mr Wooster was away, visiting a friend in the country, at the time, and knew nothing of the matter till your ladyship informed him.'

Lady Malvern gave a kind of grunt. It didn't rattle Jeeves.

'I feared Mr Wooster might be disturbed if he knew the truth, as he is so attached to his lordship and has taken such pains to look after him, so I took the liberty of telling him that his lordship had gone away for a visit. It might have been hard for Mr Wooster to believe that his lordship had gone to prison voluntarily and from the best motives, but your ladyship, knowing him better, will readily understand.'

'What!' Lady Malvern goggled at him. 'Did you say that Lord Pershore went to prison voluntarily?'

'If I might explain, your ladyship. I think that your ladyship's parting words made a deep impression on his lordship. I have frequently heard him speak to Mr Wooster of his desire to do something to follow your ladyship's instructions and collect material for your ladyship's book on America. Mr Wooster will bear me out when I say that his lordship was frequently extremely depressed at the thought that he was doing so little to help.'

'Absolutely, by Jove! Quite pipped about it!' I said.

'The idea of making a personal examination into the prison system of the country – from within – occurred to his lordship very suddenly one night. He embraced it eagerly. There was no restraining him.'

Lady Malvern looked at Jeeves, then at me, then at Jeeves again. I could see her struggling with the thing.

'Surely, your ladyship,' said Jeeves, 'it is more reasonable to suppose that a gentleman of his lordship's character went to prison of his own volition that that he committed some breach of the law which necessitated his arrest?'

Lady Malvern blinked. Then she got up.

'Mr Wooster,' she said, 'I apologize. I have done you an injustice. I should have known Wilmot better. I should have had more faith in his pure, fine spirit.'

'Absolutely!' I said.

'Your breakfast is ready, sir,' said Jeeves.

I sat down and dallied in a dazed sort of way with a poached egg.

'Jeeves,' I said, 'you are certainly a life-saver.'

'Thank you, sir.'

'Nothing would have convinced my Aunt Agatha that I hadn't lured that blighter into riotous living.'

'I fancy you are right, sir.'

I champed my egg for a bit. I was most awfully moved, don't you know, by the way Jeeves had rallied round. Something seemed to tell me that this was an occasion that called for rich rewards. For a moment I hesitated. Then I made up my mind.

'Jeeves!'

'Sir?'

'That pink tie.'

'Yes, sir?'

'Burn it.'

'Thank you, sir.'

'And, Jeeves.'

'Yes, sir?'

'Take a taxi and get me that White House Wonder hat, as worn by President Coolidge.'

'Thank you very much, sir.'

I felt most awfully braced. I felt as if the clouds had rolled away and all was as it used to be. I felt like one of those chappies in the novels who calls off the fight with his wife in the last chapter and decides to forget and forgive. I felt I wanted to do all sorts of other things to show Jeeves that I appreciated him.

'Jeeves,' I said, 'it isn't enough. Is there anything else you would like?'

'Yes, sir. If I may make the suggestion – fifty dollars.'

'Fifty dollars?'

'It will enable me to pay a debt of honour, sir. I owe it to His Lordship.'

'You owe Lord Pershore fifty dollars?'

'Yes, sir. I happened to meet him in the street the night His Lordship was arrested. I had been thinking a good deal about the most suitable method of inducing him to abandon his mode of living, sir. His lordship was a little over-excited at the time, and I fancy that he mistook me for a friend of his. At any rate, when I took the liberty of wagering him fifty dollars that he would not punch a passing policeman in the eye, he accepted the bet very cordially and won it.'

I produced my pocket-book and counted out a hundred.

'Take this, Jeeves,' I said; 'fifty isn't enough. Do you know, Jeeves, you're – well, you absolutely stand alone!'

'I endeavour to give satisfaction, sir,' said Jeeves.

4
JEEVES AND THE HARD-BOILED EGG

Sometimes of a morning, as I've sat in bed sucking down the early cup of tea and watched Jeeves flitting about the room and putting out the raiment for the day, I've wondered what the deuce I should do if the fellow ever took it into his head to leave me. It's not so bad when I'm in New York, but in London the anxiety is frightful. There used to be all sorts of attempts on the part of low blighters to sneak him away from me. Young Reggie Foljambe to my certain knowledge offered him double what I was giving him, and Alistair Bingham-Reeves, who's got a valet who had been known to press his trousers sideways, used to look at him, when he came to see me, with a kind of glittering, hungry eye which disturbed me deucedly. Bally pirates!

The thing, you see, is that Jeeves is so dashed competent. You can spot it even in the way he shoves studs into a shirt.

I rely on him absolutely in every crisis, and he never lets me down. And, what's more, he can always be counted on to extend himself on behalf of any pal of mine who happens to be to all appearances knee-deep in the bouillon. Take the rather rummy case, for instance, of dear old Bicky and his uncle, the hard-boiled egg.

It happened after I had been in America for a few months. I got back to the flat latish one night, and when Jeeves brought me the final drink he said:

'Mr Bickersteth called to see you this evening, sir, while you were out.'

'Oh?' I said.

'Twice, sir. He appeared a trifle agitated.'

'What, pipped?'

'He gave that impression, sir.'

I sipped the whisky. I was sorry if Bicky was in trouble, but, as a matter of fact, I was rather glad to have something I could discuss freely with Jeeves just then, because things had been a bit strained between us for some time, and it had been rather difficult to hit on anything to talk about that wasn't apt to take a personal turn. You see, I had decided – rightly or wrongly – to grow a moustache, and this had cut Jeeves to the quick. He couldn't stick the thing at any price, and I had been living ever since in an atmosphere of bally disapproval till I was getting jolly well fed up with it. What I mean is, while there's no doubt that in certain matters of dress Jeeves's judgement is absolutely sound and should be followed, it seemed to me that it was getting a bit too thick if he was going to edit my face as well as my costume. No one can call me an unreasonable chappie, and many's the time I've given in like a lamb when Jeeves has voted against one of my pet suits or ties; but when it comes to a valet's staking out a claim on your upper lip you've simply got to have a bit of the good old bulldog pluck and defy the blighter.

'He said that he would call again later, sir.'

'Something must be up, Jeeves.'

'Yes, sir.'

I gave the moustache a thoughtful twirl. It seemed to hurt Jeeves a good deal, so I chucked it.

'I see by the papers, sir, that Mr Bickersteth's uncle is arriving on the *Carmantic*.'

'Yes?'

'His Grace the Duke of Chiswick, sir.'

This was news to me, that Bicky's uncle was a duke. Rum, how little one knows about one's pals. I had met Bicky for the first time at a species of beano or jamboree down in Washington Square, not long after my arrival in New York. I suppose I was a bit homesick at the time, and I rather took to Bicky when I found that he was an Englishman and had, in fact, been up at Oxford with me. Besides, he was a frightful chump, so we naturally drifted together; and while we were taking a quiet snort in a corner that wasn't all cluttered up with artists and sculptors, he furthermore endeared himself to me by a most extraordinarily gifted imitation of a bull-terrier chasing a cat up a tree. But, though we had subsequently become extremely pally, all I really knew about him was that he was generally hard up, and had an uncle who relieved the strain a bit from time to time by sending him monthly remittances.

'If the Duke of Chiswick is his uncle,' I said, 'why hasn't he a title? Why isn't he Lord What-Not?'

'Mr Bickersteth is the son of His Grace's late sister, sir, who married Captain Rollo Bickersteth of the Coldstream Guards.'

Jeeves knows everything.

'Is Mr Bickersteth's father dead too?'

'Yes, sir.'

'Leave any money?'

'No, sir.'

I began to understand why poor old Bicky was always more or less on the rocks. To the casual and irreflective observer it may sound a pretty good wheeze having a duke for an uncle, but the trouble about old Chiswick was that, though an extremely wealthy old buster, owning half London and about five counties up north, he was notoriously the most prudent spender in England. He was what Americans call a hard-boiled egg. If Bicky's people hadn't left him anything and he depended on what he could prise out of the old duke, he was in a pretty bad way. Not that that explained why he was hunting me like this, because he was a chap who never borrowed money. He said he wanted to keep his pals, so never bit anyone's ear on principle.

At this juncture the door-bell rang. Jeeves floated out to answer it.

'Yes, sir. Mr Wooster has just returned,' I heard him say. And Bicky came beetling in, looking pretty sorry for himself.

'Hallo, Bicky,' I said. 'Jeeves told me you had been trying to get me. What's the trouble, Bicky?'

'I'm in a hole, Bertie. I want your advice.'

'Say on, old lad.'

'My uncle's turning up tomorrow, Bertie.'

'So Jeeves told me.'

'The Duke of Chiswick, you know.'

'So Jeeves told me.'

Bicky seemed a bit surprised.

'Jeeves seems to know everything.'

'Rather rummily, that's exactly what I was thinking just now myself.'

'Well, I wish,' said Bicky, gloomily, 'that he knew a way to get me out of the hole I'm in.'

'Mr Bickersteth is in a hole, Jeeves,' I said, 'and wants you to rally round.'

'Very good, sir.'

Bicky looked a bit doubtful.

'Well, of course, you know, Bertie, this thing is by way of being a bit private and all that.'

'I shouldn't worry about that, old top. I bet Jeeves knows all about it already. Don't you, Jeeves?'

'Yes, sir.'

'Eh?' said Bicky, rattled.

'I am open to correction, sir, but is not your dilemma due to the fact that you are at a loss to explain to His Grace why you are in New York instead of in Colorado?'

Bicky rocked like a jelly in a high wind.

'How the deuce do you know anything about it?'

'I chanced to meet His Grace's butler before we left England. He informed me that he happened to overhear His Grace speaking to you on the matter, sir, as he passed the library door.'

Bicky gave a hollow sort of laugh.

'Well, as everybody seems to know all about it, there's no need to try to keep it dark. The old boy turfed me out, Bertie, because he said I was a brainless nincompoop. The idea was that he would give me a remittance on condition that I dashed out to some blighted locality of the name of Colorado and learned farming or ranching, or whatever they call it, at some bally ranch or farm, or whatever it's called. I didn't fancy the idea a bit. I should have had to ride horses and pursue cows, and so forth. At the same time, don't you know, I had to have that remittance.'

'I get you absolutely, old thing.'

'Well, when I got to New York it looked a decent sort of place to me, so I thought it would be a pretty sound notion to stop here. So I cabled to my uncle telling him that I had dropped into a good business wheeze in the city and wanted to chuck the ranch idea. He wrote back that it was all right, and here I've been ever since. He thinks I'm doing well at something or other over here. I never dreamed, don't you know, that he would ever come out here. What on earth am I to do?'

'Jeeves,' I said, 'what on earth is Mr Bickersteth to do?'

'You see,' said Bicky, 'I had a wireless from him to say that he was coming to stay with me – to save hotel bills, I suppose. I've always given him the impression that I was living in pretty good style. I can't have him to stay at my boarding-house.'

'Thought of anything, Jeeves?' I said.

'To what extent, sir, if the question is not a delicate one, are you prepared to assist Mr Bickersteth?'

'I'll do anything I can for you, of course, Bicky, old man.'

'Then, if I might make the suggestion, sir, you might lend Mr Bickersteth – '

'No, by Jove!' said Bicky firmly. 'I never have touched you, Bertie, and I'm not going to start now. I may be a chump, but it's my boast that I don't owe a penny to a single soul – not counting tradesmen, of course.'

'I was about to suggest, sir, that you might lend Mr Bickersteth this flat. Mr Bickersteth could give His Grace the impression that he was the owner of it. With your permission I could convey the notion that I was in Mr Bickersteth's employment and not in yours. You would be residing here temporarily as Mr Bickersteth's guest. His Grace would occupy the second spare bedroom. I fancy that you would find this answer satisfactory, sir.'

Bicky had stopped rocking himself and was staring at Jeeves in an awed sort of way.

'I would advocate the dispatching of a wireless message to His Grace on board the vessel, notifying him of the change of address. Mr Bickersteth could meet His Grace at the dock and proceed directly here. Will that meet the situation, sir?'

'Absolutely.'

'Thank you, sir.'

Bicky followed him with his eye till the door closed.

'How does he do it, Bertie?' he said. 'I'll tell you what I think it is. I believe it's something to do with the shape of his head. Have you ever noticed his head, Bertie, old man? It sort of sticks out at the back!'

I hopped out of bed pretty early next morning, so as to be among those present when the old boy should arrive. I knew from experience that these ocean liners fetch up at the dock at a deucedly ungodly hour. It wasn't much after nine by the time I'd dressed and had my morning tea and was leaning out of the window, watching the street for Bicky and his uncle. It was one of those jolly, peaceful mornings that make a chappie wish he'd got a soul or something, and I was just brooding on life in general when I became aware of the dickens of a spat in progress down below. A taxi had driven up, and an old boy in a top hat had got out and was kicking up a frightful row about the fare. As far as I could make out, he was trying to get the cabby to switch from New York to London prices, and the cabby had apparently never heard of London before, and didn't seem to think a lot of it now. The old boy said that in London the trip would have set him back a shilling; and the cabby said he should worry. I called to Jeeves.

'The duke has arrived, Jeeves.'

'Yes, sir?'

'That'll be him at the door now.'

Jeeves made a long arm and opened the front door, and the old boy crawled in.

'How do you do, sir?' I said, bustling up and being the ray of sunshine. 'Your nephew went down to the dock to meet you, but you must have missed him. My name's Wooster, don't you know. Great pal of Bicky's, and all that sort of thing. I'm staying with him, you know. Would you like a cup of tea? Jeeves, bring a cup of tea.'

Old Chiswick had sunk into an arm chair and was looking about the room.

'Does this luxurious flat belong to my nephew Francis?'

'Absolutely.'

'It must be terribly expensive.'

'Pretty well, of course. Everything costs a lot over here, you know.'

He moaned. Jeeves filtered in with the tea. Old Chiswick took a stab at it to restore his tissues, and nodded.

'A terrible country, Mr Wooster! A terrible country. Nearly eight shillings for a short cab-drive. Iniquitous!' He took another look round the room. It seemed to fascinate him. 'Have you any idea how much my nephew pays for this flat, Mr Wooster?'

'About two hundred dollars a month, I believe.'

'What! Forty pounds a month!'

I began to see that, unless I made the thing a bit more plausible, the scheme might turn out a frost. I could guess what the old boy was thinking. He was trying to square all this prosperity with what he knew of poor old Bicky. And one had to admit that it took a lot of squaring, for dear old Bicky, though a stout fellow and absolutely unrivalled as an imitator of bull-terriers and cats, was in many ways one of the most pronounced fatheads that ever pulled on a suit of gents' underwear.

'I suppose it seems rummy to you,' I said, 'but the fact is New York often bucks fellows up and makes them show a flash of speed that you wouldn't have imagined them capable of. It sort of develops them. Something in the air, don't you know. I imagine that Bicky in the past, when you knew him, may have been something of a chump, but it's quite different now. Devilish efficient sort of bird, and looked on in commercial circles as quite the nib!'

'I am amazed! What is the nature of my nephew's business, Mr Wooster?'

'Oh, just business, don't you know. The same sort of thing Rockefeller and all these coves do, you know.' I slid for the door. 'Awfully sorry to leave you, but I've got to meet some of the lads elsewhere.'

Coming out of the lift I met Bicky bustling in from the street.

'Hallo, Bertie. I missed him. Has he turned up?'

'He's upstairs now, having some tea.'

'What does he think of it all?'

'He's absolutely rattled.'

'Ripping! I'll be toddling up, then. Toodle-oo, Bertie, old man. See you later.'

'Pip-pip, Bicky, dear boy.'

He trotted off, full of merriment and good cheer, and I went off to the club to sit in the window and watch the traffic coming up one way and going down the other.

It was latish in the evening when I looked in at the flat to dress for dinner.

'Where's everybody, Jeeves?' I said, finding no little feet pattering about the place. 'Gone out?'

'His Grace desired to see some of the sights of the city, sir. Mr Bickersteth is acting as his escort. I fancy their immediate objective was Grant's Tomb.'

'I suppose Mr Bickersteth is a bit bucked at the way things are going – what?'

'Sir?'

'I say, I take it that Mr Bickersteth is tolerably full of beans.'

'Not altogether, sir.'

'What's his trouble now?'

'The scheme which I took the liberty of suggesting to Mr Bickersteth and yourself has, unfortunately, not answered entirely satisfactorily, sir.'

'Surely the duke believes that Mr Bickersteth is doing well in business, and all that sort of thing?'

'Exactly, sir. With the result that he has decided to cancel Mr Bickersteth's monthly allowance, on the ground that, as Mr Bickersteth is doing so well on his own account, he no longer requires pecuniary assistance.'

'Great Scott, Jeeves! This is awful!'

'Somewhat disturbing, sir.'

'I never expected anything like this!'

'I confess I scarcely anticipated the contingency myself, sir.'

'I suppose it bowled the poor blighter over absolutely?'

'Mr Bickersteth appeared somewhat taken aback, sir.'

My heart bled for Bicky.

'We must do something, Jeeves.'

'Yes, sir.'

'Can you think of anything?'

'Not at the moment, sir.'

'There must be something we can do.'

'It was a maxim of one of my former employers, sir – as I believe I mentioned to you once before – the present Lord Bridgworth, that there is always a way. No doubt we shall be able to discover some solution of Mr Bickersteth's difficulty, sir.'

'Well, have a stab at it, Jeeves.'

'I will spare no pains, sir.'

I went and dressed sadly. It will show you pretty well how pipped I was when I tell you that I as near as a toucher put on a white tie with a dinner-jacket. I sallied out for a bit of food more to pass the time than because I wanted it. It seemed brutal to be wading into the bill of fare with poor old Bicky headed for the bread-line.

When I got back old Chiswick had gone to bed, but Bicky was there, hunched up in an arm chair, brooding pretty tensely, with a cigarette hanging out of the corner of his mouth and a more or less glassy stare in his eyes.

'This is a bit thick, old thing – what!' I said.

He picked up his glass and drained it feverishly, overlooking the fact that it hadn't anything in it.

'I'm done, Bertie!' he said.

He had another go at the glass. It didn't seem to do him any good.

'If only this had happened a week later, Bertie! My next month's money was due to roll in on Saturday. I could have worked a wheeze I've been reading about in the magazine advertisements. It seems that you can make a dashed amount of money if you can only collect a few dollars and start a chicken-farm. Jolly life, too, keeping hens!' He had begun to get quite worked up at the thought of it, but he slopped back in his chair at this juncture with a good deal of gloom. 'But, of course, it's no good,' he said, 'because I haven't the cash.'

'You've only to say the word, you know, Bicky, old top.'

'Thanks awfully, Bertie, but I'm not going to sponge on you.'

That's always the way in this world. The chappies you'd like to lend money to won't let you, whereas the chappies you don't want to lend it to will do everything except actually stand you on your head and lift the specie out of your pockets. As a lad who has always rolled tolerably freely in the right stuff, I've had lots of experience of the second class. Many's the time, back in London, I've hurried along Piccadilly and felt the hot breath of the toucher on the back of my neck and heard his sharp, excited yapping as he closed in on me. I've simply spent my life scattering largesse to blighters I didn't care a hang for; yet here was I now, dripping doubloons and pieces of eight and longing to hand them over, and Bicky, poor fish, absolutely on his uppers, not taking any at any price.

'Well, there's only one hope then.'

'What's that?'

'Jeeves.'

'Sir?'

There was Jeeves, standing behind me, full of zeal. In this matter of shimmering into rooms the man is rummy to a degree. You're sitting in the old arm chair, thinking of this and that, and then suddenly you look up, and there he is. He moves from point to point with as little uproar as a jelly-fish. The thing startled poor old Bicky considerably. He rose from his seat like a rocketing pheasant. I'm used to Jeeves now, but often in the days when he first came to me I've bitten my tongue freely on finding him unexpectedly in my midst.

'Did you call, sir?'

'Oh, there you are, Jeeves!'

'Precisely, sir.'

'Any ideas, Jeeves?'

'Why, yes, sir. Since we had our recent conversation I fancy I have found what may prove a solution. I do not wish to appear to be taking a liberty, sir, but I think that we have overlooked His Grace's potentialities as a source of revenue.'

Bicky laughed what I have sometimes seen described as a hollow, mocking laugh, a sort of bitter cackle from the back of the throat, rather like a gargle.

'I do not allude, sir,' explained Jeeves, 'to the possibility of inducing His Grace to part with money. I am taking the liberty of regarding His Grace in the light of an at present – if I may say so – useless property, which is capable of being developed.'

Bicky looked at me in a helpless kind of way. I'm bound to say I didn't get it myself.

'Couldn't you make it a bit easier, Jeeves?'

'In a nutshell, sir, what I mean is this: His Grace is, in a sense, a prominent personage. The inhabitants of this country, as no doubt you are aware, sir, are peculiarly addicted to shaking hands with prominent personages. It occurred to me that Mr Bickersteth or yourself might know of persons who would be willing to pay a small fee – let us say two dollars or three – for the privilege of an introduction, including handshake, to His Grace.'

Bicky didn't seem to think much of it.

'Do you mean to say that anyone would be mug enough to part with solid cash just to shake hands with my uncle?'

'I have an aunt, sir, who paid five shillings to a young fellow for bringing a moving-picture actor to tea at her house one Sunday. It gave her social standing among the neighbours.'

Bicky wavered.

'If you think it could be done – '

'I feel convinced of it, sir.'

'What do you think, Bertie?'

'I'm for it, old boy, absolutely. A very brainy wheeze.'

'Thank you, sir. Will there be anything further? Good night, sir.'

And he flitted out, leaving us to discuss details.

Until we started this business of floating old Chiswick as a money-making proposition I had never realized what a perfectly foul time those Stock Exchange fellows must have when the public isn't biting freely. Nowadays I read that bit they put in the financial reports about 'The market opened quietly' with a sympathetic eye, for, by Jove, it certainly opened quietly for us. You'd hardly believe how difficult it was to interest the public and make them take a flutter on the old boy. By the end of a week the only name we had on our list was a delicatessen-store keeper down in Bicky's part of the town, and as he wanted us to take it out in sliced ham instead of cash that didn't help much. There was a gleam of light when the brother of Bicky's pawnbroker offered ten dollars, money down, for an introduction to old Chiswick, but the deal fell through, owing to its turning out that the chap was an anarchist and intended to kick the old boy instead of shaking hands with him. At that, it took me the deuce of a time to persuade Bicky not to grab the cash and let things take their course. He seemed to regard the pawnbroker's brother rather as a sportsman and benefactor of his species than otherwise.

The whole thing, I'm inclined to think, would have been off if it hadn't been for Jeeves. There is no doubt that Jeeves is in a class of his own. In the matter of brain and resource I don't think I have ever met a chappie so supremely like mother made. He trickled into my room one morning with the good old cup of tea, and intimated that there was something doing.

'Might I speak to you with regard to that matter of His Grace, sir?'

'It's all off. We've decided to chuck it.'

'Sir?'

'It won't work. We can't get anybody to come.'

'I fancy I can arrange that aspect of the matter, sir.'

'Do you mean to say you've managed to get anybody?'

'Yes, sir. Eighty-seven gentlemen from Birdsburg, sir.'

I sat up in bed and spilt the tea.

'Birdsburg?'

'Birdsburg, Missouri, sir.'

'How did you get them?'

'I happened last night, sir, as you had intimated that you would be absent from home, to attend a theatrical performance, and entered into conversation between the acts with the occupant of the adjoining seat. I had observed that he was wearing a somewhat ornate decoration in his buttonhole, sir – a large blue button with the words "Boost for Birdsburg" upon it in red letters, scarcely a judicious addition to a gentleman's evening costume. To my surprise I noticed that the auditorium was full of persons similarly decorated. I ventured to inquire the explanation, and was informed that these gentlemen, forming a party of eighty-seven, are a convention from a town of the name of Birdsburg in the State of Missouri. Their visit, I gathered, was purely of a social and pleasurable nature, and my informant spoke at some length of the entertainments arranged for their stay in the city. It was when he related with a considerable amount of satisfaction and pride that a deputation of their number had been introduced to and had shaken hands with a well-known prize-fighter that it occurred to me to broach the subject of His Grace. To make a long story short, sir, I have arranged, subject to your approval, that the entire convention shall be presented to His Grace tomorrow afternoon.'

I was amazed.

'Eighty-seven, Jeeves! At how much a head?'

'I was obliged to agree to a reduction for quantity, sir. The terms finally arrived at were one hundred and fifty dollars for the party.'

I thought a bit.

'Payable in advance?'

'No, sir. I endeavoured to obtain payment in advance, but was not successful.'

'Well, anyway, when we get it I'll make it up to five hundred. Bicky'll never know. Do you suppose Mr Bickersteth would suspect anything, Jeeves, if I made it up to five hundred?'

'I fancy not, sir. Mr Bickersteth is an agreeable gentleman, but not bright.'

'All right, then. After breakfast run down to the bank and get me some money.'

'Yes, sir.'

'You know, you're a bit of a marvel, Jeeves.'

'Thank you, sir.'

'Right ho!'

'Very good, sir.'

When I took dear old Bicky aside in the course of the morning and told him what had happened he nearly broke down. He tottered into the sitting-room and buttonholed old Chiswick, who was reading the comic section of the morning paper with a kind of grim resolution.

'Uncle,' he said, 'are you doing anything special tomorrow afternoon? I mean to say, I've asked a few of my pals in to meet you, don't you know.'

The old boy cocked a speculative eye at him.

'There will be no reporters among them?'

'Reporters? Rather not. Why?'

'I refuse to be badgered by reporters. There were a number of adhesive young men who endeavoured to elicit from me my views on America while the boat was approaching the dock. I will not be subjected to this persecution again.'

'That'll be absolutely all right, Uncle. There won't be a newspaper man in the place.'

'In that case I shall be glad to make the acquaintance of your friends.'

'You'll shake hands with them, and so forth?'

'I shall naturally order my behaviour according to the accepted rules of civilized intercourse.'

Bicky thanked him heartily and came off to lunch with me at the club, where he babbled freely of hens, incubators, and other rotten things.

After mature consideration we had decided to unleash the Birdsburg contingent on the old boy ten at a time. Jeeves brought his theatre pal round to see us, and we arranged the whole thing with him. A very decent chappie, but rather inclined to collar the conversation and turn it in the direction of his home-town's new water-supply system. We settled that, as an hour was about all he would be likely to stand, each gang should consider itself entitled to seven minutes of the duke's society by Jeeves's stop-watch, and that when their time was up Jeeves should slide into the room and cough meaningly. Then we parted with what I believe are called mutual expressions of goodwill, the Birdsburg chappie extending a cordial invitation to us all to pop out some day and take a look at the new water-supply system, for which we thanked him.

Next day the deputation rolled in. The first shift consisted of the cove we had met and nine others almost exactly like him in

every respect. They all looked deuced keen and business-like, as
if from youth up they had been working in the office and catching
the boss's eye and what not. They shook hands with the old boy with
a good deal of apparent satisfaction – all except one chappie, who
seemed to be brooding about something – and then they stood off
and became chatty.

'What message have you for Birdsburg, duke?' asked our pal.

The old boy seemed a bit rattled.

'I have never been to Birdsburg.'

The chappie seemed pained.

'You should pay it a visit,' he said. 'The most rapidly growing city
in the country. Boost for Birdsburg!'

'Boost for Birdsburg!' said the other chappies reverently.

The chappie who had been brooding suddenly gave tongue.

'Say!'

He was a stout sort of well-fed cove with one of those determined
chins and a cold eye.

The assemblage looked at him.

'As a matter of business,' said the chappie – 'mind you, I'm not
questioning anybody's good faith, but, as a matter of strict business
– I think this gentleman here ought to put himself on record before
witnesses as stating that he really is a duke.'

'What do you mean, sir?' cried the old boy, getting purple.

'No offence, simply business. I'm not saying anything, mind you,
but there's one thing that seems kind of funny to me. This gentleman
here says his name's Mr Bickersteth, as I understand it. Well, if you're
the Duke of Chiswick, why isn't he Lord Percy Something? I've read
English novels, and I know all about it.'

'This is monstrous!'

'Now don't get hot under the collar. I'm only asking. I've a right to
know. You're going to take our money, so it's only fair that we should
see that we get our money's worth.'

The water-supply cove chipped in:

'You're quite right, Simms. I overlooked that when making the
agreement. You see, gentlemen, as business men we've a right to
reasonable guarantees of good faith. We are paying Mr Bickersteth
here a hundred and fifty dollars for this reception, and we naturally
want to know – '

Old Chiswick gave Bicky a searching look; then he turned to the
water-supply chappie. He was frightfully calm.

'I can assure you that I know nothing of this,' he said quite politely.
'I should be grateful if you would explain.'

'Well, we arranged with Mr Bickersteth that eighty-seven citizens of Birdsburg should have the privilege of meeting and shaking hands with you for a financial consideration mutually arranged, and what my friend Simms here means – and I'm with him – is that we have only Mr Bickersteth's word for it – and he is a stranger to us – that you are the Duke of Chiswick at all.'

Old Chiswick gulped.

'Allow me to assure you, sir,' he said in a rummy kind of voice, 'that I am the Duke of Chiswick.'

'Then that's all right,' said the chappie heartily. 'That was all we wanted to know. Let the thing go on.'

'I am sorry to say,' said old Chiswick, 'that it cannot go on. I am feeling a little tired. I fear I must ask to be excused.'

'But there are seventy-seven of the boys waiting round the corner at this moment, Duke, to be introduced to you.'

'I fear I must disappoint them.'

'But in that case the deal would have to be off.'

'That is a matter for you and my nephew to discuss.'

The chappie seemed troubled.

'You really won't meet the rest of them?'

'No!'

'Well, then, I guess we'll be going.'

They went out, and there was a pretty solid silence. Then old Chiswick turned to Bicky:

'Well?'

Bicky didn't seem to have anything to say.

'Was it true what that man said?'

'Yes, Uncle.'

'What do you mean by playing this trick?'

Bicky seemed pretty well knocked out, so I put in a word:

'I think you'd better explain the whole thing, Bicky, old top.'

Bicky's adam's apple jumped about a bit; then he started.

'You see, you had cut off my allowance, Uncle, and I wanted a bit of money to start a chicken farm. I mean to say it's an absolute cert if you once get a bit of capital. You buy a hen, and it lays an egg every day of the week, and you sell the egg, say, seven for twenty-five cents. Keep of hen costs nothing. Profit practically – '

'What is all this nonsense about hens? You led me to suppose you were a substantial business man.'

'Old Bicky rather exaggerated, sir,' I said, helping the chappie out. 'The fact is, the poor old lad is absolutely dependent on that remittance of yours, and when you cut it off, don't you know, he was pretty solidly in the soup, and had to think of some way of closing in on a bit of the ready pretty quick. That's why we thought of this hand-shaking scheme.'

Old Chiswick foamed at the mouth.

'So you have lied to me! You have deliberately deceived me as to your financial status!'

'Poor old Bicky didn't want to go to that ranch,' I explained. 'He doesn't like cows and horses, but he rather thinks he would be hot stuff among the hens. All he wants is a bit of capital. Don't you think it would be rather a wheeze if you were to – '

'After what has happened? After this – this deceit and foolery? Not a penny!'

'But – '

'Not a penny!'

There was a respectful cough in the background.

'If I might make a suggestion, sir?'

Jeeves was standing on the horizon, looking devilish brainy.

'Go ahead, Jeeves!' I said.

'I would merely suggest, sir, that if Mr Bickersteth is in need of a little ready money, and is at a loss to obtain it elsewhere, he might secure the sum he requires by describing the occurrences of this afternoon for the Sunday issue of one of the more spirited and enterprising newspapers.'

'By Jove!' I said.

'By George!' said Bicky.

'Great heavens!' said old Chiswick.

'Very good, sir,' said Jeeves.

Bicky turned to old Chiswick with a gleaming eye.

'Jeeves is right! I'll do it! The *Chronicle* would jump at it. They eat that sort of stuff.'

Old Chiswick gave a kind of moaning howl.

'I absolutely forbid you, Francis, to do this thing!'

'That's all very well,' said Bicky, wonderfully braced, 'but if I can't get the money any other way – '

'Wait! Er – wait, my boy! You are so impetuous! We might arrange something.'

'I won't go to that bally ranch.'

'No, no! No, no, my boy! I would not suggest it. I would not for a moment suggest it. I – I' think – ' He seemed to have a bit of a struggle with himself. 'I – I think that, on the whole it would be best if you returned with me to England. I – I might – in fact, I think I see my way to doing – to – I might be able to utilize your services in some secretarial position.'

'I shouldn't mind that.'

'I should not be able to offer you a salary, but, as you know, in English political life the unpaid secretary is a recognized figure – '

'The only figure I'll recognize,' said Bicky firmly, 'is five hundred quid a year, paid quarterly.'

'My dear boy!'

'Absolutely!'

'But your recompense, my dear Francis, would consist in the unrivalled opportunities you would have, as my secretary, to gain experience, to accustom yourself to the intricacies of political life, to – in fact, you would be in an exceedingly advantageous position.'

'Five hundred a year!' said Bicky, rolling it round his tongue. 'Why, that would be nothing to what I could make if I started a chicken farm. It stands to reason. Suppose you have a dozen hens. Each of the hens has a dozen chickens. After a bit the chickens grow up and have a dozen chickens each themselves, and then they all start laying eggs! There's a fortune in it. You can get anything you like for eggs in America. Fellows keep them on ice for years and years, and don't sell them till they fetch about a dollar a whirl. You don't think I'm going to chuck a future like this for anything under five hundred o' goblins a year – what?'

A look of anguish passed over old Chiswick's face, then he seemed to be resigned to it. 'Very well, my boy,' he said.

'What ho!' said Bicky. 'All right, then.'

'Jeeves,' I said. Bicky had taken the old boy off to dinner to celebrate, and we were alone. 'Jeeves, this has been one of your best efforts.'

'Thank you, sir.'

'It beats me how you do it.'

'Yes, sir?'

'The only trouble is you haven't got much out of it yourself.'

'I fancy Mr Bickersteth intends – I judge from his remarks – to signify his appreciation of anything I have been fortunate enough to do to assist him, at some later date when he is in a more favourable position to do so.'

'It isn't enough, Jeeves!'

'Sir?'

It was a wrench, but I felt it was the only possible thing to be done.

'Bring my shaving things.'

A gleam of hope shone in the man's eye, mixed with doubt.

'You mean, sir?'

'And shave off my moustache.'

There was a moment's silence. I could see the fellow was deeply moved.

'Thank you very much indeed, sir,' he said, in a low voice.

5

THE AUNT AND THE SLUGGARD

Now that it's all over, I may as well admit that there was a time during the affair of Rockmetteller Todd when I thought that Jeeves was going to let me down. Silly of me, of course, knowing him as I do, but that is what I thought. It seemed to me that the man had the appearance of being baffled.

The Rocky Todd business broke loose early one morning in spring. I was in bed, restoring the physique with my usual nine hours of the dreamless, when the door flew open and somebody prodded me in the lower ribs and began to shake the bedclothes in an unpleasant manner. And after blinking a bit and generally pulling myself together, I located Rocky, and my first impression was that it must be some horrid dream.

Rocky, you see, lived down on Long Island somewhere, miles away from New York; and not only that, but he had told me himself more than once that he never got up before twelve, and seldom earlier than one. Constitutionally the laziest young devil in America, he had hit on a walk in life which enabled him to go the limit in that direction. He was a poet. At least, he wrote poems when he did anything; but most of his time, as far as I could make out, he spent in a sort of trance. He told me once that he could sit on a fence, watching a worm and wondering what on earth it was up to for hours at a stretch.

He had his scheme of life worked out to a fine point. About once a month he would take three days writing a few poems; the other three hundred and twenty-nine days of the year he rested. I didn't know there was enough money in poetry to support a chappie, even in the way in which Rocky lived; but it seems that, if you stick to exhortations to young men to lead the strenuous life and don't shove in any rhymes, American editors fight for the stuff. Rocky showed me one of his things once. It began:

Be!
Be!
>The past is dead,
>Tomorrow is not born.
>Be today!
Today!
>Be with every nerve,
>With every fibre,
>With every drop of your red blood!
Be!
Be!

There were three more verses, and the thing was printed opposite the frontispiece of a magazine with a sort of scroll round it, and a picture in the middle of a fairly nude chappie with bulging muscles giving the rising sun the glad eye. Rocky said they gave him a hundred dollars for it, and he stayed in bed till four in the afternoon for over a month.

As regarded the future he was pretty solid, owing to the fact that he had a moneyed aunt tucked away somewhere in Illinois. It's a curious thing how many of my pals seem to have aunts and uncles who are their main source of supply. There is Bicky for one, with his uncle the Duke of Chiswick; Corky, who, until things went wrong, looked to Alexander Worple, the bird specialist, for sustenance. And I shall be telling you a story shortly of a dear old friend of mine, Oliver Sipperley, who had an aunt in Yorkshire. These things cannot be mere coincidence. They must be meant. What I'm driving at is that Providence seems to look after the chumps of this world; and, personally, I'm all for it. I suppose the fact is that, having been snootered from infancy upwards by my own aunts, I like to see that it is possible for these relatives to have a better and a softer side.

However, this is more or less of a side-track. Coming back to Rocky, what I was saying was that he had this aunt in Illinois; and, as he had been named Rockmetteller after her (which in itself, you might say, entitled him to substantial compensation) and was her only nephew, his position looked pretty sound. He told me that when he did come into the money he meant to do no work at all, except perhaps an occasional poem recommending the young man with life opening out before him with all its splendid possibilities to light a pipe and shove his feet up on the mantelpiece.

And this was the man who was prodding me in the ribs in the grey dawn!

'Read this, Bertie!' babbled old Rocky.

I could just see that he was waving a letter or something equally foul in my face. 'Wake up and read this!'

I can't read before I've had my morning tea and a cigarette. I groped for the bell.

Jeeves came in, looking as fresh as a dewy violet. It's a mystery to me how he does it.

'Tea, Jeeves.'

'Very good, sir.'

I found that Rocky was surging round with his beastly letter again.

'What is it?' I said. 'What on earth's the matter?'

'Read it!'

'I can't. I haven't had my tea.'

'Well, listen then.'

'Who's it from?'

'My aunt.'

At this point I fell asleep again. I woke to hear him saying:

'So what on earth am I to do?'

Jeeves flowed in with the tray, like some silent stream meandering over its mossy bed; and I saw daylight.

'Read it again, Rocky, old top,' I said. 'I want Jeeves to hear it. Mr Todd's aunt has written him a rather rummy letter, Jeeves, and we want your advice.'

'Very good, sir.'

He stood in the middle of the room, registering devotion to the cause, and Rocky started again:

'My dear Rockmetteller,

'I have been thinking things over for a long while, and I have come to the conclusion that I have been very thoughtless to wait so long before doing what I have made up my mind to do now.'

'What do you make of that, Jeeves?'

'It seems a little obscure at present, sir, but no doubt it becomes clearer at a later point in the communication.'

'Proceed, old scout,' I said, champing my bread and butter.

'You know how all my life I have longed to visit New York and see for myself the wonderful gay life of which I have read so much. I fear that now it will be impossible for me to fulfil my dream. I am old and worn out. I seem to have no strength left in me.'

'Sad, Jeeves, what?'
'Extremely, sir.'
'Sad nothing!' said Rocky. 'It's sheer laziness. I went to see her last Christmas and she was bursting with health. Her doctor told me himself that there was nothing wrong with her whatever. But she will insist that she's a hopeless invalid, so he has to agree with her. She's got a fixed idea that the trip to New York would kill her; so, though it's been her ambition all her life to come here, she stays where she is.'

'Rather like the chappie whose heart was "in the Highlands a-chasing of the deer", Jeeves?'
'The cases are in some respects parallel, sir.'
'Carry on, Rocky, dear boy.'

'So I have decided that, if I cannot enjoy all the marvels of the city myself, I can at least enjoy them through you. I suddenly thought of this yesterday after reading a beautiful poem in the Sunday paper about a young man who had longed all his life for a certain thing and won it in the end only when he was too old to enjoy it. It was very sad, and it touched me.'

'A thing,' interpolated Rocky bitterly, 'that I've not been able to do in ten years.'

'As you know, you will have my money when I am gone; but until now I have never been able to see my way to giving you an allowance. I have now decided to do so – on one condition. I have written to a firm of lawyers in New York, giving them instructions to pay you quite a substantial sum each month. My one condition is that you live in New York and enjoy yourself as I have always wished to do. I want you to be my representative, to spend this money for me as I should do myself. I want you to plunge into the gay, prismatic life of New York. I want you to be the life and soul of brilliant supper parties.

'Above all, I want you – indeed, I insist on this – to write me letters at least once a week, giving me a full description of all you are doing and all that is going on in the city, so that I may enjoy at second-hand what my wretched health prevents my enjoying for myself. Remember that I shall expect full details, and that no detail is too trivial to interest.
Your affectionate Aunt,
  Isabel Rockmetteller.'

'What about it?' said Rocky.

'What about it?' I said.

'Yes. What on earth am I going to do?'

It was only then that I really got on to the extremely rummy attitude of the chappie, in view of the fact that a quite unexpected mess of good cash had suddenly descended on him from a blue sky. To my mind it was an occasion for the beaming smile and the joyous whoop; yet here the man was, looking and talking as if Fate had swung on his solar plexus. It amazed me.

'Aren't you bucked?' I said.

'Bucked!'

'If I were in your place I should be frightfully braced. I consider this pretty soft for you.'

He gave a kind of yelp, stared at me for a moment, and then began to talk of New York in a way that reminded me of Jimmy Mundy, the reformer bloke. Jimmy had just come to New York on a hit-the-trail campaign, and I had popped in at Madison Square Garden a couple of days before, for half an hour or so, to hear him. He had certainly told New York some pretty straight things about itself, having apparently taken a dislike to the place, but, by Jove, you know, dear old Rocky made him look like a publicity agent for the old metrop!

'Pretty soft!' he cried. 'To have to come and live in New York! To have to leave my little cottage and take a stuffy, smelly, overheated hole of an apartment in this Heaven-forsaken, festering Gehenna. To have to mix night after night with a mob who think that life is a sort of St Vitus's dance, and imagine that they're having a good time because they're making enough noise for six and drinking too much for ten. I loathe New York, Bertie. I wouldn't come near the place if I hadn't got to see editors occasionally. There's a blight on it. It's got moral delirium tremens. It's the limit. The very thought of staying more than a day in it makes me sick. And you call this thing pretty soft for me!'

I felt rather like Lot's friends must have done when they dropped in for a quiet chat and their genial host began to criticize the Cities of the Plain. I had no idea old Rocky could be so eloquent.

'It would kill me to have to live in New York,' he went on. 'To have to share the air with six million people! To have to wear stiff collars and decent clothes all the time! To – ' He started. 'Good Lord! I suppose I should have to dress for dinner in the evenings. What a ghastly notion!'

I was shocked, absolutely shocked.

'My dear chap!' I said, reproachfully.

'Do you dress for dinner every night, Bertie?'

'Jeeves,' I said coldly. 'How many suits of evening clothes have we?'

'We have three suits of full evening dress, sir; two dinner jackets – '

'Three.'

'For practical purposes two only, sir. If you remember, we cannot wear the third. We have also seven white waistcoats.'

'And shirts?'

'Four dozen, sir.'

'And white ties?'

'The first two shallow shelves in the chest of drawers are completely filled with our white ties, sir.'

I turned to Rocky.

'You see?'

The chappie writhed like an electric fan.

'I won't do it! I can't do it! I'll be hanged if I'll do it! How on earth can I dress up like that? Do you realize that most days I don't get out of my pyjamas till five in the afternoon, and then I just put on an old sweater?'

I saw Jeeves wince, poor chap. This sort of revelation shocked his finest feelings.

'Then, what are you going to do about it?' I said.

'That's what I want to know.'

'You might write and explain to your aunt.'

'I might – if I wanted her to get round to her lawyer's in two rapid leaps and cut me out of her will.'

I saw his point.

'What do you suggest, Jeeves?' I said.

Jeeves cleared his throat respectfully.

'The crux of the matter would appear to be, sir, that Mr Todd is obliged by the conditions under which the money is delivered into his possession to write Miss Rockmetteller long and detailed letters relating to his movements, and the only method by which this can be accomplished, if Mr Todd adheres to his expressed intention of remaining in the country, is for Mr Todd to induce some second party to gather the actual experiences which Miss Rockmetteller wishes reported to her, and to convey these to him in the shape of a careful report, on which it would be possible for him, with the aid of his imagination, to base the suggested correspondence.'

Having got which off the old diaphragm, Jeeves was silent. Rocky looked at me in a helpless sort of way. He hasn't been brought up on Jeeves as I have, and he isn't on to his curves.

'Could he put it a little clearer, Bertie?' he said. 'I thought at the start it was going to make sense, but it kind of flickered. What's the idea?'

'My dear old man, perfectly simple. I knew we could stand on Jeeves. All you've got to do is to get somebody to go round the town for you and take a few notes, and then you work the notes up into letters. That's it, isn't it, Jeeves?'

'Precisely, sir.'

The light of hope gleamed in Rocky's eyes. He looked at Jeeves in a startled way, dazed by the man's vast intellect.

'But who would do it?' he said. 'It would have to be a pretty smart sort of man, a man who would notice things.'

'Jeeves!' I said. 'Let Jeeves do it.'

'But would he?'

'You would do it, wouldn't you, Jeeves?'

For the first time in our long connexion I observed Jeeves almost smile. The corner of his mouth curved quite a quarter of an inch, and for a moment his eye ceased to look like a meditative fish's.

'I should be delighted to oblige, sir. As a matter of fact, I have already visited some of New York's places of interest on my evening out, and it would be most enjoyable to make a practice of the pursuit.'

'Fine! I know exactly what your aunt wants to hear about, Rocky. She wants an earful of cabaret stuff. The place you ought to go to first, Jeeves, is Reigelheimers's. It's on Forty-second Street. Anybody will show you the way.'

Jeeves shook his head.

'Pardon me, sir. People are no longer going to Reigelheimer's. The place at the moment is Frolics on the Roof.'

'You see?' I said to Rocky. 'Leave it to Jeeves. He knows.'

It isn't often that you find an entire group of your fellow-humans happy in this world; but our little circle was certainly an example of the fact that it can be done. We were all full of beans. Everything went absolutely right from the start.

Jeeves was happy, partly because he loves to exercise his giant brain, and partly because he was having a corking time among the bright lights. I saw him one night at the Midnight Revels. He was sitting at a table on the edge of the dancing floor, doing himself remarkably well with a fat cigar. His face wore an expression of austere benevolence, and he was making notes in a small book.

As for the rest of us, I was feeling pretty good, because I was fond of old Rocky and glad to be able to do him a good turn. Rocky was perfectly contented, because he was still able to sit on fences in his pyjamas and watch worms. And, as for the aunt, she seemed tickled to death. She was getting Broadway at pretty long range, but it seemed to be hitting her just right. I read one of her letters to Rocky, and it was full of life.

But then Rocky's letters, based on Jeeve's notes, were enough to buck anybody up. It was rummy when you came to think of it. There was I, loving the life, while the mere mention of it gave Rocky a tired feeling; yet here is a letter I wrote home to a pal of mine in London:

Dear Freddie,
   Well, here I am in New York. It's not a bad place. I'm not having a bad time. Everything's not bad. The cabarets aren't bad. Don't know when I shall be back. How's everybody? Cheerio!
Yours,
   Bertie.
P.S. – Seen old Ted lately?

Not that I cared about old Ted; but if I hadn't dragged him in I couldn't have got the confounded thing on to the second page.
   Now here's old Rocky on exactly the same subject:

Dearest Aunt Isabel,
   How can I ever thank you enough for giving me the opportunity to live in this astounding city! New York seems more wonderful every day.
   Fifth Avenue is at its best, of course, just now. The dresses are magnificent!

Wads of stuff about the dresses. I didn't know Jeeves was such an authority.

I was out with some of the crowd at the Midnight Revels the other night. We took in a show first, after a little dinner at a new place on Forty-third Street. We were quite a gay party. Georgie Cohan looked in about midnight and got off a good story about Willie Collier. Fred Stone could only stay a minute, but Doug. Fairbanks did all sorts of stunts and made us roar. Ed. Wynn was there, and Laurette Taylor showed up with a party. The show at the Revels is quite good. I am enclosing a programme.
   Last night a few of us went round to Frolics on the Roof –

And so on and so forth, yards of it. I suppose it's the artistic temperament or something. What I mean is, it's easier for a chappie who's used to writing poems and that sort of tosh to put a bit of a punch into a letter than it is for a fellow like me. Anyway, there's no doubt that Rocky's correspondence was hot stuff. I called Jeeves in and congratulated him.

'Jeeves, you're a wonder!'

'Thank you, sir.'

'How you notice everything at these places beats me. I couldn't tell you a thing about them, except that I've had a good time.'

'It's just a knack, sir.'

'Well, Mr Todd's letters ought to brace Miss Rockmetteller all right, what?'

'Undoubtedly, sir,' agreed Jeeves.

And, by Jove, they did! They certainly did, by George! What I mean to say is, I was sitting in the apartment one afternoon, about a month after the thing had started, smoking a cigarette and resting the old bean, when the door opened and the voice of Jeeves burst the silence like a bomb.

It wasn't that he spoke loud. He has one of those soft, soothing voices that slide through the atmosphere like the note of a far-off sheep. It was what he said that made me leap like a young gazelle.

'Miss Rockmetteller!'

And in came a large, solid female.

The situation floored me. I'm not denying it. Hamlet must have felt much as I did when his father's ghost bobbed up in the fairway. I'd come to look on Rocky's aunt as such a permanency at her own home that it didn't seem possible that she could really be here in New York. I stared at her. Then I looked at Jeeves. He was standing there in an attitude of dignified detachment, the chump, when, if ever he should have been rallying round the young master, it was now.

Rocky's aunt looked less like an invalid than anyone I've ever seen, except my Aunt Agatha. She had a good deal of Aunt Agatha about her, as a matter of fact. She looked as if she might be deucedly dangerous if put upon; and something seemed to tell me that she would certainly regard herself as put upon if she ever found out the game which poor old Rocky had been pulling on her.

'Good afternoon,' I managed to say.

'How do you do?' she said. 'Mr Cohan?'

'Er – no.'

'Mr Fred Stone?'

'Not absolutely. As a matter of fact, my name's Wooster – Bertie Wooster.'

She seemed disappointed. The fine old name of Wooster appeared to mean nothing in her life.

'Isn't Rockmetteller home?' she said. 'Where is he?'

She had me with the first shot. I couldn't think of anything to say. I couldn't tell her that Rocky was down in the country, watching worms.

There was the faintest flutter of sound in the background. It was the respectful cough with which Jeeves announces that he is about to speak without having been spoken to.

'If you remember, sir, Mr Todd went out in the automobile with a party earlier in the afternoon.'

'So he did, Jeeves; so he did,' I said, looking at my watch. 'Did he say when he would be back?'

'He gave me to understand, sir, that he would be somewhat late in returning.'

He vanished; and the aunt took the chair which I'd forgotten to offer her. She looked at me in rather a rummy way. It was a nasty look. It made me feel as if I were something the dog had brought in and intended to bury later on, when he had time. My own Aunt Agatha, back in England, has looked at me in exactly the same way many a time, and it never fails to make my spine curl.

'You seem very much at home here, young man. Are you a great friend of Rockmetteller's?'

'Oh, yes, rather!'

She frowned as if she had expected better things of old Rocky.

'Well, you need to be,' she said, 'the way you treat his flat as your own!'

I give you my word, this quite unforeseen slam simply robbed me of the power of speech. I'd been looking on myself in the light of the dashing host, and suddenly to be treated as an intruder jarred me. It wasn't, mark you, as if she had spoken in a way to suggest that she considered my presence in the place as an ordinary social call. She obviously looked on me as a cross between a burglar and the plumber's man come to fix the leak in the bathroom. It hurt her – my being there.

At this juncture, with the conversation showing every sign of being about to die in awful agonies, an idea came to me. Tea – the good old stand-by.

'Would you care for a cup of tea?' I said.

'Tea?'

She spoke as if she had never heard of the stuff.

'Nothing like a cup after a journey,' I said. 'Bucks you up! Puts a bit of zip into you. What I mean is, restores you, and so on, don't you know. I'll go and tell Jeeves.'

I tottered down the passage to Jeeves's lair. The man was reading the evening paper as if he hadn't a care in the world.

'Jeeves,' I said, 'we want some tea.'

'Very good, sir.'

'I say, Jeeves, this is a bit thick, what?'

I wanted sympathy, don't you know – sympathy and kindness. The old nerve centres had had the deuce of a shock.

'She's got the idea this place belongs to Mr Todd. What on earth put that into her head?'

Jeeves filled the kettle with a restrained dignity.

'No doubt because of Mr Todd's letters, sir,' he said. 'It was my suggestion, sir, if you remember, that they should be addressed from this apartment in order that Mr Todd should appear to possess a good central residence in the city.'

I remembered. We had thought it a brainy scheme at the time.

'Well, it's dashed awkward, you know, Jeeves. She looks on me as an intruder. By Jove! I suppose she thinks I'm someone who hangs about here, touching Mr Todd for free meals and borrowing his shirts.'

'Extremely probable, sir.'

'It's pretty rotten, you know.'

'Most disturbing, sir.'

'And there's another thing: What are we to do about Mr Todd? We've got to get him up here as soon as ever we can. When you have brought the tea you had better go out and send him a telegram, telling him to come up by the next train.'

'I have already done so, sir. I took the liberty of writing the message and dispatching it by the lift attendant.'

'By Jove, you think of everything, Jeeves!'

'Thank you, sir. A little buttered toast with the tea? Just so, sir. Thank you.'

I went back to the sitting-room. She hadn't moved an inch. She was still bolt upright on the edge of her chair, gripping her umbrella like a hammer-thrower. She gave me another of those looks as I came in. There was no doubt about it; for some reason she had taken a dislike to me. I suppose because I wasn't George M. Cohan. It was a bit hard on a chap.

'This is a surprise, what?' I said, after about five minutes' restful silence, trying to crank the conversation up again.

'What is a surprise?'

'Your coming here, don't you know, and so on.'

She raised her eyebrows and drank me in a bit more through her glasses.

'Why is it surprising that I should visit my only nephew?' she said.

'Oh, rather,' I said. 'Of course! Certainly. What I mean is – '

Jeeves projected himself into the room with the tea. I was jolly glad to see him. There's nothing like having a bit of business arranged for one when one isn't certain of one's lines. With the teapot to fool about with I felt happier.

'Tea, tea, tea – what! What!' I said.

It wasn't what I had meant to say. My idea had been to be a good deal more formal, and so on. Still, it covered the situation. I poured her out a cup. She sipped it and put the cup down with a shudder.

'Do you mean to say, young man,' she said, frostily, 'that you expect me to drink this stuff?'

'Rather! Bucks you up, you know.'

'What do you mean by the expression, "Bucks you up"?'

'Well, makes you full of beans, you know. Makes you fizz.'

'I don't understand a word you say. You're English, aren't you?'

I admitted it. She didn't say a word. And she did it in a way that made it worse than if she had spoken for hours. Somehow it was brought home to me that she didn't like Englishmen, and that if she had had to meet an Englishman I was the one she'd have chosen last.

Conversation languished once more after that.

Then I tried again. I was becoming more convinced every moment that you can't make a real lively *salon* with a couple of people, especially if one of them lets it go a word at a time.

'Are you comfortable at your hotel?' I said.

'At which hotel?'

'The hotel you're staying at.'

'I am not staying at an hotel.'

'Stopping with friends – what?'

'I am naturally stopping with my nephew.'

I didn't get it for the moment; then it hit me.

'What! Here?' I gurgled.

'Certainly! Where else should I go?'

The full horror of the situation rolled over me like a wave. I couldn't see what on earth I was to do. I couldn't explain that this wasn't Rocky's flat without giving the poor old chap away hopelessly, because she would then ask me where he did live, and then he would be right in the soup. I was trying to recover from the shock when she spoke again.

'Will you kindly tell my nephew's manservant to prepare my room? I wish to lie down.'

'Your nephew's manservant?'

'The man you call Jeeves. If Rockmetteller has gone for an automobile ride there is no need for you to wait for him. He will naturally wish to be alone with me when he returns.'

I found myself tottering out of the room. The thing was too much for me. I crept into Jeeves's den.

'Jeeves!' I whispered.

'Sir?'

'Mix me a b-and-s, Jeeves. I feel weak.'

'Very good, sir.'

'This is getting thicker every minute, Jeeves.'

'Sir?'

'She thinks you're Mr Todd's man. She thinks the whole place is his, and everything in it. I don't see what you're to do, except stay on and keep it up. We can't say anything or she'll get on to the whole thing, and I don't want to let Mr Todd down. By the way, Jeeves, she wants you to prepare her bed.'

He looked wounded.

'It is hardly my place, sir – '

'I know – I know. But do it as a personal favour to me. If you come to that, it's hardly my place to be flung out of the flat like this and have to go to an hotel, what?'

'Is it your intention to go to an hotel, sir? What will you do for clothes?'

'Good Lord! I hadn't thought of that. Can you put a few things in a bag when she isn't looking, and sneak them down to me at the St Aurea?'

'I will endeavour to do so, sir.'

'Well, I don't think there's anything more, is there? Tell Mr Todd where I am when he gets here.'

'Very good, sir.'

I looked round the place. The moment of parting had come. I felt sad. The whole thing reminded me of one of those melodramas where they drive chappies out of the old homestead into the snow.

'Goodbye, Jeeves,' I said.

'Goodbye, sir.'

And I staggered out.

You know, I rather think I agree with those poet-and-philosopher Johnnies who insist that a fellow ought to be devilish pleased if he has a bit of trouble. All that stuff about being refined by suffering, you know. Suffering does give a chap a sort of broader and more sympathetic outlook. It helps you to understand other people's misfortunes if you've been through the same thing yourself.

As I stood in my lonely bedroom at the hotel, trying to tie my white tie myself, it struck me for the first time that there must be whole squads of chappies in the world who had to get along without a man to look after them. I'd always thought of Jeeves as a kind of natural phenomenon; but, by Jove! of course, when you come to think of it, there must be quite a lot of fellows who have to press their own clothes themselves, and haven't got anybody to bring them tea in the morning, and so on. It was rather a solemn thought, don't you know. I mean to say, ever since then I've been able to appreciate the frightful privations the poor have to stick.

I got dressed somehow. Jeeves hadn't forgotten a thing in his packing. Everything was there, down to the final stud. I'm not sure this didn't make me feel worse. It kind of deepened the pathos. It was like what somebody or other wrote about the touch of a vanished hand.

I had a bit of dinner somewhere and went to a show of some kind; but nothing seemed to make any difference. I simply hadn't the heart to go on to supper anywhere. I just went straight up to bed. I don't know when I've felt so rotten. Somehow I found myself moving about the room softly, as if there had been a death in the family. If I had anybody to talk to I should have talked in a whisper; in fact, when the telephone-bell rang I answered in such a sad, hushed voice that the fellow at the other end of the wire said 'Hallo!' five times, thinking he hadn't got me.

It was Rocky. The poor old scout was deeply agitated.

'Bertie! Is that you, Bertie? Oh, gosh! I'm having a time!'

'Where are you speaking from?'

'The Midnight Revels. We've been here an hour, and I think we're a fixture for the night. I've told Aunt Isabel I've gone out to call up a friend to join us. She's glued to a chair, with this-is-the-life written all over her, taking it in through the pores. She loves it, and I'm nearly crazy.'

'Tell me all, old top,' I said.

'A little more of this,' he said, 'and I shall sneak quietly off to the river and end it all. Do you mean to say you go through this sort of thing every night, Bertie, and enjoy it? It's simply infernal! I was just snatching a wink of sleep behind the bill of fare just now when about a million yelling girls swooped down, with toy balloons. There are two orchestras here, each trying to see if it can't play louder than the

other. I'm a mental and physical wreck. When your telegram arrived
I was just lying down for a quiet pipe, with a sense of absolute peace
stealing over me. I had to get dressed and sprint two miles to catch
the train. It nearly gave me heart-failure; and on top of that I almost
got brain fever inventing lies to tell Aunt Isabel. And then I had to
cram myself into these confounded evening clothes of yours.'

I gave a sharp wail of agony. It hadn't struck me till then that Rocky
was depending on my wardrobe to see him through.

'You'll ruin them!'

'I hope so,' said Rocky in the most unpleasant way. His troubles
seemed to have had the worst effect on his character. 'I should like
to get back at them somehow; they've given me a bad enough time.
They're about three sizes too small, and something's apt to give at
any moment. I wish to goodness it would, and give me a chance
to breathe. I haven't breathed since half past seven. Thank Heaven,
Jeeves managed to get out and buy me a collar that fitted, or I should
be a strangled corpse by now! It was touch and go till the stud broke.
Bertie, this is pure Hades! Aunt Isabel keeps on urging me to dance.
How on earth can I dance when I don't know a soul to dance with?
And how the deuce could I, even if I knew every girl in the place?
It's taking big chances even to move in these trousers. I had to tell
her I've hurt my ankle. She keeps asking me when Cohan and Stone
are going to turn up; and it's simply a question of time before she
discovers that Stone is sitting two tables away. Something's got to be
done, Bertie! You've got to think up some way of getting me out of
this mess. It was you who got me into it.'

'Me! What do you mean?'

'Well, Jeeves, then. It's all the same. It was you who suggested
leaving it to Jeeves. It was those letters I wrote from his notes that
did the mischief. I made them too good. My aunt's just been telling
me about it. She says she had resigned herself to ending her life
where she was, and then my letters began to arrive, describing the
joys of New York; and they stimulated her to such an extent that she
pulled herself together and made the trip. She seems to think she's
had some miraculous kind of faith cure. I tell you I can't stand it,
Bertie! It's got to end!'

'Can't Jeeves think of anything?'

'No. He just hangs round, saying: "Most disturbing, sir!" A fat lot
of help that is!'

'Well, old lad,' I said, 'after all, it's far worse for me than it is for
you. You've got a comfortable home and Jeeves. And you're saving a
lot of money.'

'Saving money? What do you mean – saving money?'

'Why, the allowance your aunt was giving you. I suppose she's paying all the expenses now, isn't she?'

'Certainly she is: but she's stopped the allowance. She wrote the lawyers tonight. She says that, now she's in New York, there is no necessity for it to go on, as we shall always be together, and it's simpler for her to look after that end of it. I tell you, Bertie, I've examined the darned cloud with a microscope, and if it's got a silver lining it's some little dissembler!'

'But, Rocky, old top, it's too bally awful! You've no notion of what I'm going through in this beastly hotel, without Jeeves. I must get back to the flat.'

'Don't come near the flat!'

'But it's my own flat.'

'I can't help that. Aunt Isabel doesn't like you. She asked me what you did for a living. And when I told her you didn't do anything she said she thought as much, and that you were a typical specimen of a useless and decaying aristocracy. So if you think you have made a hit, forget it. Now I must be going back, or she'll be coming out here after me. Goodbye.'

Next morning Jeeves came round. It was all so home-like when he floated noiselessly into the room that I nearly broke down.

'Good morning, sir,' he said. 'I have brought a few more of your personal belongings.'

He began to unstrap the suitcase he was carrying.

'Did you have any trouble sneaking them away?'

'It was not easy, sir. I had to watch my chance. Miss Rockmetteller is a remarkably alert lady.'

'You know, Jeeves, say what you like – this *is* a bit thick, isn't it?'

'The situation is certainly one that has never before come under my notice, sir. I have brought the heather-mixture suit, as the climatic conditions are congenial. Tomorrow, if not prevented, I will endeavour to add the brown lounge with the faint green twill.'

'It can't go on – this sort of thing – Jeeves.'

'We must hope for the best, sir.'

'Can't you think of anything to do?'

'I have been giving the matter considerable thought, sir, but so far without success. I am placing three silk shirts – the dove-coloured, the light blue, and the mauve – in the first long drawer, sir.'

'You don't mean to say you can't think of anything, Jeeves?'

'For the moment, sir, no. You will find a dozen handkerchiefs and the tan socks in the upper drawer on the left.' He strapped the suit-case and put it on a chair. 'A curious lady, Miss Rockmetteller, sir.'

'You understate it, Jeeves.'

He gazed meditatively out of the window.

'In many ways, sir, Miss Rockmetteller reminds me of an aunt of mine who resides in the south-east portion of London. Their temperaments are much alike. My aunt has the same taste for the pleasures of the great city. It is a passion with her to ride in hansom cabs, sir. Whenever the family take their eyes off her she escapes from the house and spends the day riding about in cabs. On several occasions she has broken into the children's savings bank to secure the means to enable her to gratify this desire.'

'I love to have these little chats with you about your female relatives, Jeeves,' I said coldly, for I felt that the man had let me down, and I was fed up with him. 'But I don't see what all this has got to do with my trouble.'

'I beg your pardon, sir. I am leaving a small assortment of your neckties on the mantelpiece, sir, for you to select according to your preference. I should recommend the blue with the red domino pattern, sir.'

Then he streamed imperceptibly towards the door and flowed silently out.

I've often heard that fellows after some great shock or loss have a habit, after they've been on the floor for a while wondering what hit them, of picking themselves up and piecing themselves together, and sort of taking a whirl at beginning a new life. Time, the great healer, and Nature adjusting itself and so on and so forth. There's a lot in it. I know, because in my own case, after a day or two of what you might call prostration, I began to recover. The frightful loss of Jeeves made any thought of pleasure more or less a mockery, but at least I found that I was able to have a dash at enjoying life again. What I mean is, I braced up to the extent of going round the cabarets once more, so as to try to forget, if only for the moment.

New York's a small place when it comes to the part of it that wakes up just as the rest is going to bed, and it wasn't long before my tracks began to cross old Rocky's. I saw him once at Peale's, and again at Frolics on the Roof. There wasn't anybody with him either time except the aunt, and, though he was trying to look as if he had struck the ideal life, it wasn't difficult for me, knowing the circumstances, to see that beneath the mask the poor chap was suffering. My heart bled for the fellow. At least, what there was of it that wasn't bleeding for myself bled for him. He had the air of one who was about to crack under the strain.

It seemed to me that the aunt was looking slightly upset also. I took it that she was beginning to wonder when the celebrities were going to surge round, and what had suddenly become of all those wild, careless spirits Rocky used to mix with in his letters. I didn't blame her. I had only read a couple of his letters, but they certainly gave the impression that poor old Rocky was by way of being the hub of New York night life, and that, if by any chance he failed to show up at a cabaret, the management said, 'What's the use?' and put up the shutters.

The next two nights I didn't come across them, but the night after that I was sitting by myself at the Maison Pierre when somebody tapped me on the shoulder-blade, and I found Rocky standing beside me, with a sort of mixed expression of wistfulness and apoplexy on his face. How the man had contrived to wear my evening clothes so many times without disaster was a mystery to me. He confided later that early in the proceedings he had slit the waistcoat up the back and that that had helped a lot.

For a moment I had the idea that he had managed to get away from his aunt for the evening; but, looking past him, I saw that she was in again. She was at a table over by the wall, looking at me as if I were something the management ought to be complained to about.

'Bertie, old scout,' said Rocky, in a quiet, sort of crushed voice, 'we've always been pals, haven't we? I mean, you know I'd do you a good turn if you asked me.'

'My dear old lad,' I said. The man had moved me.

'Then, for Heaven's sake, come over and sit at our table for the rest of the evening.'

Well, you know, there are limits to the sacred claims of friendship.

'My dear chap,' I said, 'you know I'd do anything in reason; but – '

'You must come, Bertie. You've got to. Something's got to be done to divert her mind. She's brooding about something. She's been like that for the last two days. I think she's beginning to suspect. She can't understand why we never seem to meet anyone I know at these joints. A few nights ago I happened to run into two newspaper men I used to know fairly well. That kept me going for a while. I introduced them to Aunt Isabel as David Belasco and Jim Corbett, and it went well. But the effect has worn off now, and she's beginning to wonder again.

Something's got to be done, or she will find out everything, and if she does I'd take a nickel for my chance of getting a cent from her later on. So, for the love of Mike, come across to our table and help things along.'

I went along. One has to rally round a pal in distress. Aunt Isabel was sitting bolt upright, as usual. It certainly did seem as if she had lost a bit of the zest with which she had started out to explore Broadway. She looked as if she had been thinking a good deal about rather unpleasant things.

'You've met Bertie Wooster, Aunt Isabel?' said Rocky.

'I have.'

'Take a seat, Bertie.' said Rocky.

And so the merry party began. It was one of those jolly, happy, bread-crumbling parties where you cough twice before you speak, and then decide not to say it after all. After we had had an hour of this wild dissipation, Aunt Isabel said she wanted to go home. In the light of what Rocky had been telling me, this struck me as sinister. I had gathered that at the beginning of her visit she had had to be dragged home with ropes.

It must have hit Rocky the same way, for he gave me a pleading look.

'You'll come along, won't you, Bertie, and have a drink at the flat?'

I had a feeling that this wasn't in the contract, but there wasn't anything to be done. It seemed brutal to leave the poor chap alone with the woman, so I went along.

Right from the start, from the moment we stepped into the taxi, the feeling began to grow that something was about to break loose. A massive silence prevailed in the corner where the aunt sat, and, though Rocky, balancing himself on the little seat in front, did his best to supply dialogue, we weren't a chatty party.

I had a glimpse of Jeeves as we went into the flat, sitting in his lair, and I wished I could have called to him to rally round. Something told me that I was about to need him.

The stuff was on the table in the sitting-room. Rocky took up the decanter.

'Say when, Bertie.'

'Stop!' barked the aunt, and he dropped it.

I caught Rocky's eye as he stooped to pick up the ruins. It was the eye of one who sees it coming.

'Leave it there, Rockmetteller!' said Aunt Isabel; and Rocky left it there.

'The time has come to speak,' she said. 'I cannot stand idly by and see a young man going to perdition!'

Poor old Rocky gave a sort of gurgle, a kind of sound rather like the whisky had made running out of the decanter on to my carpet.

'Eh?' he said, blinking.

The aunt proceeded.

'The fault,' she said, 'was mine. I had not then seen the light. But now my eyes are open. I see the hideous mistake I have made. I shudder at the thought of the wrong I did you, Rockmetteller, by urging you into contact with this wicked city.'

I saw Rocky grope feebly for the table. His fingers touched it, and a look of relief came into the poor chappie's face. I understood his feelings.

'But when I wrote you that letter, Rockmetteller, instructing you to go to the city and live its life, I had not had the privilege of hearing Mr Mundy speak on the subject of New York.'

'Jimmy Mundy!' I cried.

You know how it is sometimes when everything seems all mixed up and you suddenly get a clue. When she mentioned Jimmy Mundy I began to understand more or less what had happened. I'd seen it happen before. I remember, back in England, the man I had before Jeeves sneaked off to a meeting on his evening out and came back and denounced me in front of a crowd of chappies I was giving a bit of supper to as a useless blot on the fabric of Society.

The aunt gave me a withering up and down.

'Yes; Jimmy Mundy!' she said. 'I am surprised at a man of your stamp having heard of him. There is no music, there are no drunken, dancing men, no shameless, flaunting women at his meetings; so for you they would have no attraction. But for others, less dead in sin, he has his message. He has come to save New York from itself; to force it – in his picturesque phrase – to hit the trail. It was three days ago, Rockmetteller, that I first heard him. It was an accident that took me to his meeting. How often in this life a mere accident may shape our whole future!

'You had been called away by that telephone message from Mr Belasco; so you could not take me to the Hippodrome, as we had arranged. I asked your manservant, Jeeves, to take me there. The man has very little intelligence. He seems to have misunderstood me. I am thankful that he did. He took me to what I subsequently learned was Madison Square Garden, where Mr Mundy is holding his meetings. He escorted me to a seat and then left me. And it was not till the meeting had begun that I discovered the mistake which had been made. My seat was in the middle of a row. I could not leave without inconveniencing a great many people, so I remained.'

She gulped.

'Rockmetteller, I have never been so thankful for anything else. Mr Mundy was wonderful! He was like some prophet of old, scouring the sins of the people. He leaped about in a frenzy of inspiration till I feared he would do himself an injury. Sometimes he expressed himself in a somewhat odd manner, but every word carried conviction. He showed me New York in its true colours. He showed me the vanity and wickedness of sitting in gilded haunts of vice, eating lobster when decent people should be in bed.

'He said that the tango and the fox-trot were devices of the devil to drag people down into the Bottomless Pit. He said that there was more sin in ten minutes with a negro banjo orchestra than in all the ancient revels of Nineveh and Babylon. And when he stood on one leg and pointed right at where I was sitting and shouted "This means you!" I could have sunk through the floor. I came away a changed woman. Surely you must have noticed the change in me, Rockmetteller? You must have seen that I was no longer the careless, thoughtless person who had urged you to dance in those places of wickedness?'

Rocky was holding on to the table as if it was his only friend.

'Yes,' he stammered; 'I – I thought something was wrong.'

'Wrong? Something was right! Everything was right! Rockmetteller, it is not too late for you to be saved. You have only sipped of the evil cup. You have not drained it. It will be hard at first, but you will find that you can do it if you fight with a stout heart against the glamour and fascination of this dreadful city. Won't you, for my sake, try, Rockmetteller? Won't you go to the country tomorrow and begin the struggle? Little by little, if you use your will – '

I can't help thinking it must have been that word 'will' that roused dear old Rocky like a trumpet call. It must have brought home to him the realization that a miracle had come off and saved him from being cut out of Aunt Isabel's. At any rate, as she said it he perked up, let go of the table, and faced her with gleaming eyes.

'Do you want me to go to the country, Aunt Isabel?'

'Yes.'

'To live in the country?'

'Yes, Rockmetteller.'

'Stay in the country all the time? Never come to New York?'

'Yes, Rockmetteller; I mean just that. It is the only way. Only there can you be safe from temptation. Will you do it, Rockmetteller? Will you – for my sake?'

Rocky grabbed the table again. He seemed to draw a lot of encouragement from that table.

'I will,' he said.

'Jeeves,' I said. It was next day, and I was back in the old flat, lying in the old armchair, with my feet upon the good old table. I had just come from seeing dear old Rocky off to his country cottage, and an hour before he had seen his aunt off to whatever hamlet it was that she was the curse of; so we were alone at last. 'Jeeves, there's no place like home – what?'

'Very true, sir.'

'The jolly old roof-tree, and all sort of thing – what?'

'Precisely, sir.'

I lit another cigarette.

'Jeeves.'

'Sir?'

'Do you know, at one point in the business I really thought you were baffled.'

'Indeed, sir?'

'When did you get the idea of taking Miss Rockmetteller to the meeting? It was pure genius!'

'Thank you, sir. It came to me a little suddenly, one morning when I was thinking of my aunt, sir.'

'Your aunt? The hansom cab one?'

'Yes, sir. I recollected that, whenever we observed one of her attacks coming on, we used to send for the clergyman of the parish. We always found that if he talked to her a while of higher things it diverted her mind from hansom cabs. It occurred to me that the same treatment might prove efficacious in the case of Miss Rockmetteller.'

I was stunned by the man's resource.

'It's brain,' I said; 'pure brain! What do you do to get like that, Jeeves? I believe you must eat a lot of fish, or something. Do you eat a lot of fish, Jeeves?'

'No, sir.'

'Oh, well, then, it's just a gift, I take it; and if you aren't born that way there's no use worrying.'

'Precisely, sir,' said Jeeves. 'If I might make the suggestion, sir, I should not continue to wear your present tie. The green shade gives you a slightly bilious air. I should strongly advocate the blue with the red domino pattern instead, sir.'

'All right, Jeeves,' I said humbly. 'You know!'

6

THE RUMMY AFFAIR OF OLD BIFFY

'Jeeves,' I said, emerging from the old tub, 'rally round.'

'Yes, sir.'

I beamed on the man with no little geniality. I was putting in a week or two in Paris at the moment, and there's something about Paris that always makes me feel fairly full of *espièglerie* and *joie de vivre*.

'Lay out our gent's medium-smart raiment, suitable for Bohemian revels,' I said. 'I am lunching with an artist bloke on the other side of the river.'

'Very good, sir.'

'And if anybody calls for me, Jeeves, say that I shall be back towards the quiet evenfall.'

'Yes, sir. Mr Biffen rang up on the telephone while you were in your bath.'

'Mr Biffen? Good heavens!'

Amazing how one's always running across fellows in foreign cities – coves, I mean, whom you haven't seen for ages and would have betted weren't anywhere in the neighbourhood. Paris was the last place where I should have expected to find old Biffy popping up. There was a time when he and I had been lads about town together, lunching and dining together practically every day; but some eighteen months back his old godmother had died and left him that place in Herefordshire, and he had retired there to wear gaiters and prod cows in the ribs and generally be the country gentleman and landed proprietor. Since then I had hardly seen him.

'Old Biffy in Paris? What's he doing here?'

'He did not confide in me, sir,' said Jeeves – a trifle frostily, I thought. It sounded somehow as if he didn't like Biffy. And yet they had always been matey enough in the old days.

'Where's he staying?'

'At the Hotel Avenida, Rue du Colisée, sir. He informed me that he was about to take a walk and would call this afternoon.'

'Well, if he comes when I'm out, tell him to wait. And now, Jeeves, *mes gants, mon chapeau, et le whangee de monsieur*. I must be popping.'

It was such a corking day and I had so much time in hand that near the Sorbonne I stopped my cab, deciding to walk the rest of the way. And I had hardly gone three steps and a half when there on the pavement before me stood old Biffy in person. If I had completed the last step I should have rammed him.

'Biffy!' I cried. 'Well, well, well!'

He peered at me in a blinking kind of way, rather like one of his Herefordshire cows prodded unexpectedly while lunching.

'Bertie!' he gurgled, in a devout sort of tone. 'Thank God!' He clutched my arm. 'Don't leave me, Bertie. I'm lost.'

'What do you mean, lost?'

'I came out for a walk and suddenly discovered after a mile or two that I didn't know where on earth I was. I've been wandering round in circles for hours.'

'Why didn't you ask the way?'

'I can't speak a word of French.'

'Well, why didn't you call a taxi?'

'I suddenly discovered I'd left all my money at my hotel.'

'You could have taken a cab and paid it when you got to the hotel.'

'Yes, but I suddenly discovered, dash it, that I'd forgotten its name.'

And there in a nutshell you have Charles Edward Biffen. As vague and woollen-headed a blighter as ever bit a sandwich. Goodness knows – and my Aunt Agatha will bear me out in this – I'm no master-mind myself; but compared with Biffy I'm one of the great thinkers of all time.

'I'd give a shilling,' said Biffy wistfully, 'to know the name of that hotel.'

'You can owe it me. Hotel Avenida, Rue du Colisée.'

'Bertie! This is uncanny. How the deuce did you know?'

'That was the address you left with Jeeves this morning.'

'So it was. I had forgotten.'

'Well, come along and have a drink and then I'll put you in a cab and send you home. I'm engaged for lunch, but I've plenty of time.'

We drifted to one of the eleven cafés which jostled each other along the street and I ordered restoratives.

'What on earth are you doing in Paris?' I asked.

'Bertie, old man,' said Biffy solemnly, 'I came here to try and forget.'

'Well, you've certainly succeeded.'

'You don't understand. The fact is, Bertie, old lad, my heart is broken. I'll tell you the whole story.'

'No, I say!' I protested. But he was off.

'Last year,' said Biffy, 'I buzzed over to Canada to do a bit of salmon fishing.'

I ordered another. If this was going to be a fish-story, I needed stimulants.

'On the liner going to New York I met a girl.' Biffy made a sort of curious gulping noise not unlike a bulldog trying to swallow half a cutlet in a hurry so as to be ready for the other half. 'Bertie, old man, I can't describe her. I simply can't describe her.'

This was all to the good.

'She was wonderful! We used to walk on the boat-deck after dinner. She was on the stage. At least, sort of.'

'How do you mean, sort of?'

'Well, she had posed for artists and been a mannequin in a big dressmaker's and all that sort of thing, don't you know. Anyway, she had saved up a few pounds and was on her way to see if she could get a job in New York. She told me all about herself. Her father ran a milk-walk in Clapham. Or it may have been Cricklewood. At least, it was either a milk-walk or a boot-shop.'

'Easily confused.'

'What I'm trying to make you understand,' said Biffy, 'is that she came of good, sturdy, respectable middle-class stock. Nothing flashy about her. The sort of wife any man might have been proud of.'

'Well, whose wife was she?'

'Nobody's. That's the whole point of the story. I wanted her to be mine, and I lost her.'

'Had a quarrel, you mean?'

'No, I don't mean we had a quarrel. I mean I literally lost her. The last I ever saw of her was in the Customs sheds at New York. We were behind a pile of trunks, and I had just asked her to be my wife, and she had just said she would and everything was perfectly splendid, when a most offensive blighter in a peaked cap came up to talk about some cigarettes which he had found at the bottom of my trunk and which I had forgotten to declare. It was getting pretty late by then, for we hadn't docked till about ten-thirty, so I told Mabel to go on to her hotel and I would come round next day and take her to lunch. And since then I haven't set eyes on her.'

'You mean she wasn't at the hotel?'

'Probably she was. But – '

'You don't mean you never turned up?'

'Bertie, old man,' said Biffy, in an overwrought kind of way, 'for Heaven's sake don't keep trying to tell me what I mean and what I don't mean! Let me tell this my own way, or I shall get all mixed up and have to go back to the beginning.'

'Tell it your own way,' I said hastily.

'Well, then, to put it in a word, Bertie, I forgot the name of the hotel. By the time I'd done half an hour's heavy explaining about those cigarettes my mind was a blank. I had an idea I had written the name down somewhere, but I couldn't have done, for it wasn't on any of the papers in my pocket. No, it was no good. She was gone.'

'Why didn't you make inquiries?'

'Well, the fact is, Bertie, I had forgotten her name.'

'Oh, no, dash it!' I said. This seemed a bit too thick even for Biffy. 'How could you forget her name? Besides, you told it me a moment ago. Muriel or something.'

'Mabel,' corrected Biffy coldly. 'It was her surname I'd forgotten. So I gave it up and went to Canada.'

'But half a second,' I said. 'You must have told her your name. I mean, if you couldn't trace her, she could trace you.'

'Exactly. That's what makes it all seem so infernally hopeless. She knows my name and where I live and everything, but I haven't heard a word from her. I suppose, when I didn't turn up at the hotel, she took it that that was my way of hinting delicately that I had changed my mind and wanted to call the thing off.'

'I suppose so,' I said. There didn't seem anything else to suppose. 'Well, the only thing to do is to whizz around and try to heal the wound, what? How about dinner tonight, winding up at the Abbaye or one of those places?'

Biffy shook his head.

'It wouldn't be any good. I've tried it. Besides, I'm leaving on the four o'clock train. I have a dinner engagement tomorrow with a man who's nibbling at that house of mine in Herefordshire.'

'Oh, are you trying to sell that place? I thought you liked it.'

'I did. But the idea of going on living in that great, lonely barn of a house after what has happened appals me, Bertie. So when Sir Roderick Glossop came along – '

'Sir Roderick Glossop! You don't mean the loony-doctor?'

'The great nerve specialist, yes. Why, do you know him?'

It was a warm day, but I shivered.

'I was engaged to his daughter for a week or two,' I said, in a hushed voice. The memory of that narrow squeak always made me feel faint.

'Has he a daughter?' said Biffy absently.

'He has. Let me tell you about – '

'Not just now, old man,' said Biffy, getting up. 'I ought to be going back to my hotel to see about my packing.'

Which, after I had listened to his story, struck me as pretty low-down. However, the longer you live, the more you realize that the good old sporting spirit of give-and-take has practically died out in our midst. So I boosted him into a cab and went off to lunch.

It can't have been more than ten days after this that I received a nasty shock while getting outside my morning tea and toast. The English papers had arrived, and Jeeves was just drifting out of the room after depositing *The Times* by my bedside, when, as I idly turned the pages in search of the sporting section, a paragraph leaped out and hit me squarely in the eyeball.

As follows:-

FORTHCOMING MARRIAGES
MR C.E. BIFFEN AND MISS GLOSSOP

The engagement is announced between Charles Edward, only son of the late Mr E.C. Biffen, and Mrs Biffen, of 11 Penslow Square, Mayfair, and Honoria Jane Louise, only daughter of Sir Roderick and Lady Glossop, of 6b Harley Street, W.

'Great Scott!' I exclaimed.

'Sir?' said Jeeves, turning at the door.

'Jeeves, you remember Miss Glossop?'

'Very vividly, sir.'

'She's engaged to Mr Biffen!'

'Indeed, sir?' said Jeeves. And, with not another word, he slid out. The blighter's calm amazed and shocked me. It seemed to indicate that there must be a horrible streak of callousness in him. I mean to say, it wasn't as if he didn't know Honoria Glossop.

I read the paragraph again. A peculiar feeling it gave me. I don't know if you have ever experienced the sensation of seeing the announcement of the engagement of a pal of yours to a girl whom you were only saved from marrying yourself by the skin of your teeth. It induces a sort of – well, it's difficult to describe it exactly; but I should imagine a fellow would feel much the same if he happened to be strolling through the jungle with a boyhood chum and met a tigress or a jaguar, or what not, and managed to shin up a tree and looked down and saw the friend of his youth vanishing into the undergrowth in the animal's slavering jaws. A sort of profound, prayerful relief, if you know what I mean, blended at the same time with a pang of pity. What I'm driving at is that, thankful as I was that I hadn't had to marry Honoria myself, I was sorry to see a real good chap like old Biffy copping it. I sucked down a spot of tea and began to brood over the business.

Of course, there are probably fellows in the world – tough, hardy blokes with strong chins and glittering eyes – who could get engaged to this Glossop menace and like it, but I knew perfectly well that Biffy was not one of them. Honoria, you see, is one of those robust, dynamic girls with the muscles of a welterweight and a laugh like a squadron of cavalry charging over a tin bridge. A beastly thing to have to face over the breakfast table. Brainy, moreover. The sort of girl who reduces you to pulp with sixteen sets of tennis and a few rounds of golf and then comes down to dinner as fresh as a daisy, expecting you to take an intelligent interest in Freud. If I had been engaged to her another week, her old father would have had one more patient on his books; and Biffy is much the same quiet sort of peaceful, inoffensive bird as me. I was shocked, I tell you, shocked.

And, as I was saying, the thing that shocked me most was Jeeves's frightful lack of proper emotion. The man happening to float in at this juncture, I gave him one more chance to show some human sympathy.

'You got the name correctly, didn't you, Jeeves?' I said. 'Mr Biffen is going to marry Honoria Glossop, the daughter of the old boy with the egg-like head and the eyebrows.'

'Yes, sir. Which suit would you wish me to lay out this morning?'

And this, mark you, from the man who, when I was engaged to the Glossop, strained every fibre in his brain to extricate me. It beat me. I couldn't understand it.

'The blue with the red twill,' I said coldly. My manner was marked, and I meant him to see that he had disappointed me sorely.

About a week later I went back to London, and scarcely had I got settled in the old flat when Biffy blew in. One glance was enough to tell me that the poisoned wound had begun to fester. The man did not look bright. No, there was no getting away from it, not bright. He had that kind of stunned, glassy expression which I used to see on my own face in the shaving-mirror during my brief engagement to the Glossop pestilence. However, if you don't want to be one of the What is Wrong With This Picture brigade, you must observe the conventions, so I shook his hand as warmly as I could.

'Well, well, old man,' I said. 'Congratulations.'

'Thanks,' said Biffy wanly, and there was rather a weighty silence.

'Bertie,' said Biffy, after the silence had lasted about three minutes.

'Hallo?'

'Is it really true – ?'

'What?'

'Oh, nothing,' said Biffy, and conversation languished again. After about a minute and a half he came to the surface once more.

'Bertie.'

'Still here, old thing. What is it?'

'I say, Bertie, is it really true that you were once engaged to Honoria?'

'It is.'

Biffy coughed.

'How did you get out – I mean, what was the nature of the tragedy that prevented the marriage?'

'Jeeves worked it. He thought out the entire scheme.'

'I think, before I go,' said Biffy, thoughtfully, 'I'll just step into the kitchen and have a word with Jeeves.'

I felt that the situation called for complete candour.

'Biffy, old egg,' I said, 'as man to man, do you want to oil out of this thing?'

'Bertie, old cork,' said Biffy earnestly, 'as one friend to another I do.'

'Then why the dickens did you ever get into it?'

'I don't know. Why did you?'

'I – well, it sort of happened.'

'And it sort of happened with me. You know how it is when your heart's broken. A kind of lethargy comes over you. You get absent-minded and cease to exercise proper precautions, and the first thing you know you're for it. I don't know how it happened, old man, but there it is. And what I want you to tell me is, what's the procedure?'

'You mean, how does a fellow edge out?'

'Exactly. I don't want to hurt anybody's feelings, Bertie, but I can't go through with this thing. The shot is not on the board. For about a day and a half I thought it might be all right, but now – You remember that laugh of hers?'

'I do.'

'Well, there's that, and then all this business of never letting a fellow alone – improving his mind and so forth – '

'I know. I know.'

'Very well, then. What do you recommend? What did you mean when you said that Jeeves worked a scheme?'

'Well, you see, old Sir Roderick, who's a loony-doctor and nothing but a loony-doctor, however much you may call him a nerve specialist, discovered that there was a modicum of insanity in my family. Nothing serious. Just one of my uncles. Used to keep rabbits in his bedroom. And the old boy came to lunch here to give me the once-over, and Jeeves arranged matters so that he went away firmly convinced that I was off my onion.'

'I see,' said Biffy thoughtfully. 'The trouble is there isn't any insanity in my family.'

'None?'

It seemed to me almost incredible that a fellow could be such a perfect chump as dear old Biffy without a bit of assistance.

'Not a loony on the list,' he said gloomily. 'It's just my luck. The old boy's coming to lunch with me tomorrow, no doubt to test me as he did you. And I never felt saner in my life.'

I thought for a moment. The idea of meeting Sir Roderick again gave me a cold shivery feeling; but when there is a chance of helping a pal we Woosters have no thought of self.

'Look here, Biffy,' I said, 'I'll tell you what. I'll roll up for that lunch. It may easily happen that when he finds you are a pal of mine he will forbid the banns right away and no more questions asked.'

'Something in that,' said Biffy, brightening. 'Awfully sporting of you, Bertie.'

'Oh, not at all,' I said. 'And meanwhile I'll consult Jeeves. Put the whole thing up to him and ask his advice. He's never failed me yet.'

Biffy pushed off, a good deal braced, and I went into the kitchen.

'Jeeves,' I said, 'I want your help once more. I've just been having a painful interview with Mr Biffen.'

'Indeed, sir?'

'It's like this,' I said, and told him the whole thing.

It was rummy, but I could feel him freezing from the start. As a rule, when I call Jeeves into conference on one of these little problems, he's all sympathy and bright ideas; but not today.

'I fear, sir,' he said, when I had finished, 'it is hardly my place to intervene in a private matter affecting – '

'Oh, come!'

'No, sir. It would be taking a liberty.'

'Jeeves,' I said, tackling the blighter squarely, 'what have you got against old Biffy?'

'I, sir?'

'Yes, you.'

'I assure you, sir!'

'Oh, well, if you don't want to chip in and save a fellow-creature, I suppose I can't make you. But let me tell you this. I am now going back to the sitting-room, and I am going to put in some very tense thinking. You'll look pretty silly when I come and tell you that I've got Mr Biffen out of the soup without your assistance. Extremely silly you'll look.'

'Yes, sir. Shall I bring you a whisky-and-soda, sir?'

'No. Coffee! Strong and black. And if anybody wants to see me, tell 'em that I'm busy and can't be disturbed.'

An hour later I rang the bell.

'Jeeves,' I said with hauteur.

'Yes, sir?'

'Kindly ring Mr Biffen up on the phone and say that Mr Wooster presents his compliments and that he has got it.'

I was feeling more than a little pleased with myself next morning as I strolled round to Biffy's. As a rule the bright ideas you get overnight have a trick of not seeming quite so frightfully fruity when you examine them by the light of day; but this one looked as good at breakfast as it had done before dinner. I examined it narrowly from every angle, and I didn't see how it could fail.

A few days before, my Aunt Emily's son Harold had celebrated his sixth birthday; and, being up against the necessity of weighing in with a present of some kind, I had happened to see in a shop in the Strand a rather sprightly little gadget, well calculated in my opinion to amuse the child and endear him to one and all. It was a bunch of flowers in a sort of holder ending in an ingenious bulb attachment which, when pressed, shot about a pint and a half of pure spring water into the face of anyone who was ass enough to sniff at it. It seemed to me just the thing to please the growing mind of a kid of six, and I had rolled round with it.

But when I got to the house I found Harold sitting in the midst of a mass of gifts so luxurious and costly that I simply hadn't the crust to contribute a thing that had set me back a mere elevenpence-ha'penny; so with rare presence of mind – for we Woosters can think quick on occasion – I wrenched my Uncle James's card off a toy aeroplane, substituted my own, and trousered the squirt, which I took away with me. It had been lying around in my flat ever since, and it seemed to me that the time had come to send it into action.

'Well?' said Biffy anxiously, as I curveted into his sitting-room.

The poor old bird was looking pretty green about the gills. I recognized the symptoms. I had felt much the same myself when waiting for Sir Roderick to turn up and lunch with me. How the deuce people who have anything wrong with their nerves can bring themselves to chat with that man, I can't imagine; and yet he has the largest practice in London. Scarcely a day passes without his having to sit on somebody's head and ring for the attendant to bring the strait-waistcoat: and his outlook on life has become so jaundiced through constant association with coves who are picking straws out of their hair that I was convinced that Biffy had merely got to press the bulb and nature would do the rest.

So I patted him on the shoulder and said: 'It's all right, old man!'

'What does Jeeves suggest?' asked Biffy eagerly.

'Jeeves doesn't suggest anything.'

'But you said it was all right.'

'Jeeves isn't the only thinker in the Wooster home, my lad. I have taken over your little problem, and I can tell you at once that I have the situation well in hand.'

'You?' said Biffy.

His tone was far from flattering. It suggested a lack of faith in my abilities, and my view was that an ounce of demonstration would be worth a ton of explanation. I shoved the bouquet at him.

'Are you fond of flowers, Biffy?' I said.

'Eh?'

'Smell these.'

Biffy extended the old beak in a careworn sort of way, and I pressed the bulb as per printed instructions on the label.

I do like getting my money's worth. Elevenpence-ha'penny the thing had cost me, and it would have been cheap at double. The advertisement on the outside of the box had said that its effects were 'indescribably ludicrous', and I can testify that it was no over-statement. Poor old Biffy leaped three feet in the air and smashed a small table.

'There!' I said.

The old egg was a trifle incoherent at first, but he found words fairly soon and began to express himself with a good deal of warmth.

'Calm yourself, laddie,' I said, as he paused for breath. 'It was no mere jest to pass an idle hour. It was a demonstration. Take this, Biffy, with an old friend's blessing, refill the bulb, shove it into Sir

Roderick's face, press firmly, and leave the rest to him. I'll guarantee that in something under three seconds the idea will have dawned on him that you are not required in his family.'

Biffy stared at me.

'Are you suggesting that I squirt Sir Roderick?'

'Absolutely. Squirt him good. Squirt as you have never squirted before.'

'But – '

He was still yammering at me in a feverish sort of way when there was a ring at the front-door bell.

'Good Lord!' cried Biffy, quivering like a jelly. 'There he is. Talk to him while I go and change my shirt.'

I had just time to refill the bulb and shove it beside Biffy's plate, when the door opened and Sir Roderick came in. I was picking up the fallen table at the moment, and he started talking brightly to my back.

'Good afternoon. I trust I am not – Mr Wooster!'

I'm bound to say I was not feeling entirely at my ease. There is something about the man that is calculated to strike terror into the stoutest heart. If ever there was a bloke at the very mention of whose name it would be excusable for people to tremble like aspens, that bloke is Sir Roderick Glossop. He has an enormous bald head, all the hair which ought to be on it seeming to have run into his eyebrows, and his eyes go through you like a couple of Death Rays.

'How are you, how are you, how are you?' I said, overcoming a slight desire to leap backwards out of the window. 'Long time since we met, what?'

'Nevertheless, I remember you most distinctly, Mr Wooster.'

'That's fine,' I said. 'Old Biffy asked me to come and join you in mangling a bit of lunch.'

He waggled the eyebrows at me.

'Are you a friend of Charles Biffen?'

'Oh, rather. Been friends for years and years.'

He drew in his breath sharply, and I could see that Biffy's stock had dropped several points. His eye fell on the floor, which was strewn with things that had tumbled off the upset table.

'Have you had an accident?'

'Nothing serious,' I explained. 'Old Biffy had some sort of fit or seizure just now and knocked over the table.'

'A fit!'

'Or seizure.'

'Is he subject to fits?'

I was about to answer, when Biffy hurried in. He had forgotten to brush his hair, which gave him a wild look, and I saw the old boy direct a keen glance at him. It seemed to me that what you might call the preliminary spade-work had been most satisfactorily attended to and that the success of the good old bulb could be in no doubt whatever.

Biffy's man came in with the nose-bags and we sat down to lunch.

It looked at first as though the meal was going to be one of those complete frosts which occur from time to time in the career of a constant luncher-out. Biffy, a very C-3 host, contributed nothing to the feast of reason and flow of soul beyond an occasional hiccup, and every time I started to pull a nifty, Sir Roderick swung round on me with such a piercing stare that it stopped me in my tracks. Fortunately, however, the second course consisted of a chicken fricassee of such outstanding excellence that the old boy, after wolfing a plateful, handed up his dinner-pail for a second instalment and became almost genial.

'I am here this afternoon, Charles,' he said, with what practically amounted to bonhomie, 'on what I might describe as a mission. Yes, a mission. This is most excellent chicken.'

'Glad you like it,' mumbled old Biffy.

'Singularly toothsome,' said Sir Roderick, pronging another half ounce. 'Yes, as I was saying, a mission. You young fellows nowadays are, I know, content to live in the centre of the most wonderful metropolis the world has seen, blind and indifferent to its many marvels. I should be prepared – were I a betting man, which I am not – to wager a considerable sum that you have never in your life visited even so historic a spot as Westminster Abbey. Am I right?'

Biffy gurgled something about always having meant to.

'Nor the Tower of London.'

'No, nor the Tower of London.'

'And there exists at this very moment, not twenty minutes by cab from Hyde Park Corner, the most supremely absorbing and educational collection of objects, both animate and inanimate, gathered from the four corners of the Empire, that has ever been assembled in England's history. I allude to the British Empire Exhibition now situated at Wembley.'

'A fellow told me one about Wembley yesterday,' I said, to help on the cheery flow of conversation. 'Stop me if you've heard it before. Chap goes up to deaf chap outside the Exhibition and says, "Is this Wembley?" "Hey?" says deaf chap. "Is this Wembley?" says chap. "Hey?" says deaf chap. "Is this Wembley?" says chap. "No, Thursday," says deaf chap. Ha, ha, I mean, what?'

The merry laughter froze on my lips. Sir Roderick sort of just waggled an eyebrow in my direction and I saw that it was back to the basket for Bertram. I never met a man who had such a knack of making a fellow feel like a waste-product.

'Have you yet paid a visit to Wembley, Charles?' he asked. 'No? Precisely as I suspected. Well, that is the mission on which I am here this afternoon. Honoria wishes me to take you to Wembley. She says it will broaden your mind, in which view I am at one with her. We will start immediately after luncheon.'

Biffy cast an imploring look at me.

'You'll come too, Bertie?'

There was such agony in his eyes that I only hesitated for a second. A pal is a pal. Besides, I felt that, if only the bulb fulfilled the high expectations I had formed of it, the merry expedition would be cancelled in no uncertain manner.

'Oh, rather,' I said.

'We must not trespass on Mr Wooster's good nature,' said Sir Roderick, looking pretty puff-faced.

'Oh, that's all right,' I said. 'I've been meaning to go to the good old Exhibish for a long time. I'll slip home and change my clothes and pick you up here in my car.'

There was a silence. Biffy seemed too relieved at the thought of not having to spend the afternoon alone with Sir Roderick to be capable of speech, and Sir Roderick was registering silent disapproval. And then he caught sight of the bouquet by Biffy's plate.

'Ah, flowers,' he said. 'Sweet peas, if I am not in error. A charming plant, pleasing alike to the eye and the nose.'

I caught Biffy's eye across the table. It was bulging, and a strange light shone in it.

'Are you fond of flowers, Sir Roderick?' he croaked.

'Extremely.'

'Smell these.'

Sir Roderick dipped his head and sniffed. Biffy's fingers closed slowly over the bulb. I shut my eyes and clutched the table.

'Very pleasant,' I heard Sir Roderick say. 'Very pleasant indeed.'

I opened my eyes, and there was Biffy leaning back in his chair with a ghastly look, and the bouquet on the cloth beside him. I realized what had happened. In that supreme crisis of his life, with his whole happiness depending on a mere pressure of the fingers, Biffy, the poor spineless fish, had lost his nerve. My closely reasoned scheme had gone phut.

Jeeves was fooling about with the geraniums in the sitting-room window-box when I got home.

'They make a very nice display, sir,' he said, cocking a paternal eye at the things.

'Don't talk to me about flowers,' I said. 'Jeeves, I know now how a general feels when he plans out some great scientific movement and his troops let him down at the eleventh hour.'

'Indeed, sir?'

'Yes,' I said, and told him what had happened.

He listened thoughtfully.

'A somewhat vacillating and changeable young gentleman, Mr Biffen,' was his comment when I had finished. 'Would you be requiring me for the remainder of the afternoon, sir?'

'No, I'm going to Wembley. I just came back to change and get the car. Produce some fairly durable garments which can stand getting squashed by the many-headed, Jeeves, and then phone to the garage.'

'Very good, sir. The grey cheviot lounge will, I fancy, be suitable. Would it be too much if I asked you to give me a seat in the car, sir? I had thought of going to Wembley myself this afternoon.'

'Eh? Oh, all right.'

'Thank you very much, sir.'

I got dressed, and we drove round to Biffy's flat. Biffy and Sir Roderick got in at the back and Jeeves climbed into the front seat next to me. Biffy looked so ill-attuned to an afternoon's pleasure that my heart bled for the blighter and I made one last attempt to appeal to Jeeves's better feelings.

'I must say, Jeeves,' I said, 'I'm dashed disappointed in you.'

'I am sorry to hear that, sir.'

'Well, I am. Dashed disappointed. I do think you might rally round. Did you see Mr Biffen's face?'

'Yes, sir.'

'Well, then.'

'If you will pardon my saying so, sir, Mr Biffen has surely only himself to thank if he has entered upon matrimonial obligations which do not please him.'

'You're talking absolute rot, Jeeves. You know as well as I do that Honoria Glossop is an Act of God. You might just as well blame a fellow for getting run over by a truck.'

'Yes, sir.'

'Absolutely yes. Besides, the poor ass wasn't in a condition to resist. He told me all about it. He had lost the only girl he had ever loved, and you know what a man's like when that happens to him.'

'How was that, sir?'

'Apparently he fell in love with some girl on the boat going over to New York, and they parted at the Customs sheds, arranging to meet next day at her hotel. Well, you know what Biffy's like. He forgets his own name half the time. He never made a note of the address, and it passed clean out of his mind. He went about in a sort of trance, and suddenly woke up to find that he was engaged to Honoria Glossop.'

'I did not know of this, sir.'

'I don't suppose anybody knows of it except me. He told me when I was in Paris.'

'I should have supposed it would have been feasible to make inquiries, sir.'

'That's what I said. But he had forgotten her name.'

'That sounds remarkable, sir.'

'I said that too. But it's a fact. All he remembered was that her Christian name was Mabel. Well, you can't go scouring New York for a girl named Mabel, what?'

'I appreciate the difficulty, sir.'

'Well, there it is, then.'

'I see, sir.'

We had got into a mob of vehicles outside the Exhibition by this time, and, some tricky driving being indicated, I had to suspend the conversation. We parked ourselves eventually and went in. Jeeves drifted away, and Sir Roderick took charge of the expedition. He headed for the Palace of Industry, with Biffy and myself trailing behind.

Well, you know, I have never been much of a lad for exhibitions. The citizenry in the mass always rather puts me off, and after I have been shuffling along with the multitude for a quarter of an hour or so I feel as if I were walking on hot bricks. About this particular binge, too, there seemed to me a lack of what you might call human interest. I mean to say, millions of people, no doubt, are so constituted that they scream with joy and excitement at the spectacle of a stuffed porcupine fish or a glass jar of seeds from Western Australia – but not Bertram. No; if you will take the word of one who would not deceive you, not Bertram. By the time we had tottered out of the Gold Coast village and were working towards the Palace of Machinery, everything pointed to my shortly executing a quiet sneak in the direction of that rather jolly Planters' Bar in the West Indian section. Sir Roderick had whizzed up past this at a high rate of speed, it touching no chord in him; but I had been able to observe that there was a sprightly sportsman behind the counter mixing things out of bottles and stirring them up with a stick in long glasses that seemed to have ice in them, and the urge came upon me to see more of this man. I was about to drop away from the main body and become a straggler, when something pawed at my coat sleeve. It was Biffy, and he had the air of one who has had about sufficient.

There are certain moments in life when words are not needed. I looked at Biffy, Biffy looked at me. A perfect understanding linked our two souls.

'?'

'!'

Three minutes later we had joined the Planters.

I have never been in the West Indies, but I am in a position to state that in certain of the fundamentals of life they are streets ahead of our European civilization. The man behind the counter, as kindly a bloke as I ever wish to meet, seemed to guess our requirements the moment we hove in view. Scarcely had our elbows touched the wood before he was leaping to and fro, bringing down a new bottle with each leap. A planter, apparently, does not consider he has had a drink unless it contains at least seven ingredients, and I'm not saying, mind you, that he isn't right. The man behind the bar told us the things were called Green Swizzles; and, if ever I marry and have a son, Green Swizzle Wooster is the name that will go down on the register, in memory of the day his father's life was saved at Wembley.

After the third, Biffy breathed a contented sigh.

'Where do you think Sir Roderick is?' he said.

'Biffy, old thing,' I replied frankly, 'I'm not worrying.'

'Bertie, old bird,' said Biffy, 'nor am I.'

He sighed again, and broke a long silence by asking the man for a straw.

'Bertie,' he said, 'I've just remembered something rather rummy. You know Jeeves?'

I said I knew Jeeves.

'Well, a rather rummy incident occurred as we were going into this place. Old Jeeves sidled up to me and said something rather rummy. You'll never guess what it was.'

'No, I don't believe I ever shall.'

'Jeeves said,' proceeded Biffy earnestly, 'and I am quoting his very words – Jeeves said, "Mr Biffen" – addressing me, you understand –'

'I understand.'

'"Mr Biffen," he said, "I strongly advise you to visit the – "'

'The what?' I asked as he paused.

'Bertie, old man,' said Biffy, deeply concerned, 'I've absolutely forgotten!'

I stared at the man.

'What I can't understand,' I said, 'is how you manage to run that Herefordshire place of yours for a day. How on earth do you remember to milk the cows and give the pigs their dinner?'

'Oh, that's all right. There are divers blokes about the places – hirelings and menials, you know – who look after that.'

'Ah!' I said. 'Well, that being so, let us have one more Green Swizzle, and then hey for the Amusement Park.'

When I indulged in those few rather bitter words about exhibitions, it must be distinctly understood that I was not alluding to what you might call the more earthy portion of these curious places. I yield to no man in my approval of those institutions where on payment of a shilling you are permitted to slide down a slippery runway sitting on a mat. I love the Jiggle-Joggle, and I am prepared to take on all and sundry at Skee Ball for money, stamps, or Brazil nuts.

But, joyous reveller as I am on these occasions, I was simply not in it with old Biffy. Whether it was the Green Swizzles or merely the relief of being parted from Sir Roderick, I don't know, but Biffy flung himself into the pastimes of the proletariat with a zest that was almost frightening. I could hardly drag him away from the Whip, and as for the Switchback, he looked like spending the rest of his life on it. I managed to remove him at last, and he was wandering through the crowd at my side with gleaming eyes, hesitating between having his fortune told and taking a whirl at the Wheel of Joy, when he suddenly grabbed my arm and uttered a sharp animal cry.

'Bertie!'

'Now what?'

He was pointing at a large sign over a building.

'Look! Palace of Beauty!'

I tried to choke him off. I was getting a bit weary by this time. Not so young as I was.

'You don't want to go in there,' I said. 'A fellow at the club was telling me about that. It's only a lot of girls. You don't want to see a lot of girls.'

'I do want to see a lot of girls,' said Biffy firmly. 'Dozens of girls, and the more unlike Honoria they are, the better. Besides, I've suddenly remembered that that's the place Jeeves told me to be sure and visit. It all comes back to me. "Mr Biffen," he said, "I strongly advise you to visit the Palace of Beauty." Now, what the man was driving at or what his motive was, I don't know; but I ask you, Bertie, is it wise, is it safe, is it judicious ever to ignore Jeeves's lightest word? We enter by the door on the left.'

I don't know if you know this Palace of Beauty place? It's a sort of aquarium full of the delicately-nurtured instead of fishes. You go in, and there is a kind of cage with a female goggling out at you through a sheet of plate glass. She's dressed in some weird kind of costume, and over the cage is written 'Helen of Troy'. You pass on to the next, and there's another one doing jiu-jitsu with a snake. Sub-title, 'Cleopatra'. You get the idea – Famous Women Through the Ages and all that. I can't say it fascinated me to any great extent. I maintain that a lovely woman loses a lot of her charm if you have to stare at her in a tank. Moreover, it gave me a rummy sort of feeling of having wandered into the wrong bedroom at a country house, and I was flying past at a fair rate of speed, anxious to get it over, when Biffy suddenly went off his rocker.

At least, it looked like that. He let out a piercing yell, grabbed my arm with a sudden clutch that felt like the bite of a crocodile, and stood there gibbering.

'Wuk!' ejaculated Biffy, or words to that general import.

A large and interested crowd had gathered round. I think they thought the girls were going to be fed or something. But Biffy paid no attention to them. He was pointing in a loony manner at one of the cages. I forget which it was, but the female inside wore a ruff, so it may have been Queen Elizabeth or Boadicea or someone of that period. She was a rather nice-looking girl, and she was staring at Biffy in much the same pop-eyed way as he was staring at her.

'Mabel!' yelled Biff, going off in my ear like a bomb.

I can't say I was feeling my chirpiest. Drama is all very well, but I hate getting mixed up in it in a public spot; and I had not realized before how dashed public this spot was. The crowd seemed to have doubled itself in the last five seconds, and, while most of them had their eye on Biffy, quite a goodish few were looking at me as if they thought I was an important principal in the scene and might be expected at any moment to give of my best in the way of wholesome entertainment for the masses.

Biffy was jumping about like a lamb in the springtime – and, what is more, a feeble-minded lamb.

'Bertie! It's her! It's she!' He looked about him wildly. 'Where the

deuce is the stage-door?' he cried. 'Where's the manager? I want to
see the house-manager immediately.'

And then he suddenly bounded forward and began hammering on
the glass with his stick.

'I say, old lad!' I began, but he shook me off.

These fellows who live in the country are apt to go in for fairly
sizable clubs instead of the light canes which your well-dressed man
about town considers suitable for metropolitan use; and down in
Herefordshire, apparently, something in the nature of a knobkerrie
is *de rigueur*. Biffy's first slosh smashed the glass all to a hash. Three
more cleared the way for him to go into the cage without cutting
himself. And, before the crowd had time to realize what a wonderful
bob's-worth it was getting in exchange for its entrance fee, he was
inside, engaging the girl in earnest conversation. And at the same
moment two large policemen rolled up.

You can't make policemen take the romantic view. Not a tear did
these two blighters stop to brush away. They were inside the cage and
out of it and marching Biffy through the crowd before you had time to
blink. I hurried after them, to do what I could in the way of soothing
Biffy's last moments, and the poor old lad turned a glowing face in
my direction.

'Chiswick, 60873,' he bellowed in a voice charged with emotion.
'Write it down, Bertie, or I shall forget it. Chiswick, 60873. Her
telephone number.'

And then he disappeared, accompanied by about eleven thousand
sightseers, and a voice spoke at my elbow.

'Mr Wooster! What – what – what is the meaning of this?'

Sir Roderick, with bigger eyebrows than ever, was standing at
my side.

'It's all right,' I said. 'Poor old Biffy's only gone off his crumpet.'

He tottered.

'What?'

'Had a sort of fit or seizure, you know.'

'Another!' Sir Roderick, drew a deep breath. 'And this is the man
I was about to allow my daughter to marry!' I heard him mutter.

I tapped him in a kindly spirit on the shoulder. It took some doing,
mark you, but I did it.

'If I were you,' I said, 'I should call that off. Scratch the fixture.
Wash it out absolutely, is my advice.'

He gave me a nasty look.

'I do not require your advice, Mr Wooster! I had already arrived
independently at the decision of which you speak. Mr Wooster, you

are a friend of this man – a fact which should in itself have been sufficient warning to me. You will – unlike myself – be seeing him again. Kindly inform him, when you do see him, that he may consider his engagement at an end.'

'Right-ho,' I said, and hurried off after the crowd. It seemed to me that a little bailing-out might be in order.

It was about an our later that I shoved my way out to where I had parked the car. Jeeves was sitting in the front seat, brooding over the cosmos. He rose courteously as I approached.

'You are leaving, sir?'

'I am.'

'And Sir Roderick, sir?'

'Not coming. I am revealing no secrets, Jeeves, when I inform you that he and I have parted brass rags. Not on speaking terms now.'

'Indeed, sir? And Mr Biffen? Will you wait for him?'

'No. He's in prison.'

'Really, sir?'

'Yes. I tried to bail him out, but they decided on second thoughts to coop him up for the night.'

'What was his offence, sir?'

'You remember that girl of his I was telling you about? He found her in a tank at the Palace of Beauty and went after her by the quickest route, which was via a plate-glass window. He was then scooped up and borne off in irons by the constabulary.' I gazed sideways at him. It is difficult to bring off a penetrating glance out of the corner of your eye, but I managed it. 'Jeeves,' I said, 'there is more in this than the casual observer would suppose. You told Mr Biffen to go to the Palace of Beauty. Did you know the girl would be there?'

'Yes, sir.'

This was most remarkable and rummy to a degree.

'Dash it, do you know everything?'

'Oh, no, sir,' said Jeeves with an indulgent smile. Humouring the young master.

'Well, how did you know that?'

'I happen to be acquainted with the future Mrs Biffen, sir.'

'I see. Then you knew all about that business in New York?'

'Yes, sir. And it was for that reason that I was not altogether favourably disposed towards Mr Biffen when you were first kind enough to suggest that I might be able to offer some slight assistance. I mistakenly supposed that he had been trifling with the girl's affections, sir. But when you told me the true facts of the case I appreciated the injustice I had done to Mr Biffen and endeavoured to make amends.'

'Well, he certainly owes you a lot. He's crazy about her.'

'That is very gratifying, sir.'

'And she ought to be pretty grateful to you, too. Old Biffy's got fifteen thousand a year, not to mention more cows, pigs, hens, and ducks than he knows what to do with. A dashed useful bird to have in any family.'

'Yes, sir.'

'Tell me, Jeeves,' I said, 'how did you happen to know the girl in the first place?'

Jeeves looked dreamily out into the traffic.

'She is my niece, sir. If I might make a suggestion, sir, I should not jerk the steering wheel with quite such suddenness. We very nearly collided with that omnibus.'

7

WITHOUT THE OPTION

The evidence was all in. The machinery of the law had worked without a hitch. And the beak, having adjusted a pair of pince-nez which looked as though they were going to do a nosedive any moment, coughed like a pained sheep and slipped us the bad news. 'The prisoner, Wooster,' he said – and who can paint the shame and agony of Bertram at hearing himself so described? – 'will pay a fine of five pounds.'

'Oh, rather!' I said. 'Absolutely! Like a shot!'

I was dashed glad to get the thing settled at such a reasonable figure. I gazed across what they call the sea of faces till I picked up Jeeves, sitting at the back. Stout fellow, he had come to see the young master through his hour of trial.

'I say, Jeeves,' I sang out, 'have you got a fiver? I'm a bit short.'

'Silence!' bellowed some officious blighter.

'It's all right,' I said, 'just arranging the financial details. Got the stuff, Jeeves?'

'Yes, sir.'

'Good egg!'

'Are you a friend of the prisoner?' asked the beak.

'I am in Mr Wooster's employment, Your Worship, in the capacity of gentleman's personal gentleman.'

'Then pay the fine to the clerk.'

'Very good, Your Worship.'

The beak gave a coldish nod in my direction, as much as to say that they might now strike the fetters from my wrists; and having hitched up the pince-nez once more, proceeded to hand poor old Sippy one of the nastiest looks ever seen in Bosher Street Police Court.

'The case of the prisoner Leon Trotzky – which,' he said, giving Sippy the eye again, 'I am strongly inclined to think an assumed and fictitious name – is more serious. He has been convicted of a wanton and violent assault upon the police. The evidence of the officer has proved that the prisoner struck him in the abdomen, causing severe internal pain, and in other ways interfered with him in the execution of his duties. I am aware that on the night following the annual aquatic contest between the Universities of Oxford and Cambridge a certain licence is traditionally granted by the authorities, but aggravated acts of ruffianly hooliganism like that of the prisoner Trotzky cannot be overlooked or palliated. He will serve a sentence of thirty days in the Second Division without the option of a fine.'

'No, I say – here – hi – dash it all!' protested poor old Sippy.

'Silence!' bellowed the officious blighter.

'Next case,' said the beak. And that was that.

The whole affair was most unfortunate. Memory is a trifle blurred; but as far as I can piece together the facts, what happened was more or less this:

Abstemious cove though I am as a general thing there is one night in the year when, putting all other engagements aside, I am rather apt to let myself go a bit and renew my lost youth, as it were. The night to which I allude is the one following the annual aquatic contest between the Universities of Oxford and Cambridge; or, putting it another way, Boat-Race Night. Then, if ever, you will see Bertram under the influence. And on this occasion, I freely admit, I had been doing myself rather juicily, with the result that when I ran into old Sippy opposite the Empire I was in quite fairly bonhomous mood. This being so, it cut me to the quick to perceive that Sippy, generally the brightest of revellers, was far from being his usual sunny self. He had the air of a man with a secret sorrow.

'Bertie,' he said as we strolled along towards Piccadilly Circus, 'the heart bowed down by the weight of woe to weakest hope will cling.' Sippy is by way of being an author, though mainly dependent for the necessaries of life on subsidies from an old aunt who lives in the country, and his conversation often takes a literary turn. 'But the trouble is that I have no hope to cling to, weak or otherwise. I am up against it, Bertie.'

'In what way, laddie?'

'I've got to go tomorrow and spend three weeks with some absolutely dud – and I go further – some positively scaly friends of my Aunt Vera. She has fixed the thing up, and may a nephew's curse blister every bulb in her garden.'

'Who are these hounds of hell?' I asked.

'Some people named Pringle. I haven't seen them since I was ten, but I remember them at that time striking me as England's premier warts.'

'Tough luck. No wonder you've lost your morale.'

'The world,' said Sippy, 'is very grey. How can I shake off this awful depression?'

It was then that I got one of those bright ideas one does get round about 11.30 on Boat-Race Night.

'What you want, old man,' I said, 'is a policeman's helmet.'

'Do I, Bertie?'

'If I were you, I'd just step straight across the street and get that one over there.'

'But there's a policeman inside it. You can see him distinctly.'

'What does that matter?' I said. I simply couldn't follow his reasoning.

Sippy stood for a moment in thought.

'I believe you're absolutely right,' he said at last. 'Funny I never thought of it before. You really recommend me to get that helmet?'

'I do, indeed.'

'Then I will,' said Sippy, brightening up in the most remarkable manner.

So there you have the posish, and you can see why, as I left the dock a free man, remorse gnawed at my vitals. In his twenty-fifth year, with life opening out before him and all that sort of thing, Oliver Randolph Sipperley had become a jail-bird, and it was all my fault. It was I who had dragged that fine spirit down into the mire, so to speak, and the question now arose, What could I do to atone?

Obviously the first move must be to get in touch with Sippy and see if he had any last messages and what not. I pushed about a bit, making inquiries, and presently found myself in a little dark room with whitewashed walls and a wooden bench. Sippy was sitting on the bench with his head in his hands.

'How are you, old lad?' I asked in a hushed, bedside voice.

'I'm a ruined man,' said Sippy, looking like a poached egg.

'Oh, come,' I said, 'it's not so bad as all that. I mean to say, you had the swift intelligence to give a false name. There won't be anything about you in the papers.'

'I'm not worrying about the papers. What's bothering me is, how can I go and spend three weeks with the Pringles, starting today, when I've got to sit in a prison cell with a ball and chain on my ankle?'

'But you said you didn't want to go.'

'It isn't a question of wanting, fathead. I've got to go. If I don't my aunt will find out where I am. And if she finds out that I am doing thirty days, without the option, in the lowest dungeon beneath the castle moat – well, where shall I get off?'

I saw his point.

'This is not a thing we can settle for ourselves,' I said gravely. 'We must put our trust in a higher power. Jeeves is the man we must consult.'

And having collected a few of the necessary data, I shook his hand, patted him on the back and tooled off home to Jeeves.

'Jeeves,' I said, when I had climbed outside the pick-me-up which he had thoughtfully prepared against my coming, 'I've got something to tell you; something important; something that vitally affects one whom you have always regarded with – one whom you have always looked upon – one whom you have – well, to cut a long story short, as I'm not feeling quite myself – Mr Sipperley.'

'Yes, sir?'

'Jeeves, Mr Souperley is in the sip.'

'Sir?'

'I mean, Mr Sipperley is in the soup.'

'Indeed, sir?'

'And all owing to me. It was I who, in a moment of mistaken kindness, wishing only to cheer him up and give him something to occupy his mind, recommended him to pinch that policeman's helmet.'

'Is that so, sir?'

'Do you mind not intoning the responses, Jeeves?' I said. 'This is a most complicated story for a man with a headache to have to tell, and if you interrupt you'll make me lose the thread. As a favour to me, therefore, don't do it. Just nod every now and then to show that you're following me.'

I closed my eyes and marshalled the facts.

'To start with then, Jeeves, you may or may not know that Mr Sipperley is practically dependent on his Aunt Vera.'

'Would that be Miss Sipperley of the Paddock, Beckley-on-the-Moor in Yorkshire, sir?'

'Yes. Don't tell me you know her!'

'Not personally, sir. But I have a cousin residing in the village who has some slight acquaintance with Miss Sipperley. He has described her to me as an imperious and quick-tempered old lady . . . But I beg your pardon, sir, I should have nodded.'

'Quite right, you should have nodded. Yes, Jeeves, you should have nodded. But it's too late now.'

I nodded myself. I hadn't had my eight hours the night before, and what you might call a lethargy was showing a tendency to steal over me from time to time.

'Yes, sir?' said Jeeves.

'Oh – ah – yes,' I said, giving myself a bit of a hitch up. 'Where had I got to?'

'You were saying that Mr Sipperley is practically dependent upon Miss Sipperley, sir.'

'Was I?'

'You were, sir.'

'You're perfectly right; so I was. Well, then, you can readily understand, Jeeves, that he has got to take jolly good care to keep in with her. You get that?'

Jeeves nodded.

'Now mark this closely: The other day she wrote to old Sippy, telling him to come down and sing at her village concert. It was equivalent to a royal command, if you see what I mean, so Sippy couldn't refuse in so many words. But he had sung at her village concert once before and had got the bird in no uncertain manner, so he wasn't playing any return dates. You follow so far, Jeeves?'

Jeeves nodded.

'So what did he do, Jeeves? He did what seemed to him at the moment a rather brainy thing. He told her that, though he would have been delighted to sing at her village concert, by a most unfortunate chance an editor had commissioned him to write a series of articles on the colleges of Cambridge and he was obliged to pop down there at once and would be away for quite three weeks. All clear up to now?'

Jeeves inclined the coco-nut.

'Whereupon, Jeeves, Miss Sipperley wrote back, saying that she quite realized that work must come before pleasure – pleasure being her loose way of describing the act of singing songs at the Beckley-on-the-Moor concert and getting the laugh from the local toughs; but that, if he was going to Cambridge, he must certainly stay with her friends, the Pringles, at their house just outside the town. And she dropped them a line telling them to expect him on the twenty-eighth, and they dropped another line saying right-ho, and the thing was settled. And now Mr Sipperley is in the jug, and what will be the ultimate outcome or upshot? Jeeves, it is a problem worthy of your great intellect. I rely on you.'

'I will do my best to justify your confidence, sir.'

'Carry on, then. And meanwhile pull down the blinds and bring a couple more cushions and heave that small chair this way so that I can put my feet up, and then go away and brood and let me hear from you in – say, a couple of hours, or maybe three.

And if anybody calls and wants to see me, inform them that I am dead.'

'Dead, sir?'

'Dead. You won't be so far wrong.'

It must have been well towards evening when I woke up with a crick in my neck but otherwise somewhat refreshed. I pressed the bell.

'I looked in twice, sir,' said Jeeves, 'but on each occasion you were asleep and I did not like to disturb you.'

'The right spirit, Jeeves ... Well?'

'I have been giving close thought to the little problem which you indicated, sir, and I can see only one solution.'

'One is enough. What do you suggest?'

'That you go to Cambridge in Mr Sipperley's place, sir.'

I stared at the man. Certainly I was feeling a good deal better than I had been a few hours before; but I was far from being in a fit condition to have rot like this talked to me.

'Jeeves,' I said sternly, 'pull yourself together. This is mere babble from the sick-bed.'

'I fear I can suggest no other plan of action, sir, which will extricate Mr Sipperley from his dilemma.'

'But think! Reflect! Why, even I, in spite of having had a disturbed night and a most painful morning with the minions of the law, can see that the scheme is a loony one. To put the finger on only one leak in the thing, it isn't me these people want to see; it's Mr Sipperley. They don't know me from Adam.'

'So much the better, sir. For what I am suggesting is that you go to Cambridge, affecting actually to be Mr Sipperley.'

This was too much.

'Jeeves,' I said, and I'm not half sure there weren't tears in my eyes, 'surely you can see for yourself that this is pure banana oil. It is not like you to come into the presence of a sick man and gibber.'

'I think the plan I have suggested would be practicable, sir. While you were sleeping, I was able to have a few words with Mr Sipperley, and he informed me that Professor and Mrs Pringle have not set eyes upon him since he was a lad of ten.'

'No, that's true. He told me that. But even so, they would be sure to ask him questions about my aunt – or rather his aunt. Where would I be then?'

'Mr Sipperley was kind enough to give me a few facts respecting Miss Sipperley, sir, which I jotted down. With these, added to what my cousin has told me of the lady's habits, I think you would be in a position to answer any ordinary question.'

There is something dashed insidious about Jeeves. Time and again since we first came together he has stunned me with some apparently drivelling suggestion or scheme or ruse or plan of campaign, and after about five minutes has convinced me that it is not only sound but fruity. It took nearly a quarter of an hour to reason me into this particular one, it being considerably the weirdest to date; but he did it. I was holding out pretty firmly, when he suddenly clinched the thing.

'I would certainly suggest, sir,' he said, 'that you left London as soon as possible and remained hid for some little time in some retreat where you would not be likely to be found.'

'Eh? Why?'

'During the last hours Mrs Spenser has been on the telephone three times, sir, endeavouring to get into communication with you.'

'Aunt Agatha!' I cried, paling beneath my tan.

'Yes, sir. I gathered from her remarks that she had been reading in the evening paper a report of this morning's proceedings in the police court.'

I hopped from the chair like a jack rabbit of the prairie. If Aunt Agatha was out with her hatchet, a move was most certainly indicated.

'Jeeves,' I said, 'this is a time for deeds, not words. Pack – and that right speedily.'

'I have packed, sir.'

'Find out when there is a train for Cambridge.'

'There is one in forty minutes, sir.'

'Call a taxi.'

'A taxi is at the door, sir.'

'Good!' I said. 'Then lead me to it.'

The Maison Pringle was quite a bit of a way out of Cambridge, a mile or two down the Trumpington Road; and when I arrived everybody was dressing for dinner. So it wasn't till I had shoved on the evening raiment and got down to the drawing-room that I met the gang.

'Hullo-ullo!' I said, taking a deep breath and floating in.

I tried to speak in a clear and ringing voice, but I wasn't feeling my chirpiest. It is always a nervous job for a diffident and unassuming bloke to visit a strange house for the first time; and it doesn't make the thing any better when he goes there pretending to be another fellow. I was conscious of a rather pronounced sinking feeling, which the appearance of the Pringles did nothing to allay.

Sippy had described them as England's premier warts, and it

looked to me as if he might be about right. Professor Pringle was a thinnish, baldish, dyspeptic-lookingish cove with an eye like a haddock, while Mrs Pringle's aspect was that of one who had had bad news round about the year 1900 and never really got over it. And I was just staggering under the impact of these two when I was introduced to a couple of ancient females with shawls all over them.

'No doubt you remember my mother?' said Professor Pringle mournfully, indicating Exhibit A.

'Oh – ah!' I said, achieving a bit of a beam.

'And my aunt,' sighed the Prof, as if things were getting worse and worse.

'Well, well, well!' I said, shooting another beam in the direction of Exhibit B.

'They were only saying this morning that they remembered you,' groaned the Prof, abandoning all hope.

There was a pause. The whole strength of the company gazed at me like a family group out of one of Edgar Allan Poe's less cheery yarns, and I felt my *joie de vivre* dying at the roots.

'I remember Oliver,' said Exhibit A. She heaved a sigh. 'He was such a pretty child. What a pity! What a pity!'

Tactful, of course, and calculated to put the guest completely at his ease.

'I remember Oliver,' said Exhibit B, looking at me in much the same way as the Bosher Street beak had looked at Sippy before putting on the black cap. 'Nasty little boy! He teased my cat.'

'Aunt Jane's memory is wonderful, considering that she will be eighty-seven next birthday,' whispered Mrs Pringle with mournful pride.

'What did you say?' asked the Exhibit suspiciously.

'I said your memory was wonderful.'

'Ah!' The dear old creature gave me another glare. I could see that no beautiful friendship was to be looked for by Bertram in this quarter. 'He chased my Tibby all over the garden, shooting arrows at her from a bow.'

At this moment a cat strolled out from under the sofa and made for me its tail up. Cats always do take to me, which made it all the sadder that I should be saddled with Sippy's criminal record. I stooped to tickle it under the ear, such being my invariable policy, and the Exhibit uttered a piercing cry.

'Stop him! Stop him!'

She leaped forward, moving uncommonly well for one of her years, and having scooped up the cat, stood eyeing me with bitter defiance, as if daring me to start anything. Most unpleasant.

'I like cats,' I said feebly.

It didn't go. The sympathy of the audience was not with me. And conversation was at what you might call a low ebb, when the door opened and a girl came in.

'My daughter Heloise,' said the Prof moodily, as if he hated to admit it.

I turned to mitt the female, and stood there with my hand out, gaping. I can't remember when I've had such a nasty shock.

I suppose everybody has had the experience of suddenly meeting somebody who reminded them frightfully of some fearful person. I mean to say, by way of an example, once when I was golfing in Scotland I saw a woman come into the hotel who was the living image of my Aunt Agatha. Probably a very decent sort, if I had only waited to see, but I didn't wait. I legged it that evening, utterly unable to stand the spectacle. And on another occasion I was driven out of a thoroughly festive night club because the head waiter reminded me of my Uncle Percy.

Well, Heloise Pringle, in the most ghastly way, resembled Honoria Glossop.

I think I may have told you before about this Glossop scourge. She was the daughter of Sir Roderick Glossop, the loony-doctor, and I had been engaged to her for about three weeks, much against my wishes, when the old boy most fortunately got the idea that I was off my rocker and put the bee on the proceedings. Since then the mere thought of her had been enough to make me start out of my sleep with a loud cry. And this girl was exactly like her.

'Er – how are you?' I said.

'How do you do?'

Her voice put the lid on it. It might have been Honoria herself talking. Honoria Glossop has a voice like a lion tamer making some authoritative announcement to one of the troupe, and so had this girl. I backed away convulsively and sprang into the air as my foot stubbed itself against something squashy. A sharp yowl rent the air, followed by an indignant cry, and I turned to see Aunt Jane, on all fours, trying to put things right with the cat, which had gone to earth under the sofa. She gave me a look, and I could see that her worst fears had been realized.

At this juncture dinner was announced – not before I was ready for it.

*

'Jeeves,' I said, when I got him alone that night, 'I am no faint heart, but I am inclined to think that this binge is going to prove a shade above the odds.'

'You are not enjoying your visit, sir?'

'I am not, Jeeves. Have you seen Miss Pringle?'

'Yes, sir, from a distance.'

'The best way to see her. Did you observe her keenly?'

'Yes, sir.'

'Did she remind you of anybody?'

'She appeared to me to bear a remarkable likeness to her cousin, Miss Glossop, sir.'

'Her cousin! You don't mean to say she's Honoria Glossop's cousin!'

'Yes, sir. Mrs Pringle was a Miss Blatherwick – the younger of two sisters, the elder of whom married Sir Roderick Glossop.'

'Great Scott! That accounts for the resemblance.'

'Yes, sir.'

'And what a resemblance, Jeeves! She even talks like Miss Glossop.'

'Indeed, sir? I have not yet heard Miss Pringle speak.'

'You have missed little. And what it amounts to, Jeeves, is that, though nothing will induce me to let old Sippy down, I can see that this visit is going to try me high. At a pinch, I could stand the Prof and wife. I could even make the effort of a lifetime and bear up against Aunt Jane. But to expect a man to mix daily with the girl Heloise – and to do it, what is more, on lemonade, which is all there was to drink at dinner – is to ask too much of him. What shall I do, Jeeves?'

'I think you should avoid Miss Pringle's society as much as possible.'

'The same great thought had occurred to me,' I said.

It is all very well, though, to talk airily about avoiding a female's society; but when you are living in the same house with her, and she doesn't want to avoid you, it takes a bit of doing. It is a peculiar thing in life that the people you most particularly want to edge away from always seem to cluster round like a poultice. I hadn't been twenty-four hours in the place before I perceived that I was going to see a lot of this pestilence.

She was one of those girls you're always meeting on the stairs and in passages. I couldn't go into a room without seeing her drift in a minute later. And if I walked in the garden she was sure to leap out at me from a laurel bush or the onion bed or something. By about the tenth day I had begun to feel absolutely haunted.

'Jeeves,' I said, 'I have begun to feel absolutely haunted.'

'Sir!'

'This woman dogs me. I never seem to get a moment to myself. Old Sippy was supposed to come here to make a study of the Cambridge colleges, and she took me round about fifty-seven this morning. This afternoon I went to sit in the garden, and she popped up through a trap and was in my midst. This evening she cornered me in the morning-room. It's getting so that, when I have a bath, I wouldn't be a bit surprised to find her nestling in the soap dish.'

'Extremely trying, sir.'

'Dashed so. Have you any remedy to suggest?'

'Not at the moment, sir. Miss Pringle does appear to be distinctly interested in you, sir. She was asking me questions this morning respecting your mode of life in London.'

'What?'

'Yes, sir.'

I stared at the man in horror. A ghastly thought had struck me. I quivered like an aspen.

At lunch that day a curious thing had happened. We had just finished mangling the cutlets and I was sitting back in my chair, taking a bit of an easy before being allotted my slab of boiled pudding, when, happening to look up, I caught the girl Heloise's eye fixed on me in what seemed to me a rather rummy manner. I didn't think much about it at the time, because boiled pudding is a thing you have to give your undivided attention to if you want to do yourself justice; but now, recalling the episode in the light of Jeeves's words, the full sinister meaning of the thing seemed to come home to me.

Even at the moment, something about that look had struck me as oddly familiar, and now I suddenly saw why. It had been the identical look which I had observed in the eye of Honoria Glossop in the days immediately preceding our engagement – the look of a tigress that has marked down its prey.

'Jeeves, do you know what I think?'

'Sir?'

I gulped slightly.

'Jeeves,' I said, 'listen attentively. I don't want to give the impression that I consider myself one of those deadly coves who exercise an irresistible fascination over one and all and can't meet a girl without wrecking her peace of mind in the first half-minute. As a matter of fact, it's rather the other way with me, for girls on entering my presence are most inclined to give me the raised eyebrow and the twitching upper lip. Nobody, therefore, can say that I am a man who's likely to take alarm unnecessarily. You admit that, don't you?'

'Yes, sir.'

'Nevertheless, Jeeves, it is a known scientific fact that there is a particular style of female that does seem strangely attracted to the sort of fellow I am.'

'Very true, sir.'

'I mean to say, I know perfectly well that I've got, roughly speaking, half the amount of brain a normal bloke ought to possess. And when a girl comes along who has about twice the regular allowance, she too often makes a bee-line for me with the love-light in her eyes. I don't know how to account for it, but it is so.'

'It may be Nature's provision for maintaining the balance of the species, sir.'

'Very possibly. Anyway, it has happened to me over and over again. It was what happened in the case of Honoria Glossop. She was notoriously one of the brainiest women of her year at Girton, and she just gathered me in like a bull pup swallowing a piece of steak.'

'Miss Pringle, I am informed, sir, was an even more brilliant scholar than Miss Glossop.'

'Well, there you are! Jeeves, she looks at me.'

'Yes, sir?'

'I keep meeting her on the stairs and in passages.'

'Indeed, sir?'

'She recommends me books to read, to improve my mind.'

'Highly suggestive, sir.'

'And at breakfast this morning, when I was eating a sausage, she told me I shouldn't, as modern medical science held that a four-inch sausage contained as many germs as a dead rat. The maternal touch, you understand; fussing over my health.'

'I think we may regard that, sir, as practically conclusive.'

I sank into a chair, thoroughly pipped.

'What's to be done, Jeeves?'

'We must think, sir.'

'You think. I haven't the machinery.'

'I will most certainly devote my very best attention to the matter, sir, and will endeavour to give satisfaction.'

Well, that was something. But I was ill at ease. Yes, there is no getting away from it, Bertram was ill at ease.

*

Next morning we visited sixty-three more Cambridge colleges, and after lunch I said I was going to my room to lie down. After staying there for half an hour to give the coast time to clear, I shoved a book and smoking materials in my pocket, and climbing out of a window, shinned down a convenient water-pipe into the garden. My objective was the summer-house, where it seemed to me that a man might put in a quiet hour or so without interruption.

It was extremely jolly in the garden. The sun was shining, the crocuses were all to the mustard and there wasn't a sign of Heloise Pringle anywhere. The cat was fooling about on the lawn, so I chirruped to it and it gave a low gargle and came trotting up. I had just got it in my arms and was scratching it under the ear when there was a loud shriek from above, and there was Aunt Jane half out of the window. Dashed disturbing.

'Oh, right-ho,' I said.

I dropped the cat, which galloped off into the bushes, and dismissing the idea of bunging a brick at the aged relative, went on my way, heading for the shrubbery. Once safely hidden there, I worked round till I got to the summer-house. And, believe me, I had hardly got my first cigarette nicely under way when a shadow fell on my book and there was young Sticketh-Closer-Than-a-Brother in person.

'So there you are,' she said.

She seated herself by my side, and with a sort of gruesome playfulness jerked the gasper out of the holder and heaved it through the door.

'You're always smoking,' she said, a lot too much like a lovingly chiding young bride for my comfort. 'I wish you wouldn't. It's so bad for you. And you ought not to be sitting out here without your light overcoat. You want someone to look after you.'

'I've got Jeeves.'

She frowned a bit.

'I don't like him,' she said.

'Eh? Why not?'

'I don't know. I wish you would get rid of him.'

My flesh absolutely crept. And I'll tell you why. One of the first things Honoria Glossop had done after we had become engaged was to tell me she didn't like Jeeves and wanted him shot out. The realization that this girl resembled Honoria not only in body but in blackness of soul made me go all faint.

'What are you reading?'

She picked up my book and frowned again. The thing was one I had brought down from the old flat in London, to glance at in the train – a fairly zippy effort in the detective line called *The Trail of Blood*. She turned the pages with a nasty sneer.

'I can't understand you liking nonsense of this – ' She stopped suddenly. 'Good gracious!'

'What's the matter?'

'Do you know Bertie Wooster?'

And then I saw that my name was scrawled right across the title page, and my heart did three back somersaults.

'Oh – er – well that is to say – well, slightly.'

'He must be a perfect horror. I'm surprised that you can make a friend of him. Apart from anything else, the man is practically an imbecile. He was engaged to my Cousin Honoria at one time, and it was broken off because he was next door to insane. You should hear my Uncle Roderick talk about him!'

I wasn't keen.

'Do you see much of him?'

'A goodish bit.'

'I saw in the paper the other day that he was fined for making a disgraceful disturbance in the street.'

'Yes, I saw that.'

She gazed at me in a foul, motherly way.

'He can't be a good influence for you,' she said. 'I do wish you would drop him. Will you?'

'Well – ' I began. And at this point old Cuthbert, the cat, having presumably found it a bit slow by himself in the bushes, wandered in with a matey expression on his face and jumped on my lap. I welcomed him with a good deal of cordiality. Though but a cat, he did make a sort of third at this party; and he afforded a good excuse for changing the conversation.

'Jolly birds, cats,' I said.

She wasn't having any.

'Will you drop Bertie Wooster?' she said, absolutely ignoring the cat *motif*.

'It would be so difficult.'

'Nonsense! It only needs a little will-power. The man surely can't be so interesting a companion as all that. Uncle Roderick says he is an invertebrate waster.'

I could have mentioned a few things that I thought Uncle Roderick was, but my lips were sealed, so to speak.

'You have changed a great deal since we last met,' said the Pringle disease reproachfully. She bent forward and began to scratch the cat under the other ear. 'Do you remember, when we were children together, you used to say that you would do anything for me?'

'Did I?'

'I remember once you cried because I was cross and wouldn't let you kiss me.'

I didn't believe it at the time, and I don't believe it now. Sippy is in many ways a good deal of a chump, but surely even at the age of ten he cannot have been such a priceless ass as that. I think the girl was lying, but that didn't make the position of affairs any better. I edged away a couple of inches and sat staring before me, the old brow beginning to get slightly bedewed.

And then suddenly – well, you know how it is, I mean. I suppose everyone has had that ghastly feeling at one time or another of being urged by some overwhelming force to do some absolutely blithering act. You get it every now and then when you're in a crowded theatre, and something seems to be egging you on to shout, 'Fire!' and see what happens. Or you're talking to someone and all at once you feel, 'Now, suppose I suddenly biffed this bird in the eye!'

Well, what I'm driving at is this: at this juncture, with her shoulder squashing against mine and her black hair tickling my nose, a perfectly loony impulse came sweeping over me to kiss her.

'No, really?' I croaked.

'Have you forgotten?'

She lifted the old onion and her eyes looked straight into mine. I could feel myself skidding. I shut my eyes. And then from the doorway there spoke the most beautiful voice I had ever heard in my life:

'Give me that cat!'

I opened my eyes. There was good old Aunt Jane, that queen of her sex, standing before me, glaring at me as if I were a vivisectionist and she had surprised me in the middle of an experiment. How this pearl among women had tracked me down I don't know, but there she stood, bless her dear, intelligent old soul, like the rescue party in the last reel of a motion picture.

I didn't wait. The spell was broken and I legged it. As I went, I heard that lovely voice again.

'He shot arrows at my Tibby from a bow,' said this most deserving and excellent octogenarian.

For the next few days all was peace. I saw comparatively little of Heloise. I found the strategic value of that water-pipe outside my window beyond praise. I seldom left the house now by any other route. It seemed to me that, if only the luck held like this, I might after all be able to stick this visit out for the full term of the sentence.

But meanwhile, as they say in the movies –

The whole family appeared to be present and correct as I came down to the drawing-room a couple of nights later. The Prof, Mrs Prof, the two Exhibits and the girl Heloise were scattered about at intervals. The cat slept on the rug, the canary in its cage. There was nothing, in short, to indicate that this was not just one of our ordinary evenings.

'Well, well, well!' I said cheerily. 'Hullo-ullo-ullo!'

I always like to make something in the nature of an entrance speech, it seeming to me to lend a chummy tone to the proceedings.

The girl Heloise looked at me reproachfully.

'Where have you been all day?' she asked.

'I went to my room after lunch.'

'You weren't there at five.'

'No. After putting in a spell of work on the good old colleges I went for a stroll. Fellow must have exercise if he means to keep fit.'

'*Mens sana in corpore sano,*' observed the Prof.

'I shouldn't wonder,' I said cordially.

At this point, when everything was going as sweet as a nut and I was feeling on top of my form, Mrs Pringle suddenly soaked me on the base of the skull with a sandbag. Not actually, I don't mean. No, no. I speak figuratively, as it were.

'Roderick is very late,' she said.

You may think it strange that the sound of that name should have sloshed into my nerve centres, like a half-brick. But, take it from me, to a man who has had any dealings with Sir Roderick Glossop there is only one Roderick in the world – and this is one too many.

'Roderick?' I gurgled.

'My brother-in-law, Sir Roderick Glossop, comes to Cambridge tonight,' said the Prof. 'He lectures at St Luke's tomorrow. He is coming here to dinner.'

And while I stood there, feeling like the hero when he discovers that he is trapped in the den of the Secret Nine, the door opened.

'Sir Roderick Glossop,' announced the maid or some such person, and in he came.

One of the things that gets this old crumb so generally disliked among the better element of the community is the fact that he has a head like the dome of St Paul's and eyebrows that want bobbing or shingling to reduce them to anything like reasonable size. It is a nasty experience to see this bald and bushy bloke advancing on you when you haven't prepared the strategic railways in your rear.

As he came into the room I backed behind a sofa and commended my soul to God. I didn't need to have my hand read to know that trouble was coming to me through a dark man.

He didn't spot me at first. He shook hands with the Prof and wife, kissed Heloise and waggled his head at the Exhibits.

'I fear I am somewhat late,' he said. 'A slight accident on the road, affecting what my chauffeur termed the – '

And then he saw me lurking on the outskirts and gave a startled grunt, as if I hurt him a good deal internally.

'This – ' began the Prof, waving in my direction.

'I am already acquainted with Mr Wooster.'

'This,' went on the Prof, 'is Miss Sipperley's nephew, Oliver. You remember Miss Sipperley?'

'What do you mean?' barked Sir Roderick. Having had so much to do with loonies has given him a rather sharp and authoritative manner on occasion. 'This is that wretched young man, Bertram Wooster. What is all this nonsense about Olivers and Sipperleys?'

The Prof was eyeing me with some natural surprise. So were the others. I beamed a bit weakly.

'Well, as a matter of fact – ' I said.

The Prof was wrestling with the situation. You could hear his brain buzzing.

'He said he was Oliver Sipperley,' he moaned.

'Come here!' bellowed Sir Roderick. 'Am I to understand that you have inflicted yourself on this household under the pretence of being the nephew of an old friend?'

It seemed a pretty accurate description of the facts.

'Well – er – yes,' I said.

Sir Roderick shot an eye at me. It entered the body somewhere about the top stud, roamed around inside for a bit and went out at the back.

'Insane! Quite insane, as I knew from the first moment I saw him.'

'What did he say?' asked Aunt Jane.

'Roderick says this young man is insane,' roared the Prof.

'Ah!' said Aunt Jane, nodding. 'I thought so. He climbs down water-pipes.'

'Does what?'

'I've seen him – ah, many a time!'

Sir Roderick snorted violently.

'He ought to be under proper restraint. It is abominable that a person in his mental condition should be permitted to roam the world at large. The next stage may quite easily be homicidal.'

It seemed to me that, even at the expense of giving old Sippy away, I must be cleared of this frightful charge. After all, Sippy's number was up anyway.

'Let me explain,' I said. 'Sippy asked me to come here.'

'What do you mean?'

'He couldn't come himself, because he was jugged for biffing a cop on Boat-Race Night.'

Well, it wasn't easy to make them get the hang of the story, and even when I'd done it it didn't seem to make them any chummier towards me. A certain coldness about expresses it, and when dinner was announced I counted myself out and pushed off rapidly to my room. I could have done with a bit of dinner, but the atmosphere didn't seem just right.

'Jeeves,' I said, having shot in and pressed the bell, 'we're sunk.'

'Sir?'

'Hell's foundations are quivering and the game is up.'

He listened attentively.

'The contingency was one always to have been anticipated as a possibility, sir. It only remains to take the obvious step.'

'What's that?'

'Go and see Miss Sipperley, sir.'

'What on earth for?'

'I think it would be judicious to apprise her of the facts yourself, sir, instead of allowing her to hear of them through the medium of a letter from Professor Pringle. That is to say, if you are still anxious to do all in your power to assist Mr Sipperley.'

'I can't let Sippy down. If you think it's any good – '

'We can but try it, sir. I have an idea, sir, that we may find Miss Sipperley disposed to look leniently upon Mr Sipperley's misdemeanour.'

'What makes you think that?'

'It is just a feeling that I have, sir.'

'Well, if you think it would be worth trying – How do we get there?'

'The distance is about a hundred and fifty miles, sir. Our best plane would be to hire a car.'

'Get it at once,' I said.

The idea of being a hundred and fifty miles away from Heloise

Pringle, not to mention Aunt Jane and Sir Roderick Glossop, sounded about as good to me as anything I had ever heard.

The Paddock, Beckley-on-the-Moor, was about a couple of parasangs from the village, and I set out for it next morning, after partaking of a hearty breakfast at the local inn, practically without a tremor. I suppose when a fellow has been through it as I had in the last two weeks his system becomes hardened. After all, I felt, whatever this aunt of Sippy's might be like, she wasn't Sir Roderick Glossop, so I was that much on velvet from the start.

The Paddock was one of those medium-sized houses with a goodish bit of very tidy garden and a carefully rolled gravel drive curving past a shrubbery that looked as if it had just come back from the dry cleaner – the sort of house you take one look at and say to yourself, 'Somebody's aunt lives there.' I pushed on up the drive, and as I turned the bend I observed in the middle distance a woman messing about by a flower-bed with a trowel in her hand. If this wasn't the female I was after, I was very much mistaken, so I halted, cleared the throat and gave tongue.

'Miss Sipperley?'

She had her back to me, and at the sound of my voice she executed a sort of leap or bound, not unlike a barefoot dancer who steps on a tin-tack halfway through the Vision of Salome. She came to earth and goggled at me in a rather goofy manner. A large, stout female with a reddish face.

'Hope I didn't startle you,' I said.

'Who are you?'

'My name's Wooster. I'm a pal of your nephew, Oliver.'

Her breathing had become more regular.

'Oh?' she said. 'When I heard your voice I thought you were someone else.'

'No, that's who I am. I came up here to tell you about Oliver.'

'What about him?'

I hesitated. Now that we were approaching what you might call the nub, or crux, of the situation, a good deal of my breezy confidence seemed to have slipped from me.

'Well, it's rather a painful tale, I must warn you.'

'Oliver isn't ill? He hasn't had an accident?'

She spoke anxiously, and I was pleased at this evidence of human feeling. I decided to shoot the works with no more delay.

'Oh, no, he isn't ill,' I said, 'and as regards having accidents, it depends on what you call an accident. He's in chokey.'

'In what?'

'In prison.'

'In prison!'

'It was entirely my fault. We were strolling along on Boat-Race Night and I advised him to pinch a policeman's helmet.'

'I don't understand.'

'Well, he seemed depressed, don't you know; and rightly or wrongly, I thought it might cheer him up if he stepped across the street and collared a policeman's helmet. He thought it a good idea, too, so he started doing it, and the man made a fuss and Oliver sloshed him.'

'Sloshed him?'

'Biffed him – smote him a blow – in the stomach.'

'My nephew Oliver hit a policeman in the stomach?'

'Absolutely in the stomach. And next morning the beak sent him to the bastille for thirty days without the option.'

I was looking at her a bit anxiously all this while to see how she was taking the thing, and at this moment her face seemed suddenly to split in half. For an instant she appeared to be all mouth, and then she was staggering about the grass, shouting with laughter and waving the trowel madly.

It seemed to me a bit of luck for her that Sir Roderick Glossop wasn't on the spot. He would have been sitting on her head and calling for the strait-waistcoat in the first half-minute.

'You aren't annoyed?' I said.

'Annoyed?' She chuckled happily. 'I've never heard of such a splendid thing in my life.'

I was pleased and relieved. I had hoped the news wouldn't upset her too much, but I had never expected it to go with such a roar as this.

'I'm proud of him,' she said.

'That's fine.'

'If every young man in England went about hitting policemen in the stomach, it would be a better country to live in.'

I couldn't follow her reasoning, but everything seemed to be all right; so after a few more cheery words I said goodbye and legged it.

'Jeeves,' I said when I got back to the inn, 'everything's fine. But I am far from understanding why.'

'What actually occurred when you met Miss Sipperley, sir?'

'I told her Sippy was in the jug for assaulting the police. Upon which she burst into hearty laughter, waved her trowel in a pleased manner and said she was proud of him.'

'I think I can explain her apparently eccentric behaviour, sir. I am informed that Miss Sipperley has had a good deal of annoyance at the hands of the local constable during the past two weeks. This has doubtless resulted in a prejudice on her part against the force as a whole.'

'Really? How was that?'

'The constable has been somewhat over-zealous in the performance of his duties, sir. On no fewer than three occasions in the last ten days he has served summonses upon Miss Sipperley – for exceeding the speed limit in her car; for allowing her dog to appear in public without a collar; and for failing to abate a smoking chimney. Being in the nature of an autocrat, if I may use the term, in the village, Miss Sipperley has been accustomed to do these things in the past with impunity, and the constable's unexpected zeal has made her somewhat ill-disposed to policemen as a class and consequently disposed to look upon such assaults as Mr Sipperley's in a kindly and broadminded spirit.'

I saw his point.

'What an amazing bit of luck, Jeeves!'

'Yes, sir.'

'Where did you hear all this?'

'My informant was the constable himself, sir. He is my cousin.'

I gaped at the man. I saw, so to speak, all.

'Good Lord, Jeeves! You didn't bribe him?'

'Oh, no, sir. But it was his birthday last week, and I gave him a little present. I have always been fond of Egbert, sir.'

'How much?'

'A matter of five pounds, sir.'

I felt in my pocket.

'Here you are,' I said. 'And another five for luck.'

'Thank you very much, sir.'

'Jeeves,' I said, 'you move in a mysterious way your wonders to perform. You don't mind if I sing a bit, do you?'

'Not at all, sir,' said Jeeves.

8

FIXING IT FOR FREDDIE

'Jeeves,' I said, looking in on him one afternoon on my return from the club, 'I don't want to interrupt you.'

'No, sir?'

'But I would like a word with you.'

'Yes, sir?'

He had been packing a few of the Wooster necessaries in the old kitbag against our approaching visit to the seaside, and he now rose and stood bursting with courteous zeal.

'Jeeves,' I said, 'a somewhat disturbing situation has arisen with regard to a pal of mine.'

'Indeed sir?'

'You know Mr Bullivant?'

'Yes, sir.'

'Well, I slid into the Drones this morning for a bite of lunch, and found him in a dark corner of the smoking-room looking like the last rose of summer. Naturally I was surprised. You know what a bright lad he is as a rule. The life and soul of every gathering he attends.'

'Yes, sir.'

'Quite the little lump of fun, in fact.'

'Precisely, sir.'

'Well, I made inquiries, and he told me that he had had a quarrel with the girl he's engaged to. You knew he was engaged to Miss Elizabeth Vickers?'

'Yes, sir. I recall reading the announcement in the *Morning Post*.'

'Well, he isn't any longer. What the row was about he didn't say, but the broad facts, Jeeves, are that she has scratched the fixture. She won't let him come near her, refuses to talk on the phone, and sends back his letters unopened.'

'Extremely trying, sir.'

'We ought to do something, Jeeves. But what?'

'It is somewhat difficult to make a suggestion, sir.'

'Well, what I'm going to do for a start is to take him down to Marvis Bay with me. I know these birds who have been handed their hat by the girl of their dreams, Jeeves. What they want is complete change of scene.'

'There is much in what you say, sir.'

'Yes. Change of scene is the thing. I heard of a man. Girl refused him. Man went abroad. Two months later girl wired him "Come back, Muriel." Man started to write out a reply; suddenly found that he couldn't remember girl's surname; so never answered at all, and lived happily ever after. It may well be, Jeeves, that after Freddie Bullivant has had a few weeks of Marvis Bay he will get completely over it.'

'Very possibly, sir.'

'And, if not, it's quite likely that, refreshed by sea air and good simple food, you will get a brainwave and think up some scheme for bringing these two misguided blighters together again.'

'I will do my best, sir.'

'I knew it, Jeeves, I knew it. Don't forget to put in plenty of socks.'

'No, sir.'

'Also of tennis shirts not a few.'

'Very good, sir.'

I left him to his packing, and a couple of days later we started off for Marvis Bay, where I had taken a cottage for July and August.

I don't know if you know Marvis Bay? It's in Dorsetshire; and, while not what you would call a fiercely exciting spot, has many good points. You spend the day there bathing and sitting on the sands, and in the evening you stroll out on the shore with the mosquitoes. At nine p.m. you rub ointment on the wounds and go to bed. It was a simple, healthy life, and it seemed to suit poor old Freddie absolutely. Once the moon was up and the breeze sighing in the trees, you couldn't drag him from that beach with ropes. He became quite a popular pet with the mosquitoes. They would hang round waiting for him to come out, and would give a miss to perfectly good strollers just so as to be in good condition for him.

It was during the day that I found Freddie, poor old chap, a trifle heavy as a guest. I suppose you can't blame a bloke whose heart is broken, but it required a good deal of fortitude to bear up against this gloom-crushed exhibit during the early days of our little holiday. When he wasn't chewing a pipe and scowling at the carpet, he was sitting at the piano, playing 'The Rosary' with one finger. He couldn't play anything except 'The Rosary', and he couldn't play much of that. However firmly and confidently he started off, somewhere around the third bar a fuse would blow out and he would have to start all over again.

He was playing it as usual one morning when I came in from bathing: and it seemed to me that he was extracting more hideous melancholy from it even than usual. Nor had my sense deceived me.

'Bertie,' he said in a hollow voice, skidding on the fourth crotchet from the left as you enter the second bar and producing a distressing sound like the death-rattle of a sand-eel. 'I've seen her!'

'Seen her?' I said. 'What, Elizabeth Vickers? How do you mean, you've seen her? She isn't down here.'

'Yes, she is. I suppose she's staying with relations or something. I was down at the post office, seeing if there were any letters, and we met in the doorway.'

'What happened?'

'She cut me dead.'

He started 'The Rosary' again, and stubbed his finger on a semi-quaver.

'Bertie,' he said, 'you ought never to have brought me here. I must go away.'

'Go away? Don't talk such rot. This is the best thing that could have happened. It's a most amazing bit of luck, her being down here. This is where you come out strong.'

'She cut me.'

'Never mind. Be a sportsman. Have another dash at her.'

'She looked clean through me.'

'Well, don't mind that. Stick at it. Now, having got her down here, what you want,' I said, 'is to place her under some obligation to you. What you want is to get her timidly thanking you. What you want – '

'What's she going to thank me timidly for?'

I thought for a while. Undoubtedly he had put his finger on the nub of the problem. For some moments I was at a loss, not to say nonplussed. Then I saw the way.

'What you want,' I said, 'is to look out for a chance and save her from drowning.'

'I can't swim.'

That was Freddie Bullivant all over. A dear old chap in a thousand ways, but no help to a fellow, if you know what I mean.

He cranked up the piano once more, and I legged it for the open.

I strolled out on the beach and began to think this thing over. I

would have liked to consult Jeeves, of course, but Jeeves had disappeared for the morning. There was no doubt that it was hopeless
expecting Freddie to do anything for himself in this crisis. I'm not
saying that dear old Freddie hasn't got his strong qualities. He is
good at polo, and I have heard him spoken of as a coming man at
snooker-pool. But apart from this you couldn't call him a man of
enterprise.

Well, I was rounding some rocks, thinking pretty tensely, when I
caught sight of a blue dress, and there was the girl in person. I had
never met her, but Freddie had sixteen photographs of her sprinkled
round his bedroom, and I knew I couldn't be mistaken. She was
sitting on the sand, helping a small, fat child to build a castle. On a
chair close by was an elderly female reading a novel. I heard the girl
call her 'aunt'. So getting the reasoning faculties to work, I deduced
that the fat child must be her cousin. It struck me that if Freddie had
been there he would probably have tried to work up some sentiment
about the kid on the strength of it. I couldn't manage this. I don't
think I ever saw a kid who made me feel less sentimental. He was
one of those round, bulging kids.

After he had finished his castle he seemed to get bored with life
and began to cry. The girl, who seemed to read him like a book,
took him off to where a fellow was selling sweets at a stall. And I
walked on.

Now, those who know me, if you ask them, will tell you that I'm
a chump. My Aunt Agatha would testify to this effect. So would my
Uncle Percy and many more of my nearest and – if you like to use the
expression – dearest. Well, I don't mind. I admit it. I *am* a chump. But
what I do say – and I should like to lay the greatest possible stress on
this – is that every now and then, just when the populace has given up
hope that I will ever show any real human intelligence – I get what it is
idle to pretend is not an inspiration. And that's what happened now. I
doubt if the idea that came to me at this juncture would have occurred
to a single one of any dozen of the largest-brained blokes in history.
Napoleon might have got it, but I'll bet Darwin and Shakespeare and
Thomas Hardy wouldn't have thought of it in a thousand years.

It came to me on my return journey. I was walking back along
the shore, exercising the old bean fiercely, when I saw the fat child
meditatively smacking a jelly-fish with a spade. The girl wasn't with
him. The aunt wasn't with him. In fact, there wasn't anybody else
in sight. And the solution of the whole trouble between Freddie and
his Elizabeth suddenly came to me in a flash.

From what I had seen of the two, the girl was evidently fond of this kid: and, anyhow, he was her cousin, so what I said to myself was this: If I kidnap this young heavyweight for a brief space of time: and if, when the girl has got frightfully anxious about where he can have got to, dear old Freddie suddenly appears leading the infant by the hand and telling a story to the effect that he found him wandering at large about the country and practically saved his life, the girl's gratitude is bound to make her chuck hostilities and be friends again.

So I gathered up the kid and made off with him.

Freddie, dear old chap, was rather slow at first in getting on to the fine points of the idea. When I appeared at the cottage, carrying the child, and dumped him down in the sitting-room, he showed no joy whatever. The child had started to bellow by this time, not thinking much of the thing, and Freddie seemed to find it rather trying.

'What the devil's all this?' he asked, regarding the little visitor with a good deal of loathing.

The kid loosed off a yell that made the windows rattle, and I saw that this was a time for strategy. I raced to the kitchen and fetched a pot of honey. It was the right idea. The kid stopped bellowing and began to smear his face with the stuff.

'Well?' said Freddie, when silence had set in.

I explained the scheme. After a while it began to strike him. The careworn look faded from his face, and for the first time since his arrival at Marvis Bay he smiled almost happily.

'There's something in this, Bertie.'

'It's the goods.'

'I think it will work,' said Freddie.

And, disentangling the child from the honey, he led him out.

'I expect Elizabeth will be on the beach somewhere,' he said.

What you might call a quiet happiness suffused me, if that's the word I want. I was very fond of old Freddie, and it was jolly to think that he was shortly about to click once more. I was leaning back in a chair on the veranda, smoking a peaceful cigarette, when down the road I saw the old boy returning, and, by George, the kid was still with him.

'Hallo!' I said. 'Couldn't you find her?'

I then perceived that Freddie was looking as if he had been kicked in the stomach.

'Yes, I found her,' he replied, with one of those bitter, mirthless laughs you read about.

'Well, then – ?'

He sank into a chair and groaned.

'This isn't her cousin, you idiot,' he said. 'He's no relation at all – just a kid she met on the beach. She had never seen him before in her life.'

'But she was helping him build a sand-castle.'

'I don't care. He's a perfect stranger.'

It seemed to me that, if the modern girl goes about building sand-castles with kids she has only known for five minutes and probably without a proper introduction at that, then all that has been written about her is perfectly true. Brazen is the word that seems to meet the case. I said as much to Freddie, but he wasn't listening.

'Well, who is this ghastly child, then?' I said.

'I don't know. O Lord, I've had a time! Thank goodness you will probably spend the next few years of your life in Dartmoor for kidnapping. That's my only consolation. I'll come and jeer at you through the bars on visiting days.'

'Tell me all, old man,' I said.

He told me all. It took him a good long time to do it, for he broke off in the middle of nearly every sentence to call me names, but I gradually gathered what had happened. The girl Elizabeth had listened like an iceberg while he worked off the story he had prepared, and then – well, she didn't actually call him a liar in so many words, but she gave him to understand in a general sort of way that he was a worm and an outcast. And then he crawled off with the kid, licked to a splinter.

'And mind,' he concluded, 'this is your affair. I'm not mixed up in it at all. If you want to escape your sentence – or anyway get a portion of it remitted – you'd better go and find the child's parents and return him before the police come for you.'

'Who are his parents?'

'I don't know.'

'Where do they live?'

'I don't know.'

The kid didn't seem to know, either. A thoroughly vapid and uninformed infant. I got out of him the fact that he had a father, but that was as far as he went. It didn't seem ever to have occurred to him, chatting of an evening with the old man, to ask him his name and address. So, after a wasted ten minutes, out we went into the great world, more or less what you might call at random.

I give you my word that, until I started to tramp the place with this child, I never had a notion that it was such a difficult job restoring a son to his parents. How kidnappers ever get caught is a mystery to me. I searched Marvis Bay like a bloodhound, but nobody came forward to claim the infant. You would have thought, from the lack of interest in him, that he was stopping there all by himself in a cottage of his own. It wasn't till, by another inspiration, I thought to ask the sweet-stall man that I got on the track. The sweet-stall man, who seemed to have seen a lot of him, said that the child's name was Kegworthy, and that his parents lived at a place called Ocean Rest.

It then remained to find Ocean Rest. And eventually, after visiting Ocean View, Ocean Prospect, Ocean Breeze, Ocean Cottage, Ocean Bungalow, Ocean Nook and Ocean Homestead, I trailed it down.

I knocked at the door. Nobody answered. I knocked again. I could hear movements inside, but nobody appeared. I was just going to get to work with that knocker in such a way that it would filter through these people's heads that I wasn't standing there just for the fun of the thing, when a voice from somewhere above shouted 'Hi!'

I looked up and saw a round, pink face, with grey whiskers east and west of it, staring down at me from an upper window.

'Hi!' it shouted again. 'You can't come in.'

'I don't want to come in.'

'Because – Oh, is that Tootles?'

'My name is not Tootles. Are you Mr Kegworthy? I've brought back your son.'

'I see him. Peep-bo, Tootles, Dadda can see 'oo.'

The face disappeared with a jerk. I could hear voices. The face reappeared.

'Hi!'

I churned the gravel madly. This blighter was giving me the pip.

'Do you live here?' asked the face.

'I have taken a cottage here for a few weeks.'

'What's your name?'

'Wooster.'

'Fancy that! Do you spell it W-o-r-c-e-s-t-e-r or W-o-o-s-t-e-r?'

'W-o-o-'

'I ask because I once knew a Miss Wooster, spelled W-o- – '

I had had about enough of this spelling-bee.

'Will you open the door and take this child in?'

'I mustn't open the door. This Miss Wooster that I knew married a man named Spenser. Was she any relation?'

'She is my Aunt Agatha,' I replied, and I spoke with a good deal of bitterness, trying to suggest by my manner that he was exactly the sort of man, in my opinion, who would know my Aunt Agatha.

He beamed down at me.

'This is most fortunate. We were wondering what to do with

Tootles. You see, we have mumps here. My daughter Bootles has just developed mumps. Tootles must not be exposed to the risk of infection. We could not think what to do with him. It was most fortunate, your finding the dear child. He strayed from his nurse. I would hesitate to trust him to a stranger, but you are different. Any nephew of Mrs Spenser's has my complete confidence. You must take Tootles into your house. It will be an ideal arrangement. I have written to my brother in London to come and fetch him. He may be here in a few days.'

'May!'

'He is a busy man, of course; but he should certainly be here within a week. Till then Tootles can stop with you. It is an excellent plan. Very much obliged to you. Your wife will like Tootles.'

'I haven't got a wife!' I yelled; but the window had closed with a bang, as if the man with the whiskers had found a germ trying to escape and had headed it off just in time.

I breathed a deep breath and wiped the old forehead.

The window flew up again.

'Hi!'

A package weighing about a ton hit me on the head and burst like a bomb.

'Did you catch it?' said the face, reappearing. 'Dear me, you missed it. Never mind. You can get it at the grocer's. Ask for Bailey's Granulated Breakfast Chips. Tootles takes them for breakfast with a little milk. Not cream. Milk. Be sure to get Bailey's.'

'Yes, but – '

The face disappeared, and the window was banged down again. I lingered a while, but nothing else happened, so, taking Tootles by the hand, I walked slowly away.

And as we turned up the road we met Freddie's Elizabeth.

'Well, baby?' she said, sighting the kid. 'So Daddy found you again, did he? Your little son and I made great friends on the beach this morning,' she said to me.

This was the limit. Coming on top of that interview with the whiskered lunatic, it so utterly unnerved me that she had nodded goodbye and was half-way down the road before I caught up with my breath enough to deny the charge of being the infant's father.

I hadn't expected Freddie to sing with joy when he saw me looming up with child complete, but I did think he might have showed a little more manly fortitude, a little more of the old British bulldog spirit. He leaped up when we came in, glared at the kid and clutched his head. He didn't speak for a long time; but, to make up for it, when he began he did not leave off for a long time.

'Well,' he said, when he had finished the body of his remarks, 'say something! Heavens, man, why don't you say something?'

'If you give me a chance, I will,' I said, and shot the bad news.

'What are you going to do about it?' he asked. And it would be idle to deny that his manner was peevish.

'What can we do about it?'

'We? What do you mean, we? I'm not going to spend my time taking turns as a nursemaid to this excrescence. I'm going back to London.'

'Freddie!' I cried. 'Freddie, old man!' My voice shook. 'Would you desert a pal at a time like this?'

'Yes, I would.'

'Freddie,' I said, 'you've got to stand by me. You must. Do you realize that this child has to be undressed, and bathed, and dressed again? You wouldn't leave me to do all that single-handed?'

'Jeeves can help you.'

'No, sir,' said Jeeves, who had just rolled in with lunch. 'I must, I fear, disassociate myself completely from the matter.' He spoke respectfully, but firmly. 'I have had little or no experience with children.'

'Now's the time to start,' I urged.

'No, sir; I am sorry to say that I cannot involve myself in any way.'

'Then you must stand by me, Freddie.'

'I won't.'

'You must. Reflect, old man! We have been pals for years. Your mother likes me.'

'No, she doesn't.'

'Well, anyway, we were at school together and you owe me a tenner.'

'Oh, well,' he said in a resigned sort of voice.

'Besides, old thing,' I said, 'I did it all for your sake, you know.'

He looked at me in a curious way, and breathed rather hard for some moments.

'Bertie,' he said, 'one moment. I will stand a good deal, but I will not stand being expected to be grateful.'

Looking back at it, I can see that what saved me from Colney Hatch in this crisis was my bright idea in buying up most of the contents of the local sweet-shop. By serving out sweets to the kid practically incessantly we managed to get through the rest of that day pretty satisfactorily. At eight o'clock he fell asleep in a chair; and, having undressed him by unbuttoning every button in sight and, where there were no buttons, pulling till something gave, we carried him up to bed.

Freddie stood looking at the pile of clothes on the floor with a sort of careworn wrinkle between his eyes, and I knew what he was thinking. To get the kid undressed had been simple – a mere matter of muscle. But how were we to get him into his clothes again? I stirred the heap with my foot. There was a long linen arrangement which might have been anything. Also a strip of pink flannel which was like nothing on earth. All most unpleasant.

But in the morning I remembered that there were children in the next bungalow but one, and I went there before breakfast and borrowed their nurse. Women are wonderful, by Jove they are! This nurse had all the spare parts assembled and in the right places in about eight minutes, and there was the kid dressed and looking fit to go to a garden party at Buckingham Palace. I showered wealth upon her, and she promised to come in morning and evening. I sat down to breakfast almost cheerful again. It was the first bit of silver lining that had presented itself to date.

'And, after all,' I said, 'there's lots to be argued in favour of having a child about the place, if you know what I mean. Kind of cosy and domestic, what?'

Just then the kid upset the milk over Freddie's trousers, and when he had come back after changing he lacked sparkle.

It was shortly after breakfast that Jeeves asked if he could have a word in my ear.

Now, though in the anguish of recent events I had rather tended to forget what had been the original idea in bringing Freddie down to this place, I hadn't forgotten it altogether; and I'm bound to say that, as the days went by, I had found myself a little disappointed in Jeeves. The scheme had been, if you recall, that he should refresh himself with sea-air and simple food and, having thus got his brain into prime working order, evolve some means of bringing Freddie and his Elizabeth together again.

And what had happened? The man had eaten well and he had slept well, but not a step did he appear to have taken towards bringing about the happy ending. The only move that had been made in that direction had been made by me, alone and unaided; and, though I freely admit that it had turned out a good deal of a bloomer, still the fact remains that I had shown zeal and enterprise. Consequently I received him with a bit of hauteur when he blew in. Slightly cold. A trifle frosty.

'Yes, Jeeves?' I said. 'You wished to speak to me?'

'Yes, sir.'

'Say on, Jeeves,' I said.

'Thank you, sir. What I desired to say, sir, was this: I attended a performance at the local cinema last night.'

I raised the eyebrows. I was surprised at the man. With life in the home so frightfully tense and the young master up against it to such a fearful extent, I disapproved of him coming toddling in and prattling about his amusements.

'I hope you enjoyed yourself,' I said in rather a nasty manner.

'Yes sir, thank you. The management was presenting a super-super-film in seven reels, dealing with life in the wilder and more feverish strata of New York Society, featuring Bertha Blevitch, Orlando Murphy and Baby Bobbie. I found it most entertaining, sir.'

'That's good,' I said. 'And if you have a nice time this morning on the sands with your spade and bucket, you will come and tell me all about it, won't you? I have so little on my mind just now that it's a treat to hear all about your happy holiday.'

Satirical, if you see what I mean. Sarcastic. Almost bitter, as a matter of fact, if you come right down to it.

'The title of the film was *Tiny Hands*, sir. And the father and mother of the character played by Baby Bobbie had unfortunately drifted apart – '

'Too bad,' I said.

'Although at heart they loved each other still, sir.'

'Did they really? I'm glad you told me that.'

'And so matters went on, sir, till came a day when – '

'Jeeves,' I said, fixing him with a dashed unpleasant eye, 'what the dickens do you think you're talking about? Do you suppose that, with this infernal child landed on me and the peace of the home practically shattered into a million bits, I want to hear – '

'I beg your pardon, sir. I would not have mentioned this cinema performance were it not for the fact that it gave me an idea, sir.'

'An idea!'

'An idea that will, I fancy, sir, prove of value in straightening out the matrimonial future of Mr Bullivant. To which end, if you recollect, sir, you desired me to – '

I snorted with remorse.

'Jeeves,' I said, 'I wronged you.'

'Not at all, sir.'

'Yes, I did. I wronged you. I had a notion that you had given yourself up entirely to the pleasures of the seaside and had chucked that businesss altogether. I might have known better. Tell me all, Jeeves.'

He bowed in a gratified manner. I beamed. And, while we didn't actually fall on each other's necks, we gave each other to understand that all was well once more.

'In this super-super-film *Tiny Hands*, sir,' said Jeeves, 'the parents of the child had, as I say, drifted apart.'

'Drifted apart,' I said, nodding. 'Right! And then?'

'Came a day, sir, when their little child brought them together again.'

'How?'

'If I remember rightly, sir, he said, "Dadda, doesn't 'oo love Mummie no more?"'

'And then?'

'They exhibited a good deal of emotion. There was what I believe is termed a cut-back, showing scenes from their courtship and early married life and some glimpses of Lovers Through the Ages, and the picture concluded with a close-up of the pair in an embrace, with the child looking on with natural gratification and an organ playing "Hearts and Flowers" in the distance.'

'Proceed, Jeeves,' I said. 'You interest me strangely. I begin to grasp the idea. You mean – ?'

'I mean, sir, that, with this young gentleman on the premises, it might be possible to arrange a *dénouement* of a somewhat similar nature in regard to Mr Bullivant and Miss Vickers.'

'Aren't you overlooking the fact that this kid is no relation of Mr Bullivant and Miss Vickers?'

'Even with that handicap, sir, I fancy that good results might ensue. I think that, if it were possible to bring Mr Bullivant and Miss Vickers together for a short space of time in the presence of the child, sir, and if the child were to say something of a touching nature – '

'I follow you absolutely, Jeeves,' I cried with enthusiasm. 'It's big. This is the way I see it. We lay the scene in this room. Child, centre. Girl, l.c. Freddie up stage, playing the piano. No, that won't do. He can only play a little of "The Rosary" with one finger, so we'll have to cut out the soft music. But the rest's all right. Look here,' I said, 'this inkpot is Miss Vickers. This mug with "A Present from Marvis Bay" on it is the child. This penwiper is Mr Bullivant. Start with dialogue leading up to child's line. Child speaks line, let us say, "Boofer lady, does 'oo love Dadda?" Business of outstretched hands. Hold picture for a moment. Freddie crosses l. takes girl's hand. Business of swallowing lump in throat. Then big speech: "Ah, Elizabeth, has not this misunderstanding of ours gone on too long? See! A little child rebukes us!" And so on. I'm just giving you the general outline. Freddie must work up his own part. And we must get a good line for the child. "Boofer lady, does 'oo love Dadda?" isn't definite enough. We want something more – '

'If I might make a suggestion, sir – ?'

'Yes?'

'I would advocate the words "Kiss Freddie?" It is short, readily memorized, and has what I believe is technically termed the punch.'

'Genius, Jeeves!'

'Thank you very much, sir.'

'"Kiss Freddie!" it is, then. But, I say, Jeeves, how the deuce are we to get them together in here? Miss Vickers cuts Mr Bullivant. She wouldn't come within a mile of him.'

'It is awkward, sir.'

'It doesn't matter. We shall have to make it an exterior set instead of an interior. We can easily corner her on the beach somewhere, when we're ready. Meanwhile, we must get the kid word-perfect.'

'Yes, sir.'

'Right! First rehearsal for lines and business at eleven sharp tomorrow morning.'

Poor old Freddie was in such a gloomy frame of mind that I decided not to tell him the idea till we had finished coaching the child. He wasn't in the mood to have a thing like that hanging over him. So we concentrated on Tootles. And pretty early in the proceedings we saw that the only way to get Tootles worked up to the spirit of the thing was to introduce sweets of some sort as a sub-motive, so to speak.

'The chief difficulty, sir,' said Jeeves, at the end of the first rehearsal, 'is, as I envisage it, to establish in the young gentleman's mind a connexion between the words we desire him to say and the refreshment.'

'Exactly,' I said. 'Once the blighter has grasped the basic fact that these two words, clearly spoken, result automatically in chocolate nougat, we have got a success.'

I've often thought how interesting it must be to be one of those animal-trainer blokes – to stimulate the dawning intelligence and all that. Well, this was every bit as exciting. Some days success seemed to be staring us in the eyeball, and the kid got out the line as if he had been an old professional. And then he would go all to pieces again. And time was flying.

'We must hurry up, Jeeves,' I said. 'The kid's uncle may arrive any day now and take him away.'

'Exactly, sir.'

'And we have no understudy.'

'Very true, sir.'

'We must work! I must say this child is a bit discouraging at times. I should have thought a deaf-mute would have learned his part by now.'

I will say this for the kid, though: he was a trier. Failure didn't damp him. Whenever there was any kind of sweet in sight he had a dash at his line, and kept saying something till he had got what he was after. His chief fault was his uncertainty. Personally, I would have been prepared to risk opening in the act and was ready to start the public performance at the first opportunity, but Jeeves said no.

'I would not advocate undue haste, sir,' he said. 'As long as the young gentleman's memory refuses to act with any certainty, we are running grave risks of failure. Today, if you recollect, sir, he said "Kick Freddie!" That is not a speech to win a young lady's heart, sir.'

'No. And she might do it, too. You're right. We must postpone production.'

But, by Jove, we didn't! The curtain went up the very next afternoon.

It was nobody's fault – certainly not mine. It was just fate. Jeeves was out, and I was alone in the house with Freddie and the child. Freddie had just settled down at the piano, and I was leading the kid out of the place for a bit of exercise, when, just as we'd got onto the veranda, along came the girl Elizabeth on her way to the beach. And at the sight of her the kid set up a matey yell, and she stopped at the foot of the steps.

'Hallo, baby,' she said. 'Good morning,' she said to me. 'May I come up?'

She didn't wait for an answer. She just hopped on to the veranda. She seemed to be that sort of girl. She started fussing over the child. And six feet away, mind you, Freddie smiting the piano in the sitting-room. It was a dashed disturbing situation, take it from Bertram. At any minute Freddie might take it into his head to come out on the veranda, and I hadn't even begun to rehearse him in his part.

I tried to break up the scene.

'We were just going down to the beach.' I said.

'Yes?' said the girl. She listened for a moment. 'So you're having your piano tuned?' she said. 'My aunt has been trying to find a tuner for ours. Do you mind if I go in and tell this man to come on to us when he has finished here?'

I mopped the brow.

'Er – I shouldn't go in just now.' I said. 'Not just now, while he's working, if you don't mind. These fellows can't bear to be disturbed when they're at work. It's the artistic temperament. I'll tell him later.'

'Very well. Ask him to call at Pine Bungalow. Vickers is the name . . . Oh, he seems to have stopped. I suppose he will be out in a minute now. I'll wait.'

'Don't you think – shouldn't you be getting on to the beach?' I said.

She had started talking to the kid and didn't hear. She was feeling in her bag for something.

'The beach,' I babbled.

'See what I've got for you, baby,' said the girl. 'I thought I might meet you somewhere, so I bought some of your favourite sweets.'

And, by Jove, she held up in front of the kid's bulging eyes, a chunk of toffee about the size of the Albert Memorial!

That finished it. We had just been having a long rehearsal, and the kid was all worked up in his part. He got it right first time.

'Kiss Fweddie!' he shouted.

And the french windows opened and Freddie came out on to the veranda, for all the world as if he had been taking a cue.

'Kiss Fweddie!' shrieked the child.

Freddie looked at the girl, and the girl looked at him. I looked at the ground, and the kid looked at the toffee.

'Kiss Fweddie!' he yelled. 'Kiss Fweddie!'

'What does this mean?' said the girl, turning on me.

'You'd better give it to him,' I said. 'He'll go on till you do, you know.'

She gave the kid the toffee and he subsided. Freddie, poor ass, still stood there gaping, without a word.

'What does it mean?' said the girl again. Her face was pink, and her eyes were sparkling in the sort of way, don't you know, that makes a fellow feel as if he hadn't any bones in him, if you know what I mean. Yes, Bertram felt filleted. Did you ever tread on your partner's dress at a dance – I'm speaking now of the days when women wore dresses long enough to be trodden on – and hear it rip and see her smile at you like an angel and say, '*Please* don't apologize. It's nothing,' and then suddenly meet her clear blue eyes and feel as if you had stepped on the teeth of a rake and had the handle jump up and hit you in the face? Well, that's how Freddie's Elizabeth looked.

'*Well?*' she said, and her teeth gave a little click.

I gulped. Then I said it was nothing. Then I said it was nothing much. Then I said, 'Oh, well, it was this way.' And told her all about it. And all the while Idiot Freddie stood there gaping, without a word. Not one solitary yip had he let out of himself from the start.

And the girl didn't speak, either. She just stood listening.

And then she began to laugh. I never heard a girl laugh so much. She leaned against the side of the veranda and shrieked. And all the while Freddie, the World's Champion Dumb Brick, standing there, saying nothing.

Well, I finished my story and sidled to the steps. I had said all I had to say, and it seemed to me that about here the stage-direction 'exit cautiously' was written in my part. I gave poor old Freddie up in despair. If only he had said a word it might have been all right. But there he stood speechless.

Just out of sight of the house I met Jeeves, returning from his stroll.

'Jeeves,' I said, 'all is over. The thing's finished. Poor dear old Freddie has made a complete ass of himself and killed the whole show.'

'Indeed, sir? What has actually happened?'

I told him.

'He fluffed his lines,' I concluded. 'Just stood there saying nothing, when if ever there was a time for eloquence, this was it. He . . . Great Scott! Look!'

We had come back within view of the cottage, and there in front of it stood six children, a nurse, two loafers, another nurse, and the fellow from the grocer's. They were all staring. Down the road came galloping five more children, a dog, three men and a boy, all about to stare. And on our porch, as unconscious of the spectators as if they had been alone in the Sahara, stood Freddie and his Elizabeth, clasped in each other's arms.

'Great Scott!' I said.

'It would appear, sir,' said Jeeves, 'that everything has concluded most satisfactorily, after all.'

'Yes. Dear old Freddie may have been fluffy in his lines,' I said, 'but his business certainly seems to have gone with a bang.'

'Very true, sir,' said Jeeves.

9

CLUSTERING ROUND YOUNG BINGO

I blotted the last page of my manuscript and sank back, feeling more or less of a spent force. After incredible sweat of the old brow the thing seemed to be in pretty fair shape, and I was just reading through and debating whether to bung in another paragraph at the end, when there was a tap at the door and Jeeves appeared.

'Mrs Travers, sir, on the telephone.'

'Oh?' I said. Preoccupied, don't you know.

'Yes, sir. She presents her compliments and would be glad to know what progress you have made with the article which you are writing for her.'

'Jeeves, can I mention men's knee-length underclothing in a woman's paper?'

'No, sir.'

'Then tell her it's finished.'

'Very good, sir.'

'And, Jeeves, when you're through, come back. I want you to cast your eye over this effort and give it the O.K.'

My Aunt Dahlia, who runs a woman's paper called *Milady's Boudoir*, had recently backed me into a corner and made me promise to write her a few authoritative words for her 'Husbands and Brothers' page on 'What the Well-Dressed Man is Wearing'. I believe in encouraging aunts, when deserving; and, as there are many worse eggs than her knocking about the metrop I had consented blithely. But I give you my honest word that if I had had the foggiest notion of what I was letting myself in for, not even a nephew's devotion would have kept me from giving her the raspberry. A deuce of a job it had been, taxing the physique to the utmost. I don't wonder now that all these author blokes have bald heads and faces like birds who have suffered.

'Jeeves,' I said, when he came back, 'you don't read a paper called *Milady's Boudoir* by any chance, do you?'

'No, sir. The periodical has not come to my notice.'

'Well, spring sixpence on it next week, because this article will appear in it. Wooster on the well-dressed man, don't you know.'

'Indeed, sir?'

'Yes, indeed, Jeeves. I've rather extended myself over this little bijou. There's a bit about socks that I think you will like.'

He took the manuscript, brooded over it, and smiled a gentle, approving smile.

'The sock passage is quite in the proper vein, sir,' he said.

'Well expressed, what?'

'Extremely, sir.'

I watched him narrowly as he read on, and, as I was expecting, what you might call the love-light suddenly died out of his eyes. I braced myself for an unpleasant scene.

'Come to the bit about soft silk shirts for evening wear?' I asked carelessly.

'Yes, sir,' said Jeeves, in a low, cold voice, as if he had been bitten in the leg by a personal friend. 'And if I may be pardoned for saying so – '

'You don't like it?'

'No, sir. I do not. Soft silk shirts with evening costume are not worn, sir.'

'Jeeves,' I said, looking the blighter diametrically in the centre of the eyeball, 'they're dashed well going to be. I may as well tell you now that I have ordered a dozen of those shirtings from Peabody and Simms, and it's no good looking like that, because I am jolly well adamant.'

'If I might – '

'No, Jeeves,' I said, raising my hand, 'argument is useless. Nobody has a greater respect than I have for your judgement in socks, ties, and – I will go farther – in spats; but when it comes to evening shirts you nerve seems to fail you. You have no vision. You are prejudiced and reactionary. Hidebound is the word that suggests itself. It may interest you to learn that when I was at Le Touquet the Prince of Wales buzzed into the Casino one night with soft silk shirt complete.'

'His Royal Highness, sir, may permit himself a certain licence which in your own case – '

'No, Jeeves,' I said firmly, 'it's no use. When we Woosters are adamant, we are – well, adamant, if you know what I mean.'

'Very good, sir.'

I could see the man was wounded, and, of course, the whole episode had been extremely jarring and unpleasant; but these things have to be gone through. Is one a serf or isn't one? That's what it all boils down to. Having made my point, I changed the subject.

'Well, that's that,' I said. 'We now approach another topic. Do you know any housemaids, Jeeves?'

'Housemaids, sir?'

'Come, come, Jeeves, you know what housemaids are.'

'Are you requiring a housemaid, sir?'

'No, but Mr Little is. I met him at the club a couple of days ago, and he told me that Mrs Little is offering rich rewards to anybody who will find her one guaranteed to go light on the china.'

'Indeed, sir?'

'Yes. The one now in office apparently runs through the *objets d'art* like a typhoon, simoom, or sirocco. So if you know any – '

'I know a great many, sir. Some intimately, others mere acquaintances.'

'Well, start digging round among the old pals. And now the hat, the stick, and other necessaries. I must be getting along and handing in this article.'

The offices of *Milady's Boudoir* were in one of those rummy streets in the Covent Garden neighbourhood; and I had just got to the door, after wading through a deep top-dressing of old cabbages and tomatoes, when who should come out but Mrs Little. She greeted me with the warmth due to the old family friend, in spite of the fact that I hadn't been round to the house for a goodish while.

'Whatever are you doing in these parts, Bertie? I thought you never came east of Leicester Square.'

'I've come to deliver an article of sorts which my Aunt Dahlia asked me to write. She edits a species of journal up those stairs. *Milady's Boudoir.*'

'What a coincidence! I have just promised to write an article for her, too.'

'Don't you do it,' I said earnestly. 'You've simply no notion what a ghastly labour – Oh, but, of course, I was forgetting. You're used to it, what?'

Silly of me to have talked like that. Young Bingo Little, if you remember, had married the famous female novelist, Rosie M. Banks, author of some of the most pronounced and widely-read tripe ever put on the market. Naturally a mere article would be pie for her.

'No, I don't think it will give me much trouble,' she said. 'Your aunt has suggested a most delightful subject.'

'That's good. By the way, I spoke to my man Jeeves about getting you a housemaid. He knows all the hummers.'

'Thank you so much. Oh, are you doing anything tomorrow night?'

'Not a thing.'

'Then do come and dine with us. Your aunt is coming, and hopes to bring your uncle. I am looking forward to meeting him.'

'Thanks. Delighted.'

I meant it, too. The Little household may be weak on housemaids, but it is right there when it comes to cooks. Somewhere or other some time ago Bingo's missus managed to dig up a Frenchman of the most extraordinary vim and skill. A most amazing Johnnie who dishes a wicked *ragout*. Old Bingo has put on at least ten pounds in weight since this fellow Anatole arrived in the home.

'At eight, then.'

'Right. Thanks ever so much.'

She popped off, and I went upstairs to hand in my copy, as we boys of the Press call it. I found Aunt Dahlia immersed to the gills in papers of all descriptions.

I am not much of a lad for my relatives as a general thing, but I've always been very pally with Aunt Dahlia. She married my Uncle Thomas – between ourselves a bit of a squirt – the year Bluebottle won the Cambridgeshire; and they hadn't got halfway down the aisle before I was saying to myself, 'That woman is much too good for the old bird.' Aunt Dahlia is a large, genial soul, the sort you see in dozens on the hunting field. As a matter of fact, until she married Uncle Thomas, she put in most of her time on horseback; but he won't live in the country, so nowadays she expends her energy on this paper of hers.

She came to the surface as I entered, and flung a cheery look at my head.

'Hullo, Bertie! I say, have you really finished that article?'

'To the last comma.'

'Good boy! My gosh, I'll bet it's rotten.'

'On the contrary, it is extremely hot stuff, and most of it approved by Jeeves, what's more. The bit about soft silk shirts got in amongst him a trifle; but you can take it from me, Aunt Dahlia, that they are the latest yodel and will be much seen at first nights and other occasions where Society assembles.'

'Your man Jeeves,' said Aunt Dahlia, flinging the article into a basket and skewering a few loose pieces of paper on a sort of meat hook, 'is a washout, and you can tell him I said so.'

'Oh, come,' I said. 'He may not be sound on shirtings –'

'I'm not referring to that. As long as a week ago I asked him to get me a cook, and he hasn't found one yet.'

'Great Scott! Is Jeeves a domestic employment agency? Mrs Little wants him to find her a housemaid. I met her outside. She tells me she's doing something for you.'

'Yes, thank goodness. I'm relying on it to bump the circulation up a bit. I can't read her stuff myself, but women love it. Her name on the cover will mean a lot. And we need it.'

'Paper not doing well?'

'It's doing all right really, but it's got to be a slow job building up a circulation.'

'I suppose so.'

'I can get Tom to see that in his lucid moments,' said Aunt Dahlia, skewering a few more papers. 'But just at present the poor fathead has got one of his pessimistic spells. It's entirely due to that mechanic who calls herself a cook. A few more of her alleged dinners, and Tom will refuse to go on paying the printer's bills.'

'You don't mean that!'

'I do mean it. There was what she called a *ris de veau à la financière* last night which made him talk for three-quarters of an hour about good money going to waste and nothing to show for it.'

I quite understood, and I was dashed sorry for her. My Uncle Thomas is a cove who made a colossal pile of money out in the East, but in doing so put his digestion on the blink. This has made him a tricky proposition to handle. Many a time I've lunched with him and found him perfectly chirpy up to the fish, only to have him turn blue on me well before the cheese.

Who was that lad they used to try to make me read at Oxford? Ship – Shop – Schopenhauer. That's the name. A grouch of the most pronounced description. Well, Uncle Thomas, when his gastric juices have been giving him the elbow, can make Schopenhauer look like Pollyanna. And the worst of it is, from Aunt Dahlia's point of view, that on these occasions he always seems to think he's on the brink of ruin and wants to start to economize.

'Pretty tough,' I said. 'Well, anyway, he'll get one good dinner tomorrow night at the Littles'.'

'Can you guarantee that, Bertie?' asked Aunt Dahlia earnestly. 'I simply daren't risk unleashing him on anything at all wonky.'

'They've got a marvellous cook. I haven't been round there for some time, but unless he's lost his form of two months ago Uncle Thomas is going to have the treat of a lifetime.'

'It'll only make it all the worse for him, coming back to our steak-incinerator,' said Aunt Dahlia, a bit on the Schopenhauer side herself.

*

The little nest where Bingo and his bride had settled themselves was up in St John's Wood; one of those rather jolly houses with a bit of garden. When I got there on the following night, I found that I was the last to weigh in. Aunt Dahlia was chatting with Rosie in a corner, while Uncle Thomas, standing by the mantelpiece with Bingo, sucked down a cocktail in a frowning, suspicious sort of manner, rather like a chappie having a short snort before dining with the Borgias: as if he were saying to himself that, even if this particular cocktail wasn't poisoned, he was bound to cop it later on.

Well, I hadn't expected anything in the nature of beaming *joie de vivre* from Uncle Thomas, so I didn't pay much attention to him. What did surprise me was the extraordinary gloom of young Bingo. You may say what you like against Bingo, but nobody has ever found him a depressing host. Why, many a time in the days of his bachelorhood I've known him to start throwing bread before the soup course. Yet now he and Uncle Thomas were a pair. He looked haggard and careworn, like a Borgia who has suddenly remembered that he has forgotten to shove cyanide in the *consommé*, and the dinner gong due any moment.

And the mystery wasn't helped at all by the one remark he made to me before conversation became general. As he poured out my cocktail, he suddenly bent forward.

'Bertie,' he whispered, in a nasty, feverish manner. 'I want to see you. Life and death matter. Be in tomorrow morning.'

That was all. Immediately after that the starting-gun went and we toddled down to the festive. And from that moment, I'm bound to say, in the superior interests of the proceedings he rather faded out of my mind. For good old Anatole, braced presumably by the fact of there being guests, had absolutely surpassed himself.

I am not a man who speaks hastily on these matters. I weigh my words. And I say again that Anatole had surpassed himself. It was as good a dinner as I have ever absorbed, and it revived Uncle Thomas like a watered flower. As we sat down he was saying some things about the Government which they wouldn't have cared to hear. With the *consommé pâté d'Italie* he said but what could you expect nowadays? With the *paupiettes de sole à la princesse* he admitted rather decently that the Government couldn't be held responsible for the rotten weather, anyway. And shortly after the *caneton Aylesbury à la broche* he was practically giving the lads the benefit of his whole-hearted support.

And all the time young Bingo looking like an owl with a secret sorrow. Rummy!

I thought about it a good deal as I walked home, and I was hoping he wouldn't roll round with his hard-luck story too early in the morning. He had the air of one who intends to charge in at about six-thirty.

Jeeves was waiting up for me when I got back.

'A pleasant dinner, sir?' he said.

'Magnificent, Jeeves.'

'I am glad to hear that, sir. Mr George Travers rang up on the telephone shortly after you had left. He was extremely desirous that you should join him at Harrogate, sir. He leaves for that town by an early train tomorrow.'

My Uncle George is a festive old bird who has made a habit for years of doing himself a dashed sight too well, with the result that he's always got Harrogate or Buxton hanging over him like the sword of what's-his-name. And he hates going there alone.

'It can't be done,' I said. Uncle George is bad enough in London, and I wasn't going to let myself be cooped up with him in one of these cure-places.

'He was extremely urgent, sir.'

'No, Jeeves,' I said firmly. 'I am always anxious to oblige, but Uncle George – no, no! I mean to say, what?'

'Very good, sir,' said Jeeves.

It was a pleasure to hear the way he said it. Docile the man was becoming, absolutely docile. It just showed that I had been right in putting my foot down about those shirts.

When Bingo showed up next morning I had had breakfast and was all ready for him. Jeeves shot him into the presence, and he sat down on the bed.

'Good morning, Bertie,' said young Bingo.

'Good morning, old thing,' I replied courteously.

'Don't go, Jeeves,' said young Bingo hollowly. 'Wait.'

'Sir?'

'Remain. Stay. Cluster round. I shall need you.'

'Very good, sir.'

Bingo lit a cigarette and frowned bleakly at the wallpaper.

'Bertie,' he said, 'the most frightful calamity has occurred. Unless something is done, and done right speedily, my social prestige is doomed, my self-respect will be obliterated, my name will be mud, and I shall not dare to show my face in the West End of London again.'

'My aunt!' I cried, deeply impressed.

'Exactly,' said young Bingo, with a hollow laugh. 'You have put it in a nutshell. The whole trouble is due to your blasted aunt.'

'Which blasted aunt? Specify, old thing. I have so many.'

'Mrs Travers. The one who runs that infernal paper.'

'Oh, no, dash it, old man,' I protested. 'She's the only decent aunt I've got. Jeeves, you will bear me out in this?'

'Such has always been my impression, I must confess, sir.'

'Well, get rid of it, then,' said young Bingo. 'The woman is a menace to society, a home-wrecker, and a pest. Do you know what she's done? She's got Rosie to write an article for that rag of hers.'

'I know that.'

'Yes, but you don't know what it's about.'

'No. She told me Aunt Dahlia had given her a splendid idea for the thing.'

'It's about me!'

'You?'

'Yes, me! And do you know what it's called? It is called "How I Keep the Love of My Husband-Baby".'

'My what?'

'Husband-baby!'

'What's a husband-baby?'

'I am, apparently,' said young Bingo, with much bitterness. 'I am also, according to this article, a lot of other things which I have too much sense of decency to repeat even to an old friend. This beastly composition, in short, is one of those things they call "human interest stories"; one of those intimate revelations of married life over which the female public loves to gloat; all about Rosie and me and what she does when I come home cross, and so on. I tell you, Bertie, I am still blushing all over at the recollection of something she says in paragraph two.'

'What?'

'I decline to tell you. But you can take it from me that it's the edge. Nobody could be fonder of Rosie than I am, but – dear, sensible girl as she is in ordinary life – the moment she gets in front of a dictating machine she becomes absolutely maudlin. Bertie, that article must not appear!'

'But – '

'If it does I shall have to resign from my clubs, grow a beard, and become a hermit. I shall not be able to face the world.'

'Aren't you pitching it a bit strong, old lad?' I said. 'Jeeves, don't you think he's pitching it a bit strong?'

'Well, sir – '

'I am pitching it feebly,' said young Bingo earnestly. 'You haven't heard the thing. I have. Rosie shoved the cylinder on the dictating machine last night before dinner, and it was grisly to hear the instrument croaking out those awful sentences. If that article appears I shall be kidded to death by every pal I've got. Bertie,' he said, his voice sinking to a hoarse whisper, 'you have about as much imagination as a warthog, but surely even you can picture to yourself what Jimmy Bowles and Tuppy Rogers, to name only two, will say when they see me referred to in print as "half god, half prattling, mischievous child"?'

I jolly well could.

'She doesn't say that?' I gasped.

'She certainly does. And when I tell you that I selected that particular quotation because it's about the only one I can stand hearing spoken, you will realize what I'm up against.'

I picked at the coverlet. I had been a pal of Bingo's for many years, and we Woosters stand by our pals.

'Jeeves,' I said, 'you have heard?'

'Yes, sir.'

'The position is serious.'

'Yes, sir.'

'We must cluster round.'

'Yes, sir.'

'Does anything suggest itself to you?'

'Yes, sir.'

'What! You don't really mean that?'

'Yes, sir.'

'Bingo,' I said, 'the sun is still shining. Something suggests itself to Jeeves.'

'Jeeves,' said young Bingo, in a quivering voice, 'if you see me through this fearful crisis, ask of me what you will even unto half my kingdom.'

'The matter,' said Jeeves, 'fits in very nicely, sir, with another mission which was entrusted to me this morning.'

'What do you mean?'

'Mrs Travers rang me up on the telephone shortly before I brought you your tea, sir, and was most urgent that I should endeavour to persuade Mr Little's cook to leave Mr Little's service and join her staff. It appears that Mr Travers was fascinated by the man's ability, sir, and talked far into the night of his astonishing gifts.'

Young Bingo uttered a frightful cry of agony.

'What! Is that – that buzzard trying to pinch our cook?'

'Yes, sir.'

'After eating our bread and salt, dammit?'

'I fear, sir,' sighed Jeeves, 'that when it comes to a matter of cooks, ladies have but a rudimentary sense of morality.'

'Half a second, Bingo,' I said, as the fellow seemed about to plunge into something of an oration. 'How does this fit in with the other thing, Jeeves?'

'Well, sir, it has been my experience that no lady can ever forgive another lady for taking a really good cook away from her. I am convinced that, if I am able to accomplish the mission which Mrs Travers entrusted to me, an instant breach of cordial relations must inevitably ensue. Mrs Little will, I feel certain, be so aggrieved with Mrs Travers that she will decline to contribute to her paper. We shall therefore not only bring happiness to Mr Travers, but also suppress the article. Thus killing two birds with one stone, if I may use the expression, sir.'

'Certainly you may use the expression, Jeeves,' I said cordially. 'And I may add that in my opinion this is one of your best and ripest.'

'Yes, but I say, you know,' bleated young Bingo. 'I mean to say – old Anatole, I mean – what I'm driving at is that he's a cook in a million.'

'You poor chump, if he wasn't there would be no point in the scheme.'

'Yes, but what I mean – I shall miss him, you know. Miss him fearfully.'

'Good heavens!' I cried. 'Don't tell me that you are thinking of your tummy in a crisis like this?'

Bingo sighed heavily.

'Oh, all right,' he said. 'I suppose it's a case of the surgeon's knife. All right, Jeeves, you may carry on. Yes, carry on, Jeeves. Yes, yes, Jeeves, carry on. I'll look in tomorrow morning and hear what you have to report.'

And with bowed head young Bingo biffed off.

He was bright and early next morning. In fact, he turned up at such an indecent hour that Jeeves very properly refused to allow him to break in on my slumbers.

By the time I was awake and receiving, he and Jeeves had had a heart-to-heart chat in the kitchen; and when Bingo eventually crept into my room I could see by the look on his face that something had gone wrong.

'It's all off,' he said, slumping down on the bed.

'Off?'

'Yes; that cook-pinching business. Jeeves tells me he saw Anatole last night, and Anatole refused to leave.'

'But surely Aunt Dahlia had the sense to offer him more than he was getting with you?'

'The sky was the limit, as far as she was concerned. Nevertheless, he refused to skid. It seems he's in love with our parlourmaid.'

'But you haven't got a parlourmaid.'

'We have got a parlourmaid.'

'I've never seen her. A sort of bloke who looked like a provincial undertaker waited at the table the night before last.'

'That was the local greengrocer, who comes to help out when desired. The parlourmaid is away on her holiday – or was till last night. She returned about ten minutes before Jeeves made his call, and Anatole, I take it, was in such a state of elation and devotion and what not on seeing her again that the contents of the Mint wouldn't have bribed him to part from her.'

'But look here, Bingo,' I said, 'this is all rot. I see the solution right off. I'm surprised that a bloke of Jeeves's mentality overlooked it. Aunt Dahlia must engage the parlourmaid as well as Anatole. Then they won't be parted.'

'I thought of that, too. Naturally.'

'I bet you didn't.'

'I certainly did.'

'Well, what's wrong with the scheme?'

'It can't be worked. If your aunt engaged our parlourmaid she would have to sack her own, wouldn't she?'

'Well?'

'Well, if she sacks her parlourmaid, it will mean that the chauffeur will quit. He's in love with her.'

'With my aunt?'

'No, with the parlourmaid. And apparently he's the only chauffeur your uncle has ever found who drives carefully enough for him.'

I gave it up. I had never imagined before that life below stairs was so frightfully mixed up with what these coves call the sex complex. The personnel of domestic staffs seemed to pair off like characters in a musical comedy.

'Oh!' I said. 'Well, that being so, we do seem to be more or less stymied. That article will have to appear after all, what?'

'No, it won't.'

'Has Jeeves thought of another scheme?'

'No, but I have,' Bingo bent forward and patted my knee affection-ately. 'Look here, Bertie,' he said, 'you and I were at school together. You'll admit that?'

'Yes, but – '

'And you're a fellow who never lets a pal down. That's well known, isn't it?'

'Yes, but listen – '

'You'll cluster round. Of course you will. As if,' said Bingo with a scornful laugh, 'I ever doubted it! You won't let an old school-friend down in his hour of need. Not you. Not Bertie Wooster. No, no!'

'Yes, but just one moment. What is this scheme of yours?'

Bingo massaged my shoulder soothingly.

'It's something right in your line, Bertie, old man; something that'll come as easy as pie to you. As a matter of fact, you've done very much the same thing before – that time you were telling me about when you pinched your uncle's Memoirs at Easeby. I suddenly remembered that, and it gave me the idea. It's – '

'Here! Listen!'

'It's all settled, Bertie. Nothing for you to worry about. Nothing whatever. I see now that we made a big mistake in ever trying to tackle this job in Jeeves's silly, roundabout way. Much better to charge straight ahead without any of that finesse and fooling about. And so – '

'Yes, but listen – '

'And so this afternoon I'm going to take Rosie to a matinée. I shall leave the window of her study open, and when we have got well away you will climb in, pinch the cylinder and pop off again. It's absurdly simple – '

'Yes, but half a second – '

'I know what you are going to say,' said Bingo, raising his hand. 'How are you to find the cylinder? That's what is bothering you, isn't it? Well, it will be quite easy. Not a chance of a mistake. The thing is in the top left-hand drawer of the desk, and the drawer will be left unlocked because Rosie's stenographer is to come round at four o'clock and type the article.'

'Now listen, Bingo,' I said. 'I'm frightfully sorry for you and all that, but I must firmly draw the line at burglary.'

'But, dash it, I'm only asking you to do what you did at Easeby.'

'No, you aren't. I was staying at Easeby. It was simply a case of having to lift a parcel off the hall table. I hadn't got to break into a house. I'm sorry, but I simply will not break into your beastly house on any consideration whatever.'

He gazed at me, astonished and hurt.

'Is this Bertie Wooster speaking?' he said in a low voice.

'Yes, it is!'

'But, Bertie,' he said gently, 'we agreed that you were at school with me.'

'I don't care.'

'At school, Bertie. The dear old school.'

'I don't care. I will not –'

'Bertie!'

'I will not –'

'Bertie!'

'No!'

'Bertie!'

'Oh, all right,' I said.

'There,' said young Bingo, patting me on the shoulder, 'spoke the true Bertram Wooster!'

I don't know if it has ever occurred to you, but to the thoughtful cove there is something dashed reassuring in all the reports of burglaries you read in the papers. I mean, if you're keen on Great Britain maintaining her prestige and all that. I mean, there can't be much wrong with the morale of a country whose sons go in to such a large extent for housebreaking, because you can take it from me that the job requires a nerve of the most cast-iron description. I suppose I was walking up and down in front of that house for half an hour before I could bring myself to dash in at the front gate and slide round to the side where the study window was. And even then I stood for about ten minutes cowering against the wall and listening for police-whistles.

Eventually, however, I braced myself up and got to business. The study was on the ground floor and the window was nice and large, and, what is more, wide open. I got the old knee over the sill, gave a jerk which took an inch of skin off my ankle, and hopped down into the room. And there I was, if you follow me.

I stood for a moment, listening. Everything seemed to be all right. I was apparently alone in the world.

In fact, I was so much alone that the atmosphere seemed positively creepy. You know how it is on these occasions. There was a clock on the mantelpiece that ticked in a slow, shocked sort of way that was dashed unpleasant. And over the clock a large portrait stared at me with a good deal of dislike and suspicion. It was a portrait of somebody's grandfather. Whether he was Rosie's or Bingo's I didn't know, but he was certainly a grandfather. In fact, I wouldn't be prepared to swear that he wasn't a great-grandfather. He was a big, stout old buffer in a high collar that seemed to hurt his neck, for he had drawn his chin back a goodish way and was looking down his nose as much as to say, '*You* made me put this dam' thing on!'

Well, it was only a step to the desk, and nothing between me and it but a brown shaggy rug; so I avoided grandfather's eye and, summoning up the good old bulldog courage of the Woosters, moved forward and started to navigate the rug. And I had hardly taken a step when the south-east corner of it suddenly detached itself from the rest and sat up with a snuffle.

Well, I mean to say, to bear yourself fittingly in the face of an occurrence of this sort you want to be one of those strong, silent, phlegmatic birds who are ready for anything. This type of bloke, I imagine, would simply have cocked an eye at the rug, said to himself, 'Ah, a Pekingese dog, and quite a good one, too!' and started at once to make cordial overtures to the animal in order to win its sympathy and moral support. I suppose I must be one of the neurotic younger generation you read about in the papers nowadays, because it was pretty plain within half a second that I wasn't strong and I wasn't phlegmatic. This wouldn't have mattered so much, but I wasn't silent either. In the emotion of the moment I let out a sort of sharp yowl and leaped about four feet in a north-westerly direction. And there was a crash that sounded as though somebody had touched off a bomb.

What a female novelist wants with an occasional table in her study containing a vase, two framed photographs, a saucer, a lacquer box, and a jar of pot-pourri, I don't know; but that was what Bingo's Rosie had, and I caught it squarely with my right hip and knocked it endways. It seemed to me for a moment as if the whole world had dissolved into a kind of cataract of glass and china. A few years ago, when l legged it to America to elude my Aunt Agatha, who was out with her hatchet, I remember going to Niagara and listening to the Falls. They made much the same sort of row, but not so loud.

And at the same instant the dog began to bark.

It was a small dog – the sort of animal from which you would have expected a noise like a squeaking, slate-pencil; but it was simply baying. It had retired into a corner, and was leaning against the wall with bulging eyes; and every two seconds it chucked its head back in a kind of pained way and let out another terrific bellow.

Well, I know when I'm licked. I was sorry for Bingo and regretted the necessity of having to let him down; but the time had come, I felt, to shift. 'Outside for Bertram!' was the slogan, and I took a running leap at the window and scrambled through.

And there on the path, as if they had been waiting for me by appointment, stood a policeman and a parlourmaid.

It was an embarrassing moment.

'Oh – er – there you are!' I said. And there was what you might call a contemplative silence for a moment.

'I told you I heard something,' said the parlourmaid.

The policeman was regarding me in a boiled way.

'What's all this?' he asked.

I smiled in a sort of saint-like manner.

'It's a little hard to explain,' I said.

'Yes, it is!' said the policeman.

'I was just – er – having a look round, you know. Old friend of the family, you understand.'

'How did you get in?'

'Through the window. Being an old friend of the family, if you follow me.'

'Old friend of the family, are you?'

'Oh, very. Very. Very old. Oh, a very old friend of the family.'

'I've never seen him before,' said the parlourmaid.

I looked at the girl with positive loathing. How she could have inspired affection in anyone, even a French cook, beat me. Not that she was a bad-looking girl, mind you. Not at all. On another and happier occasion I might even have thought her rather pretty. But now she seemed one of the most unpleasant females I had ever encountered.

'No,' I said. 'You have never seen me before. But I'm an old friend of the family.'

'Then why didn't you ring at the front door?'

'I didn't want to give any trouble.'

'It's no trouble answering front doors, that being what you're paid for,' said the parlourmaid virtuously. 'I've never seen him before in my life,' she added, perfectly gratuitously. A horrid girl.

'Well, look here,' I said, with an inspiration, 'the undertaker knows me.'

'What undertaker?'

'The cove who was waiting at table when I dined here the night before last.'

'Did the undertaker wait at table on the sixteenth instant?' asked the policeman.

'Of course he didn't,' said the parlourmaid.

'Well, he looked like – By Jove, no. I remember now. He was the greengrocer.'

'On the sixteenth instant,' said the policeman – pompous ass! – 'did the greengrocer – ?'

'Yes, he did, if you want to know,' said the parlourmaid. She seemed disappointed and baffled, like a tigress that sees its prey being sneaked away from it. Then she brightened. 'But this fellow could easily have found that out by asking round about.'

A perfectly poisonous girl.

'What's your name?' asked the policeman.

'Well, I say, do you mind awfully if I don't give my name, because – '

'Suit yourself. You'll have to tell it to the magistrate.'

'Oh, no, I say, dash it!'

'I think you'd better come along.'

'But I say, really, you know, I am an old friend of the family. Why, by Jove, now I remember, there's a photograph of me in the drawing-room. Well, I mean, that shows you!'

'If there is,' said the policeman.

'I've never seen it,' said the parlourmaid.

I absolutely hated this girl.

'You would have seen it if you had done your dusting more conscientiously,' I said severely. And I meant it to sting, by Jove!

'It is not a parlourmaid's place to dust the drawing-room,' she sniffed haughtily.

'No,' I said bitterly. 'It seems to be a parlourmaid's place to lurk about and hang about and – er – waste her time fooling about in the garden with policemen who ought to be busy about their duties elsewhere.'

'It's a parlourmaid's place to open the front door to visitors. Them that don't come in through windows.'

I perceived that I was getting the loser's end of the thing. I tried to be conciliatory.

'My dear old parlourmaid,' I said, 'don't let us descend to vulgar wrangling. All I'm driving at is that there is a photograph of me in the drawing-room, cared for and dusted by whom I know not; and this photograph will, I think, prove to you that I am an old friend of the family. I fancy so, officer?'

'If it's there,' said the man in a grudging way.

'Oh, it's there all right. Oh, yes, it's there.'

'Well, we'll go to the drawing-room and see.'

'Spoken like a man, my dear old policeman,' I said.

The drawing-room was on the first floor, and the photograph was on the table by the fireplace. Only, if you understand me, it wasn't. What I mean is there was the fireplace, and there was the table by the fireplace, but, by Jove, not a sign of any photograph of me whatsoever.

A photograph of Bingo, yes. A photograph of Bingo's uncle, Lord Bittlesham, right. A photograph of Mrs Bingo, three-quarter face, with a tender smile on her lips, all present and correct. But of anything resembling Bertram Wooster, not a trace.

'Ho!' said the policeman.

'But, dash it, it was there the night before last.'

'Ho!' he said again. 'Ho! Ho!' As if he were starting a drinking-chorus in a comic opera, confound him.

Then I got what amounted to the brainwave of a lifetime.

'Who dusts these things?' I said, turning on the parlourmaid.

'I don't.'

'I didn't say you did. I said who did.'

'Mary. The housemaid, of course.'

'Exactly. As I suspected. As I foresaw. Mary, officer, is notoriously the worst smasher in London. There have been complaints about her on all sides. You see what has happened? The wretched girl has broken the glass of my photograph and, not being willing to come forward and admit it in an honest, manly way, has taken the thing off and concealed it somewhere.'

'Ho!' said the policeman, still working through the drinking-chorus.

'Well, ask her. Go down and ask her.'

'You go down and ask her,' said the policeman to the parlourmaid. 'If it's going to make him any happier.'

The parlourmaid left the room, casting a pestilential glance at me over her shoulder as she went. I'm not sure she didn't say 'Ho!' too. And then there was a bit of a lull. The policeman took up a position with a large beefy back against the door, and I wandered to and fro and hither and yonder.

'What are you playing at?' demanded the policeman.

'Just looking round. They may have moved the thing.'

'Ho!'

And then there was another bit of a lull. And suddenly I found myself by the window, and, by Jove, it was six inches open at the bottom. And the world beyond looked so bright and sunny and – Well, I don't claim that I am a particularly swift thinker, but once more something seemed to whisper 'Outside for Bertram!' I slid my fingers nonchalantly under the sash, gave a hefty heave, and up she came. And the next moment I was in a laurel bush, feeling like the cross which marks the spot where the accident occurred.

A large red face appeared in the window. I got up and skipped lightly to the gate.

'Hi!' shouted the policeman.

'Ho!' I replied, and went forth, moving well.

'This,' I said to myself, as I hailed a passing cab and sank back on the cushions, 'is the last time I try to do anything for young Bingo!'

These sentiments I expressed in no guarded language to Jeeves when I was back in the old flat with my feet on the mantelpiece, pushing down a soothing whisky-and.

'Never again, Jeeves!' I said. 'Never again!'

'Well, sir – '

'No, never again!'

'Well, sir – '

'What do you mean, "Well, sir"? What are you driving at?'

'Well, sir, Mr Little is an extremely persistent young gentleman, and yours, if I may say so, sir, is a yielding and obliging nature – '

'You don't think that young Bingo would have the immortal rind to try to get me into some other foul enterprise?'

'I should say that it was more than probable, sir.'

I removed the dogs swiftly from the mantelpiece, and jumped up, all of a twitter.

'Jeeves, what would you advise?'

'Well, sir, I think a little change of scene would be judicious.'

'Do a bolt?'

'Precisely, sir. If I might suggest it, sir, why not change your mind and join Mr George Travers at Harrogate?'

'Oh, I say, Jeeves!'

'You would be out of what I might describe as the danger zone there, sir.'

'Perhaps you're right, Jeeves,' I said thoughtfully. 'Yes, possibly you're right. How far is Harrogate from London?'

'Two hundred and six miles, sir.'

'Yes, I think you're right. Is there a train this afternoon?'

'Yes, sir. You could catch it quite easily.'

'All right, then. Bung a few necessaries in a bag.'

'I have already done so, sir.'

'Ho!' I said.

It's a rummy thing, but when you come down to it Jeeves is always right. He had tried to cheer me up at the station by saying that I would not find Harrogate unpleasant, and, by Jove, he was perfectly correct. What I had overlooked, when examining the project, was the fact that I should be in the middle of a bevy of blokes who were taking the cure and I shouldn't be taking it myself. You've no notion what a dashed cosy, satisfying feeling that gives a fellow.

I mean to say, there was old Uncle George, for instance. The medicine-man, having given him the once-over, had ordered him to abstain from all alcoholic liquids, and in addition to tool down the hill to the Royal Pump-Room each morning at eight-thirty and imbibe twelve ounces of warm crescent saline and magnesia. It doesn't sound much, put that way, but I gather from contemporary accounts that it's practically equivalent to getting outside a couple of little old last year's eggs beaten up in sea-water. And the thought of Uncle George, who had oppressed me sorely in my childhood, sucking down that stuff and having to hop out of bed at eight-fifteen to do so was extremely grateful and comforting of a morning.

At four in the afternoon he would toddle down the hill again and repeat the process, and at night we would dine together and I would loll back in my chair, sipping my wine, and listen to him telling me what the stuff had tasted like. In many ways the ideal existence.

I generally managed to fit it in with my engagements to go down and watch him tackle his afternoon dose, for we Woosters are as fond of a laugh as anyone. And it was while I was enjoying the performance in the middle of the second week that I heard my name spoken. And there was Aunt Dahlia.

'Hallo!' I said. 'What are you doing here?'

'I came down yesterday with Tom.'

'Is Tom taking the cure?' asked Uncle George, looking up hopefully from the hell-brew.

'Yes.'

'Are you taking the cure?'

'Yes.'

'Ah!' said Uncle George, looking happier than I had seen him for days. He swallowed the last drops, and then, the programme calling for a brisk walk before his massage, left us.

'I shouldn't have thought you would have been able to get away from the paper,' I said. 'I say,' I went on, struck by a pleasing idea. 'It hasn't bust up, has it?'

'Bust up? I should say not. A pal of mine is looking after it for me while I'm here. It's right on its feet now. Tom has given me a couple of thousand and says there's more if I want it, and I've been able to buy serial rights of Lady Bablockhythe's *Frank Recollections of a Long Life*. The hottest stuff, Bertie. Certain to double the circulation and send half the best-known people in London into hysterics for a year.'

'Oh!' I said. 'Then you're pretty well fixed, what? I mean, what with the Frank Recollections and that article of Mrs Little's.'

Aunt Dahlia was drinking something that smelled like a leak in the gas-pipe, and I thought for a moment that it was that that made her twist up her face. But I was wrong.

'Don't mention that woman to me, Bertie!' she said. 'One of the worst.'

'But I thought you were rather pally.'

'No longer. Will you credit it that she positively refuses to let me have that article – '

'What!'

'–purely and simply on account of some fancied grievance she thinks she has against me because her cook left her and came to me.'

I couldn't follow this at all.

'Anatole left her?' I said. 'But what about the parlourmaid?'

'Pull yourself together, Bertie. You're babbling. What do you mean?'

'Why, I understood – '

'I'll bet you never understood anything in your life.' She laid down her empty glass. 'Well, that's done!' she said with relief. 'Thank goodness, I'll be able to watch Tom drinking his in a few minutes. It's the only thing that enables me to bear up. Poor old chap, he does hate it so! But I cheer him by telling him it's going to put him in shape for Anatole's cooking. And that, Bertie, is something worth going into training for. A master of his art, that man. Sometimes I'm not altogether surprised that Mrs Little made such a fuss when he went. But, really, you know, she ought not to mix sentiment with business. She has no right to refuse to let me have that article just because of a private difference. Well, she jolly well can't use it anywhere else, because it was my idea and I have witnesses to prove it. If she tries to sell it to another paper, I'll sue her. And, talking of sewers, it's high time Tom was here to drink his sulphur-water.'

'But look here – '

'Oh, by the way, Bertie,' said Aunt Dahlia, 'I withdraw any harsh expressions I may have used about your man Jeeves. A most capable feller!'

'Jeeves?'

'Yes; he attended to the negotiations. And very well he did it, too. And he hasn't lost by it, you can bet. I saw to that. I'm grateful to him. Why, if Tom gives up a couple of thousand now, practically without a murmur, the imagination reels at what he'll do with Anatole cooking regularly for him. He'll be signing cheques in his sleep.'

I got up. Aunt Dahlia pleaded with me to stick around and watch Uncle Tom in action, claiming it to be a sight nobody should miss, but I couldn't wait. I rushed up the hill, left a farewell note for Uncle George, and caught the next train for London.

'Jeeves,' I said, when I had washed off the stains of travel, 'tell me frankly all about it. Be as frank as Lady Bablockhythe.'

'Sir?'

'Never mind, if you've not heard of her. Tell me how you worked this binge. The last I heard was that Anatole loved that parlourmaid – goodness knows why! – so much that he refused to leave her. Well, then?'

'I was somewhat baffled for a while, I must confess, sir. Then I was materially assisted by a fortunate discovery.'

'What was that?'

'I chanced to be chatting with Mrs Travers's housemaid, sir, and, remembering that Mrs Little was anxious to obtain a domestic of that description, I asked her if she would consent to leave Mrs Travers and go at an advanced wage to Mrs Little. To this she assented, and I saw Mrs Little and arranged the matter.'

'Well? What was the fortunate discovery?'

'That the girl, in a previous situation some little time back, had been a colleague of Anatole, sir. And Anatole, as is the too frequent practice of these Frenchmen, had made love to her. In fact, they were, so I understand it, sir, formally affianced until Anatole disappeared one morning, leaving no address, and passed out of the poor girl's life. You will readily appreciate that this discovery simplified matters considerably. The girl no longer had any affection for Anatole, but the prospect of being under the same roof with two young persons, both of whom he had led to assume – '

'Great Scott! Yes, I see! It was rather like putting in a ferret to start a rabbit.'

'The principle was much the same, sir. Anatole was out of the house and in Mrs Travers's service within half an hour of the receipt of the information that the young person was about to arrive. A volatile man, sir. Like so many of these Frenchmen.'

'Jeeves,' I said, 'this is genius of a high order.'

'It is very good of you to say so, sir.'

'What did Mr Little say about it?'

'He appeared gratified, sir.'

'To go into sordid figures, did he – '

'Yes, sir. Twenty pounds. Having been fortunate in his selections at Hurst Park on the previous Saturday.'

'My aunt told me that she – '

'Yes, sir. Most generous. Twenty-five pounds.'

'Good Lord, Jeeves! You've been coining the stuff!'

'I have added appreciably to my savings, yes, sir. Mrs Little was good enough to present me with ten pounds from finding her such a satisfactory housemaid. And then there was Mr Travers – '

'Uncle Thomas?'

'Yes, sir. He also behaved most handsomely, quite independently of Mrs Travers. Another twenty-five pounds. And Mr George Travers – '

'Don't tell me that Uncle George gave you something, too! What on earth for?'

'Well, really, sir, I do not quite understand myself. But I received a cheque for ten pounds from him. He seemed to be under the impression that I had been in some way responsible for your joining him at Harrogate, sir.'

I gaped at the fellow.

'Well, everybody seems to be doing it,' I said, 'so I suppose I had better make the thing unanimous. Here's a fiver.'

'Why, thank you, sir. This is extremely – '

'It won't seem much compared with these vast sums you've been acquiring.'

'Oh, I assure you, sir.'

'And I don't know why I'm giving it to you.'

'No, sir.'

'Still, there it is.'

'Thank you very much, sir.'

I got up.

'It's pretty late,' I said, 'but I think I'll dress and go out and have a bite somewhere. I feel like having a whirl of some kind after two weeks in Harrogate.'

'Yes, sir. I will unpack your clothes.'

'Oh, Jeeves,' I said, 'did Peabody and Simms send those soft silk shirts?'

'Yes, sir. I sent them back.'

'Sent them back?'

'Yes, sir.'

I eyed him for a moment. But I mean to say. I mean, what's the use?

'Oh, all right,' I said. 'Then lay out one of the gents' stiff-bosomed.'

'Very good, sir,' said Jeeves.

10

BERTIE CHANGES HIS MIND

It has happened so frequently in the past few years that young fellows starting in my profession have come to me for a word of advice, that I have found it convenient now to condense my system into a brief formula. 'Resource and Tact' – that is my motto. Tact, of course, has always been with me a *sine qua non*; while as for resource, I think I may say that I have usually contrived to show a certain modicum of what I might call *finesse* in handling those little *contretemps* which inevitably arise from time to time in the daily life of a gentleman's personal gentleman. I am reminded, by way of an instance, of the Episode of the School for Young Ladies near Brighton – an affair which, I think, may be said to have commenced one evening at the moment when I brought Mr Wooster his whisky and siphon and he addressed me with such remarkable petulance.

Not a little moody Mr Wooster had been for some days – far from his usual bright self. This I had attributed to the natural reaction from a slight attack of influenza from which he had been suffering; and, of course, took no notice, merely performing my duties as usual, until on the evening of which I speak he exhibited this remarkable petulance when I brought him his whisky and siphon.

'Oh, dash it, Jeeves!' he said, manifestly overwrought. 'I wish at least you'd put it on another table for a change.'

'Sir?' I said.

'Every night, dash it all,' proceeded Mr Wooster morosely, 'you come in at exactly the same old time with the same old tray and put it on the same old table. I'm fed up, I tell you. It's the bally monotony of it that makes it all seem so frightfully bally.'

I confess that his words filled me with a certain apprehension. I had heard gentlemen in whose employment I have been speak in very much the same way before, and it had almost invariably meant that they were contemplating matrimony. It disturbed me, therefore, I am free to admit, when Mr Wooster addressed me in this fashion. I had no desire to sever a connexion so pleasant in every respect as his and mine had been, and my experience is that when the wife comes in at the front door the valet of bachelor days goes out at the back.

'It's not your fault, of course,' went on Mr Wooster, regaining a certain degree of composure. 'I'm not blaming you. But, by Jove, I mean, you must acknowledge – I mean to say, I've been thinking pretty deeply these last few days, Jeeves, and I've come to the conclusion mine is an empty life. I'm lonely, Jeeves.'

'You have a great many friends, sir.'

'What's the good of friends?'

'Emerson,' I reminded him, 'says a friend may well be reckoned the masterpiece of Nature, sir.'

'Well, you can tell Emerson from me next time you see him that he's an ass.'

'Very good, sir.'

'What I want – Jeeves, have you seen that play called I-forget-its-dashed-name?'

'No, sir.'

'It's on at the What-d'you-call-it. I went last night. The hero's a chap who's buzzing along, you know, quite merry and bright, and suddenly a kid turns up and says she's his daughter. Left over from act one, you know – absolutely the first he'd heard of it. Well, of course, there's a bit of a fuss and they say to him "What-ho?" and he says, "Well, what about it?" and they say, "Well, *what* about it?" and he says, "Oh, all right, then, if that's the way you feel!" and he takes the kid and goes off with her out into the world together, you know. Well, what I'm driving at, Jeeves, is that I envied that chappie. Most awfully jolly little girl, you know, clinging to him trustingly and what not. Something to look after, if you know what I mean. Jeeves, I wish I had a daughter. I wonder what the procedure is?'

'Marriage is, I believe, considered the preliminary step, sir.'

'No, I mean about adopting a kid. You can adopt kids, you know, Jeeves. But what I want to know is how you start about it.'

'The process I should imagine, would be highly complicated and laborious, sir. It would cut into your spare time.'

'Well, I'll tell you what I could do, then. My sister will be back from India next week with her three little girls. I'll give up this flat and take a house and have them all to live with me. By Jove, Jeeves, I think that's rather a scheme, what? Prattle of childish voices, eh? Little feet pattering hither and thither, yes?'

I concealed my perturbation, but the effort to preserve my *sang-froid* tested my powers to the utmost. The course of action outlined by Mr Wooster meant the finish of our cosy bachelor establishment if it came into being as a practical proposition; and no doubt some men in my place would at this juncture have voiced their disapproval. I avoided this blunder.

'If you will pardon my saying so, sir,' I suggested, 'I think you are not quite yourself after your influenza. If I might express the opinion, what you require is a few days by the sea. Brighton is very handy, sir.'

'Are you suggesting that I'm talking through my hat?'

'By no means, sir. I merely advocate a short stay at Brighton as a physical recuperative.'

Mr Wooster considered.

'Well, I'm not sure you're not right,' he said at length. ' I *am* feeling more or less an onion. You might shove a few things in a suitcase and drive me down in the car tomorrow.'

'Very good, sir.'

'And when we get back I'll be in the pink and ready to tackle this pattering-feet wheeze.'

'Exactly, sir.'

Well, it was a respite, and I welcomed it. But I began to see that a crisis had arisen which would require adroit handling. Rarely had I observed Mr Wooster more set on a thing. Indeed, I could recall no such exhibition of determination on his part since the time when he had insisted, against my frank disapproval, on wearing purple socks. However, I had coped successfully with that outbreak, and I was by no means unsanguine that I should eventually be able to bring the present affair to a happy issue. Employers are like horses. They require managing. Some gentlemen's personal gentlemen have the knack of managing them, some have not. I, I am happy to say, have no cause for complaint.

For myself, I found our stay at Brighton highly enjoyable, and should have been willing to extend it, but Mr Wooster, still restless, wearied of the place by the end of two days, and on the third afternoon he instructed me to pack up and bring the car round to the hotel. We started back along the London road at about five on a fine summer's day, and had travelled perhaps two miles when I perceived in the road before us a young lady, gesticulating with no little animation. I applied the brake and brought the vehicle to a standstill.

'What,' inquired Mr Wooster, waking from a reverie, 'is the big thought at the back of this, Jeeves?'

'I observed a young lady endeavouring to attract our attention with signals a little way down the road, sir,' I explained. 'She is now making her way towards us.'

Mr Wooster peered.

'I see her. I expect she wants a lift, Jeeves.'

'That was the interpretation which I placed upon her actions, sir.'

'A jolly-looking kid,' said Mr Wooster. 'I wonder what she's doing, biffing about the high road.'

'She has the air to me, sir, of one who has been absenting herself without leave from her school, sir.'

'Hallo-allo-allo!' said Mr Wooster, as the child reached us. 'Do you want a lift?'

'Oh, I say, can you?' said the child, with marked pleasure.

'Where do you want to go?'

'There's a turning to the left about a mile farther on. If you'll put me down there, I'll walk the rest of the way. I say, thanks awfully. I've got a nail in my shoe.'

She climbed in at the back. A red-haired young person with a snub-nose and an extremely large grin. Her age, I should imagine, would be about twelve. She let down one of the spare seats, and knelt on it to facilitate conversation.

'I'm going to get into a frightful row,' she began. 'Miss Tomlinson will be perfectly furious.'

'No, really?' said Mr Wooster.

'It's a half-holiday, you know, and I sneaked away to Brighton, because I wanted to go on the pier and put pennies in the slot-machines. I thought I could get back in time so that nobody would notice I'd gone, but I got this nail in my shoe, and now there'll be a fearful row. Oh, well,' she said, with a philosophy which, I confess, I admired, 'it can't be helped. What's your car? A Sunbeam, isn't it? We've got a Wolseley at home.'

Mr Wooster was visibly perturbed. As I have indicated, he was at this time in a highly malleable frame of mind, tender-hearted to a degree where the young of the female sex was concerned. Her sad case touched him deeply.

'Oh, I say, this is rather rotten,' he observed. 'Isn't there anything to be done? I say, Jeeves, don't you think something could be done?'

'It was not my place to make the suggestion, sir,' I replied, 'but, as you yourself have brought the matter up, I fancy the trouble is susceptible of adjustment. I think it would be a legitimate subterfuge were you to inform the young lady's schoolmistress that you are an old friend of the young lady's father. In this case you could inform Miss Tomlinson that you had been passing the school and had seen the young lady at the gate and taken her for a drive. Miss Tomlinson's chagrin would no doubt in these circumstances be sensibly diminished if not altogether dispersed.'

'Well, you *are* a sportsman!' observed the young person, with considerable enthusiasm. And she proceeded to kiss me – in connexion with which I have only to say that I was sorry she had just been devouring some sticky species of sweetmeat.

'Jeeves, you've hit it!' said Mr Wooster. 'A sound, even fruity, scheme. I say, I suppose I'd better know your name and all that, if I'm a friend of your father's.'

'My name's Peggy Mainwaring, thanks awfully,' said the young person. 'And my father's Professor Mainwaring. He's written a lot of books. You'll be expected to know that.'

'Author of the well-known series of philosophical treatises, sir,' I ventured to interject. 'They have a great vogue, though, if the young lady will pardon my saying so, many of the Professor's opinions strike me personally as somewhat empirical. Shall I drive on to the school, sir?'

'Yes, carry on. I say, Jeeves, it's a rummy thing. Do you know, I've never been inside a girl's school in my life?'

'Indeed, sir?'

'Ought to be a dashed interesting experience, Jeeves, what?'

'I fancy that you may find it so, sir,' I said.

We drove on a matter of half a mile down a lane, and, directed by the young person, I turned in at the gates of a house of imposing dimensions, bringing the car to a halt at the front door. Mr Wooster and child entered, and presently a parlourmaid came out.

'You're to take the car round to the stables, please,' she said.

'Ah!' I said. 'Then everything is satisfactory, eh? Where has Mr Wooster gone?'

'Miss Peggy has taken him off to meet her friends. And cook says she hopes you'll step round to the kitchen later and have a cup of tea.'

'Inform her that I shall be delighted. Before I take the car to the stables, would it be possible for me to have a word with Miss Tomlinson?'

A moment later I was following her into the drawing-room.

Handsome but strong-minded – that was how I summed up Miss Tomlinson at first glance. In some ways she recalled to mind Mr Wooster's Aunt Agatha. She had the same penetrating gaze and that indefinable air of being reluctant to stand any nonsense.

'I fear I am possibly taking a liberty, madam,' I began, 'but I am hoping that you will allow me to say a word with respect to my employer. I fancy I am correct in supposing that Mr Wooster did not tell you a great deal about himself?'

'He told me nothing about himself, except that he was a friend of Professor Mainwaring.'

'He did not inform you, then, that he was *the* Mr Wooster?'

'*The* Mr Wooster?'

'Bertram Wooster, madam.'

I will say for Mr Wooster that, mentally negligible though he no doubt is, he has a name that suggests almost infinite possibilities. He sounds, if I may elucidate my meaning, like Someone – especially if you have just been informed that he is an intimate friend of so eminent a man as Professor Mainwaring. You might not, no doubt, be able to say offhand whether he was Bertram Wooster the novelist, or Bertram Wooster the founder of a new school of thought; but you would have an uneasy feeling that you were exposing you ignorance if you did not give the impression of familiarity with the name. Miss Tomlinson, as I had rather foreseen, nodded brightly.

'Oh, *Bertram* Wooster!' she said.

'He is an extremely retiring gentleman, madam, and would be the last to suggest it himself, but, knowing him as I do, I am sure that he would take it as a graceful compliment if you were to ask him to address the young ladies. He is an excellent extempore speaker.'

'A very good idea,' said Miss Tomlinson decidedly. 'I am very much obliged to you for suggesting it. I will certainly ask him to talk to the girls.'

'And should he make a pretence – through modesty – of not wishing – '

'I shall insist.'

'Thank you, madam. I am obliged. You will not mention my share in the matter? Mr Wooster might think I had exceeded my duties.'

I drove round to the stables and halted the car in the yard. As I got out, I looked at it somewhat intently. It was a good car, and appeared to be in excellent condition, but somehow I seemed to feel that something was going to go wrong with it – something serious – something that would not be able to be put right again for at least a couple of hours.

One gets these presentiments.

It may have been some half-hour later that Mr Wooster came into the stable-yard and I was leaning against the car enjoying a quiet cigarette.

'No, don't chuck it away, Jeeves,' he said, as I withdrew the cigarette from my mouth. 'As a matter of fact, I've come to touch you for a smoke. Got one to spare?'

'Only gaspers, I fear, sir.'

'They'll do,' responded Mr Wooster, with no little eagerness. I observed that his manner was a trifle fatigued and his eyes somewhat wild. 'It's a rummy thing, Jeeves, I seem to have lost my cigarette-case. Can't find it anywhere.'

'I am sorry to hear that, sir. It is not in the car.'

'No? Must have dropped it somewhere, then.' He drew at his gasper with relish. 'Jolly creatures, small girls, Jeeves,' he remarked, after a pause.

'Extremely so, sir.'

'Of course, I can imagine some fellows finding them a bit exhausting in – er –'

'*En masse*, sir?'

'That's the word. A bit exhausting *en masse*.'

'I must confess, sir, that that is how they used to strike me. In my younger days, at the outset of my career, sir, I was at one time page-boy in a school for young ladies.'

'No, really? I never knew that before. I say, Jeeves – er – did the – er – dear little souls *giggle* much in your day?'

'Practically without cessation, sir.'

'Makes a fellow feel a bit of an ass, what? I shouldn't wonder if they usedn't to stare at you from time to time, too, eh?'

'At the school where I was employed, sir, the young ladies had a regular game which they were accustomed to play when a male visitor arrived. They would stare fixedly at him and giggle, and there was a small prize for the one who made him blush first.'

'Oh, no, I say, Jeeves, not really?'

'Yes, sir. They derived real enjoyment from the pastime.'

'I'd no idea small girls were such demons.'

'More deadly than the male, sir.'

Mr Wooster passed a handkerchief over his brow.

'Well, we're going to have tea in a few minutes, Jeeves. I expect I shall feel better after tea.'

'We will hope so, sir.'

But I was by no means sanguine.

I had an agreeable tea in the kitchen. The buttered toast was good and the maids nice girls, though with little conversation. The parlourmaid, who joined us towards the end of the meal, after performing her duties in the school dining-room, reported that Mr Wooster was sticking it pluckily, but seemed feverish. I went back to the stable-yard, and I was just giving the car another look over when the young Mainwaring child appeared.

'Oh, I say,' she said, 'will you give this to Mr Wooster when you see him?' She held out Mr Wooster's cigarette-case. 'He must have dropped it somewhere. I say,' she proceeded, 'it's an awful lark. He's going to give a lecture to the school.'

'Indeed, miss?'

'We love it when there are lectures. We sit and stare at the poor dears, and try to make them dry up. There was a man last term who got hiccoughs. Do you think Mr Wooster will get hiccoughs?'

'We can but hope for the best, miss.'

'It would be such a lark, wouldn't it?'

'Highly enjoyable, miss.'

'Well, I must be getting back. I want to get a front seat.'

And she scampered off. An engaging child. Full of spirits.

She had hardly gone when there was an agitated noise, and round the corner came Mr Wooster. Perturbed. Deeply so.

'Jeeves!'

'Sir?'

'Start the car!'

'Sir?'

'I'm off!'

'Sir?'

Mr Wooster danced a few steps.

'Don't stand there saying "sir?" I tell you I'm off. Bally off! There's not a moment to waste. The situation's desperate. Dash it, Jeeves, do you know what's happened? The Tomlinson female has just sprung it on me that I'm expected to make a speech to the girls! Got to stand up there in front of the whole dashed collection and talk! I can just see myself! Get that car going, Jeeves, dash it all. A little speed, a little speed!'

'Impossible, I fear, sir. The car is out of order.'

Mr Wooster gaped at me. Very glassily he gaped.

'Out of order!'

'Yes, sir. Something is wrong. Trivial, perhaps, but possibly a matter of some little time to repair.' Mr Wooster being one of those easy going young gentlemen who will drive a car but never take the trouble to study its mechanism, I felt justified in becoming technical. 'I think it is the differential gear, sir. Either that or the exhaust.'

I am fond of Mr Wooster, and I admit I came very near to melting as I looked at his face. He was staring at me in a sort of dumb despair that would have touched anybody.

'Then I'm sunk! Or' – a slight gleam of hope flickered across his drawn features – 'do you think I could sneak out and leg it across country, Jeeves?'

'Too late, I fear, sir.' I indicated with a slight gesture the approaching figure of Miss Tomlinson, who was advancing with a serene determination in his immediate rear.

'Ah, there you are, Mr Wooster.'

He smiled a sickly smile.

'Yes – er – here I am!'

'We are all waiting for you in the large schoolroom.'

'But I say, look here,' said Mr Wooster, 'I – I don't know a bit what to talk about.'

'Why, anything, Mr Wooster. Anything that comes into your head. Be bright,' said Miss Tomlinson. 'Bright and amusing.'

'Oh, bright and amusing?'

'Possibly tell them a few entertaining stories. But, at the same time, do not neglect the graver note. Remember that my girls are on the threshold of life, and will be eager to hear something brave and helpful and stimulating – something which they can remember in after years. But, of course, you know the sort of thing, Mr Wooster. Come. The young people are waiting.'

I have spoken earlier of resource and the part it plays in the life of a gentleman's personal gentleman. It is a quality peculiarly necessary if one is to share in scenes not primarily designed for one's co-operation. So much that is interesting in life goes on apart behind closed doors that your gentleman's gentleman, if he is not to remain hopelessly behind the march of events, should exercise his wits in order to enable himself to be – if not a spectator – at least an auditor when there is anything of interest toward. I deprecate as vulgar and undignified the practice of listening at keyholes, but, without lowering myself to that, I have generally contrived to find a way.

In the present case it was simple. The large schoolroom was situated on the ground floor, with commodious french windows, which, as the weather was clement, remained open throughout the proceedings. By stationing myself behind a pillar on the porch or veranda which adjoined the room, I was enabled to see and hear all. It was an experience which I should be sorry to have missed. Mr Wooster, I may say at once, indubitably excelled himself.

Mr Wooster is a young gentleman with practically every desirable quality except one. I do not mean brains, for in an employer brains are not desirable. The quality to which I allude is hard to define, but perhaps I might call it the gift of dealing with the Unusual Situation. In the presence of the Unusual, Mr Wooster is too prone to smile weakly and allow his eyes to protrude. He lacks Presence. I have often wished that I had the power to bestow upon him some of the *savoir-faire* of a former employer of mine, Mr Montague-Todd, the well-known financier, now in the second year of his sentence. I have known men call upon Mr Todd with the express intention of horsewhipping him and go away half an hour later laughing heartily and smoking one of his cigars. To Mr Todd it would have been a child's play to speak a few impromptu words to a schoolroom full of young ladies; in fact, before he had finished he would probably have induced them to invest all their pocket-money in one of his numerous companies; but to Mr Wooster it was plainly an ordeal of the worst description. He gave one look at the young ladies, who were all staring at him in an extremely unwinking manner, then blinked and started to pick feebly at his coat-sleeve. His aspect reminded me of that of a bashful young man who, persuaded against his better judgement to go on the platform and assist a conjurer in his entertainment, suddenly discovers that rabbits and hard-boiled eggs are being taken out of the top of his head.

The proceedings opened with a short but graceful speech of introduction from Miss Tomlinson.

'Girls,' said Miss Tomlinson, 'some of you have already met Mr Wooster – Mr *Bertram* Wooster, and you all, I hope, know him by reputation.' Here, I regret to say, Mr Wooster gave a hideous, gurgling laugh, and, catching Miss Tomlinson's eye, turned a bright scarlet. Miss Tomlinson resumed: 'He has very kindly consented to say a few words to you before he leaves, and I am sure that you will all give him your very earnest attention. Now, please.'

She gave a spacious gesture with her right hand as she said the last two words, and Mr Wooster, apparently under the impression that they were addressed to him, cleared his throat and began to speak. But it appeared that her remark was directed to the young ladies, and was in the nature of a cue or signal, for she had no sooner spoken to them than the whole school rose to its feet in a body and burst into a species of chant, of which I am glad to say I remember the words, though the tune eludes me. The words ran as follows:

Many greetings to you!
Many greetings to you!
Many greetings, dear stranger,
Many greetings,
Many greetings,
Many greetings to you!
Many greetings to you!
To you!

Considerable latitude of choice was given to the singers in the matter of key, and there was little of what I might call co-operative effort. Each child went on till she had reached the end, then stopped and waited for the stragglers to come up. It was an unusual performance, and I, personally, found it extremely exhilarating. It seemed to smite Mr Wooster, however, like a blow. He recoiled a couple of steps and flung up an arm defensively. Then the uproar died away, and an air of expectancy fell upon the room. Miss Tomlinson directed a brightly authoritative gaze upon Mr Wooster, and he blinked, gulped once or twice, and tottered forward.

'Well, you know – ' he said.

Then it seemed to strike him that this opening lacked the proper formal dignity.

'Ladies – '

A silvery peal of laughter from the front row stopped him again.

'Girls!' said Miss Tomlinson. She spoke in a low, soft voice, but the effect was immediate. Perfect stillness instantly descended upon all present. I am bound to say that, brief as my acquaintance with Miss Tomlinson had been, I could recall few women I had admired more. She had grip.

I fancy that Miss Tomlinson had gauged Mr Wooster's oratorical capabilities pretty correctly by this time, and had come to the conclusion that little in the way of a stirring address was to be expected from him.

'Perhaps,' she said, 'as it is getting late, and he has not very much time to spare, Mr Wooster will just give you some little word of advice which may be helpful to you in after-life, and then we will sing the school song and disperse to our evening lessons.'

She looked at Mr Wooster. He passed a finger round the inside of his collar.

'Advice? After-life? What? Well, I don't know – '

'Just some brief word of counsel, Mr Wooster,' said Miss Tomlinson firmly.

'Oh, well – Well, yes – Well – ' It was painful to see Mr Wooster's brain endeavouring to work. 'Well, I'll tell you something that's often done *me* a bit of good, and it's a thing not many people know. My old Uncle Henry gave me the tip when I first came to London. "Never forget, my boy," he said, "that, if you stand outside Romano's in the Strand, you can see the clock on the wall of the Law Courts down in Fleet Street. Most people who don't know don't believe it's possible, because there are a couple of churches in the middle of the road, and you would think they would be in the way. But you can, and it's worth knowing. You can win a lot of money betting on it with fellows who haven't found it out." And, by Jove, he was perfectly right, and it's a thing to remember. Many a quid I – '

Miss Tomlinson gave a hard, dry cough, and he stopped in the middle of a sentence.

'Perhaps it will be better, Mr Wooster,' she said, in a cold, even voice, 'if you were to tell my girls some little story. What you say is, no doubt, extremely interesting, but perhaps a little – '

'Oh, ah, yes,' said Mr Wooster. 'Story? Story?' He appeared completely distraught, poor young gentleman. 'I wonder if you've heard the one about the stockbroker and the chorus-girl?'

'We will now sing the school song,' said Miss Tomlinson, rising like an iceberg.

I decided not to remain for the singing of the school song. It seemed probable to me that Mr Wooster would shortly be requiring the car, so I made my way back to the stable-yard, to be in readiness.

I had not long to wait. In a very few moments he appeared, tottering. Mr Wooster's is not one of those inscrutable faces which it is impossible to read. On the contrary, it is a limpid pool in which is mirrored each passing emotion. I could read it now like a book, and his first words were very much on the lines I had anticipated.

'Jeeves,' he said hoarsely, 'is that damned car mended yet?'

'Just this moment, sir. I have been working on it assiduously.'

'Then for heaven's sake, let's go!'

'But I understood that you were to address the young ladies, sir.'

'Oh, I've done that!' responded Mr Wooster, blinking twice with extraordinary rapidity. 'Yes, I've done that.'

'It was a success, I hope, sir?'

'Oh, yes. Oh, yes. Most extraordinarily successful. Went like a breeze. But – er – I think I may as well be going. No use outstaying one's welcome, what?'

'Assuredly not, sir.'

I had climbed into my seat and was about to start the engine, when voices made themselves heard; and at the first sound of them Mr Wooster sprang with almost incredible nimbleness into the tonneau, and when I glanced round he was on the floor covering himself with a rug. The last I saw of him was a pleading eye.

'Have you seen Mr Wooster, my man?'

Miss Tomlinson had entered the stable-yard, accompanied by a lady of, I should say, judging from her accent, French origin.

'No, madam.'

The French lady uttered some exclamation in her native tongue.

'Is anything wrong, madam?' I inquired.

Miss Tomlinson in normal mood was, I should be disposed to imagine, a lady who would not readily confide her troubles to the ear of a gentleman's gentleman, however sympathetic his aspect. That she did so now was sufficient indication of the depth to which she was stirred.

'Yes, there is! Mademoiselle has just found several of the girls smoking cigarettes in the shrubbery. When questioned, they stated that Mr Wooster had given them the horrid things.' She turned. 'He must be in the garden somewhere, or in the house. I think the man is out of his senses. Come, mademoiselle!'

It must have been about a minute later that Mr Wooster poked his head out of the rug like a tortoise.

'Jeeves!'

'Sir?'

'Get a move on! Start her up! Get going and *keep* going!'

I applied my foot to the self-starter.

'It would perhaps be safest to drive carefully until we are out of the school grounds, sir,' I said. 'I might run over one of the young ladies, sir.'

'Well, what's the objection to that?' demanded Mr Wooster with extraordinary bitterness.

'Or even Miss Tomlinson, sir.'

'Don't!' said Mr Wooster wistfully. 'You make my mouth water!'

'Jeeves,' said Mr Wooster, when I brought him his whisky and siphon one night about a week later, 'this is dashed jolly.'

'Sir?'

'Jolly. Cosy and pleasant, you know. I mean, looking at the clock and wondering if you're going to be late with the good old drinks, and then you coming in with the tray always on time, never a minute late, and shoving it down on the table and biffing off, and the next night coming in and shoving it down and biffing off, and the next night – I mean, gives you a sort of safe, restful feeling. Soothing! That's the word. Soothing!'

'Yes, sir. Oh, by the way, sir – '

'Well?'

'Have you succeeded in finding a suitable house yet, sir?'

'House? What do you mean, house?'

'I understood, sir, that it was your intention to give up the flat and take a house of sufficient size to enable you to have your sister, Mrs Scholfield, and her three young ladies to live with you.'

Mr Wooster shuddered strongly.

'That's off, Jeeves,' he said.

'Very good, sir,' I replied.